Wind Talk for Woodwinds

Wind Talk for Woodwinds

*A Practical Guide to Understanding
and Teaching Woodwind Instruments*

Mark C. Ely
Amy E. Van Deuren

OXFORD
UNIVERSITY PRESS
2009

OXFORD
UNIVERSITY PRESS

Oxford University Press, Inc., publishes works that further
Oxford University's objective of excellence
in research, scholarship, and education.

Oxford   New York
Auckland   Cape Town   Dar es Salaam   Hong Kong   Karachi
Kuala Lumpur   Madrid   Melbourne   Mexico City   Nairobi
New Delhi   Shanghai   Taipei   Toronto

With offices in
Argentina   Austria   Brazil   Chile   Czech Republic   France   Greece
Guatemala   Hungary   Italy   Japan   Poland   Portugal   Singapore
South Korea   Switzerland   Thailand   Turkey   Ukraine   Vietnam

Published by Oxford University Press, Inc.
198 Madison Avenue, New York, New York 10016
www.oup.com

Oxford is a registered trademark of Oxford University Press

Library of Congress Cataloging-in-Publication Data

Ely, Mark C.
Wind talk for woodwinds : a practical guide to understanding
and teaching woodwind instruments / Mark C. Ely and Amy E. Van Deuren
p. cm.
Includes index.
ISBN: 978-0-19-532918-6; 978-0-19-532925-4 (pbk.)
1.Brass instruments—Instruction and study.
MT18.E49 2009
788.2/193071 22   2008036363

1 3 5 7 9 8 6 4 2

Printed in the United States of America
on acid-free paper

Preface

Teaching instrumental music requires a vast working knowledge of wind instrument pedagogy. Understanding the mechanical, acoustical, and technical terminology and concepts associated with each instrument encourages and promotes communication between teachers and students and is essential for effective teaching. Teachers must have a broad pedagogical knowledge base to read, comprehend and teach pedagogical concepts effectively.

One important challenge faced by instrumental music teachers is acquiring an adequate breadth and depth of pedagogical knowledge necessary for effective teaching. Teacher training programs at most colleges and universities typically require a series of pedagogy courses designed to familiarize students with each instrument or each type of instrument. Although these courses provide a basic introduction to playing and teaching wind instruments, they cannot provide the depth and breadth necessary for successful teaching. At best, they offer a modest amount of hands-on training to enable beginning-level playing and teaching skills. As a result, the strengths and weaknesses of a teacher's ensembles are all too often a direct reflection of his or her personal strengths and weaknesses in woodwind pedagogy. Instrumental music teachers should be able to provide effective pedagogical instruction to students on every instrument.

Wind Talk for Woodwinds: A Practical Guide to Understanding and Teaching Woodwind Instruments is a one-volume reference book designed to provide instrumental music teachers, educators, practitioners, students, and professionals with a quick and easy-to-use pedagogical resource for woodwind instruments commonly used in school instrumental music programs: flute, oboe, clarinet, saxophone, and bassoon. This book is especially designed to aid instrumental music teachers in understanding frequently encountered terminology, topics, and concepts, including teaching suggestions that can be applied in the classroom. It contains information that applies to beginners and to advanced players.

Every effort has been made to be thorough and to make the information practical, applicable, and easy to understand. Each term, topic, and concept defined and discussed here meets at least one of the following three criteria: (1) it is relevant to the physical and/or acoustical characteristics of woodwind instruments, (2) it is relevant to the technical and/or physiological aspects of playing woodwind instruments, or (3) it is used to describe an accessory related to one or more woodwind instruments.

Wind Talk begins with a chapter of material common to all woodwind instruments and then has a chapter on each woodwind instrument. Each chapter contains a wide variety of pedagogical information, including terminology, related topics, concepts, and teaching suggestions. Teaching tips and key questions appear throughout each chapter. Photographs, illustrations, and musical examples also appear throughout each chapter to aid understanding or to illustrate certain concepts.

Within each chapter, the terms and topics appear in alphabetical order. For example, in the flute chapter, the first five entries are: Acoustical Properties, Action, Adjusting Pitch, Air Stream, and Alternate Fingerings/Alternates. Terms are cross-referenced when appropriate at the end of the definition or discussion using the words "See" and "See also." "See" is used to direct readers to a related term where the information is located (e.g., Instrument Parts: *See* Parts, Flute, page 138). "See also" is used to direct readers to other terms with additional relevant information that may enhance understanding.

Additional special sections appear as "Practical Tips" at the end of each instrument chapter to provide teachers with additional pedagogical information designed to further enhance teaching, learning, and musical skill development. They include:

1. Fingering Charts
2. Common Technical Faults and Corrections
3. Common Problems, Causes, and Solutions

A special section titled "General Resources for Instrumental Music Teachers" appears near the end of chapter 1. This section identifies additional references/resources for woodwind instruments in the following areas:

1. Acoustics Resources
2. Woodwind Pedagogy Books
3. General Pedagogy Web Sites
4. CD Recordings Available through Web Sites
5. Reeds, Single
6. Reeds, Double

Special sections identifying resources specific to each woodwind instrument also appear near the end of chapter 1. These include:

1. Pedagogy Books
2. Literature Resources
3. Journals/Magazines
4. Web Sites

Wind Talk for Woodwinds stands alone as an invaluable resource for practicing instrumental teachers. However, this book is also appropriate for many undergraduate and graduate courses involving woodwind pedagogy, including instrumental music methods, woodwind methods, instrumental rehearsal techniques, instrumentation and arranging, conducting, and student teaching.

Acknowledgments

We would like to express our gratitude to the many educators who contributed their time and expertise to this project, to the University of Utah musicians who graciously posed for the photographs, and to Summerhays Music for allowing us to photograph its instruments and accessories. We would also like to thank Katharine Boone, Norm Hirschy, Paul Hobson, and Suzanne Ryan at Oxford University Press for their dedication, patience, and encouragement during the production of this book.

A special "thank you!" goes to Kimberly Grundvig for her editing expertise and for her incredible attention to detail.

To our families, we would like to express our appreciation for their support and understanding during the entire process, especially during the times when we were not there.

Contents

1. Woodwind Commonalities   3

2. Flute   81
   Practical Tips   156

3. Clarinet   188
   Practical Tips   297

4. Saxophone   335
   Practical Tips   420

5. Oboe   459
   Practical Tips   563

6. Bassoon   598
   Practical Tips   679

   General Resources for Instrumental
   Music Teachers   717

   Index   729

Wind Talk for Woodwinds

Woodwind Commonalities

Acoustical Basics: Common acoustical and physical tonal characteristics of woodwind instruments. The acoustical qualities of woodwind instruments are largely determined by the design of the instrument and the manner in which tone is produced. Although the design characteristics of woodwind instruments vary greatly in some respects, they also share several fundamental design characteristics. All woodwind instruments are designed with (1) a way to set the air column in vibration; (2) an instrument tube for the vibrating air column; and (3) the use of only the first and second partials (or first and third partials on clarinet) of the harmonic series in the normal playing ranges. The way an instrument is designed contributes significantly to the overall tonal and response characteristics of that instrument. These design variables include: (1) the manner in which the air column is set in vibration; (2) the types, weight, and thickness of materials used in instrument construction; (3) the shape or flare of the instrument tubing; (4) the inner dimensions along the tubing; (5) how the tubing is bent or looped; and (6) the finish (e.g., lacquer or silver plate). The acoustical and physical tonal characteristics of each woodwind instrument are located under Acoustical Properties in each instrument chapter. See also Harmonics, page 32

Action: In general, the way keys and key mechanisms work on a particular instrument. The term "action" is used when referring to the way an instrument feels when it is played and/or the ease with which players can reach and operate the keys. Action is often described in terms of being smooth or rough, even or uneven, and heavy or light. Typically, the action on smaller woodwind instruments (flute, oboe, and clarinet) is light in comparison with the action on larger woodwind instruments (saxophone and bassoon) because their key mechanisms are smaller and lighter, and because the distance between the keys and the tone holes is much shorter. Smaller woodwind instruments are not prone to having a heavy action; however, any instrument that has not been properly adjusted, cleaned, and oiled can feel sluggish and uneven. Instruments should play with a light, even action. The keys should depress with little effort, yet spring back quickly and easily. They should never feel spongy or sluggish. In addition, weak springs can cause pads to leak, and they can cause problems with tone quality (e.g., "bobble" sounds caused by keys that bounce), response, and technical fluidity. Excessively heavy or uneven action is usually the result of poorly adjusted and/or bent key mechanisms or poorly adjusted pads. Many players prefer a light action, because it enables them to push down the keys with less finger pressure. Lightening the action, adjusting spring tension, and/or adjusting key/pad height is typically done by a knowledgeable repair technician. The bassoon is fundamentally more awkward and cumbersome than other woodwinds. The size, spacing, and complicated design of the keys and key mechanisms, and the extensive use of thumb keys on both hands throughout the range all contribute to the inherent awkwardness of a bassoon's action. Therefore, keeping the instrument properly adjusted is critical to playability.

Adjusting Pitch: The process of raising or lowering the pitch of notes. Usually, pitch is adjusted to achieve better intonation according to the musical context. Adjusting or "humoring" pitches appropriately is dependent upon three factors: (1) hearing pitch problems, (2) understanding what adjustments need to be made to correct pitch problems, and (3) having and using the skills to make the necessary adjustments. Players should be taught how to adjust pitch only after they have developed basic playing skills. In addition, tuners are very helpful for determining the appropriateness of any pitch adjustment. A general discussion of adjusting pitch is under Intonation in this chapter. A detailed discussion of adjusting pitch is under Intonation in each instrument chapter. See also Intonation, page 41

Air Column: A term used to describe the air that is vibrating inside the instrument while it is being played. The air column creates a standing wave that roughly corresponds to the frequency of the perceived pitch for a particular fingering. Acoustically, the number of divisions within the air column (nodes) determines which frequencies (partials) can be produced. Divisions of the air column are illustrated in figure 1.1. Musically, the formation of the embouchure, the speed of the air, the direction of the air stream, and the particular fingering used all help determine which partial is produced during play. See also Acoustical Basics, page 3

Air Stream: Physically, the stream of air pushed from the lungs by the diaphragm and abdominal muscles through the trachea and oral cavity into and through a musical instrument. Generally, the "air stream" refers to all of the air expelled by the player, whereas the "air column" refers only to the air inside the instrument.

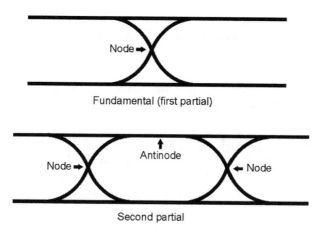

FIGURE 1.1. *Acoustical Divisions of the Air Column*

Although the physical nature of exhaling is basically the same for everyone, the ways the air stream is used on the various woodwind instruments vary significantly. These variations are discussed thoroughly in each instrument chapter.

On reed instruments, once the proper embouchure is formed, the air stream is used to set the reed, and subsequently the air column, in vibration. On flute, the air stream is split by the opposite (far) edge of the embouchure plate, setting the air column in vibration. Changes in the focus, direction, and speed of the air stream affect virtually every aspect of woodwind playing, including tone quality, intonation, dynamics, articulation, technique, and musicality.

Players often effect changes in the air stream through the use of various syllables. For example, it is common for woodwind players to think of saying "who" to help round the embouchure and warm the air stream in the middle register, "oh" for the lower register, and a firmer "who" or even "ee" for the high and altissimo registers, depending on the instrument and the pitch being played. Even oboe players, who typically use a colder, faster air stream, often think of using a "who" syllable, especially in the low and middle registers; however, their "who" syllable is firmer and smaller than the "who" syllable used on other woodwind instruments. Considerable disagreement exists as to the appropriateness of particular syllables. Teachers and players should experiment with a variety of syllables and use what yields the best results.

Although the basic concepts of producing an air stream are the same for most woodwind instruments, variations in the air stream are significant among woodwind instruments in order to produce a characteristic tone and maintain pitch control on each instrument. In addition, teachers often disagree on the appropriateness and use of certain syllables to make changes in the air stream. Specific suggestions and considerations regarding the air stream for each woodwind instrument are in each instrument chapter. A detailed discussion of the use of air and suggestions for improving the air stream can be found under Breathing/Breath Support/Air Control in this chapter.

Anchor Tonguing: An alternative method of tonguing that involves anchoring the tip of the tongue to the bottom teeth at or near the gum line. This position causes the tongue to be naturally curved or arched in the mouth. When anchor tonguing, the tongue makes contact with the reed or gum line (flute) near the middle of the tongue rather than on the tip of the tongue. Although anchor tonguing is not typically used in woodwind playing, a few clarinet and saxophone players do anchor tongue successfully. As a rule, students should not anchor tongue. See also Tonguing, page 71

Articulation/Articulative Styles: In general, the way musical phrases are to be tongued and/or slurred. Articulation is often used in conjunction with style. For example, players often refer to jazz articulations and classical articulations as separate entities. Used in this way, "articulation" refers to how pitches are tongued and released, as well as the organization of tongued and slurred notes. In performance, tones are generally started with a clean, quick, light stroke of the tongue working in conjunction with the air. Players can be taught to tongue using a "T" attack in the beginning stages. Specifically, players should think of saying the syllable "tu" because this syllable enables players to maintain an open throat and facilitates a warm, full tone quality.

With the exception of breath attacks, which are used sparingly on woodwind instruments, the sound of an articulation is determined primarily by the ways the tongue and air are used to start or attack the notes. The attack occurs when the tip of the tongue strikes the tip of the reed (saxophone and clarinet), the back of the upper teeth at or near the gum line (flute), or the tip of the bottom blade (oboe and bassoon), releasing the air behind it. As a rule, players should develop consistency and control of the "tu" syllable for articulating notes before adding other types of articulations. Other syllables, particularly "du" for legato playing, are incorporated as players gain experience. Players can vary syllables to suit their musical needs. They can also vary the strength of the attack and the amount and speed of the air, resulting in a wide variety of articulations.

Releases also play an important role in the articulation process. There are two basic ways to release or stop a tone: (1) a breath release, in which the player stops the air; and (2) a tongue cutoff, in which the player touches the tongue against

FIGURE 1.2. *Articulation/Articulative Style Markings*

the gum line or reed. In most musical contexts, breath releases are more appropriate than tongue cutoffs because tongue cutoffs tend to be harsh and abrupt; however, breath releases are more difficult to execute than tongue cutoffs because they require players to precisely control the air stream. In addition, tongue cutoffs are relatively common in jazz styles. Syllables such as "tut" are often used to facilitate tongue cutoffs. Some of the more basic articulations and articulative styles are outlined in the following list. Common articulation markings are shown in figure 1.2. See also Attacks, page 9; Breathing/Breath Support/Air Control, page 10; Releases, page 56; Tonguing, page 71

Basic Articulations/Articulative Styles

1. Basic Tongue Attack—A basic tongue attack is appropriate for most passages unless the music is marked otherwise or the style of the music calls for a particular articulation. On flute, a basic tongue attack involves interrupting the air stream by quickly striking the gum line behind the upper front teeth with the tip of the tongue using a "tu" syllable. On clarinet and saxophone, a basic tongue attack involves interrupting the air stream by quickly striking the tip of the reed with the tip of the tongue using a "tu" syllable. On oboe and bassoon, a basic tongue attack involves interrupting the air stream by quickly striking the tip of the bottom blade with the tip of the tongue using a "tu" syllable. When the tongue is not being used, it remains relatively low and relaxed in the mouth.

2. Accents—An articulation that requires placing more emphasis with the air on the beginning of the note than would normally occur on a basic tongue attack. The "tu" syllable is typically used to play accented notes. Long accents are notated by means of a ">" placed over or under the note, and short accents are notated by means of a "∧" placed over or under the note.

3. Staccato—Notated with small dots above or below each note, most staccato passages involve using a light, short pronunciation of the "tu" syllable with a quick breath release. When breath releases are

used, it is important that players "lift" off of the notes. In rapid staccato passages, tongue cutoffs are often used instead of breath releases. In such instances, the tongue placement for any successive note becomes the release for the preceding note. As long as the air stream is maintained consistently and the tongue remains light and quick, both the attacks and releases will be clean and light.

4. Legato—Notated with short horizontal lines above or below each note, most legato passages involve using a long "du" syllable for each note. In legato passages, the air stream remains constant, and the tongue lightly contacts the gum line behind the upper teeth (flute) or the tip of the reed, barely disrupting the air stream.

5. Marcato—A heavy articulation with more "bite" than a typical staccato. Marcato articulation requires a stronger pronunciation of the syllable (more air). Depending on the style (e.g., jazz), a marcato articulation may also involve using a tongue cutoff, which is an abrupt cutoff achieved by bringing the tongue back up to the gum line or reed. Marcatos are usually notated with a "∧" placed over or under the note.

6. Tenuto—Notated with a long, horizontal line over or under the note, an articulation indicating that the note (or notes) should be held for its full value. In tenuto passages, notes frequently do not have obvious release points; rather, each note is held until the articulation of the next note occurs. The distinction between tenuto and legato is not always clear; however, tenuto often refers to a specific note that is to be held out, whereas legato is used to describe the style of an entire passage.

7. Sforzando Articulation—Notated with *sfz* above or below a note, sforzando articulations are executed similarly to the piccato articulations but are slightly exaggerated. That is, sforzando articulations are generally louder and more explosive than piccato articulations. This explosiveness is typically facilitated by sudden increases in air speed. In some instances, it may be appropriate to place the tongue at the gum line behind the top teeth or on the tip of the reed, build up air pressure, and release the tongue quickly.

8. Portato—The portato, or half staccato or half legato as it is sometimes called, lies halfway between the staccato and legato articulations. In essence, the portato articulation is a lightly articulated

legato phrase with slight separations between the notes. It is notated by a slur over notes with dots above or below the note.

9. Slur—Slurs are produced when the first note of two or more in succession is tongued and the others are not. That is, air flow continues as notes are played in succession without the aid of the tongue. The fingers and air must be precisely coordinated to execute slurs accurately. In addition, finger and embouchure adjustments must be made quickly and precisely, even in slow music, to ensure a cleanly executed slur. Slurs are notated with a curved line above or below the notes to be slurred.

Attacks: The way tones are started. The word "attacks" can be misleading because it implies that players should start the tones in some kind of angry, forceful way, and, with the exception of a few instances, such attacks are musically inappropriate. There are two basic types of attacks: tongue attacks and breath attacks. However, by altering the ways the tongue and breath are used to start tones, a wide array of attacks is possible. Tongue attacks and breath attacks are described separately. See also Articulation/Articulative Styles, page 6; Releases, page 56; Tonguing, page 71

TONGUE ATTACKS

In performance, tones are generally started with a clean, quick, light stroke of the tongue working in conjunction with the air. The tip of the tongue (or slightly above the tip) should contact the gum line behind the upper teeth (flute), the tip of the reed (clarinet and saxophone), or the tip of the bottom blade (oboe and bassoon). Tongue attacks are discussed in detail under Tonguing in this chapter.

TONGUE ATTACKS AND ARTICULATIVE STYLES

As players gain experience, they can learn to use the syllable "du" or "doh" for tonguing in other styles. These syllables enable players to produce smoother, more legato attacks. Other factors that contribute to various types of attacks include: 1) the amount of air, 2) the speed of the air, and 3) the "weight" of the tongue or how hard the tongue strikes the gum line (flute) or reed. A more detailed discussion of articulative styles can be found in Articulation/Articulative Styles.

BREATH ATTACKS

Woodwind players use breath attacks far less frequently than they use tongue attacks; however, in some musical contexts or styles (e.g., a very soft, delicate entrance), tones can be started with the air alone. When executing breath attacks, players must use enough air to set the reed or air column (flute) in vibration and to achieve the intended dynamic and stylistic effects. Developing precise breath attacks is more difficult than developing precise tongue attacks, and proper execution is dependent upon several factors. The steps for executing a breath attack are listed as follows.

1. Take in air.
2. Set the embouchure.
3. Hear the pitch before actually playing it.
4. Keep the embouchure, oral cavity, and throat relatively constant while performing a breath attack.
5. Remember what it "feels" like to play that particular pitch.
6. Use enough air to start the tone.

Beats: An acoustical term used to describe the roughness that occurs when two nearly identical pitches are sounded simultaneously. Beats are frequently heard during the tuning process and are recognized as pulsations, which reflect the rapid changes in intensity or loudness. Although beats are often easier to hear when two like instruments are sounded together, they are easily audible when two unlike instruments are sounded together. As the pitches get farther apart, the beats speed up and the roughness is greater. As the pitches get closer together, the beats slow down and the roughness diminishes. See also Intonation, page 41

Bell Tones: A term used by some players for the notes produced when the keys nearest the instrument bell are closed. Bell tones are typically "long" or "closed" fingerings. For example, on clarinet, the bell tones include the lowest notes (E-natural and F-natural) and those notes that lie above the break (B-natural and C-natural).

Breathing/Breath Support/Air Control: No other factor in wind playing has greater effects on overall performance proficiency than air. In fact, the use of air affects virtually every aspect of wind playing including tone quality, intonation, dynamics, articulation, technique, and musicality. Developing proper breathing techniques and learning how to use air efficiently will not only improve tone quality, intonation, and dynamic control, which are the factors most commonly associated with air, but will also effectively eliminate many of the problems (e.g., poor response) that are often erroneously attributed to other causes.

The purpose of breathing exercises is essentially twofold: (1) to increase the amount of air taken in during one breath, and (2) to improve the efficiency of inhalation (inspiration) and exhalation (expiration) during performance. Many effective breathing exercises have been developed through the years, and imagination is about the only limitation on creating exercises to develop proper breathing habits. The physiological nature of the breathing process is summarized in the following section, along with suggested exercises, some of which are appropriate in ensemble rehearsal settings.

Physiology of Breathing: Basic Facts

1. When inhaling, air is drawn into the lungs by a vacuum created by the flattening of the diaphragm. This process results in a natural expansion of the abdominal area. It should also involve expansion all around the lower part of the torso including the chest, back, and rib cage. When exhaling, the air is pushed out of the lungs as the diaphragm rises to its "at rest" position. This process results in a natural contraction of the abdominal area. It should also involve contraction all around the lower part of the torso including the chest, back, and rib cage.

2. Some people learn to breathe inefficiently by not allowing the back and the rib cage to expand properly. Instead, movement is allowed only by the abdominal and chest areas, which limits breathing capacity. Often, the shoulders are also allowed to rise unnaturally (a very slight rise naturally occurs as the chest and abdominal regions expand), which can be detrimental to proper breathing.

3. Although breathing is a natural process, the way musicians inhale and exhale during musical performance is not. Effective musical performance typically requires that a large amount of air be taken in very quickly and let out over time in a controlled manner.

4. Breathing is more efficient when the body (neck, throat, shoulders, arms, hands, fingers, and lower body) stays relaxed. However, relaxing does not mean slouching. Breathing is more efficient when good posture is maintained.

5. The amount of air drawn in on one breath can be increased with training.

6. Lung capacity can be increased by practicing breathing exercises and by exercising regularly and staying in good physical shape.

7. Proper breathing habits and other areas of breathing can be improved through diligent practice.

Inhalation Exercises

1. Inhale slowly over four counts and focus on or "feel" what happens during the inhalation process. For now, exhale naturally. Think about what is happening during inhalation and what should be happening. Repeat the process several times.

2. Gradually decrease the inhalation time to about one second. Maintain proper mechanics of breathing as the inhalation time is lessened. Trying to break poor breathing habits takes time, thought, and effort.

3. Use a variety of strategies to help develop the "feel" for proper inhalation. Teaching suggestions for developing this feel appear separately.

Teaching Tips for Inhalation

1. Have students focus on the idea of breathing downward and on taking a "deep" breath. This idea promotes proper torso expansion and often eliminates raised shoulders. It also results in greater air intake.

2. Have students lean forward in their chairs (have them bend over at the waist if they are standing) and take a deep breath. This position basically forces students to breathe correctly and eliminates raised shoulders.

3. While leaning forward, have students place their hands around their waists (thumbs in front, fingers in back) while inhaling. This position allows students to feel the expansion.

4. Have students think of laughing deep from the belly as if saying "Ho, Ho, Ho."

5. Another way to help students feel proper breathing is to have them lie down on the floor and take a deep breath. Students will be able to feel their backs touch/push against the floor as their torsos expand properly. In addition, resting a book or similar object on their stomachs as they inhale and exhale will help students see how their stomachs rise and fall when they inhale and exhale.

6. Finally, have students stand out from a wall about a foot or so with their backs to the wall. Have them lean back slowly until their

heads touch the wall (they are now in an arched position). Have students take a deep breath. Their torsos will expand properly, and they should be able to feel this expansion easily.

Exhalation Exercises without Instruments

1. Take a deep breath and release the air with a constant "hissing" sound. The loudness of this hiss can and should be varied from one exercise to another by focusing attention on air speed.

2. Take a deep breath and blow evenly against the hand. The hand should be positioned about six inches from the mouth. Although the distance can be varied to demonstrate how the air stream expands as it gets farther from the mouth, it also becomes more difficult to feel the consistency of the air stream. This exercise provides kinesthetic feedback regarding the strength, direction, and focus of the air stream.

3. Take a deep breath and whistle a constant tone without changing its dynamic level. Changes in dynamic level indicate changes in the air stream.

4. Take a deep breath and blow air evenly through a small aperture in the lips (more resistance) and then through gradually bigger apertures (less resistance). This process helps develop control and consistency of air speed across a variety of resistances. This control and consistency is necessary in wind playing because notes tend to respond differently throughout an instrument's range.

5. Fasten a small string or thin strip of tissue paper about six inches long to a pencil. Take a deep breath, hold the pencil about six inches from the mouth and blow. If done correctly, the tissue paper will "fly" straight out away from the mouth. This exercise provides a visual guide to the consistency, power, and direction of the air stream.

6. Place a note card against a smooth surface (e.g., door, wall, window) and hold it there with a constant flow of air. Position the mouth six to ten inches from the note card. The card will begin to slide or fall as the air stream begins to fade. This exercise helps increase understanding of air focus, and it provides a visual guide to the consistency, power, and direction of the air stream.

7. Practice blowing up balloons to increase endurance.

8. Practice exhaling over a predetermined number of counts. Take a deep breath and exhale over four counts. The number of counts should be changed frequently.

Exhalation Exercises/Suggestions with Instruments

1. Take a deep breath and play one note for as long as possible while still maintaining a steady and consistent tone quality. Keep the dynamic level consistent for each tone, but change the dynamic level from one tone to the next. Focus attention on the speed and focus of the air stream. Note any changes in dynamic level, pitch, or tone quality that indicate changes in the consistency of the air stream.

2. Low woodwind instruments generally require more air volume but slower air speeds than high woodwind instruments. As a result, low woodwind players typically need to breathe more often than high woodwind players during exercises. One exception to this generalization is the flute, which requires more air to properly sustain the tone than do most other woodwind instruments.

3. Change the dynamic level on one tone in a consistent manner. For example, play one note starting at *p* and crescendo to *f* over four counts, or start at *f* and decrescendo to *p* over four counts. During this exercise, it may be helpful to think of the various dynamic levels in a natural sequence. For example, think *p, mp, mf, f, mf, mp, p* for a crescendo/decrescendo exercise over eight counts. Changing both the dynamic levels and the number of counts will help develop control of the air stream during exhalation.

4. Take a deep breath and play long tone scales while focusing on the evenness of the dynamic, tone quality, and pitch from note to note and within each note. Changes in these factors indicate changes in the air stream.

5. Think of using a warm air stream when performing each exercise. This concept applies to all woodwind instruments except the oboe. Oboe players should think of using a cool or cold air stream.

6. Play slurred, stepwise exercises at first. Gradually introduce skips and leaps, but still slur all exercises. Practice keeping the dynamic

level, tone quality, and pitch consistent while making necessary embouchure, oral cavity, and air stream adjustments for skips and leaps.

7. When slurred exercises can be played with a consistent air stream, introduce tongued exercises.

Considerations for Taking in Air

Players need to learn when and how to take a breath when they are first learning to play a musical instrument. The "when" is somewhat subjective depending on experience and training and the nature of the music to be performed; however, as a rule, players should breathe one beat before playing. This breath should be quick, smooth, and efficient, and it should be taken in the tempo of the music. The "how" is somewhat dependent upon the type of instrument played. As a general rule, breathing through the mouth corners (with as little disruption to the embouchure as possible) is the established method of taking in air. That is, on reed instruments, players should breathe such that the reed maintains contact with the center of the lower lip. On flute, the lower lip maintains contact with the embouchure plate during the inhalation process. These positions allow players to take in air while maintaining proper embouchure position.

Considerations for Developing Control of Air

Once a sufficient amount of air is being taken in on each breath, developing control of the air during exhalation is the primary concern. This control affects many areas of performance and determines to a great extent how musical the performance will or can be. For example, control of the air is a major factor in achieving a desirable tone quality. Many pedagogical terms commonly used by teachers (e.g., focus and support) relate to air. Proper use and control of air: (1) provides support for the tone in all dynamic ranges, (2) allows the muscles used for breath support to remain stable and relaxed while performing, (3) helps the embouchure muscles maintain an appropriate balance between aperture size and lip vibration, and (4) enables players to stay relaxed by reducing the need to strain other muscles to compensate for inadequate breath support. An inadequate amount of air and insufficient control of air can contribute to a tone that is weak, unsupported, unfocused, uncentered, lifeless, thin, and/or inconsistent. As a result, players must learn to control air effectively so that a rich, full tone quality can be attained and maintained. Suggestions for developing air control are listed as follows.

1. Develop proper mechanics of breathing by regularly practicing the general breathing exercises mentioned above. Use a sufficient amount of air at all times when playing.

2. Take full breaths as a rule; however, there are times when less air is needed to perform a given phrase or passage. As players mature, they should learn to judge how much air they will need to perform a given phrase musically. Making musical judgments requires practice, experience, and sensitivity to musical performance.

3. Be realistic regarding the length of phrase that can be played with one breath. As a rule, it is better to breathe more frequently and maintain good breath support than to play phrases that cannot be sustained properly on one breath.

4. Plan ample opportunities for appropriate breaths during performances. When performing, nerves and other factors can reduce a player's maximum breath capacity.

5. Play long tones daily at various dynamic levels and in all ranges.

6. Practice playing crescendi and decrescendi evenly from one dynamic level to another over a variety of counts. For example, crescendo from piano (p) to forte (f) evenly over four counts, six counts, eight counts, and so on, and decrescendo in the same manner. Varying the dynamic levels and the length of crescendi/decrescendi helps develop consistency and control of the air.

7. Practice exercises that involve sudden dynamic changes. For example, play four quarter notes so that all of the notes are at the same dynamic level except one. Players could play the first three at piano (p) and the fourth at forte (f) or play all of the notes at p except the third quarter note, which they could play at forte (f). These types of exercises are easy to devise, take very little time to perform, and are easy to vary.

8. Work on sustaining tones at the softest dynamic levels attainable. For example, decrescendo from fortissimo (ff) over eight counts to pianissimo (pp), then sustain the last note for eight more counts. This type of exercise will help develop the ability to sustain phrase endings. It is important to focus attention on what is happening with the air at each phase of the exercise in terms of tone quality and pitch.

9. Practice an entire exercise at one dynamic level, then repeat the exercise at another dynamic level. For example, play the exercise at

fortissimo (*ff*) and then at pianissimo (*pp*). Incorporating dynamic contrast in exercises will help develop consistency of the air stream, and will help maintain good tone quality and intonation at all dynamic levels.

Teaching Tips for Air Control

1. Use verbal instructions that specifically draw attention to the air stream. For example, instead of saying "play louder," say "move the air faster" or "increase air speed." In other words, relate dynamics to the speed of the air stream (the "how") rather than to the desired outcome (the "what").

2. Use phrases that relate to air speed (e.g., "faster air" and "slower air"). Air speed controls dynamics. Although phrases such as "more air" and "less air" are fine at times, phrases that relate to air speed are better because they more accurately reflect or represent what happens during performance.

3. Allow students to experiment with the air stream so that they can learn how variations in the air stream affect musical performance. Learning to recognize cause-and-effect relationships helps develop independent musicianship skills.

CONTROL OF AIR AND VIBRATO

A direct relationship exists between control of the air and vibrato. Specifically, better control of the air stream leads to a more even, pleasing vibrato. Control of the air stream is vital to the production of a diaphragmatic vibrato, since its success depends almost exclusively upon the performer's ability to produce rhythmic pulsations of the air stream in a controlled manner. Control of the air stream is also important to the production of a lip/jaw vibrato. First, it assures a more consistent response of the tones. Second, it assures a more centered tone quality during pitch fluctuation. Third, because tones with vibrato require more air to produce than those without, it assures a more uniform pulsation between tones. Fourth, it assures better control over the tone quality so that the vibrato does not dominate the tone.

CONTROL OF AIR AND ARTICULATION

Many articulation problems can also be linked to poor air control. For example, too much air causes hard, "splatty" attacks; too little air causes unclean, unresponsive attacks. Furthermore, not maintaining sufficient air speed during tongued passages results in "muddy" tonguing.

Having control of air is also necessary for clean releases. Although there are essentially two types of releases (breath releases and tongue-cutoffs), breath releases are more appropriate in most musical situations. Breath releases are more difficult to perform than tongue-cutoffs and are almost entirely dependent upon the performer's ability to control the air. Not maintaining sufficient air up to the point of release often results in untimely and unclean releases. The air should be maintained up to the point of release and then stopped quickly and cleanly. The successful performance of virtually every articulation or articulative style (staccato, legato, marcato, sforzando, accents, etc.) is dependent upon the ability to control air in some way.

CONSIDERATIONS/SUGGESTIONS FOR CONTROL OF AIR AND ARTICULATION

The following considerations/suggestions focus more specifically on developing control of air and articulation.

1. As a rule, maintain a consistent air stream while articulating. Do not let the fact that the tongue is moving affect the overall consistency of the air stream. Maintain a consistent and sufficient air stream during attacks and make necessary adjustments purposefully to enhance the attack in the appropriate manner.

2. Focus attention on the relationship between the tongue and the air stream in the tonguing process. For example, use too much tongue, no tongue, too much air, too little air, and various combinations of these variables, while trying to achieve various kinds of attacks to learn how the tongue and air stream work together. Experimenting in this manner will help develop a greater understanding of how control of the air stream affects articulation.

3. Practice various articulations at a variety of dynamic levels and tempi. Focus attention on how control of the air affects these aspects of performance.

4. Develop control of the air by changing the amount of air used to attack any particular tone. That is, attack one note with a slow air stream and the next note with a much faster air stream. Such exercises will help develop a repertoire of attacks from which to choose, depending on what type of attack is most appropriate for the musical context.

5. Practice releasing tones of varying lengths. For example, deliberately fade on a release instead of sustaining its full value. This exercise emphasizes the importance of maintaining air support during the release process.

6. Maintain an open air column. Breath releases are dependent upon stopping the air, not on closing the throat or changing the embouchure in some way. In essence, the air column is "suspended" rather than "clamped off."

7. Execute breath releases by thinking of "lifting off" of a tone. This type of release is not easy to execute. The suggestions below may facilitate "lifting off" of a tone.

Teaching Tips for Air Control

1. Have students work toward sustaining the air throughout the duration of each tone.

2. Make sure students do not change the focus of the air (and embouchure) when they stop the air. The tendency is to let the air focus fall, which causes the releases to sound dead and abrupt and also causes the pitch to change.

3. Remind students that the flow of air is stopped at the diaphragm, not from the throat and not by changing the embouchure. It is sometimes helpful to think of suspending the air column from the diaphragm as if lightly gasping.

4. Have students think of inhaling slightly on the release. Since inhaling at the point of release is very unnatural, they should not (and probably will not) actually inhale. However, thinking this way helps players stop the flow of air more quickly, maintain a consistent air column, and maintain a consistent embouchure.

Musical Use of Air/Technical Passages

It is not always possible to separate the concept of using air and the concept of controlling air, nor is it always necessary to do so. However, the distinction can be helpful. Musical decisions based on "how" and "when" involve the use of air, whereas executing these decisions involves the control of air. Based on this distinction, players learn how to use air to enhance the ability to play musically and to develop proper breath control.

One of the most common improper uses of air occurs in technical passages. Specifically, players often do not maintain a consistent air stream in technical passages. Inexperienced players may actually change the air stream on virtually every note in a passage. Not maintaining a consistent and steady air stream during technical passages can cause tones to respond poorly or "cut out." In addition, an inconsistent air stream can cause untimely attacks and releases, and coordination problems between fingers, tongue, and air stream (particularly in passages involving skips and leaps). In short, improper use of air during technical passages can greatly inhibit technical fluidity.

Using air inefficiently in technically difficult passages is generally the result of one or more of the following three things: (1) players concentrate so much on fingering the notes that they forget about air; (2) players do not maintain a consistent air stream; and/or (3) players do not focus or direct the air appropriately from one tone to the next. Suggestions/considerations on how to use air appropriately appear in the following list.

1. Associate the use of air with other aspects of wind playing (such as tone quality, pitch, dynamics, attacks, and releases) to best determine the "when" and "how" of air control.
2. Develop good habits regarding proper use of air from the very beginning so that it becomes automatic.
3. Maintain a consistent air stream throughout technical passages, making appropriate adjustments for intervals, dynamics, and so on.
4. Learn the response tendencies of your instrument. Some tones are naturally less responsive than others because of certain acoustical properties of each instrument. Sufficient air and proper focus of air are especially crucial to making "acoustically challenging" notes respond properly.
5. At first, practice technically difficult passages with slurs so that consistency of the air stream can be more easily attained. When the air stream is reasonably consistent, add in articulations.
6. Focus the air in the appropriate direction. Generally, the changes made in the direction or focus of the air stream should be minimal and consistent, unless a passage contains unusually large intervals. The specifics regarding proper focus vary among instruments.

TONE QUALITY

The success of achieving a characteristic tone quality on any instrument is particularly dependent on a player's ability to use air appropriately. General suggestions on how players can use air to affect tone quality are listed separately. See also Tone Quality, page 68

1. Play with a sufficient amount of air. Insufficient air causes a weak, unsupported tone.
2. Maintain a steady air speed in order to maintain a steady tone.
3. Develop control of air speed in all dynamic ranges to help maintain good tone quality. Specifically, maintain adequate air speed in softer dynamic ranges and other contexts when less air volume is typically used.
4. Focus the air stream appropriately throughout the instrument range to maintain a centered tone and to help control the brightness and darkness of the tone quality.
5. Control the focus of the air stream and air speed to control pitch and tone quality.

INTONATION

The success of achieving proper intonation on a particular instrument is largely dependent on a player's ability to use air appropriately. In particular, air speed and air focus are critical to playing with proper intonation. General suggestions and comments regarding breathing and intonation are outlined as follows. See also Intonation, page 41

1. Players must learn the tendencies of their particular instruments. Increasing the air speed on flute, oboe, and bassoon causes them to go sharp, whereas decreasing air speed causes the pitch to go flat. On the other hand, increasing the air speed on clarinet and saxophone causes the pitch to go flat, while decreasing air speed causes the pitch to go sharp.

2. Help players understand the relationship between air and intonation by deliberately increasing or decreasing air speed to accentuate intonation problems.

3. Players should practice long tone crescendi and decrescendi so that they can hear how changes in air speed affect intonation.

4. Once players hear and understand how air speed affects intonation, they can make appropriate changes in air speed and air direction to adjust pitch inaccuracies effectively.

5. Players must understand how to focus the air stream. In general, poor air focus causes pitch inconsistencies throughout the range. Specifically, an uncontrolled air stream typically causes an overall flatness in pitch, and an air stream that is too tight or narrow often causes the pitch to go sharp.

Performing Musically

The process of using air to create a musical performance is a holistic one. It requires using the aspects of breathing discussed above combined with all of the musical knowledge and skills that a musician has acquired through experience and training. The way air is used in a musical performance helps separate a good performance from a great one. The criteria for determining whether or not a musical performance is great are partly subjective, and many musicians would argue that some of these criteria cannot be defined at all. In fact, even the greatest performers are often unaware of the many subtle things they do with air to enhance the musicality of their performances. However, one thing is certain: great performers have superior control over the use of air in all areas of musical performance. This control enables them to incorporate a virtually infinite repertoire of musical effects and subtle shadings into their performances. As a result, players should be encouraged to become very sensitive to how air can be used to affect musicality. This awareness leads to greater musical understanding and improved performances. The following suggestions can be used to improve or enhance players' abilities to perform musically.

1. Practice sustaining phrases indefinitely while changing dynamics at will, or play the same phrase several different ways.
2. Practice releasing one phrase and starting the next phrase, both at the same dynamic level and at distinctly different dynamic levels.
3. Work on easing into entrances smoothly. Practice using light, legato attacks or even breath attacks to develop control over entrances.
4. Practice starting notes in all pitch ranges to determine how much air is required to produce a certain type of attack.
5. Vary the speed and width of the vibrato so that vibrato can be varied appropriately according to style.
6. Incorporate more rubato into phrases. An effective rubato involves using air to sustain, push, or to provide movement to the line.

7. Practice making small adjustments in air speed at various points in each phrase to achieve more subtle dynamic shadings.
8. Practice leaning on certain notes within a phrase or putting more weight on certain notes. Such musical effects require subtle increases in air speed on each note.

Care and Maintenance Accessories: A thorough discussion of care and maintenance considerations for each woodwind instrument can be found in each instrument chapter. Common woodwind instrument accessories are shown in figure 1.3.

Circular Breathing: A technique that enables players to play continuously for an extended period of time without stopping the tone. Circular breathing involves breathing through the nose periodically at the same time that stored air is being forced through the mouth with pressure from the cheeks. Some suggestions for developing circular breathing are listed separately.

Suggestions for Developing Circular Breathing

1. Learn to circular breathe using a straw and a cup of water.
2. Insert the straw into the water, take a breath, and blow air into the water, making the water bubble.
3. Let the cheeks fill with air. Close the throat by raising the tongue, and squeeze the cheeks so that the air in the mouth keeps blowing through the straw. The bubbles will continue.
4. While the cheeks are squeezing the air from the mouth, breathe in through the nose to bring air into the lungs. The cheeks will naturally deflate and return to the normal playing position.
5. Open the throat back up and blow normally.
6. Repeat this cycle indefinitely to maintain air flow.
7. With the instrument, repeat the above process. Although it typically requires more air to start and maintain a tone on an instrument than it does to blow bubbles through a straw, the basic process for circular breathing is the same.
8. Pick a note that responds easily and practice circular breathing on long tones.
9. Squeeze enough air through the cheeks to maintain the tone. Maintaining a steady air stream is the biggest challenge in this process. Circular breathing is generally more difficult on larger

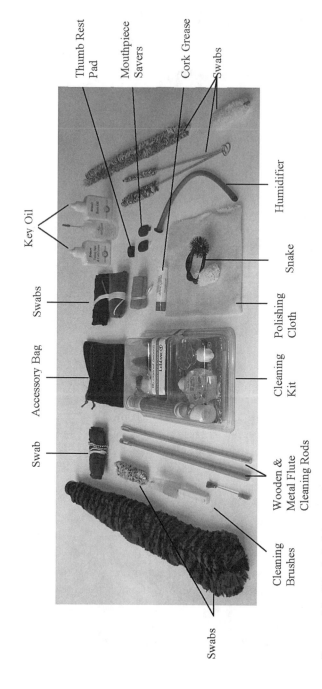

Thumb Rest
Pad

Mouthpiece
Savers

Cork Grease

Swabs

Key Oil

Humidifier

Snake

Swabs

Accessory Bag

Polishing
Cloth

Cleaning
Kit

Swab

Wooden &
Metal Flute
Cleaning Rods

Cleaning
Brushes

Swabs

FIGURE 1.3. *Woodwind Accessories*

instruments because they require more air to maintain a tone. For example, the amount of air required to keep a saxophone reed vibrating is greater than the amount of air required to keep a clarinet reed vibrating.

10. Practice quickly closing the throat, squeezing air from the mouth, and taking in air through the nose. It is important to execute this process quickly because the amount of air in the cheeks is limited. In addition, the transition from blowing normally to squeezing air from the mouth must be quick and efficient or the tone will stop.

11. Think of pushing the air from the back of the throat the moment the throat closes and the air begins to be squeezed from the cheeks.

12. Blow normally until about two-thirds of the air (or slightly more) has been expelled, and then circular-breathe. The cheeks must be able to store enough air to keep the tone going when the throat is closed.

Conical: A term used to describe the cone-shaped tubing often used in instrument construction that is relatively narrow on one end (the mouthpiece or reed end) and gradually widens toward the bell. Most woodwind instruments are conically shaped. One notable exception is the clarinet, which is basically cylindrical. See also Acoustical Basics, page 3; Cylindrical, page 25

Contemporary Techniques: See Extended/Contemporary Techniques, page 29

Cross-Fingering: In general, a specific type of fingering in which several tone holes are closed below the first open tone hole. Cross-fingerings are typically used in the high range of an instrument and are often used in conjunction with an octave key or vent key. Although the primary purpose of most cross-fingerings is to help high notes speak, they also improve tone quality and simplify fingering patterns in technical passages. High C-sharp on bassoon and high D-natural on clarinet are two common examples of cross-fingerings.

Cylindrical: A term used to describe the cylinder-shaped tubing often used in instrument construction. Unlike conical tubing, which is relatively narrow on one end and gradually widens toward the other, cylindrical tubing remains the same diameter along the entire length of tubing. Cylindrical tubes closed at one end are only capable of producing odd-numbered partials in the harmonic series. Most woodwind instruments are conically shaped; however, the clarinet is basically cylindrically shaped. See also Acoustical Basics, page 3; Acoustical Properties, page 81; Conical, page 25

Diaphragm: A thin membrane comprised of muscles and tendons that separates the chest cavity from the abdomen. The diaphragm is vital to the breathing process. At rest, the diaphragm is dome-shaped. As the diaphragm contracts, it moves downward, flattens, and expands, pushing against the abdominal organs. The rib muscles expand outward as the diaphragm contracts. This process reduces air pressure in the lungs, causing air to enter (inhalation). When the diaphragm relaxes, it resumes its original position. This process pushes on the filled air sacs in the lungs, causing exhalation. See also Breathing/Breath Support/Air Control, page 10

Dizziness/Lightheadedness: Dizziness or lightheadedness is common among beginners and is usually caused by an inefficient use of the air stream, poor breathing techniques, and excess air pressure. Dizziness or lightheadedness is common on all woodwind instruments while players are learning to control the air stream and to use air efficiently; however, it is particularly common on flute and oboe. Developing proper breathing and playing techniques, and building endurance through regular practice routines will help players overcome and avoid dizziness. In addition, beginners should take regular breaks while learning proper breathing techniques.

Double-Tonguing: See Multiple-Tonguing, page 52

Dynamic Considerations: On all wind instruments, the ability to play at a variety of dynamic levels is primarily dependent upon a player's ability to control the air stream and embouchure. Both of these factors contribute to playing with and maintaining good tone quality and intonation throughout the dynamic range. Basic dynamic considerations on woodwind instruments are listed as follows. See also Intonation, page 41

1. Maintaining a constant air stream is important at all dynamic levels. Generally, it is easier to maintain a constant air stream at louder dynamic levels and more challenging to maintain a constant air stream at softer dynamic levels. That is, players have a tendency to reduce air speed when reducing air volume. If air speed is reduced too much, tone quality and pitch suffer. A constant air stream is critical to achieving consistent tone quality and pitch throughout a wide dynamic range.

2. Generally, an increase in air speed and air volume is accompanied by an increase in dynamic level, and a decrease in air speed and volume is accompanied by a decrease in dynamic level.

3. At louder dynamic levels, flutes, oboes, and bassoons tend to go sharp. It is important to make slight adjustments in embouchure and/or air focus to compensate for this natural tendency. Relaxing the embouchure, opening the oral cavity, dropping the jaw, increasing the aperture size, and focusing the air steam downward slightly will all lower pitch. Often, these adjustments go hand in hand. That is, relaxing the embouchure automatically causes the jaw to drop, the aperture size to increase, and the air stream to be focused downward. Only slight adjustments are necessary in most cases. Players should maintain embouchure focus and tonal control at all times.

   At louder dynamic levels, clarinets and saxophones tend to go flat. It is important to make slight adjustments in embouchure and/ or air focus to compensate for this natural tendency. Firming the embouchure, raising the jaw, decreasing the size of the aperture and oral cavity, and focusing the air stream upward slightly will all raise pitch. Again, these adjustments often go hand in hand. That is, firming the embouchure automatically causes the jaw to rise, the aperture size to decrease, and the air stream to be focused upward. Only slight adjustments are necessary in most cases. Players should maintain embouchure focus and tonal control at all times.

4. At softer dynamic levels, flutes, oboes, and bassoons tend to go flat. It is important to make slight adjustments in embouchure and/or air focus to compensate for this natural tendency. Firming the embouchure, focusing the oral cavity appropriately, raising the jaw, decreasing size of the aperture and oral cavity, and focusing the air steam upward slightly will all raise pitch. Often, these adjustments go hand in hand. That is, firming the embouchure automatically causes the jaw to rise, the aperture size to decrease, and the air stream to be focused upward. Only slight adjustments are necessary in most cases. Players should maintain embouchure focus and tonal control at all times.

   At softer dynamic levels, clarinets and saxophones tend to go sharp. It is important to make slight adjustments in embouchure and/or air focus to compensate for this natural tendency. Relaxing the embouchure, dropping the jaw, increasing the size of the aperture and oral cavity, and focusing the air steam downward slightly will all lower pitch. Again, these adjustments go hand in hand. That is, relaxing the embouchure automatically causes the jaw to drop, the aperture size to increase, and the air stream to be focused downward. Only slight adjustments are necessary in most cases. Players should maintain embouchure focus and tonal control at all times.

5. When playing very loudly or softly, players sometimes lose embouchure control and tonal focus. In such instances, the tone quality suffers and the pitch actually goes flat. Maintaining proper playing mechanics at all dynamic levels is critical to tonal control and focus.

Endurance/Stamina: The ability to play for extended periods of time without tiring. Virtually every aspect of performance can affect endurance, including: (1) embouchure formation, (2) proper use of air, (3) reed strength (except flute), (4) reed aperture or tip opening (except flute), (5) playing range, (6) dynamic range, (7) head joint and/or lip plate (flute), (8) mouthpiece type/construction (clarinet and saxophone), (9) instrument type/condition, (10) instrument position, (11) posture, (12) musical style, (13) bore size and shape, and (14) performance environment. In addition, because endurance develops over time, pacing of personal practice sessions, ensemble rehearsals, and performances should be an ongoing concern of players and teachers. Although players vary in their innate abilities to play for extended periods of time, endurance can be increased through conscientious practice over time. Suggestions and considerations for improving endurance are listed separately in this section.

Considerations/Suggestions Regarding Endurance and Stamina

1. Warm up properly each day, and warm up with endurance development in mind. Practicing long tones and long tone exercises at all dynamic levels will help players develop endurance.
2. Maintain a relaxed embouchure, and avoid putting excessive pressure on the mouthpiece and/or reed.
3. Start the warm-up in the middle register (where playing is generally most comfortable) and gradually expand the range upward and downward.
4. Rest between exercises when warming up. As a general rule, rest approximately the length of the exercise just played.

5. Incorporate low notes and high notes into the warm-up period to help build endurance and develop range.
6. Gradually extend the length of practice sessions to train the muscles to adjust to extended periods of play without wearing them out or tearing them down unnecessarily.
7. Practice in all ranges, but avoid playing in the high range for extended periods of time. Playing in the high range for extended periods is very demanding on the embouchure muscles and does not simulate normal playing. Almost all pieces require players to play in all ranges, not just the high range. As a result, it is important that players learn to play in the high range "on demand" after not playing in that range for some time.
8. When practicing, take frequent, short breaks rather than rushing from one exercise or solo to the next. However, periodically playing for an extended period of time without a break also helps increase endurance.
9. Practice until moderately tired and then practice a few minutes longer to increase endurance. Practicing when physically exhausted is counterproductive because it often reinforces poor playing habits.

Teaching Tips for Endurance

1. Plan rehearsals so that players get adequate rest and easier playing tasks after rehearsing pieces that are physically demanding.
2. When programming for performances, alternate between easier pieces and more challenging pieces in terms of range and endurance. Many directors place the most challenging pieces in the middle of the program when players are fully warmed up but before they have begun to tire.

Extended/Contemporary Techniques: In general, ways of producing sounds on an instrument that are not traditionally characteristic of the instrument or not typically called for in standard literature. Extended or contemporary techniques are often used to expand, enhance, or otherwise "color" the traditional sounds of an instrument. Less frequently, a composer may require a player to rely solely on extended techniques when performing a particular piece. Woodwind instruments can produce a wide array of unique and interesting sounds that may be called for in contemporary literature. Some of these techniques are easy to master, whereas others are challenging. Some extended techniques for woodwind instruments are described separately here.

Extended/Contemporary Techniques for Woodwind Instruments

1. Using the Mouthpiece (Clarinet and Saxophone) or Reed (Oboe and Bassoon) Alone—Players can produce a variety of sounds/ effects with the mouthpiece or reed alone, including sirens, squawks, glissandos, squeals, crows, and chirps.

2. Using the Head Joint Alone (Flute)—Players can produce a variety of sounds/effects with the head joint alone. For example, placing the palm of the right hand over the end of the head joint lowers the pitch by one octave. In addition, shifting the position of the right-hand index finger inside the end of the head joint enables players to produce a variety of pitches and/or effects including a slide-whistle effect, glissandos, scoops, and falls. Players can produce a variety of sound effects with the head joint by varying air speed and direction, embouchure and lip tension, and tongue action.

3. Singing/Speaking While Playing—By adding vocal sounds to the instrument's sound, a player can add his or her own harmony or pedal tones.

4. Altissimo/Extended Range—Playing in the extreme ranges of the instrument may be used for variety and interest, even though some of these notes do not sound particularly beautiful. Altissimo notes are produced by using special fingerings and/or by altering the embouchure, air, throat, and oral cavity. A detailed discussion of altissimo notes is located under Altissimo/Extended Range in each instrument chapter.

5. Multiphonics—Playing more than one "tone" or frequency at the same time. Multiphonics can be achieved by playing one pitch while singing another. Multiphonics can also be produced by using special fingerings and/or by altering the embouchure, air, throat, and oral cavity.

6. Percussive Techniques—Tapping on, slapping, or otherwise using a woodwind instrument in a percussive manner.

7. Growl—Literally, making a growl sound into the instrument. Growls may be executed while playing pitches, or players may simply make a growling sound into the instrument without pitches being played.

8. Slap Tongue—A tonguing technique that produces a "slapping" or "popping" effect on the attacks. It is produced by pressing the tongue hard against the reed, gum line or roof of the mouth (flute), building up air pressure, and then releasing the tongue quickly.

Another method of producing a slap tongue effect on flute is to close the throat, build up air pressure, and then open the throat quickly.

9. Flutter Tonguing—A technique that involves rolling or fluttering the tongue rapidly while producing a tone. Flutter tonguing uses the same motion of the tongue that is used when pronouncing a rolling "r."

10. Half-Holes—A performance technique that typically involves partially covering a tone hole either directly with one finger (open tone holes) or by depressing a key/pad down about half way (plateau keys). Half-holes enable players to play quarter-tones and other microtones in contemporary literature.

11. Circular Breathing—A technique that enables players to play continuously for an extended period of time without stopping the tone. Circular breathing involves breathing through the nose periodically while stored air is being forced through the mouth with pressure from the cheeks. See also Circular Breathing, page 23

12. Playing while Singing—Most commonly associated with flute playing, a technique that involves humming (with the voice) and playing an instrument at the same time. Players can produce several effects including unisons, intervals, chords (by producing resultant or subjective tones), and other polyphonic effects.

13. Key Clicks—Literally, slapping the keys down without actually playing the instrument. Key clicks can be executed randomly, or players can finger a particular note and slap the keys down without playing that note. A variety of effects can be produced using different fingerings.

14. Tongue Rams—On flute, a technique that involves covering the embouchure hole with the mouth and sealing it with the tongue while tonguing. Tongue rams sound pizzicato-like.

15. Quarter Tones and other Microtones—Tones smaller than a half step. Microtones are normally produced by using special fingerings, making air, embouchure, and oral cavity adjustments, and/or employing half-hole techniques.

16. Airy Tones—On flute, a technique that involves producing airy tones by blowing a diffuse air stream above the embouchure hole.

Players can produce a variety of effects including "hissing" and "whooshing sounds" by altering the air stream.

17. Air Tones—A technique that involves fingering notes and blowing air into an instrument without actually producing tones.

18. Muted Tones—Inserting various objects into an instrument can produce a variety of muting effects. Most "mutes" tend to dampen, muffle, or deaden the tone.

Flutter Tonguing: A technique that involves rolling or fluttering the tongue rapidly while producing a tone. Flutter tonguing uses the same motion of the tongue that is used when pronouncing a rolling "r." Players who cannot roll their tongues may use a throat growl as a substitute.

Fundamental: An acoustical term used to describe the lowest partial or frequency in the harmonic series that can be produced by any particular vibrating system. The fundamental is the lowest note (partial) that can be produced given the length of the instrument's tube. For example, when a flute player fingers and plays a low C (or B-natural if the instrument has a B foot joint), that note is a fundamental. The C-natural (or B-natural) one octave higher than the fundamental is the second partial. Most woodwind instruments use only the first (fundamental) and second partials in the normal playing range; however, because the clarinet overblows the twelfth, it uses predominantly the first and third partials. See also Harmonics, page 32

Harmonics: Acoustically, the term "harmonics" is used to describe all of the tone partials above the fundamental. On woodwind instruments, the term "harmonic" is usually used to describe any pitch that can be produced with the same fingering used to produce the fundamental. The term "harmonic" refers to higher pitches played with fingerings normally used for lower pitches. Based on the harmonic series, it is possible to produce harmonics (or partials) using low-note fingerings on every wind instrument. Players can get higher pitches (harmonics) to speak by increasing air speed, firming the embouchure, and/or taking more reed in the mouth. For example, by fingering low B-flat on saxophone and making adjustments in the areas mentioned above, players can produce a B-flat one octave higher, a top-line F-natural a twelfth higher, a B-flat two octaves higher, and so on. These notes are all part of the harmonic series based on the low B-flat fundamental. Unlike brass instruments, which use several harmonics in the normal playing range, woodwind instruments typically only use the first and second partials (or first and third partials on clarinet because it only produces odd partials). In

FIGURE 1.4. *Harmonic Series on C*

the altissimo range, all of the notes are actually harmonics and not fundamental pitches. Rather than using low-note fingerings for all of these notes, players find certain fingerings that provide the best tonal response and pitch characteristics on their instruments. The harmonic series on C-natural appears in figure 1.4.

Instrument Selection: Choosing an instrument is one of the most important components of success in instrumental performance. The type, quality, and condition of an instrument affect virtually every aspect of wind playing and are critical to the overall success of any playing experience. High-quality instruments and instruments that are in proper working condition can greatly enhance performance, whereas low-quality instruments or instruments in poor condition inhibit performance and foster poor playing habits. Regardless of whether an instrument is student-line, intermediate, or professional, several good options are available. When possible, a teacher's advice can be helpful when selecting an instrument. Several suggestions and considerations for choosing woodwind instruments are listed separately.

General Considerations for All Woodwind Instruments

1. New or Used—New instruments from reputable music stores are typically the safest assurance of getting a quality instrument. Check the warranty and repair policies and the store's policies for trading up to a more advanced instrument. Reputable music stores often carry several used instruments and can accommodate a variety of budgets and playing levels. Players can also buy high-quality used instruments at reasonable prices by shopping other venues, such as consignment stores and the Internet. However, finding a good used instrument can be time-consuming, and the risk of getting an inadequate instrument increases considerably. Being knowledgeable about the instrument is critical to successfully acquiring a good used instrument.

2. Appropriate Instrument for Ability Level—Well-constructed student-line instruments are appropriate for beginners because

they are built for ease of play and durability. In addition, because student-line instruments are designed specifically for younger players, their key mechanisms are often easier to reach and manipulate. As players mature, they outgrow their student-line instruments and should switch to more advanced models. Typically, intermediate instruments are sufficient for most high school players' needs; however, advanced high school players who plan on pursuing a music-related career after high school graduation should consider purchasing professional instruments that will serve their future needs.

Check Overall Instrument Condition

1. Keys and Pads—Look for bent keys and keys that are not covering tone holes properly. Worn pads can be replaced; however, bent key mechanisms, excessive wear and tear, uneven key heights, and poor key alignment are indications that the instrument has not been cared for properly.

2. Rods—Bent rods are sometimes difficult to detect, so check them carefully. The rods should be straight, and the key mechanisms should operate freely. Instruments should be checked carefully for wear or excessive play around posts and pivot screws.

3. Dents and Dings—Check for dents and dings. An instrument that has several dents should be avoided because it indicates that it has not been properly cared for. Dents may also affect tone quality and pitch to varying degrees depending on their location and size.

4. Solder Spots or Other Evidence of Major Repair—An instrument that appears to have been repaired is not necessarily a "bad" instrument; however, the instrument should be checked closely to ensure that the repairs were done properly.

5. Corks and Felts—Excess key noise is often caused by missing corks or felts. Corks and felts can be replaced easily and inexpensively.

6. Plating Condition (Lacquer or Silver)—The amount and condition of the plating is an indication of how much an instrument has been used. A small amount of wear is normal, especially where the hands and fingers make contact with the instrument.

7. Springs—Keys that do not open and close properly, pad cups that remain closed or have little or no tension when keys are depressed,

and/or an uneven "feel" or action overall are indications that the instrument has loose or broken springs. Although replacing loose springs is a simple process, replacing springs and adjusting spring tension should be handled by an experienced repair technician. In addition, if an instrument has several spring-related problems, it often indicates that poor-quality materials were used to construct the instrument.

Play-Test

When acquiring a new or used instrument, the instrument should be play-tested. Play-testing is critical to ensure a good "fit" between the instrument and player. Student-line instruments are not typically play-tested before beginners rent or buy them; however, a knowledgeable teacher or player can and should play-test each instrument before it is rented or purchased.

1. When possible, take an experienced player or teacher with you when play-testing an instrument. Another listener can be very helpful when that person is knowledgeable about the instrument being tested.
2. Take a tuner to check pitches throughout the instrument's range. Check pitches initially and as the instrument warms up over time. Make the tuner an integral part of the entire play-test.
3. Take familiar music to the play-test. Include slow, lyrical selections and fast, technical selections. In addition, include different styles of music.
4. If possible, play-test several instruments and compare them. After selecting a particular make and model, play several instruments and select the best one.
5. First impressions are important; however, impressions formed over a longer period of time are generally more reliable.
6. Saxophone and Clarinet—When possible, use several familiar mouthpieces and reeds so that valid comparisons can be made regarding the instruments being tested. An instrument may play much better with one mouthpiece than it does with another. Avoid trying too much new equipment at once. It is generally a good idea to play-test new instruments and new mouthpieces separately.
7. Bassoon and English Horn—When possible, take several bocals and reeds so that valid comparisons can be made regarding the instruments being tested. An instrument may play much better with one bocal/reed combination than it does with another.

Flute Specific Considerations

1. Instrument Key—With the exception of some older flutes, flutes today are pitched in C.
2. Head Joint Cork—The head joint cork should fit snugly in the head joint, yet it should be relatively easy to adjust. If the head joint cork is too loose, it will move on its own during normal play, negatively affecting intonation and response. The open end of the head joint is particularly susceptible to dents, so check it carefully.

Flute Extras

Intermediate and professional flutes are generally (but not always) open-hole models, and they are generally made with higher quality materials than student-line flutes. In addition, intermediate and professional flutes are typically equipped with more features or optional key work than student-line flutes. Optional equipment available on intermediate and professional flutes is listed separately.

1. Open hole, French model Key Design
2. French pointed arms
3. White gold springs
4. B foot joint
5. High-C facilitator ("Gizmo" key)
6. Split-E mechanism
7. Soldered tone holes
8. In-line G key
9. Precious metals (silver, gold, platinum)

Clarinet Specific Considerations

1. Instrument Key—Soprano clarinets are available in several keys, most commonly B-flat and A. Choose a clarinet in the key that is appropriate for the musical context for which it will be used. For the overwhelming majority of players in school instrumental programs, the B-flat clarinet is the appropriate choice.

2. Condition of Wood or Plastic—Clarinets are prone to cracking, especially wooden clarinets. Check carefully for new cracks and for cracks that have been repaired. Although cracks can be repaired successfully in some instances, it is best not to purchase an instrument that has been cracked.

Clarinet Extras

Intermediate and professional clarinets are generally (but not always) made of high-density wood, and they are generally made with higher quality materials than are student-line clarinets. In addition, intermediate and professional clarinets are typically equipped with more features or optional key work than student-line clarinets. Optional equipment typically available on intermediate and professional clarinets is listed separately.

1. Silver or silver-plated keys
2. Polycylindrical bore
3. Double skin or Gore-tex pads
4. High-density wood (typically grenadilla)
5. Undercut tone holes
6. Offset trill keys
7. Auxiliary A-flat to E-flat key
8. Adjustable thumb rest
9. Adjustable bridge mechanism
10. Blue steel springs

Oboe Specific Considerations

1. Instrument Key—Oboes are pitched in C. English horns are pitched in F.
2. Condition of Wood or Plastic—Oboes are prone to cracking, especially wooden oboes. Check carefully for new cracks and for cracks that have been repaired. Although some cracks can be repaired successfully, it is best not to purchase an instrument that has been cracked.

Oboe Extras

Intermediate and professional oboes are generally (but not always) made of high-density wood, and they are generally made with higher quality materials than student-line oboes. In addition, intermediate and professional oboes are typically equipped with more features than student-line oboes. Consider the key work and features of each instrument carefully because instruments in the same price range may be very differently equipped. Optional equipment typically available on intermediate and professional oboes is listed separately.

1. High-density wood (typically grenadilla)
2. Modified or Simplified Conservatory (some extra key work)

3. Full Conservatory (full complement of key work)
4. Silver-plated or silver keys
5. Silver or gold posts
6. Philadelphia D key
7. Third octave key
8. Split D ring
9. Metal-lined tenons
10. Blue steel springs

Saxophone Specific Considerations

1. Instrument Key—Virtually all saxophones are in the key of E-flat (alto and baritone) or B-flat (soprano and tenor). Some older instruments that look like small tenor saxophones may actually be C melody saxophones.

2. Lacquer Condition—The amount and condition of the lacquer on a used saxophone can be an indication of the amount of wear and tear on the instrument. Most often, saxophones will have worn lacquer where the fingers contact the instrument. In addition, scratches are common around the neck strap ring and below the thumb rest where belt buckles, buttons, and so on rub against the finish.

3. Neck—The neck should fit comfortably and snugly in the body of the instrument, and it should not move from side to side when the screw is tightened. The rod that extends from the body and slides under the octave key mechanism on the neck is susceptible to damage. Pressing the octave key should operate the key mechanism freely, and the octave key pad should cover the vent hole properly.

Saxophone Extras

Intermediate and professional saxophones are generally (but not always) made of high-quality brass, and they are generally made with higher quality materials than student-line instruments. In addition, intermediate and professional saxophones are typically equipped with more features than student-line saxophones. Optional equipment typically available on intermediate and professional saxophones is listed as follows.

1. High F-sharp key
2. Low A key (baritone)

3. Tilted spatula keys
4. Rolled tone holes
5. Custom lacquer
6. Engraving

Bassoon Specific Considerations

1. Instrument Key—Bassoons are pitched in C. Contrabassoons are pitched in C and sound one octave lower than the bassoon.
2. Condition of Wood or Plastic—Bassoons are prone to cracking, especially wooden bassoons. Check carefully for new cracks and for cracks that have been repaired. Although cracks can be repaired successfully in some instances, it is best not to purchase an instrument that has been cracked.

BASSOON EXTRAS

Intermediate and professional bassoons are generally (but not always) made of high-density wood, and they are generally made with higher quality materials than student-line bassoons. In addition, intermediate and professional bassoons are typically equipped with more features than student-line bassoons. Optional equipment typically available on intermediate and professional bassoons is listed as follows.

1. Lined tone holes
2. Whisper key locks (right- and left-hand)
3. Whisper key mechanism
4. Extra keys (automatic G ring key; A-flat/B-flat trill key on boot joint; E/F-sharp trill key; High D, E, and F keys)
5. Silver-plated keys
6. Extra rollers
7. Lined boot joint

Instrument Stands: In general, stands used to hold instruments that are assembled but not being played. Several styles of stands are available for woodwind instruments. Most flute, clarinet, and oboe stands consist of a simple peg or cone over which the instrument can be placed, holding it securely in an upright position. The peg or cone is fitted onto a base (with or without legs), which sits on the floor. Bases are available with several pegs to hold more than one instrument. Most bassoon stands consist of a U-shaped arm that cradles the body of the bassoon above the butt joint and a cuplike arm that cradles the bottom of the butt joint, holding the bassoon securely in an angled upright position. Some stands are designed to enable players to play the bassoon without having to support the weight of the instrument with a seat strap or neck strap. Such stands are relatively uncommon for bassoon. However, because contrabassoons are so large and heavy, instrument stands that support the weight of the instrument are essential for young players. Most saxophone stands are designed with two U-shaped arms that cradle the top of the bell below the flare and the bottom of the bell above the crook, holding the instrument securely in an upright position. Instrument stands are often used when a player is doubling on more than one instrument and switching instruments during performance. In addition, there are stands available for the baritone (and bass) saxophone that hold the instrument in playing position, enabling players to play the instrument without having to support the weight of the instrument with a neck strap. These stands can be helpful, especially to young players. Various types of instrument stands are shown in figure 1.5.

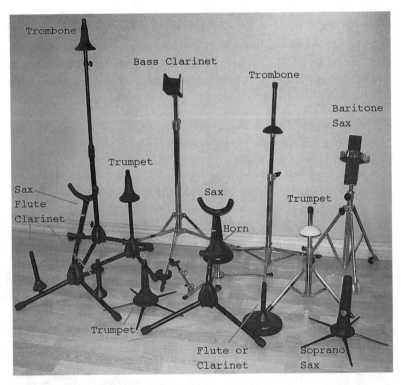

FIGURE 1.5. *Instrument Stands*

Instrument stands are often used when a player is doubling on more than one instrument and switching instruments during performance. Advanced players also use instrument stands to hold their instruments during short breaks between extended practice sessions. Setting an instrument in a stand is preferable to laying the instrument down on a chair or standing it upright on the bell without a stand. Although generally safe to use, instrument stands can be knocked or pushed over easily, which can cause damage to the instrument, so care must be taken when using them.

Intonation: Generally, the ability to play in tune in a melodic and harmonic context. In ensemble playing, the most important factors in achieving intonation accuracy are the aural skills to hear beats or roughness, and the physical skills to make appropriate adjustments. The sections below can help players (1) understand the factors that affect intonation, (2) learn the pitch tendencies of their instruments, and (3) learn how to adjust pitch. The specific pitch tendencies of each instrument are provided in each instrument chapter under Intonation. General factors/considerations that affect all woodwind instruments are described separately in this section.

General Factors/Considerations That Affect Intonation

1. Tuning—It is absolutely crucial to warm up the instrument thoroughly before tuning. Tuning before the instrument is properly warmed up is one of the most common causes of poor intonation. Tuning procedures for each instrument are located in their respective chapters.

2. Tone Production—Playing with proper intonation is directly linked to good tone production. That is, a player with a strong air stream, proper air support, and a good embouchure is likely to play with proper intonation. Conversely, a player with a weak air stream, poor air support, and a poor embouchure is likely to play with poor intonation. A detailed discussion of tone production is under Tone Production in each instrument chapter.

3. Instrument Design—All instruments will have mechanical flaws that prevent them being capable of "perfect" intonation. That is, acoustically perfect wind instruments do not exist; however, some instruments have inherently better intonation than others. In addition, pitch tendencies are frequently inconsistent from one

instrument to the next. As a result, players must learn the pitch tendencies of each instrument they play.

4. Mouthpieces—Mouthpieces affect intonation to a marked degree. For example, mouthpieces with high baffles tend to play sharper and are more inconsistent than mouthpieces with low or medium baffles. A detailed discussion of mouthpiece characteristics is under Mouthpiece/Mouthpieces in this chapter.

5. Reeds—Reeds affect intonation to a marked degree. For example, hard reeds (double and single) tend to play sharper than soft reeds. A detailed discussion of reeds is under Reeds, Single in chapter 3.

6. Temperature—The pitch of woodwind instruments goes sharper as the temperature of the air column and surrounding air rises and goes flatter as the temperature of the air column and surrounding air falls. Blowing warm air into instruments during long rest periods can help minimize pitch variations; however, slight adjustments are usually necessary to compensate for pitch changes that occur during rehearsals and performances. In addition, changes in pitch that result from changes in temperature are not consistent across all woodwind instruments. Larger instruments change pitch at different rates of speed and to different degrees than smaller instruments. A summary of these differences appears as follows.

   A. The relationship between instrument size and the degree of pitch deviation is directly proportional. As a result, larger woodwind instruments (e.g., saxophone or bassoon) will ultimately go sharper than smaller instruments (e.g., clarinet or flute) will as they warm up over time. In other words, by the end of a one-hour rehearsal, if the instruments were not warmed-up and tuned properly before rehearsing, the saxophone will have gone sharper than the clarinet.

   B. The relationship between instrument size and the speed at which instruments warm up and go sharp is directly proportional. For example, flutes warm up and go sharp faster than clarinets, and clarinets warm up and go sharp faster than saxophones.

   C. The relationship between instrument size and the speed at which instruments cool down is also directly proportional. That is, instruments that warm up quickly also cool down quickly, and instruments that warm up slowly take longer to cool down.

Key Questions

Q: Should students work on intonation or tone quality first?

A: Tone quality. Developing a good, consistent tone quality first will minimize the adjustments players will have to make later on. Adjustments will then be made primarily because of problems inherent in their instruments and in the equal tempered scale, and not because of player-created problems. In short, although achieving good tone quality necessarily promotes better intonation, achieving better intonation does not necessarily promote better tone quality.

Q: Are all instruments out of tune? Why is it necessary to adjust pitch?

A: Yes, all instruments are out of tune. Due to the complexity of musical harmony and the infinite number of tone combinations, it is impossible to perform without the presence of beats except in the simplest harmonies. To produce beatless harmony, intervals must correspond to simple, whole-number frequency ratios (e.g., 1:2, 2:3, 3:4 etc.); that is, they must align mathematically. The equal temperament tuning system, which is the tuning system used predominantly in Western music, is not based on whole-number ratios; however, the just intonation tuning system is. In practical terms, the result of using a "just" scale is playing in tune, without beats. Although this seems ideal, just intonation is only possible for the simplest pieces in one key; it does not permit free modulation to all other keys. Maintaining whole-number frequency ratios on every scale degree in all keys would require instruments to play over seventy different pitches per octave to accommodate the various harmonic possibilities. As a result, just intonation is not a practical tuning system.

Equal temperament does not maintain whole-number ratios throughout the scale. Instead, it is a compromise system that divides the octave into twelve equal semitones of 100 cents. Equal temperament facilitates modulation to all keys while maintaining a reasonable sense of "in-tune-ness." However, as might be expected, everything is out of tune just a little. The problems caused by using equal temperament are because it does not account for true mathematical relationships between certain intervals.

Considerations regarding temperament and tuning make it impossible to construct the "perfect" instrument. As a result, slight adjustments are necessary throughout the playing range based on musical contexts if an acceptable level of intonation is to be maintained.

Teaching Tips for Improving Intonation

Basic Objectives—Students Should Strive to:

1. produce a good, consistent tone quality,
2. hold a steady tone over several counts,
3. hear beats when they are present,
4. adjust or "humor" pitches to eliminate beats,
5. become aware of inherent problems with their instruments, and
6. anticipate potential pitch problems and hear pitches in their heads before playing.

Eliminating Beats

1. Arrange a demonstration so that students can learn to hear the beats.
2. Use two like instruments at first and play unisons.
3. Let one player's tone serve as a guide tone while the other player makes adjustments to eliminate the beats.
4. If a player hears the beats but does not know which direction to go to eliminate the beats, tell him or her to guess. If the beats get slower, he or she is moving in the right direction. If the beats get faster, he or she is going in the wrong direction.
5. Have one player adjust pitch slowly in both directions against a steady tone to alter the speed of the beats intentionally.
6. Once players can eliminate beats in unisons, work with octaves, fifths, fourths, and thirds. Later, practice eliminating beats in simple chords.
7. Work on eliminating beats using unlike instruments.
8. Practice eliminating beats in small ensemble settings starting with trios and moving to quartets, quintets and so on. Generally, small ensembles are more effective than large ensembles for improving intonation accuracy.

Exercises to Help Develop Better Intonation

1. Work with a tuner. Players can practice playing long tones while watching a tuner to help develop tonal consistency and pitch accuracy. To check development of pitch accuracy, regularly have students turn away from the tuner (or close their eyes), play a pitch, and then check the tuner to see how closely they have matched the reference tone.

2. Play "I play/You play" games. Practicing matching pitches with a variety of instruments provides excellent ear-training.
3. Have students sing pitches before playing them. This technique helps students hear pitches in their heads before playing them.
4. Play a pitch and have students sing a particular interval above or below the pitch you play; then have them play the pitch they sang on their instruments.
5. Repeat attacks and releases with space in between to develop muscular and tonal accuracy and consistency.
6. Have students keep notebooks on intonation problems and solutions for their particular instruments. These notebooks should include such information as:
   A. how to tune their instruments,
   B. how to adjust pitch,
   C. what pitches tend to be out of tune on their instruments, and
   D. how dynamics affect intonation.

Key/Pad Height: The distance between the keys/pads and the tone holes. Key/pad height affects both tone quality and intonation. The key/pad height in the main key stack should be consistent throughout the instrument. Uneven key/pad height causes problems with action, intonation, and response. In addition, if keys/pads are too close to the tone holes, the pitch will be flat and the tone will be muffled. If the keys/pads are too far from the tone holes, the pitch tends to be sharp and the tone tends to be bright and uncentered. In general, key/pad height should be adjusted by an experienced repair technician.

Mouthpiece/Mouthpieces: Saxophone and clarinet mouthpieces are designed to facilitate reed vibration in such a way that the vibration may be controlled by the embouchure and by the air flow to produce a characteristic tone quality and the proper pitch. Players insert the mouthpiece in the mouth, form a basic embouchure, and blow air into the tip opening and around the reed. The air causes the reed to vibrate, which sets the air column inside the instrument in vibration. A woodwind mouthpiece consists of several components. The shape, size, and dimensions of these components and the materials from which a mouthpiece is made all significantly affect tonal and response characteristics. A woodwind mouthpiece consists of several components. These components are described separately below and are shown in figures 1.6 and 1.7. A comparison of saxophone and clarinet mouthpieces and reeds is shown in figure 1.8.

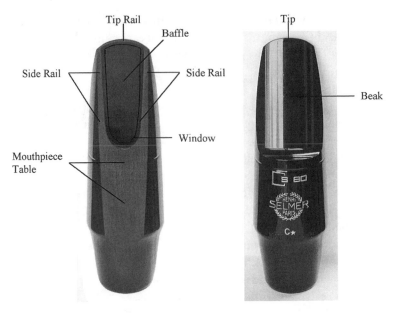

FIGURE 1.6. *Parts of a Saxophone Mouthpiece*

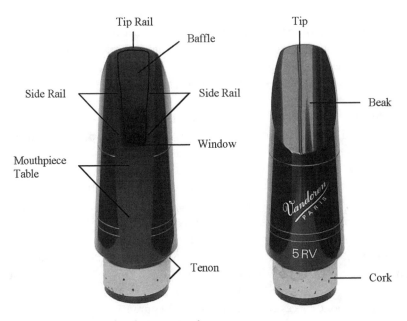

FIGURE 1.7. *Parts of a Clarinet Mouthpiece*

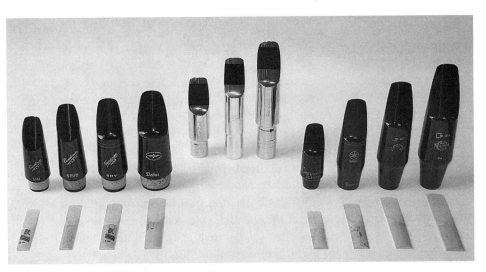

FIGURE 1.8. *Comparison of Mouthpieces and Reeds (Left to Right): E-flat Soprano Clarinet, B-flat Soprano Clarinet, Alto Clarinet, Bass Clarinet, Alto Saxophone (Metal), Tenor Saxophone (Metal), Baritone Saxophone (Metal), Soprano Saxophone, Alto Saxophone, Tenor Saxophone, and Baritone Saxophone*

Mouthpiece Components/Considerations

1. Baffle—The part of a mouthpiece opposite the mouthpiece window, or the underneath side (inside, top) of a mouthpiece. The baffle greatly affects tone quality. High baffles reduce the size of the chamber and leave less space between the reed and the mouthpiece than low baffles, which causes less resistance. As a result, mouthpieces with high baffles tend to have a brighter, "edgier" sound and better projection than mouthpieces with low baffles. Conversely, low baffles increase the size of the chamber and leave more space between the reed and the mouthpiece than high baffles, which causes more resistance. As a result, mouthpieces with low baffles tend to have a darker, mellower sound and less projection than mouthpieces with high baffles. Many mouthpieces designed for jazz playing have high baffles, while most mouthpieces designed for classical playing have relatively low baffles.

2. Beak—The outside top part of the mouthpiece that slants downward toward the tip. The top teeth rest on the beak.

3. Bore/Throat—A term used to describe the part of a mouthpiece that fits over the neck cork (saxophone) or into the barrel joint

(clarinet) and runs into the mouthpiece chamber. Bore is a term more commonly associated with brass mouthpieces. Most woodwind players refer to this area as the throat.

4. Chamber—The inside of a mouthpiece where the tone resonates. The chamber generally refers to the most open portion of the mouthpiece opposite the mouthpiece table window. As a rule, the bigger or more open the chamber is, the darker the tone will be and the more resistance the mouthpiece will have. Mouthpieces with small chambers have less resistance and often produce tones that are bright, small, thin, and edgy. In addition, small chambers limit dynamic contrast and tonal control. Finally, the shape of the chamber's sidewalls also affects tone. Generally, mouthpieces with straight side walls are brighter, whereas mouthpieces with curved side walls are darker. A variety of mouthpiece chambers and chamber/throat windows is shown in figure 1.9.

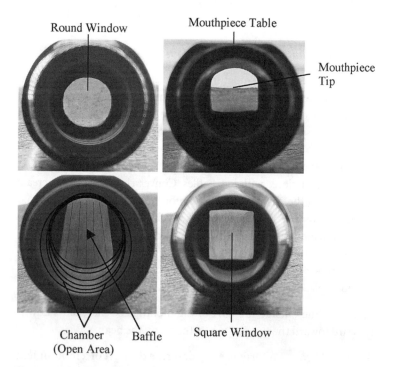

FIGURE 1.9. *Comparison of Mouthpiece Throats and Chambers*

5. Cork (Clarinet)—On clarinet, the mouthpiece tenon, which is inserted into the barrel joint, is covered with cork. This cork helps ensure a snug and secure fit and an airtight seal between joints.

6. Facing/Lay—A term used to describe the amount of bend, curve, or slope of a mouthpiece table toward the tip of the mouthpiece. The facing (also called the lay) refers to both the length of the bend (measured from the point the mouthpiece table starts to bend to the tip) and the steepness of the slope. The facing determines the size of the tip opening. Facings vary greatly; however, they are almost always categorized as "short," "medium," or "long." Most players prefer mouthpieces with medium facings. Generally, short-lay mouthpieces do not provide enough resistance for experienced players, and they tend to have small tip openings, resulting in a smaller dynamic range, less tonal control, and poor intonation. Long-lay mouthpieces often provide too much resistance, and they tend to have large tip openings, which usually necessitates the use of softer reeds. Unless the embouchure is well developed, controlling the tone quality and intonation of a long-lay mouthpiece is difficult. In addition, long-lay mouthpieces are very unforgiving with reeds that warp in dry climates, resulting in a variety of response problems and squeaks. A comparison of mouthpiece facings is shown in figure 1.10.

7. Rails/Side Rails—The two edges along the sides of the mouthpiece table that extend from the bottom of the mouthpiece window to the tip rail. The side rails should have even, uniform dimensions

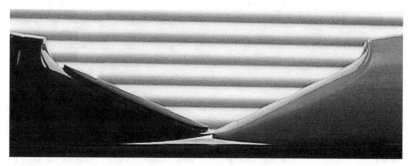

FIGURE 1.10. *Comparison of Mouthpiece Facings (Lays)*

and should be free from nicks and scrapes. Damaged side rails make the tone difficult to control and often cause squeaking and poor tone quality.

8. Table—The flat underside of a mouthpiece on which the reed lies. It is imperative that the mouthpiece table be flat and smooth. A warped and/or damaged table makes the tone difficult to control and often causes squeaking.

9. Tip Opening—The opening between the tip of the reed and the mouthpiece tip rail. The tip opening is a significant factor in determining the amount of resistance a mouthpiece will offer and the type of tone produced on an instrument. As a rule, a wider tip opening increases the amount of resistance the mouthpiece/reed combination will have and increases the potential for a full tone. Conversely, a narrower tip opening lessens the amount of resistance a mouthpiece/reed combination will have and reduces the potential for a full tone.

10. Tip Rail—The narrow flat area at the end of the mouthpiece table. The tip rail should be smooth and flat, and it should be free from nicks and scrapes. Damaged tip rails make the tone difficult to control and often cause squeaking and poor tone quality because the reed is unable to close properly against the mouthpiece. Tip rails that are too wide produce a dead tone with little flexibility. Tip rails that are too narrow or uneven tend to be bright and inconsistent and are more likely to squeak.

11. Window/Table Opening—The open area of a mouthpiece cut out of the mouthpiece table and opposite the baffle. The flat side of the reed covers the window. The term "window" is also occasionally used to refer to the opening between the throat and the chamber.

General Considerations for Selecting a Mouthpiece

The size and shape of each mouthpiece component greatly affect tonal and response characteristics. Mouthpieces vary considerably in materials, construction, and design. As a result, making hard-and-fast rules about mouthpieces is tenuous. Nonetheless, the following general statements and considerations may help with mouthpiece selection.

1. Good mouthpieces should respond freely throughout the range, and enable players to produce a full, warm, characteristic tone quality, and facilitate proper intonation.
2. Good mouthpieces are not prone to squeaking. That is, most good reeds will respond properly on a good mouthpiece.
3. Mouthpieces should feel comfortable inside the mouth to aid tone production and to avoid player fatigue. Mouthpieces should offer some resistance, but not so much that it forces players to bite or otherwise strain the embouchure.

MATERIAL CONSIDERATIONS

Several materials are commonly used to make mouthpieces. The material from which a mouthpiece is made greatly affects tonal and response characteristics; however, it is difficult to make generalizations about those characteristics based solely on material. For example, a metal mouthpiece may have a bright sound or a dark sound depending on a variety of factors, including the shape and size of the chamber, facing, baffle, and tip opening. The most common materials used for clarinet and saxophone mouthpieces are discussed in the next section.

1. Hard Rubber—Hard rubber is the most popular material for both clarinet and saxophone mouthpieces. Its overall resonance, feel, and response are excellent. In addition, hard rubber is fairly stable and not as susceptible to warping or wearing as plastic or wood. However, hard rubber can be brittle and is prone to cracking or breaking if dropped or hit, especially in cold weather. In addition, hard rubber tends to discolor over time. It also discolors when exposed to certain soap chemicals or when it is washed with hot water. Although this discoloration is unsightly, discoloration alone does not affect a mouthpiece's overall response and tone.

2. Plastic/Acrylic—Plastic/acrylic is most commonly used in student-line mouthpieces. Plastic is prone to warping and wearing and is not a good choice for intermediate or advanced players. Generally, plastic mouthpieces do not produce the warm, rich, full tone quality that hard rubber mouthpieces do; however, plastic mouthpieces are very affordable and quite durable, although they may chip or break if dropped or hit.

3. Metal—Metal (most commonly brass with gold or silver plating) is used extensively for saxophone mouthpieces, but much less

for clarinet mouthpieces. Generally, metal mouthpieces produce a brighter, more piercing tone quality than rubber mouthpieces and are common in jazz settings. Metal mouthpieces are generally smaller in circumference than hard rubber mouthpieces. As a result, metal mouthpieces often feel different in the mouth than rubber or plastic mouthpieces. Alto saxophone players doubling on tenor or baritone often prefer metal mouthpieces because their smaller size feels more comfortable inside the mouth. Metal mouthpieces are more durable and stable overall than other mouthpieces; however, they may still be scratched or damaged if they are not cared for properly. In addition, metal mouthpieces are generally more expensive than plastic or hard rubber mouthpieces.

4. Crystal—Crystal is used primarily for clarinet mouthpieces. Crystal is a very stable material, and the mouthpiece will not warp or wear; however, it is also very brittle and easily damaged.

5. Wood—Mouthpieces were originally made of wood, particularly clarinet mouthpieces. Although wood mouthpieces often have a warm tone, they do not project very well. Wooden mouthpieces are still available for clarinet today, but they are a specialty item.

Multiple-Tonguing: A type of tonguing that involves using multiple-syllabic patterns to tongue rapidly. That is, instead of using a single "tu" or "du" syllable when tonguing, players will use two or more syllables in specific patterns. The two types of multiple-tonguing are discussed in the next section.

Double-Tonguing and Triple-Tonguing

The most common syllable patterns used to double-tongue are "tu-ku" or "du-gu." The most common syllable patterns used to triple-tongue are "tu-tu-ku" and its counterpart "du-du-gu," or "tu-ku-tu" and its counterpart "du-gu-du." The choice of which syllable pattern to use is largely dependent upon which pattern works best for a particular student.

Some players believe that the "gu" syllable is pronounced farther forward in the mouth than the "ku" syllable, which improves tonal response, so they prefer the "du-gu" pattern to the "tu-ku" pattern. Players who learn to double-tongue using a "tu-ku" or "du-gu" pattern may find it advantageous to continue the basic double-tonguing pattern when triple-tonguing. As a result, they triple-tongue using a "tu-ku-tu" "ku-tu-ku" or "du-gu-du" "gu-du-gu" pattern even

FIGURE 1.11. *Double-Tonguing Patterns*

FIGURE 1.12. *Triple-Tonguing Patterns*

though it causes a "ku" or "gu" syllable to occur on the first note of every other triple note group. Common patterns for double- and triple-tonguing are shown in figures 1.11 and 1.12.

Multiple-tonguing is not common on woodwind instruments, except for flute; however, some clarinet players use multiple-tonguing regularly. It can make faster tongued passages easier and cleaner when well executed. Players are encouraged to develop good single-tonguing technique before working on double- or triple-tonguing. The primary challenges with multiple-tonguing are: (1) making the secondary syllable ("ku" or "gu") sound clear and distinct, and (2) coordinating the fingers with the tongue in technical passages. Suggestions for developing double- and triple-tonguing are listed in this section.

Suggestions for Learning to Multiple-Tongue

1. When first learning to double-tongue or triple-tongue, say or speak the appropriate pattern without the instrument. For example, if learning to triple-tongue, practice saying one of the triple patterns (whichever is easiest to repeat) mentioned above.

2. Keep the "gu" syllable forward in the mouth and use minimal tongue motion. Because the "gu" syllable is generally less responsive and softer than the "du" syllable, players need to articulate the "gu" syllable with greater emphasis so that the tonguing sounds even. Use plenty of air, work for evenness of response, and do not move the jaw.

3. Practice repeating the "gu" syllable several times in succession to develop a "feel" for it.

4. Still without the instrument, form a basic embouchure and blow air as if playing the instrument and "articulate" the air with the

"du-gu" (double-tonguing) or the "du-du-gu" or "du-gu-du" (triple-tonguing) syllables. Practice without the instrument until control is gained.

5. With the instrument, practice double-tonguing (or triple-tonguing) on one pitch in a comfortable range. Do not practice multiple-tonguing in a melodic context. While learning to multiple-tongue, practice repeating the duple (or triple) pattern on one pitch. Later, switch to another pitch, but keep practicing the pattern on only that pitch.

6. Alternate one or two duple (or triple) patterns with eighth-notes or quarter-notes as shown in the following examples.

7. Gradually build endurance on one note until it is comfortable to play at least one full measure of sixteenth-note duples (or triples) in common time.

8. As endurance is gained, change notes for each measure and gradually extend the range outward (both up and down) from the original pitch until control is gained throughout the range.

Key Questions

Q: Do high school players need to know how to multiple-tongue?

A: Probably. Some advanced solo and some large ensemble pieces contain very rapid sixteenth-note passages that cannot be single-tongued. In such instances, the ability to double-tongue is essential. However, multiple-tonguing is not a substitute for good single-tonguing, and for most of the ensemble literature players should not need to tongue faster than they can single-tongue.

Q: When is it appropriate to use multiple-tonguing?

A: Ideally, players would be able to single-tongue as fast as or faster than their slowest multiple-tongue speed, so that musical context would dictate which tonguing technique to use. However, the reality is that many players have a gap between their fastest comfortable single-tongue speed and their slowest comfortable multiple-tongue speed. When musical passages require tonguing speeds in this gap, players should develop their single-tongue speed in most instances.

Q: What is a good single-tongue speed for junior high and senior high school players?

A: The answer to this question is somewhat subjective; however, experience has shown that a reasonable goal for junior high players is to tongue sixteenth-note repeated patterns between mm100 and mm120. High school players should be able to tongue sixteenth-note repeated patterns between mm120 and mm144. Generally, professional players can single-tongue sixteenth notes between mm160 and mm168.

Overblow: An acoustical term used to describe the physical act or process of producing higher partials on an instrument by increasing air speed and wind pressure and/or by opening and closing strategically placed vent holes/keys on the instrument's tube. On brass instruments, overblowing simply refers to playing a pitch other than the fundamental, and it is not uncommon for brass instruments to produce several partials or pitches using only one fingering or slide position (trombone). Most woodwind instruments overblow at the octave. That is, the same basic fingerings used for the lower pitches can also be used to produce pitches one octave higher. Oboe, saxophone, and bassoon players use octave keys or vent keys to facilitate this process, and flute players rely on changes in embouchure, air speed, and focus to overblow the octave. The clarinet is unique in that it overblows a twelfth. That is, when a player uses the same basic fingering and depresses the register key, the pitch will jump a twelfth higher rather than an octave higher. "Overblow" is also a term used to describe the act of blowing too hard into an instrument, resulting in a raucous tone that lacks focus.

Overtones: A common but somewhat outdated term for the tones that sound above the fundamental in a complex tone. The terms overtones, harmonics, and partials are all used to describe components of a complex tone and are often incorrectly used interchangeably. Overtones only include the upper partials of a complex tone, not the fundamental. Partials, on the other hand, refer to any part of a complex tone including the fundamental. Harmonics refer to any partial of a complex tone whose frequency is an integral multiple of the fundamental frequency. See also Acoustical Basics, page 3; Harmonics, page 32

Pads: The soft material in the key cups that provides the seal on the tone hole. Generally, pads consist of the following components: (1) the backing, (2) the padding material, (3) the skin, and, on larger pads, (4) a resonator. The thickness of the skin, the surface finish, and how porous the skin is all affect the quality of the seal. The felt of the pad is typically either woven or needle felt. The thickness of the pad should conform to the height and depth of the key cup. The card or backing adds stiffness to the pad; however, because some tone holes may not be perfectly flat (especially on bassoon), the pad backing must be a flexible material, such as cork. Resonators also affect tone. Metal resonators, such as those found on some saxophone pads, produce a brighter tone than plastic resonators. Perhaps the most important aspect of pads is proper installation and fit. If pads are installed and adjusted so that they seal the tone hole properly, the instrument will play as it was designed to (assuming all other mechanicals are in proper working order).

Pitch Tendencies: Generally, the tendency for any note to deviate from a specified standard, usually the equal tempered scale based on a reference frequency of A = 440. That is, when players talk about the pitch tendencies of their instruments, they are almost always talking about how sharp or flat certain notes are relative to an equal tempered scale. The term "pitch tendency" is most commonly used to refer to pitch deviations that are an inherent part of an instrument's design. In many instances, pitch tendencies are consistent on a given instrument regardless of the make or model of the instrument. For example, most flutes are sharp on third-space C-sharp and most saxophones are sharp on fourth-line D-natural. The pitch tendencies of each woodwind instrument are under Intonation in each instrument chapter. See also Intonation, page 41; Temperament, page 61

Plateau Model/System: A key design system that uses covered tone holes rather than open tone holes. That is, rather than the tone holes being covered completely by the fingers alone, tone holes are covered by pads. In some plateau key designs, the fingers must cover vent holes in the pad cups even though pads cover some or most of the tone holes. Oboes and flutes are often designed with these open-hole key mechanisms. Because the tone holes on saxophone are so large, they are built entirely on the plateau system. That is, every tone hole is covered completely by a pad.

Releases/Cutoffs: The ways a tone can be stopped. There are two basic ways to release or stop a tone: (1) a breath release, where the player stops the air, and (2) a tongue cutoff, where the player touches the tongue against the reed (clarinet, saxophone, oboe, and bassoon) or the gum line (flute). In most musical contexts, breath releases are more appropriate than tongue cutoffs; however, breath releases are more difficult to execute than tongue cutoffs because they require the player to precisely control the air stream. During a breath release, the air is stopped quickly and precisely to produce consistent, clean releases. Proper air speed and support must be maintained up to the point of release to avoid untimely and unclean releases. In contrast, tongue cutoffs require simply placing the tongue on the reed or the gum line to stop the air. While easier to execute than breath releases, tongue cutoffs are often too abrupt, harsh, and unrefined for most musical contexts. Beginners often develop tongue cutoffs because they are easy to execute; however, they should be encouraged to use breath releases as part of building a solid technical foundation. Included in this section are suggestions for executing releases on woodwind instruments. See also Articulation/Articulative Styles, page 6; Attacks, page 9; Breathing/Breath Support/Air Control, page 10; Resistance, page 141; Response, page 141

Breath Releases

1. When stopping the air, players should think of "lifting" off of the note. This concept enables players to direct and focus the air stream properly and prevents the pitch from going flat or drop-ping on releases.
2. In addition to "lifting" off of the note, players must stop the air immediately at the precise point of release to avoid "dropping off" or going flat on the release.
3. Players should maintain an open pathway from the diaphragm and lungs to the mouthpiece, reed, or head joint. Avoid using the throat as a valve. The throat stays open. Closing the throat is a common problem among wind players. Saying the syllable "ah," taking a light "gasp" of air, and holding the air stream in posi-tion helps players feel and understand how the air stream can be stopped or suspended intact, rather than being disrupted by the tongue or throat. When the air stream is stopped properly, the air is ready to flow again immediately when needed. The proper use of air is controlled by the muscles involved in the breathing process, and not by changes in the throat or embouchure.

Tongue Cutoffs

1. Tongue cutoffs are appropriate in some jazz styles or in heavy marcato or staccato passages which require more "bite" on releases. Tongue cutoffs may also be used in staccato or marcato passages at faster tempi. Tongue cutoffs are executed by placing the tongue on the reed or the gum line. The harder the tongue hits the reed or the gum line, the more abrupt and harsh the release will be.
2. Some players use tongue cutoffs in soft, slow passages, particularly on phrase endings. If the tongue touches the reed or the gum line lightly, these releases may sound fine; however, when using tongue cutoffs, it is very easy to touch the reed (or gum line) too harshly,

resulting in abrupt, sloppy releases. It is usually more effective to use breath releases in this context because they consistently produce more musical results.

Teaching Tips for Releases

1. Players must maintain a consistent embouchure while releasing tones. Changing the embouchure on releases will affect both pitch and tone quality.
2. Players must maintain a constant air stream until the point of release. Decreasing or increasing air speed before the point of release affects pitch, tone quality, and the clarity of the release.
3. Occasionally, flute players will release tones by closing off the aperture, using a "tup" syllable. This type of release produces abrupt cutoffs similar in sound to tongue cutoffs. Generally, aperture releases are not appropriate on woodwind instruments.

Key Questions

Q: If breath releases should be used most of the time, why do players gravitate toward tongue cutoffs?

A: Because tongue cutoffs are easier to execute. The proper execution of breath releases requires a great deal of control and practice.

Q: How are breath releases used in fast technical passages?

A: They are not. When players tongue sixteenth-note patterns, the notes are often moving too fast to control breath releases for each note. As a result, the tongue placement for any successive note becomes the release for the preceding note. As long as the air stream is maintained consistently, both the attacks and releases will be clean.

Serial Number: The number stamped on instruments by the maker or manufacturer that provides identification for the instrument. The serial number may provide a great deal of information about the instrument, including the date and place of manufacture and the history of ownership. In addition to serial numbers, some schools and other institutions may add numbers or markings to track instruments using their own systems. When purchasing a used instrument, it is advisable to check for a legible serial number. Serial numbers are usually in conspicuous places on the instrument.

Spring Hook Tool: A tool used to remove springs from or to place springs into their proper positions. See also Springs, page 59

Springs: Springs are relatively short lengths of strong metal wire or flat spring steel that hold an instrument's keys either open or shut, depending on key design. Springs can be round or flat and are made out of stainless steel, gold alloy, or even platinum alloy. While the material springs are made of does not affect tone quality, it can affect key action and the durability of the key alignment significantly. It is not uncommon for springs to come loose, particularly on student-line instruments. When an instrument suddenly stops responding properly, a loose spring is often the cause. Players can usually tell that a spring has come off of a particular key because that key will be in a closed position without being depressed. Springs are relatively easy to position using a spring hook tool but can lose tension or break if manipulated too much. If springs are damaged or broken, a qualified repair technician can replace them. When a spring hook tool is not available, players may be able to use the eraser end of a pencil to replace the spring. The eraser helps keep the spring from sliding while being positioned. A crochet hook can also be used to replace springs. See also Spring Hook Tool, page 59

Staggered Breathing: A technique used during performance whereby players do not breathe at the same time. Staggered breathing is very effective in long, sustained passages and with long tones where continuity of sound is desired. When staggered breathing is appropriate, players typically plan who will breathe where in a passage.

Stamina: See Endurance/Stamina, page 28

Swab: An accessory designed to clean and dry the inside of an instrument's joints after the instrument is played. Typically, swabs are made of a soft, absorbent cloth, such as cotton or silk. One common swab consists of a string attached to an absorbent cloth. These swabs typically have a plastic covered weight on one end of the string. The weight is dropped through the instrument joints, and the string is used to pull the cloth through the joint. Another type of swab is inserted into the instrument or joint and left there (e.g., a "Pad Saver" or "Shove It" swab). Such swabs vary in length and width according to the type of instrument tube or joint the swab is designed for. These one-piece swabs are convenient; however, they are also problematic. When players place these swabs into the instrument or joints and leave them there, the moisture on the swab is held near or against the pads. Over time, this moisture will damage the pads prematurely. Players can use these types of swabs effectively by inserting them into the joints to absorb the moisture and then removing them immediately. Some players remove the swabs, wipe them off, and then reinsert them back into the instrument or joints.

Technique: In general, the manner and ability with which players use the technical skills involved in playing an instrument. Most commonly, the term is used to describe the physical actions involved in musical performance, and often specifically refers to technical passages. Virtually every pedagogical aspect of woodwind playing (acoustical, physical, and mental) affects technique. Developing technical proficiency is most commonly associated with finger facility, fluidity, and coordination, although the ability to play with a high level of technical accuracy is also dependent upon having control over factors related to tone production and articulation. Instrument-specific and technique-specific considerations are discussed throughout each instrument chapter under Technique. General suggestions for developing technical proficiency are provided in the following section.

General Suggestions for Developing Technical Proficiency

Developing technical proficiency requires mastering fundamental skills on an instrument. That is, the proper use of air, embouchure, tongue, body, fingers, and instrument are all needed for developing a high level of technical proficiency. Although learning to coordinate the fingers is an important component of proper technique, finger coordination must complement other fundamentals of playing. Considerations for developing technical proficiency are listed as follows.

1. Maintain proper hand, holding, and instrument position, and maintain proper playing posture.
2. Develop a proper embouchure.
3. Develop proper breathing habits and learn to use air efficiently.
4. Develop proper tonguing skills. Tongue speed and tongue placement significantly affect technique.
5. Develop finger-tongue coordination. The ability to articulate cleanly in a variety of contexts and styles is vital to proper technique.
6. As a rule, work slow to fast. That is, practice technical passages slowly at first. Once control is gained, increase speed gradually.
7. Maintain proper playing habits as the speed increases. Stay relaxed and minimize finger movement. Playing faster or trying "harder" to play technical passages does not mean to tongue harder, blow harder, and/or let the fingers fly out of control.

8. Practice often with a metronome to help ensure steadiness of tempo and rhythmic accuracy. Setting the metronome at a variety of speeds for a given exercise helps develop technical control.

9. Use alternate fingerings when appropriate because they often make playing technically challenging passages easier.

Temperament: Generally, the way scale degrees are tuned or pitched within a given tuning system. Many tuning systems have been developed through the years including Pythagorean, just intonation, meantone, and equal temperament. The two most relevant systems to achieving proper intonation in Western music are just intonation and equal temperament.

Just intonation is a tuning system built entirely on mathematical relationships. That is, the intervals in a just scale all correspond to simple, whole-number frequency ratios based on a fundamental (tonic) frequency. As a result, intervals and simple chords produce beatless harmonies. The problem with just intonation is that it does not permit free modulation. As a result, tuning instruments to any "just" scale (based on one fundamental frequency) is not practical.

Equal temperament is the most commonly used system in the Western world. It divides the octave into twelve equal parts (one semitone equals 100 cents). The biggest advantage of equal temperament is that it enables modulation in all keys without glaring intonation problems. The biggest disadvantage is that it naturally results in many intonation problems in ensemble playing.

The use of equal temperament inherently causes some pitch problems because the system does not account for true mathematical relationships between intervals. For example, assume that an ensemble ends a piece on a concert B-flat chord. Even if every player in the ensemble is playing his or her pitches perfectly true to the equal tempered scale, the chord will not sound in tune. That is, there will be beats or roughness between various combinations of pitches. General descriptions of these two tuning systems appear below, and a comparison of these systems is shown in figure 1.13. See also Harmonics, page 32; Intonation, page 41

Equal	0	100	200	300	400	500	600	700	800	900	1000	1100	1200
Just	0	112	204	316	386	498	603	702	814	884	1018	1088	1200
Cent Deviation	0	12	4	16	14	2	3	2	14	16	18	12	0

FIGURE 1.13. *Temperament Comparison Scale*

CHARACTERISTICS OF JUST INTONATION

1. The use of the word "just" means pure or natural. Just intervals are related mathematically so that when they are sounded, beats are not present. That is, the intervals involved all correspond to simple, whole-number frequency ratios.
2. The just intonation tuning system has advantages over equal temperament. However, for a wind instrument to use this system, it would need to be able to produce dozens of pitches per octave in order to permit free modulation, which is not practical. In addition, the idea of playing without beats in all passages is not possible. Problems associated with modulation will arise in all but the simplest harmonies.

Characteristics of Equal Temperament

1. Equal temperament is a compromise scale in which all semitones are equal to 100 cents. As a result, tuning an instrument in equal temperament is a process of mistuning all of the intervals except the unisons and octaves. This compromise necessarily means that beats are built into the system.
2. In the equal tempered scale, none of the intervals of the harmonic series will divide evenly into the octave or any octave expansion. As a result, every note within the octave is out of tune to some degree.
3. Musically, the most noticeable problem is that the thirds are badly mistuned. Major thirds are sharp by fourteen cents and minor thirds are flat by sixteen cents.
4. Equal temperament is accepted almost universally as a method of tuning because it permits complete freedom of modulation to all keys.

Key Questions

Q: Are all instruments out of tune? Why is it necessary to adjust pitch?

A: Yes, all instruments are out of tune. Due to the complexity of musical harmony and the infinite number of tone combinations, it is impossible to perform without the presence of beats except in the simplest harmonies. To produce beatless harmony, intervals must correspond to simple, whole-number frequency ratios (e.g., 1:2, 2:3, 3:4 etc.); that is, they must align mathematically. The equal temperament tuning system is not based on whole-number ratios; however, the just intonation tuning system is. In practical terms, the result of using a "just" scale is playing in tune, without beats. Although this seems ideal, just intonation is only possible for the simplest pieces in one key; it does not permit free modulation to all other keys. As a result, just intonation is not a practical tuning system.

Equal temperament does not maintain whole-number ratios throughout the scale. Instead, it is a compromise system that divides the octave into twelve equal semitones of 100 cents. Equal temperament facilitates modulation to all keys while maintaining a reasonable sense of "in-tuneness." However, most of the pitches are out of tune to a degree. As a result, players must learn to adjust pitches in order to eliminate beats in ensemble settings no matter how expensive the instrument.

Tone Holes: Literally, the holes in an instrument tube that may be opened or closed, effectively changing the length of the tube. Tone holes enable different pitches to be produced on a woodwind instrument. Tone holes vary in size, shape, and placement according to predetermined specifications and significantly affect the tonal characteristics of an instrument. Instruments with open-hole designs require that the fingers cover at least some (or part) of the tone holes. In closed-hole designs, pads are used to cover the tone holes. The height of the pads from the tone holes is important to tone quality and intonation. If the pads and/or fingers are too close to the tone holes, the pitch will be flat and the tones muffled. If the pads and/or fingers are too far from the tone holes, the pitch tends to be sharp and the tones brighter and uncentered.

Tone Production: The term used to describe how tone is produced on an instrument. Virtually every pedagogical aspect of wind playing (acoustical, physical, and mental) affects tone quality. Developing good fundamentals of tone production and a mature, characteristic tone quality are arguably the most important aspects of wind playing. A thorough discussion of tone production fundamentals can be found under Embouchure in each instrument chapter. Instrument-specific suggestions for tone production are discussed thoroughly throughout each instrument chapter under Tone Production and other relevant terms. The following information includes several suggestions and considerations for tone production on woodwind instruments. See also Tone Quality, page 68

Tonal Concept/Tone Quality

Develop a concept of "good" tone and the type of tone quality desired. Several suggestions/considerations for developing this concept are listed separately.

1. Listen to advanced players and high quality recordings to develop concepts of tone in different styles and contexts.
2. Take lessons from a knowledgeable teacher whose tone quality can provide an exemplary model.
3. Attend clinics, workshops, and master classes when possible. Be an active participant when possible for helpful feedback.
4. Attend recitals and concerts to hear live performances in different venues.

Teaching Tips for Developing Tonal Concepts

1. In a classroom setting, characterize or describe each student's tone quality aloud on a regular basis using appropriate terminology.
2. Talk freely with students about the factors that affect tone production (e.g., air; embouchure; oral cavity) to help students develop tonal concepts and musical independence.
3. Allow students to experiment with tone production. For example, let them deliberately make changes in embouchure, air, oral cavity, mouthpiece placement, and so on, and discuss the tonal changes with them. At first, have students exaggerate these changes. Later, make these changes subtler.
4. Encourage students to learn "what" tone to listen for and "how" to affect tone, so that they will be able to practice tone production without a teacher being there. After all, students often spend more time practicing alone than they do in the presence of a knowledgeable teacher.

Basic Playing Considerations

Fundamental aspects of playing have a significant effect on tone production and tone quality. These aspects are encountered in daily rehearsal settings and during practice. If properly addressed and reinforced, players are more likely to produce a consistent, characteristic tone. These considerations are listed separately.

1. Assemble instruments properly.
2. Maintain proper hand, holding, and instrument position, and maintain proper playing posture.
3. Place music stands in positions that do not interfere with basic playing positions. In addition, each stand should be raised to a height that enables players to see the director without compromising good posture and playing position.

4. Arrange the chairs so that players are able to maintain proper playing positions without being cramped or crowded.

Tonal Consistency and Control

Tonal consistency and control are critical factors in tone production for two primary reasons. First, they enable players to play evenly throughout the range of the instrument. Second, they indicate that players are developing a proper "set" for facial muscles and embouchure, and that the head joint (flute), reed, or reed/mouthpiece combination are appropriate for the ability level of the player. When the facial muscles are not properly developed or the head joint (flute), reed, or reed/mouthpiece combination is inappropriate, it is common for the tone to be inconsistent and uncontrolled.

Embouchure

Maintain proper embouchure formation at all times. Proper mechanics of embouchure are critical to tone production. Although many fine players' embouchures vary slightly from a classic or standard embouchure, the basic embouchure mechanics for each instrument have withstood the test of time, and should be the starting point for virtually all woodwind players. Developing a mature, characteristic tone on an instrument requires time and practice to properly develop the facial muscles used to form a good embouchure. Detailed embouchure considerations are under Embouchure in each instrument chapter. General considerations for developing tone production are listed in the next section.

Breathing/Breath Support/Air Control

Develop proper breathing techniques and learn how to use air efficiently. Proper use of air is critical to good tone production. That is, a mature, characteristic tone cannot be achieved without proper control of breathing, good breath support, and proper focus of the air stream. Basic breathing considerations for good tone production are listed separately. A detailed discussion of breathing is located under Breathing/Breath Support/Air Control in this chapter. Basic breathing considerations for good tone production are listed as follows.

1. When inhaling, take a full breath and expand the waistline in all directions. Proper expansion also involves the chest, back, and rib cage. "Fill" from the bottom up.

2. Maintain good posture, and keep the body relaxed during inhalation and exhalation.

3. As a rule, use a warm air stream on woodwind instruments, except for the oboe, which requires a cold air stream. Keep the air stream moving forward to support the tone.

4. Move the air stream sufficiently fast to support the tone at all dynamic levels. Dynamics and phrasing are controlled by the volume and speed of the air.

5. Control pitch and pitch placement by making slight changes in air speed and focus.

6. Think of blowing the air through the instrument rather than merely into the instrument.

7. Minimize tongue movement when articulating to avoid unnecessarily disrupting the air stream.

Tonguing/Attacks

The use of the tongue can greatly affect tone production. Improper tonguing techniques can alter embouchure and impair air flow, which compromises tone production. A detailed discussion of tonguing is under Tonguing in this chapter. Basic tonguing considerations for good tone production are listed as follows.

1. On flute, the tongue should strike the gum line behind the top teeth. On clarinet and saxophone, the tip of the tongue should strike the tip of the reed. On oboe and bassoon, the tip of the tongue should strike the tip of the bottom blade. In all cases, the tongue should strike lightly and quickly.

2. Beginners can be taught to tongue using a "T" attack. Specifically, players should think of saying the syllable "tu" or "toh" because these syllables help players maintain an open throat and help create a warm, full tone quality.

3. As players gain experience and develop consistency and control of the tongue, they can learn to use the syllable "du" or "doh" for tonguing in legato passages. These syllables enable players to produce smoother, more legato attacks. Gaining control of the tongue is critical to tonguing effectively across a variety of musical styles.

Instrument/Equipment Considerations

Using appropriate equipment is critical to success in woodwind instrument performance. Several important factors to consider include the quality and condition of the instrument, the "fit" of the head joint (flute), reed, or reed/mouthpiece combination to the player, and the adjustment of accessories such as neck straps, seat straps, and thumb rests. Considerations regarding the instrument in relation to tone production are listed as follows.

1. Play on equipment (head joint; instrument; mouthpiece; reed; etc.) that matches each player's level of performance and experience. Beginners should use equipment appropriate for beginners. As players mature, they should experiment with more advanced equipment. Tone production is maximized when players play on appropriate equipment.
2. Play instruments that are in proper working order. Playing on instruments that are not working properly causes players to develop poor habits that can take weeks, months, or even years to break.
3. Properly care for and maintain instruments. Developing a proper maintenance routine is an important part of playing wind instruments.
4. Reed players: rotate and replace reeds regularly. Reeds that are chipped, cracked, or simply worn out will produce unsatisfactory tonal and response characteristics.

Vibrato

Vibrato is an important factor in tone production for players as they advance, whereas it is not a factor in tone production for beginners. Typically, vibrato is added when the fundamentals of good tone production have been mastered. A detailed discussion of vibrato is under Vibrato in this chapter. General considerations for vibrato are listed as follows.

1. Add vibrato to a full, well-centered tone according to the musical style being performed.
2. Use vibrato to enhance tone quality, not to cover up a poor tone.
3. Use vibrato appropriately. Flute, oboe, and bassoon players use a diaphragmatic vibrato, while saxophone players use a jaw vibrato. Although clarinet players typically do not use vibrato in concert band or classical playing, a jaw vibrato is often used in jazz playing.

Teaching Tips for Tone Production

1. Prepare mentally before producing a tone. Players can either play without thinking and hope for acceptable results, or they can

prepare the mind, body, and the instrument for musical performance. The latter approach will result in more consistent sounds and more accurate pitches.

2. Make sure players are "set" before they play. Create an environment conducive to good focus and readiness to learn, and insist that players consistently execute the fundamentals that are taught.

3. Make sure players can "hear" pitches before they play them (audiation) to facilitate pitch placement and tonal accuracy. Have students sing pitches regularly before playing to internalize pitch awareness. See also Intonation, page 41

4. Teach (or practice) from a musical perspective. Do not separate concepts of tone production from the mechanics of performance. For example, when working on fingerings, relate those fingerings to particular pitches and tonal characteristics. When working on breathing and using air, relate those processes to pitch, tone quality, and tonal consistency.

5. Consider adopting a "Sound Before Sight" approach to teaching and practicing in order to facilitate tone production and tone quality.

Tone Quality: The characteristic timbre associated with an instrument. From a mechanical standpoint, tone quality is dependent upon several factors involving the design of the mouthpiece, reed, head joint, instrument bore, neck, bocal, and the materials used in the construction of the instrument. From a player's standpoint, tone quality is largely dependent upon two factors: (1) the use of air, which is discussed under Breathing/Breath Support/Air Control and (2) the embouchure and oral cavity, which are discussed under Embouchure and Tone Production.

Several terms are often used to describe tone quality; however, players do not always use terminology consistently. Furthermore, certain tonal characteristics are relative. For example, what may be considered a bright, inappropriate tone in one style (e.g., classical) may be considered a relatively dark, appropriate tone in another style (e.g., jazz). One effective way to understand the variances in tone quality is to listen to a wide variety of players and styles, preferably with an experienced teacher or player. Common terms associated with tone quality and used to characterize tone quality are identified and described separately. See also Breathing/Breath Support/Air Control, page 10; Embouchure, page 104; Mouthpiece/Mouthpieces, page 45; Tone Production, page 63

Terms Associated with Tone Quality

1. Center—A term commonly used to describe the center of a tone or the tonal center. When a tone is centered, it possesses tonal

characteristics that are spread somewhat evenly above and below a perceived center.

2. Core—A term commonly used to describe the resonant fullness and depth of a tone or how "solid" a tone is perceived to be. Tones with a good core are generally perceived to have a good tonal center as well; however, centered tones do not always possess a good core, especially when the tone quality is weak.

3. Color—A term used almost exclusively to describe the brightness or darkness of a tone. When the higher partials in a tone are predominant, the tone is considered bright. When the lower partials in a tone are predominant, the tone is considered dark.

4. Edge—A term used to describe a particularly noticeable or penetrating "twang" or high-pitched "buzz" in the tone. "Edgy" is often used when describing bright tone colors because it also involves the prominence of higher partials in the tone. In fact, many bright tones do have an "edge" to them; however, an edge is an audible entity in and of itself and may be present even in a darker tone.

5. Intensity—Physically, intensity refers to the power of a tone or the energy emitted from a tone. The intensity of a tone is directly related to how much air is being used and how well a tone projects. Musically, intensity is also used to describe softer tones that project and resonate largely because of a well-supported air stream.

6. Resonance—A term used to describe the vibrating fullness of a tone. Tones with a big core and a full complement of partials are generally considered resonant. Resonant tones project well and usually have a ringing quality about them even though they may not be particularly loud. There is a direct relationship between the resonance of a tone and the amount of air supporting it, even though not all tones that are supported are resonant.

7. Timbre—A physical or acoustical term for tone quality that describes the relationship between the various partials and transient effects (e.g., the sound of the tongue hitting the reed) created by such things as attacks or vibrato. Generally speaking, timbre is the characteristic sound (or sounds) that enables us to distinguish one instrument from another.

TERMS USED TO DESCRIBE TONE QUALITY

1. Bright—A tone is considered bright when the higher partials in a tone are predominant.
2. Dark—A tone is considered dark when the lower partials in a tone are predominant.
3. Fuzzy—A tone that has nonmusical extraneous "noises" in the tone. Fuzziness can be caused by several factors including poor embouchure formation, poor air control, bad reeds, poor instrument condition, improper air focus, and other fundamental problems.
4. Clear or Pure—A tone in which very few (if any) extraneous "noises" are present in the tone.
5. Focused—A term often used interchangeably with "centered" to describe a tone that remains steady and consistent. "Focused" is often used to describe the appropriateness of the direction and shape of the air stream on a particular tone.
6. Thin—A weak, small, pinched tone, or a tone that lacks depth and core. Woodwind players sometimes play with a thin tone when they "bite" or pinch the reed, when the lip aperture (flute) or tip opening is too small, and/or when players use a weak air stream.
7. Weak—A term used to describe a tone that has inadequate air volume and air speed. That is, the tone is unsupported.
8. Big—A full tone with a good core. A big tone is almost always accompanied by good breath support.
9. Small—A tone that lacks partials or depth even though the air support may be adequate.
10. Warm—A term usually used to describe a dark tone in which the lower partials are more dominant than the upper partials. Warm tones are generally calming or pleasing to hear and they lack any kind of edge or brightness.
11. Airy or Breathy—A tone that has a lot of audible air in the tone. An airy tone can have several causes, including reeds that are too hard, air escaping through the mouth corners, and unfocused embouchures.
12. Fat—A tone that seems to spread out from a tonal center more than normal. Fat tones generally contain a full complement of strong partials on both sides of the center.
13. Round—A tone that is centered and focused. Round tones generally have a good core to them as well.

14. Muffled or Dead—A tone that sounds stuffy and small. Muffled tones lack higher partials and sound dull. Reed players produce muffled or dead tones when they use reeds that do not vibrate properly.
15. Vibrant or Lively—A tone that sounds alive and energetic. A vibrant tone contains a full complement of partials and is characteristic of a vibrating mechanism (e.g., a reed) that is vibrating freely and rapidly.
16. Harsh—A tone that accentuates undesirable partials or transients, causing the tone to be unpleasant. Harsh tones are often caused by an uncontrolled air stream and/or poor embouchure formation. Some saxophone and clarinet mouthpieces can produce a harsh tone.

Tonguing: The process of articulating notes using the tongue in some manner. There are several ways to tongue notes depending on the desired effect or style. In performance, tones are generally started with a quick, light stroke of the tongue working in conjunction with the air. When tonguing, the tip of the tongue strikes the tip of the reed or bottom blade (clarinet, saxophone, oboe, and bassoon) or gum line (flute) behind the upper teeth.

Players and teachers sometimes disagree as to how the tongue should actually move during the tonguing process. Some teachers describe the movement as up and down, and others describe the movement as forward and backward. In reality, the tongue moves both up and down and forward and backward to varying degrees; however, as a teaching concept, the idea of moving the tongue up and down rather than forward and backward may minimize unnecessary and inefficient tongue motion. On the other hand, some players develop a slow or sluggish action when they think of moving the tongue up and down. The choice of how to approach tonguing action should be based on what works for a particular student.

Beginners can be taught to tongue using a "T" attack. Specifically, players should think of saying the syllable "tu" because this syllable enables players to maintain an open throat and to produce a warm, full tone quality.

As players gain experience and develop consistency and control of the tongue, they can learn to use the syllable "du" for tonguing in legato passages. This syllable enables players to produce smoother, more legato attacks. Gaining control of the tongue is critical to tonguing effectively across a variety of musical styles.

The inability to tongue efficiently can often be linked to poor air control. For example, too much air often contributes to hard, "splatty" attacks, and too little air often contributes to unresponsive attacks. Maintaining a consistent air stream improves tonguing. Some suggestions and considerations for teaching tonguing appear separately. See also Articulation/Articulative Styles, page 6; Attacks, page 9; Releases/Cutoffs, page 56

Suggestions and Considerations for Tongue Position

1. Initially, the tongue should be down in the mouth in a relaxed position. For most people, a relaxed tongue will be rather flat with the tip positioned just behind the bottom teeth.
2. To prepare the tongue for tonguing, the tip of the tongue should be raised upward and brought back slightly so that the tip will be in a position to contact the reed or gum line (flute) quickly and efficiently.
3. When tonguing, players should think of moving only the tip. Moving the entire tongue contributes to a slow, sluggish tonguing action and harsh, muddy attacks.
4. Tonguing with the tip of the tongue also results in a minimal disruption of the air stream. Keeping this disruption to a minimum is important because the air actually works in conjunction with the tongue to create clean attacks. That is, the tongue and the air work together in the tonguing process.
5. In fast, tongued passages, it is important to keep the air stream moving. A constant air stream facilitates clean attacks and tonguing speed, and it helps maintain good tone quality. Thinking of maintaining the air stream and cutting or slicing it with the tongue can be a helpful analogy.

Double-Tonguing and Triple-Tonguing

Multiple-tonguing techniques involve using syllable patterns to enable performers to tongue duple or triple patterns rapidly. A detailed discussion of multiple-tonguing is under Multiple-Tonguing in this chapter.

Key Questions

Q: Does the "tip" of the tongue really strike the "tip" of the reed?

A: Probably not, for several reasons. First, the tongue is very soft. The moment the tongue touches the reed, it will flatten out to some degree no matter how lightly it touches. Second, the reed is vibrating rapidly and the idea that one specific place on the tongue would always strike the reed is not realistic. Finally, because the tongue is starting below the reed and moving up toward the reed tip, the tongue may actually contact the reed slightly below the tip and slightly on top of the tongue.

However, the concept of placing the tip of the tongue on the tip of the reed is a sound teaching concept because when students hear phrases such as "slightly below the tip" or "slightly on top of the tongue," they have a tendency to exaggerate these suggestions, which causes tonguing problems.

Q: Can players use their tongues correctly during the tonguing process and still have unsatisfactory attacks?

A: Yes. Many times players do not set their embouchures properly before the initial attack. In such cases, attacks may be out of focus and "splatty" despite the fact that players may actually be using the tongue properly. Hearing the pitch ahead of time and setting the embouchure accordingly is essential to proper tonguing. The tongue, embouchure, and air stream work together in the tonguing process.

Teaching Tips Regarding Tonguing

1. When tonguing rapidly, it is a common mistake to close the throat and to tense up. Tension actually slows down the tonguing process and should be avoided. As the tongue moves faster, it is important to maintain a proper embouchure, an open air column, and a consistent air speed.

2. Jaw movement in tongued passages is one of the most common problems among young players, especially on saxophone and bassoon. This "jawing" motion can easily distort attacks and often causes problems with tone quality, pitch, and tonguing speed. Players who move their jaws when tonguing are usually tonguing too hard and/or moving the tongue too much. The tonguing motion should be short, light, and quick and should only involve the tip of the tongue. As a rule, there should be no jaw movement during the tonguing process.

3. The following exercise may help players develop an understanding of where and how hard/easy the tongue strikes the reed.
   A. While playing a long tone, touch the reed with the tongue as lightly as possible and hold it there without stopping the tone. Of course, it is virtually impossible to maintain a tone while touching the reed with the tongue no matter how lightly the

tongue touches the reed. The tone will stop the moment the tongue touches the reed tip. Using a very light tonguing action will help produce clean attacks.

4. Have students think of moving the air and the tongue together. Technically, the attack occurs when the tip of the tongue is removed from the reed or gum line (flute), releasing the air behind it. However, when tonguing, it is helpful to think of coordinating the air stream with the tongue movement. The idea of building up air pressure and then releasing the tongue creates harsh, uncontrolled attacks; the air and the tongue must work together.

Triple-Tonguing: See Multiple-Tonguing, page 52

Vibrato: The regular fluctuation of pitch and/or intensity around a tonal center that is often used to enhance the tone. Two types of vibrato are commonly used in woodwind playing: (1) jaw vibrato, and 2) diaphragmatic vibrato, which is sometimes described as a diaphragmatic/throat vibrato. Jaw vibrato results in regular pitch fluctuations around a tonal center, whereas diaphragmatic vibrato results in regular intensity (loudness) fluctuations around a tonal center. Saxophone players typically use a jaw vibrato. Flute and oboe players use a diaphragmatic or diaphragmatic/throat vibrato. Bassoon players often use a combination of jaw and diaphragmatic vibrato. Clarinet players do not typically use vibrato; however, when vibrato is needed for certain musical styles, a jaw vibrato is used. Steps for developing a pleasing vibrato are listed in "Basic Considerations."

Basic Considerations

1. Vibrato should only be used when the musical style calls for it.
2. Vibrato should enhance the tone, not dominate it.
3. Players should not work on vibrato until they can maintain a good characteristic tone on their instruments. Do not add vibrato on top of a poor tone.
4. Players should learn to control the speed and/or the width of the vibrato for greater musical effect.
5. Diaphragmatic vibrato affects intensity to a much greater degree than it affects pitch. In contrast, jaw vibrato affects pitch to a much greater degree than it affects intensity.
6. The decision to use vibrato, the speed of vibrato, and the width of vibrato are all determined by the musical style.
7. It is important to maintain a tonal center and add vibrato around this tonal center. That is, conceptually, a "basic" vibrato is spread evenly

around the tonal center, even though it is much easier to go below the tonal center than it is to go above it. Different effects can be achieved by altering these proportions. For example, in certain jazz styles, it is common to get more "bottom" (i.e., to stay below the tonal center) than "top" (i.e., to stay above the tonal center) in the vibrato.

Developing a Jaw Vibrato on Saxophone/Clarinet

1. Without the instrument, form a proper embouchure and say the syllable "wa."

2. Again without the instrument, say a series of "wa" syllables in an even manner. Pay attention to the upward and downward movement of the jaw.

3. With the instrument, play a tone in the middle register (top-line F-sharp is an excellent starting note on sax and clarinet) with a nice, open tone quality without vibrato. Hold this tone for two counts before adding vibrato for all beginning exercises. The tonal center must remain unchanged when vibrato is added, and the pulsations must be focused around this tonal center.

4. Using a metronome, play the same tone, hold it for two counts at mm60, and then play one pulsation ("wa") per beat for four counts. Each pulsation must be played evenly over one count. Exaggerate the width of each pulsation when practicing one or two pulsations per beat. Making the pulsations wide and "ugly" sounding helps gain muscle control over the process in the early stages of vibrato development. The tonal center may be temporarily lost during this exercise; however, when control is gained and the speed is increased to three or four pulsations per beat, the width of the pulsations should become narrower and more focused, and the tonal center will be reestablished.

5. Progress in a stepwise manner. When one pulsation per beat at mm60 is mastered, play two pulsations per beat, then three, then four, and so on. Keep pulsations even throughout each exercise to develop smooth vibrato and to maintain a tonal center.

6. Practice these pulsations on tones in the middle register at first. Gradually expand the range upward and downward, keeping in mind that vibrato is more difficult to produce in the lower and higher registers than it is in the middle register.

Sharp

Pitch
Center

Flat

FIGURE 1.14. *Concept of Jaw Vibrato Fluctuation around a Tonal Center*

7. Alternate playing tones with and without vibrato so that the tonal center is constantly referenced. For example, play a tone without vibrato and then play the same tone with vibrato. After producing pulsations on individual tones, play long tone scales and alternate playing tones with and without vibrato.

8. After practicing pulsations on individual notes, begin using vibrato on whole-note scales. Instead of playing a straight tone for two counts, begin using vibrato immediately after the initial attack.

9. Play long tones without vibrato frequently so that the ability to hear the tonal center is maintained.

10. With jaw vibrato, strive to keep the pitch level of the tonal center maintained while the differences created by the pulsations are evenly spaced around this tonal center, as shown in figure 1.14. In reality, it is much easier to go below the tonal center than it is to go above it. "Top," or going above the tonal center, gives the sound brilliance. "Bottom," or going below the tonal center, gives the sound depth. Too much "bottom" results in a flat-sounding, dull vibrato, while too much "top" results in a pinched, choppy vibrato.

11. Develop vibrato by practicing a certain number of pulsations per beat. This technique allows players to gain control over the pulsations in the vibrato. For learning purposes, a metronomic pulsation is clearly more technical than musical. However, most players learn to use a rate and amount of vibrato that is musical. That is, players incorporate vibrato appropriately according to musical context, not according to tempo alone. Ultimately, most players use a rate of vibrato around six pulsations at mm60 or four pulsations at mm72, depending on musical style and individual preferences.

Developing a Diaphragmatic or Diaphragmatic/Throat Vibrato on Flute

1. Without the instrument, form a proper embouchure and pulse the air using a "who" or "oo" syllable.

2. Again without the instrument, say a series of "who" or "oo" syllables in an even manner. Keep the throat open and the embouchure and jaw steady. Exaggerate movement in the diaphragm when saying these syllables.

3. With the instrument, play a tone in the middle register (third-line B-natural is an excellent starting note) with a nice, open tone quality without vibrato. Using a metronome, hold the tone for two counts at mm60, and then play one pulsation per beat for four counts. Each pulsation must be played evenly over one count. Exaggerate the push of each pulsation when practicing two pulsations per beat. This exaggeration will result in a change in dynamic level from loud to soft; this change is normal. Exaggerating the push helps gain muscle control over the process in the early stages of vibrato development. The tonal center may be lost temporarily during this exercise; however, when control is gained and the speed increased to three or four pulsations per beat, the evenness of the pulsations should become more focused, and the tonal center will be reestablished.

4. Using a metronome, play the same tone, hold it for two counts at mm60, and then play two pulsations per beat for four counts keeping in mind the same considerations stated above.

5. Continue to progress in a stepwise manner. When one pulsation per beat at mm60 is mastered, play two pulsations per beat, then three, and so on up to about six pulsations per beat. Keep pulsations even throughout each exercise to develop smooth vibrato and to maintain a tonal center. Using the diaphragm alone, players can typically achieve about two pulsations before the throat muscles are activated to some degree. As the speed increases, listen for glottal sounds that indicate the throat is closing. The throat should remain open at all times.

6. Practice these pulsations on tones in the middle register at first. Gradually expand the range upward and downward, keeping in mind that vibrato is more difficult to produce in the lower and higher registers than it is in the middle register.

7. After practicing pulsations on individual notes, begin using vibrato on whole-note scales. Instead of playing a straight tone for two counts, begin using vibrato immediately after the initial attack.

8. Also, play long tones without vibrato frequently so that the ability to hear the tonal center is maintained.

9. Develop vibrato by practicing a certain number of pulsations per beat. This technique enables players to gain control over the technique. For learning purposes, a metronomic pulsation is clearly more technical than musical. However, most players learn to use a rate and amount of vibrato that is musical. That is, players incorporate vibrato appropriately according to musical context, not according to tempo alone. Ultimately, most players use a rate of vibrato around six pulsations at mm60 or four pulsations at mm72, depending on musical style and individual preferences.

Developing a Diaphragmatic or Diaphragmatic/Throat Vibrato on Oboe/Bassoon

1. Without the instrument, form a proper embouchure and pulse the air using a "who" or "oo" syllable.

2. Still without the instrument, pulse the air stream by repeating a "who" syllable in an even manner. Keep the throat open and the embouchure and jaw steady. Think of "bumping" or "pulsing" each syllable quickly and abruptly from the abdomen. Exaggerate each pulsation or bump in the diaphragm when saying these syllables. These pulsations or bumps will be the foundation of a good vibrato. In the beginning stages, it may help to practice vibrato on the reed alone.

3. With the instrument, play a tone in the middle register with a nice, open tone quality without vibrato. Third-line B-natural is an excellent starting note on oboe, and fourth-line F-natural is an excellent starting note on bassoon. Using a metronome, hold the tone for two counts at mm60 and then play one pulsation per beat for four counts. Each pulsation must be played evenly over one count. Exaggerate the "push" of each pulsation when practicing one or two pulsations per beat. This exaggeration will result in a change in dynamic level from loud to soft; this change is normal. Exaggerating the push or "bump" helps gain muscle control over the process in the early stages of vibrato development. The tonal center may be lost temporarily during this exercise; however, when control is gained and the speed is increased to three or four pulsations per beat, the evenness of the pulsations should become more focused, and the tonal center will be reestablished.

4. Using a metronome, play the same tone, hold it for two counts at mm60, and then play two pulsations per beat for four counts keeping in mind the same considerations stated above.

5. Continue to progress in a stepwise manner. When two pulsations per beat at mm60 are mastered, increase the number of pulsations to three per beat, and so on up to about six pulsations per beat. Keep the pulsations even throughout each exercise. Using the diaphragm alone, players can typically achieve about two pulsations before the throat muscles are activated to a degree. It is this activation of the throat muscles that leads many teachers to describe oboe vibrato as a throat vibrato; however, it is not a throat vibrato because the air originates from the diaphragm rather than the throat. On the other hand, because the throat is involved to a degree, diaphragmatic vibrato may be more accurately described as a diaphragmatic/throat vibrato. As the speed of the vibrato increases, listen for glottal sounds, which indicate the throat is closing. The throat should remain relatively open at all times.

6. Practice these pulsations on tones in the middle register at first. Gradually expand the range upward and downward, keeping in mind that vibrato is more difficult to produce in the lower and higher registers than it is in the middle register.

7. After practicing pulsations on individual notes, begin using vibrato on whole-note scales. Instead of playing a straight tone for two counts, begin using vibrato immediately after the initial attack.

8. Play long tones without vibrato frequently so that the ability to hear the tonal center is maintained.

9. Develop vibrato by practicing a certain number of pulsations per beat. This technique allows players to gain control over the vibrato. For learning purposes, a metronomic pulsation is clearly more technical than musical; however, most players learn to use a rate and amount of vibrato that is musical. That is, players incorporate vibrato appropriately according to musical context, not according to tempo alone. Ultimately, most players use a rate of vibrato around six pulsations at mm60 or four pulsations at mm72, depending on musical style and individual preferences.

Key Questions

Q: What is a "singing" vibrato?

A: Advanced players sometimes describe their vibrato as a sympathetic vibrato. That is, they feel the pulsations originating around the larynx and in the neck/upper chest area rather than in the diaphragmatic region. These players often refer to this vibrato as a "singing" vibrato. In reality, the air stream always begins at the diaphragm. Players who use a "singing" vibrato have simply learned to control the air stream by using the muscles in the throat area, thus eliminating the need to pulse the air from the diaphragm. This type of vibrato often develops naturally after years of playing and should never be taught to beginners.

2

Flute

Acoustical Properties: The acoustical and physical tonal characteristics of an instrument that affect its sound quality. Although the head joint is slightly conical, the flute is essentially a cylindrical tube that is open on both ends. Sound is produced when air is blown against the sharp edge of the embouchure hole, causing the air column inside the instrument to vibrate. Players can produce different octaves or partials by changing air speed and direction. Harmonically speaking, the flute produces the purest tone of any wind instrument; that is, the sound wave is almost sinusoidal at times. The flute's tone quality blends well with other instruments; however, it is also easily masked by the complex tones (i.e., tones that contain many partials) produced by other wind instruments. Modern flutes are most commonly made of nickel silver (also called German silver, an alloy consisting of copper, zinc, and nickel), silver plate, or solid silver. Many professional flute makers use a wide variety of metal and wood in their flutes, including yellow gold, rose gold, platinum, and grenadilla wood. These materials offer players the option of choosing an instrument that inherently produces a particular quality of sound.

The flute overblows the octave. That is, most of the fingerings used in the lower octave are used in the middle octave with the exception of D-natural and E-flat, which are slightly modified. Only the first (fundamental) and second partials are used for the majority of the normal playing range. See also Acoustical Basics, page 3; Construction and Design, page 99; Harmonics, page 32

Key Questions

Q: Why doesn't the flute have an octave key or register like the saxophone and clarinet?

A: Practically speaking, the tube of the instrument must be open on both ends to overblow the octave without an octave key. The clarinet and saxophone are closed at one end because the reed and mouthpiece are in the mouth. The flute is open at both ends (the embouchure hole is the opening at the head joint end) and is therefore capable of overblowing the octave without the assistance of an octave key. Air speed and air direction largely determine the harmonic produced.

Q: If the flute overblows the octave, why are many of the fingerings different from one octave to the next?

A: Different fingerings are used in the second octave because they produce a better tone quality, are better in tune, and/or are more responsive. For example, fourth-line D-natural and top-space E-flat are particularly stuffy if the left-hand index finger is not raised.

Action: See Action, page 3

Adjusting Pitch: The process of raising or lowering the pitch of notes. A general discussion of adjusting pitch is under Intonation in chapter 1. Specific suggestions for adjusting pitch on flute are under Intonation in this chapter.

Air Stream: Physically, the stream of air pushed from the lungs by the diaphragm and abdominal muscles through the trachea and oral cavity into and through a musical instrument. Although the physical nature of exhaling is basically the same for everyone, the ways the air stream is used to play particular instruments vary widely. A general discussion of the air stream and breathing is under Air Stream and Breathing/Breath Support/Air Control in chapter 1. In addition, the effects of the air stream on pitch are under Intonation in this chapter. Specific comments regarding the flute air stream appear separately.

On flute, players generally blow a warm air stream through a small aperture in the lips across and into the embouchure hole. The air stream strikes the sharp back edge of the embouchure hole, which splits the air stream and sets the air column inside the instrument in vibration. The air stream must be consistent and steady, and there must be sufficient air speed and volume to support the tone. The direction of the air stream changes according to range, and the relationship between air and embouchure is direct. Specifically, the air must be focused upward as the scale ascends and downward as the scale descends, and the embouchure must firm and loosen accordingly. In other words, the focus of the air changes slightly throughout the range of the instrument in conjunction with changes in embouchure. As a general rule, the air stream is directed downward more in the low range than it is in the middle range and downward more in the middle range than it is in the high range. Pitch and tone quality determine the appropriateness of air direction.

The direction of the air stream can be moved up or down to adjust the pitch of individual tones. For example, the low range of most flutes tends to be flat, while the high range tends to be sharp. Raising the air stream sharpens the pitch, while lowering the air stream flattens the pitch. Adjustments to the air stream can be made with slight movements of the lips, jaw, and/or head. In addition, there may be a few instances where players may roll the flute in or out slightly, effectively altering the direction of the air stream.

The way the air stream moves through and exits the mouth also affects tone quality and color. For example, a more "hollow" or "pure" tone quality can be achieved by using a lip aperture with a round "O" shape as if saying "who." A brighter sound that projects farther may be achieved by using a more oval aperture and by directing the air toward specific areas of the embouchure hole that emphasize the desired partials. In general, regardless of the desired tone color, the tongue remains low in the mouth and the cheeks remain flat so that the air stream is not disrupted unnecessarily.

The piccolo uses the same general principles as the flute except that it requires a faster air stream and a smaller aperture to accommodate the instrument's smaller embouchure hole. Most flute players who double on piccolo also find that they place the piccolo slightly higher on the lip (closer to the lip aperture) than they do the flute. See also Air Stream, page 4; Breathing/Breath Support/Air Control, page 10; Embouchure, page 104; Intonation, page 129

Alternate Fingerings/Alternates: Fingerings not considered standard or basic that can be used to facilitate or enhance musical performance. Alternate fingerings are most often used to minimize awkward fingerings or to improve intonation in specific musical contexts. The choice of when and which alternate fingerings to use should ultimately be determined by the musical result. That is, does using the alternate fingering improve the musicality of the performance?

Developing command of alternate fingerings is important so that players can use the most appropriate fingering in a given situation. Learning alternate fingerings can be awkward at first. Practicing patterns, passages, scales, and other exercises in which alternate fingerings can be incorporated is helpful. Practice alternate fingerings slowly and deliberately, focusing on only one or two alternates at a time.

The alternate fingerings described are appropriate for players who are fundamentally sound. Examples of when to use these alternates are shown in figure 2.1. When appropriate, suggestions and comments regarding alternate fingerings have been included. A complete fingering chart that includes alternate fingerings

Figure 2.1. *Alternate Fingerings*

is in the "Practical Tips" section at the end of this chapter. See also Intonation, page 129; Technique, page 144

Common Alternate Fingerings for Flute

1. Alternate F-sharp (first-space or top-line)—Instead of fingering F-sharp with the ring finger of the right hand (6), players sometimes choose to finger F-sharp with the middle finger of the right hand (5). This alternate fingering can facilitate playing fast

technical passages, but is more often used when trilling from E-natural to F-sharp or from F-sharp to G-natural. It is important to note that this alternate F-sharp fingering is not a substitute for the regular fingering.

2. Alternate B-flat (third-line or above the staff)—Instead of fingering B-flat with the index fingers of both hands (1-4), players can simply depress the B-flat thumb key with the left thumb and avoid depressing the right-hand index finger (4) altogether. The D-sharp key remains depressed in both fingerings. The B-flat alternate fingering eliminates the need to coordinate both hands when playing certain intervals (e.g., from B-flat to G-natural).

3. C-Sharp Trill Key—An optional trill key above and to the left of the B-flat chromatic (bis) key on the right hand. Contexts in which the C-sharp trill key can be used are listed as follows.
   A. When playing from B-natural to C-sharp in the first and second octaves, using the C-sharp trill key eliminates the two-fingered trill on the left hand.
   B. For an alternate C-sharp in the first and second octaves, finger B-natural and add the C-sharp trill key.
   C. When trilling C-natural to C-sharp in the first and second octaves, play C-natural and trill with the C-sharp key.
   D. When trilling high F-sharp to G-sharp, play high F-sharp and trill with the C-sharp key.
   E. When trilling high G-natural to A-flat, play high G-natural and trill with the C-sharp key.

4. Long C-natural and Long C-sharp (third-space)—Players sometimes choose to use the low fingerings for these pitches and simply overblow them slightly. Although the tone quality and pitch are not usually as good as the regular fingerings, these alternates may match the quality of the fourth-line D-natural in certain contexts (e.g., softer passages) better than the regular fingerings.

Leaving Fingers Down to Facilitate Technical Playing

1. The left-hand little finger may remain depressed on the G-sharp key when playing fast passages involving left-hand fingerings, because leaving it depressed does not affect pitches above the G-sharp to a marked degree. However, the left-hand little finger may not be left down when playing fast passages involving right-hand fingerings

because the notes will not speak properly if this key is depressed on pitches below G-sharp.

2. When playing B-flat, C-natural, or C-sharp in the second and third octave, any or all of the right-hand fingers can be left down.

Key Questions

Q: When should students begin using alternate fingerings?

A: Students who are fundamentally sound can begin using alternate fingerings when opportunities arise to incorporate them into rehearsals and performances. By the time students are in high school, they should be using alternate fingerings regularly.

Q: Is it better to adjust pitch by making embouchure adjustments or by using special fingerings or adding keys?

A: It depends on the musical context. Generally, if using alternate fingerings improves the musicality of a performance, then use them.

Altissimo/Extended Range: A term sometimes used for the notes in the high range and/or the extreme high range of an instrument. The normal flute range generally includes all notes up to C-natural two octaves above the third-space C-natural (i.e., double high C-natural). The range of notes above double-high C-natural to high F-natural is sometimes referred to as the extended or altissimo range, although "altissimo" is a term more often applied to the saxophone or clarinet than to the flute. Players typically begin working on the altissimo range after they have developed excellent control and facility throughout the normal range of the instrument. Producing altissimo notes successfully involves making several adjustments including using altissimo fingerings, adjusting the embouchure formation, and changing the speed, focus, and direction of the air stream. Some suggestions for developing the altissimo range appear separately.

Suggestions for Developing the Altissimo Range

1. Work on altissimo after developing a good, consistent tone quality throughout the normal range of the instrument.
2. Embouchure/Oral Cavity Suggestions
   A. Firm the embouchure and pull the mouth corners back slightly, decreasing the size of the lip aperture.
   B. Arch and pull the tongue back slightly as if saying "ee."

3. Air Stream Comments/Suggestions

    Altissimo success hinges on the ability to make the air move fast on a narrowly focused plane. To get air moving faster than in the normal range, follow these steps.

    A. Focus the oral cavity and air stream as if saying "ee."

    B. Increase air speed.

    C. Direct the air upward so that less air is going into the embouchure hole.

4. Start with high C-sharp and D-natural and work upward. These notes respond relatively easily for most players.

5. When first working on altissimo, use breath attacks and slur from one note to the next. Once control is gained, try tonguing the notes. Make sure that the tongue is light and quick; it should disrupt the air stream minimally.

Key Questions

Q:　Do high school students really need to have control over the altissimo range?

A:　No. Most pieces appropriate for high school instrumental music programs do not include notes above double high C-natural. However, pieces may include the range from high A-natural (two octaves above second-space A-natural) to high C-natural. Students should not begin working in the altissimo range before good fundamentals are developed because altissimo practice can cause bad habits such as pinching or overblowing.

Q:　When should students being to learn altissimo?

A:　Advanced students who are fundamentally sound can begin working on the altissimo range at the high school level, preferably under the guidance of a knowledgeable teacher.

Alto Flute: See Instrument Family and Playing Considerations, page 122

Arm: The connecting piece between the bar and the key cup. Two configurations are typically used for flute arms: Y arms and French pointed arms. Y arms are shaped like a "Y," and the pad cup is cradled in the crook of the arm. Y arms are usually found on beginning and some intermediate instruments. A French pointed arm is essentially a straight bar that extends over the pad cup, ending in a point in the middle of the pad cup. French pointed arms are usually found on professional and some intermediate model flutes.

Articulated Keys: Keys that automatically open or close more than one tone hole or key mechanism by design. Articulated keys can facilitate technique and help produce a more even scale throughout the instrument's playing range. For example, when the right-hand index finger depresses the 4-key, two other keys are also depressed.

Articulation: See Articulation/Articulative Styles, page 6

Assembly: The manner in which an instrument is put together before being played. Proper assembly is important to playability, instrument care, and maintenance. Teaching students to carefully assemble their instruments using a defined assembly procedure can help significantly reduce wear and tear. The flute can be assembled efficiently and safely using the steps listed. Figures 2.2 and 2.3 can be used to guide the assembly process. See also Hand/Holding/Instrument/Playing Positions and Posture, page 113

1. The flute should be assembled while standing (when the case is securely resting on a chair or table) or while kneeling (when the case is sitting on the floor). Flutes should not be assembled in the player's lap. Although flutes are small, the parts can easily be dropped and damaged. Before handling the flute, make sure that all of the connecting joints are clean. Wipe them with a soft, clean

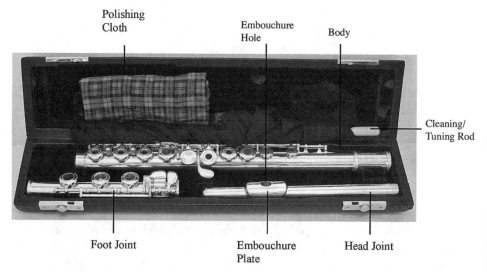

FIGURE 2.2. *Flute Before Assembly*

FIGURE 2.3. *C-foot Flute Assembled*

cloth to remove excess dirt and grime if necessary. Avoid putting unnecessary pressure on the keys, bars, rods, and other delicate mechanisms during assembly.

2. Grasp the head joint firmly with the left hand just below the embouchure plate. Grasp the instrument body with the right hand near the top, away from the key mechanisms.

3. Connect the head joint and body by using a gentle back-and-forth twisting motion while pushing the joints together. Align the embouchure hole with the main key stack as shown in figure 2.3. This position may be adjusted slightly to suit individual tastes. Many players make a small mark on the head joint and the body so that lining up the instrument during assembly is easier.

4. When assembling the head joint and body, do not insert the head joint into the body all the way. Most flutes are designed to be played with the head joint pulled out between one-eighth and one-quarter inch; however, the exact placement of the head joint varies from one instrument to another and is determined through individual experimentation and experience. Check the head joint placement regularly with a tuner. Most players visually memorize the "normal" position of the head joint, and make additional small adjustments when tuning and playing.

5. Grasp the foot joint firmly with the right hand, and avoid putting pressure on key mechanisms. Grasp the instrument body with the left hand near the top of the main body, away from the key mechanisms.

6. Connect the foot joint to the rest of the flute using a gentle back-and-forth twisting motion. Position the foot joint so that the post/rod is centered with the last pad cup on the flute body, as shown in figure 2.5.

Attacks: A detailed discussion of attacks is under Attacks in chapter 1. See also Releases/Cutoffs, page 56; Tonguing, page 71

Balance and Blend Considerations: In general, woodwind instruments are less homogeneous than brass instruments. As a result, they do not always blend together as well as brass instruments in ensemble settings. To enhance blend, some instrumental teachers recommend using the same instrument brand or

FIGURE 2.4. *Embouchure Hole Alignment*

FIGURE 2.5. *C-foot Joint Alignment*

model. In addition, because the flute does not project well in the low and middle ranges, more flutes are needed to achieve proper ensemble balance.

In a typical wind band with fifty to sixty players, six to eight flutes are often recommended as a good number for balance considerations. The number of flute players in any wind group depends largely on the type of sound desired, the number of instruments available, and the strength of flute players in the program.

Key Questions

Q: If I use six flute players in my ensemble, how many players should I put on each part?

A: Put three players on each part.

FIGURE 2.6. *B Foot Joint*

Q: If I use eight flute players in my ensemble, how many players should I put on each part?

A: It depends on the strength of your players; however, as a rule, put the same number of players on each part (i.e., four on first and four on second). If the top four or five players are particularly strong, placing three players on first and five players on second may provide better balance.

B Foot Joint: A foot joint that extends the range of the flute downward to low B-natural. B foot joints are longer than C foot joints and have an extra key (see fig. 2.6). Although optional on some student-line and intermediate flutes, B foot joints are standard on most professional flutes. See also Foot Joint, page 111

Bass Flute: The lowest commonly found instrument in the flute family. The bass flute sounds one octave below the C flute. Typically, the bass flute consists of four joints: the head joint, a J-shaped joint that extends the head joint tube and connects to the body, the body, and the foot joint. Bass flutes are also equipped with a hand rest for the left hand. The bass flute does not have the carrying power of other low-pitched instruments and is used primarily in flute choirs, other flute ensembles, and some jazz settings. See also Instrument Family and Playing Considerations, page 122

Beats: See Beats, page 10

Bell Tones: See Bell Tones, page 10

Bennett: See Flute Scales, page 111

Bis: Also called the chromatic or lever B-flat key, a term used to describe the small alternate B-flat key to the left of the F key (4). The bis key may be used as an alternate fingering for B-flat (instead of T, 1-4, use T, 1-bis). It is also used as a trill key. See also Alternate Fingerings/Alternates, page 83

Body: The long section of the flute that contains most of the keys. Most C flutes and alto flutes have three sections: the head joint, the body, and the foot joint. Piccolos typically have only two sections: the head joint and the body. See also Parts, Flute, page 138; Wall Thickness, page 155; Materials in Flute Making, page 136

Boehm System: The key system developed by Theobald Boehm (1794–1881) on which the modern flute is based. Boehm's system involved redesigning the traditional eight-key flute to improve technical playing. By the late 1830s, ring keys and the right-hand trill keys were prominent features of Boehm's flutes. By the end of the 1840s, flutes were made of metal and had a conical bore, much like the modern flute. Boehm's system was widely adopted on some woodwind instruments (flute, clarinet, and saxophone) and has greatly influenced modifications on other woodwind instruments (oboe).

Bore, Instrument: In general, a term used to describe the inside shape and dimensions of an instrument's tube. Bore is sometimes used when describing specific parts of a woodwind or brass mouthpiece. Bore is not a term commonly associated with flute playing. See also Acoustical Properties, page 81; Conical, page 99; Cylindrical, page 102

Break: The point at which there is a register shift on an instrument. On flute, the break occurs at fourth-line D-natural. There are three main challenges for players when crossing the break. The first challenge is coordinating the fingers. The break involves moving from an open fingering (with few tone holes covered) to a closed fingering (with most tone holes covered). As a result, a great deal of finger movement must be precisely coordinated. The second challenge is maintaining an even tone quality across the break because the notes just before the break engage a short section of tubing, whereas the notes just over the break engage a long section of tubing. Maintaining a consistent tone quality with such a large physical change in tube length requires subtle adjustments of the embouchure and air stream. The third challenge is playing in tune across the break. The pitch on traditional scale flutes tends to be sharp on most of the notes just before the break. Players must make appropriate adjustments in the air stream and embouchure on these sharp notes and then readjust quickly for the notes just over the break, which are typically better in tune. See also Crossing the Break, page 100; Technique, page 144

Breath Attacks: See Attacks, page 90

Breathing/Breath Support/Air Control: See Breathing/Breath Support/Air Control, page 10; Circular Breathing, page 23

Briccialdi Key: The left thumb key that sounds B-flat when depressed. The invention of this key is credited to Guilio Briccialdi (1818–1881), an Italian flutist and composer. The Briccialdi key is engaged by sliding the left thumb toward the head joint. Although this key provides a very useful alternate fingering for regular B-flat (1-4), it is not the best choice in passages with frequent shifts between B-natural and B-flat. Developing facility with both B-flat fingerings greatly enhances technical proficiency.

C Foot Joint: The traditional flute foot joint that extends the low range of the flute downward to low C-natural. The C foot joint is typically found on student-line flutes and is less commonly found on intermediate and professional flutes. See also B Foot Joint, page 93; Foot Joint, page 111

C-Sharp Trill Key: An optional trill key located above and to the left of the B-flat bis key on the right hand. Contexts in which the C-sharp trill key can be used are described under Alternate Fingerings/Alternates in this chapter.

Care and Maintenance: Taking proper care of the flute is essential for achieving high performance levels. One of the most important aspects of daily care and maintenance is carefully cleaning out the flute after each playing session. Players typically keep a cloth or swab in the case for cleaning the instrument. The best swabs are made from soft, absorbent materials, such as cotton or silk. Swabs should be big enough to fill the inside of the flute when inserted, but not so big that they are difficult to use. Thread the cloth through the eye of the cleaning rod, and wrap the cloth around the rod to avoid damaging the instrument tube. Insert the rod (eye end first) into one end of each joint and push the swab through and out the other end of the joint. Remove the swab from the eye and pull the swab through the joint. Repeat this process for each joint. Some players insert the rod end of the cleaning rod into the joint and pull it (and the cloth behind it) through the joint. A plastic or wooden cleaning rod can help prevent scratches to the inside of the flute. Swab the head joint by working the rod and swab back and forth inside the joint.

While swabbing the flute after each playing session is important, other aspects of care and maintenance are also important for keeping the instrument in top playing condition. Most of the maintenance suggestions are relevant to secondary school students, and many of them simply involve establishing a daily routine. See also Care and Maintenance Accessories, page 23

Routine Maintenance

1. Assemble and disassemble the flute in the same manner each day.
2. Clean the joints (inside and outside) regularly so that excess pressure can be avoided during the assembly/disassembly processes.
3. Maintain proper hand/holding/instrument position while playing. Flutes should be rested in an upright position. When the flute is rested in a horizontal or semihorizontal position, water tends to run into tone holes.
4. Carry the instrument securely in an upright position to minimize the chance of banging the instrument into music stands, chairs, or into other instruments.
5. When placing the instrument in its case, lay the sections down gently in their proper locations, then swab out the moisture one joint at a time.
6. Remove excess moisture on the pads with a piece of ungummed cigarette paper or a dollar bill. Ultimately, pads that are not allowed to dry properly between playing sessions and pads that accumulate the most moisture will need to be replaced more often than other pads.
7. Wipe the outside of the flute with a dry, soft cloth to remove excess moisture, fingerprints, and/or dust. Do not use silver polish or other cleaners on the flute.

Other Maintenance

1. Remove the dust from under the key mechanisms once every couple of weeks or so with a small, soft paintbrush.
2. If excessive key noise is heard during regular play, oil the key mechanisms with woodwind key oil. These clacking sounds are often caused by metal-to-metal contact, which results in excessive wear of the key mechanisms. As a rule, the key mechanisms should be oiled lightly once a month or so.
3. Rinse out the head joint with warm (not hot) soapy water two or three times a year to remove accumulated grime. Remove the cork stopper before rinsing the head joint.

Considerations

1. Buy a well-made and well-fitted case; a good case is essential to maintaining instrument condition. Some flute cases also include case covers, which add additional protection.
2. Avoid subjecting the flute to extreme temperature and humidity changes. Pads, corks, and felts have a tendency to loosen as the instrument contracts and expands in response to the temperature. Never leave the instrument in an uncontrolled environment.
3. Wipe the flute with a soft cloth to keep the outside clean. Do not clean the outside of the flute or the keys with silver polish or other similar polish. Polish damages key mechanisms, ruins pads, and gums up tone holes.
4. Check the position of the cork stopper regularly and adjust as necessary. There will be times when the cork stopper will fit tighter or looser than usual. These differences are normal because as humidity increases, cork expands; as humidity decreases, cork contracts.

Cases, Instrument: Generally, the cases that come with most flutes are the best cases for everyday use, especially for young players. These hard cases protect the instrument well and are designed to "fit" particular instruments. This design secures instruments properly in the case and provides adequate storage for a cleaning rod and a soft cloth. Student-line flute cases generally have carrying handles and no outer case cover. Intermediate and professional flutes often come with French style cases that are slimmer than student-line cases. French style cases typically do not have carrying handles; therefore, they usually come with a case cover with handles that zips around the entire case, providing added protection and storage. Several cases from aftermarket manufacturers are also available. These cases are available in a variety of configurations, including standard replacement cases, combination flute and piccolo cases, cases with storage for small "extras" such as a tuner or metronome, and cases that are designed like backpacks. In addition to stand-alone flute cases and cases that hold both a flute and a piccolo, many saxophone cases and gig bags are designed to hold a flute or a flute case. Manufacturers of aftermarket instrument cases and bags include Pro Tec, SKB, Reunion Blues, Gator, Cavallaro, and Gig.

Key Questions

Q: Are all cases well constructed and designed?

A: No. Students should not purchase cases without checking them out thoroughly. Many cases do not protect instruments properly. Inspect each case for adequate padding, sturdy and secure hinges, latches, and handles, and a proper fit for the instrument. A case that does not fit the instrument well or a poorly constructed case will not adequately protect the instrument, which may result in damaged equipment. Typical problems with flute cases include latches that do not stay fastened securely, which allows the instrument to fall out when the case is picked up, and worn padding, which allows the instrument to move excessively while in the case.

Chimney: See Riser, page 142

Choosing an Instrument: See Instrument Selection, page 33

Cleaning/Tuning Rod: An accessory used to help clean the inside of an instrument's joints. Cleaning rods are usually made of metal or wood and have an eye or slot at one end that holds the corner of a cloth swab. Typically, the cloth is pushed through one end of the joint to the other with the rod. The cloth is then removed from the rod and pulled through the joint with the hand. The cleaning rod is also used for tuning. It has a mark or line on one end that is used to check the position of the cork stopper in the head joint. When inserted into the head joint as far as it will go, this mark should appear in the center of the embouchure hole. If the mark is not centered, the cork stopper must be adjusted appropriately. The proper position of the cork stopper is critical to good intonation. See also Cork Stopper, page 100

Clefs: The treble clef is used to notate music for all flutes.

Closed G-sharp Key: A G-sharp key that remains closed until activated by depressing the G-sharp key with the left-hand little finger. Most modern flutes are equipped with a closed G-sharp key. The closed G-sharp key is configured so that the left-hand little finger is not depressing a key most of the time. It is important to maintain good hand position and not allow the little finger of the left hand to droop underneath the G-sharp key or float high above the G-sharp key. Many antique flutes were equipped with an open G-sharp key, which required the left-hand little finger to be actively involved in depressing the G-sharp key most of the time. See also Open G-sharp Key, page 137

Closed-Hole Model: See Plateau Model Flutes, page 138

Conical: A term used to describe the cone-shaped tubing often used in instrument construction that is relatively narrow on one end and gradually widens toward the other. At first glance the flute may look cylindrical; however, the head joint is actually conical. See also Acoustical Basics, page 3; Acoustical Properties, page 81; Cylindrical, page 102

Construction and Design: The modern flute is pitched in C, and the piccolo is pitched in C one octave above the flute. Although the head joint is slightly conical, the rest of the flute is cylindrical. Flutes can be made of a variety of materials, including nickel silver, silver, gold, wood, and even platinum. A nickel silver or silver flute may be plated with silver or gold. In addition, it is quite common for the head joint to be made of different materials than the body and foot joint. For example, some intermediate flutes are made with a solid silver head joint and a silver-plated body and foot joint. Springs may also be made of a variety of materials, including stainless steel, copper, silver, or gold.

Student-line flutes are typically closed-hole models with a C foot joint and an offset G key (third-finger left-hand key), so that smaller hands can reach the G key more easily. These instruments are usually made of nickel silver and may be silver-plated, have drawn tone holes and "Y" arms attaching the keys to the rods. Intermediate flutes may include a sterling silver head joint, or a sterling silver head joint, body, and foot joint (the key work is often silver-plated). Many intermediate flutes are open-hole models, and may have either an offset G key or an inline G key, and most are also equipped with a B foot joint. Professional flutes are available with a wide variety of options and for a wide range of prices. In addition to the options typically available for intermediate flutes, professional flutes are more commonly made with soldered tone holes and French-pointed arms attaching the keys to the rods. A professional flute is also more likely to have "extras" such as a split E key or a "Gizmo" key (high C facilitator). It is also more likely to be constructed with more precious metals, which may include gold (or more rarely, platinum) in addition to, or instead of, silver. The most common places for gold to appear on a flute are in the springs and on the lip plate.

The tubing on flutes, particularly professional flutes, is available in a variety of thicknesses, each producing different tonal qualities. Silver flutes are most commonly available in .014 inches (thin wall), .016 inches (medium wall), and .018 inches (thick wall). As a rule, flutes with thin walls produce a brighter sound, and flutes with thick walls produce a darker sound.

The head joint affects tone quality and intonation significantly and is an important component of the flute. Players can improve the tonal characteristics of their instruments significantly and less expensively by investing in a new head joint rather than purchasing a new instrument. When considering a new head joint, make sure that it will fit into the flute body for which it is intended. The diameter of flute joints is not universal, and a new head joint may have to be adjusted to fit properly. The head joint should also be a good "fit" for the player. Try several head joints to see which one works best. See also Acoustical Basics, page 3; Acoustical Properties, page 81; Head Joint, page 121

Cooper Scale: See Flute Scales, page 111

Cork Stopper: A cork in the head joint just beneath the end cap. The position of the cork stopper is critical to good intonation. It should be checked regularly because it can move over time, especially if it is not fitted very tightly. To check the cork stopper position, use the end of the cleaning rod that has a tuning mark on it. Insert the rod into the head joint as far as it will go and look through the embouchure hole. The tuning mark should be in the middle of the embouchure hole. Adjust the cork if necessary. To move the cork closer to the end cap, twist the end cap. To move the cork closer to the embouchure hole, unscrew the end cap slightly and push down on it. Avoid adjusting the cork stopper by taking off the end cap and/or pushing it from either end with the cleaning rod.

> *Key Questions*
>
> Q: Can I use any cleaning rod on any flute to check the cork stopper?
>
> A: Generally, yes. Modern flutes are designed with 17mm of space between the end of the stopper and the center of the embouchure hole, and most cleaning rods are marked to accommodate this distance. However, it is possible that a particular tuning rod may not be accurate. If a problem is suspected, check the tuning rod against another and make sure that the rod has a mark at the 17mm point.

Crossing the Break: Playing any note below fourth-line D-natural to any note above fourth-line D-natural or playing any note above fourth-line D-natural to any note below fourth-line D-natural is considered crossing the break. However, crossing the break usually refers to performing intervals close in proximity to fourth-line D-natural. For example, playing from C-sharp to D-natural, C-natural to D-natural, C-natural to D-sharp, B-natural to D-natural, B-natural to D-sharp, and so on is commonly referred to as crossing the break. Crossing the break is sometimes technically problematic on flute because it requires players to play from an open note (where few keys are depressed) to a closed note (where most keys are depressed). Preparing the right hand simplifies the problems inherent in crossing the break, while causing only slight changes in tone quality and intonation. Suggestions for crossing the break and preparing the right hand appear in the following section. See also Break, page 94; Technique, page 144

Preparing the Right Hand/Suggestions for Crossing the Break

1. When playing from open C-sharp to fourth-line D-natural, put the right-hand fingers (4-5-6) down when playing the C-sharp.
2. When playing from C-sharp to D-sharp, put the right-hand fingers (4-5-6) down when playing the C-sharp.
3. When playing from C-sharp to E-natural, put the right-hand fingers (4-5) down when playing the C-sharp.
4. When playing intervals back and forth across the break, the appropriate fingers can be left down. For example, when playing from D-natural to C-sharp and back to D-natural, the right-hand fingers (4-5-6) can be left down.

Crossing the Break: Other Problematic Intervals

Playing across the break from C-natural to D-natural, C-natural to D-sharp, B-natural to D-natural, A-natural to D-natural, and so on is also problematic. Because preparing the right hand is not a practical option with these intervals, it is especially important to maintain proper hand position and practice precise finger coordination. Common examples of crossing the break appear in figure 2.7.

Leave 4-5-6 Down   Leave 5-6 Down   Leave 4-5-6 Down   Leave 4-5 Down

Figure 2.7. *Crossing the Break. Prepare the right hand by depressing the appropriate right-hand keys on the lower note in each grouping.*

Teaching Tips for Crossing the Break

1. Make sure players keep their fingers as close as possible to the keys and in the ready position at all times. Proper finger position will improve finger coordination.
2. Practice these intervals slowly at first, and work on one interval at a time. When students can play from C-sharp to D-natural, C-sharp to D-sharp, C-sharp to E-natural in isolation, then have them play two together, then three, and so on.
3. When learning to play these intervals, tonguing each note can facilitate response; however, tonguing can also mask problems with finger coordination. It is important that students practice these intervals using slurs across the break. Students will often make changes in air, embouchure, throat, and so on to compensate for poor finger coordination when playing across the break. Such compensations are unnecessary. In addition, maintaining a steady air stream and a consistent embouchure when playing across the break is essential.

Curved Head Joint: A head joint that curves in a U-shape to minimize the distance between the embouchure hole and the keys on the left hand. Curved head joints are commonly found on bass flutes, sometimes found on alto flutes, and occasionally found on C flutes. Curved head joints are available on C flutes for younger players, or players who cannot otherwise reach the keys comfortably (see fig. 2.8). See also Head Joint, page 121

Curved Lip Plate: A lip plate that is curved to better fit the contours of the lips. Most lip plates on the market are straight; however, more flute makers are now offering curved lip plates. Whether or not to play on a curved lip plate is a matter of personal preference.

Cylindrical: A term used to describe the cylinder-shaped tubing often used in instrument construction. Unlike conical tubing, which is relatively narrow on one end and gradually widens toward the other, cylindrical tubing remains the same diameter along the entire length of tubing. Although at first glance the flute may look cylindrical, the head joint is actually conical. See also Acoustical Basics, page 3; Acoustical Properties, page 81; Conical, page 99

Deveau Scale: See Flute Scales, page 111

Diaphragm: See Breathing/Breath Support/Air Control, page 10; Diaphragm, page 26

FIGURE 2.8. *Curved Head Joint (Bass Flute)*

Dizziness/Lightheadedness: See Dizziness/Lightheadedness, page 26

Double-Tonguing: A technique that enables performers to tongue duple patterns rapidly. See also Multiple-Tonguing, page 52

Doubling Considerations: See Instrument Family and Playing Considerations, page 122

Drawn Tone Holes: Drawn tone holes are constructed by drawing up the metal around the tone hole to create a rim on which the pad rests. That is, the body of the flute and the tone holes are crafted out of the same piece of metal tubing. Most student-line and intermediate flutes have drawn tone holes. Most drawn tone holes are also rolled at the top. See also Soldered Tone Holes, page 142; Tone Holes, page 147

Dynamic Considerations: See Dynamic Considerations, page 26; Intonation, page 129

Embouchure: The flute can be a relatively difficult instrument on which to initially create a sound. Although the embouchure is not difficult to form, the combination of embouchure formation, placement on the lip plate, and proper air speed and direction can make producing a flute sound somewhat challenging. Steps and suggestions for forming a fundamentally sound flute embouchure are described in the following section. Proper embouchures for various flutes are shown in figures 2.9 through 2.13. Embouchure considerations for piccolo, alto flute, and bass flute are discussed under Instrument Family and Playing Considerations. See also Instrument Family and Playing Considerations, page 122

The "Kiss, Roll, and Drop" Method of Teaching the Flute Embouchure

1. With the lips together lightly (as if preparing a light kiss), position the head joint against the lips so that the embouchure hole is centered. Make sure that the embouchure hole is centered with the lips by feeling the embouchure hole lightly with the tongue.
2. Bring the mouth corners down and back slightly. The lower lip may become smoother, but should not become stretched or tight. The lower lip remains relaxed.
3. Roll the head joint forward until the embouchure hole is almost parallel to the floor. The edge of the embouchure hole maintains contact with the lower lip, and the lower lip should cover one-quarter to one-third of the hole, depending on the thickness and shape of the player's lips.
4. Drop the head joint down from the center position slightly, depending on the thickness and shape of the player's lips.
5. Allow the upper lip to relax slightly and blow a stream of air through the lips, forming a hole in the center of the lips (lip aperture). Direct this air stream across the embouchure hole toward the opposite edge of the hole. It may help to think of saying the syllable "poo" when blowing. The lip aperture should be relatively small (about one-eighth of an inch high, and no wider than the embouchure hole). The lip aperture should look more like a diamond than an oval.

General Considerations for Flute Embouchure

1. Use only the head joint when first learning to produce a tone. Learning to produce a tone while also learning to hold the flute

FIGURE 2.9. *Embouchure*

FIGURE 2.10. *Bass Flute Embouchure*

FIGURE 2.11. *Embouchure in the Low Range*

FIGURE 2.12. *Embouchure in the Middle Range*

FIGURE 2.13. *Embouchure in the High Range*

properly is particularly challenging for young players. A variety of sounds can be produced with the head joint alone. For example, placing the palm of the right hand over the end of the head joint lowers the pitch by one octave. In addition, shifting the position of the right-hand index finger inside the end of the head joint produces a variety of pitches. Playing musical games by varying the finger position inside the head joint is a good exercise when playing on the head joint alone. Finally, players can produce a variety of partials by varying air speed and direction, which helps develop important concepts regarding the relationships between air, embouchure, tone quality, and pitch.

2. Make sure that the edge of the embouchure hole rests approximately where the red area of the lower lip meets the skin. Players with thicker lips may require a slightly higher lip placement.

3. Avoid spitting. In an effort to push air out of a relatively small lip aperture, some players have a tendency to spit. Although the inside of the mouth should feel moist, keep the moisture away from the lip aperture.

4. Play with a relaxed embouchure. Although the corners of the mouth are somewhat firm in the high range, the flute embouchure is not tight or tense; it is relaxed. A tight embouchure limits pitch flexibility and negatively affects tone quality.

5. Rest the lip plate comfortably against the lower lip. It should not be pressed forcefully against the lip.

6. Do not puff the cheeks. Players should relax the cheeks slightly to help produce a richer tone, especially in the low register and into the lower part of the middle register. Puffing the cheeks distorts pitch and tone quality.

7. In general, move the head joint, not the head, to obtain the correct flute position for producing a tone. The player's head should remain straight at all times.

8. Make sure that the actual opening of the lip aperture is no wider than the embouchure hole of the flute. An aperture that is too large causes an excessively airy, unfocused tone quality.

9. Take frequent breaks. Beginners often complain of dizziness, lightheadedness, or tingling in the limbs. These sensations are

normal and should disappear as embouchures are developed and control is gained over air speed, direction, and focus. Frequent short breaks can minimize these sensations.

Key Questions

Q: Is the same basic embouchure used for all flutes?

A: Yes. However, there are differences. On alto and bass flute, the lip aperture is somewhat larger to accommodate the larger embouchure hole, and the embouchure is slightly looser when playing in the lower range. Furthermore, the lower flutes are generally less resistant because of the larger embouchure holes. It may help to think of the syllable "who" when playing these flutes. On the other hand, the piccolo requires a very fast air stream pushed through a small lip aperture and is challenging to play with good intonation and blend. Even experienced flute players may experience dizziness and tingling in the limbs when first playing the piccolo. In general, the intonation tendencies of most traditional scale modern flutes are exaggerated on piccolo. In addition, the piccolo projects well and stands out in any ensemble.

Q: Can students with braces play the flute?

A: Yes. However, students may encounter some challenges for a period of time after getting braces. For example, it is common for the tone to become airy and less focused and for the high notes to become more difficult to produce after getting braces. Many players experience pain or discomfort, especially when they first get braces and for a week or so after they have their braces adjusted. Some players find it advantageous to use wax or other materials to relieve pain. A dentist can recommend the best kind of wax for students who play musical instruments. In addition, players will have to readjust their embouchures after the braces are removed. When possible, it is a good idea for players to take some time off (usually a couple of weeks) after their braces are removed. This time off will allow players to "forget" the feel of the embouchure used when playing with braces. When players begin playing again, it will be easier for them to adjust to playing without braces.

Q: Can students with uneven teeth, an underbite, or thick lips play the flute?

A: Yes. Although these physical attributes are traditionally considered a disadvantage to playing the flute, players who are highly motivated to play flute can overcome almost any abnormality. The best predictor of flute success is the ability of the student to produce an acceptable sound on the head joint. That is, regardless of less-than-ideal physical attributes, if the student is able to produce an acceptable sound on the head joint, there is no reason he or she should not play flute.

Q: Is it acceptable to play the flute with the lip aperture "off center?"

A: Rarely. In most cases, the best embouchure position will be in the center of the lips. One of the few exceptions may be a player who has a pronounced cupid's bow or dip in the center of the upper lip. He or she may not be able to form an even, round hole in the lips at the center and may have better success with an off-center lip aperture.

Embouchure Hole: The hole in the head joint that air is blown into and across. On most modern flutes, the embouchure "hole" is really comprised of two holes: one in the lip plate, and one in the head joint tube. These two holes are connected by means of a riser (or chimney), which gives depth to the embouchure hole. Most embouchure holes are basically round or oval; however, some holes are designed with a slightly square shape. See also Lip Plate, page 136; Riser, page 142

Embouchure Plate: See Lip Plate, page 136

End Cap: The cap at the end of the head joint. The end cap is typically screwed onto a threaded rod at the top of the cork. Twisting or pulling on the end cap affects the position of the cork stopper, which can flatten or sharpen the overall pitch of the instrument. See also Cork Stopper, page 100

Endurance/Stamina: See Endurance/Stamina, page 28

Exhalation/Exhaling: See Breathing/Breath Support/Air Control, page 10

Extended/Contemporary Techniques: In general, ways of producing sounds on an instrument that are not traditionally characteristic of the instrument or not typically called for in standard literature. A detailed discussion of these techniques is found under Extended/Contemporary Techniques in chapter 1. See also Extended/Contemporary Techniques, page 29

Family: See Instrument Family and Playing Considerations, page 122

Flute Scales: A term referring to the placement and size of tone holes and the resulting pitch tendencies of each note. "Old scale flutes," or flutes with a traditional scale, are based on a reference pitch of roughly A = 435 and use a shorter head joint to achieve A = 440 (or A = 442, or A = 444). Most of these flutes possess at least some of the pitch tendencies discussed under Intonation. "New scale" flutes have been redesigned in terms of tone hole size and placement to compensate for many of the inherent pitch tendencies found in the traditional (old) scale flutes. Several makers have developed their own flute scales, most notably Albert Cooper, Lewis Deveau, and William Bennett. Many newer flutes have adopted a new scale and may exhibit fewer and less severe pitch tendencies than traditional scale flutes. However, many players still choose to play on older flutes, learning to make the appropriate adjustments. Regardless of the scale of any given flute, it is important to learn the individual pitch tendencies of each instrument because a perfectly in tune flute does not exist.

Flutter Tonguing: A technique that involves rolling or "fluttering" the tongue rapidly while producing a tone. Flutter tonguing uses the same motion of the tongue that is used when pronouncing a rolling "r." Players who cannot roll their tongues may use a throat growl as a substitute. See also Extended/Contemporary Techniques, page 29

Foot Joint: The small joint that contains the right-hand little-finger keys. Flute foot joints are available in C or B. Flutes with a C foot joint are capable of playing downward to a low C-natural, while flutes with a B foot joint are capable of playing downward to a low B-natural. C foot joints are most commonly found on student-line flutes, while low B foot joints are most commonly found on intermediate and professional flutes. Although many advancing flute players prefer the extended range of the low B foot joint, some advanced players actually prefer the C foot joint for acoustical reasons. The piccolo does not have a foot joint. The lowest note of the piccolo is D-natural, and the only pinky key is the E-flat key, which is on the body of the piccolo.

French Case: A sleek, small, thin flute case that is very compact, typically having no handle. French cases are often carried in case covers, and are commonly used with intermediate and professional flutes. See also Cases, Instrument, page 97

French Model Flute: Also called an open-hole flute, a French model flute has keys that are open in the middle where the fingers cover them. French model flutes have open key work for the second and third finger keys of the left hand, and the first, second, and third fingers of the right hand as is shown in figure 2.14. Most

FIGURE 2.14. *B Foot French Model (Open Hole) Flute*

intermediate and professional flutes are French model flutes. Some disagreement
exists as to whether a French model flute is better than a plateau model (closed-
hole) flute. Advantages of a French model flute include: (1) it has a better tone
quality than does a plateau model (according to some players); (2) it is possible
to use the half-hole technique to achieve in-between pitches; and (3) the open-
hole design encourages good hand and finger position. Disadvantages of a French
model flute include: (1) it causes hand and wrist strain (according to some players)
because such an exact hand position must be maintained during play; and (2) it

has a less desirable tone quality than does a closed-hole flute (according to some players). See also Plateau Model Flutes, page 138

Fundamental: See Fundamental, page 32

Gizmo Key: Also called a high-C facilitator, a small extra key to the right of the low C-natural and B-natural rollers on flutes with a low B foot joint. The gizmo key closes the low B-natural tone hole, which provides a clear response for the fourth octave C-natural.

Gold: See Materials in Flute Making, page 136

Half-Holes: A performance technique in which the player typically covers half (or part) of a tone hole with one finger. Open-hole flutes work especially well for traditional half-holes, although the pitch can be similarly altered with a closed-hole flute by using the embouchure and/or pushing the key about halfway down. Using half-holes enables players to play quarter tones in contemporary literature. Half-holes can also be used to execute certain trills. See also Extended/ Contemporary Techniques, page 29; French Model Flute, page 111; Plateau Model Flutes, page 138

Hand/Holding/Instrument/Playing Positions and Posture: Holding the flute properly, maintaining good hand position, and maintaining proper playing position are key factors in developing good technique, facility, and ease of playing. In addition, good hand position, holding position, and playing position will reduce muscle fatigue and help players avoid physical problems, such as carpal tunnel syndrome. The majority of the flute's weight is supported by the left-hand index finger and the right thumb. Balancing the instrument, particularly when few or no fingers are depressed, can be somewhat challenging. Suggestions for appropriate hand/holding/instrument/playing positions and posture are listed in this section.

Left-Hand Position

1. The index finger contacts the underneath side of the flute between the first knuckle (large knuckle at the hand) and the second knuckle. Essentially, the flute rests on the first knuckle as if sitting on a shelf, and the index finger supports the flute by wrapping around and slightly underneath it. The index finger curves around the flute and the finger pad covers the C key as shown in figures 2.15 and 2.16.

FIGURE 2.15. *Hand Position (Back View)*

FIGURE 2.16. *Hand Position (Front View)*

2. The left thumb rests on the B key on the underneath back side of the flute just above the first knuckle. The thumb must remain ready to operate the B-flat key as shown in figure 2.17.

3. The fingers curve around the flute from underneath and rest naturally on the keys. The fingers remain no more than one-fourth of an inch from the keys, and they cross the instrument at a slightly downward angle.

4. The index finger is positioned on the C key (1), the middle finger is positioned on the A key (2), and the ring finger is positioned on the G key (3). The finger pads should cover any open tone holes. Even if playing a closed-hole flute, place the finger pads (not the tips) inside the round centers of the keys for proper hand position.

5. The little finger touches the G-sharp key lightly and remains ready to operate this key when needed. Many players develop the bad habit of letting the little finger droop underneath the G-sharp key or float high above the G-sharp key. Letting the little finger droop or float out of position creates extra tension in the hand and increases the distance the little finger must travel to operate

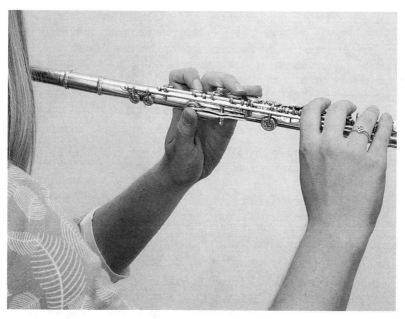

FIGURE 2.17. *Left Thumb on B-flat Key*

the G-sharp key. Both of these factors negatively affect technical proficiency.

6. The wrist has an inward bend.

Right-Hand Position

1. The right thumb supports the flute, so its position is very important. The right thumb pad is placed on the underneath side of the flute between the index and middle fingers. The left-most acceptable position of the right thumb is underneath the index finger, and the right-most acceptable position is underneath the middle finger, depending on the player. The thumb should not extend too far from underneath the flute (the tip of the thumb protruding to the front) because that position hinders technical proficiency.

2. The fingers curve around the flute and rest naturally on the keys as if forming a "C." The fingers remain no more than one-fourth of an inch from the keys, and they cross the instrument at right angles.

3. The index finger is positioned on the F key (4), the middle finger is positioned on the E key (5), and the ring finger is positioned on the D key (6). The finger pads should cover any open tone holes. Even if playing a closed-hole flute, place the finger pads (not the tips) inside the round centers of the keys for proper hand position.

4. The little finger should touch the E-flat key lightly and should remain ready to operate the pinky keys (E-flat, low C-natural, low C-sharp, and low B-natural).

5. The wrist remains virtually straight; however, a very slight inward bend is acceptable.

Holding/Instrument Position

1. There are two common standing positions. The first is to stand with the feet parallel to the music stand. The second is to stand with the feet at about a 30- to 45-degree angle to the right of the music stand and then rotate the upper body so that the flute is almost parallel to the music stand. Some teachers believe that this position fosters a more open chest cavity by pulling the left arm out away from the chest area.

2. In the sitting position, the feet and body can be positioned parallel to or at a slight angle to the music stand. A common alternate position preferred by some teachers is to sit with the hips and legs rotated at a 30- to 45-degree angle toward the right of the music stand as stated above.

3. Hold the elbows out away from the body so that the flute is almost, but not quite, parallel to the floor. Keep the elbows and arms out away from the body to encourage proper breathing techniques.

4. Hold the head so that the lips are parallel to the embouchure plate. The head may be tilted slightly to the right to achieve this position.

5. Avoid slouching. Slouching brings the elbows into the body, lowers the flute toward the floor, and causes the head to tilt significantly. Proper playing positions are shown in figures 2.18 and 2.19. Proper playing positions for the bass flute and piccolo are shown in figures 2.20, 2.21, and 2.22.

FIGURE 2.18. *Flute Playing Position (Front View)*

FIGURE 2.19. *Flute Playing Position (Side View)*

FIGURE 2.20. *Bass Flute Playing Position (Front View)*

FIGURE 2.21. *Piccolo Playing Position (Front View)*

Posture

1. Sit up straight (but avoid being rigid or tense) with feet flat on the floor.

2. Avoid tension or tightness in the playing position because tension negatively affects both the mental and physical aspects of playing the flute.

3. Keep the head relaxed. A slight tilt to the right is acceptable so that the lips remain parallel with the embouchure plate.

4. Hold the right arm out from the body with the elbow pointing slightly downward and backward away from the music stand. The

FIGURE 2.22. *Piccolo Playing Position (Side View)*

arm is bent at about a 90-degree angle, so that the wrist remains straight. Maintaining good right arm position is a challenge for many flute players. Avoid developing poor posture habits that result from resting the right arm on the back of the chair. Whether sitting or standing, develop the muscle strength necessary to hold the flute in the correct position for a long period of time.

5. Position the music stand carefully. Many posture problems result from poor placement of the music stand. Place the music stand in a position that enables comfortable and easy viewing of both the music and the teacher/director while playing with proper posture. The most common problem is for music stands to be too low. The most detrimental problem is for music stands to be placed too far to one side, forcing players to abandon good playing positions. Sharing music stands often creates this problem.

6. Accord each player ample performance space. Posture problems often result from players sitting too close together in ensemble settings. Players should have enough room to hold the flute at the

proper angle. Turning chairs slightly can help players avoid hitting each other with their instruments.

Harmonics: See Harmonics, page 32

Head Joint: The joint at the top of the flute that contains the lip plate, embouchure hole, cork stopper, and end cap. In essence, the head joint is the mouthpiece of the flute because it is where the mouth blows air into (and across) the instrument. Head joints are considered the heart of the flute sound, and they may be upgraded to improve tonal response. In addition, some advanced players have more than one head joint for different playing situations. Head joints must be properly fitted to the instrument for which they are intended because flutes vary in circumference. A wide variety of head joints is available, and players should play-test several for fit, feel, and responsiveness before purchasing one. Particular attributes that affect a head joint's playability include: (1) the materials from which the tube, riser, and lip plate are made, and (2) the cut and shape of the embouchure hole. See also Embouchure Hole, page 116; Lip Plate, page 136; Riser, page 142

Head Joint Angle: The head joint remains parallel to the lips. See also Instrument Angle, page 122

High C Facilitator: See Gizmo Key, page 113

History: The flute has been around in various forms since ancient times; however, the key system on which the modern flute is based was developed by Theobald Boehm (1794–1881) in the 1800s. Boehm's system involved redesigning the traditional eight-key flute to improve technique. By the late 1830s, ring keys, right-hand trill keys, and enlarged tone holes were prominent features of Boehm's flutes. In addition, the original Boehm flutes were equipped with an open G-sharp key. By the end of the 1840s, flutes were made of metal and had a conical bore, much like the modern flute. In addition, the closed G-sharp key replaced the open G-sharp key. Through the years, several keys and articulated keys have been added, and flute makers have experimented with different scales, materials, and head joint designs.

Inline G: A term used to describe a G key mechanism that is in line with the other primary keys on flute. Flutes with inline G keys are appropriate for mature players and are typically available on intermediate and professional flutes, rather than on student-line flutes. Flutes with offset G keys are generally more appropriate for players with small hands because the offset G key is easier to reach.

Regardless of whether a flute has an inline G key or an offset G key, it plays the same acoustically. Whether or not to play a flute with an inline G key is a matter of personal preference. See also Offset G, page 137

Instrument Angle: The flute is held so that the foot joint is lowered slightly from a parallel position toward the floor. In addition, the foot joint is pushed out slightly away from the player.

Instrument Brands: Several brands of flutes are available from which to choose. Some makers carry several models to accommodate a wide range of playing skills and budgets. Other makers carry models that are particularly suited to certain skill levels, budgets, and playing situations. Used instruments are also a good option for many players, and used instruments made by reputable manufacturers are available. When searching for an inexpensive or used instrument, beware of "off" brands and instrument models (even with reputable brands) that have not performed up to a high standard. The following list includes several reputable flute manufacturers. Although this list is not exhaustive, it does provide a good starting point for research. See also Instrument Selection, page 33

Flute Manufacturers

Altus; Armstrong; Artley; Brannen; Emerson; Gemeinhardt; Haynes; Jupiter; Mateki; Miyazawa; Muramatsu; Nomata; Pearl; Powell; Prima Sankyo; Trevor James, and Yamaha.

Instrument Family and Playing Considerations: The basic modern flute family includes the four flutes shown in figure 2.23. These include the piccolo, C Flute, alto flute in G, and bass flute. In addition, some older band music may include parts written for D-flat flute, E-flat flute, or D-flat piccolo, although these instruments are not widely used. With the exception of the C flute, these instruments are transposing; that is, their written pitches are different than their sounding pitches. However, the alto flute is the only flute not pitched in C (the piccolo and bass flute transpose at the octave). Other flutes are available, including contrabass flutes pitched in G and C, but they are rarely used.

All of the flutes use the same basic fingering system and have a similar written range. The major difference between these instruments is their size and sounding ranges. What follows are some suggestions for playing the piccolo, alto flute, and bass flute, including a chart of written and sounding ranges of the various instruments.

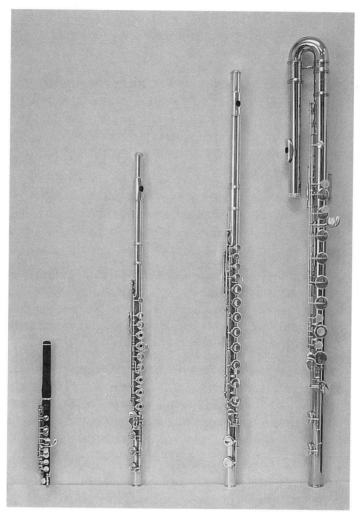

FIGURE 2.23. *Flute Family (Left to Right): Piccolo, Flute, Alto Flute, and Bass Flute*

PICCOLO

The piccolo is the smallest member of the flute family and sounds one octave higher than written. The piccolo has a low range that extends downward to low D-natural rather than to low C-natural (or B-natural) as other flutes do. The piccolo has a piercing high tone that cuts through virtually any ensemble. The piccolo is the most challenging flute to play for several reasons. First, it is the most difficult flute to play in tune. Pitch tendencies can vary greatly from instrument to instrument. Some piccolos may exhibit the pitch tendencies of flutes (only more exaggerated), while other piccolos may have the opposite pitch tendencies. Piccolos are popular in marching bands and are used frequently in outdoor settings, where the pitch is even harder to control. The smaller embouchure required to play the piccolo makes it more challenging to articulate passages and produce a clear tone. Players with large hands and/or fingers may find that the keys on the piccolo are too small and close together to play comfortably. Suggestions and considerations for playing the piccolo are listed separately. A size comparison between the piccolo and flute is shown in figure 2.24.

1. Piccolo players are often required to play fast, embellished passages. The piccolo is well suited to this type of playing, although the small keys can present challenges to players with large hands.

2. Because of the smaller embouchure hole, the piccolo requires less air but a faster air stream than the C flute. Many piccolos sound flat much of the time because players do not maintain proper air speed. In addition, inexperienced piccolo players may experience dizziness, lightheadedness, or tingling in the limbs.

3. Producing a clear piccolo tone can be challenging. "Airiness," which is common among beginners, is often caused by a lip aperture that is too large. As a rule, the aperture should not be wider than the embouchure hole, and it should be about an eighth of an inch high. Players can use a mirror to check aperture size.

4. The piccolo is typically not held at a downward angle like the flute. It is typically held parallel to the floor. In addition, the body rotation required for the flute is not required for the piccolo.

5. The piccolo is less forgiving than the flute. That is, small changes in embouchure, lip placement, and air stream on piccolo can affect tone quality and pitch to a greater degree than small changes on flute.

6. Piccolos are typically made of wood, plastic, or metal as can been seen in figures 2.25 and 2.26. Wooden piccolos tend to sound warmer and darker than metal piccolos. Plastic piccolos are durable, but they do not project as well or produce as good a tone as either wood or metal. The choice of piccolos is a matter of personal preference and often depends on the use for which the instrument is intended.

FIGURE 2.24. *C Piccolo (Metal) and C Flute*

ALTO FLUTE

The alto flute is the only commonly used modern flute that is not pitched in C. Therefore, it may present challenges for players who have never played a transposing instrument. The alto flute transposes to a key not common among transposing instruments. The alto flute is pitched in G, a fourth lower than the C flute.

FIGURE 2.25.   *C Piccolo (Metal)*

Players used to hearing and seeing music in C may find it unsettling at first to hear and see music in G. The alto flute has a dark tone quality with only moderate projection. Alto flutes are typically available with a C foot joint. Both curved and straight head joints are available on alto flutes. Alto flutes are significantly longer than C flutes; however, a player with average arm length should be able to hold an alto flute with a straight head joint. The alto flute is primarily a "color" instrument and is used in flute choirs, other flute ensembles, and in some jazz ensembles. The alto flute is occasionally used in band or orchestra settings. Suggestions and considerations for playing alto flute are listed separately.

FIGURE 2.26. *C Piccolo (Wooden)*

1. The alto flute embouchure is slightly larger, longer, and more relaxed than the C flute embouchure. Like the other flutes, the embouchure should not be wider than the embouchure hole.
2. The alto flute requires more air to play than the C flute. In addition, the oral cavity and throat are more open on alto flute. Thinking "who" when producing a tone can help focus the air stream appropriately.
3. Because players are required to use more air on alto flute, they may experience some dizziness, lightheadedness, or tingling in the limbs when they first start playing the instrument. These sensations are normal and should disappear as embouchures are developed and control is gained over air speed, direction, and focus. Frequent short breaks can minimize these sensations.

4. Notes over the break (especially from fourth-space E-natural) are noticeably "stuffier" on alto flute than they are on C flute. Players can adjust embouchure, air speed, and air direction to help improve the tone quality of these notes.

5. The response of the alto flute is slower than the C flute, and it takes more air. As a result, playing fast, technical passages is more difficult on alto flute than on C flute.

Bass Flute

The bass flute is pitched in C and sounds one octave lower than the C flute. It has a very dark, deep tone, but has minimal projection. Bass flutes are available with C or B foot joints. Bass flutes have an extra U-shaped joint between the body and the head joint that redirects the head joint back toward the foot joint. In effect, the bass flute has a curved head joint, which allows players to reach the keys comfortably. Like the alto flute, the bass flute is primarily a "color" instrument and is used in flute choirs, other flute ensembles, and in some jazz ensembles. The bass flute is generally not used in band or orchestra settings. Suggestions and considerations for playing the bass flute are listed separately.

1. The bass flute embouchure is slightly larger, longer, and more relaxed than the alto flute embouchure. Like the other flutes, the embouchure should not be wider than the embouchure hole.

2. The bass flute requires more air than the alto flute. In addition, the oral cavity and throat are more open on the bass flute. Thinking "who" or "oh" when producing a tone can help focus the air stream appropriately.

3. Because players are required to use more air on bass flute, they may experience some dizziness, lightheadedness, or tingling in the limbs when they first start playing the instrument. These sensations are normal and should disappear as embouchures are developed and control is gained over air speed, direction, and focus. Frequent short breaks can minimize these sensations.

4. Notes over the break, especially from fourth space E-natural can feel and sound very stuffy. Producing clean higher notes (G-natural and above) can also be challenging. Players can adjust embouchure, air speed, and air direction to help improve the tone quality of these notes.

5. Bass flutes respond slower than alto or C flutes. As a result, playing fast, technical passages tend to sound "muddy." The typical role

for the bass flute is to play simple bass lines or lyrical melodies; however, playing fast technical passages is certainly possible on bass flute.

Instrument Parts: See Parts, Flute, page 138

Instrument Position: See Hand/Holding/Instrument Playing Positions and Posture, page 113

Instrument Ranges: See Range, page 140

Instrument Selection: See Instrument Brands, page 122; Instrument Selection, page 33

Instrument Sizes: See Instrument Family and Playing Considerations, page 122

Instrument Stands: See Instrument Stands, page 39

Intonation: Generally, the degree of "in-tuneness" in a melodic and a harmonic context. In ensemble playing, the most important factors in achieving intonation accuracy are: (1) hearing intonation problems, (2) understanding what adjustments need to be made to correct intonation problems, and (3) having the skills to make the necessary adjustments. A detailed general discussion of Intonation is in chapter 1. Specific suggestions for helping players better understand the pitch tendencies of the flute and how to make appropriate pitch adjustments are outlined separately. See also Flute Scales, page 111; Intonation, page 41; Temperament, page 61; Tuning/Tuning Note Considerations, page 152

GENERAL COMMENTS FOR ADJUSTING PITCH

Adjusting pitch is the process of raising or lowering the pitch of notes. Comments and suggestions for adjusting pitch are outlined as follows.

1. Embouchure/Air Stream—The embouchure and air stream can be altered in several subtle ways to adjust or humor pitches. As players progress, they learn to make embouchure adjustments for certain pitches as part of standard technique. Common embouchure/air stream adjustments are described in the following list.
   A. To lower or flatten the pitch, focus the air stream downward. As a rule, the farther downward the pitch is directed,

the flatter the pitch will be. The air stream can be focused downward by moving the lower lip and/or jaw back slightly. If further adjustment is needed, lowering the head slightly to redirect the air or rolling the flute inward slightly will further drop the pitch; however, these techniques should be used sparingly.

B. To raise or sharpen the pitch, focus the air stream upward. As a rule, the farther upward the pitch is directed, the sharper the pitch will be. The air stream can be focused upward by moving the lower lip and/or jaw forward slightly. If further adjustment is needed, raising the head slightly to redirect the air or rolling the flute outward slightly will further raise the pitch; however, these techniques should be used sparingly.

C. As a rule, the smaller and tighter the lip aperture is, the faster the air and the sharper the pitch will be. Conversely, the larger and looser the lip aperture is, the slower the air and the flatter the pitch will be.

D. Only slight changes in the air stream and embouchure should be made when adjusting pitch. Large-scale changes affect tone quality, control, and focus.

2. Alternates/Adding Keys—If slight changes in the air stream and embouchure do not bring the desired pitches in tune, adding keys to regular fingerings or using alternate fingerings may help adjust pitch. On the other hand, adding keys and using alternates to adjust pitch is not always practical. As a general rule, tonal considerations, technical considerations, and tempo largely dictate the appropriateness of such adjustments. Finally, adding keys or using alternates to adjust pitch often negates or minimizes the need to make changes in air stream or embouchure. In general, flute players use fewer alternate fingerings and added fingers to adjust pitch than other woodwind players.

3. Dynamics/Air Speed—Changes in dynamics and air speed affect pitch, sometimes significantly. Considerations regarding dynamics and air speed are described as follows.

A. When playing loudly and increasing air speed, the pitch tends to go sharp. Adjust by focusing the air stream downward and/or relaxing the embouchure slightly, increasing aperture size. Proper air speed and control is maintained at all times. Do not overblow.

B. When playing softly and decreasing air speed, the pitch tends to go flat. Adjust by focusing the air stream upward and/or firming the embouchure slightly, decreasing aperture size. Even at softer dynamic levels, the air stream must move fast enough to sustain and support the pitch. Not using enough air or using an air stream that is too slow causes the pitch to go flat.

4. Mechanical—If all notes seem out of tune, check the cork in the head joint for proper placement. The mark on the end of the cleaning rod should be visible in the middle of the embouchure hole. If it is not exactly centered, adjust the cork. The position of this cork should be checked regularly. Other mechanical design characteristics that affect intonation are described as follows.

A. The flute is not designed to be in tune when the head joint is pushed in as far as it will go. As a result, head joint is pulled out slightly when the instrument is properly tuned. Inserting a head joint all the way into the body can cause significant overall intonation problems. The precise placement of the head joint is determined by using a tuner.

B. The E-flat key is depressed on most of the notes in the normal playing range. Depressing this key appropriately helps maintain pitch and tone quality.

C. Pad height affects pitch. If pads are too low, the pitch will be flat. If pads are too high, the pitch will be sharp. If pad height appears to be a problem, have it checked by a repair technician.

D. Leaks and other mechanical problems affect pitch. Check the flute regularly for leaks, loose and/or broken springs, and missing corks or felts. Maintaining the instrument in good repair is essential for good intonation.

5. Instrument Position—Instrument position can affect intonation significantly. Considerations regarding instrument position are described as follows.

A. The correct angle of the flute in relation to the head is down and out slightly, so that the air crosses the embouchure hole at a slight angle. Deviations from this position can cause both pitch and tonal inconsistencies.

B. If the head joint is rolled in too far (too much lip covers the embouchure hole), the pitch will be flat. If the head joint is rolled out too far (too little lip covers the embouchure hole), the pitch will be sharp. Check for proper placement of the embouchure hole and head joint in relation to the body and key work. Some players mark the body and head joint once the best alignment is determined in order to maintain consistency each time the instrument is assembled.

C. If the embouchure plate is too low on the lip, the pitch will be flat. If the embouchure plate is too high on the lip, the pitch will be sharp. Ensure proper placement of the embouchure plate on the lower lip.

TUNING THE FLUTE

A detailed description of how to tune the flute is under Tuning/Tuning Note Considerations in this chapter.

PITCH TENDENCIES

Pitch tendencies of instruments refers to the tendency for notes to deviate from a specified standard, usually the equal tempered scale based on a reference frequency of A = 440. That is, when players talk about the pitch tendencies of their instruments, they are almost always talking about how sharp or flat certain notes are in reference to a modern, equal-tempered tuner. Comments and suggestions regarding pitch tendencies are outlined in this section. A summary of these tendencies is presented in figures 2.27 and 2.28.

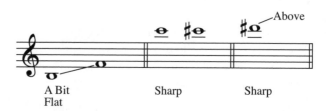

FIGURE 2.27. *Intonation Tendencies (General)*

FIGURE 2.28. *Intonation Tendencies (Specific)*

General Range/Register Tendencies—Flat Pitches

1. Flutes tend to play flat in the low range (between low B-natural and first-space F-natural).

   Adjustment 1—Increase air speed and focus the air stream upward slightly by moving the lower lip forward slightly.

   Adjustment 2—Decrease aperture size and increase air speed slightly.

   Adjustment 3—If other adjustments do not raise the pitch sufficiently, lift the head slightly, cover less embouchure hole with the lip, and/or roll the flute outward slightly.

General Range/Register Tendencies—Sharp Pitches

1. Flutes tend to play sharp in the high range (above high C-natural) with the exception of high D-natural, which tends to be flat.

   Adjustment 1—Relax the embouchure and focus the air stream downward slightly by moving the lower lip back slightly.

   Adjustment 2—Increase aperture size and decrease air speed slightly.

   Adjustment 3—If other adjustments do not lower the pitch sufficiently, lower the head slightly, cover more embouchure hole with the lip, and/or roll the flute inward slightly.

Specific Pitch Tendencies—Making Adjustments for Problem Pitches

1. Third-space C-natural tends to be sharp, and third-space C-sharp tends to be very sharp.
2. High C-natural, C-sharp, and D-sharp (above the staff) tend to be sharp.

   Adjustments for Numbers 1 and 2

   Adjustment 1—Relax the embouchure and focus the air stream downward slightly by moving the lower lip back slightly.

   Adjustment 2—Increase aperture size and decrease air speed slightly.

   Adjustment 3—If other adjustments do not lower the pitch sufficiently, drop the head slightly, cover more embouchure hole with the lip, and/or roll the flute inward slightly.

Adjustment 4—Adding the right-hand fingers (4-5-6) may help lower the pitch of the upper and lower octave C-natural and C-sharp.

3. Fourth-line D-natural and D-sharp tend to be slightly flat. Make sure that the left-hand index finger is not depressed on these notes.

4. Fourth-space E-natural tends to be slightly flat.

Adjustments for Numbers 3 and 4

Adjustment 1—Increase air speed and focus the air stream upward slightly by moving the lower lip forward slightly.

Adjustment 2—Decrease aperture size and increase air speed slightly.

Adjustment 3—If other adjustments do not raise the pitch sufficiently, lift the head slightly, cover less embouchure hole with the lip, and/or roll the flute outward slightly.

5. High D-natural above the staff can be manipulated easily with air direction and tends to go flat if players make adjustments for the upper register too early.

6. B-flat two octaves above the staff tends to be flat.

Adjustments for Numbers 5 and 6

Adjustment 1—Maintain an upward air direction for these notes. Direct the air stream slightly upward by moving the lower lip forward slightly.

Adjustment 2—Decrease aperture size and increase air speed slightly.

Adjustment 3—If other adjustments do not raise the pitch sufficiently, lift the head slightly, cover less embouchure hole with the lip, and/or roll the flute outward slightly.

ADDING FINGERS TO ADJUST INTONATION

Players can depress other keys in addition to the regular fingering to adjust pitch. An outline of basic fingering adjustments appears separately.

1. Adding the right-hand index finger, middle finger, and/or ring finger (4-5-6) to the third-space and high C-natural and C-sharp fingerings will lower the pitch.

2. Adding the G-sharp key (left-hand little finger) to the middle and high B-natural, C-natural, and C-sharp can help raise the pitch on some flutes.

USING ALTERNATE FINGERINGS TO ADJUST INTONATION

It is common for players to use alternate fingerings to adjust pitch. A list of basic alternates and their typical relationships to the corresponding regular fingerings appears separately.

1. Alternate B-flat (thumb B-flat) tends to be slightly flatter than regular B-flat.
2. The chromatic B-flat tends to be flatter than regular B-flat.
3. Alternate top-line F-sharp (using 5 instead of 6) tends to be flat.
4. Long C-natural and C-sharp tend to be flat.

Key Questions

Q: Is it safe to assume that my flute probably has the intonation tendencies described above?

A: Probably, but not necessarily. The frequencies produced by the overtone series on the flute naturally do not correspond exactly to the frequencies required by equal temperament tuning, a tuning system in which each note is compromised somewhat to facilitate modulation. The accuracy of the scale for equal temperament tuning on each individual flute is largely the result of the placement, size, and design of the tone holes and mechanisms. Recently (in the last fifteen to twenty years), many makers have made significant adjustments to the flute scale to accommodate a higher standard pitch (A = 440). Newer flutes with modern scale modifications may not exhibit many of the intonation tendencies common with traditional scale flutes. To check a flute's scale, first play the low C-natural. Overblow the low C-natural to sound the third-space C-natural. Do not make adjustments to your embouchure to tune the octaves. Without changing embouchure, change the fingering to the normal fingering for third-space C-natural. There will be a noticeable change in tone quality. Repeat this process for C-sharp. If the normal C-natural and C-sharp sound sharper than the harmonics, then the flute is most likely a "traditional" scale flute, and it will likely exhibit many of the intonation tendencies described above. If the two C-naturals are in tune, then the flute may be built on a different scale, and the individual tendencies of that flute may be markedly different than those tendencies normally encountered.

Key Cups: Metal cups above the tone holes that house the pads. Key cups may cover the entire tone hole or they may be open in the middle.

Key/Pad Height: See Key/Pad Height, page 45

Lip Plate: Also called embouchure plate, the raised plate on the head joint that contains the embouchure hole. The lip plate surrounds the riser, which is connected to the tube of the head joint. The embouchure plate is contoured to fit comfortably under the lower lip to facilitate good embouchure placement. Lip plates are found on virtually all metal head joints and may or may not be found on wooden head joints. Most wooden piccolos do not have embouchure plates largely because the wood is thick enough to cut the embouchure hole without adding a riser. See also Riser, page 142

Low B Key: An auxiliary key available on some flutes that extends the range of the instrument down one half step from low C-natural to low B-natural. Flutes with a low B key also have a slightly longer foot joint to accommodate this additional key. Low B keys are available on most intermediate and professional model flutes. The low B key is just above the low C roller and is played by the right-hand little finger. When depressed, it closes the low B-natural tone hole on the foot joint. See also B Foot Joint, page 93

Lightheadedness: See Dizziness/Lightheadedness, page 26

Materials in Flute Making: A variety of materials is common in modern flute making, and each material affects the overall sound of the instrument. Most student-line flutes are made of nickel silver, which actually contains no silver at all. Also called German silver, it is an alloy consisting of copper, zinc, and nickel. Nickel silver is very durable and more resistant to denting than silver is, yet it still produces a characteristic flute tone. Flutes may also be made partially or entirely of sterling silver, which produces a richer tone but is not as durable as nickel silver. Gold is also used in flute making, most commonly in the lip plate, riser, springs (gold alloy), and tubing. Gold adds warmth and richness to the tone, but also adds significant cost to the instrument. Platinum has also been used in flute making, but the tone is considered "cold" by many professional players. Recently, wooden flutes and head joints have become popular. Some players use a wooden head joint on a metal flute. Grenadilla wood is the most commonly used wood for flutes and head joints. Wooden flutes are more resistant than metal flutes; however, they also have a warmer, darker tone quality. Choosing a flute made of a particular material is typically a matter of personal preference (regarding sound and response) and budget. Trying several flutes made from a variety of materials can help players hear and feel the differences to determine which flute is best for their needs.

Multiphonics: See Extended/Contemporary Techniques, page 29

Multiple-Tonguing: See Multiple-Tonguing, page 52

Nickel Silver: See Materials in Flute Making, page 136

Octave Key: One unique feature of the flute relative to other woodwind instruments is the absence of an octave key. Unlike other woodwind instruments, the flute is an open tube. That is, it is open at the embouchure hole on one end and at the foot joint (or first open hole) on the other end. Other woodwind instruments are closed tubes, in that the reed or mouthpiece/reed combination is inserted into the mouth, closing off the tube at one end. This unique feature enables flute players to overblow the octave without an octave key.

Offset G: A term used to describe a G key mechanism that is not in line with the other primary keys on flute. This offset design is more comfortable for smaller players because the key is positioned where the third finger of the left hand naturally lies, making the G key easier to reach. Most student-line flutes have offset G keys, as do many intermediate and professional flutes. Regardless of whether a flute has an inline G key or an offset G key, it plays the same acoustically. Whether or not to play a flute with an offset G key is largely a matter of hand size and personal preference. See also Inline G, page 121

Open G-Sharp Key: A type of key design that makes the extra G-sharp tone hole unnecessary. Flutes with open G-sharp keys are constructed so that the key mechanisms operated by the left-hand third finger are reversed compared to most modern flutes. In an open G-sharp key design, the traditional G-sharp fingering (1-2-3 G-sharp key) is actually used to finger G-natural, and the traditional G-natural fingering (1-2-3) is used to finger G-sharp. In addition, all notes below G-natural require that the G-sharp key be depressed. One benefit of this key arrangement is that the G-sharp key functions like the split E mechanism, so that when players play high E-natural, they can simply leave the G-sharp key depressed. Flutes with open G-sharp keys are most commonly found on antique flutes; however, some newer flutes have open G-sharp keys.

Open-Hole Model: See French Model Flute, page 111

Optional Keys/Key Mechanisms: Keys or key mechanisms that are not standard to the essential functioning of the flute, but that make playing easier. Optional keys on the flute include the Gizmo key (high C-facilitator), the C-sharp trill key, the split E mechanism, and the G/A trill key. While these keys can make certain aspects of technique and pitch easier, flutes without these optional keys are fully functional and capable of producing the full range of notes and trills. See also Construction and Design, page 99; Gizmo Key, page 113; C-Sharp Trill Key, page 95; Split E Mechanism, page 143

Overblow: See Overblow, page 55

Overtones: See Overtones, page 55

Pad Height: See Key/Pad Height, page 45

Parts, Flute: The parts of a flute are identified in figure 2.29.

Piccolo: See Instrument Family and Playing Considerations, page 122

Pitch Adjustment: See Intonation, page 129; Tuning/Tuning Note Considerations, page 152

Pitch Tendencies: Generally, the tendency for any note to deviate from a specified standard, usually the equal tempered scale based on a reference frequency of A = 440. That is, when players talk about the pitch tendencies of their instruments, they are almost always talking about how sharp or flat certain notes are in reference to a modern, equal tempered scale. The term pitch tendency is most commonly used to refer to pitch deviations that are an inherent part of an instrument's design. In many instances, pitch tendencies are consistent on a given instrument (e.g., most flutes or most trumpets) regardless of the make or model of the instrument. For example, most flutes tend to play sharp in the high range. The pitch tendencies of the flute are discussed under Intonation in this chapter. See also Temperament, page 61; Tuning/Tuning Note Considerations, page 152

Plateau Model Flutes: Also called closed-hole flutes, instruments where the tone holes are covered by pads rather than by the fingertips. Most student-line flutes are plateau model instruments, while most (but not all) intermediate and professional flutes are open-hole instruments. Some disagreement exists regarding whether or not a plateau model flute is better than an open-hole or French model flute. Players who prefer plateau model flutes believe that they: (1) alleviate hand and wrist strain; (2) provide better tone quality; and 3) allow pitches to be manipulated by making embouchure adjustments or by partially depressing the keys, so that the half-hole technique is unnecessary. Players who prefer open-hole (French

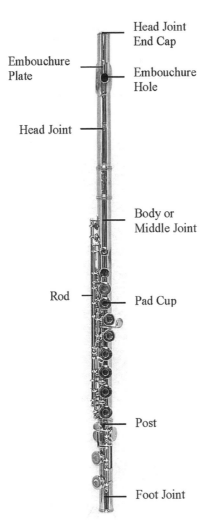

FIGURE 2.29. *Parts of a Flute*

model) flutes believe that they: (1) produce a better sound; (2) allow the player to more easily produce microtones; and (3) promote better hand and finger position. See also Plateau Model/System, page 56; French Model Flute, page 111

Platinum: See Materials in Flute Making, page 136

Playing Position: See Hand/Holding/Instrument/Playing Positions and Posture, page 113

Posture: See Hand/Holding/Instrument/Playing Positions and Posture, page 113

Preparing the Right Hand: See Crossing the Break, page 100

Range: In general, the distance from the lowest note to the highest note on a given instrument. In addition, players and teachers often refer to the different registers (roughly by octave) of the flute in terms of range: low range, middle range, and high range. The written and sounding ranges of the flute appear separately and are summarized in figure 2.30. See also Register/Registers, page 140; Transpositions, page 151

> *Key Questions*
>
> Q: What ranges are recommended for elementary, junior high/middle school, and senior high students?
>
> A: A student's range varies according to experience and ability level. Once the fundamentals of tone production and embouchure formation are mastered, range can be extended systematically. Suggested ranges for each level are presented as follows.
>   Elementary: Low C-natural to third octave C-natural
>   Junior High: Low C-natural to third octave G-natural
>   Senior High: Low C-natural (or B-natural) to fourth octave C-natural

Register/Registers: Groups of notes that share certain tonal characteristics usually related to pitch range, timbre, and/or manner of production. Players vary in their description of registers. Some players and teachers use the term "register" interchangeably with the term "range" to describe the playing ranges of the instrument. Furthermore, players and teachers also use terms such as "high" and

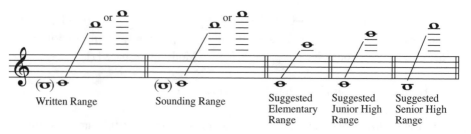

Figure 2.30. *Range*

"low" indiscriminately, or at least relatively, depending upon the musical context. Ultimately, delineating registers commonly used by junior high students, senior high students, college students, and professional players is a subjective process that varies according to the criteria used for delineation. Nonetheless, it seems reasonable to divide the flute range into four registers. These registers are listed separately and are notated in figure 2.31. See also Range, page 140

1. Low Register—From low C-natural (or B-natural) to first-space F-sharp.
2. Middle Register—From second-line G-natural to top-line F-sharp.
3. High Register—From G-natural (just above the staff) to high G-natural.
4. Altissimo Register—All notes above double high G-natural.

Releases/Cutoffs: See Releases/Cutoffs, page 56

Resistance: In general, the counteraction of the embouchure hole, riser, and instrument to the incoming air stream. The term is also used to describe how easily an instrument responds. The amount of resistance provided by the instrument dictates the amount of air and support needed to start and maintain a steady tone. The material and construction of the embouchure hole, riser, and flute all contribute to the resistance felt by the player.

The materials of the head joint and flute significantly affect resistance. Wooden flutes are more resistant than metal flutes, and thin-walled flutes are less resistant than thick-walled flutes. Flutes that respond quickly are considered less resistant, and flutes that respond slowly are considered more resistant. Tone quality and resistance are also related. Flutes with warmer, darker tone qualities tend to be more resistant, whereas flutes with brighter, more projecting tone qualities tend to be less resistant. The amount of resistance also affects the ability to create subtle tonal nuances on flute. As a rule, a more resistant flute (e.g., one made of wood) is

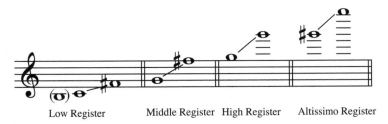

Low Register   Middle Register High Register   Altissimo Register

FIGURE 2.31. *Register/Registers*

less capable of producing a wide range of tonal nuances, while a less resistant flute (e.g., one made of silver) is capable of producing a wide variety of tonal nuances. See also Breathing/Breath Support/Air Control, page 10; Materials in Flute Making, page 136; Wall Thickness, page 155

Response: The way the instrument air column vibrates as a result of the player's air stream and embouchure. The term is also used to refer to the ease with which the notes "speak" or sound. Some notes respond easier than others, depending on how much of the tube is closed and the range of the notes being played. Notes in the extreme high or low range tend not to respond as well as notes in the middle range. The quality and condition of the flute, the head joint, and a player's ability to control the air speed and air volume greatly affect response. See also Resistance, page 141

Riser: Also called the chimney, the riser is in the embouchure hole and connects the embouchure plate to the head joint tube. The riser gives the embouchure hole depth. This depth enables players to have control over air direction and, ultimately, tonal response. During play, the air stream is directed toward the opposite edge of the embouchure hole. On contact, part of the air stream is directed above the embouchure hole, while the other part is directed downward into the flute by the riser, setting the air column in vibration. Many wooden flutes do not have built-up risers because the thickness of the wood provides sufficient depth in the embouchure hole to allow tone production and control.

Rolled Tone Holes: Tone holes that have a small roll around the rim to prevent excess wear on the pad. Drawn tone holes are typically also rolled. See also Drawn Tone Holes, page 103; Soldered Tone Holes, page 142; Tone Holes, page 147

Selecting an Instrument: See Instrument Brands, page 122; Instrument Selection, page 33

Slap Tongue: A tonguing technique that produces a harsh tonguing effect on the attacks. Slap tonguing is sometimes used as a special effect in both jazz and contemporary literature and is often produced by pressing the tongue hard against the roof of the mouth, building up air pressure, and then releasing the tongue quickly. Another method of producing a slap tongue effect is to close the throat, build up air pressure, and then open the throat quickly. See also Extended/Contemporary Techniques, page 29

Soldered Tone Holes: Soldered tone holes are made by soldering a piece of metal around the tone hole to create a rim on which the pad rests. That is, the body of the flute and the tone holes are crafted out of separate pieces of metal. Soldered tone holes are typically found on handmade flutes. See also Drawn Tone Holes, page 103; Rolled Tone Holes, page 142; Tone Holes, page 147

Sounding Range: See Instrument Family and Playing Considerations, page 122; Range, page 140; Transpositions, page 151

Split E Mechanism: An optional arm that only depresses the key immediately to the right of the G-sharp key when fingering the high E-natural ("split E"). E-natural is a challenging note on most flutes (especially at softer dynamic levels) because two extra keys are vented compared to the fingering one octave lower. The split E mechanism closes an unnecessarily vented key, which significantly improves the response and intonation of high E-natural.

Spring Hook Tool: See Spring Hook Tool, page 59

Springs: See Springs, page 59

Staggered Breathing: See Staggered Breathing, page 59

Stamina: See Endurance/Stamina, page 28

Stands: See Instrument Stands, page 39

Starting Note/Range, The Best: Most players will have excellent results starting somewhere in the middle range and working their way upward to higher notes and downward to lower notes. Many method books start players on fourth-line D-natural and top-space E-flat. These notes enable students to securely hold the flute while playing, and they respond well to moderate air flow and breath support. In addition, these pitches require players to raise the right-hand index finger, which helps them develop proper fingering habits from the beginning. This starting note range is shown is figure 2.32.

Sterling Silver: See Materials in Flute Making, page 136

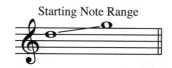

FIGURE 2.32. *Starting Note Range*

Stopper: See Cork Stopper, page 100

Swab: See Swab, page 59; Care and Maintenance, page 95

Technique: In general, the manner and ability with which players use the technical skills involved in playing an instrument. Most commonly, the term is used to describe the physical actions involved in playing an instrument, and often specifically refers to technical passages. Virtually every pedagogical aspect of woodwind playing (acoustical, physical, and mental) affects technique. General technical considerations for all woodwind instruments are in chapter 1. The suggestions and considerations apply specifically to the flute. When appropriate, readers are directed to relevant terms in the book where particular topics are addressed in detail. See also Alternate Fingerings/Alternates, page 83; Technique, page 60

General Technical Considerations/Concerns for Flute Players[1]

1. Flute keys are small, light, close to the tone holes, and comfortably spaced. In addition, the fingerings tend to follow intuitive or logical patterns. As a result, playing technically difficult passages quickly and efficiently on flute is easier than on larger instruments.
2. Because flutes require a slightly different focus on most of the notes throughout the range, the ability to control and make subtle changes in the air stream is essential for technical and tonal development.

Specific Technical Considerations/Concerns for Flute Players

1. E-flat Key—A common problem in flute playing is not using the E-flat key appropriately. The E-flat key should remain depressed throughout most of the normal range except on low B-natural, C-natural, C-sharp, and D-natural, and on fourth-line D-natural. Lifting the little finger off of the E-flat key on other notes affects pitch and tone quality.

2. Left-hand Index Finger—The left-hand index finger is raised on D-natural and E-flat in the second octave on flute. Keeping the index finger down on these notes is a common problem in flute playing. If the index finger is not raised, these notes tend to be fuzzy, unfocused, and out of tune.

3. Left-hand Little Finger—The left-hand little finger should lightly touch or remain slightly above the G-sharp key at all times. Players

commonly let the little finger droop underneath the G-sharp key or float high above the G-sharp key. Letting the little finger droop or float out of position creates extra tension in the hand and increases the distance the little finger must travel to operate the G-sharp key. Both of these factors negatively affect technical proficiency.

4. F-sharp Fingering—F-sharp in the first two octaves is played with the ring finger (6) of the right hand. It is common to develop the bad habit of using the middle finger (5) on the right hand for the F-sharp (the fingering used for saxophone and clarinet). The middle finger F-sharp is an alternate that is generally used when playing trills from E-natural to F-sharp, and is occasionally used in very fast technical passages; however, its tone quality and intonation make this alternate an unacceptable choice in most contexts. Saxophone and clarinet players who double on flute often make the mistake of using the middle finger for F-sharp.

5. Losing Instrument Balance when Playing C-natural and C-sharp—A common problem with beginners is to lose instrument balance when playing C-natural and C-sharp because the left thumb is lifted off of the instrument for these notes. Players must learn to balance the flute with the right hand (thumb and little finger), to maintain the contact point between the flute and the left-hand index first finger, and to maintain the contact point between the lower lip and the embouchure plate.

6. Right Thumb—Players often develop the habit of placing the thumb too high, too low, or too far onto on the body of the instrument, making it difficult to finger the instrument properly. Not placing the thumb properly is extremely detrimental to technique, especially in rapid passages. The thumb should be placed on the flute body between and opposite the right-hand index and middle fingers.

7. Crossing the Break—Crossing the break can be as problematic on flute as it is on other woodwind instruments. The primary considerations are with instrument balance, right- and left-hand coordination, and finger/hand position. The main challenge with crossing the break is moving from an open fingering (where few keys are depressed) to a closed fingering (where many keys are depressed), requiring coordination of hands and fingers. For

example, the interval from third-space C-natural to fourth-line D-natural requires players to coordinate finger movement from 1-D-sharp key (C-natural) to Thumb-2-3 4-5-6 (D-natural). Crossing the break becomes even more challenging for players who have switched from a closed-hole flute to an open-hole flute and are in the process of learning how to properly cover the tone holes. See also Crossing the Break, page 100

8. Trill Fingerings—Because flutes are required to trill more than other instruments, it is important to learn trill fingerings. A special trill fingering chart is near the end of this chapter.

9. High Range—Notes above third-octave E-flat require awkward fingerings that can be challenging to coordinate. In addition, playing in the high register requires a faster air stream and greater embouchure support to maintain good tone quality, pitch, and dynamic control. Practicing scales, arpeggios, and etudes in the high range can help smooth out fingering problems.

10. Alternate Fingerings/Alternates—Like other woodwind players, flute players learn to use alternate fingerings. The choice of fingerings should be determined by musical considerations including tone quality, intonation, and smoothness of the phrase. Although new fingerings seem awkward initially, developing control over all fingerings including alternates is crucial to technical proficiency. See also Alternate Fingerings/Alternates, page 83

11. Skips and Leaps—Executing skips and leaps can be challenging for flute players. As with crossing the break, coordinating the fingers as well as making proper embouchure adjustments are critical to executing skips and leaps effectively. Maintaining proper hand positions, keeping the fingers close to the keys at all times, and minimizing excess finger motion will help players execute skips and leaps cleanly. Suggestions for executing skips and leaps effectively are listed as follows. See also Crossing the Break, page 100

    A. The primary technical consideration with skips and leaps is the need to make adjustments in embouchure, air, and aperture from note to note. In the middle register these adjustments are relatively subtle; however, from the low register to the high register these adjustments can be significant, and the timing of these adjustments is critical to smoothly executing skips and leaps.

B. As a general rule, when ascending to higher pitches, the embouchure needs to be firmer, the air speed needs to be faster, the air stream needs to be directed higher, and the aperture needs to be smaller to help the high pitches speak properly. When descending to lower pitches, players must reverse these adjustments.

C. The adjustments in embouchure, air, and aperture must be balanced. That is, increasing air speed significantly without changing air direction or aperture size may cause a higher pitch to sound, but it may also create problems with pitch and tone quality. Decreasing aperture size without making appropriate changes in air speed, direction, and focus may also create problems with pitch and tone quality. As a rule, players should balance the adjustments in embouchure tension, air speed, air direction, and aperture size rather than make large-scale changes in one or two of these variables.

D. Learning to make appropriate embouchure (firmness), air (direction, speed, focus), and aperture (size) adjustments is crucial to playing skips and leaps smoothly and efficiently. The appropriateness of any adjustment is based on the resultant tone quality and pitch placement.

Thumb Rests: Typically, flutes are not constructed with thumb rests. However, several right thumb rests are available today as auxiliary equipment. These thumb rests attach to the underneath side of the flute where the right thumb is normally positioned and are adjustable to better fit players' hands. In addition, these thumb rests open the hand, which may enhance finger flexibility. See also Hand/Holding/Instrument/Playing Positions and Posture, page 113

Tone Holes: The holes in the instrument tube that may be opened or closed in various combinations to produce different pitches. Tone holes are cut into the body of the flute and then built up by either drawing the tubing up around the tone hole or by soldering a separate piece of metal to the tone hole. Building up a wall around the tone hole creates a flat surface on which the pad can rest. Soldered tone holes are typically found on handmade flutes and are traditionally thought to be better than drawn tone holes because the thickness of the flute body is not in danger of being compromised and because the surface on which the pad rests is thought to be more even. However, with modern technology, those problems rarely occur with quality instruments from reputable makers. See also Drawn Tone Holes, page 103; Soldered Tone Holes, page 142

Tone Production: The term used to describe how tone is produced on an instrument. General considerations for woodwind tone production are discussed under Tone Production in chapter 1. Specific considerations for flute tone production and terms included in this chapter that address tone production appear in the following section.

TONAL CONCEPT/TONE QUALITY

Develop a concept of "good" flute tone and the type of tone quality desired. Listening to advanced players and high-quality recordings can help develop appropriate tonal concepts. In addition, taking lessons from a knowledgeable teacher who provides an exemplary model during lessons is invaluable. See also Tone Production, page 160

1. Use appropriate equipment (instrument and head joint). Players should play on equipment that matches their level of performance and experience. As players mature, they should experiment with several advanced instruments and head joints under the guidance of a knowledgeable teacher to find the right combination for them.

2. Keep the air stream consistent and steady to support the tone. The direction of the air stream changes according to range. Specifically, the air must be focused upward as the scale ascends and downward as the scale descends, and the embouchure must firm and loosen accordingly. In other words, the focus of the air changes slightly throughout the range of the instrument in conjunction with changes in embouchure. As a general rule, the air stream is directed downward more in the low range than it is in the middle range and downward more in the middle range than it is in the high range. Pitch and tone quality determine the appropriateness of air direction.

EMBOUCHURE

Maintain proper embouchure formation at all times. Proper mechanics of embouchure are critical to tone production. Although many fine players' embouchures vary slightly from a classic or standard embouchure, the fundamental characteristics have withstood the test of time. Achieving a mature, characteristic tone on any wind instrument requires time and practice to develop the physical and aural skills necessary for proper tone production. A brief summary of embouchure considerations for good tone production appears as follows. See also Embouchure, page 104

1. The mouth corners remain relatively relaxed and are drawn slightly downward. A pout is more appropriate than a smile.
2. The lips form an oval-shaped or diamond-shaped aperture as if saying "oo" with a slight pout. The lip aperture should be no wider than the embouchure hole.
3. The lips remain relaxed, and the embouchure plate rests gently against the lower lip.
4. The chin remains flat, but not tight.
5. The air is focused toward the opposite edge of the embouchure hole.
6. Maintain a consistent embouchure.

BREATHING AND AIR

A thorough discussion of breathing and air is in chapter 1. See Breathing/Breath Support/Air Control, page 10; Tone Production, page 160

VIBRATO

While vibrato is not a factor in tone production for beginners and intermediate players, it is a factor in tone production for more advanced players. Typically, vibrato is added after the fundamentals of good tone production have been mastered. Considerations for vibrato are listed as follows. See also Vibrato, page 154

1. Add vibrato to a full, well-centered tone according to the musical style being performed.
2. Use vibrato to enhance tone quality, not to cover up poor tone quality.
3. Use a diaphragmatic vibrato.

Specific Tonal Considerations/Concerns for Flute Players

1. Low Notes—Low notes tend to crack easily, and using a strong tonguing motion can inhibit the initial response of these notes. As a result, beginners can initially practice getting low notes to respond using breath attacks. In addition, experiment with the direction, focus, and speed of the air stream until the notes respond easily.

2. High Notes/Embouchure—As notes get higher, players need to increase air speed, firm their embouchures, decrease aperture size, and narrow the focus of the air stream and oral cavity to achieve proper tonal response, tone quality, and pitch. Notes above high C-natural become increasing more difficult to play with good tone quality and intonation. The adjustments in embouchure, air, and aperture must be balanced. That is, increasing air speed significantly without changing air direction or aperture size may cause a higher pitch to sound, but it will also create problems with pitch and tone quality. Decreasing aperture size without making appropriate changes in air speed, direction, and focus will also create problems with pitch and quality. As a rule, players must balance the adjustments in embouchure tension, air speed, air direction, and aperture size, rather than making large-scale changes in one or two of these variables.

3. Technical Considerations—Players must raise the left-hand index finger on D-natural and E-flat in the second octave. Keeping the index finger down on these notes causes them to be fuzzy, unfocused, and out of tune. In addition, the E-flat key should remain depressed throughout most of the normal range except on low B-natural, C-natural, C-sharp, and D-natural, and on fourth-line D-natural. Lifting the little finger off of the E-flat key on other notes affects pitch and tone quality.

Tone Quality: The characteristic sound associated with an instrument regarding tone color or timbre, and consistency, focus, and control of the air stream. The tone quality of the flute varies from low and mellow to high and piercing. Compared to other woodwind instruments, the flute's tone is much more consistent throughout the range. From a mechanical standpoint, tone quality is dependent upon several factors involving the design of the instrument, the materials used in the construction of the flute, and, most important, the head joint, which is discussed under Head Joint in this chapter. From a player's standpoint, tone quality is largely dependent upon two factors: (1) the use of air, which is discussed in detail under Tone Production and Breathing/Breath Support/Air Control; and (2) the embouchure and oral cavity, which is discussed in detail under Tone Production and Embouchure. Common terms associated with tone quality and common terms used to describe tone quality are identified and described under Tone Quality in chapter 1. See also Breathing/Breath Support/Air Control, page 10; Tone Quality, page 68

Key Questions

Q: Should I work on tone quality or intonation first?

A: Tone quality. If players cannot play with a good, consistent tone quality, working on intonation is counterproductive.

Tonguing: See Tonguing, page 71

Transpositions: The relationship between the written and sounding ranges of an instrument. The C flute is a non-transposing instrument. That is, the flute sounds as written. As a result, when a flute plays a written C-natural, the sounding pitch is concert C-natural. However, other members of the flute family are transposing instruments. What follows is a list of transpositions. A summary of notated transpositions is shown in figure 2.33. See also Range, page 140

Flute Transposition

1. The C flute sounds as written.
2. The C piccolo sounds one octave higher than written and one octave above the flute. It is one of the few instruments that transposes upward.
3. The alto flute in G sounds a fourth lower than written. As a result, when it plays a third-space C-natural, it sounds a concert G-natural a fourth below the written C-natural.
4. The bass flute sounds one octave lower than written, and one octave below the C flute.

Trill Keys: Two small keys between the first and second, and second and third keys of the right hand. The trill keys are primarily used for trills and in some

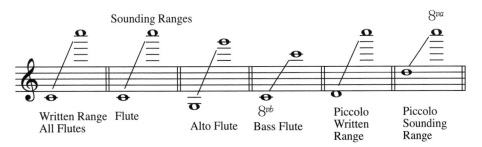

FIGURE 2.33. *Flute Transpositions*

third-octave and altissimo fingerings. The first trill key is operated with the middle finger and the second trill key is operated by the ring finger. Operating these keys with the wrong fingers is a common mistake. See also "Practical Tips," page 156

Triple-Tonguing: A technique that enables performers to tongue triple patterns rapidly. See also Multiple-Tonguing, page 52

Tuning/Tuning Note Considerations: Tuning any instrument is a process that involves making mechanical adjustments (e.g., pulling out or pushing in a mouthpiece, slide, or instrument joint) so that the instrument will produce pitches that are in tune with a predetermined standard (typically A = 440). Tuning notes refer to specific pitches that are good to tune to on any given instrument. Considerations have been given to the notes most commonly used for tuning wind groups. Adjusting pitch and adjusting for pitch tendencies of the flute are discussed under Intonation. Considerations for tuning the flute appear in the following section.

Tuning the Flute

1. Most flutes are designed to be in tune (at A = 440) when the head joint is pulled out slightly from the body (typically about 1/8 to 1/4 inch). This design feature enables players to raise the pitch if necessary by pushing the head joint in slightly.

2. Players can raise or lower the pitch by adjusting the position of the head joint. Pulling out the head joint lowers the pitch, while pushing in the head joint raises the pitch. Generally, only small adjustments (no more than 1/4 inch) should be made for tuning purposes. The need to make large adjustments is often an indication of problems in other areas such as embouchure, air focus, and instrument condition. In addition, pulling the head joint out excessively negatively affects the overall intonation of the instrument, resulting in an uneven scale from note to note. Playing in tune under these circumstances is virtually impossible.

3. The cork stopper in the head joint can significantly affect intonation. Although not a tuning device per se, its position is crucial to maintaining proper intonation. Technically, the cork stopper should be positioned 17mm from the center of the embouchure

hole. This position can be checked by making sure that the line on the cleaning/tuning rod is centered with the embouchure hole when the rod is inserted properly into the head joint as shown in figures 2.34 and 2.35.

4. Because the natural overtones do not correspond exactly with the frequencies of the equal tempered scale, the intonation of the flute (and of every other instrument for that matter) is compromised. In addition, the wavelengths of the pitches produced by the flute are shorter than those produced by most other instruments because the pitches (frequencies) in the normal playing range are higher. As a result, the interference (beats) occurring between two near-unison tones is more noticeable to listeners. This acoustical phenomenon is one reason that the flutes often seem to be more out of tune than other wind instruments.

Tuning Note Considerations

1. Concert B-flat—An excellent tuning note; however, because this note is fairly high, players must maintain good air support for an accurate tuning assessment. In addition, concert B-flat is susceptible to the natural tendency of the flute to go flat at softer dynamic levels and sharp at louder dynamic levels. As a result, players should tune at a mezzo-forte (mf) dynamic level.

2. Concert A-natural—An excellent tuning note; however, because this note is fairly high, players must maintain good air support for an accurate tuning assessment. In addition, concert A-natural is susceptible to the natural tendency of the flute to go flat at softer

FIGURE 2.34. *Correct Position of Tuning Rod Mark*

FIGURE 2.35. *Tuning Rod Inserted into the Head Joint*

dynamic levels and sharp at louder dynamic levels. As a result, players should tune at a mezzo-forte (mf) dynamic level.

3. Concert F-natural—Top-line F-natural is an excellent tuning note, and it is not as susceptible to the natural tendency of the flute to go flat at softer dynamic levels and sharp at louder dynamic levels as B-flat or A-natural.

Vibrato: Two types of vibrato are commonly used in woodwind playing: jaw vibrato and diaphragmatic vibrato (sometimes described as a diaphragmatic/

throat vibrato). Jaw vibrato results in regular pitch fluctuations around a tonal center, whereas diaphragmatic vibrato results in regular intensity (loudness) fluctuations around a tonal center. Nearly all flute players use a diaphragmatic vibrato (or diaphragmatic/throat vibrato). Steps for developing vibrato are under Vibrato in chapter 1. See also Vibrato, page 74

Wall Thickness: The thickness of the metal used to construct the instrument tube. Many flutes, particularly professional flutes, are available in a variety of wall thicknesses, typically ranging from .014 inch to .020 inch. Generally, a thinner wall yields a brighter sound, while a thicker wall yields a darker tone. Wall thickness is a matter of personal preference. Wall thickness also pertains to head joints, and many head joints are available in a variety of thicknesses.

Wing Lip Plate: A lip plate that is built up on the ends to help players find and maintain better position on the flute. Although wing lip plates are available for all types of flutes, they can be especially helpful on alto or bass flutes because they are typically not played every day, and because the wings help the player adjust to the larger embouchure hole.

Written Range: The basic written range for all flutes is the same regardless of key or size; it is the sounding ranges that vary from instrument to instrument. Flute music is written in the treble clef. The basic written range of all flutes is from low B-natural or C-natural below the staff (depending on the foot joint of the instrument) to double high C-natural above the staff. This range can be extended to the F-sharp above double high C-natural using altissimo/harmonic fingerings and overtones. In addition, the piccolo can only play down to low D-natural. Suggested ranges for different playing levels are under Range. See also Instrument Family and Playing Considerations, page 122; Range, page 140; Transpositions, page 151

PRACTICAL TIPS

FINGERING CHARTS

Flute Basic Fingerings

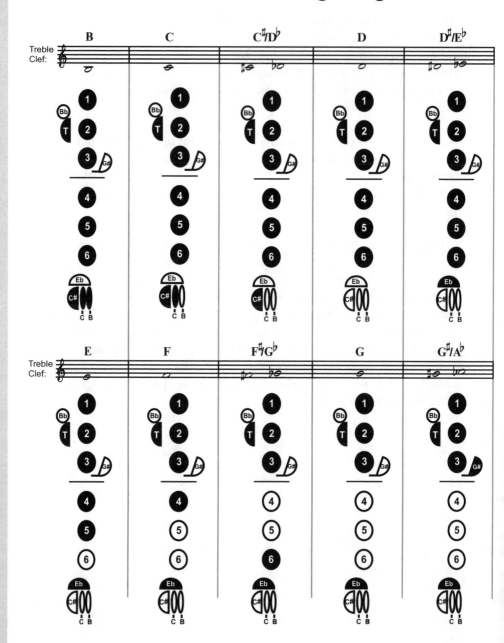

Flute Basic Fingerings

Flute Basic Fingerings

Flute Basic Fingerings

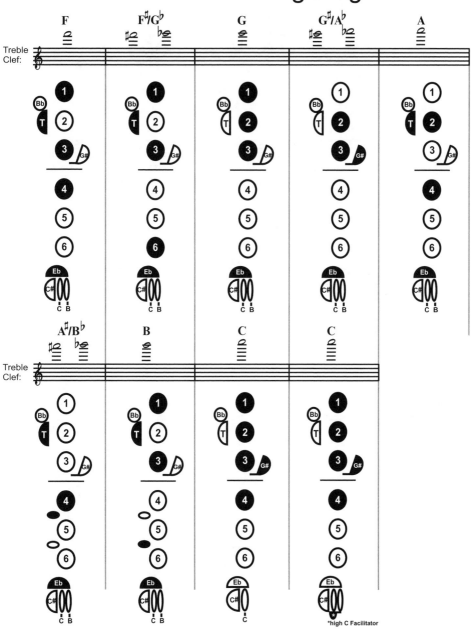

Flute Alternate Fingerings

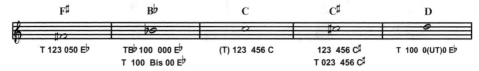

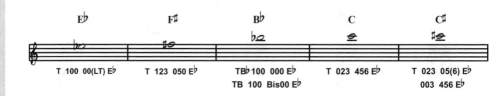

F♯	B♭	C	C♯	D
T 123 050 E♭	TB♭ 100 000 E♭	(T) 123 456 C	123 456 C♯	T 100 0(UT)0 E♭
	T 100 Bis 00 E♭		T 023 456 C♯	

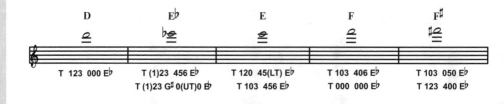

E♭	F♯	B♭	C	C♯
T 100 00(LT) E♭	T 123 050 E♭	TB♭ 100 000 E♭	T 023 456 E♭	T 023 05(6) E♭
		TB 100 Bis00 E♭		003 456 E♭

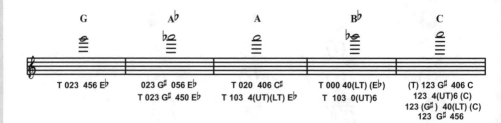

D	E♭	E	F	F♯
T 123 000 E♭	T (1)23 456 E♭	T 120 45(LT) E♭	T 103 406 E♭	T 103 050 E♭
	T (1)23 G♯ 0(UT)0 E♭	T 103 456 E♭	T 000 000 E♭	T 123 400 E♭

G	A♭	A	B♭	C
T 023 456 E♭	023 G♯ 056 E♭	T 020 406 C♯	T 000 40(LT) (E♭)	(T) 123 G♯ 406 C
	T 023 G♯ 450 E♭	T 103 4(UT)(LT) E♭	T 103 0(UT)6	123 4(UT)6 (C)
				123 (G♯) 40(LT) (C)
				123 G♯ 456

Flute Altissimo Fingerings

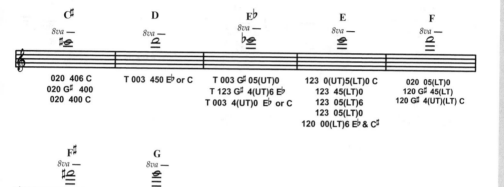

C♯	D	E♭	E	F
8va —	*8va —*	*8va —*	*8va —*	*8va —*
020 406 C	T 003 450 E♭ or C	T 003 G♯ 05(UT)0	123 0(UT)5(LT)0 C	020 05(LT)0
020 G♯ 400		T 123 G♯ 4(UT)6 E♭	123 45(LT)0	120 G♯ 45(LT)
020 400 C		T 003 4(UT)0 E♭ or C	123 05(LT)6	120 G♯ 4(UT)(LT) C
			123 05(LT)0	
			120 00(LT)6 E♭ & C♯	

F♯	G
8va —	*8va —*
T 023 G♯ 056	T 023 G♯ 0(UT)50
T 020 05(LT)	
T 103 40(LT)6	

Flute Special Trill Fingerings

Trills performed with regular fingerings are not included

Flute Special Trill Fingerings

Trills performed with regular fingerings are not included

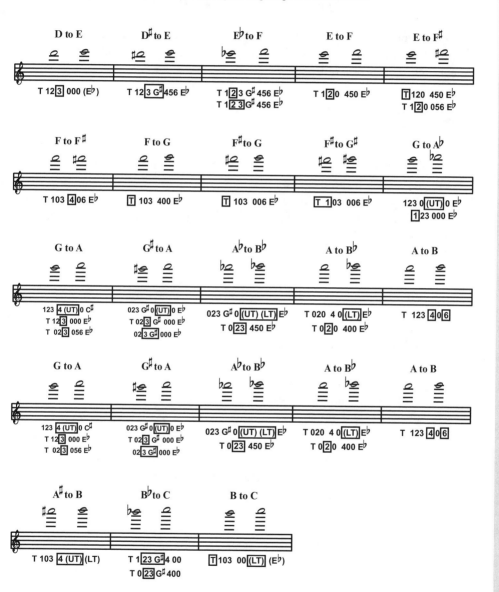

Common Technical Faults and Corrections

Many problems in wind playing result from basic faults in the following areas: (1) instrument assembly, (2) embouchure formation, and (3) hand/holding/playing positions and posture. The following section provides information on how to correct technical faults frequently encountered in flute performance. Headings appear in alphabetical order.

Assembly

Fault 1:　Improperly aligning the head joint.

Correction:　Align the embouchure hole with the center of the main key stack. The head joint may be rolled inward or outward slightly from this position depending on the embouchure and lip formation of the player. Let the overall pitch, response, and tonal characteristics determine the exact position of the head joint.

Fault 2:　Improperly aligning the foot joint.

Correction:　Align the post/rod on the foot joint with the center of the main key stack on the instrument body. Many beginners assemble the foot joint incorrectly, lining up the rods on the foot joint and body. This position places the keys operated by the right-hand little finger out of comfortable reach.

Fault 3:　Placing unnecessary pressure on the keys while assembling and handling the flute.

Correction:　Avoid placing pressure on the keys whenever possible when assembling or handling the flute. Grasp the body of the flute near the head joint, where there is little key work. When assembling the body and foot joint, grasp the foot joint underneath the key work and place as little pressure as possible on the keys.

Fault 4:　Not pushing head joint far enough onto the body.

Correction:　Make sure that the head joint and the inside of the body where the head joint is inserted are clean and dry. Assemble the head joint and body with a back-and-forth twisting motion. Most flutes are designed to play in tune at A = 440 when the head joint is pulled out approximately one-eighth to one-fourth of an inch. Use a tuner to determine the exact placement of the head joint.

Embouchure Formation

FAULT 1: Not aligning the lips and embouchure plate/hole so that they are parallel.

CORRECTION: Make sure that the lips are parallel with the embouchure hole. This positioning requires that the head and the flute form a 90-degree angle. If the flute is held at a slight downward angle, then the head must be tilted slightly to keep the lips parallel to the embouchure hole.

FAULT 2: Covering too much or not enough of the embouchure hole with the lower lip.

CORRECTION: Cover about one-fourth to one-third of the embouchure hole with the lower lip. Make slight adjustments as necessary to achieve the best tone and response.

FAULT 3: Focusing the air incorrectly.

CORRECTION: Make sure that the air is directed toward the opposite edge of the embouchure hole. Air that is directed too high or too low will produce an undesirable sound or tone quality.

FAULT 4: Holding the lower lip too tightly.

CORRECTION: Allow the lower lip to remain flexible (as if pouting). Pull the mouth corners slightly downward to encourage this formation.

FAULT 5: Directing too much air to the top and sides of the embouchure hole (wasted air).

CORRECTION: Use a mirror to check the embouchure formation and the size of the lip aperture. The lip aperture should be no wider than the embouchure hole. Focus the air stream toward the opposite side of the embouchure hole.

FAULT 6: Creating a vapor trail that is off to one side.

CORRECTION: Use a mirror to make sure that the lip aperture is centered with the embouchure hole and that the top lip is not splitting the air stream in half.

Hand/Holding/Instrument Playing Positions and Posture

FAULT 1:   Holding the flute at an improper angle.

CORRECTION: Tilt the flute slightly downward at the foot joint. It should also be pushed slightly outward at the foot joint away from the body.

FAULT 2:   Tilting the head too much to the right.

CORRECTION: Tilt the head only slightly so that the embouchure can remain parallel to the embouchure plate/hole.

FAULT 3:   Slouching.

CORRECTION: Sit up straight, keep the chin in a normal position (not up or down), keep the eyes straight ahead, and keep the shoulders and back straight but relaxed to avoid tension.

FAULT 4:   Holding the elbows too far from or too close to the body.

CORRECTION: Hold the elbows out from the body in a relaxed, comfortable position. When the elbows are in the proper position, the right wrist will be nearly straight, and the left upper arm does not touch the body.

FAULT 5:   Resting the right arm on the back of the chair.

CORRECTION: Turn the chair so that the back of the chair is out of the way of the right arm, and adjust the music stand so that the music can be seen without compromising proper playing position.

FAULT 6:   Holding the left-hand index finger incorrectly.

CORRECTION: Rest the flute at the base of left-hand index finger. Slightly bend the index finger and the left wrist.

FAULT 7:   Placing the left thumb on the body of the instrument for support.

CORRECTION: Position the left thumb so that it rests on the B key on the underneath side of the flute between the index and middle fingers.

FAULT 8:   Holding the fingers straight or in a "locked" position.

CORRECTION: Slightly curve the fingers so that a U- or C-shape is formed between the thumb and fingers.

FAULT 9:   Placing the right-hand little finger on the wrong key or allowing it to float or droop out of position.

CORRECTION: Position the right-hand little finger lightly on the E-flat key in the default position. Slide or shift the right-hand little finger to the other keys when necessary.

FAULT 10:   Pushing the right thumb too far under the flute.

CORRECTION: Place the right thumb underneath the flute for support, but be careful to not extend it so far underneath the flute that it pulls the fingers of the right hand back, which can inhibit technical proficiency.

FAULT 11:   Bending the right wrist.

CORRECTION: Hold the right wrist straight. A bent wrist is often a result of the right elbow being too high or too low.

FAULT 12:   Holding the left-hand little finger underneath the G-sharp key or allowing it to float or droop out of position.

CORRECTION: Lightly touch or rest the left-hand little finger just above the G-sharp key in the ready position to minimize finger movement and improve technical proficiency.

FAULT 13:   Holding the fingers too far from keys/tone holes.

CORRECTION: Position the fingers as close as possible without distorting the sound and/or affecting the pitch. Keeping the fingers close to the keys will help eliminate the tendency to slap the fingers down. On open-hole flutes, players must keep their fingers close to the tone holes or keys, but they must leave enough room above the tone holes for the air to escape freely.

COMMON PROBLEMS, CAUSES, AND SOLUTIONS FOR FLUTE

Problems in wind instrument playing relate to some aspect of sound. That is, incorrect assembly is not a problem; poor tone quality or squeaking are problems.

Incorrect assembly is simply one common cause of such problems. Understanding this distinction makes it easier to solve problems. The following section provides information on solving problems frequently encountered in flute performance. The main headings are: Articulation Problems, Intonation Problems, Performance/Technical Problems, and Tone Quality and Response Problems.

Articulation Problems

PROBLEM: Audible dip or scoop in pitch during initial attacks.

CAUSE 1:   Excessive movement of the embouchure (especially the jaw) while tonguing.

SOLUTION 1:   Use light, quick movements of the tongue and maintain a consistent embouchure. Use a "tu" syllable, not a "twa" syllable. Practice tonguing in front of a mirror and use the visual feedback to help eliminate jaw movement.

CAUSE 2:   Embouchure not set properly before the attack.

SOLUTION 2:   Allow enough time to be physically and mentally set before the attack. That is, the embouchure must be set properly for the note being played. When the embouchure is too tight or too loose for a particular note at the point of attack, players will make an immediate adjustment or shift to correct the pitch. This shift causes an audible dip or scoop in the attack.

PROBLEM: Heavy, thick, and/or sluggish attacks.

CAUSE 1:   Too much tongue on the attacks coupled with a slow tonguing action.

SOLUTION 1:   Minimize tongue movement. Use a light, quick tonguing action and make sure the tip of the tongue strikes the gum line behind the top teeth. Think of moving only the tip of the tongue during the tonguing process and use a "tu" attack for normal tonguing.

CAUSE 2:   Tonguing between the teeth.

SOLUTION 2:   The tip of the tongue strikes the back of the upper teeth at or near the gum line. Make sure the tongue is pulled back or arched slightly in the mouth to begin the tonguing process. This position places the tongue slightly higher in the mouth to start. Think of moving only the tip of the tongue quickly and lightly.

CAUSE 3:   Tongue disrupting the air stream.

SOLUTION 3:   Make sure the tongue is pulled back or arched slightly in the mouth to begin the tonguing process, and increase the quickness of the tongue strike against gum line. If the tongue is too low or too high in the mouth, or if the tongue moves too slowly, the air stream is disrupted, causing sluggish attacks.

PROBLEM: Mistimed attacks (tongue, embouchure, air).

CAUSE 1:   Tongue and air stream not coordinated.

SOLUTION 1:   Practice coordinating the tongue and the air stream by attacking one note at a time. Think of starting the tongue and the air at the same time on attacks. Although it is the release of the tongue from the gum line that actually starts a tone, the air stream and the tongue must work together.

CAUSE 2:   Embouchure not set properly before the attack.

SOLUTION 2:   Allow enough time to be physically and mentally set before the attack. That is, the embouchure must be set properly for the note being played. An embouchure that is improperly formed for the note being played can delay the response of the attack.

CAUSE 3:   Too much embouchure movement during attacks.

SOLUTION 3:   Maintain embouchure formation and avoid using a "jaw-ing" action. The embouchure must be set properly for the note being played. Think of moving only the tip of the tongue.

CAUSE 4:   Player not set to play.

SOLUTION 4:   Maintain proper playing positions (physical readiness), and internally hear the pitches before playing them (mental readiness).

PROBLEM: Inability to execute clean slurs.

CAUSE 1:   Inconsistent air stream.

SOLUTION 1:   Do not change the air stream from note to note. Instead, blow a consistent stream of air and simply move the fingers. On flute, it is generally not necessary to adjust the air stream drastically for various pitches in slurred passages unless large intervals are involved; however, adjustments in air speed and air volume should be made as necessary to accommodate the dynamic level.

CAUSE 2:   Too much embouchure movement throughout a slurred passage.

SOLUTION 2:   Use the same basic embouchure throughout the entire passage. Making large shifts in embouchure for various notes disrupts the air stream and is usually unnecessary on flute unless large intervals are involved.

CAUSE 3:   Fingers not coordinated.

SOLUTION 3:   Keep the fingers close to the keys and depress them quickly and smoothly from note to note. Avoid excess finger movement, and avoid "slapping" the keys.

CAUSE 4:   Player not set to play.

SOLUTION 4:   Maintain proper playing positions (physical readiness), and internally "hear" the pitches before playing them (mental readiness).

PROBLEM: Inability to execute clean releases.

CAUSE 1:   Inappropriate use of tongue cutoffs.

SOLUTION 1:   Use breath releases rather than tongue cutoffs in most musical contexts because tongue cutoffs tend to be harsh and abrupt. Tongue cutoffs are appropriate in some jazz styles.

CAUSE 2:   Not stopping the air at the point of release.

SOLUTION 2:   Practice maintaining an open air column from the diaphragm into the instrument, and stop the air by suspending it midstream as if lightly gasping. Using the throat as a valve and pushing the air on releases both prevent clean releases.

CAUSE 3:   Not "lifting" on the release.

SOLUTION 3:   Think of gasping lightly on the release and directing the air stream upward. Thinking this way helps stop the flow of air quickly while maintaining an open air column. Be sure to maintain a consistent embouchure during the release. Another technique is to direct the air stream upward while decreasing the volume (but maintaining air speed). The tone should stop slightly before the air stops. This type of release is often made easier by using a "whisp of smoke" analogy.

CAUSE 4:   Closing off the embouchure and/or throat, or using the embouchure and/or throat as a valve for stopping the air.

SOLUTION 4:   Think of gasping lightly on the release and directing the air stream upward. The embouchure and throat remain unchanged on breath releases; it is the air that is stopped to release a tone. Thinking this way helps stop the flow of air quickly while maintaining an open air column, an open throat, and a proper embouchure.

PROBLEM: Inability to execute a controlled accent.

CAUSE 1:   Not balancing the air stream and tongue appropriately.

SOLUTION 1:   On an accented note, "lift off" of the air; that is, think of gasping lightly and directing the air stream upward on the release. On most accents, the weight of the tongue is not increased on the attack. Rather, the accent is produced by a sudden increase in air. As a rule, do not use tongue cutoffs on accented notes.

CAUSE 2:   Too much tongue on releases in staccato passages with repeated accents.

SOLUTION 2:   Tongue each note consistently and evenly. In rapid patterns, the release of each note (except the first) in the pattern becomes the attack for each subsequent note. If each note is tongued consistently, the releases will take care of themselves.

Intonation Problems

PROBLEM: Pitch generally flat in all registers.

CAUSE 1:   Head joint pulled out too far.

SOLUTION 1:   Determine the appropriate head joint placement by using a tuner, and put a line or mark on the head joint. Position the head joint at this line each time the instrument is assembled, and then make small adjustments as needed.

CAUSE 2:   Lip aperture too large, too wide, and/or uncentered.

SOLUTION 2:   Make sure that the opening in the lips is no wider than the embouchure hole and that the lips are centered on the embouchure plate to achieve the most accurate pitch. Use a mirror to check the size of the lip aperture. If the lip aperture is too large, think of decreasing the imaginary circle of air into the instrument, while still maintaining an open air stream. That is, use a slightly more focused air stream.

CAUSE 3:   Not enough air.

SOLUTION 3:   Blow a controlled, steady air stream through a properly formed embouchure, and increase the speed of the air stream slightly. Form the embouchure as if saying "who" or "oh," firm the mouth corners slightly (in a downward direction), and blow a steady stream of warm air into and across the embouchure hole.

CAUSE 4:   Not compensating for the natural tendency of the flute to go flat in soft passages.

SOLUTION 4:   Raise the direction of the air stream slightly to compensate for the drop in pitch and maintain adequate air speed (even though less air is being used).

CAUSE 5:   Air stream directed downward too much.

SOLUTION 5:   Raise the air stream by making slight adjustments in the lips and jaw, rolling the flute outward, or even lifting the head upward slightly. Small adjustments are usually more effective than large adjustments.

CAUSE 6:   Slouching.

SOLUTION 6:   When seated, sit up straight (but avoid being rigid or tense) with feet flat on the floor. Sit toward the front edge of the chair. Hold the flute up so that the head does not have to tilt too far to the right to maintain the proper angle with the instrument.

CAUSE 7:   Holding the flute at an incorrect angle.

SOLUTION 7:   Hold the flute at an angle roughly perpendicular to the head. If the flute is pointed to the ground, the embouchure's ability to blow properly into and across the embouchure hole is compromised and can cause the pitch to be flat.

CAUSE 8:   Head tilted too far to the right.

SOLUTION 8:   Bring the flute up to the mouth and hold it so that the head and flute are roughly perpendicular. Players should not have to reach forward or downward for the embouchure plate. Such reaching affects breathing and the embouchure's ability to blow properly into and across the embouchure hold and can cause the pitch to be flat.

CAUSE 9:   Pads are too close to the tone holes.

SOLUTION 9:   Have a knowledgeable repair technician adjust the pads to the proper height.

CAUSE 10:   Insufficient air support.

SOLUTION 10:   Use adequate air speed and air volume to support the tone.

CAUSE 11:   Too much lower lip covering the lip plate.

SOLUTION 11:   Cover about one-fourth or one-third of the embouchure hole with the lower lip. Too much lower lip results in a muffled, fuzzy tone that is generally flat.

PROBLEM: Pitch generally sharp in all registers.

CAUSE 1:   Head joint pushed in too far.

SOLUTION 1:   Determine the appropriate head joint placement by using a tuner, and put a line or mark on the head joint. Position the head joint at this line each time the instrument is assembled, and then make small adjustments as needed.

CAUSE 2:   Lip aperture too small, too narrow, and/or uncentered.

SOLUTION 2:   Open the lip aperture and relax the embouchure. The lip aperture should be centered with the embouchure hole to achieve the most accurate pitch. Use a mirror to check the size of the lip aperture. If the lip aperture is too small, think of increasing the imaginary circle of air into the instrument, while still maintaining an open air stream. That is, use a slightly more open air stream.

CAUSE 3:   Not compensating for the natural tendency to go sharp as more air is used.

SOLUTION 3:   Lower the direction of the air stream slightly to compensate for the rise in pitch, and use a more open oral cavity.

CAUSE 4:   Air stream directed upward too much.

SOLUTION 4:   Direct the air stream downward into the embouchure hole and/or roll the head joint inward slightly. Cover more of the embouchure hole with the lower lip.

CAUSE 5:   Holding the flute at an incorrect angle.

SOLUTION 5:   Hold the flute so that the foot joint is lowered slightly from a parallel position toward the floor. In addition, the foot joint is pushed out slightly away from the player.

CAUSE 6:   Pads are too far from tone holes.

SOLUTION 6:   Have a knowledgeable repair technician adjust the pads to the proper height.

CAUSE 7:   Too little lower lip covering the lip plate.

SOLUTION 7:   Cover about one-fourth to one-third of the embouchure hole with the lower lip. Not using enough lower lip results in a bright, harsh, uncontrollable tone that is generally sharp.

PROBLEM: Pitch is inconsistent throughout the playing range.

CAUSE 1:   Inconsistent air stream.

SOLUTION 1:   Do not change the air stream drastically from note to note. Instead, blow a consistent stream of air and make small adjustments based on the pitches being played. Adjustments in air speed, air volume, and air direction should be made as necessary to accommodate the dynamic level and pitches involved.

CAUSE 2:   Inconsistent embouchure.

SOLUTION 2:   Maintain a good basic embouchure. Practice playing long tones to develop the embouchure muscles, and concentrate on keeping the embouchure consistent at all times. Use a mirror on a regular basis to check embouchure formation and lip aperture size until proper habits are formed.

CAUSE 3:   Lack of proper breath support.

SOLUTION 3:   Work on breathing exercises with and without the flute to help develop breath support. Take full breaths and practice playing long tones at all dynamic levels. Focus on maintaining a consistent air speed appropriate for each dynamic level. Practice extensively at softer dynamic levels because it is harder to maintain proper breath support at softer dynamic levels than it is at louder dynamic levels. In addition, breath support is often compromised when playing technical passages, because players tend to focus on technique at the expense of proper breath support. Practice maintaining breath support in technical passages.

CAUSE 4:   Slouching.

SOLUTION 4:   When seated, sit up straight (but avoid being rigid or tense) with feet flat on the floor. Sit toward the front edge of the chair. Allow adequate space around the chair to hold the flute at the proper angle. When standing, stand straight and position the feet about shoulder width apart.

CAUSE 5:   Shifting the angle at which the flute is held.

SOLUTION 5: Hold the flute so that the foot joint is lowered slightly from a parallel position toward the floor. In addition, the foot joint is pushed out slightly away from the player.

PROBLEM: Playing out of tune without adjusting.

NOTE: A detailed account of adjusting pitch is located under Intonation in chapter 1.

CAUSE 1: Inability to hear beats or roughness.

SOLUTION 1: Focus on hearing the beats or pulsations that occur when pitches are out of tune. Play long tone unisons with other players and listen for beats. Deliberately playing extremely flat and sharp to accentuate the beats will help players learn to hear beats.

CAUSE 2: Not knowing how to adjust pitch on the instrument.

SOLUTION 2: Adjust pitch involving the head joint/instrument position, embouchure, throat, oral cavity, air stream, and alternate fingerings. There are several ways to do this. Players need to learn how each of these factors affects pitch.

CAUSE 3: The physical skills necessary to adjust pitch on the instrument are not developed.

SOLUTION 3: Practice adjusting pitch every day and continue developing embouchure skills. Relax and tighten the embouchure, focus the air stream upward and downward, open and close the throat and oral cavity, and try alternate fingerings. In addition, incorporate long tone exercises into each practice session. Learn "what does what" so that appropriate adjustments can be made when necessary.

Performance/Technical Problems

PROBLEM: Sloppy playing in tongued technical passages.

CAUSE 1: Tongue and fingers are not coordinated.

SOLUTION 1: Practice simple interval exercises slowly with a metronome, and make sure that the tongue and fingers move together. Keep the fingers close to the keys during these exercises to avoid excessive finger movement. As control is gained, progress to more difficult exercises, and continue to practice with a metronome. Gradually speed up the exercises, but make sure that proper finger-tongue coordination is maintained.

CAUSE 2:   Tonguing speed too slow.

SOLUTION 2:   Using a metronome, start by practicing a variety of simple rhythm patterns on isolated pitches at a slow tempo. Gradually increase the speed and difficulty of the exercises. The tip of the tongue strikes the back of the upper teeth at or near the gum line. Keep the tongue motion light and quick. Periodically, practice tonguing slightly faster than is comfortable. Develop control and rhythmic precision by changing the tempo frequently.

PROBLEM: Sloppy playing overall.

CAUSE   1:   Poor   Hand/Holding/Instrument/Playing   Positions   and Posture.

SOLUTION 1:   Make sure that the playing basics are maintained at all times. A detailed explanation of these playing basics is under Hand/Holding/Instrument/Playing Positions and Posture.

CAUSE 2:   Poor instrument action.

SOLUTION 2:   Make sure the key mechanisms have been properly adjusted, cleaned, and oiled. Excessively sloppy or uneven action is usually the result of poorly adjusted key mechanisms, poorly adjusted pads, and/or bent key mechanisms. In addition, make sure the springs are in proper working condition. Weak springs sometimes bobble or bounce, which inhibits technical fluidity.

CAUSE 3:   Using awkward fingerings.

SOLUTION 3:   Use alternate fingerings when appropriate to maximize technical fluidity. Preparing the right hand when crossing the break contributes significantly to clean playing.

PROBLEM: Speed of the fingers seems slow in technical passages.

CAUSE 1:   Tenseness in the fingers and hands.

SOLUTION 1:   Practice tough passages slowly at first to gain control, and focus on staying relaxed; trying too hard or forcing the fingers to move during technical passages slows down the fingers. Gradually increase the tempo of the passage, and develop the habit of staying relaxed at all tempos.

PROBLEM: An excessive amount of key noise can be heard when the keys are depressed.

CAUSE 1:   Key mechanisms need to be oiled.

SOLUTION 1:   Oil the mechanisms. As a rule, the key mechanisms should be oiled lightly once a month or so. Clacking sounds are often caused by metal-to-metal contact, which results in excessive wear of the key mechanisms.

CAUSE 2:   Pushing keys down too hard or "slapping" the keys.

SOLUTION 2:   Use only enough finger pressure to seal the pads (or fingers) against the tone holes. Stay relaxed, and think of playing smoothly and efficiently. Keeping the fingers close to the keys will help eliminate the tendency to slap the fingers down.

CAUSE 3:   Missing corks or felts.

SOLUTION 3:   Replace missing corks or felts and adjust key height appropriately. Sometimes the corks or felts that prevent metal-to-metal contact (and also help regulate proper key height) fall off. In such cases, the clacking is quite noticeable, and the affected key or keys will often appear out of line with the rest of the keys in the stack.

PROBLEM: Skips and leaps not clean.

CAUSE 1:   Not coordinating the fingers.

SOLUTION 1:   Practice simple interval exercises slowly with a metronome, and focus on moving the tongue and fingers together. Keep the fingers close to the keys during these exercises to avoid excessive finger movement. It may also help to slur all exercises because tonguing often covers up poor finger coordination. As control is gained, progress to more difficult exercises and continue to practice with a metronome. Gradually speed up the exercises, making sure that proper finger-tongue coordination is maintained.

CAUSE 2:   Air stream not maintained properly.

SOLUTION 2:   Do not focus on skips and leaps at the expense of proper breath support; focus on maintaining breath support in all technical passages. Improper use of air in passages involving skips and leaps causes coordination problems between the tongue, fingers, and air stream. Maintain a consistent air stream at all dynamic levels.

CAUSE 3:   Air stream not adjusted properly.

SOLUTION 3:   When skips and leaps are significant, change air direction along with a change in air speed. When skips and leaps are ascending, increase air speed and direct air upward during the interval change. When skips and leaps are descending, decrease air speed and direct air down into the embouchure hole during the interval change.

PROBLEM: Poor finger-tongue coordination.

CAUSE 1:   Poor playing habits resulting from playing passages too fast, too soon.

SOLUTION 1:   Practice simple interval exercises slowly with a metronome, and focus on moving the tongue and fingers together. Keep the fingers close to the keys during these exercises to avoid excessive finger movement. Slur all exercises because tonguing often covers up poor finger coordination. As control is gained, progress to more difficult exercises. Continue to practice with a metronome, and continue to slur the exercises.

CAUSE 2:   Air stream not maintained properly.

SOLUTION 2:   Maintain a consistent air stream at all dynamic levels. Improper use of air in technical passages causes coordination problems between the tongue, fingers, and air stream. Players tend to focus on technique at the expense of proper breath support. Focus on maintaining breath support at all times until proper support becomes automatic.

PROBLEM: Uneven finger movement within the beat.

CAUSE 1:   Poor control of individual fingers.

SOLUTION 1:   Use a metronome and practice exercises that isolate each finger. Practice these exercises slowly and deliberately at first and gradually increase tempo, while always focusing on control. Playing fast is one thing; playing with control is another. The ring fingers and the little fingers are particularly problematic, so work on these fingers extensively.

CAUSE 2:   Poor coordination of cross fingerings.

SOLUTION 2:   Use a metronome and practice exercises that isolate problematic combinations of fingerings. When more awkward fingerings are mixed with less awkward fingerings in technical passages, uneven finger movement within the beat often occurs. Practice these exercises slowly and deliberately at first and gradually increase tempo, while always focusing on control.

Tone Quality and Response Problems

PROBLEM: The tone is small and weak.

CAUSE 1:   Lack of sufficient air, air speed, and/or breath support.

SOLUTION 1:   Use more air, increase air speed, and keep the air stream consistent. Maintain a consistent embouchure to more efficiently utilize air. Take full breaths and practice playing long tones at all dynamic levels. Focus on maintaining a consistent air speed appropriate for each dynamic level. Practice extensively at softer dynamic levels because it is harder to maintain proper breath support at softer dynamic levels than it is at louder dynamic levels.

CAUSE 2:   Lip aperture too small and/or uncentered.

SOLUTION 2:   Keep the opening in the lips no wider than the embouchure hole and be sure to center the lips on the embouchure plate to achieve the fullest sound. Use a mirror to check the size and placement of the lip aperture. If the lip aperture is too small, think of increasing the size of the imaginary circle of air into the instrument. That is, use a slightly more open air stream.

CAUSE 3:   Tight or closed throat.

SOLUTION 3:   Relax or open the throat as if saying "ah." Saying the syllable "ah" and shifting to an "oh" syllable while exhaling will open the throat and oral cavity and keep the embouchure round. Do not tighten or close the throat while articulating; the throat should remain open at all times.

PROBLEM: An unfocused tone quality.

CAUSE 1:   Improper direction of the air stream.

SOLUTION 1:   Direct the air stream across and slightly down into the embouchure hole. The opening in the lips should be no wider than the embouchure hole and should be centered on the embouchure hole to achieve the fullest sound. Use a mirror to check the size and placement of the lip aperture. The syllable "oh" is slightly more open than the syllable "who." The resulting tone quality dictates which syllable is most appropriate.

CAUSE 2: Lip aperture too large and/or wide and/or uncentered.

SOLUTION 2: Make sure that the opening of the lips is no wider than the embouchure hole and that the lips are centered on the embouchure plate to achieve the most accurate pitch. Use a mirror to check the size of the lip aperture. If the lip aperture is too large, think of decreasing the imaginary circle of air into the instrument, while still maintaining an open air stream. That is, use a slightly more focused air stream.

CAUSE 3: Not enough or too much lower lip covering the lip plate.

SOLUTION 3: Cover about one-fourth to one-third of the embouchure hole with the lower lip. Too much lower lip results in a muffled, fuzzy tone that is generally flat in pitch. Not enough lower lip results in a bright, uncontrollable tone that is generally sharp in pitch. Both are unfocused and undesirable.

PROBLEM: Lack of tone control.

CAUSE 1: Embouchure is inconsistent.

SOLUTION 1: Form a good basic embouchure and make sure that the bottom lip covers one-fourth to one-third of the embouchure hole. Practice playing long tones to develop the embouchure muscles, and focus on keeping the embouchure consistent at all times. Use a mirror on a regular basis to check embouchure formation and placement on the lip plate until proper habits are formed.

CAUSE 2: Inconsistent breath support and/or control of the air stream.

SOLUTION 2: Practice breathing exercises with and without the flute to help develop breath support. Take full breaths and practice playing long tones at all dynamic levels. Focus on maintaining a consistent air speed appropriate for each dynamic level. Practice extensively at softer dynamic levels because it is harder to maintain proper breath support at softer dynamic levels than it is at louder dynamic levels. Maintain breath support in technical passages. That is, breath support is often compromised when playing technical passages because players focus on technique at the expense of proper breath support.

CAUSE 3: Inconsistent hand/holding/instrument/playing positions and posture.

SOLUTION 3: Develop and follow a daily routine of checking hand and instrument positions so that maintaining proper positions becomes habit.

Proper placements of the left and right thumbs and proper instrument angle are particularly important for tone control. Practice while sitting and standing so that good habits are developed in both playing positions. A detailed discussion of these playing basics is under Hand/Holding/Instrument/Playing Positions and Posture.

CAUSE 4:   Inconsistencies in the oral cavity and/or tongue positions.

SOLUTION 4:   The throat should remain open as if saying "ah," and the tongue should remain relatively flat and relaxed in the mouth when slurring and drawn back slightly (arched) in the mouth when tonguing. Unnecessary movement and tension of the throat and tongue disrupts the air stream and can affect tone control, tone quality, and pitch.

CAUSE 5:   Lip aperture too large, too wide, and/or uncentered.

SOLUTION 5:   Make sure that the opening of the lips is no wider than the embouchure hole and that the lips are centered on the embouchure plate. Use a mirror to check the size of the lip aperture. If the lip aperture is too large, think of decreasing the imaginary circle of air into the instrument, while still maintaining an open air stream. That is, use a slightly more focused air stream.

CAUSE 6:   Not enough lower lip covering the lip plate.

SOLUTION 6:   Cover about one-fourth to one-third of the embouchure hole with the lower lip. Not using enough lower lip results in a bright, harsh, uncontrollable tone that is generally sharp.

CAUSE 7:   Too much lower lip covering the lip plate.

SOLUTION 7:   Players should cover about one-fourth to one-third of the embouchure hole with the lower lip. Too much lower lip results in a muffled, fuzzy tone that is generally flat and difficult to control.

PROBLEM: Lack of dynamic control.

CAUSE 1:   Insufficient control of the air stream and/or insufficient breath support throughout the dynamic range.

SOLUTION 1:   Practice playing long tones at one dynamic level over a set number of counts. When long tones can be played evenly at one dynamic level, practice playing long tones at different dynamic levels. Later, practice playing crescendi and decrescendi on long tones evenly over a set number of counts from one dynamic level to another. The softest and loudest dynamic levels can be particularly problematic. Practicing at softer and louder dynamic levels is particularly important for tonal control.

CAUSE 2:   Making unnecessary embouchure adjustments when changing dynamics.

SOLUTION 2:   Keep the embouchure relatively stable and consistent during play, making only slight adjustments for range and pitch tendencies. These adjustments include moving the lower lip, jaw, head, and/or flute slightly to redirect air downward or upward. Maintain adequate air speed regardless of dynamic level. As a rule, the lip aperture becomes slightly smaller in softer dynamic ranges and slightly larger in louder dynamic ranges.

PROBLEM: The low notes do not respond well.

CAUSE 1:   Leaks in the pads.

SOLUTION 1:   Check for leaks and replace any worn-out pads. Pad leaks are most noticeable on low notes, because for low notes to respond well, all of the pads on the instrument must seal properly.

CAUSE 2:   Embouchure and/or throat too tight.

SOLUTION 2:   Drop the jaw slightly and open the throat as much as possible. The embouchure should be relaxed. Start on second-line G-natural and work chromatically downward playing half notes or whole notes. Maintain a consistent tone quality on each note and notice the degree to which the embouchure relaxes and opens for the lowest notes.

CAUSE 3:   Not enough air and/or air stream too slow.

SOLUTION 3:   Use a little less air to start the tone, and then increase air speed and volume to keep the tone sounding. Low notes on the flute can be challenging to initially produce, and they can sound lifeless if they are not supported by a strong air stream. Practice long tones on low notes to learn how much air each low note can take before it starts to crack.

CAUSE 4:   Articulation too harsh.

SOLUTION 4:   When learning low notes, do not tongue notes until they respond. Low notes tend to crack easily. Using a strong tonguing motion can inhibit the initial response of the note. When notes respond, practice tonguing exercises to learn the degree of attack appropriate for each low note.

PROBLEM: The high notes do not respond well.

CAUSE 1:   Inadequate air support.

SOLUTION 1:   Provide a faster air stream. Practice playing long tones on high notes to develop good air speed. Start on top-space G-natural and work chromatically upward playing half notes or whole notes. Maintain a consistent tone quality on each note and focus on the degree to which the air speed is increased to maintain the tone the higher notes. Begin with a forte dynamic level because it is easier to push air faster if more air is being used. As the high range develops, practice high notes at soft dynamic levels, making sure to maintain tone quality and intonation.

CAUSE 2:   Embouchure too relaxed.

SOLUTION 2:   Firm the embouchure slightly. Use the same basic embouchure in the high range that is used in the middle range, and then focus the oral cavity slightly for the particular note being played. Direct the air stream upward slightly.

CAUSE 3:   Embouchure unfocused or undeveloped.

SOLUTION 3:   Practice playing long tones to develop embouchure muscles. Notes in the middle range should sound focused and clear before working on high notes. Increase range gradually.

PROBLEM: A thin, pinched tone.

CAUSE 1:   Inadequate air support.

SOLUTION 1:   Use more air and maintain a consistent air speed. Practice long tones to develop the ability to sustain the air. It may be helpful to think of increasing the imaginary circle of air into the instrument. That is, use a slightly more open air stream.

CAUSE 2:   Undeveloped embouchure.

SOLUTION 2:   Practice long tones to develop embouchure muscles. Maintain a consistent embouchure while playing.

CAUSE 3:   Too much lower lip covering the lip plate.

SOLUTION 3:   Cover about one-fourth to one-third of the embouchure hole with the lower lip. Too much lower lip results in a muffled, fuzzy tone that is generally flat and difficult to control.

CAUSE 4:   Improper focus of the air stream.

SOLUTION 4:   Make minor adjustments with the lips, jaw, head and/or flute to maintain consistent tone quality and pitch regardless of range and dynamic level. Focusing the air stream at too high an angle can result in a spread tone. Focusing the air stream at too low an angle can result in a thin tone.

CAUSE 5:   Lip aperture is too small.

SOLUTION 5:   Check the opening in the lips; it should be no wider than the embouchure hole. Use a mirror to check the size of the lip aperture. If necessary, make the lip aperture slightly wider and/or larger to let more air through. Practice long tones, and change the size of the lip aperture to notice the effect that aperture size has on tone quality.

CAUSE 6:   Instrument is improperly positioned, causing the embouchure to be off-center or improperly angled.

SOLUTION 6:   Reposition the instrument so that the embouchure and lip plate are parallel to each other. Make sure that the lip aperture is centered on the embouchure hole.

PROBLEM: Grunting or guttural noises can be heard during normal play.

CAUSE 1:   Closing the glottis when coughing or swallowing is normal; however, players sometimes develop the habit of closing the throat to stop the air and opening it to release the air (especially when articulating), which results in a grunting sound. Closing the throat or glottis and using it as a valve to control air flow negatively affects releases, tone quality, and pitch.

SOLUTION 1:   Maintain an open throat as if saying "ah," and learn to control the flow of the air from the diaphragm. Do not use the throat to articulate.

PROBLEM: An airy tone quality.

CAUSE 1:   Lip aperture too large and/or wide.

SOLUTION 1:   Make sure that the opening in the lips is no wider than the embouchure hole. Use a mirror to check the size of the lip aperture. Think of decreasing the imaginary circle of air into the instrument, while still maintaining an open air stream. That is, use a slightly more focused air stream.

CAUSE 2:   Not enough lower lip covering the lip plate.

SOLUTION 2:   Cover about one-fourth to one-third of the embouchure hole with the lower lip. Not using enough lower lip results in a bright, airy, uncontrollable tone that is generally sharp.

CAUSE 3:   Undeveloped embouchure.

SOLUTION 3:   Practice long tones to develop embouchure muscles. Maintain a consistent embouchure while playing.

CAUSE 4:   Leaks in the instrument.

SOLUTION 4:   Have a repair technician check for leaks and replace any worn out and/or leaking pads.

CAUSE 5:   The height of the pads above the tone holes is incorrect.

SOLUTION 5:   Adjust the pad height and play the instrument after each adjustment to determine if appropriate adjustments have been made. Pad height should be adjusted by a knowledgeable repair technician.

PROBLEM: Cracking notes.

CAUSE 1:   Articulation too harsh.

SOLUTION 1:   Learn how hard attacks can be before the tone cracks. Practice articulations lightly at first, gradually using stronger attacks until the tone cracks.

CAUSE 2:   Embouchure not properly set for the note being played.

SOLUTION 2:   Learn the ways the embouchure needs to be set for every note throughout the range. Cracking notes because the embouchure is not properly set is most common when slurring over large intervals.

CAUSE 3:   Hitting keys unintentionally.

SOLUTION 3:   Maintain proper hand position and finger placement. Cover tone holes with the pads of the fingers. Move the fingers and hands as little as possible when moving from note to note.

CAUSE 4:   Leaks in the instrument.

SOLUTION 4:   Have a repair technician check for leaks and replace any worn out and/or leaking pads.

CAUSE 5:   Loose and/or detached springs.

SOLUTION 5:　Reposition springs with a spring hook tool or crochet hook. If the key still does not work properly, the spring has probably lost adequate tension. Loose or worn springs can sometimes be tightened by reseating them and/or by bending them gently in the appropriate direction. Broken springs must be replaced.

PROBLEM:　A slightly delayed response of certain notes during slurred intervals, or the wrong pitch is sounding even though the fingering is correct.

CAUSE 1:　Pad or pads sticking. Pads absorb moisture during normal play. This moisture attracts dirt and food particles. These particles collect in and around the tone holes and on the pads (particularly in the creases), causing pads to stick. In addition, sugar from certain beverages also causes pads to stick.

SOLUTION 1:　Clean the pads and tone holes. For a quick fix, place a thin sheet of tissue paper, cigarette paper, or a dollar bill (preferably a clean one) between the sticking pad and tone hole. Close the pad lightly, and pull the paper through. Cleaning pads in this way is fairly common among advanced players. Various types of "no-stick" powder are also available. These powders do work for a very short period of time; however, they are often quite messy, and they create more problems in the long run because they simply add to the particles already collected on the pads and inside the tone holes. Generally, powders should not be used to free sticking pads. Ultimately, the instrument may need to be taken apart and cleaned thoroughly by a repair technician, and sticking pads may need to be replaced. Players should not eat or drink (except water) while playing to avoid pad and instrument damage.

CAUSE 2:　The crease in the pad is too deep, causing the pad to bind against the tone hole edge.

SOLUTION 2:　Replace the pad.

CAUSE 3:　The outside layer of a pad is torn, causing the pad to bind against the tone hole edge.

SOLUTION 3:　Replace the pad.

CAUSE 4:　A rod is bent.

SOLUTION 4:   Have a repair technician straighten the rod. Bent rods can cause key mechanisms to stick. Often, players can feel a bump or hitch in the mechanism, indicating that a bent rod is the source of the problem.

CAUSE 5:   A spring has come off, a spring is broken, or a spring is loose or worn out.

SOLUTION 5:   Put the spring back into place using a spring hook tool. A pencil, small screwdriver, or crochet hook can also be used to replace springs in some cases, but they are not nearly as effective. Spring hook tools are easy to use, inexpensive, and are an excellent investment. Loose or worn springs can sometimes be tightened by reseating them and/or by bending them gently in the appropriate direction. Broken springs must be replaced.

CAUSE 6:   Pivot (post) screws are loose. Pivot screws work themselves loose periodically, creating problems with the alignment of key mechanisms. The area around pivot screws can also get gummed up by accumulating dirt and other foreign materials, resulting in sticky key mechanisms.

SOLUTION 6:   Clean pivot screws and surrounding areas. Place a drop of key oil on the screws and threads, and tighten the screws snugly. Placing a small amount of nail polish on screw heads and rods that frequently work themselves loose will help hold them in place.

3

Clarinet

Acoustical Properties: The acoustical and physical tonal characteristics of an instrument that affect its sound quality. The clarinet is cylindrical, made of wood (sometimes plastic or metal), and has a key design similar to other woodwind instruments. Tone is produced by the vibration of a single reed attached to a mouthpiece. These design characteristics result in a sound that accentuates odd partials (1, 3, 5, and so on). For this reason, the clarinet overblows the twelfth rather than the octave when the register key is depressed. For example, the fingering that produces a middle C-natural (T, 1-2-3) without the register key will produce a G-natural above the staff when the register key is depressed. Only the first (fundamental) and third partials (the clarinet only produces the odd partials in the harmonic series) are used for the majority of the normal playing range. See also Acoustical Basics, page 3; Construction and Design, page 211; Harmonics, page 32

Key Questions

Q: Why doesn't the clarinet overblow the octave like the saxophone?

A: Acoustically, both the clarinet and the saxophone are tubes closed at one end (i.e., the mouthpiece end) and open at the other end (i.e., the bell). However, the clarinet is generally cylindrically shaped and the saxophone is conically shaped. Predominantly, it is this design difference that affects partial strength, and ultimately, instrument timbre. The result of this design difference is that the saxophone produces the second partial (an octave)when overblown, whereas the clarinet produces the third partial (a twelfth) when overblown.

Action: See Action, page 3

Adjusting Pitch: The process of raising or lowering the pitch of notes. A general discussion of adjusting pitch is under Intonation in chapter 1. Specific suggestions for adjusting pitch on clarinet are under Intonation in this chapter.

Air Stream: Physically, the stream of air pushed from the lungs by the diaphragm and abdominal muscles through the trachea and oral cavity into and through a musical instrument. Although the physical nature of exhaling is basically the same for everyone, the ways the air stream is used to play particular instruments vary widely. A general discussion of the air stream and breathing is under Air Stream and Breathing/Breath Support/Air Control in chapter 1. In addition, the effects of the air stream on pitch are under Intonation in this chapter. Specific comments regarding the clarinet air stream appear separately in this chapter.

Clarinet players can surround the reed with warm air as if saying "who" or "oh" in the low register, "who" in the middle register, and "ee" in the extreme high register, and they can think of pushing the air through the clarinet. Syllables can help effect the proper focus and position of the throat, oral cavity, and air stream. The use of and transition from one syllable to the next occurs gradually during normal play and is based on the tone quality at any given time. For example, if players need to open up the tone, "oh" is more appropriate than "who," and "who" is more appropriate than "ee." Considerable disagreement exists as to the appropriateness of particular syllables. Teachers and players should experiment with a variety of syllables and use what yields the best results. In addition, for pitches in the high range, players may need to firm the embouchure slightly without "biting." Most clarinet players flatten the chin and pull the mouth corners back slightly more in the high range, while increasing air speed. Ultimately, precise changes in embouchure, oral cavity, and the use of air are dictated by tone quality and intonation concerns.

On clarinet, the direction of the air stream changes according to range. Specifically, players need to focus the air slightly downward in the low range and slightly upward as the range ascends. There is a direct relationship between air and embouchure. The air must be focused upward as the scale ascends and downward as the scale descends, and the embouchure must firm and loosen accordingly. In other words, the focus of the air changes slightly throughout the normal playing range of the instrument in conjunction with changes in embouchure. It is important that embouchure changes be minimal. The idea of focusing the air around the reed and making slight adjustments throughout the normal playing range of the instrument is a sound teaching concept on clarinet. Players must use a tuner and listen carefully to determine the appropriate adjustments in air and embouchure.

As a rule, the air stream on the lower clarinets is much more open than it is on B-flat soprano clarinet. The use of the syllable "oh" or "who" in the low and middle registers and "who" or "ee" from the upper part of the middle register to the high register is appropriate. See also Air Stream, page 4; Breathing/Breath Support/Air Control, page 10; Intonation, page 238

Albert System: Also called the "simple" system, a system of clarinet key work developed by Eugene Albert (1816–1890), who was a student of Adolphe Sax (1814–1894). The Albert system is a derivative of the early-nineteenth-century thirteen-key system developed by Iwan Müller and is related to the Oehler system used by most German and Austrian clarinetists. Albert system clarinets have fewer rings and fewer fingering options than Boehm system clarinets. In addition, the right-hand holes are spaced farther apart on Albert system clarinets, and the keys operated by the right-hand little finger are similar to those found on the saxophone. The most distinguishing feature on many (but not all) Albert system clarinets is that the register key wraps around the instrument. That is, the register key is operated by the left thumb, but it is vented on the top of the instrument. Although not commonly played today and not manufactured for the past half a century, Albert system clarinets are played mainly by clarinetists who perform Eastern European and Turkish folk music and by some New Orleans–style jazz players. These musicians sometimes prefer the Albert system due to the ease of slurring notes provided by unkeyed tone holes.

Alternate Fingerings/Alternates: Fingerings not considered standard or basic that can be used to enhance musical performance. Alternate fingerings are most often used to minimize awkward fingerings or to improve intonation in specific musical contexts. The choice of when and which alternate fingerings to use should ultimately be determined by the musical result. That is, does using the alternate fingering improve the musicality of the performance?

Developing command of alternate fingerings is important so that players can use the most appropriate fingering in a given situation. Learning alternate fingerings can be awkward at first. Practicing patterns, passages, scales, and other exercises in which alternate fingerings can be incorporated is helpful. Practice alternate fingerings slowly and deliberately, focusing on only one or two alternate fingerings at a time.

The alternate fingerings described are appropriate for players who are fundamentally sound. Examples of when to use these alternates are shown in figure 3.1. When appropriate, suggestions and comments regarding alternate fingerings have been included. A complete fingering chart that includes alternate fingerings is in "Practical Tips." See also Intonation, page 238; Technique, page 284

FIGURE 3.1. *Alternate Fingerings*

Common Alternate Fingerings for Clarinet

Because many of the same basic fingerings are used in two registers a twelfth apart (the only addition being the register key in the high octave), some of the alternate fingerings described are applicable to notes in both registers. To avoid redundancy, these alternate fingerings have been combined in the following list.

1. Alternate B-natural (below the staff) or Alternate F-sharp (top-line)—An alternate used in chromatic passages to simplify finger movement. Using standard fingerings when playing from B-flat to B-natural to C-natural (or F-natural to F-sharp to G-natural) is awkward because of the "flip" between the index (4) and middle fingers (5) of the right hand. To avoid this "flip," players can play the B-natural (or F-sharp) by using the fingering for B-flat (or F-natural) and simply adding the sliver key. The sliver key is between the fifth and sixth tone holes and is depressed with the ring (third) finger of the right hand (6). Alternate B-natural (F-sharp) should be used in ascending and descending chromatic passages and when trilling between B-flat and B-natural (F-natural and F-sharp).

2. Alternate E-flat (first-line) or Alternate B-flat (above the staff): Chromatic Fingering—Using standard fingerings (involving the right hand side key) when playing from D-natural to E-flat to E-natural (or A-natural to B-flat to B-natural) can be a bit awkward because of the coordination problems that often occur between the right and left hands. For a smoother transition, players can finger the E-flat (or B-flat) by substituting the sliver key for the side key. The sliver key is between the second and third tone holes and is depressed with the ring (third) finger (3) of the left hand. This fingering is most often used in chromatic passages. It should be mentioned that the chromatic (or left-hand) E-flat is usually better in tune and has a better tone quality than other alternate E-flat fingerings.

3. Alternate E-flat (first-line) or Alternate B-flat (above the staff)—There are two other common alternates for E-flat or B-flat. The first alternate is to finger E-flat (or B-flat) using the left thumb and index fingers of both hands (1-4). This alternate is particularly useful when players need to play rapidly from first-line E-natural to E-flat (or high B-natural to B-flat) or when playing from low B-flat to E-flat (or top-line F-natural to high B-flat).

The second alternate is to finger E-flat (or B-flat) using the left thumb and index finger and the right-hand middle finger (1-5). This alternate is particularly useful when playing from E-flat (or B-flat) to F-sharp or when playing from low B-natural to E-flat (or top-line F-sharp to B-flat). The only difference between the E-flat and B-flat fingerings (a twelfth apart) is that the register key is used on B-flat.

4. Alternate F-sharp (first-space)—In chromatic passages or when trilling from F-natural to F-sharp, F-sharp can be fingered with the thumb and the two bottom side keys on the right hand (depressed with the side of the index finger). This fingering avoids having to shift rapidly between the left thumb alone (F-natural) and the index finger alone (F-sharp), which is awkward.

5. Alternate F-natural (above the staff)—One of the most common alternates in the high range is the long-F fingering. This alternate F-natural is fingered with the thumb (T) and register (R) key plus 1-2-3-C-sharp key of the left hand, and 4-5-6 of the right hand. This alternate tends to be sharp.

6. Alternate F-sharp (above the staff)—One of the most common alternates in the high range is the long-F-sharp fingering. This alternate F-sharp is fingered with the thumb (T) and register (R) key and 1-2 of the left hand, and 4-5-6-G-sharp key of the right hand. This alternate tends to be very sharp.

Fourth-Finger or Little-Finger Alternate Fingerings for Clarinet

1. Alternate B-natural (third-line) or Low E-natural–Alternate C-natural (third-space) or Low F-natural–Alternate C-sharp (third-space) or Low F-sharp—Third-line B-natural, third-space C-natural, and third-space C-sharp can all be fingered two ways. On these three notes, the thumb and register key and the index, middle, and ring fingers are down on both hands (T, R, 1-2-3 4-5-6); however, players can choose which little finger (right-hand or left-hand) will be used to complete the fingering for each note.

   Low E-natural, low F-natural, and low C-sharp (the notes a twelfth below those mentioned above) use the same basic fingerings and can also be fingered two ways. On these three notes, the thumb and the index, middle, and ring fingers are down on both hands (T, 1-2-3 4-5-6). Players have the same option mentioned above regarding which little finger (right-hand or left-hand) will be used to complete the fingering for each note.

In summary, all of the notes listed above can be fingered two ways. In every instance, the thumb (and register key for the higher notes) and the index, middle, and ring fingers are down on both hands. Players can choose to complete each fingering with either the left-hand or the right-hand little finger key.

Leaving Fingers Down to Facilitate Technical Playing

1. Players sometimes leave the left-hand G-sharp/C-sharp key (little finger) down when playing certain intervals or when playing a fast passage centered around G-sharp (or C-sharp) because leaving it down does not affect the other pitches to a marked degree. For example, when playing a passage from G-sharp to high B-natural to G-sharp to F-sharp to G-sharp, the G-sharp key can be left down throughout.

2. When playing from open G-natural, G-sharp, A-natural, or B-flat to third-line B-natural, players can put the right-hand fingers (4-5-6-B-key) down when playing the G-natural, G-sharp, A-natural, or B-flat.

3. When playing from open G-natural, G-sharp, A-natural, or B-flat (i.e., the throat tones) to third-space C-natural or fourth-line D-natural, put the appropriate right-hand fingers down when playing the G-natural, G-sharp, A-natural, or B-flat. The idea is to put down the right-hand fingers that will be used to finger the next note in advance.

4. When playing intervals back and forth across the break, the appropriate right-hand fingers can be left down. For example, when playing from A-natural to B-natural and back to A-natural, 4, 5, 6 and the B key can be left down. In addition, 2 and/or 3 of the left hand can also be left down on many clarinets, which further simplifies crossing the break.

Key Questions

Q: When should students begin using alternate fingerings?

A: Students who are fundamentally sound can begin using alternate fingerings when opportunities arise to incorporate them into rehearsals and performances. By the time students are in high school, they should be using alternate fingerings regularly.

Q: Is it better to adjust pitch by making embouchure adjustments or by using special fingerings or adding keys?

A: It depends on the musical context. Generally, if using alternate fingerings improves the musicality of a performance, then use them.

Altissimo/Extended Range: In general, a term sometimes used for the notes in the high range and/or the extreme high range of an instrument. On clarinet, the altissimo range extends from high C-sharp upward to about high G-natural. In the standard literature for clarinet, the altissimo range is most commonly heard in advanced works. Players typically begin working on the altissimo range after they have developed excellent control and facility throughout the normal range of the instrument. Producing altissimo notes successfully involves making several adjustments including using altissimo fingerings, adjusting the embouchure and oral cavity, and changing the speed, focus, and direction of the air stream. Some suggestions for developing the altissimo range are outlined separately in this section.

General Suggestions for Developing the Altissimo Range

1. Work on altissimo after developing a good, consistent tone quality throughout the normal range of the instrument.
2. Use a slightly harder reed than normal. Using soft reeds makes it difficult to produce altissimo notes with good pitch and tone quality.
3. For notes above high C-sharp, use the E-flat/A-flat key as a vent key. The addition of this key will help response, tone quality, and pitch.
4. Learn different fingerings for each note in the altissimo range, and experiment with new fingerings. The "best" fingering for any particular player or instrument should be determined through trial and error.
5. Start with high C-sharp and D-natural because these notes respond relatively easily for most players.

Practice Suggestions for Developing the Altissimo Range

1. Practice altissimo slowly and deliberately.
2. Listen carefully, and use a tuner to check pitch.

3. Warm up properly before working on altissimo, and cool down properly with some long tones and/or slow playing in the low range to help the embouchure relax.

4. When first working on altissimo, use breath attacks (but do not move the tongue), and slur from one note to the next. Once control is gained, try tonguing the notes. Make sure that the tongue is light and quick; it should disrupt the air stream minimally.

5. Start with high C-sharp and D-natural because these notes respond relatively easily for most players, their fingerings are relatively simple, and their fingerings follow an intuitive pattern.

6. Start on a note that responds relatively well and that you know is "right," and then work upward one note at a time.

7. After a modest amount of control is gained, play simple tunes to help gain tonal control and pitch accuracy.

8. Limit the amount of time spent working on altissimo during each practice session. Working on altissimo can damage reeds, and excessive practice in this range can tire the embouchure. As a rule, ten to fifteen minutes of altissimo work during a practice session is sufficient, especially in the early stages of altissimo development.

Embouchure/Oral Cavity Suggestions

1. Point the chin downward, and firm the embouchure.

2. Firm the lower lip and pull the mouth corners back slightly to help the response, especially in the initial stages. Some teachers describe this process as flexing the lip muscles. Keep such adjustments minimal.

3. Take a little more mouthpiece into the mouth, so that the lower lip is applying more pressure to a thicker, stiffer part of the reed. The teeth may actually be slightly farther apart when playing altissimo notes as a result of taking more mouthpiece into the mouth. This position may facilitate response.

4. Apply more pressure near the center of the reed with the bottom lip but do not "bite" the reed.

5. Experiment with different oral cavity and/or throat positions by using a variety of syllables. For example, arch and pull the tongue back slightly as if saying "ee," "eh," or "ah" to facilitate response.

6. Practice to develop a faster air stream and an open throat; both are crucial to playing in the altissimo range.

Air Stream Comments/Suggestions

1. Think of using a cold air stream. The air must move faster in the altissimo range than in the normal range.
2. Focus the air stream as if saying "ee" (or "hee" if using breath attacks). Players may feel the tongue curve so that the sides of the tongue actually touch the teeth.
3. Initially, think of focusing the air in a direction parallel to the plane of the reed. If the desired response is not obtained, focus the air stream sharply downward. This downward focus splits the air stream in such a way that less of the air stream is actually passing over the top of the reed, yet the air passing over the reed is moving faster.
4. If low tones are still being produced, use a fast but unfocused air stream while saying "hee" or "heh," and let the air come out of the mouth corners slightly. Once control is gained, players should be able to produce altissimo notes without letting air escape through the mouth corners.
5. Focus on making the air move fast on a narrowly focused plane. Faster air speed is essential to playing in the altissimo range.

Key Questions

Q: Do high school students really need to have control over the altissimo range?

A: Yes and no. Yes, because some pieces appropriate for high school instrumental music programs include the lower altissimo notes. For example, the range from high C-natural to high E-natural above the staff is fairly common. No, because the middle-to-upper altissimo range is rarely encountered in the high school repertoire. Working on the altissimo range too soon can cause bad habits such as biting and overblowing.

Q: When should students begin to learn altissimo?

A: Advanced students who are fundamentally sound can begin working on the altissimo range in high school, preferably under the guidance of a knowledgeable teacher.

Alto Clarinet: See Instrument Family and Playing Considerations, page 232

Anchor Tonguing: See Anchor Tonguing, page 6

Articulated Keys: Keys that automatically open or close more than one tone hole or key mechanism by design. Articulated keys make technique easier and help produce a more even scale throughout the instrument's playing range. On clarinet, the key rings perform articulated functions. For example, in several instances when a finger closes an open tone hole, it also depresses a key ring connected to a rod that activates other key mechanisms. In addition, the little-finger keys on both hands are articulated so that players can complete certain fingerings using either the left- or the right-hand little fingers, depending on which fingering is more appropriate for the context.

Articulation: See Articulation/Articulative Styles, page 6

Arundo Donax: See Cane/Cane Color, page 206

Assembly: The manner in which an instrument is put together before being played. Proper assembly is important to playability, instrument care, and maintenance. Teaching students to carefully assemble their instruments using a defined assembly procedure can help significantly reduce wear and tear. The clarinet can be assembled efficiently and safely using the steps listed as follows. Figures 3.2 and 3.3 can be used to guide the assembly process. See also Hand/Holding/Instrument Playing Positions and Posture, page 224

1. The clarinet should be assembled while standing (when the case is securely resting on a chair or table) or while kneeling (when the case is sitting on the floor). Clarinets should not be assembled in the player's lap. Although clarinets are small, the parts can easily be dropped and damaged.

2. Put the reed in the mouth (tip side first) and soak thoroughly while assembling the clarinet. Before placing the reed on the mouthpiece, turn the reed around and soak the heel end of the reed, being careful not to damage the reed tip. It is important to soak the entire reed, even though only the tip end of the reed is inserted into the mouth while playing. Many advanced players soak their reeds in cups of water, although this method of soaking is often not practical in school settings.

3. If the corks feel dry, apply cork grease to them before continuing with the assembly process. Rub the cork grease into the cork with the thumb and index finger. If the corks are new, it may be

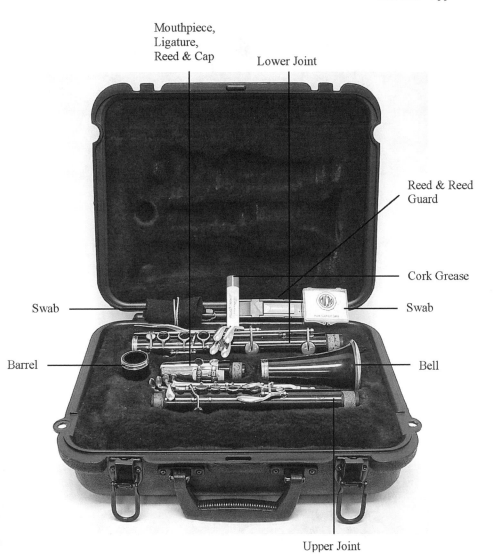

Figure 3.2. *B-flat Clarinet before Assembly*

necessary to apply cork grease every time the instrument is assembled for the first few weeks. As the corks become conditioned, they will not need to be greased as often.

4. Grasp the lower joint (the longer of the two main joints) with the right hand in a way that does not put pressure on the keys.

FIGURE 3.3. *B-flat Clarinet Assembled*

5. Grasp the bell with left hand and attach it to the lower joint with a slight back-and-forth twisting motion. Rest this assembly on the leg with the bell down.

6. Grasp the upper joint (the shorter of the two main joints) with the left hand and depress the keys as if fingering middle C-natural (T, 1-2-3). This position raises the bridge key at the bottom of the joint and prevents damage to the key mechanism when connecting the upper and lower joints. Avoid putting excessive pressure on the keys, and make sure that the bridge keys are properly aligned.

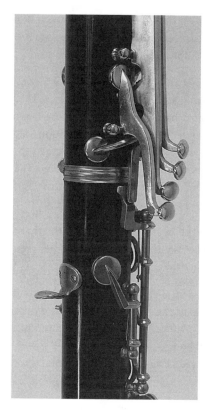

FIGURE 3.4. *Bridge Key Alignment*

7. Attach the upper and lower joints with a slight back-and-forth twisting motion. Make sure to push the two joints together all the way, and make sure that the bridge keys are properly aligned as shown in figure 3.4. There should not be excessive movement between the joints. If the joints are loose and/or the cork is cracked and worn, the corks should be replaced. Maintain a proper seal so that the instrument responds appropriately.

8. While holding the top of the upper joint with one hand, grasp the barrel with the other hand and attach the barrel to the upper joint with a slight back-and-forth twisting motion. Make sure to push the two joints together all the way.

9. While holding the clarinet with one hand where the top of the upper joint and barrel joint join, grasp the mouthpiece (without

the ligature) with the other hand and attach it to the barrel joint with a slight back-and-forth twisting motion. Center the mouthpiece table with the register key.

10. Loosen the ligature screws if they are not already loose and carefully slide the ligature (large end first) over the mouthpiece. The screws on most basic ligatures should be near the flat table on the underside of the mouthpiece (traditional ligature); however, some ligatures are designed with the screws (or screw) near the top of the mouthpiece (inverted ligature). The ligature should slide down below the window opening in the mouthpiece table loosely, leaving plenty of room for the reed.

11. Gently push the ligature back toward the tip of the mouthpiece just enough so that the reed can be slid between the ligature and the mouthpiece table, flat side down.

12. Align the reed so that it is centered on the mouthpiece table and so that the tip of the reed is slightly below the tip of the mouthpiece. When centered properly on the mouthpiece, a small bit of black should be visible over the top of the reed. Avoid touching the tip of the reed. Make reed adjustments by controlling the reed at the heel end and near the vamp and shoulders.

13. Slide the ligature down over the reed so that it is positioned just below the U-shape cut or scrape and tighten the ligature screws snugly as shown in figure 3.5. Do not overtighten.

Attacks: A detailed discussion of attacks is under Attacks in chapter 1. See also Releases/Cutoffs, page 56; Tonguing, page 71

Back Pressure: Air pressure that builds up inside the oral cavity and lungs during normal play. With the exception of oboe players, clarinet players experience more back pressure than other woodwind players do because of the small tip opening. While playing, clarinet players often use more air than can pass through the tip opening, causing the excess air to "back up" inside the oral cavity. As a result, players can find themselves struggling to get rid of excess air. Some players develop the habit of letting this excess air escape through the mouth corners causing an unmusical hissing sound. Although nothing can totally eliminate back pressure, playing on good reeds and mouthpieces, developing proper breathing

FIGURE 3.5. *Reed and Ligature Placement*

habits, learning to use air efficiently, and phrasing properly all help lessen back pressure.

Baffle: The part of a mouthpiece opposite the mouthpiece window, or the underneath side (inside, top) of a mouthpiece. A detailed discussion of the mouthpiece baffle is under Mouthpiece/Mouthpieces in chapter 1. See also Mouthpiece/Mouthpieces, page 247

Balance and Blend Considerations: In general, woodwind instruments are less homogeneous than are brass instruments. As a result, they do not always blend together as well as brass instruments in ensemble settings. To enhance blend, some instrumental teachers recommend using the same brand and/or model of instruments. In addition, different mouthpieces and/or reeds may be used to achieve different balances and blends, depending on the ensemble. For example, players may use one mouthpiece/reed setup in a wind ensemble setting and a different mouthpiece/reed setup in jazz band or orchestra.

In a typical wind band with fifty to sixty players, six to eight soprano clarinets and one or two bass clarinets are often recommended as a good number for balance considerations. The number of soprano clarinet players in any wind group depends largely on the type of sound desired, the number of instruments available, and the strength of clarinet players in the program.

Key Questions

Q: If I use six clarinet players in my ensemble, how many players should I put on each part?

A: As a general rule, put an equal number of players on each part. When the music calls for four parts, put a strong player on each part and double the parts that need to be brought out the most (usually first and second).

Q: How many alto, bass, and contra clarinet players should I have?

A: Some directors choose not to use alto clarinets primarily because the alto clarinet part is almost always doubled by other instruments. One bass clarinet player should suffice; however, two players can add support to the low winds. One contra player is sufficient.

Barrel: The relatively short joint that connects the mouthpiece and the upper joint. Although most clarinets are purchased with only one barrel, many advanced players have two or three barrels for various performing situations. Barrels vary in length and design and can greatly affect pitch, tone quality, and response. In addition, some barrels are adjustable. For example, the CLiCK barrel can be adjusted (lengthened or shortened) by clicking a thumb wheel. Each click changes the length by one millimeter. The standard barrel length is 66mm. Although some players use adjustable barrels, many professional players prefer the tone quality of traditional, non-adjustable barrels. Makers of aftermarket barrels include Moennig, DEG (Accubore) and Backun. See also Tuning Rings, page 294; Tuning/Tuning Note Considerations, page 294

Bass Clarinet: See Instrument Family and Playing Considerations, page 232

Beak: A term sometimes used to describe the outside top part of a mouthpiece that slants downward toward the tip. The top teeth rest on the beak. See also Mouthpiece/Mouthpieces, page 247

Beats: See Beats, page 10

Bell Tones: See Bell Tones, page 10

Blanks, Reed: Precut but unfinished pieces of cane that can be purchased by players who want to make or finish their own reeds. See also Reeds, Single, page 265

Boehm System: The fingering system originally developed by Theobald Boehm (1794–1881) on which most modern woodwinds are constructed. Hyacinthe Klosé (1808–1880) and Louis-Auguste Buffet (1816–1884) took the Boehm system and created a key system for clarinet based on the Boehm system between 1839 and 1843. Among the most significant additions by Klosé and Buffet were the duplicate keys for both the left and right hands, which significantly improved technical playing. The full Boehm clarinet, or French system clarinet as it is sometimes called, had several improvements over the older design including a seventh ring, an articulated C-sharp/G-sharp key, an E-flat key, and an alternate A-flat/E-flat key.

Bore, Instrument: In general, a term used to describe the inside shape and dimensions of an instrument's tube. See also Acoustical Properties, page 188; Bore/Throat, Mouthpiece, page 205; Conical, page 210; Cylindrical, page 214

Bore, Mouthpiece: A term sometimes used to describe the part of a mouthpiece that fits into the barrel and runs back into the mouthpiece chamber. Most clarinet players refer to this area as the "throat." "Bore" is a term more commonly associated with brass mouthpieces. See also Mouthpiece/Mouthpieces, page 247

Bore/Throat, Mouthpiece: A term used to describe the part of a mouthpiece that fits into the barrel joint and runs into the mouthpiece chamber. "Bore" is a term more commonly associated with brass mouthpieces. Most woodwind players refer to this area as the "throat." See also Mouthpiece/Mouthpieces, page 247

Break: The point at which a player must engage the register key mechanism. On clarinet, the break occurs at third-line B-natural. For example, playing from second-space A-natural to third-line B-natural and vice versa involves crossing the break. The term "break" is also used to describe playing from the lower octave to the upper octave simply by depressing the register key (i.e., playing twelfths). For example, playing from low G-natural (T, 1-2-3 4-5-6) to fourth-line D-natural (T, OK, 1-2-3 4-5-6) involves crossing the break. Advanced players also use the term "break" to describe playing from a note below high C-sharp to high C-sharp or a note above high C-sharp in the altissimo register. This "upper break" occurs on high C-sharp because the fingerings necessary to produce the upper partials (i.e., the altissimo pitches) become less patterned or intuitive. In addition, changes in embouchure, oral cavity, air speed, and air focus are more pronounced. See also Crossing the Break, page 212; Technique, page 284

Breathing/Breath Support/Air Control: See Breathing/Breath Support/Air Control, page 10; Circular Breathing, page 23

Butt, Reed: A term sometimes used for the bottom end or heel end of a single reed. See also Reeds, Single, page 265

Cane/Cane Color: The material from which a reed is constructed, and the color, tint, or cast that a particular reed has. A detailed discussion of cane is under Reeds, Single in this chapter. See also Reeds, Single, page 265

Care and Maintenance: Taking proper care of the clarinet is essential for achieving high performance levels. Most of the following maintenance suggestions are relevant to secondary school students, and many of them simply involve establishing a daily routine. See also Care and Maintenance Accessories, page 23

Routine Maintenance

1. Assemble and disassemble the clarinet properly each day.

2. Grease the corks regularly so that excess pressure can be avoided during the assembly/disassembly processes.

3. Maintain proper hand/holding/instrument position while playing. When resting, hold the clarinet in a safe position. The basic resting position is to stand the instrument straight up and rest the bell on one leg (usually the right leg).

4. Put the mouthpiece cap over the mouthpiece/reed assembly and carry the instrument securely in an upright position to minimize the chance of banging the instrument into music stands, chairs, or other instruments.

5. When placing the instrument in its case, lay the sections down gently in their proper locations, and then run the swab through each individual joint. When swabbing out joints, insert and pull

the swab from the large end to the small end of each joint several times. Excess moisture should also be wiped from the tenons. The bell does not collect much moisture and does not need to be swabbed daily.

6. Remove excess water from the instrument regularly. When playing for long periods of time, moisture sometimes collects in the tone holes, especially the smaller holes in the top part of the upper joint (i.e., register key, side keys, and throat tone keys). Players can blow forcefully into these tone holes to remove excess water. If this action does not remove the excess water, players may use a soft pipe cleaner or cigarette paper to remove excess water from tone holes.

7. Rest the clarinet in an upright position. When the clarinet is rested in a horizontal or semi-horizontal position, water tends to run into tone holes.

8. Remove excess water on pads off with a piece of ungummed cigarette paper, a dollar bill, or other absorbent material. Ultimately, pads that receive the most moisture will need to be replaced more often than will other pads because the excess moisture causes them to harden and lose their proper seal.

9. Wipe off the outside of the clarinet with a dry, soft cloth to remove excess moisture, fingerprints, dust, and so on.

10. Remove excess moisture from the reed by gently wiping it off against a soft cloth or by gently wiping the reed (from heel to tip) against the heel of the hand. Store reeds in a reed guard or case to avoid damaging them.

Key Questions

Q: Some sources suggest that swabs should be pulled from the small end to the large end of each joint so that the swab does not get stuck. How should students swab their clarinets?

A: Pulling the swab from the small end compresses the swab, preventing it from absorbing moisture properly throughout the length of the joint. Students should pull the swab from the large end to the small end of the joint because the swab absorbs moisture more efficiently; however, students must not force the swab through the small end of the joint because it can get stuck.

Other Maintenance

1. Remove the dust from under the key mechanisms once every couple of weeks or so with a small, soft paintbrush.

2. If excessive key noise is heard during regular play, oil the key mechanisms. As a rule, the key mechanisms should be oiled lightly once a month or so. These clacking sounds are generally caused by metal-to-metal contact, which results in excessive wear of the key mechanisms.

3. Clean out the tone holes every month or so to remove excess dirt, lint, and grime that has collected over time. A Q-tip can be used for this purpose. Care must be taken not to damage the tone holes and the key mechanisms during the cleaning process.

4. With wooden clarinets, oil the bore, the exterior of the clarinet, and the bell with bore oil once or twice a year. Make sure that the oil does not get on the pads. When oiling the bore, place a small amount of oil on a soft cloth and run the cloth through each joint several times as if swabbing the instrument.

5. Once or twice a year, wipe off the corks with a soft, clean cloth. Cork grease tends to attract dirt creating a build-up on the corks. Some players use alcohol to clean cork, but alcohol should be used only by knowledgeable players. After being cleaned, apply a small amount of cork grease to the corks and rub it in well using the thumb and index finger.

6. Mouthpieces should be washed with warm soapy water once every couple of weeks to remove undesirable particles. Avoid getting the cork wet during the cleaning process. Never use hot water to clean mouthpieces! Hot water can easily warp and discolor mouthpieces.

Considerations

1. Invest in a well-made and well-fitted case. It will prove essential to maintaining instrument condition. Some clarinet cases also include case covers, which add additional protection.

2. Avoid subjecting clarinets to extreme temperature and humidity changes. Wooden clarinets are more likely to crack or split when exposed to extreme temperature and humidity changes,

especially when cold instruments are warmed up too quickly. In addition, pads, corks, and felts have a tendency to loosen as the instrument contracts and expands in response to temperature and humidity. Never leave the instrument in an uncontrolled environment.

3. If an instrument is cold, let it warm up gradually. Do not warm up clarinets by blowing warm air into them. The sudden change in temperature could cause the inside of the clarinet to expand faster than the outside, causing it to crack.

4. Make repairs promptly. Small cracks that have not gone through to the bore or that do not go through a tone hole should be repaired immediately. Larger cracks or splits may or may not be able to be repaired properly.

5. Do not clean keys with silver polish or other similar polish. Polish damages key mechanisms, ruins pads, and gums up tone holes.

6. Do not use swabs with a weighted string for cleaning/drying mouthpieces. First, because the mouthpiece is relatively thin, the weight itself can easily break, chip, or crack the mouthpiece, especially the tip. Second, drawing the string over the tip and tip rail can cut into these surfaces over time and ruin the mouthpiece. Third, drawing the swab through the mouthpiece can wear down the interior and actually reshape the chamber over time, changing the way the mouthpiece responds.

7. Apply cork grease if the joints are tighter than normal during assembly and disassembly. Wrap cigarette paper or Teflon tape around the corks if the joints are too loose. Humidity affects cork. As a result, there will be times when the joints will feel tighter or looser than others during assembly and disassembly. As the humidity increases, cork expands; as humidity decreases, cork contracts. These differences are normal.

8. Do not use wooden clarinets for marching band!

Cases, Instrument: Generally, the cases that come with most clarinets are the best cases to use, especially for young players. These hard cases protect the instrument well and are designed to fit particular instruments. This design secures the instrument properly in the case and provides adequate storage for reeds, mouthpieces, and accessories.

Nonetheless, there is a variety of instrument cases on the market today designed to suit a variety of needs. Commonly called "gig" bags or "carry-alls," these cases are available in a variety of designs and are readily available for B-flat clarinet. The materials used for gig bags vary. Generally, the shell consists of synthetic-covered rigid plastic or wood, molded plastic, or leather. The interiors are typically lined with high-density foam. Other features of gig bags may include shoulder straps, carrying handles, and accessory pockets. Other hard cases are also available. One popular hard case design holds a B-flat clarinet and an A clarinet, because many professional symphony players use both instruments. Some auxiliary hard cases are designed to hold additional instruments, such as a clarinet, flute and/or saxophone. Performers who frequently double on flute and saxophone may find these cases more convenient than regular cases. Companies that make cases include Altieri, Pro Pac, Pro Tec, SKB, and Gator.

Key Questions

Q: Are all cases well constructed and designed?

A: No. Students should not purchase cases without checking them out thoroughly. Many cases do not protect instruments properly. Inspect each case for adequate padding, sturdy and secure hinges and handles, and a proper fit for the instrument. A case that does not fit the instrument well or a poorly constructed case will not adequately protect the instrument, which may result in damaged equipment.

Cases, Reed: See Reed Holders/Guards/Cases, page 255

Chamber: The inside of a mouthpiece where the tone resonates. The chamber generally refers to the most open portion of the mouthpiece opposite the mouthpiece table window. See Mouthpiece/Mouthpieces, page 247

Choosing an Instrument: See Instrument Selection, page 33

Clefs: The treble clef is used to notate music for all clarinets; however, it is not unheard of to notate low passages for the bass, contrabass, contra-alto, and contrabass clarinets in bass clef.

Conical: A term used to describe the cone-shaped tubing often used in instrument construction that is relatively narrow on one end (e.g., the mouthpiece end) and gradually widens toward the bell. Clarinets are predominantly cylindrical rather than conical, despite having small bells that flare outward. See also Acoustical Basics, page 3; Acoustical Properties, page 188; Cylindrical, page 214

Construction and Design: The clarinet family consists of a wide variety of instruments pitched in several keys. The clarinets most commonly used in band settings are pitched in B-flat and E-flat and include the E-flat soprano, B-flat soprano, E-flat alto, B-flat bass, E-flat contra-alto, and B-flat contrabass. The A soprano clarinet, which is pitched one half step below the B-flat soprano clarinet, is frequently used in orchestral and chamber music settings.

Today, the Boehm system (or French system) clarinet is considered standard. Generally, most clarinets have seventeen keys and six rings. Student-line instruments are typically made of plastic with nickel-plated key work and synthetic pads. Intermediate and professional instruments may be made of wood (typically grenadilla), hard rubber, or a more "eco-friendly" composite material (e.g., Green Line), which tolerates extreme weather conditions better than wood. These clarinets may have silver-plated, nickel-plated, or silver key work and the pads may be made of synthetic material, double skin, or Gore-Tex. Intermediate and professional clarinets are available with optional keys. The alternate E-flat/A-flat key is the most common optional key, although some or all of the other keys considered part of the "Full Boehm" system might be included on an intermediate or professional instrument. The Full Boehm system includes a low E-flat key, an E-flat/A-flat lever, an alternate G-sharp/C-sharp trill key, and an additional ring on the lowest open hole in the upper joint.

Clarinets are available in different bore sizes and shapes, which significantly affect sound quality and other tonal characteristics. Large-bore clarinets have the potential for a fuller sound than small-bore clarinets; however, small-bore clarinets are more appropriate for beginners because they produce a more focused tone with less effort, are generally more responsive and easier to control, and their tone holes are sometimes easier to cover. The medium-bore clarinet displays some of the characteristics of both large- and small-bore clarinets and is the most popular choice for general use. Most student-line instruments have a cylindrical bore, while many intermediate and professional instruments have a "poly-cylindrical" bore, or a bore that is slightly tapered through the upper and lower joints. This taper contributes to a warmer, fuller, more rounded tone quality.

Barrels are another significant design component of the clarinet. The length and shape of the barrel significantly affects pitch and tone quality. Players can improve the tonal characteristics of their instruments significantly and less expensively by investing in a new barrel rather than purchasing a new instrument. Advanced players often have more than one barrel for different playing situations. The choice of barrels is a matter of personal preference.

The mouthpiece is also a critical component of the clarinet. Mouthpiece choice is a matter of personal preference, and there is no one-size-fits-all mouthpiece. Trying several mouthpieces is important when selecting an appropriate mouthpiece for any given player. Experimenting with a wide variety of mouthpieces also deepens players' understanding of tone production and response. It is common for advanced players to have more than one mouthpiece for different playing situations. Finding a good "fit" between the mouthpiece, the instrument, and the player is critical to proper tonal and technical development. See also Acoustical Basics, page 3; Acoustical Properties, page 188; Mouthpiece/Mouthpieces, page 247

Contra-alto Clarinet: See Instrument Family and Playing Considerations, page 232

Contrabass Clarinet: See Instrument Family and Playing Considerations, page 232

Cracks: See Care and Maintenance, page 206

Crossing the Break: Technically, playing from any note below third-line B-natural to third-line B-natural or above (or vice versa) involves crossing the break; however, crossing the break usually refers to performing intervals close in proximity to third-line B-natural. For example, going from B-flat to B-natural, B-flat to C-natural, A-natural to B-natural, A-natural to C-natural, G-natural to B-natural, and so on is commonly referred to as "crossing the break." Crossing the break on clarinet can be challenging, especially for young players. The primary considerations when crossing the break are maintaining instrument finger/hand position, coordinating the fingers, and covering the tone holes properly.

The main challenge with crossing the break is moving from an open fingering (where few keys are depressed) to a closed fingering (where many keys are depressed), requiring players to coordinate fingers and to seal the tone holes properly. Crossing the break involves using the register key and coordinating the left thumb with the other fingers while covering tone holes completely. In addition, because the clarinet is heavier than the flute or oboe and is held out to the front of the player (usually without a neck strap), it may be more challenging to master crossing the break on clarinet than on other instruments. Preparing the right hand simplifies the problems inherent in crossing the break, while causing only slight changes in tone quality and intonation. On many instruments, preparing the right hand actually improves both tone quality and pitch. Suggestions for crossing the break and preparing the right hand appear in the following list.

Examples of Crossing the Primary Break

Prepare the right hand by depressing the appropriate right-hand keys
on the lower note in each grouping

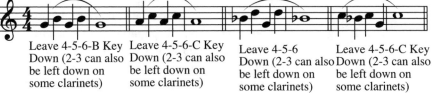

Leave 4-5-6-B Key
Down (2-3 can also
be left down on
some clarinets)

Leave 4-5-6-C Key
Down (2-3 can also
be left down on
some clarinets)

Leave 4-5-6
Down (2-3 can also
be left down on
some clarinets)

Leave 4-5-6-C Key
Down (2-3 can also
be left down on
some clarinets)

FIGURE 3.6. *Crossing the Break*

Common examples of crossing the break appear in figure 3.6. See also Break, page
205; Secondary Break, page 281; Technique, page 284

Preparing the Right Hand/Suggestions for Crossing the Break

1. When playing from open G-natural, G-sharp, A-natural, or
   B-flat to third-line B-natural, players can put the right-hand fin-
   gers (4-5-6, B-key) down when playing the G-natural, G-sharp,
   A-natural, or B-flat.

2. When playing from open G-natural, G-sharp, A-natural, or B-flat
   to third-space C-natural or fourth-line D-natural, players can
   put the appropriate right-hand fingers down when playing the
   G-natural, G-sharp, A-natural, or B-flat. The general idea is to put
   down the right-hand fingers that will be used on the next note in
   advance.

3. When playing intervals back and forth across the break, the appropriate fingers can be left down. For example, when playing from
   A-natural to B-natural and back to A-natural, 4-5-6 and the B key
   can be left down.

Teaching Tips for Crossing the Break

1. Make sure students keep their fingers close to the keys and in the
   ready position at all times. Proper finger position will improve finger coordination and minimize excess finger movement.

2. Practice these intervals slowly at first, and work on one interval
   at a time. When students can play from G-natural to B-natural,
   G-sharp to B-natural, A-natural to B-natural, and B-flat to

B-natural in isolation, have them play two intervals together, then three, and so on.

3. When learning to play these intervals, tonguing each note can improve response; however, tonguing can also mask problems with finger coordination. Therefore, it is important that students practice these intervals using slurs across the break. Students will often make changes in air, embouchure, throat, and so on to compensate for poor finger coordination when playing across the break. Such compensations are unnecessary. In addition, maintaining a steady air stream and a consistent embouchure when playing across the break is essential.

Cut, Reed: Also called the "vamp" or "scrape," the U-shaped area of a single reed, where the bark has been removed. On a single-cut reed, the U-shaped area has been cut from a reed blank. The other areas of the reed retain the original bark. On a double-cut reed, the U-shaped area constitutes the first cut, and then additional bark is removed from the area just behind and to the sides of the U-shaped area, constituting the second cut. See also Reeds, Single, page 265

Cylindrical: A term used to describe the cylinder-shaped tubing often used in instrument construction. Unlike conical tubing, which is relatively narrow on one end and gradually widens toward the other, cylindrical tubing remains the same diameter along the entire length of tubing. All clarinets are predominantly cylindrical despite the fact that the bell flares outward slightly. See also Acoustical Basics, page 3; Acoustical Properties, page 188; Conical, page 210

Diaphragm: See Breathing/Breath Support/Air Control, page 10; Diaphragm, page 26

Dizziness/Lightheadedness: See Dizziness/Lightheadedness, page 26

Double-Cut Reeds: One of two basic types of cuts available for single reeds, primarily used for saxophone and clarinet playing. In addition to the initial U-shaped cut characteristic of a single-cut reed, a double-cut reed has additional bark removed. This additional bark is removed from the area just behind and to the sides of where the original cut begins. Rico Royal and Vandoren reeds are double-cut reeds. Compared to single-cut reeds, double-cut reeds are thought to be more responsive, to last longer, and to produce a bigger, darker tone quality. Double-cut reeds are typically more expensive than single-cut reeds. See also Reeds, Single, page 265

Double-Lip Embouchure: A nontraditional single-reed embouchure that involves having both the upper and lower lips (thus the term "double-lip") rolled over the teeth, similar to a double reed embouchure. The double-lip embouchure is usually inappropriate for most players, although a few players use this embouchure successfully. The tone is more difficult to control with a double-lip embouchure, and a double-lip embouchure is less flexible than a traditional clarinet embouchure. See also Embouchure, page 215

Double-Tonguing: A technique that enables performers to tongue duple patterns rapidly. See also Multiple-Tonguing, page 52

Doubling Considerations: See Instrument Family and Playing Considerations, page 232

Dutch Rush: Also called reed rush, horsetail, file grass, and shave grass, a natural fiber that can be used to smooth cane and to remove small amounts of cane in the reed making and/or adjusting process. See Reeds, Single, page 265

Dynamic Considerations: See Dynamic Considerations, page 26; Intonation, page 238

E-flat Soprano Clarinet: See Instrument Family and Playing Considerations, page 232

Embouchure: The clarinet is a relatively easy instrument on which to initially create a sound. That is, the basic embouchure is relatively easy to form, and the beginning reed/mouthpiece combination typically responds easily; however, some aspects of the clarinet embouchure can be challenging to form properly. For example, many beginners "bunch" their chins rather than play with flat chins. Learning to make appropriate adjustments according to range is also challenging. The steps for forming a fundamentally sound clarinet embouchure are described in the following list. Proper embouchures are shown in figure 3.7. A proper bass clarinet embouchure is shown in figure 3.8. General embouchure considerations for members of the clarinet family are described under Instrument Family and Playing Considerations. See also Instrument Family and Playing Considerations, page 232

1. Put lips together lightly.

2. Gently stretch the lower lip against the bottom teeth. The mouth corners will naturally come back slightly in a flexed position.

FIGURE 3.7. *Embouchure*

3. Drop the jaw slightly, separating the lips and teeth.

4. Insert enough of the mouthpiece into the mouth to allow the
   end of the reed to rest lightly on the lower lip. Make sure that
   the mouthpiece is centered in the mouth. The mouthpiece enters
   the mouth at an upward angle. As a general rule, the bell of the

FIGURE 3.8. *Bass Clarinet Embouchure*

clarinet extends outward between the knees in the seated position. The exact angle will ultimately be determined by the tone quality.

5. Push the mouthpiece into the mouth about three-eights of an inch, allowing the reed to push the bottom lip over the bottom teeth. The exact amount of mouthpiece in the mouth will ultimately be determined by the tone quality.

6. The upper teeth should rest lightly on top of the mouthpiece. Firm the upper lip slightly and gently push down on the top of the mouthpiece.

7. Position the lips as if saying "who." This position causes the lips to seal around the mouthpiece and helps bring the mouth corners in. No air should escape through the mouth corners.

8. The chin remains flat and pointed downward. The cheeks should be in a natural position and not puffed out. Generally, the clarinet embouchure is slightly firmer and less rounded than an alto saxophone embouchure.

Key Questions

Q: Is the same basic embouchure used for all clarinets?

A: Yes and no. Although many basic aspects of embouchure formation are the same for all clarinets, there are also several important differences. In general, as the size of the mouthpiece increases, the openness of the embouchure increases and the firmness of the embouchure decreases. Therefore, bass and contrabass embouchures are more open and relaxed than the alto embouchure, and much more open and relaxed than the B-flat and E-flat soprano embouchures. Overall, E-flat soprano players use a noticeably firmer embouchure. When playing the low clarinets, it is also helpful to focus the air downward more than on B-flat soprano clarinet, especially in the low range. It can also be challenging to focus the air correctly to get high notes (typically above top-space G-natural) to respond properly. In contrast, the E-flat soprano clarinet requires a noticeably firmer embouchure than the lower clarinets. The E-flat soprano clarinet embouchure is the most challenging for two reasons: (1) it is the most difficult clarinet to play in tune; and (2) it is the most difficult clarinet on which to produce an even scale. That is, the E-flat soprano clarinet requires more adjustments throughout the range of the instrument than other clarinets. Regardless of which clarinet is being played, players must learn to make adjustments in the embouchure, oral cavity, and air stream throughout the entire range of the instrument according to the intonation tendencies of each specific instrument.

Q: How much pressure should the bottom teeth exert on the lower lip?

A: In general, a small amount on the lower clarinets and a modest amount on B-flat soprano clarinets. Most of the pressure on the reed is applied and supported by the facial muscles; however, the lower teeth and jaw do contribute to embouchure support. Players who are out of shape or who play an excessive amount without building up their embouchure muscles often develop soreness on the inside of their lower lip where the lip makes contact with the teeth. In addition, slightly more pressure is used on E-flat soprano clarinet than on other clarinets.

Q: What can be done to prevent soreness of the lower lip?

A: Strengthen the embouchure muscles by practicing long tones and long tone exercises regularly and by extending practice time gradually over a period of weeks. Also, avoid excessively long practice sessions. Distributed practice is more effective than massed practice.

Q: What can be done to relieve soreness of the lower lip?

A: Some players place a small piece of folded paper over their lower teeth to prevent the teeth from cutting into the lower lip. Cellophane and cigarette paper are two types of paper used for this purpose. Other players have their dentists make removable pads or covers for their lower teeth. These covers last much longer than paper and conform to the shape of an individual's teeth. In addition to preventing or relieving pain or discomfort, covering the lower teeth can "even out" the teeth, applying a more even pressure across the reed and improving tone quality.

Q: Should players with crooked, uneven teeth play clarinet?

A: Players who are highly motivated to play clarinet can overcome almost any abnormality; however, crooked, uneven teeth can be problematic. If the upper teeth are uneven, placing them on top of the mouthpiece is difficult because teeth that extend farther down will contact the mouthpiece first. Placing a rubber pad on top of the mouthpiece can help. These pads are available at most music stores. If the lower teeth are uneven, the pressure applied to the lower lip/reed will be uneven. Having a dentist make a cover for the lower teeth may help in this regard. In addition, players with crooked, uneven teeth often learn that if they play off-center such that the mouthpiece is no longer centered in the mouth, they will get a better sound. In a few instances, playing off-center may be perfectly acceptable; however, this is the exception and not the rule.

Teaching Tips for Embouchure Formation

1. The firmness of the clarinet embouchure does not remain the same throughout the entire range of the instrument. As a rule, the embouchure is firmer in the high range and more relaxed in the low range. However, in many cases, these changes are slight. In fact, some professional players keep their embouchures very consistent throughout the normal playing range, making adjustments predominantly for pitch and tone color.

2. The idea of applying equal pressure around the mouthpiece, sometimes called the "drawstring effect," is a sound teaching concept because it enables students to understand the need for a round embouchure. In reality, more pressure is applied to the reed from the lower lip, teeth, and surrounding muscles than is applied to the top of the mouthpiece from the upper lip, teeth, and surrounding muscles. However, students who take this analogy too literally may actually apply too much pressure from the top lip.

3. For teaching purposes, telling beginners to smile as a means of producing an embouchure is generally inappropriate. It detracts

from the drawstring analogy or roundness concept and usually results in embouchures that are too tight. When appropriate, students can be instructed to "bring their mouth corners back slightly," or "firm the mouth corners" without being told to smile. In some cases, it may be more appropriate to have students flex their mouth corners and actually bring them forward slightly.

4. If students can play twelfths (middle C-natural to G-natural, D-natural to A-natural, E-natural to B-natural, etc.) by pushing the register key and without making significant embouchure adjustments, then the embouchure pressure is appropriate. If there is too little pressure, the upper pitch will not respond properly and/or will be flat and out of focus. If there is too much embouchure pressure, the lower pitch will not respond when the register key is disengaged; instead, the same pitch that sounded when the register key was depressed will be heard (i.e., the upper pitch). In reality, a very slight increase in embouchure pressure may be necessary to help center the upper note; however, this information is more useful to students after they develop appropriate concepts regarding embouchure formation.

5. Students with moderate to severe overbites often appear to be taking too much mouthpiece in the mouth, while students with a moderate to severe underbite often appear to be taking too little mouthpiece in the mouth. Unless these students are having problems with tone production, tone quality, and tonguing, their "appearances" are acceptable.

6. Students should use a mirror to check their embouchure formations and placement of the mouthpiece. Using a mirror regularly in the beginning stages will help students develop proper playing habits.

End Pin/Spike: An adjustable metal rod attached to the instrument and designed to help support the weight of the instrument. End pins are commonly used on the alto and bass clarinets and are absolutely essential for contrabass clarinets. A bass clarinet with an end pin is shown in figure 3.9.

End Rail: See Tip Rail, Mouthpiece, page 288

Endurance/Stamina: See Endurance/Stamina, page 28

Exhalation/Exhaling: See Breathing/Breath Support/Air Control, page 10

FIGURE 3.9. *Bass Clarinet with an End Pin*

Extended/Contemporary Techniques: In general, ways of producing sounds on an instrument that are not traditionally characteristic of the instrument or not typically called for in standard literature. A detailed discussion of these techniques is found under Extended/Contemporary Techniques in chapter 1. See also Extended/Contemporary Techniques, page 29

F-sharp Key: Clarinets have an alternate F-sharp key between the middle and ring fingers (5-6) of the right hand. This alternate key (or sliver key) is opened using the ring finger (6) of the right hand. For example, when playing top-line F-natural, players can simply push the sliver key to produce an F-sharp. This alternate fingering is commonly used in chromatic passages and for executing trills. In the low range, this same fingering combination (minus the register key), results in an alternate fingering for low B-natural. This alternate is helpful in making the low B-flat to B-natural transition. Alternate F-sharp should be used in ascending and descending chromatic passages and when trilling from F-natural and F-sharp. Alternate B-natural should be used in ascending and descending chromatic passages and when trilling between B-flat and B-natural. See also Alternate Fingerings/Alternates, page 190; B Key, page 93

Facing/Lay: A term used to describe the amount of bend, curve, or slope of a mouthpiece table toward the tip of the mouthpiece. A detailed discussion of the mouthpiece facing is under Mouthpiece/Mouthpieces in chapter 1. See also Mouthpiece/Mouthpieces, page 247

> *Key Questions*
>
> Q: What kind of facing should my students' mouthpieces have?
>
> A: A medium facing.

Family: See Instrument Family and Playing Considerations, page 232

Flutter Tonguing: A technique that involves rolling or fluttering the tongue rapidly while producing a tone. Flutter tonguing uses the same motion of the tongue that is used when pronouncing a rolling "r." Players who cannot roll their tongues may use a throat growl as a substitute. See also Extended/Contemporary Techniques, page 221

French Reed: See Reeds, Single, page 265

Fundamental: See Fundamental, page 32

German Reed: A style of reed whose primary characteristics are a thick heart, thin tip, and slightly narrow width. See Reeds, Single, page 265

Grain, Reed: The natural fibers in reed cane. The grain or fibers of a reed can be fine, medium, coarse, or a combination of the three. By comparing several reeds, players can easily learn to see the variations in the grain. Reeds that contain too many coarse grains typically do not respond well, feel rough on the lip, and produce an unsatisfactory tone quality. Reeds that contain too many fine grains are often inconsistent and tend to wear out quickly. See also Reeds, Single, page 265

Half-Holes: A performance technique that typically involves covering half (or part) of a tone hole with one finger. Using half-holes is an advanced technique that requires great control and precision. On clarinet, half-holes can be produced in two ways. First, when pitches are normally produced by completely covering tone holes with the fingers, a half-hole can be produced by only partially covering the appropriate tone hole. Second, when pitches are normally produced by depressing a key/pad combination, half-holes can be produced by depressing the appropriate key (or keys) down about halfway. The half-hole technique can be used in several ways. First, half-holes can be used to smooth out skips and leaps when playing certain intervals. For example, when playing from fourth-space E-natural to high C-sharp or from top-line F-natural to high D-natural, using a half-hole on the left-hand index finger on the upper notes may facilitate this transition. Second, using half-holes enables players to play quarter tones and to create other effects in contemporary literature. Third, half-holes can also be used in the performance of certain trills. Finally, half-holes can be used to adjust pitch. Using half-holes is an advanced technique that requires great control and precision. See also Extended/ Contemporary Techniques, page 221

Half-hole Key, Low Clarinets: The low clarinets (alto, bass, contra-alto, and contrabass) are designed with a half-hole key for the first hole on the upper joint (index finger) similar to the half-hole key on the oboe. The purpose of this key is to enhance a player's ability to execute half-holes in the high range. Half-holes are executed by rolling the index finger down slightly, uncovering the small vent hole normally covered by the index finger as shown in figure 3.10. Using half-holes

Figure 3.10. *Bass Clarinet Half-Hole Position*

on the low clarinets in the high register beginning with high C-sharp improves response, tone quality, and intonation. The upper clarinets (E-flat soprano, B-flat soprano, and A clarinet) do not have half-hole keys.

Hand/Holding/Instrument/Playing Positions and Posture: Holding the clarinet properly and maintaining good hand position and playing position are key factors in developing good technique, facility, and ease of playing. In addition, good hand position, holding position, and playing position will reduce muscle fatigue and help players avoid physical problems, such as carpal tunnel syndrome. Suggestions for appropriate hand/holding/instrument/playing positions and posture are listed as follows.

Left-Hand Position

1. The left hand is on top (upper joint) with the thumb positioned just behind the thumb (F) hole and slightly touching (or almost touching) the register key as shown in figure 3.11. The thumb is positioned at an upward angle (diagonal) at about 1 o'clock so that it can operate the register key with a simple rocking motion while covering the F hole as shown in figure 3.12.

Figure 3.11. *Hand Position*

FIGURE 3.12. *Thumb Positions*

2. The fingers curve slightly around the clarinet as if forming an open "C" or as if holding a ball. The fingers remain close to the tone holes or rings, and they cross the instrument at right angles.

3. The index, middle, and ring fingers are positioned on or above the first, second, and third tone holes (1-2-3), respectively. Open tone holes are covered with the pads of the fingers, rather than the tips of the fingers.

4. The little finger touches the E key lightly and remains ready to operate the little-finger keys (C-sharp, F-natural, E-natural, and F-sharp).

5. The wrist remains virtually straight.

Right-Hand Position

1. The right hand is on bottom (lower joint) with the thumb positioned on the back side of the clarinet under the thumb rest. The thumb rest should contact the thumb between the thumbnail and the first joint with the ball of the thumb against the clarinet, and the thumb should remain relatively straight as shown in figure 3.16.

2. The fingers curve slightly around the clarinet as if forming an open "C" or as if holding a ball. The fingers should remain close to the tone holes or rings, and they cross the instrument at right angles.
3. The index, middle, and ring fingers are positioned on or above the fourth, fifth, and sixth tone holes (4-5-6), respectively. Open tone holes are covered with the pads of the fingers, rather than the tips of the fingers.
4. The little finger touches the F key lightly and remains ready to operate the little-finger keys (F-sharp, G-sharp, E, and F).
5. The wrist remains virtually straight.

Holding/Instrument Position (B-flat Soprano)

1. The weight of the clarinet is supported by the right thumb. Balance of the instrument is controlled primarily by the right thumb, to a lesser degree by the left thumb, and by the embouchure when the instrument is being played.
2. The bell is held out from the body at about a 35- to 40-degree angle. As a general point of reference, the bell of the clarinet is positioned between knees; small adjustments can be made based on each player's tone quality. As a rule, the clarinet is held slightly closer to the body than the oboe.
3. The clarinet is centered with the body.
4. The elbows are held away from the body in a relaxed manner, and the wrists remain straight. Proper playing positions for the B-flat clarinet are shown in figures 3.13 and 3.14.

Holding/Instrument Position (The Low Clarinets)

1. The low clarinets are played in the seated position. Players should sit near the front edge of the chair so that the bottom of the bell can be brought back slightly so that the mouthpiece enters the mouth at a slightly upward angle (more similar to a saxophone than a B-flat soprano clarinet).

2. The weight of the low clarinets is supported by an end pin, although the alto clarinet is sometimes supported by a neck strap. Balance of the instrument is controlled primarily by maintaining proper instrument position and by the embouchure when the instrument is being played. Balance is controlled to a lesser degree by the right and left thumbs.

FIGURE 3.13. *Playing Position (Front View)*

3. The low clarinets are centered with the body or turned slightly to the left to minimize the inward bend of the right wrist/hand.

4. The elbows are held away from the body in a relaxed manner. Proper playing positions for the bass clarinet and the contra-alto clarinet are shown in figures 3.15 and 3.16.

Posture

1. Sit up straight (but avoid being rigid or tense) with feet flat on the floor. Sit toward the front edge of the chair while in the seated playing position. If the instrument touches the front of the chair, move farther forward on the chair.

2. Avoid being tense or tight in the playing position because tension negatively affects both the mental and physical aspects of playing the clarinet.

3. Keep the head straight and relaxed. Bring the clarinet mouthpiece to the mouth. Do not reach for the mouthpiece.

FIGURE 3.14. *Playing Position (Side View)*

4. Position the music stand carefully. The music stand should be in a position that enables each player reading from the stand to read the music comfortably and easily and to see the teacher/director while maintaining proper playing posture. The most common problem is for music stands to be too low. The most detrimental problem is for music stands to be placed too far to one side, forcing players to abandon good playing positions. Players who share music stands often experience this problem.

5. Make sure the instrument angle is correct. When the instrument is too close or too far from the body, players cannot support the reed properly, resulting in poor tone quality, tone control, and intonation.

Harmonics: See Harmonics, page 32

Heart: The center portion of the reed extending from just behind the tip toward the shoulders. When held up to a light, the heart can be seen as a symmetrically shaded U-shaped area. See also Reeds, Single, page 265

FIGURE 3.15. *Playing Position Bass Clarinet*

Heel: Also called the butt, the end of a single reed opposite the tip. The heel has an arch-shaped curve (arc). The arc is determined by the diameter of the cane from which the reed was made. See also Reeds, Single, page 265

History: The clarinet was invented in the early 1700s either by Johann Christoph Denner (1655–1707) or by his son Jakob (1681–1785) in Nüremberg. A modification of an instrument called the chalumeau, the clarinet was the first reed instrument to use a cylindrical bore. The original clarinets were pitched in C or D, had three joints, six finger holes, two keys, and were made of boxwood. Because of a limited range, clarinets were soon made in other keys including A, B-flat, B, E-flat, F, and G. The mouthpiece was fitted with a single reed held in place with twine. The barrel was added in the 1750s, and the flared bell was added around 1790. The clarinet underwent many additional changes through the years. Most of the changes involved the addition of key mechanisms and the modification of

FIGURE 3.16. *Playing Position Contra-alto*

the fingering system. The modern clarinet was developed in the first half of the nineteenth century, largely through the efforts of Iwan Müller (1786–1854) and later Hyacinthe Klosé (1808–1880) and Louis-Auguste Buffet (1816–1884). The clarinet was originally a solo instrument, and did not become a standard part of the orchestra until the middle of the nineteenth century. The first bass clarinet was invented in the 1770s, although it did not become standard until the 1830s, with Adolphe Sax's saxophone-shaped design.

Instrument Angle: The clarinet is held out from the body at about a 35- to 40-degree angle. When the clarinet is held too close to the body, the tone tends to be small and pinched because the pressure the reed is increased. When the clarinet is held too far from the body, the tone tends to be out of focus or spread because the pressure on the reed is decreased. In both instances, problems result from uneven embouchure pressure being applied to the reed.

Key Questions

Q: How does the instrument angle of the clarinet compare to the instrument angle of the oboe?

A: As a rule, the clarinet is held slightly closer to the body than the oboe.

Q: Do all players hold the clarinet at the same angle?

A: No. Experienced players may find that holding the instrument out slightly more or slightly less from the body improves their tone quality. However, beginners should be taught to hold the instrument at about a 35- to 40-degree angle. As they gain experience, they can experiment to see if a slightly different angle improves their tone quality.

Q: Is the instrument angle the same for all clarinets?

A: No. The bell of the low clarinets is actually brought back slightly toward the body slightly during play, and the mouthpiece enters the mouth at a straighter angle than the B-flat soprano clarinet. The angle of the low clarinets is more similar to the angle of the saxophone than it is to the B-flat soprano clarinet.

Instrument Brands: Several brands of clarinets are available from which to choose. Some makers carry several models to accommodate a wide range of playing skills and budgets. Other makers carry models that are particularly suited to certain skill levels, budgets, and playing situations. Used instruments are also a good option for many players, and used instruments made by reputable manufacturers are available. When searching for an inexpensive or used instrument, beware of "off" brands and instrument models (even with reputable brands) that have not performed up to a high standard. The list includes several reputable clarinet manufacturers. Although this list is not exhaustive, it does provide a good starting point for research. See also Instrument Selection, page 33

Clarinet Manufacturers

Buffet; Bundy (Selmer); Eaton; Jupiter; Leblanc; Noblet (Leblanc); Patricola; Rossi; Selmer; Vito (Leblanc); and Yamaha.

Instrument Family and Playing Considerations: The clarinet family includes the E-flat soprano, B-flat soprano, A soprano, E-flat alto, B-flat bass, E-flat contra-alto (sometimes called E-flat contrabass), and B-flat contrabass. Much of the literature written for secondary school music ensembles includes only the B-flat soprano, the E-flat alto, and the B-flat bass clarinets.

The most commonly used clarinet in high school ensembles is the B-flat soprano clarinet. The B-flat bass clarinet is the second most commonly used clarinet in high school ensembles, followed by the E-flat contra-alto and the E-flat soprano clarinets. Alto clarinet parts are usually included in most band literature; however, these parts are almost always doubled by other instruments. In addition, because of the limited availability of instruments and players, the alto clarinet is often not used at all in school ensembles. The A soprano clarinet is primarily an orchestral instrument; however, it is occasionally used in wind ensembles. Although fairly common at the university level, the E-flat soprano clarinet is not commonly used in high school ensembles. The most common members of the clarinet family are shown in figure 3.17.

FIGURE 3.17. *Basic Clarinet Family (Left to Right): E-flat Soprano, B-flat Soprano, A Clarinet, E-flat Alto Clarinet, and B-flat Bass Clarinet)*

All clarinets are transposing instruments. That is, their written pitches are different than their sounding pitches. Specifically, when a B-flat soprano clarinet plays a written C-natural, the sounding pitch is one step lower than written (concert B-flat). When an E-flat alto clarinet plays its written C-natural, it sounds a major sixth lower than written (concert E-flat). The E-flat contra-alto clarinet sounds an octave and a major sixth lower than written and one octave lower than the E-flat alto clarinet. The B-flat bass clarinet sounds an octave and a major second lower than written and one octave lower than the B-flat soprano clarinet. The B-flat contrabass clarinet sounds two octaves and a major second lower than written and one octave lower than the B-flat bass clarinet. The E-flat soprano clarinet is one of the few instruments that transposes upward. It sounds a minor third higher than written, and it sounds one octave higher than the E-flat alto clarinet. Another clarinet fairly common in advanced orchestral literature (but not commonly played at the secondary school level) is the A clarinet. The A clarinet sounds a minor third lower than written, or one half step lower than the B-flat soprano clarinet. Because it is only slightly longer than the B-flat soprano, the same mouthpiece can be used to play both instruments. The extended family of clarinets is shown in figure 3.18.

All of the Boehm or French system clarinets have the same basic fingering system and the same basic written range, with a few minor exceptions. The lower clarinets (alto, bass, contra-alto, and contrabass) are designed with a half-hole key for the first hole on the upper joint (left-hand index finger) similar to the half-hole key on the oboe. The purpose of this key is to help players half-hole in the high range. Half-holes are executed by rolling the index finger down slightly uncovering the small vent hole normally covered by the index finger. Using half-holes on the low clarinets in the high register beginning with high C-sharp improves response, tone quality, and intonation. The upper clarinets (E-flat soprano, B-flat soprano, and A clarinet) do not have half-hole keys. What follow are some suggestions for playing the clarinets and a chart of their written and sounding ranges.

E-flat Soprano Clarinet

The E-flat soprano clarinet is challenging to play for several reasons. First, getting a good steady tone quality is more difficult on soprano than on other clarinets, especially from the middle of the register upward. The frequency of these pitches coupled with the smaller reed size contributes significantly to the unsteadiness and unevenness of tone and pitch, and even slight changes in the embouchure, oral cavity, and air stream can affect tone quality and pitch to a marked degree. Second, it is very difficult to play in tune. Players must learn to make embouchure changes or adjustments throughout the entire range of the instrument according

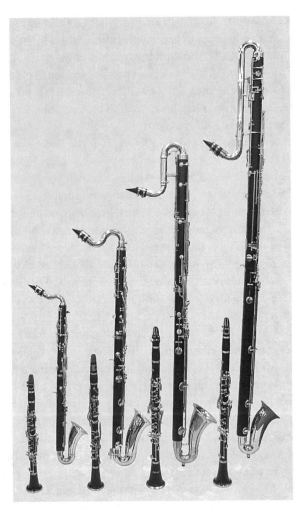

FIGURE 3.18. *Extended Clarinet Family (Left to Right): E-flat Soprano, E-flat Alto, C Clarinet, B-flat Bass, B-flat Soprano, E-flat Contra-alto, A Clarinet, B-flat Contrabass Clarinet*

to the intonation tendencies of each specific instrument. Furthermore, these adjustments often vary significantly from one reed/mouthpiece combination to another. Players must hear the pitches before playing them, and they must learn what adjustments are necessary to play them in tune. That is, players must develop muscle memory or kinesthetic feel in order to produce an even scale. Finally, the smaller key design can make playing technical passages more difficult for players with large hands. Players must learn to adapt to these differences and minimize excess finger motion. Suggestions and considerations for playing E-flat soprano clarinet are listed as follows.

1. Because the keys are smaller and closer together, executing fast, technical passages smoothly requires greater efficiency of finger movement. Keeping the fingers close to the keys and minimizing unnecessary finger movement are essential for technical proficiency.

2. The tones often respond more easily and quickly overall because of the smaller reed/mouthpiece combination. As a result, the timing necessary to coordinate the tongue and the fingers can be problematic. Players switching from one of the low clarinets may have to adjust to the response characteristics of the soprano to coordinate the tongue and fingers, especially in the low range.

3. It is harder to center the tone on E-flat soprano than on any other clarinet. As a result, intonation and pitch accuracy are much more difficult to control. Setting the embouchure appropriately for each note before it is played and adjusting pitch are particularly important for E-flat soprano clarinet players.

4. Players may need to use a slightly harder reed on E-flat soprano than they use on the other clarinets to produce a rounder, more stable tone and to achieve better intonation.

ALTO AND BASS CLARINETS

The alto and bass clarinets present several challenges to players. First, playing in tune throughout the entire playing range is more difficult on alto and bass than it is on B-flat soprano. Second, both the alto and bass are larger, heavier, and more cumbersome than the B-flat soprano, which can inhibit technical playing. In addition, players may find that the increased weight causes fatigue and discomfort in the neck and back after only a short period of time. For these reasons, end pins are recommended over neck straps for supporting the low clarinets. Third, producing a warm, rich, full tone on the throat tones and in the upper range is more challenging on alto and bass than on B-flat soprano clarinet. Fourth, the low clarinets require more air, especially in the low range. Finally, pitch adjustments may be slightly exaggerated on the low clarinets because of the larger instrument size. Suggestions and considerations for playing alto and bass clarinets are listed here.

1. The alto clarinet embouchure is more relaxed than the B-flat soprano embouchure, and the bass clarinet embouchure is more relaxed than the alto clarinet embouchure. In addition, the mouthpiece enters the mouth at a slightly straighter angle on the lower clarinets.

2. Generally, the oral cavity is more open on the low clarinets because of the larger mouthpiece/reed combination.

3. The throat tones (G-natural, G-sharp, A-natural, and A-sharp) can sound and/or feel especially stuffy on some low clarinets. In addition, notes in the high range tend to be weak and less responsive. These notes often feel worse to players than they sound. Although nothing can totally eliminate the stuffy sensation, using a good embouchure, good breath support, and a good reed/mouthpiece combination can greatly improve the quality of these notes.

4. The pitch tendencies of the low clarinets parallel the tendencies of the B-flat soprano; however, these pitch tendencies will often be exaggerated on the low clarinets. In addition, making pitch adjustments on larger instruments often requires greater changes in air, embouchure, and/or oral cavity than pitch adjustments on smaller instruments. That is, making the same adjustment on the B-flat soprano and the B-flat bass will result in a greater pitch change on the B-flat soprano.

5. Pitches in the low range can be sharper on the low clarinets than they are on the B-flat soprano clarinet. As a result, it is usually necessary to drop the jaw, open the oral cavity, and/or focus the air stream slightly downward to play these notes in tune.

6. Because of the larger reed/mouthpiece combination and instrument size, more air is required on alto and bass clarinets.

7. Generally, a slightly softer reed may be used on alto and bass to facilitate response. For example, a player who normally uses a number 3½ strength reed on B-flat soprano, may use a number 2½ or 3 reed on bass. In addition, the embouchure must remain relaxed and open to compensate for the softer reed's natural tendency toward an edgy, reedy sound.

E-flat Contra-alto and B-flat Contrabass Clarinets

The greatest challenge faced by contra clarinet players is coping with the instrument's large size. The contra clarinets respond relatively easily with an appropriate reed/mouthpiece combination and proper breath support; however, they generally require much more air than the other clarinets. Intonation problems parallel those for the other clarinets, but may be slightly greater overall. As a result, playing a contra clarinet in tune requires players to have good listening skills and the ability to adjust pitch appropriately. When switching from B-flat soprano to one of the contra clarinets, players learn to adjust to the increased size of the mouthpiece/reed combination and to the increased amount of time it sometimes takes for notes to respond, especially in the low range. The contra clarinets are almost always played in a seated position. Players often use a stool to sit higher off the floor to achieve a better playing position. Because of the instruments' size, end pins or instrument stands are essential. Suggestions and considerations for playing the contra clarinets are listed here.

1. The embouchure is more relaxed and open on the contra clarinets than it is on the other clarinets.

2. Slightly more mouthpiece should be taken into the mouth on the contra clarinets, and the mouthpiece enters the mouth at a slightly straighter angle than it does on the B-flat soprano.

3. The contra clarinets require more air than the other clarinets.

4. It may be necessary to drop the jaw slightly to get the low notes to respond properly.

5. The adjustments in the embouchure, oral cavity, and air stream are slightly greater on the contra clarinets because of the larger reed/mouthpiece combination and overall instrument size. Making proper adjustments requires more air and a more concentrated effort to focus the air stream accordingly.

6. The contra clarinets tend to be sharp in all ranges; however, if the reeds are too soft, they will be noticeably flat in the high range.

7. The tone quality on contra clarinets tends to be more inconsistent throughout the playing range than it is on the other clarinets. Generally, the low range sounds rich and full, the middle range

sounds somewhat less resonant and the upper range is thin and small. Better consistency can be achieved as players gain experience and try different reed/mouthpiece combinations.

8. The contras respond more slowly than the other clarinets because of the larger reed/mouthpiece combination and overall instrument size, making tonguing more challenging. Players should increase air speed while continuing to use a "tip of the tongue to the tip of the reed" approach to tonguing.

9. Because of the contras' size, playing fast, technical passages is more challenging. Players should minimize finger motion and not let the fingers "fly" off of the keys. In addition, because the keys are relatively large and heavy compared to the other clarinets, it is common for contra players to "slap" the keys down rather than to depress the keys efficiently.

10. As with the bass clarinet, a slightly softer reed may be used on contras to facilitate response; however, the embouchure must remain relaxed and open to compensate for the softer reed's tendency toward an edgy sound. If the reed is too soft, tone quality will suffer dramatically, especially in the upper range.

Instrument Parts: See Parts, Clarinet, page 250

Instrument Position: See Hand/Holding/Instrument Playing Positions and Posture, page 224

Instrument Ranges: See Range, page 252

Instrument Selection: See Instrument Brands, page 232; Instrument Selection, page 33

Instrument Sizes: See Instrument Family and Playing Considerations, page 232

Instrument Stands: See Instrument Stands, page 39

Intonation: Generally, the degree of "in-tuneness" in a melodic and a harmonic context. In ensemble playing, the most important factors in achieving intonation accuracy are: (1) hearing intonation problems, (2) understanding what adjustments need to be made to correct intonation problems, and (3) having the skills to make the necessary adjustments. A detailed general discussion of Intonation is in chapter 1. Specific suggestions for helping players better understand the pitch tendencies of the clarinet and how to make appropriate pitch adjustments are outlined in the following section. See also Intonation, page 41; Temperament, page 61; Tuning/Tuning Note Considerations, page 294

General Comments for Adjusting Pitch

Adjusting pitch is the process of raising or lowering the pitch of notes. Comments and suggestions for adjusting pitch are outlined here.

1. Embouchure/Air Stream—The embouchure and air stream can be altered in several subtle ways to adjust or humor pitches. As players progress, they learn to make embouchure adjustments for certain pitches as part of standard technique. Common embouchure/air stream/oral cavity adjustments are described as follows.

   A. To lower or flatten the pitch, focus the air stream downward. As a rule, the farther downward the pitch is directed, the flatter the pitch will be. The air stream may be focused downward by making slight changes in the oral cavity (i.e., a slightly more open focus) and/or by making slight adjustments in embouchure (i.e., a slightly lowered jaw).

   B. To raise or sharpen the pitch, focus the air stream upward. As a rule, the farther upward the pitch is directed, the sharper the pitch will be. The air stream may be focused downward by making slight changes in the oral cavity (i.e., a slightly smaller focus) and/or by making slight adjustments in embouchure (i.e., a slightly raised jaw).

   C. As a rule, the firmer the embouchure, the sharper the pitch will be. Conversely, the looser the embouchure, the flatter the pitch will be. The embouchure can be firmed by increasing embouchure pressure around the reed and loosened by decreasing embouchure pressure around the reed. Changes in embouchure pressure and air speed are facilitated by thinking of using a cold or a warm air stream. A warm air stream tends to decrease air speed and relax the embouchure, which flattens the pitch. A cold air stream tends to increase air speed and firm the embouchure, which sharpens the pitch. Generally, clarinet players use a warmer air stream than oboe players and a colder air stream than saxophone players.

   D. Only slight changes in air stream and embouchure should be made when adjusting pitch. Large-scale changes affect tone quality, control, and focus.

2. Throat/Oral Cavity—A tight, restricted throat causes the pitch to go sharp. An open throat generally results in the best tone quality on clarinet. Open the throat as if saying "ah," and the pitch will drop. In addition, the tone quality will improve. Changes and adjustments in the oral cavity affect both tone quality and pitch and are usually accomplished by thinking of saying certain syllables such as "oh," "oo," "ah," and "ee." That is, the use of syllables is effective in altering pitch and tone quality; however, be aware that using syllables often causes changes in embouchure and air flow as well. Understanding the relationships and balances among the embouchure, air stream, throat, and oral cavity is important to players and teachers.

3. Alternates/Adding Keys—If slight changes in the embouchure, oral cavity, and air stream do not bring the desired pitches in tune, adding keys to regular fingerings or using alternate fingerings may help bring certain pitches in tune. On the other hand, adding keys and using alternates to adjust pitch are not always practical. As a rule, tonal considerations, technical considerations, and tempi largely dictate the appropriateness of such adjustments. Finally, adding keys or using alternates to adjust pitch often negate the need to make changes in air stream or embouchure.

4. Dynamics/Air Speed—Changes in dynamics/air speed affect pitch, sometimes significantly. Considerations regarding dynamics/air speed are described as follows.
   A. When playing loudly and increasing air speed, the pitch tends to go flat. Adjust by keeping the air direction parallel to the reed plane, focusing the air stream upward slightly, and/or firming the embouchure slightly. Proper air speed and control is maintained at all times. Do not overblow.
   B. When playing softly and decreasing air speed, the pitch tends to go sharp. Adjust by focusing the air stream downward slightly, opening the oral cavity, and/or relaxing the embouchure slightly. Even at softer dynamic levels, the air stream must move fast enough to sustain and support the pitch.

5. Mechanical—Mechanical design characteristics and instrument condition affect intonation and are described as follows.
   A. Pad height affects pitch. If pads are too low, the pitch will be flat. If pads are too high, the pitch will be sharp. Make sure instruments are properly adjusted.

B. The clarinet is not designed to be in tune when all of the joints are pushed together as far as they will go. As a result, the barrel joint (mouthpiece or other joints depending on your preferred method of tuning) is usually pulled out slightly when the instrument is properly tuned. The precise placement of the barrel joint (or other joints) can be determined by using a tuner.

C. Leaks and other mechanical problems affect pitch. Check the clarinet regularly for leaks, loose and/or broken springs, and missing corks or felts. Maintaining the instrument is essential for good intonation.

6. Mouthpieces—Mouthpieces can have a significant effect on pitch. Until players gain experience and understand what type of sound and feel they wish to achieve, the best solution is to have players use a hard rubber mouthpiece with a medium lay, a medium bore, and a medium-sized chamber. In addition, stating hard and fast rules that are applicable to all mouthpieces is tenuous; however, several useful generalizations can be made. These generalizations and are listed as follows.

A. Close-lay mouthpieces tend to play sharper than open-lay mouthpieces.

B. Small-chamber mouthpieces tend to play sharper than large-chamber mouthpieces.

C. Mouthpieces with high baffles tend to play sharper than mouthpieces with low baffles.

D. Plastic mouthpieces tend to play sharper than hard rubber mouthpieces.

E. Small-bore mouthpieces tend to play sharper than large-bore mouthpieces.

F. If the bore of the mouthpiece does not match the bore of the clarinet, the pitch may be inconsistent and difficult to control.

7. Reeds—Hard reeds tend to play sharp, especially in soft passages. In addition, players tend to firm the embouchure to control a harder reed, which further raises pitch. Soft reeds tend to play flat, especially in loud passages. When players try to relax and maintain a good embouchure, tone and pitch are difficult to control because soft reeds do not provide enough resistance against or counteraction to the embouchure pressure. On the other hand, when players "bite" too hard, the reed closes toward the mouthpiece, reducing the size of the tip opening and resulting in a small,

pinched tone or no tone at all. Players should use a reed strength that provides a modest amount of resistance in the middle register.

8. Barrel Length—If a clarinet is noticeably flat when all of the joints are pushed together as far as they will go and the mouthpiece/reed combination is appropriate, players can try a shorter barrel. If a clarinet is noticeably sharp when the barrel is pulled out excessively far, players can try a longer barrel. It is quite common for advanced players to have several barrels that can be used in different musical contexts. Using A = 440 as a standard, the clarinet should play in tune when the barrel (whatever the length may be) is pulled out slightly. The standard barrel length for B-flat soprano clarinet is 66mm.

9. Instrument Angle—When the clarinet is held too close to the body, the tone tends to be small and pinched and the pitch tends to be sharper because the pressure on the reed is increased. When the clarinet is held too far from the body, the tone tends to be out of focus or spread and the pitch tends to be flatter because the pressure on the reed is decreased. In both instances, problems result from uneven embouchure pressure being applied to the reed. Exaggerated instrument angles in or out from the body flatten pitch because the reed is not supported properly. The clarinet is held out from the body at about a 35- to 40-degree angle.

Tuning the Clarinet

A detailed description of how to tune the clarinet is under Tuning/Tuning Note Considerations in this chapter.

Pitch Tendencies

Pitch tendencies refers to the tendency for certain notes on an instrument to deviate from a specified standard, usually the equal tempered scale based on a reference frequency of A = 440. That is, when players talk about the pitch tendencies of their instruments, they are almost always talking about how sharp or flat certain notes are in reference to equal temperament. Comments and suggestions regarding pitch tendencies are outlined in the following list. A summary of these tendencies is presented in figures 3.19 and 3.20.

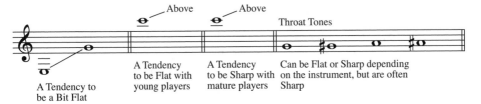

FIGURE 3.19. *Intonation Tendencies (General)*

FIGURE 3.20. *Intonation Tendencies (Specific)*

General Range/Register Tendencies—Flat Pitches

1. Clarinets tend to play flat in the low range (between low E-natural and open G-natural), especially when playing loudly.

    Adjustment 1—Focus the air stream upward slightly.

    Adjustment 2—Think of using an "oo" syllable or even an "ee" syllable to help focus the oral cavity, and maintain appropriate flex in the embouchure muscles.

    Adjustment 3—If these notes are still flat, firm the embouchure slightly, but do not bite or pinch the reed.

2. Inexperienced players tend to play flat in the high/altissimo register (above high C-natural) because their embouchures are not developed properly for playing in that range and because their concepts of adjusting pitch are not developed.

    Adjustment 1—Focus the air stream upward slightly.

    Adjustment 2—Firm the embouchure. Do not bite or pinch the reed excessively and close the tip opening.

    Adjustment 3—Think of using an "oo" or "ee" syllable rather than and "oh" syllable to help focus the oral cavity, and maintain appropriate flex in the embouchure muscles.

    Adjustment 4—Increase air speed.

    Adjustment 5—Be sure to add the low E-flat key (right-hand little finger) as a vent key for notes above high C-sharp.

General Range/Register Tendencies—Sharp Pitches

1. Experienced players tend to play sharp in the high/altissimo register (high C-natural and above) because they tend to over compensate or "bite" the reed too much rather than adjusting air speed and focus.

     Adjustment 1—Focus the air stream downward slightly.

     Adjustment 2—Relax the embouchure (lower the jaw slightly), but maintain embouchure support, flex, and focus.

     Adjustment 3—Think of using an "oo" syllable rather than an "ee" syllable to help focus the oral cavity.

Throat Tone Considerations

1. The throat tones (G-natural, G-sharp, A-natural, A-sharp) are inconsistent. Depending on the particular instrument, throat tones may be a little sharp or flat. Usually, throat tones will be sharp.

2. The throat tones are flat.

     Adjustment 1—Focus the air stream upward slightly.

     Adjustment 2—Increase air speed for proper support.

     Adjustment 3—Firm the embouchure slightly, but do not "bite" or "pinch" the reed. Think of using an "oo" syllable rather than and "oh" syllable to help focus the oral cavity, and maintain appropriate flex in the embouchure muscles.

     Adjustment 4—Add the two bottom side keys of the right hand to raise the pitch (but sometimes this adjustment raises pitch too much!). The two keys are depressed at the same time by the side of the index finger. Adding keys or using alternate fingerings to adjust pitch often negates or minimizes the need to make changes in the air stream or embouchure.

3. The throat tones are sharp

     Adjustment 1—Focus the air stream downward slightly.

     Adjustment 2—Relax the embouchure (lower the jaw slightly), but maintain embouchure support, flex, and focus.

     Adjustment 3—When the throat tones are sharp, depress fingers on the right hand (i.e., covering holes 4-5-6) to help lower the pitch and focus the tone. Players can depress one, all, or a combination of the right-hand fingers to adjust pitch appropriately according to the tendencies of their instruments. On some throat tones, covering holes of the left hand (2-3) may also help lower the pitch. Finally, some players like to close the low C-key (right-hand little finger) when playing throat tones. Players can experiment to see which combination works best on their instruments. In addition, adding keys or using alternate fingerings to adjust pitch often negates or minimizes the need to make changes in the air stream or embouchure.

Specific Pitch Tendencies—Making Adjustments for Problem Pitches

1. Low E-natural and F-natural (below the staff) tend to be quite flat.
2. Middle C-natural tends to be a little flat.
3. First-line E-flat and E-natural, and first-space F-natural and F-sharp can be flat.

   Adjustments for Numbers 1, 2, and 3

      Adjustment 1—Focus the air stream upward slightly.

      Adjustment 2—Firm the embouchure slightly, but do not bite or pinch the reed. Think of using an "oo" syllable rather than and "oh" syllable to help focus the oral cavity, and maintain appropriate flex in the embouchure muscles.

      Adjustment 3—On first-line E-natural and first-space F-natural and F-sharp, add the lowest side key of the right hand to raise the pitch (use the side of the index finger). If the pitch needs to be raised further, add the C-sharp/G-sharp key (left-hand little finger). In addition, adding keys or using alternate fingerings to adjust pitch often negates the need to make changes in the air stream or embouchure.

4. Low A-natural and B-natural (below the staff) tend to be sharp.
5. High B-natural and C-natural (above the staff) tend to be sharp.

   Adjustments for Numbers 4 and 5

      Adjustment 1—Relax the embouchure (lower the jaw slightly), but maintain embouchure support, flex, and focus.

      Adjustment 2—Focus the air stream downward slightly.

      Adjustment 3—For the low notes, think of using a "who" or "oh" syllable to help focus the oral cavity. For the high notes, think of using an "oo" or even an "ee" syllable to help focus the oral cavity.

ADDING FINGERS TO ADJUST FOR INTONATION PROBLEMS

Players can depress other keys in addition to the regular fingering to adjust pitch. An outline of basic fingering adjustments appears here.

1. On high D-natural (above the staff), make sure the index finger of the right hand is depressed.
2. On low A-natural and B-natural, letting the ring finger partially block the air coming out of the G tone hole (6) will lower the pitch.
3. The throat tones can be adjusted using the fingerings in various combinations as described above.
4. When playing high C-natural (thumb and register key), depressing the low F or C key with the right-hand little finger may improve tone and intonation.

USING ALTERNATE FINGERINGS TO ADJUST INTONATION

It is common for players to use alternate fingerings to adjust pitch. An outline of basic alternates and their typical relationships to the corresponding regular fingerings appears here.

1. Alternate low B-natural (fork fingering w/sliver key) tends to be slightly sharper than regular B-natural (middle finger right hand).
2. Alternate top-line F-sharp (fork fingering w/sliver key) tends to be slightly sharper than regular F-sharp (middle finger right hand).
3. Alternate E-flat/B-flat (1-4 and 1-5) tend to be flat.
4. Alternate F–natural and F-sharp above the staff tend to be sharp.

Inverted Ligature: Ligatures designed so that the screw or screws that secure the reed against the mouthpiece are on top of the mouthpiece. In contrast, traditional ligatures are designed so that the screw or screws that secure the reed against the mouthpiece are on the bottom of the mouthpiece next to the reed. See also Ligature, page 247

Key/Pad Height: See Key/Pad Height, page 45

Knife: See Reed Knife, page 256

Lay, Mouthpiece: See Facing/Lay, page 222; Mouthpiece/Mouthpieces, page 247

Lay, Reed: The scraped or shaped portion of a single reed that extends from the U-shaped cut (or first cut on a double-cut reed) to the tip. Various areas of the lay are referred to with different terminology when discussing reed adjustment. These areas include the tip, channels, rails, and heart. Each area contributes in a specific way to overall response, tone, and intonation. To a large extent, the lay determines the reed's potential for good tone quality and response. It is important that the lay is even, smooth, and symmetrically tapered from the center to the edges of the blade. See also Reeds, Single, page 265

Ligature: A device that holds a single reed onto the mouthpiece. See Ligature, page 390

Lightheadedness: See Dizziness/Lightheadedness, page 26

Mouthpiece/Mouthpieces: A detailed discussion of mouthpieces is in chapter 1. This discussion provides valuable information regarding mouthpiece selection. Specific suggestions for clarinet mouthpieces are listed in the following section. It is not possible to discuss all of the mouthpieces on the market today, nor is it possible to know which mouthpiece will work best for a particular player without play-testing each mouthpiece under a variety of playing conditions. As a result, the suggestions are certainly not absolute; however, they can serve as a starting point for players and teachers in their search for the right mouthpiece. A comparison of mouthpieces and reeds is shown in figure 3.21. See also Mouthpiece/Mouthpieces, page 45

Key Questions

Q: Given all of the above considerations, what should I look for when selecting a mouthpiece for my students?

A: As a rule, start players with a small to medium-size mouthpiece (chamber, facing, etc.). As players mature, they can experiment with mouthpieces that have bigger chambers or more open facings to help produce a bigger, richer tone.

Q: What are some good beginning mouthpieces?

A: Mouthpiece suggestions for clarinet are outlined in this section.

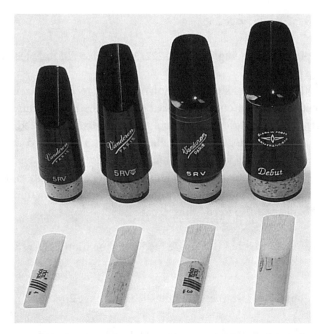

FIGURE 3.21. *Mouthpiece and Reed Comparisons (Left to Right): E-flat Soprano, B-flat Soprano, E-flat Alto Clarinet, and B-flat Bass Clarinet.*

CLARINET MOUTHPIECES

Beginning Mouthpieces

Clark Fobes Debut; Hite Premiere 111; Morgan RM6 or Protone; Selmer Standard HS; and Yamaha Standard 3C or 4C.

Intermediate Mouthpieces

Vandoren B45 or B45 Lyre; Clark Fobes 2M or AL; Borbeck 8, 11, or 13; Morgan RM10 or RM15; Yamaha Standard 5C or 6C; Yamaha Custom 4C or 5C; Hite Artist Series Model M41 or D; Selmer CP100; Vandoren M13 or M13 Lyre; Vandoren 5RVLyre or B40 Lyre; and Bay H2.

Advanced Mouthpieces

Clark Fobes Cicero or Pro Series 11-14; Borbeck 11, 13, or 14; Vandoren M13, M13 Lyre, or M 15; Vandoren 5RV; Hite D or J; Morgan J5 or RM28; Bay H2 or

H3, Gregory Smith Kaspar or Chedeville; and Lomax Classic A-4, A4+, A5, or Symphonie "Elite" S2 or S3.

Mouthpiece/Reed Angle: The clarinet is held out from the body at about a 35- to 40-degree angle. With smaller players, this angle places the clarinet between the knees; however, the clarinet should not be supported or held by the knees. When the clarinet is held too close to the body, the tone tends to be smaller and pinched and the pitch tends to be sharper because the pressure on the reed is increased. When the clarinet is held too far from the body, the tone tends to be out of focus or spread and the pitch tends to be flatter because the pressure on the reed is decreased. In both instances, problems result from uneven embouchure pressure being applied to the reed. Exaggerated instrumental angles in or out from the body cause flatness in pitch because the reed is not supported properly. See also Instrument Angle, page 230

Multiphonics: See Extended/Contemporary Techniques, page 221

Multiple-Tonguing: See Multiple-Tonguing, page 52

Neck: On the low clarinets, the curved metal joint that connects the mouthpiece with the instrument body. The neck significantly affects tonal characteristics, response, and pitch. In addition, the curvature of the neck affects the angle at which the mouthpiece enters the mouth. Generally, the mouthpiece enters the mouth at a straighter angle on the low clarinets than it does on the B-flat clarinet. Players can use the neck that comes with the instrument as long as it provides a comfortable playing angle and excellent tonal control. The neck may also be pulled out somewhat to tune the overall pitch of the instrument. Some professional model clarinets have necks designed with tuning mechanisms to facilitate tuning.

Neck Strap: A strap positioned around the player's neck that attaches to the clarinet strap ring via a clip or hook. Neck straps have become increasingly popular among soprano clarinet players in recent years because they help support the weight of the instrument and they alleviate much of the stress placed on the right thumb during normal play. Neck straps are especially useful while inexperienced players are developing proper playing positions. One disadvantage of the neck strap is that it can limit a player's control over instrument angle. As a result, players often balance the weight distribution between the neck strap and the right thumb. Neck straps are typically made of nylon or leather and are adjustable so that the clarinet can be positioned properly.

Octave Keys: Clarinets do not have octave keys because they overblow a twelfth rather than an octave. Instead, clarinets have one register key. See Register Key, page 278

Optional Keys/Key Mechanisms: Keys or key mechanisms not necessary to the essential functioning of the clarinet, but that make playing easier. Optional keys on the B-flat soprano clarinet include the alternate A-flat/E-flat lever, and the C-sharp/G-sharp with trill key extension. Adjustable thumb rests are also a common option on clarinets, although the thumb rest is not technically a key. Some professional bass clarinets have a range to low E-flat, and they are equipped with a double register key. While optional keys can make certain aspects of technique and pitch easier, clarinets without these and other optional keys are fully functional and capable of producing the full range of notes and trills. See also Construction and Design, page 211

Overblow: See Overblow, page 55

Overtones: See Overtones, page 55

Pad Height: See Key/Pad Height, page 45

Parts, Clarinet: The parts of a clarinet are identified in figure 3.22.

Pitch Adjustment: See Intonation, page 238; Tuning/Tuning Note Considerations, page 294

Pitch Tendencies: Generally, the tendency for any note to deviate from a specified standard, usually the equal tempered scale based on a reference frequency of A = 440. That is, when players talk about the pitch tendencies of their instruments, they are almost always talking about how sharp or flat certain notes are in reference to a modern, equal tempered scale. The term pitch tendency is most commonly used to refer to pitch deviations that are an inherent part of an instrument's design. In many instances, pitch tendencies are consistent on a given instrument (e.g., most clarinets or most trumpets) regardless of the make or model of the instrument. For example, most clarinets are sharp in the high range. The pitch tendencies of clarinets are discussed under Intonation in this chapter. See also Intonation, page 238; Temperament, page 61; Tuning/Tuning Note Considerations, page 294

Plastic Reeds: See Synthetic Reeds, page 283

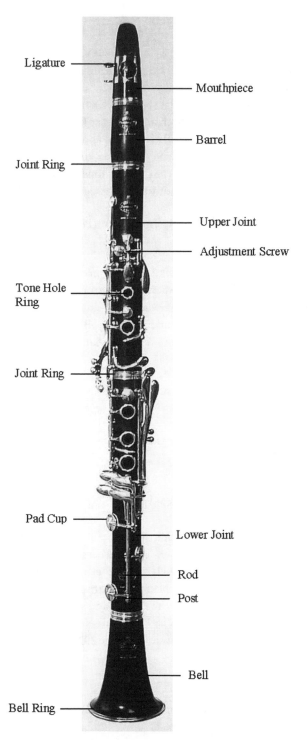

Ligature

Mouthpiece

Barrel

Joint Ring

Upper Joint

Adjustment Screw

Tone Hole
Ring

Joint Ring

Pad Cup

Lower Joint

Rod

Post

Bell

Bell Ring

FIGURE 3.22. *Parts of a Clarinet*

Plateau Model/System: Also called a closed-hole system, a key design where the tone holes are covered by pads rather than by the fingertips. The low clarinets are generally constructed using a plateau system because the tone holes are too big to be covered by the fingertips. The B-flat soprano clarinet is not constructed using a plateau system because the left thumb and primary fingers (T, 1-2-3 4-5-6) cover open tone holes, even though the other tone holes are covered by pads. Plateau model soprano clarinets are available; however, they are not recommended because the closeness of the pads to the primary tone holes affects tonal response and pitch. "Plateau model" is a term most often associated with flutes.

Playing Position: See Hand/Holding/Instrument/Playing Positions and Posture, page 224

Poly-Cylindrical Bore: A bore design on intermediate and professional clarinets that incorporates different sized cylinders throughout the instrument bore. That is, the size of the cylindrical bore changes throughout the instrument to provide more harmonics in the sound and better overall intonation. Clarinets with a poly-cylindrical bore are slightly more resistant than traditional cylindrical bore clarinets.

Posture: See Hand/Holding/Instrument/Playing Positions and Posture, page 224

Preparing the Right Hand: See Crossing The Break, page 212

Rails, Reed: The side edges of a single reed. See also Reeds, Single, page 265

Rails/Side Rails, Mouthpiece: See Side Rails, Mouthpiece, page 281

Range: In general, the distance from the lowest note to the highest note on a given instrument. In addition, players and teachers often refer to the different registers (roughly by octave) of the clarinet in terms of range: low range (also called chalumeau), middle range (includes the throat tones), high range (also called clarion), and altissimo range. The written and sounding ranges of the clarinets appear in the following section and are summarized in figure 3.23. See also Register/Registers, page 279; Transpositions, page 292

Key Questions

Q: What ranges are recommended for elementary, junior high/middle school, and senior high students?

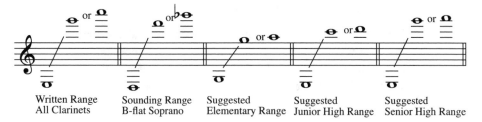

| Written Range
All Clarinets | Sounding Range
B-flat Soprano | Suggested
Elementary Range | Suggested
Junior High Range | Suggested
Senior High Range |

FIGURE 3.23. *Range*

A: A student's range varies according to experience and ability level. After the fundamentals of tone production and embouchure formation are mastered, range can be extended systematically. Suggested ranges for each level are as follows.

Elementary: Low G-natural to G-natural or A-natural (just above staff)
Junior High: Low E-natural to high C-natural or D-natural
Senior High: Low E-natural to high G-natural or A-natural

Reed: See Reeds, Single, page 265

Reed Blanks: Unfinished reeds. Reed blanks may be purchased by players interested in making, or more accurately shaping and refining, their own reeds. Companies offering reed blanks have made the initial cuts from the cane, so that the blank is the correct size and width. Although most professional clarinet and saxophone players use commercially made reeds, uncut cane is available to players who want to make their own reeds. See also Reeds, Single, page 265

Reed Care: Taking proper care of reeds is an important part of single reed playing. It can also be challenging (and expensive), especially for beginners. The suggestions will help prevent reed damage.

HANDLING REEDS

Physical damage to reeds often results from trying to position or reposition the reed on the mouthpiece. Damage also occurs frequently from hitting the reed against something or someone in a normal rehearsal setting. It is advisable to develop proper habits for handling reeds in the beginning stages.

1. Hold the instrument properly when at rest. This position protects the reed.

2. Develop the habit of holding the reed at the heel end.

3. Make adjustments in reed alignment without touching the tip in any way. Adjust the position of the reed on the mouthpiece by loosening the ligature and pushing lightly on the bark, the heel, and the sides of the reed.

4. Cover the reed and mouthpiece with a mouthpiece cap when resting for long periods. Note that some caps (especially the metal ones) may have sharp ridges inside the top of the cap, which can actually cause damage to the reed and mouthpiece. Damage typically occurs when players try to push the mouthpiece cap too far onto the mouthpiece/reed combination.

5. Remove the reed from the mouthpiece and soak it in the mouth or a container of water when resting for extended periods of time, particularly in dry climates.

Extending Reed Life

In addition to developing proper habits in handling reeds, other steps can also be taken to extend reed life and keep reeds in optimal playing condition. The suggestions may help extend the life and maintain the playing quality of single reeds.

1. Breaking in Reeds—Condition new reeds slowly. Play on new reeds for a few minutes each day for several days and then gradually play them for longer period. Playing too long on new reeds shortens reed life.

2. Rotate Reeds—Rather than play on the same reed every day, alternate or rotate three or four reeds.

3. Rinse Reeds and Wipe Excess Moisture off of Reeds before Storing Them—This process will minimize the amount of dust and other materials that typically cling to wet surfaces and will help keep reeds clean.

4. Avoid Eating and Drinking (Except Water) during Practice Sessions—Eating and drinking causes foreign substances to collect on the inside and outside of the reed and will inhibit performance and prematurely age the reed.

5. Do Not Handle Reeds with Dirty Hands—Handle reeds with clean hands to avoid a build-up of oil and grime. Even with clean hands

and careful handling, reeds will occasionally look dirty, especially when they are older. That is, some discoloration occurs with normal use.

REED DAMAGE

Reeds are delicate and easily damaged. Beginners often damage reeds by hitting them against something or someone, or by trying to align the reed on the mouthpiece by pushing against the reed tip. Among more advanced players, the ligature is a common source of reed damage. Players often damage the reed by attempting to slide the ligature over the reed after it has been positioned on the mouthpiece instead of placing the ligature on first and sliding the reed between the ligature and mouthpiece. The suggestions listed under Handling Reeds above may help prevent reed damage.

Reed Clipper/Trimmer: A device designed to clip or trim the tip of a reed. Clipping a reed makes it feel and play harder or more resistant because the reed tip is slightly thicker after being clipped. In addition, clipping reeds may result in a darker, warmer tone quality. Reed clippers are often used to make soft reeds more resistant or to extend the life of old reeds. Some clippers are designed to match certain brands of reeds and/or mouthpieces, and choosing the "right" reed clipper can be challenging. Clippers that have fine adjustment screws enable users to achieve a high degree of accuracy in centering and clipping the reed properly. Reed clippers are often used as a measure of last resort, and do not work on every reed. That is, reed clippers are most often used to extend the usefulness of reeds that would otherwise be discarded. Reed clippers are available commercially for most single reed instruments. Brands available include Cordier, Pisoni, Prestini, Roy Seaman, and Vandoren.

Reed Holders/Guards/Cases: Devices designed to hold and protect one or more reeds. Reed cases are important because they contribute to the playability and longevity of reeds. When reeds are purchased in bulk, they typically come in small cardboard boxes and may or may not be individually packaged. The packaging from the reed manufacturer is generally inadequate for reed storage because it does not allow adequate ventilation for the reed and it generally does not provide a flat surface for the reed. Most commercially made reed holders are made of plastic, wood, and/or leather; however, some of the older holders were made of metal. In most instances, reeds are placed or slid onto flat surfaces (sometimes grooved) and held in place near the top of the vamp. The flat surface helps reeds retain their shape while they dry, and the grooves help air reach the underneath side of a reed.

Saxophone and clarinet reed holders typically hold two or four reeds; however, reed holders that hold several reeds are also common.

Key Questions

Q: Should all of my students have reed holders for their reeds?

A: Yes. Reed holders prolong reed life by helping prevent warping, chipping, and breaking.

Reed Knife: A knife specifically designed to shape and adjust reeds. Reed knives can be purchased at many local music stores and are useful for removing large or small amounts of cane depending upon the skill of the user. A single-edged razor blade can also be used instead of a reed knife but it is not as convenient, and it is significantly harder to control than a reed knife. Skillful use of a reed knife takes practice. Much of what can be accomplished with a reed knife can also be accomplished with extra fine grit sandpaper (400 or 600). Commercially made knives are available under such brand names as Bhosys, Fox, Herder, Jende, Landwell, Muncy, Pisoni, Prestini, Vitry, and Weiner. See also Reed Making and Adjustment, page 256

Key Questions

Q: Do clarinet and saxophone students need reed knives?

A: No. First, commercially made reeds suitable for all playing levels are readily available. Players usually play on several reeds and find the ones that work well for them. Second, even advanced players who like to adjust their reeds typically make only minor adjustments to reeds. Minor adjustments can be made easily using only extra fine grit sandpaper (400 or 600). Finally, students should not have reed knives at school. They are extremely sharp and potentially dangerous.

Reed Making and Adjustment: Making single reeds is a complex process that requires specific tools and materials in addition to at least a modest amount of training and supervision. The information provided separately in this section does not discuss the details of reed making and is not intended to teach someone how to make reeds. Rather, its purpose is to provide a more in-depth understanding of reeds, reed adjustment, and the reed-making process. Adjusting single reeds is not a complicated task; however, it does require some of the tools and materials discussed. In addition, the more players experiment with reed adjustment, the better the adjustments are likely to be. The information and suggestions discussed should help players make reed adjustments with a reasonable expectation of success. Single reed tools are shown in figures 3.24.

Tools and Materials

1. Dial-Indicator/Micrometer—A tool used by some reed makers to determine the thickness throughout various areas of a reed or cane to aid in making or duplicating reeds. A dial indicator can measure cane or finished reeds to a hundredth of a millimeter, and is one of several "high-tech" tools available for reed making. Other such tools include hardness testers and tools to measure cane flexibility ("flextor tools").

2. Plate Glass—A piece of flat plate glass provides an excellent surface for working on reeds. It can be relatively small as long as it provides ample room to work. A two-by-three-inch piece provides adequate space and is also portable.

3. Reed Clipper/Trimmer—Reed clippers are available commercially for most single reed instruments. The brand should be chosen carefully because some clippers are designed to match certain brands of reeds and/or mouthpieces. In addition, good clippers have a fine adjustment screw that enables a high degree of accuracy in centering and positioning the reed properly. Commercially made clippers are available under such brand names as Cordier, Pisoni, Prestini, Roy Seaman, and Vandoren.

4. Reed Knife—Reed knives can be purchased at many local music stores and are useful for removing large or small amounts of cane. A single-edged razor blade can also be used instead of a reed knife, but it is not as convenient and it lacks the control of a reed knife.

5. Reed Machines/Profiler—Machines designed to copy or duplicate another reed.

6. Reed Resurfacer—A tool used to resurface single reeds. Resurfacers are generally made of tempered glass with an etched surface that functions like fine sandpaper, enabling players to even out or flatten the reed table. Reed resurfacers come with a reed stick that enables players to make fine reed adjustments to the lay of the reed.

7. Sandpaper/Dutch Rush—Materials used to remove small amounts of cane from a reed. Although both wet and dry sandpaper can

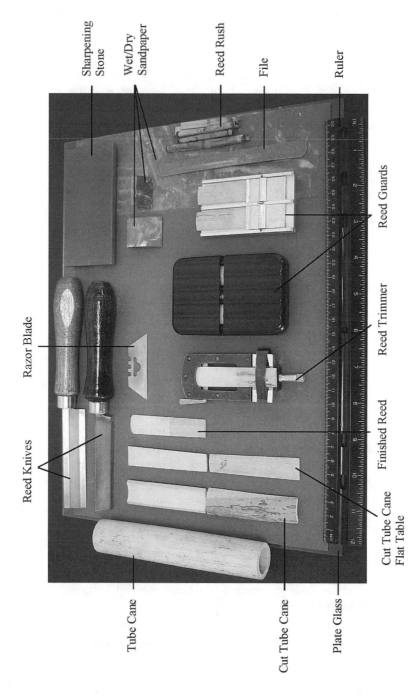

Sharpening Stone

Wet/Dry Sandpaper

Reed Rush

File

Ruler

Reed Guards

Razor Blade

Reed Trimmer

Reed Knives

Finished Reed

Cut Tube Cane
Flat Table

Tube Cane

Cut Tube Cane

Plate Glass

FIGURE 3.24. *Single Reed Tools*

258

be used to adjust reeds, wet sandpaper is more practical. Fine-grit sandpaper such as number 400 (fine), 600 (very fine), or 800 (extremely fine) should be used. The finer paper provides more control by enabling smaller amounts of cane to be removed safely. Dutch rush (also called reed rush, horsetail, file grass, and shave grass) can also be used to remove small amounts of cane; however, because it removes so little cane, Dutch rush is typically used to finish or polish the lay of a reed and to close reed pores. Dutch rush is available commercially, but it is fairly easy to find growing around swampy areas throughout the United States. Dutch rush should be wetted and flattened before using.

General Suggestions for Adjusting Single Reeds

Most reed adjustments entail: (1) resurfacing the table or flat underside portion of a reed of a reed, and/or (2) removing cane from the top, cut portion of a reed. Resurfacing the table can be accomplished by using a reed resurfacer or by using a piece of 400- or 600-grit sandpaper placed on a flat surface. Removing cane from the top of a reed is usually accomplished by scraping it with a reed knife or by sanding it with sandpaper or Dutch (reed) rush. The tools used to make reed adjustments are largely dependent upon how players wish to alter a particular reed. Learning the nuances of reed adjustment can be challenging. That is, players may make all of the "right" adjustments to a reed, yet the reed may still not respond well. The suggestions pertain to adjusting reeds that are too hard because the only effective adjustment for a reed that is too soft is to clip off some of the tip with a reed clipper.

1. Before making any adjustment, make sure the reed has good face validity. That is, check visually to make sure the reed looks good from all angles. Check the cane color, grain, heart, lay, cut, tip, shoulders, rails, and heel.

2. Perform the light test. Hold the reed up to the light and make sure the heart looks relatively good. As a rule, it is a waste of time working on a reed that looks unusually uneven, poorly cut, and/or if the cane appears to be of poor quality.

3. Before assuming that a reed needs adjusting, make sure it is thoroughly soaked in water (five minutes or so) before being tested. Generally, reeds that are played on before being thoroughly soaked do not play well. In addition, new reeds absorb water faster

than older reeds. As a result, new reeds do not need to be soaked as long.

4. Give reeds a chance to break in before making wholesale adjustments. Make small adjustments over several days and play on the reed after each adjustment. As a rule, do not make too many adjustments in one playing session.

5. Before scraping cane from the lay, consider the fact that scraping cane from the lay thins the reed, and this action cannot be undone.

6. Because reeds can be uneven (warped) on the flat underside (table), the first adjustment is to even out or flatten the reed table. Players can even out the table using a reed resurfacer or by laying a piece of 400- or 600-grit sandpaper on top of a piece of plate glass and gently drawing the reed across the sandpaper from heel to tip. Moisten two or three fingers slightly and spread them evenly over the surface of the reed with light pressure. Apply pressure evenly along the reed surface while drawing the reed lightly across the sandpaper. Check the underside of the reed often to see whether the surface is becoming even. Players can use the writing (brand name and/or number) on the underside of the reed as a guide during this process. For example, if part of this writing remains dark while the rest begins to lighten, that is visual confirmation that the table was not even. Keep sanding the table until the writing (or cane) appears uniform. After sanding, rub the table of the reed on the non-grit side of the sandpaper to polish and seal it. Finally, rinse the reed and test it after making adjustments.

7. Sometimes the pores or fiber ends on new reeds may not be closed sufficiently, causing problems with tone quality, control, and responsiveness. Many players elect to close off these pores by "polishing" the vamp. That is, players can close the pores by rubbing the vamp from shoulder to tip with their finger or thumb several times. The reed should be soaked thoroughly before closing the pores, and the finger or thumb should be kept slightly moist during this process. Some players prefer to use Dutch rush or very fine sandpaper (wet/dry 600- or 800-grit) to close the pores instead of their fingers alone. Sanding the lay lightly with Dutch rush or very fine sandpaper and then rubbing it with the thumb will not

only close the pores but will also make the reed feel very smooth against the lower lip.

8. Make large adjustments with a reed knife and small adjustments with fine sandpaper or Dutch rush.

9. When possible, place the reed to be adjusted on a small piece of plate glass as backing. The glass helps support the reed evenly across the width of the reed, which helps players sand or scrape the reed in a more uniform manner.

GENERAL SUGGESTIONS FOR SCRAPING/SANDING SINGLE REEDS

Place the reed on a small piece of plate glass when sanding or scraping. The glass helps support the reed evenly across the width of the reed, which helps players sand or scrape the reed in a more uniform manner. The suggestions are intended to help players understand the basic techniques or methods of scraping single reeds. Figures 3.25 and 3.26 show various parts of a single reed.

1. Direction—Scrape or sand from the shoulders to the tip. That is, scrape with the grain rather than against it.

2. Table—Generally, the first adjustment is to even out or flatten the table by drawing a thoroughly soaked reed across a piece of fine sandpaper several times from heel to tip as described in number 6 above.

3. Shoulders—Generally, the second adjustment occurs at the shoulders. It is important to maintain symmetry when scraping and to gradually thin the shoulders toward the rails from the center of the reed. It is usually not possible to use the light as a guide to determine the evenness or symmetry at the shoulders because the cane is too thick. Players often determine symmetry visually, or they use measuring devices (micrometers) to determine thicknesses at various points along the shoulders.

4. Vamp—Generally, after the table and shoulders have been adjusted, adjustments are made in the vamp. Removing cane from the vamp generally helps the reed respond more freely while maintaining the reed's ability to produce a good tone.

5. Heart—Avoid scraping too much cane (if any) from the heart; however, the heart should appear balanced and symmetrical when held up to a light.

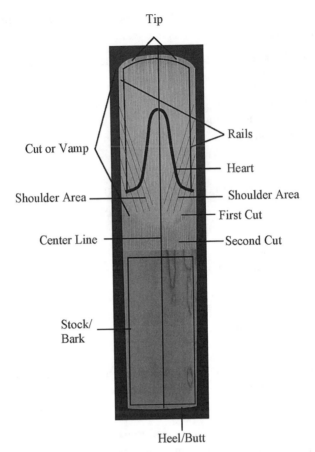

FIGURE 3.25. *Parts of a Single Reed*

6. Tip—The tip is the thinnest portion of the reed. As a rule, thin the tip by using fine sandpaper or Dutch rush rather than by scraping the tip with a reed knife. If it is necessary to scrape the tip with a reed knife, use very light strokes and a reed knife that has a straight-angle edge, while resting the reed on a flat surface.

Specific Suggestions for Adjusting Single Reeds

1. Characteristic: The reed feels/responds too hard.
    Adjustment 1—Before doing anything, make sure the reed is thoroughly soaked and rubbed flat to eliminate warping. Even out or flatten the reed table as described in number 6 above under General Suggestions for Adjusting Single Reeds.

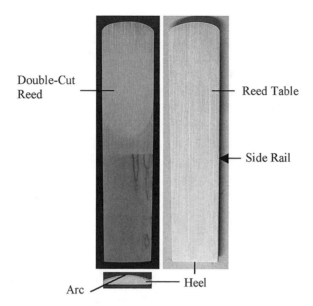

FIGURE 3.26. *Parts of a Single Reed*

Adjustment 2—If the reed is still too hard, scrape or sand the top of the shoulders and the vamp. Make sure to remove the same amount of cane on both sides of the center ridge while maintaining symmetry.

Adjustment 3—If the reed is still too hard, scrape or sand farther down on the shoulders and the vamp.

Adjustment 4—If the reed is still too hard, thin the heart area lightly and blend it in with the tip using fine sandpaper.

Adjustment 5—If the reed is still too hard, thin the tip lightly using extremely fine sandpaper (800 grit) or Dutch rush.

2. Characteristic: The reed feels too soft.

Adjustment 1—Before trimming the reed, push the reed up past the tip a little farther than normal. This extra distance causes a thicker part of the reed tip to close against the tip opening making the reed feel harder.

Adjustment 2—Before doing anything, make sure that the reed is thoroughly soaked. Using a reed clipper, trim the tip of the reed slightly.

3. Characteristic—The tone quality is poor and difficult to control, and the response is inconsistent throughout the range, even though the reed looks good.

Adjustment 1—Before doing anything, make sure the reed is thoroughly soaked and rubbed flat to eliminate warping. Then, check the reed for balance. Ideally, both halves of the reed should be symmetrical. That is, the left side of the reed should be a mirror image of the right side. Two basic tests can help determine if the two sides are balanced.

First, hold the reed (preferably soaked) up to a light and look at both sides of the reed as described earlier. Checking the shape of the heart and lay can often reveal inconsistencies in the reed's symmetry.

Second, with the reed thoroughly soaked, push the index finger lightly against each corner of the reed to help determine if one corner bends more easily than the other. If one corner is thicker than the other, that corner will provide more resistance against finger pressure than the thinner corner will.

After testing the reed, scrape or sand cane from the blade in the appropriate locations (thicker portions) to obtain balance and consistency.

Adjustment 2—Test the reed to see if there is leakage from the sides of the reed between the mouthpiece table and the reed. If there is leakage, check the reed table for evenness and adjust as described in number 6 above under General Suggestions for Adjusting Single Reeds. Sometimes, simply resoaking the reed will solve the problem.

4. Characteristic—The reed plays sharp, even though the reed looks good.

Adjustment 1—Reeds generally play sharp when they are too hard. Thin the reed as described in number 1 above in this section.

5. Characteristic—The reed plays flat, even though the reed looks good.

Adjustment 1—Reeds generally play flat when they are too soft. Adjust as described in number 2 above in this section.

6. Characteristic—Low notes do not respond well.

Adjustment 1—Check the tip opening. Usually an opening that is too large causes response problems, especially in the low range. Sand the reed table slightly to reduce the size of the tip opening.

Adjustment 2—Thin the tip slightly with fine sandpaper.

7. Characteristic—Reed is buzzy.

Adjustment 1—Thin the sides of the reed and make sure that the reed is symmetrical.

Adjustment 2—Reshape the tip corners to match the mouth-
piece, keeping the reed symmetrical.
8. Characteristic—Tone lacks depth.
Adjustment 1—The reed is not vibrating well beyond the tip.
Blend the tip with the heart by scraping/sanding back of the
tip into the windows and around the heart area.
Adjustment 2—If adjustment 1 does not help, discard the reed.
The heart is too thin.

Reed/Mouthpiece Angle: The mouthpiece enters the mouth at about a 35- to
40-degree angle. See Instrument Angle, page 230

Reed Tools: See Reed Making and Adjustment, page 256

Reeds, Single: Physically, the vibrating mechanism that sets the air column in
vibration on reed instruments. Reeds are the single most important factor in
determining tonal and response characteristics on reed instruments. They are
largely responsible for determining the type of tone quality, the type of response,
and the amount of tone control players can achieve. Reeds are traditionally made
of cane and more recently made of synthetic materials. Most single reed players
do not make their own reeds; however, many advanced players do adjust their
reeds. See also Synthetic Reeds, page 283

PHYSICAL DEMANDS OF A REED

A musical tone is produced when air sets the reed in vibration. The tone produced
by the vibrating reed is determined by the length of the air column and instrument to which the mouthpiece/reed combination is attached. This length varies
according to the fingering being used at any given time. Research shows that the
reed actually closes off the aperture periodically when a tone is being produced,
resulting in short bursts of air being emitted into the instrument rather than a
continuous air stream. This fact illustrates the importance of proper reed balance
during performance. Because the vibrating reed literally beats against the mouthpiece during vibration, the lay of the mouthpiece and the size of tip opening both
affect the responsiveness of the reed.

REED VIBRATION

During performance, the reed vibrates continually at ever-changing frequencies. These changes are often extreme. For example, to produce a low C-natural

on the alto saxophone, the reed must vibrate at approximately 155 hertz (Hz). An octave leap (third-space C-natural) would require the reed to vibrate twice as fast (approximately 310 Hz), and a two-octave leap (high C-natural) would require the reed to vibrate at approximately 620 Hz. Since the ability of a reed to vibrate equally well at all frequencies is more of an ideal than a reality, performers are constantly searching for reeds that approach this ideal.

REED CANE

Reeds are made from a cane called Arundo donax, a tall reed that resembles bamboo. Arundo donax has a hard outer layer, called the bark or rind that provides strength and stability for the reed tube and a softer inner layer that, when exposed by scraping away the bark, is flexible and vibrates easily. Reed cane also contains a chemical called "lignin," which adds to the material's elastic and flexible quality. Several factors affect the quality of the cane, including the climate, soil, irrigation, fertilization, and time of harvest. It is generally believed that the best cane is grown in southern France.

Cane plants can reach twenty feet in height and are harvested every couple of years. Once cut, cane plants are dried and their branches are removed. They are then dried or "sunned," which gives the cane its golden color. The cane plants are aged for as long as two years before being used for reeds.

Reed cane consists of many fibers, which are like hollow tubes held together by a moisture absorbent pithlike substance. Several qualities inherent in any piece of cane can affect the quality and type of reed that it may produce, including age, hardness, stiffness, resiliency, density, grain, and flexibility.

Reed makers use a variety of methods to determine whether a particular piece of cane will result in a "good" reed, including assessing the color of the cane. The most preferred cane has yellow or purple-yellow bark. Green to deep green cane indicates that the cane is not aged properly. Brown cane indicates that the cane is older; however, brown cane can still be used to produce good reeds. White or gray cane is generally too old to be used for reed making. Reed makers also assess the quality of the cane while they are working on reeds, gauging how the material feels as it is being "worked." Regardless of which testing methods a reed maker uses, exactly which pieces of cane to use is a matter of personal preference, and different reed makers will prefer different pieces of cane, depending on the playing characteristics they prefer.

Cane of various diameters is needed to produce a variety of reed sizes to accommodate the various single reed instruments. For example, clarinet reeds require one diameter and baritone saxophone reeds require another because of their size difference. Differences in reed sizes are shown in figure 3.27. Once the

Clarinet Reeds   Saxophone Reeds

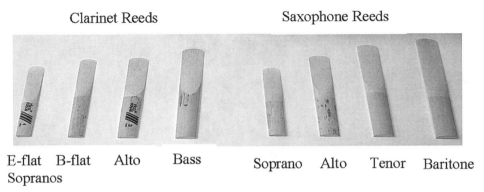

E-flat   B-flat   Alto   Bass   Soprano   Alto   Tenor   Baritone
Sopranos

FIGURE 3.27. *Reed Size Comparisons*

appropriate diameter for a particular reed type is chosen, the cane is cut into pre-determined lengths. Then, from these hollow tubes a section of the tube is cut off to make a reed blank. This reed blank then goes through a machine finishing process. Terminology commonly used to describe single reeds is listed here. Figure 3.28 shows the various parts of a reed.

Parts of a Reed

1. Cut/Vamp—The area of the reed from which the bark has been removed starting with the U-shape edge (or W-shape edge on some reeds) and running toward the tip of the reed. On a double-cut reed, bark is also removed from the area around the U-shape edge.
2. Heart—The center portion of the reed extending from just behind the tip toward the shoulders. When held up to a light, the heart can be seen as a symmetrically shaded U-shaped area.
3. Heel/Butt—The end of the reed (cane) farthest from the tip that has the arch-shaped curve or arc. This arc is determined by the diameter of the cane from which the reed was made.
4. Lay—A general term used to describe the scraped or shaped part of the reed that extends from the U-shaped cut to the tip. Some players refer to various portions of the lay more specifically, especially in relationship to reed adjustment. These portions include the tip, rails (or sides), heart, and shoulders.
5. Rails/Sides—The side edges of the reed.
6. Shoulders—The back portions of a reed that extend from the U-shaped cut toward the lay. Each reed has two shoulders, one on each side of the reed center.

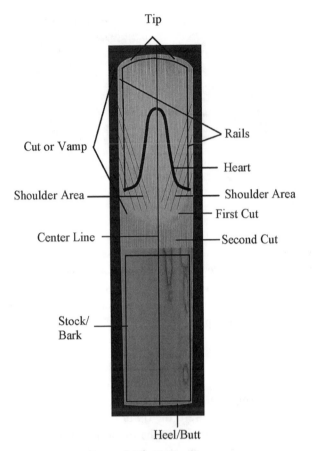

FIGURE 3.28. *Parts of a Single Reed*

7. Stock—The part of the reed that has the bark on it.
8. Table—The flat underside of the reed that lies against the mouthpiece table.
9. Tip—The very thin area of a reed that extends from the end of the reed slightly back.

Playing Characteristics of a Good Reed

1. Responds freely and easily over the entire range of the instrument.
2. Plays all octaves of the instrument reasonably well in tune without significant adjustments in embouchure or lip pressure.

3. Responds well in all dynamic ranges of the instrument.

4. Produces an appropriate amount of resistance to wind pressure.

5. Facilitates all types of articulations throughout the range of the instrument.

What to Look for When Selecting a Good Reed

1. Cane Color—Cane that has a golden-yellowish cast is desirable. Reeds that are a bright yellow, have a slight greenish cast, or have dark brown streaks in the vamp indicate that the cane may not have been aged properly or that the cane was of poor quality. Brown spots or flecks in the stock are common and should appear somewhat evenly spaced throughout.

2. Grain—The grain of a reed can be fine, medium, or coarse. Reeds that contain predominately coarse grains typically do not respond well, feel rough on the lip, and tend to produce an unsatisfactory tone quality. Reeds that contain fine grains are often inconsistent and tend to wear out quickly. Cane that has a predominantly medium grain with fine and coarse grains interspersed evenly throughout will generally yield more consistent results. Also, the grain should run straight from the heel to the tip. Figure 3.29 shows reeds with fine, medium, and coarse grains.

3. Heart—For the most part, the quality of the heart is dependent upon the cut or vamp. One common test that can be performed to see if the heart is symmetrical is to hold the reed up to the light so that you can see the various light and dark shades. In a perfect world, a U-shaped area of darkness extending from the bark down toward the reed tip will be visible. This area should be centered with the sides of the reed and should be surrounded by evenly spaced, lighter areas near the tip and on both sides. Generally, the lighter areas represent softer (thinner) sections, and the darker (thicker) areas represent harder sections of the reed. If these areas are symmetrical, the reed has a reasonably good chance of producing a good tone quality. Unfortunately, although this test is a relatively good check, cane is not always consistent in color. That is, a reed may look "bad" and play well, or a reed may look "good" and play poorly.

The reeds in figures 3.30 through 3.33 are highlighted with a light. The heart, grain, and other features are plainly visible,

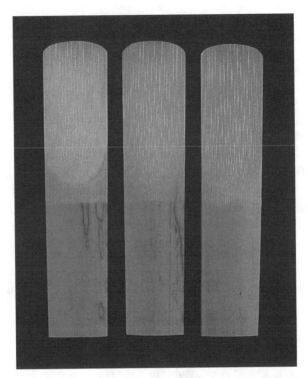

FIGURE 3.29. *Fine Grain, Medium Grain, and Coarse Grain*

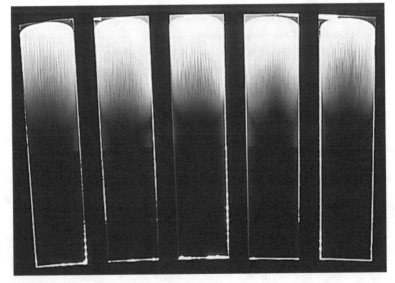

FIGURE 3.30. *Light Highlighting Areas of Five Double-Cut Reeds*

FIGURE 3.31. *Reeds Highlighted by Low Light*

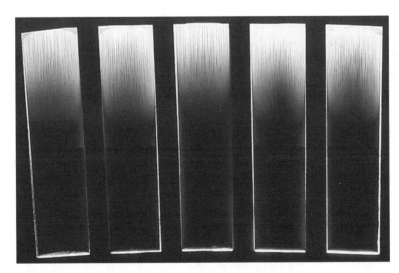

FIGURE 3.32. *Reeds Highlighted by Moderate Light*

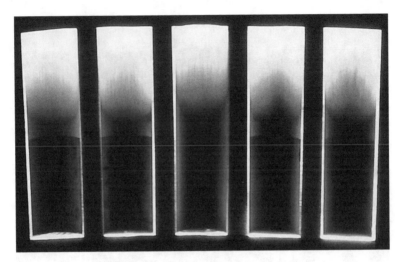

FIGURE 3.33. *Reeds Highlighted by Intense Light*

and the symmetry of the reeds (or lack of symmetry) can also be seen. In these figures, the fourth reed from the left has the most symmetrical heart and the best overall shape. The differences in shading, which generally correspond to the thickness of the cane, can help players understand the importance of reed balance. Figures 3.31, 3.32, and 3.33 are illustrative of reed balance and symmetry. Figure 3.31 shows reeds under low light. The evenness (or unevenness) of the grain, the symmetry (or asymmetry) of the vamp, and the thickness of various portions of the reed from the shoulders to the tip are visible. Figure 3.32 shows five reeds under moderate light. Four of the reeds are double-cut reeds; however, the center reed is a single-cut reed. The light showing through the edges of the second cut (double-cut reeds) is not visible on the single-cut reed (which only has one cut). This difference enables double-cut reeds to vibrate more freely. In addition, it is clear that the single-cut reed has a much flatter heart than the double-cut reeds (i.e., there is no hint of a U-shape). Figure 3.33 shows the reeds under intense light. The shape, cut, and symmetry of each reed are apparent. In addition, the light shining through near the edges of each reed may help players understand how the entire reed vibrates (or can vibrate) during play.

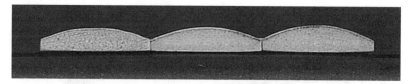

FIGURE 3.34. *Heels: Low, Medium, and High Arc*

4. Heel—Checking the heel of a reed for symmetry is one of the easiest tasks to perform. The heel must have a moderate arch (not too flat and not too high) with an even thickness on both sides. If the arc is too flat, the cane diameter from which the reed was cut was too large. If the arc is too high, the cane diameter from which the reed was cut was too small. A reed that is noticeably thicker on one side than the other almost certainly will cause performance problems and should be avoided. Figure 3.34 shows variations in heel arcs.

5. Ridge/Spine—A term used for the center "hump" of a reed. "Ridge" is a term more frequently associated with double reeds.

6. Tip—The tip of a reed is crucial to producing a good tone quality. Its thickness and flexibility must be even across the width of the reed. Holding the reed up to the light can provide useful information regarding tip thickness and evenness. Some players test the tip's flexibility by lightly pressing on both sides of the tip with the thumb or index finger and comparing the amount of pressure needed to flex the reed on both sides. There are also devices available that measure this degree of flexibility. Although such devices are useful, there is no substitute for playing on a reed to determine its ultimate potential.

7. Vamp/Cut—To a large extent, the vamp determines the reed's potential for a good tone quality. It is important that the vamp is even and symmetrical. Make sure the U-shape cut is even. That is, the bark on both sides of the reed should be uniform, and the shoulders should be tapered symmetrically on both sides. Ideally, when held up to the light, increased lightness toward the edges of the reed should be visible. Commercial devices that can measure the thicknesses of various parts of a reed are available; these devices can be useful in determining the evenness or symmetry of a reed. Figure 3.35 show how reeds can be cut at different points.

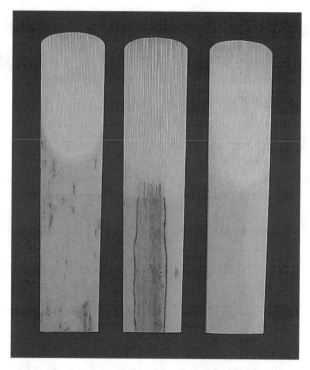

Figure 3.35. *High, Medium, and Low Cuts*

Figure 3.36 shows how reeds can be cut off center, or higher on one side than another. Figure 3.37 shows three common cuts or reed types. Figure 3.38 shows why double-cut reeds are likely to vibrate more freely than single-cut reeds.

Reed Strength

There are basically two systems for identifying reed strength. The first is a numbering system. For example, one company employs a numbering system in which reeds are numbered as follows: 1 (very soft), 2 (soft), 3 (medium soft), 4 (medium), 5 (medium hard), and 6 (hard). The second system does not use numbers. Instead it simply uses words to designate reed strength. For example, one company designates reed strength as soft, medium-soft, medium, medium-hard, and hard.

Unfortunately, both systems are unreliable and inconsistent to some degree because a reed strength designation does not indicate a specific reed hardness, but rather a range of hardness. For example, a number 2½ reed may actually be

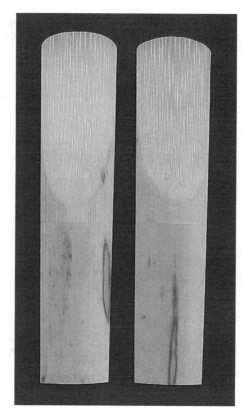

FIGURE 3.36. *Cuts off Center*

closer to a number 2 or a number 3 reed depending on the individual reed. As a result, there is no guarantee that three number 2½ reeds will play the same. In fact, there is a great chance that they will be significantly different. The only way to know how a reed responds is to play on it, and even then, it will change over time. Despite these inconsistencies, designating reed strength in some manner does provide players with a general idea of how hard a reed is likely to be.

PROBLEMATIC REED TYPES

Single reeds may display one or more problematic playing characteristics used to categorize reeds including dead, hard, hollow, soft, and uncontrollable. Because reeds are often inconsistent, it is important to evaluate a reed's performance over time before determining its ultimate fate. Playing consistency is a key factor in determining which reeds will work well, which reeds may work well with

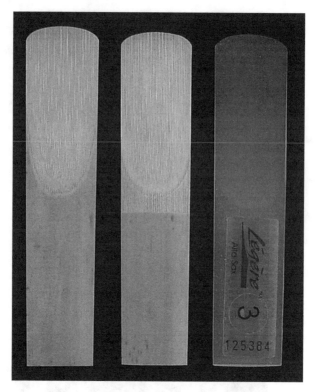

FIGURE 3.37. *Single-Cut, Double-Cut, and Plastic Reeds*

adjustments, and which reeds will probably never work well. It is important to note that a reed that does not respond well on a particular day may not be a "bad" reed. In fact, a reed may perform poorly on any particular day because of relatively minor factors such as weather conditions or simply not being soaked properly before being played. Experienced players rarely discard reeds after the first playing. Some players keep reeds for years, hoping they will be playable at some point. Various problematic reed types are described as follows.

1. Dead, Lifeless Reeds—After a reed has been played on for an extended time, tone quality and control begin to deteriorate. That is, the reed just does not seem to vibrate properly. Older reeds often sound dull and lifeless. At this point, nothing can be done to bring the reed back, and it should be discarded. Sometimes, even a new reed can have these qualities, especially if the cane it was made from is too old or of poor quality. Reeds with many dark brown streaks seem particularly prone to these tendencies.

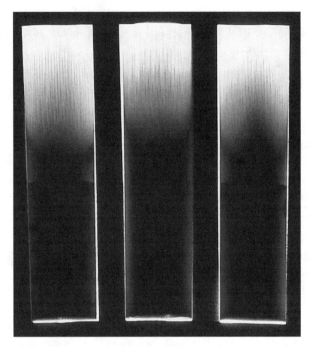

FIGURE 3.38. *Highlights of Two Double-Cut Reeds and One Single-Cut Reed (center)*

2. Hard Reeds—Hard reeds are characterized by a consistently "airy" sound and typically have response problems (especially in the low range) that make proper articulation difficult. Hard reeds also require much more air to produce a tone, which can negatively affect breathing and phrasing, and they tend to play sharp. Hard reeds tend to be consistent over time; however, they do tend to soften after they have been played on a few times. As a result, a reed that is a little too hard when first played may be just about right after a breaking-in period. If a reed does not soften adequately after a reasonable breaking-in period (some reeds actually feel harder after being played on a few times), it may need to be sanded or scraped.

3. Hollow Reeds—Some reeds may respond well and may even yield a consistent tone quality, yet lack a "core" to the sound. That is, the tone sounds hollow. A hollow sound is generally the result of an unbalanced reed. More specifically, the heart of the reed is usually

thin in areas and/or is not symmetrical. With these types of reeds, nothing can be done to give fullness to the sound, and the reed should be discarded.

4. Soft Reeds—Soft reeds are characterized by a consistently thin, pinched, reedy tone and often cause intonation problems. Players will often pinch the reed to the point of closing off the tip opening completely, which stops the flow of air into the instrument. Pushing the reed up a little past the tip of the mouthpiece may improve the tone quality somewhat because it places a thicker part of reed over the tip rail. In addition, clipping the tip of the reed may improve the overall tone quality of the reed; however, this practice is not widespread because the results are often unsatisfactory.

5. Squeaky, Uncontrollable Reeds—Reeds that squeak or feel as though they are going to squeak or break make control of the tone difficult. Uncontrollable reeds are often cracked or chipped, may be unbalanced (thicker on one side than the other, cut unevenly, etc.) or have some other inherent flaw. If a reed squeaks or is uncontrollable, and the reed looks good, problems are usually caused by warping or by not soaking the reed sufficiently. During periods of low humidity, reeds tend to dry out quickly, causing the reed to pull away from the mouthpiece. Warping causes poor reed response, poor tone quality, and squeaks or chirps.

   Figure 3.39 shows some common reed problems. The reed on the left has nicks in the tip. It also has dirt and lipstick stains on the lay and vamp. The middle reed is worn out. The light-colored flecks throughout the lay and vamp indicate that the fibers are broken down. In addition, the reed has nicks in the tip and a sliver missing from the right side rail near the tip. The four indents from the ligature are clearly present on the stock. The reed on the right also has broken-down fibers. It also has mildew and mold stains in the heart, a sliver missing from the left side rail near the tip, and a yellowish cast from the heart to the tip from being wet for extended periods of time.

Register Key: On clarinet, the register key mechanism is operated by the left thumb. When depressed, the clarinet produces a tone a twelfth higher than the tone produced by the same fingering without the register key. For example, the fingering for middle C-natural is T-1-2-3. Adding the register key causes the

FIGURE 3.39. *Common Reed Problems: Left (Dirt and Lipstick); Middle (Worn Out, Cane Fibers Broken Down, Reed Chipped); Right (Worn Out, Fibers Broken Down, Mildew/Mold Stains)*

pitch to jump a twelfth, producing a G-natural above the staff. The register key is depressed for all notes higher than and including third-line B-natural.

Register/Registers: Groups of notes that share certain tonal characteristics usually related to pitch range, timbre, octave considerations, and/or manner of production. Players vary in their description of registers. For example, some players consider the notes between middle C-natural and G-natural above the staff to be the middle register. And although some players refer to the altissimo register for those notes that lie above high C-natural, others refer to the altissimo register for those notes above high E-natural or F-natural. Finally, some players use the term register interchangeably with the term "range" to describe the playing ranges of the instrument. Ultimately, delineating registers commonly used by junior high students, high school students, college-level players, and professional players is a subjective process that varies according to the criteria used for delineation.

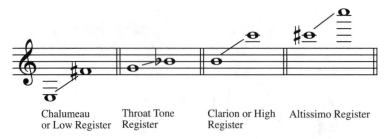

FIGURE 3.40.   *Register/Registers*

Nonetheless, it seems reasonable to divide the clarinet range into four registers. These registers are listed here and are notated in figure 3.40. See also Range, page 252

1. Low Resister or Chalumeau—From low E-natural to first-space F-sharp.
2. Throat Tone Register—From second-line G-natural to third-line B-flat.
3. High or Clarion Register—From third-line B-natural to high C-natural.
4. Altissimo Register—All notes above high C-natural.

Releases/Cutoffs: See Releases/Cutoffs, page 56

Resistance: In general, the counteraction of the reed, mouthpiece, and clarinet to the incoming air stream. A detailed discussion of resistance is under Resistance in chapter 4. See Resistance, page 402

Resonance Keys: Keys sometimes added to regular fingerings to improve the tonal response, tone quality, and/or pitch of certain notes. For example, when playing throat tones, players sometimes cover the right-hand tone holes to make the throat tones more resonant and to improve pitch. In addition, some bass clarinets are equipped with a low G-natural resonance key to improve tonal response, tone quality, and pitch. See also Speaker Keys, page 282

Response: The way a reed vibrates as a result of the player's air stream and embouchure. The term response is also used to refer to the ease with which the notes sound or speak. Some notes respond more easily than others, depending on how much of the tube is closed and how much air speed is needed to set the reed in vibration. Notes in the extreme high or low range tend not to respond as well as

FIGURE 3.41. *Secondary Break*

notes in the middle range, and the response of the throat tones is often inconsistent. The quality and condition of the clarinet, the reed/mouthpiece combination, and a player's ability to control the air speed and air volume greatly affect reed response. See also Resistance, page 280

Ring Inserts: See Tuning Rings, page 294

Secondary Break: A term used by advanced players to describe playing from a note below high C-sharp (above the staff) to high C-sharp or a note above high C-sharp in the altissimo register. The secondary break occurs at high C-sharp because the fingerings necessary to produce the upper partials (i.e., the altissimo pitches) become less patterned or intuitive at this point. Examples involving the secondary break are shown in figure 3.41. See also Break, page 205; Crossing the Break, page 212

Secondary Throat Tones: A term used by some players to describe the range of notes between and including first-line E-flat and first-space F-sharp. These notes lie at the top of the chalumeau range and just below the throat tones and often display the same characteristics of true throat tones. See also Throat Tones, page 287

Selecting an Instrument: See Instrument Brands, page 232; Instrument Selection, page 33

Shank, Mouthpiece: A term sometimes used to describe the part of a mouthpiece that fits into the barrel and runs into the mouthpiece bore. Clarinetists often refer to this area as the mouthpiece throat. "Shank" is a term more commonly associated with brass mouthpieces. See also Mouthpiece/Mouthpieces, page 247

Shoulders: The areas that surround the heart of a single reed. The shoulders extend back toward the heel of the reed. See also Reeds, Single, page 265

Side Rails, Mouthpiece: The two edges along the sides of the mouthpiece table that extend from the bottom of the mouthpiece window to the tip rail. The side rails should have even, uniform dimensions and should be free from nicks and scrapes. Damaged side rails make the tone difficult to control and often cause squeaking and poor tone quality. See also Mouthpiece/Mouthpieces, page 247

Single-Cut Reeds: Reeds that have one visible slice or cut from the stock to form the vamp. That is, the bark has been removed from the U-shape to the tip. All of the outer bark surrounding the U-shape to the heel of the reed is intact. The standard reeds made by Rico and LaVoz are single-cut reeds. See also Reeds, single, page 265; Double-Cut Reeds, page 214

Slap Tongue: A tonguing technique that produces a "slapping" or "popping" effect on the attacks. Slap tonguing is sometimes used as a special effect in both jazz and contemporary literature and is produced by pressing the tongue hard against the reed to close or nearly close the tip opening, building up air pressure, and then releasing the tongue quickly. See also Extended/Contemporary Techniques, page 221

Sounding Range: See Instrument Family and Playing Considerations, page 232; Range, page 252; Transpositions, page 292

Speaker Keys: Generally, a term used for keys that help notes respond or "speak" when depressed. Speaker keys can be special keys (e.g., bassoon flick keys) or they can be regular keys (e.g., an octave key). On clarinet, the register key is the most obvious speaker key. See also Resonance Keys, page 280

Spring Hook Tool: See Spring Hook Tool, page 59

Springs: See Springs, page 59

Squeaks: Undesirable, accidentally produced partials that sometimes sound during normal play. Squeaks can be caused by several factors. Some of the most common causes of squeaks include: (1) fingers not covering tone holes properly, (2) poor or dry reeds, (3) poor embouchure formation, (4) overblowing, and/or (5) accidentally hitting side keys. Squeaking is a common problem for beginners as they learn to control their embouchures and the instrument. A more detailed discussion regarding the causes of squeaks is in "Practical Tips."

Staggered Breathing: See Staggered Breathing, page 59

Stamina: See Endurance/Stamina, page 28

Stands: See Instrument Stands, page 39

Starting Note/Range, The Best: Most players will have excellent results starting on second-line G-natural (open) and working their way downward note by note to middle C-natural (1-2-3). This five-note range is ideal for several reasons. First, it is relatively easy to produce a tone in this range. Second, the fingerings in this range are relatively simple and intuitive. Third, this range provides teachers with the opportunity to point out that as more holes are covered, the tones get lower. These relationships make this range ideal for simple ear training exercises. Finally, adding one finger at a time in a comfortable range enables players to cover each tone hole properly. That is, players learn to cover the tone holes more efficiently when they proceed in a logical step-by-step manner. This starting note range is shown is figure 3.42. It is interesting to note that because band method books must accommodate beginners on a variety of instruments, they often do not have players start on the above sequence of notes.

Stock: The part of a reed that has bark on it. See also Reeds, Single, page 265

Swab: See Swab, page 59; Care and Maintenance, page 206

Synthetic Reeds: Reeds made from synthetic, man-made materials instead of traditional cane. A variety of synthetic reeds are available today. These reeds last longer and are more durable than cane reeds. In addition, they do not need to be moist to respond; therefore, they do not dry out. However, the sound produced by synthetic reeds is not the same quality as the sound produced by cane reeds, and the vast majority of players prefer cane reeds. In addition, synthetic reeds are difficult if not impossible to adjust. Despite the sound difference, many players find synthetic reeds useful in some situations. For example, synthetic reeds are useful when players are doubling on other instruments and the instrument must respond immediately with little or no preparation. Synthetic reeds are also suitable for marching band, when the weather conditions are often less than ideal. Some of the most commonly used synthetic reeds are marketed under the names Legere, Bari, Fibracell, and Hahn. See also Reeds, Single, page 265

FIGURE 3.42. *Starting Note Range*

Table, Mouthpiece: The flat underside of a mouthpiece on which the reed lies. It is imperative that the mouthpiece table be flat and smooth. A warped and/or damaged table makes the tone difficult to control and often causes squeaks. See also Mouthpiece/Mouthpieces, page 247

Technique: In general, the manner and ability with which players use the technical skills involved in playing an instrument. Most commonly, the term is used to describe the physical actions involved in playing an instrument, and often specifically refers to technical passages. Virtually every pedagogical aspect of woodwind playing (acoustical, physical, and mental) affects technique. General technical considerations for all woodwind instruments are under Technique in chapter 1. The suggestions and considerations apply specifically to the clarinet. When appropriate, readers are directed to relevant terms in the book where particular topics are addressed in detail. See also Alternate Fingerings/Alternates, page 190; Technique, page 60

General Technical Considerations/Concerns for Clarinet Players

1. Because clarinet keys are small, light, and comfortably spaced, clarinets are capable of playing technically difficult passages more quickly and efficiently than some of the larger instruments. However, beginners often have trouble covering the holes properly. As a result, technical proficiency can be problematic in the first few months of play.

2. The little-finger keys are used extensively on clarinet. Beginners often have trouble coordinating their little fingers with the other fingers and covering the tone holes properly at the same time. Practicing slowly at first and adding only one finger at a time can help players develop these skills appropriately.

3. Players often have trouble with the right-hand side keys because reaching these keys requires the hands and/or fingers to shift slightly away from the "home" position. In many instances, players actually straighten or lock the fingers and lose track of the "home" keys altogether. In addition, these keys are very close together and they are quite small, so players often depress the wrong key (or keys) accidentally. Working with the side keys slowly and deliberately to develop finger coordination, timing, and placement is extremely important to technical development.

Specific Technical Considerations/Concerns for Clarinet Players

1. Alternate Fingerings/Alternates—Clarinet players use several alternate fingerings. In fact, the clarinet probably has more alternates than any other woodwind instrument. The choice of fingerings should be determined by musical considerations including tone quality, intonation, and smoothness of the phrase. Although new fingerings may seem awkward initially, developing control over all fingerings is crucial to technical proficiency. See also Alternate Fingerings/Alternates, page 190

2. Right- and Left-hand Key Clusters (Little-Finger Keys)—Players need to learn how and when to use fingerings involving the little fingers on both hands for smoothness of technique, especially the fourth-finger or little-finger alternate fingerings described under Alternate Fingerings/Alternates. Working on the little-finger keys slowly and deliberately to develop finger coordination and control is extremely important to technical development. Learning to shift properly from one key to another in the key clusters is also crucial to technical proficiency. See also Alternate Fingerings/Alternates, page 190

3. Left Thumb—A common problem among clarinet players is improper left thumb position. The proper position of the left thumb is at an angle with the thumbnail pointing at approximately 1 o'clock, so that it can both cover the F-hole and operate the register key with a simple rocking motion. If the thumb is not angled properly, reaching the register key with an efficient rocking motion becomes very difficult if not impossible. An improper left thumb position is extremely detrimental to technique, especially in rapid passages.

4. Right Thumb—Players often develop the habit of placing the thumb too far under the thumb rest, making it difficult to cover the tone holes properly. Not placing the thumb properly under the rest hinders technical proficiency, especially in rapid passages. The thumb should be placed under the rest between the thumbnail and first joint with the ball of the thumb against the clarinet.

5. Crossing the Break/Preparing the Right Hand—Crossing the break can be challenging on the clarinet, especially with young players. The primary considerations are with instrument finger/

hand position, finger coordination, and covering the tone holes properly. The main challenge with crossing the break is playing from a note where few keys are depressed to a note where many keys are depressed, requiring coordination of hands and fingers. In addition, because the clarinet is heavier than the flute or oboe, and is held out to the front of the player (usually without a neck strap) it is more challenging to master crossing the break on clarinet than on other instruments. Maintaining proper hand positions, keeping the fingers close to the keys/tone holes at all times, and minimizing excess finger motion will help make crossing the break easier. See also Crossing the Break, page 212

6. Trill Fingerings—Because clarinet players are required to trill often, it is important to learn the special trill fingerings. A special trill fingering chart is in "Practical Tips" at the end of this chapter.

7. High/Altissimo Range—Clarinet players are required to play in the high range frequently. Therefore, technical proficiency is limited if players do not learn to play in this range. As notes ascend, players may need to increase air speed, firm their embouchures slightly, and focus the air and oral cavity for the pitch or pitches being played to achieve proper tonal response. The response of notes above high C-natural becomes increasingly more difficult as the range ascends. In addition, the fingerings for notes above high C-natural can be increasingly more difficult and less intuitive. Practicing scales, arpeggios, and etudes can help smooth out fingering problems in the high register. See also Altissimo/Extended Range, page 195

8. Skips and Leaps—Executing skips and leaps can cause clarinet players problems. As with crossing the break, coordinating the fingers becomes key to executing skips and leaps effectively. Maintaining proper hand positions, keeping the fingers close to the keys at all times, and minimizing excess finger motion will help players execute skips and leaps cleanly. Suggestions for executing skips and leaps effectively are listed here. See also Crossing the Break, page 212

   A. The primary technical consideration with skips and leaps is the need to make adjustments in embouchure, air, and oral cavity from note to note. In the low and middle registers, these adjustments are relatively subtle; however, from the low register to the high register, these adjustments are significant.

B. The clarinet overblows the twelfth rather than an octave, which creates unique problems for clarinet players when executing skips and leaps. That is, clarinet players cannot simply learn fingerings for one octave and transfer them to the next octave (with some minor adjustments) like other woodwind players. For example, the fingering for low A-natural produces the E-natural a twelfth above when the register key is depressed.

C. As a rule, when ascending, the embouchure needs to be firmer, the air speed needs to be faster, the air direction needs to be raised, and the oral cavity must be slightly more focused. When descending to lower pitches, players must reverse these adjustments.

D. The adjustments in embouchure, air, and oral cavity must be balanced. That is, increasing air speed significantly without changing the embouchure or air direction may help a higher pitch to sound, but it will also create problems with pitch and tone quality. Likewise, increasing embouchure tension without making appropriate changes in air speed, direction, and focus will also create problems with pitch and quality. As a rule, players must balance the adjustments in embouchure tension, air speed, air direction, and the oral cavity, rather than making large-scale changes in one or two of these variables.

E. Learning to make appropriate embouchure (firmness), air (direction, speed, focus), and oral cavity (focus) adjustments is crucial to playing skips and leaps smoothly and efficiently. The appropriateness of any adjustment is based on the resultant tone quality and pitch placement.

Temperament: See Temperament, page 61

Throat Tones: A group of pitches in the middle register extending from second-line G-natural to third-line B-flat. Few tone holes are covered when playing throat tones, and the air escapes from the tone holes after begin pushed through a very short length of tubing. As a result, throat tones tend to be weak and difficult to play in tune. In addition, they often do not match the tone quality of the notes around them. Players who use air properly will have greater success making the throat tones sound full. Intermediate and advanced players make instrument adjustments, employ alternate fingerings, and try a variety of mouthpieces and barrels, all for the sake of improving the throat tones. Some players consider the first-space F-natural and F-sharp, and the first-line E-natural and E-flat to be throat tones or secondary throat tones as well. Although these pitches display some of the same characteristics as the primary throat tones, they are not as problematic as the throat-tones above open G-natural. The throat tones are shown in figure 3.43.

Throat/Bore, Mouthpiece: A term used to describe the part of a mouthpiece that fits into the barrel joint. Most clarinet players use the term "throat" when describing this part of the mouthpiece. "Bore" is a term more commonly associated with brass mouthpieces. See also Mouthpiece/Mouthpieces, page 247

Thumb Rest: A metal or plastic rest attached to the back of the clarinet under which the right thumb is positioned while the instrument is being played. Thumb rests are often rubber coated for comfort. Adjustable thumb rests are also available. These thumb rests can be adjusted up or down to better fit the players' hands. See also Hand/Holding/Instrument/Playing Positions and Posture, page 224

Timbre: See Tone Quality, page 291

Tip Opening: The opening between the tip of the reed and the mouthpiece tip rail. The tip opening is a significant factor in determining the amount of resistance a mouthpiece will offer and the type of tone produced on an instrument. As a rule, a wider tip opening increases the amount of resistance the mouthpiece/ reed combination will have. However, a wider tip opening also increases the potential for a bigger, fuller tone. Conversely, a more narrow tip opening lessens the amount of resistance a mouthpiece/reed combination will have and reduces the potential for a bigger, fuller tone. See also Mouthpiece/Mouthpieces, page 247; Resistance, page 280

Tip Rail, Mouthpiece: The narrow flat area at the end of the mouthpiece table. The tip rail should be smooth and flat, and it should be free from nicks and scrapes. A damaged tip rail makes the tone difficult to control and often causes squeaking and poor tone quality because the reed is unable to close properly against the mouthpiece. Tip rails that are too wide produce a dead tone with little flexibility.

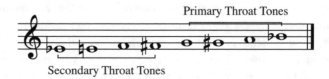

FIGURE 3.43. *Throat Tones*

Tip rails that are too narrow or uneven tend to be bright and inconsistent, and are more likely to squeak. See also Mouthpiece/Mouthpieces, page 247

Tip, Reed: The very thin area of a single reed that extends from the end of the reed slightly back. Generally, the tip of a reed closes off against the mouthpiece tip rail. See also Reeds, Single, page 265

Tone Holes: See Tone Holes, page 63

Tone Production: The term used to describe how tone is produced on an instrument. General considerations for woodwind tone production are discussed under Tone Production in chapter 1. Specific considerations for clarinet tone production and some of the terms included within the clarinet chapter that address tone production appear in the following section.

Tonal Concept/Tone Quality

Develop a concept of "good" clarinet tone and the type of tone quality desired. Listening to advanced players and high quality recordings can help develop appropriate tonal concepts. In addition, taking lessons from a knowledgeable teacher who provides an exemplary model during lessons is invaluable. See Tone Production, page 63

1. Use appropriate equipment (instrument; mouthpiece; reed; ligature; barrel). Players should play on equipment that matches their level of performance and experience. As players mature, they should experiment with several advanced mouthpieces, ligatures, reeds, and barrels under the guidance of a knowledgeable teacher to find the right combination for them.

2. Strive for a consistent tone quality and evenness of scale in all ranges and develop control of the air stream at all dynamic levels. Thinking of certain syllables can help set the proper focus or position of the throat, oral cavity, and air stream. Maintain an open throat and oral cavity in the low to middle registers as if saying the syllable "ah" or "oh." Gradually change this syllable to an "oo" syllable to obtain a more appropriate focus of the air stream in the middle register. As players ascend into the high range, a slightly firmer "oo" syllable is needed to focus tone properly. In the extreme high range, players sometimes think of using an "ee" syllable to help focus the air stream appropriately.

EMBOUCHURE

Maintain proper embouchure formation at all times. Proper mechanics of embouchure are critical to tone production. Although many fine players' embouchures vary slightly from a classic or standard embouchure, the fundamental characteristics have withstood the test of time. Achieving a mature, characteristic tone on any wind instrument requires time and practice to develop the physical and aural skills necessary for proper tone production. A brief summary of embouchure considerations for good tone production appears in the following list. See also Embouchure, page 215

1. The mouth corners are drawn inward toward reed, and the mouth corners remain firm (not tight).
2. The lips surround the mouthpiece as if saying "who."
3. The lower lip is curled over the bottom teeth, and the jaw is lowered slightly. The lower lip remains flexed against the reed and is supported by the bottom teeth/jaw and surrounding muscles. Players should not put too much pressure on the lower lip with the teeth.
4. The chin remains flat, but not tight. Do not puff the cheeks.
5. The upper teeth rest on top of the mouthpiece.
6. A consistent embouchure is maintained.

BREATHING AND AIR

A thorough discussion of breathing and air is in chapter 1. See Breathing/Breath Support/Air Control, page 10; Tone Production, page 63

VIBRATO

While vibrato is not a factor in tone production for beginners and intermediate players, it is a factor in tone production for more advanced players. Clarinet players traditionally do not use vibrato in concert playing or classical style. A jaw vibrato is often used by clarinet players in certain jazz styles. See also Vibrato, page 296

Specific Tonal Considerations/Concerns for Clarinet Players

1. High Notes—As notes get higher, players need to increase air speed, firm the embouchure, and adjust the throat and oral cavity to achieve proper tonal response, tone quality, and pitch. Notes above high C-natural become increasingly more difficult to play

with good tone quality and intonation. In addition, the fingerings in the high range become increasingly complex and less intuitive. There is frequently more than one fingering for the same note above high F-natural. Players typically experiment to find the fingering that works best for them.

2. Throat Tones—Producing a good tone quality on the throat tones is challenging. Suggestions for improving the tone quality of these notes are under Throat Tones. See also Throat Tones, page 287

3. Embouchure—The firmness of the clarinet embouchure does not remain the same throughout the entire range of the instrument. As a rule, the embouchure is slightly firmer in the high range and slightly more relaxed in the low range. These adjustments are often minimal in the normal playing range. See also Embouchure, page 215

4. Reed—Players need to use appropriate reed strengths. Harder reeds are more resistant than softer reeds. A certain amount of resistance is needed to maintain a steady, rich tone quality and proper intonation. When reeds are too soft, the tone is thin and "quivery," and pitch is difficult to control. When reeds are too hard, the tone is airy, response is poor, pitch control suffers, and players' embouchures tire quickly. Reeds need to be hard enough to push back against the lower lip pressure to create a stable tone but not so hard that players have to "fight" the reed. See also Reeds, Single, page 265

Tone Quality: The characteristic sound associated with an instrument regarding tone color or timbre, and consistency, focus, and control of the air stream. The clarinet is an unusual instrument because it produces only odd partials. In addition, the reed gives the clarinet a great deal of pitch flexibility. As a result, achieving a full, consistent tone quality throughout the entire range of the instrument can be challenging. From a mechanical standpoint, tone quality is dependent upon several factors including instrument design, materials used in instrument construction, and, most important, the reed/mouthpiece combination, which is discussed under Reeds, Single, in this chapter and under Mouthpiece/Mouthpieces in chapter 1. From a player's standpoint, tone quality is largely dependent upon three factors: (1) the use of air, which is discussed in detail under Tone Production and Breathing/Breath Support/Air Control in chapter 1; and (2) the embouchure and oral cavity, which is discussed in detail under Tone Production and Embouchure.

Common terms associated with tone quality and common terms used to describe tone quality are identified and described under Tone Quality in chapter 1. See also Breathing/Breath Support/Air Control, page 10; Tone Quality, page 68

Key Questions

Q: Should I work on tone quality or intonation first?

A: Tone quality. If players cannot play with a good, consistent tone quality, working on intonation is counterproductive.

Tonguing: See Tonguing, page 71

Transpositions: The relationship between the written and sounding ranges of an instrument. Clarinets are transposing instruments. That is, clarinets do not sound as written. Members of the clarinet family, with only a few exceptions, are either in the keys of B-flat or E-flat. What follows is a list of clarinet transpositions. Summaries of transpositions for high and low clarinets are shown in figures 3.44 and 3.45. See also Range, page 252

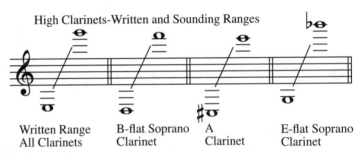

FIGURE 3.44. *High Clarinet Transpositions*

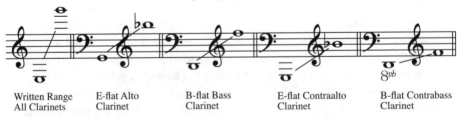

FIGURE 3.45. *Low Clarinet Transpositions*

CLARINET TRANSPOSITIONS

1. The E-flat soprano clarinet sounds a minor third higher than written. As a result, when it plays a written third-space C-natural, it sounds a concert E-flat a minor third higher than the written C-natural. It is one of the few instruments that transposes upward. The E-flat soprano clarinet sounds one octave higher than the E-flat alto clarinet and two octaves higher than the E-flat contra-alto clarinet.

2. The B-flat soprano clarinet sounds a major second lower than written. As a result, when it plays a written third-space C-natural, it sounds a concert B-flat one whole step lower than the written C-natural. The B-flat soprano clarinet sounds one octave higher than the bass clarinet and two octaves higher than the contrabass clarinet.

3. The E-flat alto clarinet sounds a major sixth lower than written. As a result, when it plays a written third-space C-natural, it sounds a concert E-flat a major sixth lower than the written C-natural. The E-flat alto clarinet sounds one octave lower than the E-flat soprano clarinet and one octave higher than the E-flat contra-alto clarinet. It transposes like the E-flat alto saxophone.

4. The B-flat bass clarinet sounds an octave and a major second lower than written. As a result, when it plays a written third-space C-natural, it sounds a concert B-flat a major ninth below the written C-natural. The bass clarinet sounds one octave lower than the B-flat soprano clarinet and one octave higher than the B-flat contrabass clarinet.

5. The A clarinet sounds a minor third lower than written. As a result, when it plays a written third-space C-natural, it sounds a concert A-natural a minor third lower than the written C-natural.

6. The E-flat contra-alto clarinet sounds an octave and a major sixth lower than written. As a result, when it plays a written third-space C-natural, it sounds a concert E-flat an octave and a major sixth below the written C-natural. The contra-alto sounds one octave lower than the E-flat alto clarinet.

7. The B-flat contrabass clarinet sounds two octaves and a major second lower than written. As a result, when it plays a written

third-space C-natural, it sounds a concert B-flat two octaves and a major second below the written C-natural. The contrabass clarinet sounds one octave lower than the B-flat bass clarinet and two octaves lower than the B-flat soprano clarinet.

Triple-Tonguing: A technique that enables performers to tongue triple patterns rapidly. See also Multiple-Tonguing, page 52

Tuning Rings: Thin rings usually made of plastic, fiberglass, or other synthetic materials that can be inserted between the barrel and upper joint to fill in the gap created when the barrel is pulled out. Professional players sometimes have sets of tuning rings, where each ring varies in thickness. Most sets contain two or three rings. Some players believe that tuning rings contribute to better tone quality and pitch consistency, and other players believe that they make no difference or that the difference is negligible. Companies that make tuning rings include AccuBore, Buffet, Howarth, Leblanc, and Muncy.

Tuning/Tuning Note Considerations: Tuning any instrument is a process that involves making mechanical adjustments (e.g., pulling out or pushing in a mouthpiece, slide, or instrument joint) so that the instrument will produce pitches that are in tune with a predetermined standard (e.g., A = 440). Tuning notes refer to specific pitches that are good to tune to on any given instrument. Considerations have been given to the notes most commonly used for tuning wind groups. Adjusting pitch and adjusting for pitch tendencies of the clarinet are discussed under Intonation. Considerations for tuning the clarinet appear separately in this section.

Tuning the Clarinet

1. Most clarinets are designed to be in tune (using A = 440 as a standard) when the barrel is pulled out slightly from the upper joint. This design feature enables players to raise the pitch if necessary by pushing the barrel in slightly.

2. As a general rule, players should tune at the barrel. That is, players can raise or lower the pitch by adjusting the position of the barrel in the upper joint. Pulling the barrel out will make the overall pitch flatter, while pushing the barrel in will make the overall pitch sharper. Generally, only small adjustments (no more than a quarter of an inch) need to be made for tuning purposes. The need to make large adjustments is often an indication of problems in other areas such as embouchure or air focus.

3. Advanced players often own more than one barrel joint. In such cases, making tuning adjustments may simply be a matter of using a different barrel. A shorter barrel makes the overall pitch go sharp, whereas a longer barrel makes the overall pitch go flat.

4. Advanced players sometimes insert tuning rings into the gap created when the barrel is pulled out for tuning purposes. Tuning rings fill in the gap created in the bore (inside the clarinet) and may eliminate acoustical problems that can result from simply pulling the barrel joint.

5. If the barrel has to be pulled out more than one-fourth of an inch to play in tune, the scale from note to note will probably be uneven. In this case, it may be better to divide the distance by three and make adjustments in three locations. Specifically, pull the barrel joint out from the upper joint, pull the upper joint out from the lower joint, and pull the lower joint out from the bell. Pull each joint one-third the total distance needed to play in tune. Pulling the upper joint often helps adjust the pitch more evenly throughout the normal playing range. In addition, while pulling the bell may help the pitch of third-space C-natural and third-line B-natural, it may also affect the pitch of low F-natural and low E-natural.

Tuning Note Considerations

1. Concert B-flat (written C-natural)—Third-space C-natural is an excellent tuning note. Low C-natural can be a little bit flat, and high C-natural tends to be sharp. Neither should be used as tuning notes.

2. Concert A-natural (written B-natural)—Third-line B-natural is a good tuning note. Low B-natural can be a bit flat, and high B-natural tends to be sharp. Neither should be used as tuning notes.

3. Concert F-natural (written G-natural)—A poor tuning note in all ranges.

Vamp: The area of the reed from which the bark has been removed starting at the U-shaped cut and extending toward the heart of the reed. In other words, the vamp is the sloped area of the lay between the shoulders and the heart. See also Reeds, Single, page 265

Vibrato: Clarinetists seldom use vibrato when playing classical or concert style music. However, in jazz or dance band styles, a jaw vibrato, like the vibrato used by saxophonists, is often used. Steps for developing vibrato are under Vibrato in chapter 1. See also Vibrato, page 74

Window, Mouthpiece: The open area of a mouthpiece cut out of the mouthpiece table and opposite the baffle. The flat side of reed covers the window. The term "window" is also occasionally used to refer to the opening between the throat and the chamber. See also Mouthpiece/Mouthpieces, page 247

Written Range: The written range for all clarinets is the same regardless of key or size; it is the sounding ranges that vary from instrument to instrument. Furthermore, most clarinet music is written in the treble clef; however, some low passages on bass clarinet and the contra clarinets are written in bass clef. The basic written range of all clarinets is from low E-natural (below the staff) to high G-natural one octave above the staff. Advanced players extend this range upward to high C-natural or D-natural depending on the demands of a particular piece. Suggested ranges for different playing levels are under Range. See also Instrument Family and Playing Considerations, page 232; Range, page 252; Transpositions, page 292

Clarinet Basic Fingerings

Clarinet Basic Fingerings

Clarinet Basic Fingerings

Clarinet Basic Fingerings

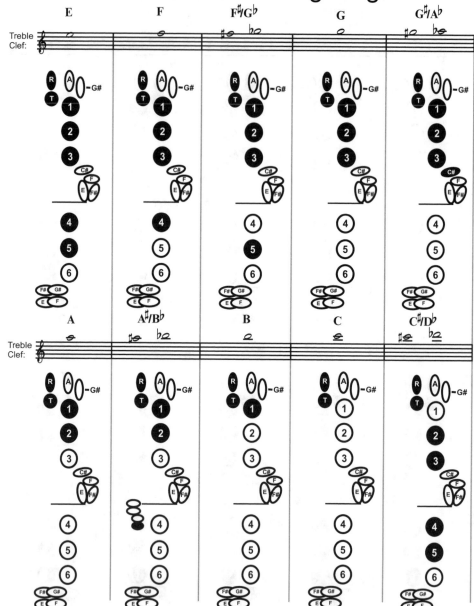

Clarinet Basic Fingerings

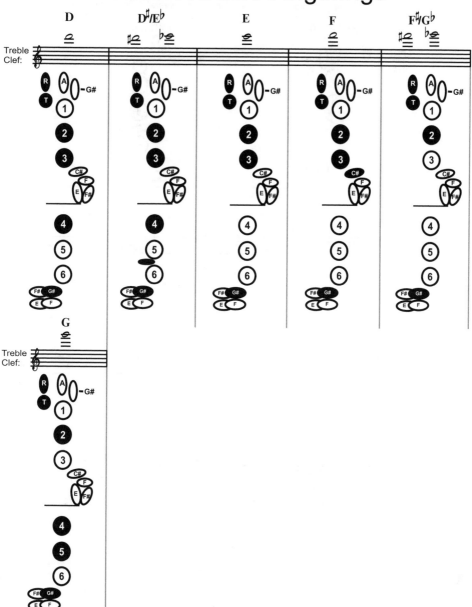

Clarinet Alternate Fingerings

The alternate fingerings shown below do not include the addition of right-hand fingers to facilitate throat tones

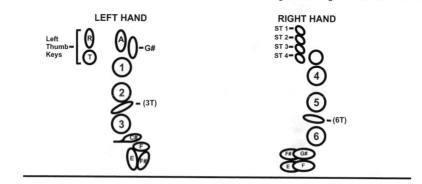

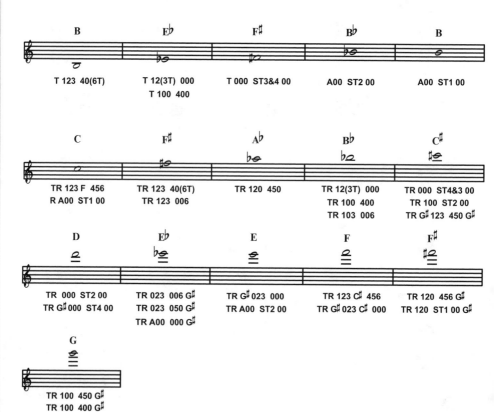

B	Eb	F♯	Bb	B
T 123 40(6T)	T 12(3T) 000	T 000 ST3&4 00	A00 ST2 00	A00 ST1 00
	T 100 400			

C	F♯	Ab	Bb	C♯
TR 123 F 456	TR 123 40(6T)	TR 120 450	TR 12(3T) 000	TR 000 ST4&3 00
R A00 ST1 00	TR 123 006		TR 100 400	TR 100 ST2 00
			TR 103 006	TR G♯ 123 450 G♯

D	Eb	E	F	F♯
TR 000 ST2 00	TR 023 006 G♯	TR G♯ 023 000	TR 123 C♯ 456	TR 120 456 G♯
TR G♯ 000 ST4 00	TR 023 050 G♯	TR A00 ST2 00	TR G♯ 023 C♯ 000	TR 120 ST1 00 G♯
	TR A00 000 G♯			

G
TR 100 450 G♯
TR 100 400 G♯
TR 023 450 G♯

Clarinet Altissimo Fingerings

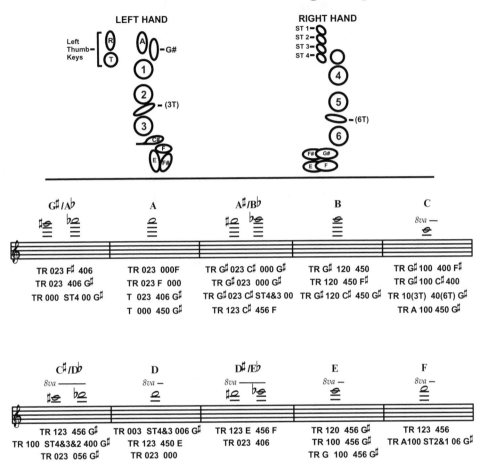

G♯/A♭

TR 023 F♯ 406
TR 023 406 G♯
TR 000 ST4 00 G♯

A

TR 023 000F
TR 023 F 000
T 023 406 G♯
T 000 450 G♯

A♯/B♭

TR G♯ 023 C♯ 000 G♯
TR G♯ 023 000 G♯
TR G♯ 023 C♯ ST4&3 00
TR 123 C♯ 456 F

B

TR G♯ 120 450
TR 120 450 F♯
TR G♯ 120 C♯ 450 G♯

C

TR G♯ 100 400 F♯
TR G♯ 100 C♯ 400
TR 10(3T) 40(6T) G♯
TR A 100 450 G♯

C♯/D♭

TR 123 456 G♯
TR 100 ST4&3&2 400 G♯
TR 023 056 G♯

D

TR 003 ST4&3 006 G♯
TR 123 450 E
TR 023 000

D♯/E♭

TR 123 E 456 F
TR 023 406

E

TR 120 456 G♯
TR 100 456 G♯
TR G 100 456 G♯

F

TR 123 456
TR A100 ST2&1 06 G♯

Clarinet Special Trill Fingerings

Trills performed with regular fingerings are not included

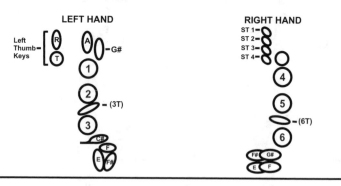

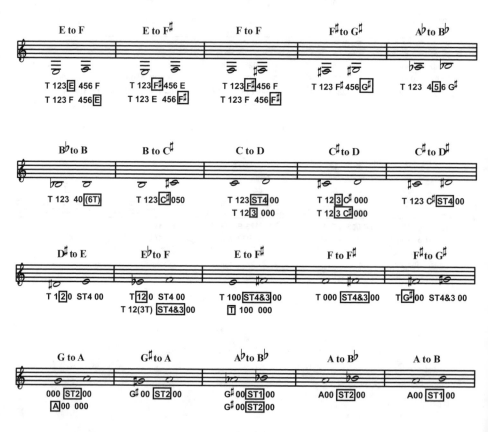

Clarinet Special Trill Fingerings

Trills performed with regular fingerings are not included

COMMON TECHNICAL FAULTS AND CORRECTIONS

Many problems in wind playing result from basic faults in the following areas: (1) instrument assembly, (2) embouchure formation, and (3) hand/holding/playing positions and posture. The following section provides information on how to correct technical faults frequently encountered in clarinet performance. Headings appear in alphabetical order.

Assembly

FAULT 1:   Not properly aligning the bridge keys between the upper and lower joints.

CORRECTION: Align the bridge keys properly during assembly. The upper joint bridge key will rest lightly on top of the lower joint bridge key. Make sure that the left hand keys are depressed on the upper joint so that the upper joint bridge key is raised to avoid bending bridge keys during assembly.

FAULT 2:   Not pushing the mouthpiece far enough into the barrel.

CORRECTION: Push the mouthpiece into the barrel all the way. The pitch is then adjusted by pushing or pulling the barrel into or out of the upper joint.

FAULT 3:   Improperly aligning the mouthpiece.

CORRECTION: Make sure the mouthpiece table (i.e., where the reed is placed) is lined up with the left thumb (F) hole. The mouthpiece alignment is correct when the player can keep his or her head straight (not tilted to one side) when playing.

FAULT 4:   Handling the instrument carelessly and putting unnecessary pressure on the keys and rods.

CORRECTION: Avoid unnecessary pressure on rods and keys by holding the upper and lower joints the way they are held when the instrument is being played. In other words, depress 1-2-3 (left hand) on the upper joint, and depress 4-5-6 (right hand) on the lower joint. Make sure that the corks are well greased. Assembling the clarinet while seated or standing next to the playing location will minimize unnecessary handling.

FAULT 5:   Not pushing the joints of the clarinet together all of the way.

CORRECTION: Push the joints in all the way when the clarinet is first assembled. Pitch adjustments are then made by pulling the barrel joint out until the desired pitch is achieved. If the clarinet is badly out of tune, other joints are sometimes pulled out slightly as well. Make sure that the corks are well greased so that the joints will go together and come apart relatively easily.

FAULT 6:   Improperly aligning the reed on the mouthpiece table.

CORRECTION: The reed should be centered on the mouthpiece table between the side rails and slightly below the tip rail. As a general rule, a very small amount of black (tip rail) should be showing above the tip of the reed. Pushing the reed up slightly past the tip slightly can improve tone quality of soft reeds and raise the pitch slightly.

FAULT 7:   Positioning the ligature improperly.

CORRECTION: Place the ligature slightly below the U-shaped cut of the reed and tighten just enough to hold the reed in place. Overtightening the ligature affects tone quality and reed response, and it will strip the ligature threads quickly.

FAULT 8:   Sliding the ligature over the reed/mouthpiece assembly.

CORRECTION: Make sure that the ligature is placed over the mouthpiece before the reed is placed or positioned on the mouthpiece table. While holding up the ligature toward the tip of the mouthpiece with the left hand, slide the reed between the ligature and the mouthpiece table and position the ligature slightly below the U-shaped cut. Align the reed properly and tighten the ligature screws enough to hold the reed in place. Using this method of placing the reed on the mouthpiece will help prevent chipped reeds.

Embouchure Formation

FAULT 1:   Not putting enough bottom lip over the teeth.

CORRECTION: See that the red part of the bottom lip is not visible (or is barely visible) at the point where the reed contacts the bottom lip; however, the amount of bottom lip over the teeth varies from player to player.

FAULT 2:   Taking too much mouthpiece into the mouth.

CORRECTION: Make sure that the mouthpiece is inserted into the mouth about one-third of the length of the beak. The exact position depends upon the player and the mouthpiece, and slight adjustments can be made based on tone quality and response.

FAULT 3:   Not firming the mouth corners and/or embouchure not sealing around the mouthpiece.

CORRECTION: Firm and flex the mouth corners, but do not draw them back excessively into a smiling position; the lip should be gently stretched against the bottom teeth, and the mouth corners should come back slightly. The clarinet embouchure is firmer than the saxophone embouchure. Players should think of surrounding the mouthpiece with even pressure from all sides (i.e., a drawstring effect) and form a seal around the reed so that air does not escape through the mouth corners.

FAULT 4:   Forming an embouchure that is too tight, or "biting."

CORRECTION: The clarinet embouchure is firmer than the saxophone embouchure; however, if the embouchure is too tight, the tone will be small and pinched. In addition, a tight embouchure can cause discomfort in the jaw. Relax the embouchure, lower the jaw slightly, and think of using warmer air.

FAULT 5:   Air escaping through the mouth corners.

CORRECTION: Air escapes when the surrounding muscles are not supporting inwardly toward the mouthpiece. Forming a proper embouchure will eliminate this problem. Players should think of surrounding the mouthpiece with even pressure from all sides (i.e., a drawstring effect) and form a seal around the reed so that air does not escape through the mouth corners.

FAULT 6:   Puffing the cheeks.

CORRECTION: Focus the air stream around the reed and through the tip opening. The mouth corners provide support inwardly toward the mouthpiece, and the chin should remain flat.

FAULT 7:   Top teeth not resting on the mouthpiece.

CORRECTION: Rest the top teeth lightly on top of the mouthpiece without biting into the mouthpiece. If players find this placement uncomfortable, a thin rubber pad can be placed on top of the mouthpiece.

FAULT 8: Putting too much pressure on top of the mouthpiece with the top teeth.

CORRECTION: Rest the top teeth on top of the mouthpiece lightly without biting the mouthpiece. Too much pressure results when players force the head downward. Players should maintain proper position of the head during play.

Hand/Holding/Instrument Playing Positions and Posture

FAULT 1: Elbows too far from or too close to the body while playing.

CORRECTION: Elbows should be held out from the body in a relaxed, comfortable position.

FAULT 2: Elbows resting on knees while playing.

CORRECTION: Elbows should be held out from the body in a relaxed, comfortable position. Younger, smaller players sometimes rest their arms on their knees when they get tired. Take frequent breaks to eliminate fatigue and encourage proper playing positions at all times.

FAULT 3: Holding the clarinet at an improper angle causing problems with hand position and embouchure.

CORRECTION: The clarinet should be centered with the body and held out at about a 35- to 40-degree angle. This angle will put the clarinet somewhere between the knees depending on the size of the student. The exact placement is determined by the tone quality. The angle of the clarinet is the same, whether the player is standing or sitting. On the lower clarinets, position the end pin slightly back of vertical toward the player. On the lower clarinets, the mouthpiece enters the mouth almost straight, with only a slightly upward angle.

FAULT 4: Head tilted too much to one side.

CORRECTION: Keep the head straight at all times. Make certain that the mouthpiece is not twisted to one side and that the mouthpiece table and reed are aligned with the left hand thumb (F) hole.

FAULT 5:   Slouching.

CORRECTION: Sit up (or stand) straight, keep the chin in a normal position (not up or down), keep the eyes straight ahead, and keep the shoulders and back straight but relaxed.

FAULT 6:   Resting the bell of the clarinet on the knees or holding the bell of the clarinet with the knees.

CORRECTION: Sit farther forward on the chair and keep the feet flat on the floor with the knees apart. Center the clarinet between the knees. This position helps ensure a proper mouthpiece angle and a better overall playing position.

FAULT 7:   Not placing the left thumb on the thumb rest at the proper angle.

CORRECTION: The left thumb should be placed at an angle (approximately 1 o'clock) so that it can cover the thumb (F) hole and operate the register key simultaneously with a small rocking motion.

FAULT 8:   Fingers are straight or "locked."

CORRECTION: Fingers should be slightly curved so that a C shape is formed between the thumb and fingers.

FAULT 9:   Allowing the right-hand or left-hand little finger to droop or float out of position.

CORRECTION: Lightly touch or rest the right-hand and left-hand little fingers just above the D-sharp (G-sharp in the lower octave) and G-sharp keys (C-sharp in the lower octave), respectively, to minimize finger movement and encourage technical proficiency.

FAULT 10:   Pushing the right thumb too far under the thumb rest.

CORRECTION: See that the right thumb contacts the thumb rest between the thumbnail and the knuckle with the ball of the thumb resting against the clarinet. Depending on the make or type of clarinet and the placement of the thumb rest, the thumb may contact the thumb rest slightly below the knuckle. The right thumb supports the majority of he clarinet's weight, so proper positioning is essential.

FAULT 11: Bending the wrists.

CORRECTION: Keep the wrists relatively straight; however, a slight bend is normal. An excessively bent wrist is often the result of the instrument being too close or too far from the body and/or an improperly assembled instrument. Make sure that the upper and lower joint bridge keys are aligned and that the mouthpiece table and reed are aligned with the left thumb (F) hole. Also, make sure that the elbows are properly positioned.

FAULT 12: Holding the fingers too far from keys.

CORRECTION: Keep the fingers close to the keys while playing to eliminate unnecessary motion. Keeping the fingers close to the keys facilitates proper playing technique. On open holes, players must keep their fingers close to the tone holes or keys, but they must leave enough room above the tone holes for the air to escape freely.

FAULT 13: Improperly adjusting the neck strap.

CORRECTION: If a neck strap is used, adjust the neck strap so that the mouthpiece comes directly to the mouth when the proper playing position has been established. The neck strap is improperly adjusted if players have to reach up or down for the mouthpiece. The adjustment mechanism on the neck strap can slide out of place during play. As a result, players typically need to make small adjustments periodically to maintain the position of the neck strap.

COMMON PROBLEMS, CAUSES, AND SOLUTIONS FOR CLARINET

Problems in wind instrument playing relate to some aspect of sound. That is, incorrect assembly is not a problem; poor tone quality or squeaking is a problem. Incorrect assembly is simply one common cause of such problems. Understanding this distinction makes it easier to apply effective solutions to problems. The following section provides information on solving problems frequently encountered in clarinet performance. The main headings are: Articulation Problems, Intonation Problems, Performance/Technical Problems, and Tone Quality and Response Problems.

Articulation Problems

PROBLEM: Audible dip or scoop in pitch during initial attacks.

CAUSE 1: Excessive movement of the embouchure (especially the jaw and tongue) while tonguing.

SOLUTION 1:   Use light, quick movements of the tongue and maintain a consistent embouchure. Use a "tu" syllable not a "twa" syllable. Practice tonguing in front of a mirror and use the visual feedback to help eliminate jaw movement.

CAUSE 2:   Embouchure not set properly before the attack.

SOLUTION 2:   Allow enough time to be physically and mentally set before the attack. That is, the embouchure must be set properly for the note being played. When the embouchure is too tight or too loose for a particular note at the point of attack, players will make an immediate adjustment or shift to correct the pitch. This shift causes an audible dip or scoop in the attack.

PROBLEM: Heavy, thick, and/or sluggish attacks.

CAUSE 1:   Too much tongue contacting the reed on the attacks coupled with a slow tonguing action.

SOLUTION 1:   Minimize tongue movement. Use a light, quick tonguing action and make sure the tip of the tongue strikes the tip of the reed (or slightly below the tip) as described under Tonguing in chapter 1. Think of moving only the tip of the tongue during the tonguing process and use a "tu" attack for normal tonguing.

CAUSE 2:   Tonguing too far down on the reed.

SOLUTION 2:   The tip of the tongue strikes the tip of the reed. Make sure the tongue is pulled back or arched slightly in the mouth (i.e., positioned high in the oral cavity) to begin the tonguing process. This position places the tongue slightly higher in the mouth to start. Think of moving only the tip of the tongue quickly and lightly.

CAUSE 3:   Tongue disrupting the air stream.

SOLUTION 3:   Make sure the tongue is pulled back or arched slightly in the mouth to begin the tonguing process, and increase the quickness of the tongue strike against the tip of the reed. If the tongue is too low or too high in the mouth, or if the tongue moves too slowly, the air stream is disrupted, causing sluggish attacks.

PROBLEM: Mistimed attacks (tongue, embouchure, air).

CAUSE 1:   Tongue and air stream not coordinated.

SOLUTION 1: Practice coordinating the tongue and the air stream by attacking one note at a time. Think of starting the tongue and the air at the same time on attacks. Although it is the release of the tongue from the reed that actually starts a tone, the air stream and the tongue must work together.

CAUSE 2: Embouchure not set properly before the attack.

SOLUTION 2: Allow enough time to be physically and mentally set before the attack. That is, the embouchure must be set properly for the note being played. An embouchure that is too tight or too loose for the note being played can delay the response of the attack.

CAUSE 3: Too much embouchure movement during attacks.

SOLUTION 3: Set the embouchure properly for the note being played. Maintain embouchure formation and avoid using a "jawing" action. Think of moving only the tip of the tongue.

CAUSE 4: Player not set to play.

SOLUTION 4: Maintain proper playing positions (physical readiness), and internally hear the pitches before playing them (mental readiness).

PROBLEM: Inability to execute clean slurs.

CAUSE 1: Inconsistent air stream.

SOLUTION 1: Do not change the air stream from note to note. Instead, blow a consistent stream of air and simply move the fingers. On clarinet, it is generally necessary to adjust the air stream for various pitches in slurred passages if they involve large interval movement. In addition, adjustments in air speed and air volume should be made as necessary to accommodate the dynamic level.

CAUSE 2: Too much embouchure movement throughout a slurred passage.

SOLUTION 2: Use the same embouchure throughout the entire passage unless large intervals are being played. In general, making large shifts in embouchure for various notes disrupts the air stream and is often unnecessary on clarinet.

CAUSE 3: Fingers not coordinated.

SOLUTION 3:   Keep the fingers close to the keys and depress them quickly and smoothly from note to note. Avoid excess finger movement, and avoid "slapping" the key rings and tone holes.

CAUSE 4:   Player not set to play.

SOLUTION 4:   Maintain proper playing positions (physical readiness), and internally "hear" the pitches before playing them (mental readiness).

PROBLEM: Inability to execute clean releases.

CAUSE 1:   Inappropriate use of tongue cutoffs.

SOLUTION 1:   Use breath releases rather than tongue cutoffs in most musical contexts because tongue cutoffs tend to be harsh and abrupt. Tongue cutoffs are appropriate in some jazz styles.

CAUSE 2:   Putting the tongue back on the reed too hard on tongue cutoffs.

SOLUTION 2:   Make sure that the players are not using too much tongue, which distorts the attacks. When tongue cutoffs are appropriate (e.g., some jazz styles), the tongue should make a modest amount of contact on the tip of the reed. The rest of the "attack" consists of a sudden increase in air.

CAUSE 3:   Not stopping the air at the point of release.

SOLUTION 3:   Practice maintaining an open air column from the diaphragm into the instrument, and stop the air by suspending it midstream as if lightly gasping. Using the throat as a valve and/or pushing the air on releases both prevent clean releases.

CAUSE 4:   Not "lifting" on the release.

SOLUTION 4:   Think of gasping lightly on the release and directing the air stream upward. Thinking this way helps stop the flow of air quickly while maintaining an open air column. Make sure to maintain a consistent embouchure during the release.

CAUSE 5:   Closing off the embouchure and/or throat, or using the embouchure and/or throat as a valve for stopping the air.

SOLUTION 5:   Think of gasping lightly on the release and directing the air stream upward. Thinking this way helps stop the flow of air quickly while maintaining an open air column, an open throat, and a proper embouchure. The embouchure and throat should remain unchanged on breath releases; it is the air that is stopped to release a tone.

PROBLEM: Inability to execute a controlled accent.

CAUSE 1:   Not balancing the air stream and tongue appropriately.

SOLUTION 1:   On an accented note, "lift off" of the air; that is, think of gasping lightly and directing the air stream upward on the release. As a rule, do not use tongue cutoffs on accented notes. On most accents, the weight of the tongue is not increased on the attack. Rather, the accent is produced by a sudden increase in air.

CAUSE 2:   Too much tongue on releases in staccato passages with repeated accents.

SOLUTION 2:   Think of tonguing each note consistently and evenly, and the releases will take care of themselves. In rapid patterns, the release of each note (except the first) in the pattern becomes the attack for each subsequent note.

Intonation Problems

PROBLEM: Pitch generally flat in all registers.

CAUSE 1:   Barrel pulled out too far.

SOLUTION 1:   Determine the appropriate barrel placement by using a tuner, and note the approximate position. Position the barrel in the same place each time the instrument is assembled, and then make small adjustments as needed. Some players use tuning rings to ensure the same barrel position each time the clarinet is assembled.

CAUSE 2:   Embouchure too loose.

SOLUTION 2:   Think of surrounding the reed with warm air as if saying "who," and firm the embouchure slightly. Think of decreasing the imaginary circle of air into the instrument, while still maintaining an open air stream. That is, use a slightly more focused air stream. Make sure the top lip pushes gently down onto the top of the mouthpiece.

CAUSE 3:   Too much air, or overblowing.

SOLUTION 3:   Use a controlled, steady air stream, and slow the air stream slightly.

CAUSE 4:   Not compensating for the natural tendency of the clarinet to go flat in loud passages.

SOLUTION 4:   Raise the direction of the air stream slightly to compensate for the drop in pitch, and use a more focused oral cavity. It may be necessary to firm the embouchure slightly on pitches that are significantly flat, especially in the fortissimo dynamic range. Make sure players are not taking too much mouthpiece into the mouth.

CAUSE 5:   Air stream directed downward too much.

SOLUTION 5:   Surround the reed with warm air as if saying "who" and think of keeping the air parallel to the plane of the reed. For a more narrow focus, think of blowing air through and around the tip opening and saying the syllable "ee," which positions the tongue higher in the mouth.

CAUSE 6:   Slouching.

SOLUTION 6:   When seated, sit up straight (but avoid being rigid or tense) with feet flat on the floor. Sit toward the front edge of the chair. When standing, stand straight (avoid being tense or rigid) and position the feet about shoulder width apart. Do not rest the clarinet on the front of the chair or on the knees.

CAUSE 7:   Holding the clarinet at an incorrect angle.

SOLUTION 7:   The clarinet should be held at a 35- to 40-degree angle away from the body. If the clarinet is held too far from the body, the pitch tends to go flat because the pressure on the reed is decreased. That is, the embouchure's ability to support the reed properly is compromised and the pitch will be flat.

CAUSE 8:   Head tilted downward or forward too much.

SOLUTION 8:   Bring the mouthpiece directly to the mouth. Players should not have to reach upward or downward for the mouthpiece. Reaching for the mouthpiece impairs the embouchure's ability to support the reed properly and causes the pitch to be flat.

CAUSE 9:   Pads are too close to the tone holes.

SOLUTION 9:   Have a knowledgeable repair technician adjust the pads to the proper height.

CAUSE 10:   Reed is too soft.

SOLUTION 10:   Using harder reeds will offer more resistance and raise the pitch. Soft reeds tend to play flat.

CAUSE 11:   Joints not properly assembled.

SOLUTION 11:   While the barrel is designed to be pulled out slightly for tuning purposes, the other joints of the clarinet should generally be pushed together all the way. If the clarinet is very sharp, it may be appropriate to pull out some of the joints (other than the barrel) slightly.

PROBLEM: Pitch generally sharp in all registers.

CAUSE 1:   Barrel pushed in too far.

SOLUTION 1:   Determine the appropriate barrel placement by using a tuner, and note the approximate position. Position the barrel in the same place each time the instrument is assembled, and then make small adjustments as needed. Some players use tuning rings to ensure the same barrel position each time the clarinet is assembled.

CAUSE 2:   Embouchure too tight or biting.

SOLUTION 2:   Relax the embouchure and lower the jaw slightly. Make sure the mouth corners are drawn inward rather than pulled back and that the lower lip is not stretched too tightly over the teeth. It may be helpful to think of increasing the imaginary circle of air into the instrument. That is, use a slightly more open air stream.

CAUSE 3:   Too little air.

SOLUTION 3:   Use a controlled, steady air stream, and increase air speed.

CAUSE 4:   Not compensating for the natural tendency to go sharp as less air is used.

SOLUTION 4:   Lower the direction of the air stream slightly to compensate for the rise in pitch and use a more open oral cavity. It may be necessary to relax the embouchure and lower the jaw slightly on pitches that are significantly sharp, especially in the pianissimo dynamic range.

CAUSE 5:   Air stream directed upward too much.

SOLUTION 5:   Surround the reed with warm air as if saying "who" and maintain a consistent air stream. It may help to think of blowing air through and around the tip opening.

CAUSE 6:   Holding the clarinet at an incorrect angle.

SOLUTION 6:   Hold the clarinet at a 35- to 40-degree angle away from the body. If the clarinet is held too close to the body, the pitch tends to go sharp because the pressure on the reed is decreased. That is, when the mouthpiece angle causes too much lower lip pressure on the reed, the pitch goes sharp.

CAUSE 7:   Pads are too far from tone holes.

SOLUTION 7:   Have a knowledgeable repair technician adjust the pads to the proper height.

CAUSE 8:   Reed is too hard.

SOLUTION 8:   Using softer reeds will offer less resistance and lower the pitch. Hard reeds tend to play sharp.

PROBLEM: Pitch is inconsistent throughout the playing range.

CAUSE 1:   Inconsistent air stream.

SOLUTION 1:   Do not change the air stream from note to note. Instead, blow a consistent stream of air and simply move the fingers. On clarinet, it is generally necessary to adjust the air stream for various pitches in slurred passages if they involve large interval movement. In addition, adjustments in air speed and air volume should be made as necessary to accommodate the dynamic level.

CAUSE 2:   Inconsistent embouchure.

SOLUTION 2:   Form a good basic embouchure and make sure that there is enough bottom lip over the teeth. Practice playing long tones to develop the embouchure muscles, and concentrate on keeping the embouchure consistent at all times. Use a mirror on a regular basis to check embouchure formation until proper habits are formed.

CAUSE 3:   Lack of proper breath support.

SOLUTION 3:   Work on breathing exercises with and without the clarinet to help develop breath support. Take full breaths and practice playing long tones at all dynamic levels. Focus on maintaining a consistent air speed appropriate for each dynamic level. Practice extensively at softer dynamic levels because it is harder to maintain proper breath support at softer dynamic levels than it is at louder dynamic levels. In addition, breath support is often compromised when playing technical passages, because players tend to focus on technique at the expense of

proper breath support. Practice maintaining breath support in technical passages.

CAUSE 4: Slouching.

SOLUTION 4: When seated, sit up straight (but avoid being rigid or tense) with feet flat on the floor. Sit toward the front edge of the chair. When standing, stand straight (avoid being tense or rigid) and position the feet about shoulder width apart. Do not rest the clarinet on the front of the chair or on the knees.

CAUSE 5: Shifting the angle at which the clarinet is held.

SOLUTION 5: Hold the clarinet at a 35- to 40-degree angle away from the body. If the clarinet is held too close to the body or too far away from the body, the embouchure's ability to support the reed properly is comprised and the pitch will be inconsistent.

PROBLEM: Pitch is inconsistent throughout the playing range.

CAUSE 1: Inconsistent air stream.

SOLUTION 1: Do not change the air stream from note to note. Instead, blow a consistent stream of air and simply move the fingers. On clarinet, it is generally necessary to adjust the air stream for various pitches in slurred passages if they involve large interval movement. In addition, adjustments in air speed and air volume may need to be made to accommodate the dynamic level.

PROBLEM: Playing out of tune without adjusting.

NOTE: A detailed account of adjusting pitch is under Intonation in chapter 1.

CAUSE 1: Inability to hear beats or roughness.

SOLUTION 1: Focus on hearing the beats or pulsations that occur when pitches are out of tune. Play long tone unisons with other players and listen for beats. Deliberately playing extremely flat and sharp to accentuate the beats will help players learn to hear beats.

CAUSE 2: Not knowing how to adjust pitch on the instrument.

SOLUTION 2: Consider various options. There are several ways to adjust pitch involving the mouthpiece position, embouchure, throat, oral cavity, air stream, and alternate fingerings. Players need to learn how each of these factors affects pitch.

CAUSE 3:   The physical skills necessary to adjust pitch on the instrument are not developed.

SOLUTION 3:   Practice adjusting pitch every day and continue developing embouchure skills. Relax and tighten the embouchure, focus the air stream upward and downward, open and close the throat and oral cavity, and try alternate fingerings. Learn "what does what" so that appropriate adjustments can be made when necessary.

Performance/Technical Problems

PROBLEM: Sloppy playing in tongued technical passages.

CAUSE 1:   Tongue and fingers not coordinated.

SOLUTION 1:   Practice simple interval exercises slowly with a metronome, and make sure that the tongue and fingers move together. Keep the fingers close to the keys during these exercises to avoid excessive finger movement. As control is gained, progress to more difficult exercises and continue to practice with a metronome. Gradually speed up the exercises, but make sure that proper finger-tongue coordination is maintained.

CAUSE 2:   Tonguing speed too slow.

SOLUTION 2:   Using a metronome, start by practicing a variety of simple rhythm patterns on isolated pitches at a slow tempo. Gradually increase the speed and difficulty of the exercises. Use a "tip to tip" (tip of the tongue to the tip of the reed) technique and keep the tongue motion light and quick. Periodically, practice tonguing slightly faster than is comfortable. Develop control and rhythmic precision by changing the tempo frequently.

PROBLEM: Sloppy playing overall.

CAUSE 1:   Poor Hand/Holding/Instrument/Playing Positions and Posture.

SOLUTION 1:   Make sure that the playing basics are maintained at all times. Detailed discussion of these playing basics is under Hand/Holding/Instrument/Playing Positions and Posture.

CAUSE 2:   Poor instrument action.

SOLUTION 2:   Make sure the key mechanisms have been properly adjusted, cleaned, and oiled. Excessively heavy or uneven action is usually a result of poorly adjusted key mechanisms, poorly adjusted pads, and/ or bent key mechanisms. In addition, make sure the springs are in proper working condition. Weak springs sometimes bobble or bounce, which inhibits technical fluidity.

CAUSE 3: Awkward fingerings.

SOLUTION 3:   Use alternate fingerings when appropriate to maximize technical fluidity. Preparing the right hand when crossing the break and using basic chromatic fingerings contribute significantly to clean playing.

PROBLEM: Speed of the fingers seems slow in technical passages.

CAUSE 1: Tenseness in the fingers and hands.

SOLUTION 1:   Practice tough passages slowly at first to gain control, and focus on staying relaxed; trying too hard or forcing the fingers to move during technical passages slows down the fingers. Gradually increase the tempo of the passage, and develop the habit of staying relaxed at all tempos.

PROBLEM: An excessive amount of key noise can be heard when the keys are depressed.

CAUSE 1: Key mechanisms need to be oiled.

SOLUTION 1:   Oil the mechanisms. As a rule, the key mechanisms should be oiled lightly once a month or so. Clacking sounds are often caused by metal-to-metal contact, which results in excessive wear of the key mechanisms.

CAUSE 2: Pushing keys down too hard or slapping the keys.

SOLUTION 2:   Use only enough finger pressure to seal the pads (or fingers) against the tone holes. Stay relaxed, and think of playing smoothly and efficiently. Keeping the fingers close to the keys will help eliminate the tendency to slap the fingers down.

CAUSE 3: Corks or felts are missing.

SOLUTION 3:   Sometimes the corks or felts that prevent metal-to-metal contact (and also help regulate proper key height) fall off. In such cases, the clacking is quite noticeable and the affected key or keys will often appear out of line with the rest of the keys in the stack. Replace missing corks or felts and adjust height appropriately.

PROBLEM: Skips and leaps not clean.

CAUSE 1:   Fingers not coordinated.

SOLUTION 1:   Practice simple interval exercises slowly with a metronome, and focus on moving the tongue and fingers together. Keep the fingers close to the keys during these exercises to avoid excessive finger movement. It may also help to slur all exercises because tonguing often covers up poor finger coordination. As control is gained, progress to more difficult exercises and continue to practice with a metronome. Gradually speed up the exercises, making sure that proper finger-tongue coordination is maintained.

CAUSE 2:   Air stream not maintained properly.

SOLUTION 2:   Using air improperly in passages with skips and leaps causes coordination problems with the tongue, fingers, and air stream. Maintain a consistent air stream at all dynamic levels. Players tend to focus on skips and leaps at the expense of proper breath support. Focus on maintaining breath support in all technical passages.

CAUSE 3:   Improper left thumb (register key) action.

SOLUTION 3:   Make sure that the left thumb covers the thumb (F) hole at an angle such that the thumbnail is directed at approximately 1 o'clock (or slightly toward 12 o'clock). This position allows the thumb to reach the register key with a simple rocking motion, rather than a jumping motion. Using a jumping motion and having the left thumb out of position hinders technique, especially in rapid passages, and it often causes squeaks.

PROBLEM: Poor finger-tongue coordination.

CAUSE 1:   Poor playing habits resulting from playing too fast, too soon.

SOLUTION 1:   Practice simple interval exercises slowly with a metronome, and focus on moving the tongue and fingers together. Keep the fingers close to the keys during these exercises to avoid excessive finger movement. Slur all exercises because tonguing often covers up poor finger coordination. As control is gained, progress to more difficult exercises. Continue to practice with a metronome, and continue to slur the exercises.

CAUSE 2:   Air stream not maintained properly.

SOLUTION 2:   Maintain a consistent air stream at all dynamic levels; improper use of air in technical passages causes coordination problems between the tongue, fingers, and air stream. Players tend to focus on technique at the expense of proper breath support. Focus on maintaining breath support until proper support becomes automatic.

| PROBLEM: | Uneven finger movement within the beat. |

| CAUSE 1: | Poor control of individual fingers. |

SOLUTION 1:   Playing fast is one thing; playing with control is another. Make sure proper hand positions are maintained. Use a metronome and practice exercises that isolate each finger. Practice these exercises slowly and deliberately at first and gradually increase tempo, while always focusing on control. The ring fingers and the little fingers can be particularly problematic, so work on these fingers extensively.

| CAUSE 2: | Poor coordination of cross-fingerings. |

SOLUTION 2:   Make sure proper hand positions are maintained; when more awkward fingerings are mixed with less awkward fingerings in technical passages, uneven finger movement within the beat often occurs. Use a metronome and practice exercises that isolate problematic combinations of fingerings. Practice these exercises slowly and deliberately at first and gradually increase tempo, while always focusing on control.

Tone Quality and Response Problems

| PROBLEM: | The tone is small and weak. |

| CAUSE 1: | Lack of sufficient air, air speed, and/or breath support. |

SOLUTION 1:   Use more air, increase air speed, and keep the air stream consistent. Take full breaths and practice playing long tones at all dynamic levels. Focus on maintaining a consistent air speed appropriate for each dynamic level. Practice extensively at softer dynamic levels because it is harder to maintain proper breath support at softer dynamic levels than it is at louder dynamic levels.

| CAUSE 2: | Embouchure too tight, or biting. |

SOLUTION 2:   Relax the embouchure and/or lower the jaw slightly. Think of saying "who" and surround the reed with warm air. Think of increasing the size of the imaginary circle of air into the instrument. That is, use a slightly more open air stream.

CAUSE 3:   Tight or closed throat.

SOLUTION 3:   Relax or open the throat as if saying "ah." Saying the syllable "ah" and shifting to an "oo" syllable while exhaling will open the throat and oral cavity and keep the embouchure round.

PROBLEM: An unfocused tone quality.

CAUSE 1:   Improper direction of the air stream.

SOLUTION 1:   Direct the air stream toward the tip opening. Surround the reed with warm air as if saying "who" to relax the embouchure, and keep the air parallel to the reed plane.

CAUSE 2:   Embouchure too loose.

SOLUTION 2:   Think of surrounding the reed with warm air as if saying "who," and firm the embouchure slightly. Think of decreasing the imaginary circle of air into the instrument. That is, use a slightly more focused air stream.

CAUSE 3:   Mouthpiece is not centered in the mouth.

SOLUTION 3:   Use a mirror on a regular basis to check mouthpiece placement until proper habits are formed.

CAUSE 4:   Not enough bottom lip over the teeth, making embouchure control inconsistent.

SOLUTION 4:   Put more of the lower lip over the teeth and listen for improved tone quality. Very little red (if any) should be showing at the point where the lip contacts the reed.

CAUSE 5:   Mouthpiece enters the mouth at an incorrect angle.

SOLUTION 5:   Bring the clarinet to the mouth. Do not reach upward or downward for the mouthpiece. Adjust the angle of the clarinet so that it is at a 35- to 40-degree angle away from the body. If the mouthpiece enters at an improper angle, the embouchure's ability to support the reed properly is impaired and the tone will be unfocused.

PROBLEM: Lack of tone control.

CAUSE 1:   Embouchure is inconsistent.

SOLUTION 1:   Form a good basic embouchure and make sure that there is enough bottom lip over the teeth. Practice playing long tones to develop the embouchure muscles, and focus on keeping the embouchure consistent at all times. Use a mirror on a regular basis to check embouchure formation until proper habits are formed. Sometimes, a player's embouchure is unstable because the reed is too soft to provide sufficient resistance against the embouchure pressure, resulting in a "quivery" tone. Using a harder reed may help stabilize the embouchure.

CAUSE 2: Inconsistent breath support and/or control of the air stream.

SOLUTION 2: Practice breathing exercises with and without the clarinet to help develop breath support. Take full breaths and practice playing long tones at all dynamic levels, keeping the air moving around the reed. Focus on maintaining a consistent air speed appropriate for each dynamic level. Practice extensively at softer dynamic levels because it is harder to maintain proper breath support at softer dynamic levels than it is at louder dynamic levels. Maintain breath support in technical passages. That is, breath support is often compromised when playing technical passages because players tend to focus on technique at the expense of proper breath support.

CAUSE 3: Inconsistent hand/holding/instrument/playing positions and posture.

SOLUTION 3: Develop and follow a daily routine so that maintaining proper positions becomes habit. Proper placements of the left and right thumbs and proper adjustment of the instrument angle are particularly important for tone control. A detailed discussion of these playing basics is under Hand/Holding/Instrument/Playing Positions and Posture.

CAUSE 4: Inconsistent throat and/or tongue positions.

SOLUTION 4: Keep the throat open and the tongue relatively flat and relaxed in the mouth when slurring, and keep it drawn back slightly (arched) in the mouth when tonguing. Unnecessary movement and tension of the throat and tongue disrupts the air stream and can affect tone control, tone quality, and pitch.

CAUSE 5: Mouthpiece does not enter the mouth straight on.

SOLUTION 5: Make sure the mouthpiece and clarinet are centered with the lips and body so that the mouthpiece enters the mouth at a straight angle. Sometimes, placing the music stand too far off to one side causes the mouthpiece to enter the mouth at a diagonal.

CAUSE 6: Mouthpiece baffle is too high.

SOLUTION 6:   Consider using a mouthpiece with a medium baffle; it will be much easier to control and will result in a much warmer tone quality.

PROBLEM: Lack of dynamic control.

CAUSE 1:   Insufficient control of the air stream and/or insufficient breath support throughout the dynamic range.

SOLUTION 1:   Practice playing long tones at one dynamic level over a set number of counts. When long tones can be played evenly at one dynamic level, practice playing long tones at different dynamic levels. Later, practice playing crescendi and decrescendi on long tones evenly over a set number of counts from one dynamic level to another. The softest and loudest dynamic levels can be particularly problematic. As a result, practicing at softer and louder dynamic levels is particularly important for tonal control.

CAUSE 2:   Making unnecessary embouchure adjustments when changing dynamics.

SOLUTION 2:   Keep the embouchure relatively stable and consistent regardless of the dynamic level. Exceptions include: (1) in the pianissimo range, relax the embouchure slightly to compensate for the tendency of the pitch to go sharp; and (2) in the fortissimo range, firm the embouchure slightly to compensate for the tendency of the pitch to go flat.

CAUSE 3:   Using inappropriate reed strengths.

SOLUTION 3:   Use reeds that are commensurate with playing experience. Reeds that are too hard are difficult to control and tend to respond poorly or "cut out" at softer dynamic levels. Reeds that are too soft restrict the ability to play loudly.

PROBLEM: The low notes do not respond well.

CAUSE 1:   Leaks in the pads.

SOLUTION 1:   Check for leaks and replace any worn-out pads. The larger pads on the lower keys tend to leak more than smaller pads. Check the larger pads often for leakage.

CAUSE 2:   Reed is too hard.

SOLUTION 2:   Using a slightly softer reed will offer less resistance and will improve response in the low range.

Cause 3:   Not enough air and/or air stream too slow.

SOLUTION 3:   Use more air and increase air speed on the initial attacks for low notes. Once the note has responded, less air is needed to keep the tone sounding. Find a balance and adjust air accordingly.

Cause 4:   Embouchure too tight or "Biting."

SOLUTION 4:   Relax the embouchure and lower the jaw slightly in the low range and maintain an open throat and oral cavity. Focus for the particular note being played. Low notes do require more air than high notes.

PROBLEM: The high notes do not respond well.

Cause 1:   Reed is too soft.

SOLUTION 1:   Move up in reed strength. The reed needs to provide enough resistance to vibrate at higher frequencies. In addition, soft reeds "close off" more easily under embouchure pressure in the high range than do hard reeds.

Cause 2:   Embouchure too tight, or biting.

SOLUTION 2:   Relax the embouchure. Drop the jaw slightly to open the embouchure. As a rule, do not tighten too much in the high range. Use the same basic embouchure in the high range that is used in the middle range, and then focus the oral cavity slightly for the particular note being played.

Cause 3:   Overblowing.

SOLUTION 3:   Focus on the note being played and use a controlled air stream. There is no need to blow harder in the high range; however, slight adjustments in the oral cavity do need to be made. Practice playing familiar tunes in the high range to develop control.

PROBLEM: A loud, raucous, squawky tone.

Cause 1:   Too much mouthpiece in the mouth.

SOLUTION 1:   Take less of the mouthpiece in the mouth. Only about one-third of the beak should be inserted into the mouth. Players with a pronounced underbite tend to appear as though they are not taking enough mouthpiece in the mouth, whereas players with an overbite tend may look as if they are taking too much mouthpiece in the mouth. Let the tone quality be the determining factor for the best mouthpiece placement.

CAUSE 2:   Too much air with an unfocused embouchure.

SOLUTION 2:   Use a proper embouchure. Think of surrounding the reed with warm air as if saying "who." It may also help to think of decreasing the imaginary circle of air into the instrument. That is, use a slightly more focused air stream. Focus the throat and oral cavity for the pitch being played.

CAUSE 3:   Improper focus of the air stream.

SOLUTION 3:   Think of blowing air through and around the tip opening. Think of surrounding the reed with air as if saying "who." Experiment with air direction until the best tone quality is achieved. If the air is still out of focus, think of saying "ee" to further focus the air stream.

PROBLEM: A thin, pinched tone.

CAUSE 1:   Embouchure is too tight.

SOLUTION 1:   Relax the embouchure and surround the reed with warm air as if saying "who." Let the tone quality dictate which syllable is more appropriate. Make sure the mouth corners are drawn inward rather than back and that the lower lip is not stretched too tightly over the teeth. It may be helpful to think of increasing the imaginary circle of air into the instrument. That is, use a slightly more open air stream.

CAUSE 2:   Reed is too soft.

SOLUTION 2:   Discard old reeds and/or move up in reed strength. Using reeds that are too soft causes players to "bite," resulting in a thin, pinched tone. As reeds wear out, they tend to soften. A reed that is too hard may "break in" after being played.

CAUSE 3:   Too little mouthpiece in the mouth.

SOLUTION 3:   Insert a third of the beak (or slightly more) into the mouth and check the resulting tone. The exact amount of mouthpiece in the mouth is determined by the tone quality.

CAUSE 4:   Improper focus of the air stream.

SOLUTION 4:   Direct the air stream toward the tip opening and parallel to the reed plane. Think of surrounding the reed with a steady stream of warm air as if saying "who," and think of blowing the air stream through the instrument. Focusing the air stream at too high an angle can result in a thin tone. Focusing the air stream at too low an angle can result in a spread tone.

CAUSE 5:   Using beginner-level mouthpieces.

SOLUTION 5:   Move up as needed. Beginner-level mouthpieces respond easily for beginners, but they do not provide enough resistance for mature players. They tend to sound thin, small, and pinched. Mature players need more advanced mouthpieces. Advanced mouthpieces are made from better materials, and they are available in a wide variety of chambers and tip openings so that they can be matched to the player's level.

CAUSE 6:   Instrument is improperly positioned, putting excessive pressure on the reed.

SOLUTION 6:   Reposition the instrument so that it is at a 35- to 40-degree angle away from the body.

CAUSE 7:   Not using a sufficient amount of air and/or the air stream is too slow, and the player is biting to compensate.

SOLUTION 7:   Increase air speed and the amount of air being used, while maintaining an appropriate embouchure.

PROBLEM: Grunting or guttural noises can be heard during normal play.

CAUSE 1:   Closing the throat or glottis when coughing or swallowing is normal; however, players sometimes develop the habit of closing the throat to stop the air and opening it to release the air, which results in a grunting sound. Closing the throat and using it as a valve to control air flow negatively affects releases, tone quality, and pitch.

SOLUTION 1:   Maintain an open throat as if saying "ah" and learn to control the flow of the air from the diaphragm.

PROBLEM: A reedy/buzzy tone.

CAUSE 1:   Reed is too soft.

SOLUTION 1:   Move up in reed strength. Soft reeds can sound reedy/buzzy. Players can also move the reed up slightly past the tip to improve the tone quality and pitch of soft reeds. Players who have played for two or three years should use medium (number 3) or medium hard or hard (number 3½) reeds.

CAUSE 2:   Reed is in poor condition.

SOLUTION 2:   Use a reed that has good balance and a good cut. Also, make sure the reed has not been damaged.

CAUSE 3:   Poor mouthpiece/reed combination.

SOLUTION 3:   Replace beginner-level mouthpieces with more advanced mouthpieces after a few years of playing. In addition, use double-cut reeds (3 or 3½) with advanced mouthpieces for a more mature sound.

PROBLEM: An airy tone quality.

CAUSE 1:   Reed is too hard.

SOLUTION 1:   Use a softer reed. As a rule, beginners should use soft reeds (1½ or 2), intermediate players should use medium reeds (2½ or 3), and advanced players should use medium hard reeds (3½ or 4) depending on the mouthpiece being played.

CAUSE 2:   Air escaping from the mouth corners.

SOLUTION 2:   Focus on keeping the mouth corners inward toward the mouthpiece, and use a proper embouchure at all times. Air escapes from the mouth corners when the surrounding muscles are not supporting inwardly toward the mouthpiece. Letting air escape from the mouth corners can become a habit.

CAUSE 3:   Leaks in the instrument.

SOLUTION 3:   Have a repair technician check for leaks and replace any worn out and/or leaking pads.

CAUSE 4:   The height of the pads above the tone holes is incorrect.

SOLUTION 4:   Adjust the pad height and play the instrument after each adjustment to determine if appropriate adjustments have been made. Pad height should be adjusted by a knowledgeable repair technician.

PROBLEM: The tone sounds dead and lifeless, and the pitch is flat.

CAUSE 1:   The reed is too old and/or too soft.

SOLUTION 1:   Discard the reed and use a new one. Reeds do wear out relatively quickly, even though they may still look good. As a rule, after a reed has been played on consistently for a couple of weeks, it begins to

deteriorate. Visible signs of aging include a dirty or dingy look to the reed with nicks or chips in the tip. Old reeds that have been left on the mouthpiece consistently also may have black spots on them as well as an unpleasant musty odor.

PROBLEM: Squeaks/squeaking.

CAUSE 1:   Fingers not covering the holes properly.

SOLUTION 1:   Maintain proper hand/finger positions. When properly positioned, there is no need to depress the keys excessively.

CAUSE 2:   Reed is too dry and/or is warped.

SOLUTION 2:   Soak the reeds thoroughly before playing. To prevent reeds from drying out and warping during rehearsals, wet them periodically with the mouth or water. During prolonged periods of resting, a mouthpiece cap can prevent reeds from drying out. Store reeds in a reed guard or reed case immediately after playing to help prevent warping.

CAUSE 3:   Unfocused/unstable embouchure.

SOLUTION 3:   Practice long tones to strengthen the embouchure muscles, and concentrate on eliminating unnecessary embouchure movement, especially when playing skips and leaps. The embouchure should remain relatively constant at all times.

CAUSE 4:   Reed poorly constructed and/or in poor condition (cracked, chipped, unbalanced, etc.).

SOLUTION 4:   Use a good reed that has not been damaged. Although a sound can be produced on a cracked or chipped reed, such reeds do not allow the reed to close off against the mouthpiece tip rail, which can cause squeaks. Store reeds in a reed guard or reed case immediately after playing to help prevent damage.

CAUSE 5:   Poorly constructed and/or damaged mouthpiece.

SOLUTION 5:   Replace it. The side rails and tip rail of the mouthpiece should be even, smooth, and free of chips or cracks. In addition, hairline cracks in the beak of the mouthpiece cause squeaks and can be very difficult to detect.

CAUSE 6:   Too much mouthpiece in the mouth.

SOLUTION 6:   Take less of the mouthpiece in the mouth. Only about a third of the beak (or slightly more) should be inserted into the mouth. Too much mouthpiece in the mouth causes squeaks, and it results in a "squawky" harsh sound.

CAUSE 7:   Hitting side keys.

SOLUTION 7:   Maintain proper hand position. Inadvertently hitting the left hand G-sharp key with the side of the left hand or the side keys with the side of the right hand can cause squeaks. Maintain proper hand and finger position to avoid hitting these keys accidentally.

CAUSE 8:   Leaks in the instrument.

SOLUTION 8:   Have a repair technician check for leaks and replace any worn- out and/or leaking pads.

CAUSE 9:   Clarinet out of adjustment.

SOLUTION 9:   Have the clarinet adjusted so that the keys work properly. The keys work together in a precise manner to produce each tone. If the keys are not opening and closing properly, squeaks can occur.

PROBLEM: Gurgling sounds on certain pitches.

CAUSE 1:   Water has accumulated in one of the vent or tone holes.

SOLUTION 1:   Remove the water by blowing a fast, narrow stream of air into the appropriate vent hole. Some players use cigarette paper to remove water from the vent holes.

CAUSE 2:   Water has accumulated in the mouthpiece and/or the barrel.

SOLUTION 2:   Draw out excess condensation from the mouthpiece regularly. During long periods of play, take the barrel and mouthpiece off the instrument and swab them thoroughly.

CAUSE 3:   Poor reed/mouthpiece combination. Not all reeds "fit" onto every mouthpiece properly. An improper fit can cause gurgling sounds, especially in the low range. These gurgling or warbling sounds are not the result of excess water.

SOLUTION 3:   Try a different reed/mouthpiece combination.

PROBLEM: A slightly delayed response of certain notes during slurred intervals, or the wrong pitch is sounding even though the fingering is correct.

> CAUSE 1:   Pad or pads sticking. Pads absorb moisture during normal play. This moisture attracts dirt and food particles. These particles collect in and around the tone holes and on the pads (particularly in the creases), causing pads to stick. In addition, sugar from certain beverages also causes pads to stick.

SOLUTION 1:   Clean the pads and tone holes. For a "quick fix," place a thin sheet of tissue paper, cigarette paper, or a dollar bill (preferably a clean one) between the sticking pad and tone hole. Close the pad lightly, and pull the paper through. Cleaning pads in this way is fairly common among advanced players. Various types of "no-stick" powder are also available. These powders do work for a very short period of time; however, they are often quite messy, and they create more problems in the long run because they simply add to the particles already collected on the pads and inside the tone holes. Generally, powders should not be used to free sticking pads. Ultimately, the instrument may need to be taken apart and cleaned thoroughly by a repair technician, and sticking pads may need to be replaced. Players should not eat or drink (except water) while playing to avoid pad and instrument damage.

> CAUSE 2:   The crease in the pad is too deep, causing the pad to bind against the tone hole edge.

SOLUTION 2:   Replace the pad.

> CAUSE 3:   The outside layer of a pad is torn, causing the pad to bind against the tone hole edge.

SOLUTION 3:   Replace the pad.

> CAUSE 4:   A rod is bent.

SOLUTION 4:   Have a repair technician straighten the rod. Bent rods can cause key mechanisms to stick. Often, players can feel a bump or hitch in the mechanism, indicating that a bent rod is the source of the problem.

> CAUSE 5:   A spring has come off, a spring is broken, or a spring is loose or worn out.

SOLUTION 5:   Put the spring back into place using a spring hook tool. A pencil, small screwdriver, or crochet hook can also be used to replace springs in some cases, but they are not nearly as effective. Spring-hook tools are easy to use, inexpensive, and are an excellent investment. Loose or worn springs can sometimes be tightened by reseating them and/or by bending them gently in the appropriate direction. Broken springs must be replaced.

CAUSE 6:   Pivot (post) screws are loose. Pivot screws work themselves loose periodically, creating problems with the alignment of key mechanisms. The area around pivot screws can also get gummed up by accumulating dirt and other foreign materials, resulting in sticky key mechanisms.

SOLUTION 6:   Clean pivot screws and surrounding areas. Place a drop of key oil on the screws and threads, and tighten the screws snugly. Placing a small amount of nail polish on screw heads and rods that frequently work themselves loose will help hold them in place.

4

Saxophone

Acoustical Properties: The acoustical and physical tonal characteristics of an instrument that affect its sound quality. Although the saxophone is considered a woodwind instrument, it is also commonly referred to as a "hybrid" instrument because is shares characteristics of both brass and woodwind instruments. Specifically, it is made of brass and has a conical instrument tube; however, the vibration of a single reed produces the sound and the key design is similar to other woodwind instruments. These design characteristics result in a flexible sound that blends well with both brass and woodwind instruments. This inherent flexibility enables the saxophone to adapt to a wide range of musical styles and ensemble settings.

The saxophone overblows the octave; that is, most of the fingerings used in the lower octave are used in the middle octave with the addition of one of its two octave vents or holes. Only the first (fundamental) and second partials are used for the majority of the normal playing range. See also Acoustical Basics, page 1; Construction and Design, page 357; Harmonics, page 32

Key Questions

Q: If the saxophone overblows the octave, why does it have only two octave vent holes?

A: Theoretically, for the saxophone to play every octave "in tune" naturally, it would need to have a separate octave vent hole for every note, which would not be practical. The practical solution is to strategically place two octave vent holes so that all octaves are reasonably well in tune. This positioning is a compromise between what would be ideal and what is practical.

Action: See Action, page 1

Adjusting Pitch: The process of raising or lowering the pitch of notes. A general discussion of adjusting pitch is under Intonation in chapter 1. Specific suggestions for adjusting pitch on saxophone are under Intonation in this chapter.

Air Stream: Physically, the stream of air pushed from the lungs by the diaphragm and abdominal muscles through the trachea and oral cavity into and through a musical instrument. Although the physical nature of exhaling is basically the same for everyone, the ways the air stream is used to play particular instruments vary widely. A general discussion of the air stream and breathing is under Air Stream and Breathing/Breath Support/Air Control in chapter 1. In addition, the effects of the air stream on pitch are under Intonation in this chapter. Specific comments regarding the saxophone air stream appear in another section.

Saxophone players can surround the reed with warm air as if saying "who" or "oh" and think of pushing the air through the saxophone. "Who" is most appropriate for players who need a more focused air stream, while "oh" is most appropriate for players who need a more open air stream. Considerable disagreement exists as to the appropriateness of particular syllables. Teachers and players should experiment with a variety of syllables and use what yields the best results. Ultimately, the tone quality determines which syllable is more appropriate.

Although the direction of the air stream may change slightly in the extreme high range (slightly higher) and in the extreme low range (slightly lower), the concept of focusing the air around the reed throughout the entire range of the instrument is a sound teaching concept on saxophone. This general idea works well for alto, tenor, and baritone saxophones. On soprano saxophone, the focus of the air changes throughout the range of the instrument in conjunction with changes in the embouchure and oral cavity, similar to the changes made on clarinet. Typically, the air must be focused upward as the scale ascends and downward as the scale descends, and the embouchure must firm and loosen accordingly. Players should use a tuner and listen carefully to determine the appropriate adjustments in air and embouchure. See also Air Stream, page 4; Breathing/Breath Support/Air Control, page 10; Intonation, page 382

Alternate Fingerings/Alternates: Fingerings not considered standard or basic that can be used to facilitate or enhance musical performance. Alternate fingerings are most often used to minimize awkward fingerings or to improve intonation in specific musical contexts. The choice of when and which alternate fingerings to use should ultimately be determined by the musical result. That is, does using the alternate fingering improve the musicality of the performance?

Developing command of alternate fingerings is important so that players can use the most appropriate fingering in a given situation. Learning alternate fingerings can be awkward at first. Practicing patterns, passages, scales, and other exercises in which alternate fingerings can be incorporated is helpful. Practice alternate fingerings slowly and deliberately, focusing on only one or two alternate fingerings at a time.

The alternate fingerings described in the following section are appropriate for players who are fundamentally sound. Examples of when to use these alternates are shown in Figure 4.1. When appropriate, suggestions and comments regarding alternate fingerings have been included. A complete fingering chart that includes alternate fingerings is in "Practical Tips" at the end of this chapter. See also Intonation, page 382; Technique, page 408

Common Alternate Fingerings for Saxophone

1. Alternate Side-F-sharp (first-space and top-line)—An alternate fingering used in chromatic passages (i.e., F-natural to F-sharp to G-natural) and to trill between F-natural and F-sharp. Side F-sharp is fingered with the right-hand index finger (4) plus the alternate side F-sharp key, which is beneath the right-hand palm and depressed with the right-hand ring finger (6). Using side F-sharp allows players to avoid flipping between the index (4) and middle fingers (5) of the right hand when regular fingerings are used. The only difference in the two alternate fingerings is that the octave key is depressed on the upper F-sharp.

2. Alternate Side-C-natural (third-space and above the staff)—An alternate fingering used in chromatic passages (i.e., B-natural to C-natural to C-sharp) and to trill between B-natural and C-natural. Side C-natural is fingered with the left-hand index finger (4) plus the alternate side C key, which is above the side B-flat key and depressed with the side of the right-hand index finger. Using side C-natural allows players to avoid flipping between the index (1) and middle fingers (2) of the left hand when regular fingerings are used. The only difference in the two alternate fingerings is that the octave key is depressed on the upper C-natural.

3. Alternate bis B-flat (third-line and above the staff)—An alternate fingering used to eliminate the coordination problems caused by using the regular B-flat fingering in certain contexts. For example, playing from G-natural to B-flat using regular fingers involves coordinating fingers on both hands, including a side key. Bis B-flat is fingered by positioning the left-hand index finger (1) over two

FIGURE 4.1. *Alternate Fingerings*

keys at once. That is, the index finger is lowered slightly so that it depresses both the B-natural key and the smaller key (bis key) immediately below the B key at the same time. In flat keys, most players maintain this position for extended periods of time, and they actually use bis B-flat more than the regular B-flat fingering. In fact, advanced players often use bis B-flat more than they use the regular fingering in most musical contexts. The only difference in the two alternate fingerings is that the octave key is depressed on the upper B-flat.

4. Alternate Front F-natural (high F-natural)—An alternate fingering used to eliminate the coordination problems caused by using the regular high F-natural fingering in certain contexts. Alternate high F-natural is fingered by depressing the left-hand middle finger (2) and the top key in the left-hand stack (alternate F-key) with the left-hand index finger (1). This alternate is typically used when playing from high C-natural to high F-natural because it involves adding only one key (and no side or palm keys) to the C-natural fingering.

5. Alternate Front E-natural (high E-natural)—An alternate fingering used to eliminate the coordination problems caused by using the regular high E-natural fingering in certain contexts. Alternate high E-natural is fingered by depressing the left-hand middle and ringer fingers (2-3) and the top key in the left-hand stack (alternate F-key) with the left-hand index finger (1). This alternate is sometimes used when playing from high C-natural to high E-natural because it involves adding only two keys (and no side or palm keys) to the C-natural fingering.

6. Alternate 1-5 B-flat (third-line and high B-natural)—An alternate fingering occasionally used when playing from F-sharp to B-flat. This alternate is fingered with the index finger of the left hand and the middle finger of the right hand (1-5). Saxophone players can use this fingering in fast, technical passages to simplify finger movement; however, because shifting from F-sharp to bis B-flat is also relatively simple and because bis B-flat is a much better sounding pitch than 1-5 B-flat, players often opt to use bis B-flat instead of the 1-5 B-flat.

7. Alternate 1-4 B-flat (third-line and high B-flat)—An alternate fingering occasionally used when playing from F-natural to B-flat. This alternate is fingered with the index fingers of both hands (1-4).

Saxophone players do not use this fingering very often because it is quite flat. In addition, because shifting from F-natural to bis B-flat is also relatively simple and because bis B-flat is a much better sounding pitch than 1-4 B-flat, players often opt to use bis B-flat instead of 1-4 B-flat.

8. Alternate Side D-natural (fourth-line and high D-natural)—An alternate fingering occasionally used in fast passages when playing from C-natural to D-natural. This alternate simply involves adding the high E-flat palm key to the regular C-natural fingering (2). This fingering is only used in fast passages or when trilling.

9. Long C-sharp (third-space)—An alternate occasionally used in very soft passages when playing from third-space C-sharp to fourth-line D-natural. Long C-sharp is fingered like the low C-sharp fingering (1-2-3 4-5-6-C-sharp key) plus the octave key. Although the pitch is usually quite sharp, this alternate often matches the tone quality of the D-natural better than the regular fingering.

Leaving Fingers Down to Facilitate Technical Playing

1. Players sometimes leave the left-hand G-sharp key (little finger) down when playing certain intervals or when playing fast passages centered around G-sharp because leaving it down does not affect the other pitches to a marked degree. For example, when playing a passage from G-sharp to top-line F-sharp to G-sharp to D-sharp, the G-sharp key can be left down throughout.

2. When playing across the break (e.g., from third-space C-sharp to fourth-line D-natural or from third-space C-sharp to top-space E-natural), players can leave the right-hand fingers down. On some saxophones, players can also leave down the left-hand ring finger (3) and the octave key.

3. When playing from low C-sharp, low B-natural, or low B-flat to G-sharp, players can leave the low-note key down for the G-sharp rather than rolling the little finger from the low-note key to the G-sharp key.

Key Questions

Q: When should players begin using alternate fingerings?

A: Players who are fundamentally sound can begin using alternate fingerings when opportunities arise to incorporate them into rehearsals and performances. By the time students are in high school, they should be using alternate fingerings regularly.

Q: Is it better to adjust pitch by making embouchure and oral cavity adjustments or by using special fingerings or adding keys?

A: It depends on the musical context. Generally, if using alternate fingerings improves the musicality of a performance, then use them.

Altissimo/Extended Range: In general, a term sometimes used for the notes in the high range and/or the extreme high range of an instrument. On saxophone, the altissimo range extends from high F-sharp (or high G on instruments that have a high F-sharp key) upward about one octave. In the standard literature for saxophone, the altissimo range is most commonly heard in advanced works. In addition, many jazz players use the altissimo range during improvised solos. Players typically begin working on the altissimo range after they have developed excellent control and facility throughout the normal range of the instrument. Because altissimo notes are not produced by the same manner of reed vibration as the rest of the saxophone range, producing altissimo notes involves several special techniques. These include: using altissimo fingerings, adjusting the embouchure formation and oral cavity, and changing the speed, focus, and direction of the air stream. Some suggestions for developing the altissimo range are outlined as follows.

General Suggestions for Developing the Altissimo Range

1. Work on altissimo after developing a good, consistent tone quality throughout the normal range of the instrument.
2. Use a slightly harder reed than normal.
3. When beginning work on the altissimo range, approach as if learning a new instrument.
4. Learn different fingerings for each note in the altissimo range. The "best" fingering for any particular player or instrument can be determined through trial and error.

Practice Suggestions for Developing the Altissimo Range

1. Practice altissimo slowly and deliberately.
2. Listen carefully, and use a tuner to check pitch.
3. Warm up properly before working on altissimo, and cool down properly with some long tones and/or slow playing in the low range to help the embouchure relax.

4. When first working on altissimo, use breath attacks and slur from one note to the next. Once control is gained, try tonguing the notes. Make sure that the tongue movement is light and quick; the tongue should disrupt the air stream minimally.
5. Start with high A-natural, B-natural, or C-natural. These notes respond relatively easily for most players.
6. Start on a note that responds relatively well and that you know is "right," and then work upward one note at a time.
7. After a modest amount of control is gained, play simple tunes to help gain tonal control and pitch accuracy.
8. Limit the amount of time spent working on altissimo during each practice session. Working on altissimo can ruin reeds, and excessive practice in this range can damage the embouchure. As a rule, ten to fifteen minutes of altissimo work during a practice session is sufficient, especially in the early stages of altissimo development.

Embouchure/Oral Cavity Suggestions

1. Move the jaw slightly forward, flatten the chin, and firm the embouchure. Keep embouchure adjustments minimal.
2. Tighten (stretch) the lower lip and pull the mouth corners back slightly to improve response, especially in the initial stages. Again, keep such adjustments minimal.
3. Use less lower lip over the reed.
4. Take a little more mouthpiece into the mouth so that the lower lip is applying more pressure to a thicker, stiffer part of the reed. The teeth may actually be slightly farther apart when playing altissimo notes as a result of taking more mouthpiece into the mouth. This position improves response.
5. Apply more pressure near the center of the reed with the bottom lip, but do not "bite" the reed.
6. Experiment with different oral cavity and/or throat positions by using a variety of syllables. For example, arch and pull the tongue back slightly as if saying "ee" when ascending.
7. Practice producing harmonics (or overtones) on low note fingerings to help develop the ability to adjust the oral cavity and the air stream appropriately.
8. A faster air stream is crucial to playing in the altissimo range.

Air Stream Comments/Suggestions

1. Think of using a cold air stream, as the air must move faster in the altissimo range than in the normal range.
2. Focus the air stream as if saying "ee" (or "hee" if using breath attacks). Players may feel the tongue curve so that the sides of the tongue actually touch (or almost touch) the teeth.
3. Focus the air stream sharply downward. This downward focus splits the air stream in such a way that less of the air stream is actually passing over the top of the reed, yet the air passing over the reed is moving faster.
4. If low "tones" are still being produced, use a fast, but unfocused air stream while saying "hee" or "heh" and let the air escape from the mouth corners slightly. Once control is gained, players should be able to produce altissimo notes without letting air escape through the mouth corners.
5. Focus on making the air move fast on a narrowly focused plane. Faster air speed is essential to playing in the altissimo range.

Key Questions

Q: Do high school students really need to have control over the altissimo range?

A: No. Very few pieces appropriate for high school instrumental music programs include the altissimo range. Working on the altissimo range too soon can foster bad habits such as biting and overblowing.

Q: When should students being to learn altissimo?

A: Advanced students who are fundamentally sound can begin working on the altissimo range at the high school level, preferably under the guidance of a knowledgeable teacher.

Anchor Tonguing: See Anchor Tonguing, page 6

Articulated Keys/Articulated G-sharp Key: Keys that automatically open or close more than one tone hole or key mechanism by design. Articulated keys enhance technique and help produce a more even scale throughout the instrument's playing range. On modern saxophones, the G-sharp key is an articulated key. It has a metal plate or bar connected to it that extends downward behind the other keys in the left-hand key cluster (C-sharp key, low B key and low B-flat key) and causes the G-sharp key to open any time one of the other keys is depressed. On older model saxophones, pressing down the G-sharp key was the only way to open it. The articulated G-sharp key enhances technique and can eliminate having to slide or roll the left-hand little finger from one of the other keys in the cluster to the G-sharp key.

Articulation: See Articulation/Articulative Styles, page 6

Assembly: The manner in which an instrument is put together before being played. Proper assembly is important to playability, instrument care, and maintenance. Teaching students to carefully assemble their instruments using a defined assembly procedure can help significantly reduce wear and tear. The saxophone can be assembled efficiently and safely using the following steps. Figures 4.2 and 4.3 can be used to guide the assembly process. See also Hand/Holding/Instrument/Playing Positions and Posture, page 367

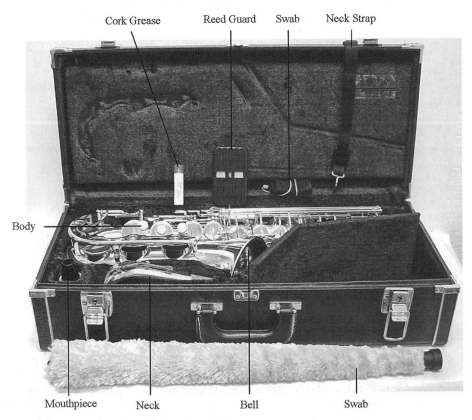

FIGURE 4.2. *Saxophone before Assembly*

1. Before handling the saxophone, place the neck strap around the neck.

2. Put the reed in the mouth (tip side first) and soak thoroughly while assembling the saxophone. Before placing the reed on the mouthpiece, turn the reed around and soak the heel end of the reed, being careful not to damage the reed tip. It is important to soak the entire reed, even though only the tip end of the reed is inserted into the mouth while playing. Many advanced players soak their

FIGURE 4.3. *Saxophone Assembled*

reeds in cups of water, although this method of soaking is often not practical in school settings.

3. If the neck cork feels dry, apply cork grease before continuing with the assembly process. Rub the cork grease into the cork with the thumb and index finger. If the cork is new, it may be necessary to apply cork grease every time the instrument is assembled for the first few weeks. As the cork becomes conditioned, it will not need to be greased as often.

4. Grasp the bell with the left hand and the top of the saxophone body near the end plug with the right hand and stand the main instrument body upright in the case. Position the instrument body so that the bell is facing the left back corner of the case. This position enables the left hand to firmly and safely hold the bell and to maneuver the saxophone during the assembly process. Remove the end plug with the right hand.

5. Loosen the screw at the top of the instrument body if it is not already loose and insert the neck into the receiver with a gentle back-and-forth twisting motion. Avoid handling or touching the octave key mechanism during the assembly process. Align the neck with the center of the bell as shown in figure 4.4 and tighten the screw snugly. Do not overtighten.

6. While supporting the neck with the left hand, gently place the mouthpiece onto the neck (flat-side down). When placing the mouthpiece onto the neck, support the neck with the left hand. Place the left thumb on the underneath side of the neck just behind the cork and hold the neck securely between the thumb and index fingers. Gently wrap the other fingers around the neck without touching the octave key mechanism. Make sure the neck cork is well greased, and use a gentle back-and-forth twisting motion while pushing the mouthpiece straight onto the neck cork. Do not pull downward when placing the mouthpiece onto the neck. Usually, about two thirds of the cork will be covered by the mouthpiece; however, the exact placement can vary widely from one instrument and/or mouthpiece to another. Check the mouthpiece placement regularly with a tuner.

7. Grasp the saxophone by the bell with the left hand, remove the saxophone from the case, and hook it to the neck strap.

FIGURE 4.4. *Neck/Mouthpiece Alignment with Body*

8. While sitting, rest the saxophone across the lap so that the bell faces left. This position enables players to reach the mouthpiece easily.

9. Loosen the ligature screws if they are not already loose and carefully slide the ligature (large end first) over the mouthpiece. The screws on most basic ligatures should be near the flat table on the underside of the mouthpiece (traditional ligature); however, some ligatures are designed with the screws near the top of the mouthpiece (inverted ligature). The ligature should slide down below the window opening in the mouthpiece table loosely, leaving plenty of room for the reed.

10. Gently push the ligature back toward the tip of the mouthpiece just enough so that the reed can be slid between the ligature and the mouthpiece table, flat side down as shown in figure 4.5.

11. Align the reed so that it is centered on the mouthpiece table and so that the tip of the reed is slightly below the tip of the mouthpiece, as shown in figure 4.6. When centered properly on the mouthpiece, a small bit of black should be visible over the top of the reed. Avoid touching the tip of the reed. Make reed adjustments by controlling the reed at the heel end and near the vamp and shoulders.

12. Slide the ligature down over the reed so that it is positioned just below the U-shape cut or scrape and tighten the ligature screws snugly as shown in figure 4.7. Do not overtighten.

Attacks: The way tones are started. A detailed discussion of attacks is under Attacks in chapter 1. See also Releases/Cutoffs, page 56; Tonguing, page 71

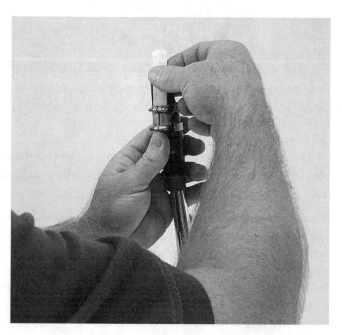

FIGURE 4.5. *Positioning Ligature for Reed Placement*

Back Pressure: Air pressure that builds up inside the oral cavity and lungs during normal play. In the course of normal playing, players use more air than can go through the tip opening, causing the excess air to "back up" inside the oral cavity. As a result, players often find themselves struggling to get rid of excess air. Although not a major problem on saxophone, players can experience excessive back pressure when they use beginning level mouthpieces and/or reeds that are too soft. Playing on good reeds, using air efficiently, and phrasing properly will reduce back pressure; however, nothing can eliminate it totally.

Baffle: The part of a mouthpiece opposite the mouthpiece window, or the underneath side (inside, top) of a mouthpiece. A detailed discussion of the mouthpiece baffle is under Mouthpiece/Mouthpieces in chapter 1. See also Mouthpiece/Mouthpieces, page 392

Balance and Blend Considerations: In general, woodwind instruments are less homogeneous than brass instruments. As a result, they do not always blend

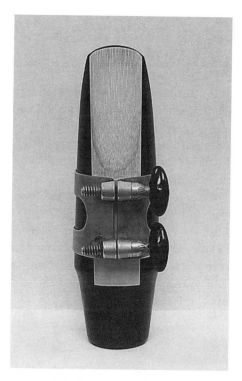

FIGURE 4.6. *Proper Reed Placement*

FIGURE 4.7. *Reed, Mouthpiece, Ligature, Neck Alignment*

together as well as brass instruments do in ensemble settings. To enhance blend, some instrumental teachers recommend using the same brand or model of instruments. In addition, different mouthpieces and/or reeds may be used to achieve different balances and blends, depending on the ensemble. For example, if the director wants the saxophone section to have a brighter sound in jazz band, players may use mouthpieces with slightly higher baffles than the mouthpieces they use in concert band. In general, a brighter and "edgier" tone quality is harder to blend and balance than a full, warm tone quality.

In a typical wind band with fifty to sixty players, four to six saxophones are often recommended as a good number for balance considerations. The number of saxophone players in any wind group depends largely on the type of sound desired, the number of instruments available, and the strength of saxophone players in the program.

Key Questions

Q: If I use four saxophone players in my ensemble, how many players should I put on each part?

A: Put one player on each part. That is, have one first alto, one second alto, one tenor, and one baritone.

Q: If I use six saxophone players in my ensemble, how many players should I put on each part?

A: Put two players on first alto, two players on second alto, one player on tenor, and one player on baritone. However, if you have a particularly strong alto player, use only one first alto player and double the tenor part.

Baritone Saxophone: See Instrument Family and Playing Considerations, page 376

Bass Saxophone: See Instrument Family and Playing Considerations, page 376

Beak: A term sometimes used for the outside top part of a mouthpiece that slants downward toward the tip. See also Mouthpiece/Mouthpieces, page 392

Beats: See Beats, page 10

Bell Tones: See Bell Tones, page 10

Bis: A term used to describe the small alternate B-flat key just below the B key (1) as shown in figure 4.8. The bis key is depressed with the left-hand index finger by pushing down both the B key (1) and the bis key at the same time. While bis B-flat is a useful alternate to the traditional B-flat fingering (1-2-side B-flat key), it does not work well in passages that require rapid shifts between B-flat and B-natural or between B-flat and C-natural. See also Alternate Fingerings/Alternates, page 336

Blanks, Reed: Precut but unfinished pieces of cane that can be purchased by players who want to make or finish their own reeds. See also Reeds, Single, page 265

Bore, Instrument: In general, a term used to describe the inside shape and dimensions of an instrument's tube. See also Acoustical Properties, page 335; Bore/Throat, Mouthpiece, page 351; Conical, page 357; Cylindrical, page 360

Bore/Throat, Mouthpiece: A term used to describe the part of a mouthpiece that fits over the neck cork and runs back into the mouthpiece chamber. "Bore" is a term more commonly associated with brass mouthpieces. Most woodwind

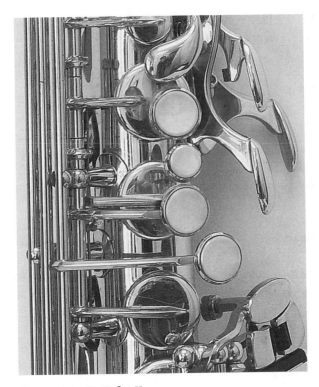

FIGURE 4.8. *Bis B-flat Key*

players refer to this area as the "throat." See also Mouthpiece/Mouthpieces, page 392

Break: The point at which a player must engage the octave key mechanism. On saxophone, the primary break occurs at fourth-line D-natural. Advanced players sometimes refer to a secondary break that occurs when transitioning from the high end of the regular range to the altissimo register. For saxophones without a high F-sharp key, this break occurs at high F-sharp. For saxophones equipped with a high F-sharp key, this break occurs at high G-natural. The break occurs at this point because the fingerings necessary to produce the upper partials (i.e., the altissimo pitches) become less patterned or intuitive. In addition, changes in embouchure, oral cavity, air speed, and air focus are more pronounced. See also Crossing the Break, page 358; Technique, page 408

Breathing/Breath Support/Air Control: See Breathing/Breath Support/Air Control, page 10; Circular Breathing, page 23

Butt, Reed: A term sometimes used for the bottom end or heel end of a single reed. See Reeds, Single, page 265

Cane/Cane Color: The material from which a reed is constructed, and the color, tint, or cast that a particular reed has. The most desirable reeds are made from cane that has a golden-yellowish cast. Reeds that are a bright yellow, have a slight greenish cast, or have dark brown streaks in the vamp indicate that the cane may not have been aged properly or that the cane was of poor quality to begin with. Brown spots or flecks in the stock (uncut exterior portion of a reed) are common and should appear somewhat evenly spaced throughout the area. In *The Art of Saxophone Playing*, Larry Teal suggests a couple of tests that can be performed on cane to help tell whether it has been aged properly. For example, if the thumbnail is pressed into the stock of the reed and nothing happens, the cane is probably too old. If the stock feels very soft and marks easily, the cane is too green. Properly aged cane should feel springy when the thumbnail is pressed against it. Teal also suggests that properly cured cane will develop a dark streak just below the stock when the heel of the reed is placed in water for a few minutes. The streak should be brownish-orange. If the streak is greenish or yellowish or simply not visible, he suggests that the cane is not ready for adjustment. Finally, after wetting a reed, blow on the heel of the reed. If small bubbles appear on the vamp, the reed is too porous. Teal suggests that it is a good idea to select a reed that resists the passage of air through its tubes, but does not completely close it off. See also Reeds, Single, page 265

Care and Maintenance: Taking proper care of the saxophone is essential for achieving high performance levels. Most of the maintenance suggestions below are relevant to secondary school students, and many of them simply involve establishing a daily routine. See also Care and Maintenance Accessories, page 23

Routine Maintenance

1. Assemble and disassemble the saxophone properly each day.

2. Grease the neck cork regularly so that excess pressure can be avoided during the assembly/disassembly processes.

3. Maintain proper hand/holding/instrument position while playing. When resting, hold the saxophone in a safe position. The basic resting position is to stand the instrument straight up and rest the bottom of the bell on the leg. Angling the saxophone across the lap and resting the saxophone on the outside of the bell is another

relatively common resting position; however, this position allows excess condensation to run down onto the palm key pads.

4. Put the mouthpiece cap over the mouthpiece/reed assembly and carry the instrument securely in an upright position to minimize the chance of banging the instrument into music stands, chairs, or other instruments.

5. When placing the instrument in its case, lay the sections down gently in their proper locations, then swab out the moisture one joint at a time. When swabbing out joints, insert and pull the swab from the large end to the small end of each joint several times.

6. When moisture collects in the octave vent holes, blow forcefully into them to remove excess water. If this action does not work, a soft pipe cleaner can be inserted carefully into the vent holes to remove excess moisture.

7. Dry off excess water on pads with a piece of ungummed cigarette paper, a dollar bill, or other absorbent material. Ultimately, pads that receive the most moisture will need to be replaced more often than other pads because the excess moisture causes them to harden and lose their proper seal.

8. Wipe off the outside of the saxophone with a dry, soft cloth to remove excess moisture, fingerprints, dust, and so on.

9. Remove excess moisture from the reed by gently wiping it off against a soft cloth or by gently wiping the reed (from heel to tip) against their pant's leg. Store reeds in a reed guard or case to avoid damaging them.

Key Questions

Q: Some sources suggest that swabs should be pulled from the small end to the large end of the neck so that the swab does not get stuck. How should students swab the neck?

A: Pulling the swab from the small end compresses the swab, preventing it from absorbing moisture properly throughout the length of the joint. Students should pull the swab from the large end to the small end of the neck because the swab absorbs moisture more efficiently; however, students must not force the swab through the small end of the joint because it can get stuck.

Other Maintenance

1. Remove the dust from under the key mechanisms once every couple of weeks or so with Q-tips or a small, soft paintbrush.

2. If excessive key noise is heard during regular play, oil the mechanisms. As a rule, the key mechanisms should be oiled lightly once a month or so. These clacking sounds are often caused by metal-to-metal contact, which results in excessive wear of the key mechanisms.

3. Clean out the tone holes every month or so to remove excess dirt, lint, and grime that has collected. A toothpick, pipe cleaner, or Q-tip can be used for this purpose. Care must be taken not to damage the tone holes and the key mechanisms during cleaning.

4. Once or twice a year, wipe the neck cork with a soft, clean cloth. Cork grease tends to attract dirt creating a buildup on the corks. Some players use alcohol to clean cork, but alcohol should be used only by experienced players. After they are cleaned, apply a small amount of cork grease to the cork and rub it in well using the thumb and index finger.

5. Wash mouthpieces with warm soapy water once every couple of weeks to remove undesirable particles. Never use hot water! Hot water can easily warp and discolor mouthpieces.

Considerations

1. A well-made and well-fitted case is essential to maintaining instrument condition. Some saxophone cases also include case covers, which add additional protection.

2. Avoid subjecting the saxophone to extreme temperature and humidity changes. Pads, corks, and felts have a tendency to loosen as the instrument contracts and expands in response to temperature and humidity. Never leave the instrument in an uncontrolled environment.

3. Do not clean keys with brass polish or other similar polish. Polish damages key mechanisms, ruins pads, and gums up tone holes.

4. Swabs with a weighted string should not be used for cleaning/ drying mouthpieces for three main reasons. First, because the

mouthpiece is relatively thin, the weight can easily break, chip, or crack the mouthpiece, especially the tip. Second, drawing the string over the tip and tip rail can cut into these surfaces over time and ruin the mouthpiece. Third, drawing the swab through the mouthpiece can wear down the interior and actually reshape the chamber over time, changing the way the mouthpiece responds.

5. Humidity affects cork. As the humidity increases, cork expands; as humidity decreases, cork contracts. As a result, there will be times when the neck cork will feel tighter or looser than others during the assembly/disassembly processes. These differences are normal. If the mouthpiece fits too loosely, cigarette paper or Teflon tape can be wrapped around the cork to make the mouthpiece fit better.

Cases, Instrument: Generally, the cases that come with most saxophones are the best cases for everyday use, especially for young players. These hard cases protect the instrument well and are designed to fit particular instruments. This design secures the instrument properly in the case and provides adequate storage for the neck, neck strap, mouthpieces, reeds, and cleaning accessories.

Nonetheless, there is a variety of instrument cases on the market today designed to suit a variety of needs. Some of the more popular cases for saxophone are shaped or contoured like a saxophone. Commonly called "gig" bags, these cases are available in a variety of designs and are available for soprano, alto, and tenor saxophones. A modified version of this design is also made for the baritone saxophone and is referred to as a contoured case. The materials used for gig bags vary. Generally, the shell consists of synthetic-covered rigid plastic or wood, molded plastic, or leather. The interiors are typically constructed from lined high-density foam padding. Other features of gig bags may include shoulder straps, carrying handles, and accessory pockets. Other hard cases are available as well. Some auxiliary hard cases are designed to hold additional instruments, such as a flute and/or a clarinet. Performers who frequently double on flute and clarinet may find these cases more convenient than regular cases. Finally, some baritone saxophone hard cases have wheels attached to them, making them easier to transport. Companies that make cases include Altieri, Pro Pac, Pro Tec, SKB, Yamaha, Weiner, Bam, Cavallaro, Selmer, Tuxedo, and Wolfpak.

Key Questions

Q: Are all cases well constructed and designed?

A: No. Players should not purchase cases without checking them out thoroughly. Many cases do not protect instruments properly. Inspect each case for adequate padding, sturdy and secure hinges and handles, and a proper fit for the instrument. A case that does not fit the instrument well or a poorly constructed case will not adequately protect the instrument, which may result in damage.

Cases, Reed: See Reed Holders/Guards/Cases, page 255

Chamber: The inside of a mouthpiece where the tone resonates. The chamber generally refers to the most open portion of the mouthpiece opposite the mouthpiece table window. See also Mouthpiece/Mouthpieces, page 392

Choosing an Instrument: See Instrument Selection, page 33

Clefs: The treble clef is used to notate music for all saxophones.

Conical: A term used to describe the cone-shaped tubing often used in instrument construction that is relatively narrow on one end (e.g., the mouthpiece end) and gradually widens toward the bell. All saxophones are conical. See also Acoustical Basics, page 3; Acoustical Properties, page 335; Cylindrical, page 360

Construction and Design: The saxophone family consists of several instruments pitched in B-flat or E-flat. The saxophones most commonly used in band settings are pitched in B-flat and E-flat and include the B-flat soprano, E-flat alto, B-flat tenor, and E-flat baritone.

All saxophones are conical-bore instruments made of brass and played with a single reed. This "hybrid" construction results in a very flexible tone quality that blends well with both woodwind and brass instruments. The tone holes are too far apart and too big to be covered properly by the fingers; therefore, all saxophones are closed-hole instruments. That is, they are constructed using a plateau system in which tone holes are covered by pads rather than by a player's fingers.

Student-line saxophones are not equipped with optional keys. Intermediate and professional saxophones are usually equipped with a high F-sharp key, and most intermediate and professional baritone saxophones have a low A key. Intermediate and professional saxophones also use high-quality materials, which contribute to improved tonal and response characteristics, overall pitch, and durability.

Necks are another significant design component of saxophones. The design of the neck significantly affects pitch and tone quality. Players can improve the tonal characteristics of their instruments significantly and less expensively by investing in a new neck rather than purchasing a new instrument. Advanced players often have more than one neck for different playing situations, and some saxophones (especially sopranos) can be purchased with two necks. The choice of necks is a matter of personal preference.

The mouthpiece is also a critical component of the saxophone. Mouthpiece choice is a matter of personal preference and there is no one-size-fits-all mouthpiece. Trying several mouthpieces is important when selecting an appropriate mouthpiece for any given player. Experimenting with a wide variety of mouthpieces also deepens players' understanding of tone production and response. It is common for advanced players to have more than one mouthpiece for different playing situations and styles. Finding a good "fit" between the mouthpiece, the instrument, and the player is critical to proper tonal and technical development. See also Acoustical Basics, page 3; Acoustical Properties, page 335; Mouthpiece/Mouthpieces, page 392

Crossing the Break: Technically, playing from any note below fourth-line D-natural to fourth-line D-natural or above is crossing the break; however, crossing the break usually refers to performing intervals close in proximity to fourth-line D-natural. For example, going from C-sharp to D-natural, C-natural to D-natural, C-natural to D-sharp, B-natural to D-natural, B-natural to D-sharp, and so on is commonly referred to as crossing the break. Crossing the break is sometimes problematic on the saxophone because players are required to play from an open fingering (where few keys are depressed) to a closed fingering (where many keys are depressed), requiring coordination of hands and fingers. In addition, crossing the break involves using the octave key and coordinating the left thumb with the other fingers. Preparing the right hand simplifies the problems inherent in crossing the break, while causing only slight changes in tone quality and intonation. Suggestions for crossing the break and preparing the right hand appear below. See also Break, page 352; Technique, page 408

Preparing the Right Hand/Suggestions for Crossing the Break

1. When playing from open C-sharp to fourth-line D-natural, put the right-hand fingers (4-5-6) down when playing the C-sharp. On most saxophones, players can also leave down the left-hand ring finger (3) and the octave key when playing this interval.

2. When playing from C-sharp to D-sharp, put the right-hand fingers (4-5-6) and the D-sharp key down when playing the

C-sharp. On most saxophones, players can also leave down the left-hand ring finger (3) and the octave key when playing this interval.

3. When playing from C-sharp to E, put the right-hand index and middle fingers (4-5) down when playing the C-sharp. On most saxophones, players can also leave down the left-hand ring finger (3) and the octave key when playing this interval.

Crossing the Break: Other Problematic Intervals

1. Playing across the break from C-natural to D-natural, C-natural to D-sharp, B-natural to D-natural, A-natural to D-natural, and so on is also problematic. Because preparing the right hand is not a practical option with these intervals, it is important to maintain proper hand position and practice precise finger coordination. Common examples of crossing the break appear in figure 4.9.

Teaching Tips for Crossing the Break

1. Make sure students keep their fingers as close as possible to the keys and in the ready position at all times. Proper finger position will improve finger coordination.

2. Practice these intervals slowly at first, and work on one interval at a time. When students can play from C-sharp to D-natural, C-sharp to D-sharp, C-sharp to E-natural in isolation, have them play two together, then three, and so on.

Examples of Crossing the Break

Prepare the right hand by depressing the appropriate right-hand keys on the lower note in each grouping

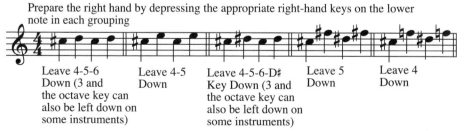

Leave 4-5-6
Down (3 and
the octave key can
also be left down on
some instruments)

Leave 4-5
Down

Leave 4-5-6-D♯
Key Down (3 and
the octave key can
also be left down on
some instruments)

Leave 5
Down

Leave 4
Down

FIGURE 4.9. *Crossing the Break*

3. When learning to play these intervals, tonguing each note can improve response; however, tonguing can also mask problems with finger coordination. As a result, it is important that students practice these intervals using slurs across the break. Students will often make changes in air, embouchure, throat, and so on in order to compensate for poor finger coordination when playing across the break. Such compensations are unnecessary. In addition, maintaining a steady air stream and a consistent embouchure when playing across the break is essential.

Cut, Reed: Also called the vamp or scrape, the U-shaped area of a single reed, where the bark has been removed. On a single-cut reed, the U-shaped area has been cut from a reed blank. The other areas of the reed retain the original bark. On a double-cut reed, the U-shaped area constitutes the first cut, and then additional bark is removed from the area just behind and to the sides of the U-shaped area, constituting the second cut. See also Reeds, Single, page 265

Cylindrical: A term used to describe the cylinder-shaped tubing often used in instrument construction. Unlike conical tubing, which is relatively narrow on one end and gradually widens toward the other, cylindrical tubing remains the same diameter along the entire length of tubing. All saxophones are conical, not cylindrical. See also Acoustical Basics, page 3; Acoustical Properties, page 335; Conical, page 357

Diaphragm: See Breathing/Breath Support/Air Control, page 10; Diaphragm, page 26

Dizziness/Lightheadedness: See Dizziness/Lightheadedness, page 26

Double-Cut Reeds: One of two basic types of cuts available for single reeds, primarily used for saxophone and clarinet playing. In addition to the initial U-shaped cut characteristic of a single-cut reed, a double-cut reed has additional bark removed. This additional bark is removed from the area just behind and to the sides of where the original cut begins. Rico Royal, Vandoren (traditional), and Hemke reeds are double-cut reeds. Compared to single-cut reeds, double-cut reeds are thought to be more responsive, to last longer, and to produce a bigger, darker tone quality. Double-cut reeds are typically more expensive than single-cut reeds. See also Reeds, Single, page 265

Double-Tonguing: A technique that enables performers to tongue duple patterns rapidly. See also Multiple-Tonguing, page 52

Doubling Considerations: See Instrument Family and Playing Considerations, page 376

Dutch Rush: Also called reed rush, horsetail, file grass, and shave grass, a natural fiber that can be used to smooth cane and to remove small amounts of cane in the reed making and/or adjusting process. See also Reeds, Single, page 265

Dynamic Considerations: See Dynamic Considerations, page 26; Intonation, page 382

Embouchure: The saxophone is a relatively easy instrument on which to initially create a sound. The basic embouchure is relatively easy to form, and the beginning reed/mouthpiece combination typically responds easily. However, because of its tonal flexibility, developing an even tone quality throughout the range of the saxophone and controlling intonation is arguably more difficult on saxophone than on any other wind instrument. The steps for forming a fundamentally sound saxophone embouchure are described in the following list. Proper embouchures are shown in figure 4.10. Embouchure considerations for specific saxophones are described under Instrument Family and Playing Considerations. See also Instrument Family and Playing Considerations, page 376

1. Put the lips together lightly.
2. Gently stretch the lower lip against the bottom teeth. The mouth corners will naturally come back slightly.
3. Drop the jaw slightly, separating the lips and teeth.
4. Insert enough mouthpiece into the mouth to allow the end of the reed to rest lightly on the lower lip. Make sure that the mouthpiece is centered in the mouth. The mouthpiece enters the mouth at a slightly upward angle. The exact angle will ultimately be determined by the tone quality.
5. Push the mouthpiece into the mouth about three-eighths to one-half inch, allowing the reed to push the bottom lip over the bottom teeth. The exact amount of mouthpiece in the mouth will ultimately be determined by the tone quality.
6. The upper teeth should rest lightly on top of the mouthpiece.
7. Position the lips as if saying "who." This position causes the lips to seal around the mouthpiece and helps bring the mouth corners in. No air should escape through the mouth corners.
8. The chin remains flat, but not stretched too tightly. The cheeks should be in a natural position and not puffed out. Generally, the saxophone embouchure is less firm and slightly more rounded than a clarinet embouchure.

FIGURE 4.10. *Embouchure*

Key Questions

Q: Is the same basic embouchure used for all saxophones?

A: Yes and no. While many basic aspects of embouchure formation are the same for all saxophones, there are also several important differences. In general, as the size of the mouthpiece increases, the openness of the embouchure increases and the firmness of the embouchure decreases. Therefore, tenor and baritone embouchures are more open and relaxed than the alto embouchure and much more open and relaxed than the soprano embouchure. Overall, soprano players use a noticeably firmer embouchure. Furthermore, players may need to focus the air downward slightly more in the low range and upward slightly more in the high range on tenor and baritone than they do on alto. The soprano embouchure is the most challenging saxophone to play for two reasons: (1) it is the most difficult saxophone to play in tune; and (2) it is the most difficult saxophone on which to produce and even scale. That is, the B-flat soprano saxophone requires more adjustments throughout the range of the instrument than other saxophones. In addition, they need to relax the embouchure as the pitch descends and firm the embouchure as the pitch ascends to varying degrees. Regardless of which saxophone is being played, players must learn to make adjustments in the embouchure, oral cavity, and air stream throughout the entire range of the instrument according to the intonation tendencies of each specific instrument. However, when teaching students (particularly beginners), it is helpful to tell them that the saxophone embouchure should remain the same throughout the entire range of the instrument. This teaching technique takes the focus off of tightening and loosening the embouchure and helps students focus attention on air stream and oral cavity adjustments.

Q: How much pressure should the bottom teeth exert on the lower lip?

A: In general, a small amount. Most of the pressure on the reed is applied and supported by the facial muscles. However, the lower teeth and jaw do contribute to embouchure support. Players who are out of shape or who play an excessive amount without building up their embouchure muscles often develop soreness on the inside of their lower lip where the lip makes contact with the teeth. In addition, slightly more pressure is used on soprano saxophone than on other saxophones.

Q: What can be done to prevent soreness of the lower lip?

A: Strengthen the embouchure muscles by practicing long tones and long tone exercises regularly and by extending practice time gradually over a period of weeks. Also, avoid excessively long practice sessions. Distributed practice is more effective than massed practice.

Q: What can be done to relieve soreness of the lower lip?

A: Some players place a small piece of folded paper over their lower teeth to prevent the teeth from cutting into the lower lip. Cellophane and cigarette paper are two types of paper used for this purpose. Other players have their dentists make removable pads or covers for their lower teeth. These covers last much longer than paper and conform to the shape of an individual's teeth. In addition to preventing or relieving pain or discomfort, covering the lower teeth can create a more even contact surface for the reed, resulting in improved tone quality.

Q: Should players with crooked, uneven teeth play saxophone?

A: Players who are highly motivated to play saxophone can overcome almost any abnormality; however, crooked, uneven teeth can be problematic. If the upper teeth are uneven, placing them on top of the mouthpiece is difficult because teeth that extend farther down will contact the mouthpiece first. Placing a rubber pad on top of the mouthpiece can help. These pads are available at most music stores. If the lower teeth are uneven, the pressure applied to the lower lip/reed will be uneven. Having a dentist make a cover for the lower teeth may help in this regard. In addition, players with crooked, uneven teeth often learn that if they play off-center such that the mouthpiece is no longer centered in the mouth, they will get a better sound. In a few instances, playing off-center may be perfectly acceptable; however, this is the exception and not the rule.

Q: Is the same basic embouchure used for classical and jazz styles?

A: Yes. However, most jazz players will drop the jaw more than classical players and support the reed to a greater degree with the lower lip and surrounding muscles. This embouchure change gives players more flexibility with pitch and tone quality, and it enables players to produce subtones. However, it can also result in bunched chin muscles and a protruding lower lip. Neither is necessary, and both should be avoided.

Teaching Tips for Embouchure Formation

1. When teaching embouchure, tell students that the alto saxophone embouchure should remain the same throughout the entire range

of the instrument even though slight embouchure changes may be required for certain pitches in the very high and low ranges. Telling beginners that slight changes are needed in these ranges is generally counterproductive because students tend to exaggerate these changes.

2. The idea of applying equal pressure around the mouthpiece, sometimes called the drawstring effect, is a sound teaching concept because it enables students to understand the need for a round embouchure. In reality, more pressure is applied to the reed from the lower lip, teeth, and surrounding muscles than is applied to the top of the mouthpiece from the upper lip, teeth and surrounding muscles. Students who take this analogy too literally may actually apply too much pressure from the top lip.

3. If students can play octaves in the low and middle range (e.g., first-line E-natural to top-space E-natural or first-space F-natural to top-line F) simply by depressing the octave key and without making embouchure adjustments, then the embouchure pressure is appropriate. If there is too little pressure, the upper octave pitch will not respond properly and/or will be flat and out of focus. If there is too much embouchure pressure, the lower pitch will not respond when the octave key is released.

4. Students with moderate to severe overbites often appear to take too much mouthpiece in the mouth, whereas students with moderate to severe underbites often appear to take too little mouthpiece in the mouth. Unless these students are having problems with tone production, tone quality, and tonguing, their "appearances" are acceptable.

5. Students should use a mirror to check their embouchure formations and placement of the mouthpiece. Using a mirror regularly in the beginning stages will help students develop proper playing habits.

6. Teachers should not see embouchure movement, even when students use vibrato. Students often develop the habit of moving the jaw back and forth as they tongue. This "jawing" motion is common, and students sometimes change their embouchure for virtually every note. As a result, players develop an uneven, inconsistent tone quality throughout the range. Unnecessary jaw movement is detrimental to tone quality, intonation, articulation, and technique.

Endurance/Stamina: See Endurance/Stamina, page 28

Exhalation/Exhaling: See Breathing/Breath Support/Air Control, page 10

Extended/Contemporary Techniques: In general, ways of producing sounds on an instrument that are not traditionally characteristic of the instrument or not typically called for in standard literature. A detailed discussion of these techniques is found under Extended/Contemporary Techniques in chapter 1. See also Extended/Contemporary Techniques, page 29

Facing/Lay: A term used to describe the amount of bend, curve, or slope of a mouthpiece table toward the tip of the mouthpiece. A detailed discussion of the mouthpiece facing is under Mouthpiece/Mouthpieces in chapter 1. See also Mouthpiece/Mouthpieces, page 392

> *Key Questions*
>
> Q: What kind of facing should my students' mouthpieces have?
>
> A: A medium facing.

Family: See Instrument Family and Playing Considerations, page 376

Flutter Tonguing: A technique that involves rolling or fluttering the tongue rapidly while producing a tone. Flutter tonguing uses the same motion of the tongue that is used when pronouncing a rolling "r." Players who cannot roll their tongues may use a throat growl as a substitute. See also Extended/Contemporary Techniques, page 29

French Reed: See Reeds, Single, page 265

F-sharp Key: Saxophones have an alternate F-sharp key across from the low F and E keys of the right hand toward the right-hand side keys. This alternate key is opened using the ring finger (6) of the right hand. Alternate F-sharp should be used in ascending and descending chromatic passages and when trilling from F-natural and F-sharp. See also Alternate Fingerings/Alternates, page 336; High F-sharp Key, page 375; Optional Keys/Key Mechanisms, page 398

Fundamental: See Fundamental, page 32

German Reed: A style of reed whose primary characteristics are a thick heart, thin tip, and slightly narrow width. See Reeds, Single, page 265

Grain, Reed: The natural fibers in reed cane. The grain or fibers of a reed can be fine, medium, coarse, or a combination of the three. By comparing several reeds, players can easily learn to see the variations in the grain. Reeds that contain too many coarse grains typically do not respond well, feel rough on the lip, and produce an unsatisfactory tone quality. Reeds that contain too many fine grains are often inconsistent and tend to wear out quickly. See also Reeds, Single, page 265

Half-Holes: A performance technique that typically involves covering half (or part) of a tone hole with one finger. On saxophone, instead of partially covering a tone hole with one finger, players can push a key or keys down about half way to create a half-hole. Using half-holes enables players to play quarter tones in contemporary literature. Half-holes can also be used to facilitate the performance of trills and to adjust pitch. Using half-holes is an advanced technique that requires great control and precision. See also Extended/Contemporary Techniques, page 29

Hand/Holding/Instrument/Playing Positions and Posture: Holding the saxophone properly and maintaining good hand position and playing position are key factors in developing good technique, facility, and ease of playing. In addition, good hand position, holding position, and playing position will reduce muscle fatigue and help players avoid physical problems, such as carpal tunnel syndrome. Suggestions for appropriate hand/holding/instrument/playing positions and posture are listed as follows.

Left-Hand Position

1. The left hand is on top of the instrument with the thumb at an upward angle (diagonal) across the thumb rest and the octave key at about 2 o'clock.

2. The left thumb remains virtually straight (but not locked) and in the position described above while in the resting position. When the octave key is being used, the thumb remains in contact with the thumb rest while "rocking" to depress the octave key. The middle thumb joint acts as a hinge during this process. Do not let players lose contact with the thumb rest and "jump" up to the octave key. Even on baritone saxophones with a low A key, the thumb remains in this angled position as is shown in figures 4.11 and 4.12.

3. The fingers curve slightly around the saxophone as if forming an open "C" or as if holding a ball. The fingers remain no more than

FIGURE 4.11. *Thumb Positions*

FIGURE 4.12. *Baritone Sax Left Thumb Position*

one-fourth of an inch from keys, and they cross the instrument at right angles or slightly downward.

4. The index finger is positioned on the B key, the middle finger is positioned on the C key, and the ring finger is positioned on the G key.

5. The little finger touches the G-sharp key lightly and remains ready to operate the little-finger keys (G-sharp, C-sharp, low B-natural, and low B-flat).

6. The wrist remains virtually straight.

Right-Hand Position

1. The right hand is on bottom with the thumb positioned beneath the thumb rest between the thumbnail and the first joint. The thumb should remain straight while playing.
2. The fingers curve slightly around the saxophone as if forming an open "C" or as if holding a ball. The fingers remain no more than one-fourth to three-eighths of an inch from the keys, and they cross the instrument at right angles or slightly downward.
3. The wrist remains virtually straight; however, a very slight inward bend is acceptable.
4. The index finger is positioned on the F key, the middle finger is positioned on the E key, and the ring finger is positioned on the D key.
5. The little finger touches the E-flat key lightly and remains ready to operate the little-finger keys (E-flat and low C). Proper hand positions are shown in figure 4.13.

Holding/Instrument Position (Soprano, Alto, Tenor, Baritone)

1. The weight of the saxophone is supported by the neck strap. Balance of the instrument is controlled primarily by maintaining proper instrument position and by the embouchure when the instrument is being played. Balance is controlled to a lesser degree by the right and left thumbs. In the seated position, the right leg (if the instrument is held to the side) or the left leg (if the instrument is held in front) also helps balance the saxophone. The right thumb does not hold the weight of the instrument. Proper playing positions are shown in figures 4.14, 4.15, 4.16, and 4.17.

FIGURE 4.13. *Hand Position*

FIGURE 4.14. *Front Playing Position (Front View)*

FIGURE 4.15. *Front Playing Position (Side View)*

FIGURE 4.16. *Side Playing Position (Front View)*

FIGURE 4.17. *Side Playing Position (Side View)*

2. When the neck strap is properly adjusted, the mouthpiece comes directly to the mouth.

3. The elbows are held away from the body in a relaxed manner.

4. When seated or standing, the tenor and baritone saxophones should be held on the right side of the body in the side position. Younger, smaller players should also hold the alto saxophone in the side position. In this position, the saxophone rests on the side of the right leg with the bottom of the bell drawn back slightly. The mouthpiece must be turned to the right so that the head stays straight while playing. In the side position, players should sit forward toward the right side of the chair to avoid hitting the saxophone against the side of the chair.

5. Older, larger players should hold the alto saxophone between the legs in the front position. Players should sit near the front edge of the chair so that the bottom of the bell can be brought back far enough to rest against the body without hitting the chair. Resting

the saxophone against the body is important because it removes unnecessary pressure on the right thumb. The bell should be turned slightly to the left to minimize the inward bend of the right wrist/hand. Do not let the bell of the saxophone rest on top of the chair, and do not support the weight of the saxophone with the right thumb. Tenor and baritone saxophones should be held in the side position.

6. The curved soprano saxophone is held in front as described above. However, the instrument position for the straight soprano is unique among the saxophones. The straight soprano is held out from the body similar to the playing position for oboe, or slightly farther out than the playing position for clarinet. Although neck straps are commonly used to help hold and support the instrument, the angle required for playing the soprano saxophone results in much more pressure/weight on the right thumb. For this reason, players should avoid playing for extended periods of time, especially when they feel discomfort in the hand, wrist, or arm.

   Many soprano saxophones are designed with bent or curved necks. Sopranos with curved necks create less tension on the right hand, wrist, and arm than sopranos with straight necks because they reduce the angle from the body, resulting in a more comfortable playing position. Some instruments come with a straight and a curved neck. Most saxophonists will play on both necks, compare tone qualities and intonation tendencies, and then use the neck they prefer. There seems to be very little consistency between necks and/or instruments regarding tone quality and/or intonation tendencies. Sometimes the straight neck yields a better tone quality and intonation tendencies, and sometimes the curved neck yields better results. When the necks are comparable, players should use the curved neck.

Posture

1. Sit up straight (but avoid being rigid or tense) with feet flat on the floor. Sit toward the front edge of the chair while in the seated playing position. If the instrument touches the front of the chair, move farther forward on the chair. If the instrument touches the right side of the chair (when the instrument is held to the side), move toward the right side of the chair and/or turn slightly to the left.

2. Avoid being tense or tight in the playing position because tension negatively affects both the mental and physical aspects of playing the saxophone.

3. Keep the head straight and relaxed. Many saxophone players tilt their heads to the left side while playing. This position is unacceptable. Players should turn their mouthpieces so that their heads are straight in the playing position. Bring the saxophone mouthpiece to the mouth. Do not reach for the mouthpiece.

4. Ensure proper placement of the music stand. The music stand should be in a position that enables each player reading from the stand to read the music comfortably and easily and to see the teacher/director while maintaining proper playing posture. The most common problem is for music stands to be too low. The most detrimental problem is for music stands to be placed too far to one side, forcing players to abandon good playing positions. Players who share music stands often experience this problem.

5. Maintain proper instrument angle. When the instrument is too close or too far from the body, players cannot support the reed properly resulting in poor tone quality, poor tone control, and poor intonation.

6. Adjust the neck strap appropriately. When the neck strap is too low, players have to reach down for it. When the neck strap is too high, players have to reach up for it. In both situations, the head and neck are out of position, which can cause problems with tone quality, breath support, and technique.

Harmonics: Acoustically, the term "harmonics" is used to describe all of the tone partials above the fundamental. On saxophone, the term is usually used to describe any pitch that can be produced with the same fingering used to produce the fundamental. In other words, a harmonic is a higher pitch produced with a fingering normally used to produce a lower pitch. For example, by fingering low B-flat on saxophone and making adjustments in the air, embouchure, and oral cavity, players can produce a B-flat one octave higher, a top-line F-natural a twelfth higher, a B-flat two octaves higher, and so on. These notes are all part of the harmonic series based on the low B-flat fundamental. Many saxophone players practice playing harmonics as a means of developing tonal control and the altissimo range. See also Harmonics, page 32

Heart: The center portion of the reed extending from just behind the tip toward the shoulders. When held up to a light, the heart can be seen as a symmetrically shaded U-shaped area. See also Reeds, Single, page 265

Heel: Also called the butt, the end of a single reed opposite the tip. The heel has an arch-shaped curve (arc). The arc is determined by the diameter of the cane from which the reed was made. See also Reeds, Single, page 265

High F-sharp Key: An alternate side key that extends the range of the saxophone upward a half step from high F-natural to high F-sharp. High F-sharp keys are found on virtually all newer intermediate and professional model saxophones and on some student-line instruments. The high F-sharp key is typically between the side B-flat key and the right-hand key stack and just above the alternate low F-sharp key. It is operated by the second (5) or third finger (6) of the right hand, depending on key placement and the size of a player's hands.

High G-Key: An auxiliary key available on some soprano saxophones that extends the range of the instrument upward to high G-natural.

History: The saxophone was invented in the early 1840s and patented in 1846 by an instrument maker from Brussels named Adolph Sax (1814–1894). Sax wanted to invent a new instrument that was a cross between woodwind and brass instruments. This new instrument was conical and made of brass yet fitted with a single-reed mouthpiece. The basic idea was to have an instrument that could produce both woodwind and brass tonal characteristics and blend the families together. The result was an instrument that could be adapted for use in a wide variety of musical settings. Saxophones were first used primarily in the French military bands; however, they have since been incorporated in a wide range of ensembles and are suited to a wide range of musical styles. Although not considered a traditional orchestral instrument, many composers such as Ravel, Gershwin, and Bizet have written orchestral pieces that include the saxophone, and the saxophone has become a relatively common addition to symphony orchestras.

Instrument Angle: The mouthpiece enters the mouth at a slightly upward angle. When the saxophone is held too close to the body, the tone tends to be small and pinched because the pressure on the reed is increased. When the saxophone is held too far from the body, the tone tends to be out of focus or spread because the pressure on the reed is decreased. In both instances, problems result from uneven embouchure pressure being applied to the reed.

Key Questions

Q: How does the instrument angle of the saxophone compare to the instrument angle of the clarinet?

A: The saxophone mouthpiece enters the mouth at a straighter angle than the clarinet.

Q: Is the instrument angle the same for all saxophones?

A: No. The angle is relatively the same for the alto, tenor, and baritone saxophones; however, the soprano saxophone is angled at about a 40- to 45-degree angle, similar to an oboe.

Instrument Brands: Several brands of saxophones are available from which to choose. Some makers carry several models to accommodate a wide range of playing skills and budgets. Other makers carry models that are particularly suited to certain skill levels, budgets, and playing situations. Used instruments are also a good option for many players, and used instruments made by reputable manufacturers are available. When searching for an inexpensive or used instrument, beware of "off" brands and instrument models (even with reputable brands) that have not performed up to a high standard. The list includes several reputable saxophone manufacturers. Although this list is not exhaustive, it does provide a good starting point for research. See also Instrument Selection, page 33

Saxophone Manufacturers

Cannonball; Guardala; Jupiter; Keilworth; L.A. Sax; Selmer; Vito; Yamaha; and Yanagasawa

Instrument Family and Playing Considerations: The saxophone family includes the B-flat soprano (curved and straight), the E-flat alto, the B-flat tenor, and the E-flat baritone. These saxophones, shown in figure 4.18, form the basic saxophone quartet and are commonly used in concert bands, jazz ensembles, and wind ensembles. In addition, the B-flat bass saxophone is commonly used in advanced saxophone ensembles, and parts for the bass are relatively common in some of the older band literature. All of these saxophones are transposing instruments. That is, their written pitches are different than their sounding pitches. Specifically, when a soprano saxophone plays a written C-natural, the sounding pitch is one whole-step lower than written (concert B-flat). When an alto saxophone plays its written C-natural, it sounds a major sixth lower than written (a concert E-flat). The tenor saxophone sounds an octave and a major second lower than written and one octave lower than the B-flat soprano saxophone. The baritone saxophone sounds an octave and a major sixth lower than written and one octave lower than the alto saxophone. Other saxophones not commonly heard include the sopranino in F and E-flat, the soprano in C, the mezzo-soprano in F, the C-melody (shown in figure 4.19), and the contrabass in E-flat.

All of the saxophones have the same fingering system and the same basic written range. The major difference between instruments is their size. What follow are some suggestions for playing the soprano, alto, tenor, and baritone saxophones and a chart of written and sounding ranges of the various instruments.

Soprano Saxophone

The soprano saxophone is the most challenging saxophone to play for several reasons. First, it is the most difficult saxophone to play in tune. Players must learn to

FIGURE 4.18. *Saxophone Family (Left to Right): B-flat Soprano (curved), E-flat Alto, B-flat Soprano (straight), B-flat Tenor, and E-flat Baritone*

FIGURE 4.19. *C Melody Compared to the Alto and Tenor Saxophones*

make adjustments in the embouchure, oral cavity, and air stream throughout the entire range of the instrument according to the intonation tendencies of each specific instrument. Furthermore, these adjustments often vary significantly from one reed/mouthpiece combination to another. Second, holding a steady tone or pitch is more difficult on soprano than on other saxophones, especially in the high range. The high frequency of these pitches coupled with the smaller reed size contributes greatly to the unsteadiness of tone and pitch, and even slight changes in the embouchure, oral cavity, and air stream can affect tone quality and pitch to a marked degree. Players must hear the pitches before playing them, and they must learn what adjustments are necessary to play them in tune. That is, players must develop muscle memory or kinesthetic feel in order to produce an even scale. Finally, the palm key arrangement of some soprano saxophones, especially some of the older models, can make playing technical passages extremely difficult if not impossible. Suggestions and considerations for playing soprano are listed as follows.

1. Because the keys are smaller and closer to the tone holes, the soprano has a greater potential for playing fast, technical passages smoothly.

2. The tones often respond easier and faster overall because of the smaller reed/mouthpiece combination. Players switching from tenor or baritone may have to adjust to the response characteristics of the soprano in order to coordinate the tongue and fingers, especially in the low range.

3. It is harder to center the tone on soprano than on any other saxophone. As a result, intonation and pitch accuracy is much more difficult to control. Setting the embouchure appropriately for each note before it is played and the ability to adjust pitch are particularly important for soprano saxophone players.

4. The soprano saxophone mouthpiece may be angled downward slightly more than the other saxophones when playing a straight soprano.

5. Players may need to use a slightly harder reed on soprano than they use on the other saxophones to effect a rounder, more stable tone and better intonation.

6. Curved sopranos typically have more intonation problems than straight sopranos, and their key design often makes playing fast, technical passages challenging.

Key Questions

Q: Which is better, a straight or a curved soprano?

A: "Better" is a relative term; however, most professional players play straight sopranos. Straight sopranos tend to play better in tune, they have a darker, more consistent tone quality throughout the range, and their key design makes it easier to play technical passages.

Tenor Saxophone

The tenor saxophone presents several challenges to players. First, playing in tune throughout the entire playing range is more difficult on tenor than on alto. Second, the tenor is somewhat larger, heavier, and more cumbersome than the alto or soprano. As a result, players may find that the increased weight causes fatigue and discomfort in the neck and back after only a short period of time. In addition, smaller players may find it uncomfortable to play the tenor while standing. Third, playing low notes on tenor is more challenging than playing low notes on alto or soprano. Getting a warm, rich, smooth tone on notes below low D-natural requires a well-developed embouchure, good control of the air stream, and a well-adjusted instrument. Finally, players can maintain a relatively consistent embouchure throughout the playing range with only slight adjustments for the extreme high and low range, which is much more similar to playing alto than soprano. However, the adjustments on tenor may be slightly more exaggerated than those on alto because of the larger instrument size. Suggestions and considerations for playing tenor are listed as follows.

1. The tenor embouchure is slightly more relaxed than the alto embouchure.

2. Generally, the oral cavity is more open on tenor than it is on alto because of the larger mouthpiece/reed combination.

3. Notes around the break (C-natural, C-sharp, D-natural, D-sharp) tend to sound and/or feel slightly stuffy on tenor. A-natural above the break can also be a particularly stuffy note. These notes usually feel worse to players than they sound. Although nothing can totally eliminate the stuffy sensation, using a good embouchure, good breath support, and a good reed/mouthpiece combination can greatly improve the quality (and feel) of these notes.

4. The pitch tendencies of the tenor parallel the tendencies of the alto; however, tones may be slightly more out of tune on tenor, depending on the instrument. In addition, the high notes on tenor are sometimes flat instead of sharp (especially with soft reeds). Using proper air and embouchure focus can help maintain pitch. Making pitch adjustments on larger instruments often requires greater changes in air, embouchure, and/or oral cavity than pitch adjustments on smaller instruments. That is, making the same adjustment on an alto and a tenor will result in a greater pitch change on the alto.

5. Low B-natural and low B-flat tend to be sharp. As a result, it is usually necessary to open the oral cavity, focus the air stream downward slightly, and/or lower the jaw slightly to play these notes in tune, especially on tenor.

6. Because of the larger reed/mouthpiece combination and instrument size, more air is required on tenor.

7. Generally, a slightly softer reed may be used on tenor to facilitate response. For example, a player who normally uses a number 3½

strength reed on alto, may use a number 3 reed on tenor. In addition, the embouchure must remain relaxed and open to compensate for the softer reed's natural tendency toward an edgy, reedy sound.

BARITONE SAXOPHONE

The greatest challenge faced by baritone saxophone players is coping with the instrument's large size. The baritone responds relatively easily with an appropriate reed/mouthpiece combination and proper breath support; however, it generally requires much more air than the other saxophones. Intonation tendencies parallel those for alto and tenor, but they may be slightly greater overall, especially in the low and high ranges. As a result, playing a baritone saxophone in tune requires players to have good listening skills and the ability to adjust pitch appropriately. When switching from alto or tenor to baritone, players learn to adjust to the increased size of the mouthpiece/reed combination and to the increased amount of time it sometimes takes for notes to respond, especially in the low range. Although the baritone may be played while sitting or standing, standing for too long can cause extreme fatigue and discomfort in the neck, back, shoulders, and legs, especially for younger, smaller players. Finally, the baritone is particularly susceptible to damage. Players can easily bend the neck if they do not support it properly with the left hand while attaching or adjusting the mouthpiece. Suggestions and considerations for playing baritone are listed as follows.

1. The embouchure is more relaxed and open on baritone than it is on other saxophones.

2. The baritone requires more air than the other saxophones.

3. Dropping the jaw slightly and adjusting the oral cavity (more open) may be necessary in some contexts to get low notes to respond properly.

4. The adjustments in the embouchure, oral cavity, and air stream are slightly greater on baritone because of the larger reed/mouthpiece combination and overall instrument size. Making proper adjustments requires more air and a more concentrated effort to focus the air stream accordingly.

5. The baritone tends to be sharp in all ranges; however, if the reeds are too soft, it will be noticeably flat in the high range.

6. The tone quality on baritone tends to be more inconsistent throughout the playing range than on alto and tenor. Generally,

the low range sounds rich and full, the middle range sounds somewhat less resonant, and the upper range is thin and small. Better consistency can be achieved as players gain experience and try different reed/mouthpiece combinations.

7. The baritone responds slower than the other saxophones because of the larger reed/mouthpiece combination and overall instrument size, making articulation more challenging. Players should increase air speed while continuing to use a "tip of the tongue to the tip of the reed" approach to tonguing.

8. Because of the baritone's size, playing fast, technical passages is more challenging. Players should minimize finger motion and not let the fingers "fly" off of the keys. In addition, because the keys are relatively large and heavy compared to the other saxophones, it is common for baritone players to "slap" the keys down rather than to depress the keys efficiently because of their weight and size.

9. As with the tenor, a slightly softer reed may be used on baritone to improve response; however, the embouchure must remain relaxed and open to compensate for the softer reed's tendency toward an edgy sound. If the reed is too soft, tone quality and pitch will suffer dramatically in the upper range.

Instrument Parts: See Parts, Saxophone, page 399

Instrument Position: See Hand/Holding/Instrument Playing Positions and Posture, page 367

Instrument Ranges: See Range, page 401

Instrument Selection: See Instrument Brands, page 376; Instrument Selection, page 33

Instrument Sizes: See Instrument Family and Playing Considerations, page 376

Instrument Stands: See Instrument Stands, page 39

Intonation: Generally, the degree of "in-tuneness" in a melodic and a harmonic context. In ensemble playing, the most important factors in achieving intonation accuracy are: (1) hearing intonation problems, (2) understanding what adjustments need to be made to correct intonation problems, and (3) having the skills to make the necessary adjustments. A detailed general discussion of Intonation is in chapter 1. Specific suggestions for helping players better understand the pitch tendencies of the saxophone and how to make appropriate pitch adjustments are outlined separately in this section. See also Intonation, page 41; Temperament, page 61; Tuning/Tuning Note Considerations, page 417

General Comments for Adjusting Pitch

Adjusting pitch is the process of raising or lowering the pitch of notes. Comments and suggestions for adjusting pitch are outlined as follows.

1. Embouchure/Air Stream—The embouchure and air stream can be altered in several subtle ways to adjust or humor pitches. As players progress, they learn to make embouchure adjustments for certain pitches as part of standard technique. Common embouchure/air stream/oral cavity adjustments are described as follows.

   A. To lower or flatten the pitch, focus the air stream downward. As a rule, the farther downward the pitch is directed, the flatter the pitch will be. The air stream may be focused downward by making slight changes in the oral cavity. Typically, these changes involve creating a slightly more open focus (as if saying "ah") and/or by lowering the jaw slightly.

   B. To raise or sharpen the pitch, focus the air stream upward. As a rule, the farther upward the pitch is directed, the sharper the pitch will be. The air stream can be focused upward by making slight changes in the embouchure and/or oral cavity. Typically, these changes involve creating a slightly smaller focus (as if saying "oo") and/or raising the jaw slightly.

   C. As a rule, a firmer embouchure results in a sharper pitch and a looser embouchure results in a flatter pitch. The embouchure can be firmed by increasing embouchure pressure around the reed and loosened by decreasing embouchure pressure around the reed. Changes in embouchure pressure and air speed are made by thinking of using a cold or a warm air stream. A warm air stream tends to decrease air speed and relax the embouchure, which flattens the pitch. A cold air stream tends to increase air speed and firm the embouchure, which sharpens the pitch. Generally, saxophone players use a warmer air stream than oboe players or clarinet players and a more consistent and open air stream throughout the range of the instrument.

   D. Only slight changes in air stream and embouchure should be made when adjusting pitch. Large-scale changes affect tone quality, control, and focus.

2. Throat/Oral Cavity—A tight, restricted throat causes the pitch to go sharp. An open throat generally results in the best tone quality on saxophone. Open the throat as if saying "ah" and the pitch will drop. In addition, the tone quality will improve. Changes and adjustments in the oral cavity affect both tone quality and pitch and are usually accomplished by having players think of saying certain syllables such as "oh," "oo," "ah," and "ee." The use of such syllables is effective in altering pitch and tone quality; however, be aware that using syllables often causes accompanying changes in embouchure and air flow as well. Understanding the relationships and balances among the embouchure, air stream, throat, and oral cavity is important to players and teachers.

3. Alternates/Adding Keys—If slight changes in the embouchure, oral cavity, and air stream do not bring the desired pitches in tune, adding keys to regular fingerings or using alternate fingerings may help bring certain pitches in tune. On the other hand, adding keys and using alternates to adjust pitch is not always practical. As a general rule, tonal considerations, technical considerations, and tempi largely dictate the appropriateness of such adjustments. Finally, adding keys or using alternates to adjust pitch often negates the need to make changes in air stream or embouchure.

4. Dynamics/Air Speed—Changes in dynamics/air speed affect pitch, sometimes significantly. Considerations regarding dynamics/air speed are described as follows.

   A. When playing loudly and increasing air speed, the pitch tends to go flat. Adjust by focusing the air stream upward slightly and/or firming the embouchure slightly. Air speed and control is maintained at all times. Do not overblow.

   B. When playing softly and decreasing air speed, the pitch tends to go sharp. Adjust by focusing the air stream downward slightly, opening up the oral cavity, and/or relaxing the embouchure slightly. Even at softer dynamic levels, the air stream must move fast enough to sustain and support the pitch.

5. Mechanical—Mechanical design characteristics and instrument condition affect intonation and are described as follows.

   A. Pad height affects pitch. If pads are too low, the pitch will be flat. If pads are too high, the pitch will be sharp. Make sure instruments are properly adjusted.

   B. The saxophone is not designed to be in tune when the mouthpiece is pushed all of the way onto the neck cork nor when the mouthpiece is pulled all of the way toward the end of the neck cork. Generally, the mouthpiece should be pushed about two-thirds of the way onto the cork to start, and then adjustments can be made from that point. The precise placement of the mouthpiece can be determined by using a tuner.

   C. Leaks and other mechanical problems affect pitch. Check the saxophone regularly for leaks, loose and/or broken springs, and missing corks or felts. Maintaining the instrument in good repair is essential for good intonation.

6. Mouthpieces—Mouthpieces can have a significant effect on pitch. Until players gain experience and understand what type of sound and feel they wish to achieve, the best solution is to have players use a hard rubber mouthpiece with a medium lay, a medium bore, and a medium-sized chamber. In addition, stating hard and fast rules that are applicable to all mouthpieces is tenuous; however, several useful generalizations can be made. These generalizations are listed here.

   A. Close-lay mouthpieces tend to play sharper than open-lay mouthpieces.

   B. Small-chamber mouthpieces tend to play sharper than large-chamber mouthpieces.

   C. Mouthpieces with high baffles tend to play sharper than mouthpieces with low baffles.

   D. Metal mouthpieces tend to play sharper than plastic mouthpieces, and plastic mouthpieces tend to play sharper than hard rubber mouthpieces.

   E. Small-bore mouthpieces tend to play sharper than large-bore mouthpieces.

7. Reeds—Hard reeds tend to play sharp, especially in soft passages. In addition, players tend to firm the embouchure to control a harder reed, which further raises pitch. Soft reeds tend to play flat, especially in loud passages. In situations where players

try to relax and maintain a good embouchure, tone and pitch are difficult to control because soft reeds do not provide enough resistance against or counteraction to the embouchure pressure. On the other hand, when players bite too hard, the reed closes toward the mouthpiece, reducing the size of the tip opening and resulting in a small, pinched tone or no tone at all. Players should use a reed strength that provides a modest amount of resistance in the middle register.

8. Neck—Occasionally a saxophone will be noticeably flat or sharp overall regardless of the mouthpiece/reed setup. In some cases, the neck cork may be too thin or too thick, which prevents the mouthpiece from being adjusted properly. In other cases, a new (or different) saxophone neck may be necessary. If a saxophone is equipped with two necks (a common option on some newer instruments), try them both and check the pitch with a tuner. The length and overall dimensions of the neck contribute to pitch (and tonal) differences in necks, and the best way to tell if one neck is better than another for a particular saxophone is to play on them.

9. Instrument Angle—When the saxophone mouthpiece enters the mouth at a slightly smaller angle (closer to the body, more like a clarinet), the tone tends to be small and pinched and the pitch tends to be sharp because the pressure on the reed is increased. When the saxophone mouthpiece enters the mouth at a slightly larger angle (i.e., a straighter angle), the tone tends to be out of focus or spread and the pitch tends to be flat because the pressure on the reed is decreased. In both instances, problems result from uneven embouchure pressure being applied to the reed. Exaggerated instrument angles in or out from the body cause a flatness in pitch because the reed is not supported properly. The saxophone mouthpiece should enter the mouth at a slightly upward angle.

Tuning the Saxophone

A detailed description of how to tune the saxophone is under Tuning/Tuning Note Considerations in this chapter.

Pitch Tendencies

Pitch tendencies refers to the tendency for notes to deviate from a specified standard, usually the equal tempered scale based on a reference frequency of A = 440.

FIGURE 4.20. *Intonation Tendencies (General)*

Specific Pitch Tendencies

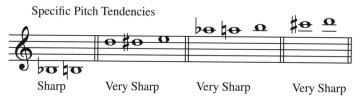

FIGURE 4.21. *Intonation Tendencies (Specific)*

That is, when players talk about the pitch tendencies of their instruments, they are almost always talking about how sharp or flat certain notes are in reference to equal temperament. Comments and suggestions regarding pitch tendencies are outlined in the following list. A summary of these tendencies is presented in figures 4.20 and 4.21.

General Range/Register Tendencies—Flat Pitches

1. Saxophones tend to play flat between low D-natural and first-space F-natural, especially when playing loudly.

    Adjustment 1—Focus the air stream upward slightly.

    Adjustment 2—Think of using a slightly firmer "oo" syllable to help focus the embouchure and oral cavity.

    Adjustment 3—If these notes are still flat, firm the embouchure slightly, but do not bite or pinch the reed.

General Range/Register Tendencies—Sharp Pitches

1. Saxophones tend to play sharp between low B-flat and low C-sharp.
2. Saxophones tend to play sharp in the high range (high A-natural and above).

    Adjustments for Numbers 1 and 2

    Adjustment 1—Focus the air stream downward slightly.

Adjustment 2—If these notes are still sharp, relax the embouchure slightly, but maintain embouchure focus.

Adjustment 3—Using a more open syllable such as "ah" or "oh" will help focus the oral cavity and lower the pitch.

Adjustment 4—Remind players that they do not need to tighten the embouchure in the high range. Maintain an open oral cavity and a relaxed embouchure.

Specific Pitch Tendencies—Making Adjustments for Problem Pitches

1. Low B-flat and low B-natural tend to be sharp.
2. Fourth-line D-natural, D-sharp, and top-space E-natural tend to be quite sharp.
3. High A-natural, B-natural, C-sharp, and D-natural tend to be quite sharp.

Adjustments for Numbers 1, 2, and 3

Adjustment 1—Focus the air stream downward slightly.

Adjustment 2—Relax the embouchure slightly, but maintain embouchure focus.

Adjustment 3—Using a more open syllable such as "oh" or "ah" will help focus the oral cavity and lower the pitch.

Adjustment 4—On high A-natural, adding the ring finger (6) of the right hand will lower the pitch; however, it often lowers the pitch too much. In addition, adding keys or using alternate fingerings to adjust pitch often negates or minimizes the need to make changes in the air stream or embouchure.

Adjustment 5—On high C-sharp and D-natural, adding the index finger (4) of the right hand will lower the pitch. If, in a particular passage, the C-sharp or D-natural is preceded and/or followed by an F-sharp, the middle finger (5) can be added instead of the index finger (4) to facilitate a smooth transition.

4. Low D-natural and first-space F-natural tend to be slightly flat.
5. Third-space C-natural tends to be moderately flat.
6. Third-space C-sharp tends to be quite flat.

Adjustments for Numbers 4, 5, and 6

> Adjustment 1—Focus the air stream upward slightly.
> Adjustment 2—If these notes are still flat, firm the embouchure slightly, but do not bite or pinch the reed.
> Adjustment 3—Think of using a slightly firmer "oo" syllable to help focus the embouchure and oral cavity.
> Adjustment 4—On third-space C-sharp, adding the middle side key of the right hand (use the side of the index finger) will raise the pitch. Again, adding keys or using alternate fingerings to adjust pitch often negates or minimizes the need to make changes in the air stream or embouchure.

ADDING FINGERS TO ADJUST FOR INTONATION PROBLEMS

Players can depress other keys in addition to the regular fingering to adjust pitch. An outline of basic fingering adjustments appears as follows.

1. Adding the right-hand ring finger (6) to the regular high A-natural fingering will lower the pitch. Be aware that this addition may lower the pitch too much on some instruments.
2. Adding the right-hand index finger (4) to the regular high C-sharp and high D-natural fingerings will lower the pitch.
3. Adding the side C key to third-space C-sharp will raise the pitch. Be aware that this addition may raise the pitch too much on some instruments.

USING ALTERNATE FINGERINGS TO ADJUST INTONATION

It is common for players to use alternate fingerings to adjust pitch. An outline of basic alternates and their typical relationships to the corresponding regular fingerings appears as follows.

1. Bis B-flat is slightly sharper than regular B-flat.
2. Side F-sharp is slightly flatter than regular F-sharp.
3. Side C-natural is slightly flatter than regular C-natural.
4. Front E-natural and F-natural are usually sharper than regular E-natural and F-natural.

Inverted Ligature: Ligatures designed so that the screws (or screw) that secure the reed against the mouthpiece are on top of the mouthpiece. In contrast, traditional ligatures are designed so that the screws (or screw) that secure the reed against the mouthpiece are on the bottom of the mouthpiece next to the reed. See also Ligature, page 390

Key/Pad Height: See Key/Pad Height, page 45

Lay, Mouthpiece: See Facing/Lay, page 366; Mouthpiece/Mouthpieces, page 392

Lay, Reed: The scraped or shaped portion of a single reed that extends from the U-shaped cut (or first cut on a double-cut reed) to the tip. Various areas of the lay are referred to with different terminology when discussing reed adjustment. These areas include the tip, channels, rails, and heart. Each area contributes in a specific way to overall response, tone, and intonation. To a large extent, the lay determines the reed's potential for good tone quality and response. It is important that the lay be even, smooth, and symmetrically tapered from the center to the edges of the blade. See also Reeds, Single, page 265

Ligature: A device that holds a single reed onto a clarinet or saxophone mouthpiece. There are a wide variety of ligatures on the market today, some with very elaborate designs. Most ligatures fall into two general types: regular and inverted. Regular ligatures are designed so that the screws (or screw) that secure the reed onto the mouthpiece are on the bottom of the mouthpiece next to the reed. Inverted ligatures are designed so that the screws (or screw) that secure the reed onto the mouthpiece are on top of the mouthpiece. Traditionally, ligatures were made of metal; however, a wide variety of materials are used to make ligatures today, including leather, cloth, vinyl, wire, and rubber. The general principle of more recent ligature designs is to maximize the vibration of the reed by placing minimal, even pressure on the stock of the reed. Most ligatures are designed to be positioned slightly below the U-shaped cut on the reed. Ligatures should only be tightened enough to hold the reed securely in place. Overtightening ligatures can strip the screw threads and adversely affect reed response, tone quality, and pitch. Over-tightening ligatures is a common problem with younger or inexperienced players.

Key Questions

Q: Does the type and quality of ligature used really make a significant difference in the tone quality, response, and overall playability of a reed?

A: Yes. Ligatures can affect tone quality and response to a marked degree. In the beginning stages, the ligatures that come with the instruments are fine. As players become more advanced, a higher quality ligature is a good investment, especially when paired with an advanced mouthpiece.

Q: How can I choose a high quality ligature? What are some high-quality ligatures?

A: There are many fine ligatures on the market today, and the best way to choose a ligature is to play several and pick the one that sounds the best. High-quality ligatures place even pressure on the reed at all contact points and should appear symmetrical in design. High quality ligatures that have withstood the test of time include BG, Bonade, Buffet, Harrison, Rovner, and Vandoren.

Lightheadedness: See Dizziness/Lightheadedness, page 26

Low A Key: An auxiliary key available on baritone saxophones that extends the range of the instrument down one half step from low B-flat to low A-natural. Baritone saxophones with a low A key also have a slightly longer bell to accommodate this additional key. Low A keys are found on virtually all intermediate and professional model baritone saxophones and on some student-line instruments. The low A key is just below the left thumb rest as shown in figures 4.22 and 4.23. When depressed, it closes the low A tone hole on the bell of the saxophone.

FIGURE 4.22. *Baritone Sax Low A Thumb Position*

FIGURE 4.23. *Baritone Sax Low A Key*

Mouthpiece/Mouthpieces: A detailed discussion of mouthpieces is in chapter 1. This discussion provides valuable information regarding mouthpiece selection. Specific suggestions for saxophone mouthpieces are listed in the following section. It is not possible to discuss all of the mouthpieces on the market today, nor is it possible to know which mouthpiece will work best for a particular player without play-testing each mouthpiece under a variety of playing conditions. As a result, the suggestions are certainly not absolute; however, they can serve as a starting point for players and teachers in their quest for the "right" mouthpiece. A comparison of mouthpieces and reeds is shown in figure 4.24. See also Mouthpiece/Mouthpieces, page 45

Key Questions

Q: Given all of the above considerations, what should I look for when selecting a mouthpiece for my students?

A: As a rule, start players with a small- to medium-sized mouthpiece (chamber, facing, etc.). As players mature, they can experiment with mouthpieces that have bigger chambers or more open facings to help produce a bigger, richer tone.

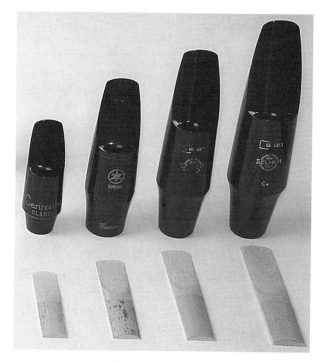

FIGURE 4.24. *Mouthpiece and Reed Comparisons (Left to Right): B-flat Soprano, E-flat Alto, B-flat Tenor, and E-flat Baritone*

Q: What are some good mouthpieces for saxophone?

A: Classical and jazz mouthpiece suggestions for each saxophone are out-lined in the following sections.

SOPRANO SAXOPHONE CLASSICAL MOUTHPIECES

Beginning Mouthpieces

Rousseau Classic 3R; Rousseau NC3; Yamaha Standard 3C or 4C; Vandoren S27 or SL3; Yamaha Custom 3C or 4C; and Morgan Protone.

Intermediate Mouthpieces

Selmer C*; Rousseau Classic 4R; Rousseau NC4; Vandoren S15 or SL4; Yamaha Standard 5C or 6C; Yamaha Custom 4C or 5C; and Vandoren Optimum SL3.

Advanced Mouthpieces

Selmer S-80 C*, C**, or D; Rousseau Classic 4R or 5R; Rousseau NC4 or NC5; and Vandoren Optimum SL3 or SL4.

ALTO SAXOPHONE CLASSICAL MOUTHPIECES

Beginning Mouthpieces

Rousseau Classic 3R; Rousseau NC3; Yamaha Standard 3C or 4C; Yamaha Custom 3C or 4C; Brilhart Ebolin 3 or 4; Clark W. Fobes Debut; Morgan 2C or Protone; Hite Premier 117; Selmer Goldentone 3; and Vandoren A15 or A17.

Intermediate Mouthpieces

Selmer S-80 C*; Rousseau Classic 4R or NC4; Selmer Larry Teal; Yamaha Standard 5C or 6C; Yamaha Custom 4C or 5C; Morgan 3C or 4C; Caravan Medium Chamber; Selmer S-90 170 or 180; Hite Premier 5* or 6*; Hite 127; Vandoren Optimum AL3; and Vandoren A25, A27, or A28.

Advanced Mouthpieces

Selmer S-80 C* or C** or D; Rousseau Classic 4R or 5R; Rousseau NC4, or Vandoren A35; Vandoren Optimum AL3, AL4; Caravan Large Chamber; Morgan 4C or 6C; and Selmer S-90 190.

TENOR SAXOPHONE CLASSICAL MOUTHPIECES

Beginning Mouthpieces

Rousseau Classic 3R; Rousseau NC3; Selmer Goldentone 3; Yamaha Standard 3C or 4C; Yamaha Custom 3C or 4C; Hite Premier 118; Vandoren T15 or T27; Brilhart Ebolin 3 or 4; Clark W. Fobes Debut; and Selmer S-90 170.

Intermediate Mouthpieces

Rousseau Classic 4R; Rousseau NC4; Selmer S-80 C*; Yamaha Custom 5C or 6C; Yamaha Standard 5C, 6C, or 7C; Vandoren T20 or T25; Brilhart Ebolin 4 or 5; Selmer S-90 180 or 190; Hite 128; and Morgan 3C.

Advanced Mouthpieces

Selmer S-80 C* or C**; Rousseau Classic 4R or 5R; Rousseau NC4 or NC5; Selmer Soloist D or E; Morgan 6C; Vandoren T25 or T35; and Vandoren Optimum TL3.

BARITONE SAXOPHONE CLASSICAL MOUTHPIECES

Beginning Mouthpieces

Rousseau Classic 3R; Rousseau NC3; Yamaha Standard 4C; Brilhart Ebolin 3 or 4; Clark W. Fobes Debut; and Morgan 3C.

Intermediate Mouthpieces

Selmer S-80 C*; Rousseau Classic 4R, 5R or NC4; Selmer Larry Teal; Yamaha Standard 5C or 6C; Selmer Soloist C*, C**, or D; Dukoff D5 or D6; Morgan 3C or 4C; Vandoren B25 or B27; Hite 129; Morgan Protone; and Vandoren Optimum BL3.

Advanced Mouthpieces

Selmer S-80 C* or C**; Rousseau Classic 6R, 7R, or NC5; Vandoren B35 or B75; and Vandoren Optimum BL4.

SOPRANO SAXOPHONE JAZZ MOUTHPIECES

Beginning Mouthpieces (Jazz)

Meyer 5 (Hard Rubber); Vandoren V16 S6 (Hard Rubber); Vandoren S25 (Hard Rubber); Otto Link 5 (Gold Plated Metal or Hard Rubber); Rousseau Studio Jazz SJ6 or SJ7 (Hard Rubber); and Selmer D (Hard Rubber).

Intermediate/Advanced Mouthpieces (Jazz)

Meyer 5, 6, 7, or 8 (Hard Rubber); Vandoren V16 S7 or S8 (Hard Rubber); Jody Jazz (Hard Rubber); Vandoren S35 (Hard Rubber); Otto Link 5, 6, 7, 8, or 9 (Gold Plated Metal or Hard Rubber); Rousseau Studio Jazz SJ7 or SJ8 (Hard Rubber); Selmer E, F, or G (Metal); and Berg Larsen 65/1, 65/2 or 70/1 (Hard Rubber).

Alto Saxophone Jazz Mouthpieces

Beginning Mouthpieces

Meyer 5 (Hard Rubber); Vandoren V16 A5 (Hard Rubber); Otto Link 5 (Hard Rubber or Metal); Vandoren Java A35 or A45 (Hard Rubber); Rousseau JDX 4 or 5 (Hard Rubber); and Beechler 5 (Metal).

Intermediate/Advanced Mouthpieces

Meyer 5, 6, 7, or 8 (Hard Rubber); Vandoren V16 A6, A7, or A8 (Hard Rubber); Otto Link 7, 8, or 9 (Hard Rubber or Metal); Vandoren Java A45, A55, or A75; Rousseau JDX 5, 6, or 7 (Hard Rubber); Berg Larsen 80/2M, 85/2M, 90/0M, 95/0M, or 100/0M (Hard Rubber or Metal); Selmer D, E or F (Hard Rubber or Metal); and Beechler 5, 6, or 7 (Hard Rubber); and Beechler M5, M6, or M7 (Metal).

Tenor Saxophone Jazz Mouthpieces

Beginning Mouthpieces (Jazz)

Meyer 5 (Hard Rubber); Vandoren V16 T45; Berg Larsen 85 95/1, 95/2, 95/3, 100/0, 100/1, 100/2, 100/3, 105/1, 105/2, 105/3, 110/1, 2 (Hard Rubber); Otto Link 5 (Gold Plated Metal or Hard Rubber); Vandoren Java Jazz T45 (Hard Rubber); Rousseau SJ4 and SJ5 (Hard Rubber); Rousseau JDX5 (Hard Rubber); Selmer Paris Jazz C (Metal); Vandoren Java Jazz T45; and Guardala Crescent.

Intermediate/Advanced Mouthpieces (Jazz)

Meyer 5, 6, 7, or 8 (Hard Rubber); Vandoren V16 T55, T75, T77, or T95; Berg Larsen 100 110/0, 110/1, 115/0, 115/1, or 120/2 (Hard Rubber or Metal); Otto Link 6, 7, or 8 (Gold Plated Metal or Hard Rubber); Rousseau SJ6, JDX6, 7, or 8; Selmer Paris Jazz C or D (Metal); Jody Jazz DV 7 or 8 (Metal); Otto Link "Master Link" (Hard Rubber); Vandoren Java Jazz T55, T75, T95, or T97 (Hard Rubber); Guardala MB (Hard Rubber); Lawton 7, 8 or 10*B (Metal); Beechler 8 or 9; and Guardala Brecker.

Baritone Saxophone Jazz Mouthpieces

Beginning Mouthpieces

Meyer 5M (Hard Rubber); Berg Larsen 80 100/0, 100/1, 100/2, 100/3, (Hard Rubber); Otto Link 5 (Gold Plated Metal or Hard Rubber); Otto Link Tone Edge 5* (Hard Rubber); Vandoren B75 (Hard Rubber); and Lawton 6.

Intermediate/Advanced Mouthpieces

Meyer 5M, 6M, 7M, or 8M (Hard Rubber); Berg Larsen Bronze 100 110/0, 110/1, 110/2, 110/3, 115/0, 115/1/ 120/0, or 120/1; Otto Link 6, 7, or 8 (Gold Plated Metal or Hard Rubber); Vandoren B95 (Hard Rubber); Otto Link Tone Edge 6*, 7*, or 8* (Hard Rubber); and Lawton 6 or 7.

Mouthpiece/Reed Angle: The mouthpiece enters the mouth at a slightly upward angle. When the saxophone is held too close to the body, the tone tends to be small and pinched and the pitch tends to be sharper because the pressure on the reed is increased. When the saxophone is held too far from the body, the tone tends to be out of focus or spread, and the pitch tends to be flatter because the pressure on the reed is decreased. In both instances, problems result from uneven embouchure pressure being applied to the reed. Exaggerated instrumental angles in or out from the body cause flatness in pitch because the reed is not supported properly. See also Instrument Angle, page 375

Multiphonics: See Extended/Contemporary Techniques, page 29

Multiple-Tonguing: See Multiple-Tonguing, page 52

Mutes: A velvet-wrapped "donut-shaped" ring inserted into the saxophone bell at various angles to affect tone quality and pitch. Mutes generally soften or muffle the tone by absorbing some of the higher partials in the tone. As a result, mutes make the tone softer and darker. Mutes flatten the pitch of the low notes (especially low B-natural and B-flat) to varying degrees depending on the placement of the mute. The closer the mute is to the bell tone holes, the flatter the pitch will be. Some players also place handkerchiefs inside the bell to mute the tone. Although handkerchiefs will certainly mute the tone, they often interfere with the response of the low notes. Muting the saxophone is considered an advanced technique and is usually done by only the most experienced players. In addition, practice mutes designed to make the saxophone quieter when practicing are also available.

Neck: The part of the saxophone that connects the top of the instrument body and the mouthpiece. On most saxophones, with the exception of some older instruments (especially older curved sopranos), the neck is detachable from the body of the instrument. Because the neck is relatively small and because of the octave key, the neck is particularly susceptible to damage if handled carelessly or improperly. Most hard-shell saxophone cases include a compartment for the neck; however, if a player has a "gig bag" or other contoured case, it is common to wrap the neck carefully in a cloth and store it in the bell of the saxophone. Storing the neck in auxiliary pockets on a gig bag can damage the neck. Any dings or dents in the neck or damage to the octave key mechanism can negatively affect the overall playability of the saxophone.

Neck Strap: A strap positioned around the player's neck that attaches to a strap ring on the saxophone via a clip or hook. The neck strap supports the majority of the saxophone's weight. Neck straps are typically made of nylon or leather and are adjustable so that the saxophone can be positioned properly. Playing the saxophone without a neck strap is awkward and uncomfortable. It also promotes bad habits and makes the instrument more susceptible to damage. Most soprano saxophones are equipped with a ring for the neck strap, and many players, both experienced and inexperienced, use a neck strap to reduce fatigue. One disadvantage of the neck strap on soprano is that it can limit a player's control over instrument angle, especially with straight-neck sopranos. As a result, players often balance the weight distribution between the neck strap and the right thumb. In addition, shoulder harnesses are available for the alto, tenor, and baritone saxophones. These harnesses are designed to distribute the weight of the instrument, reducing the strain that can be caused by neckstraps.

Octave Keys: On saxophone, the octave key mechanism is operated by the left thumb. Depending on the note being played, one of two vents will open when the octave key mechanism is depressed, producing a tone one octave higher than the tone produced by the same fingering without the octave key. The first octave key vent hole is near the top of the body on the right side. This vent hole is opened when playing from fourth-line D-natural to G-sharp above the staff. The second octave key vent hole is generally on top of the neck; however, on some saxophones, it is actually on the underneath side of the neck. The second octave key vent hole is opened when playing high A-natural and above.

Optional Keys/Key Mechanisms: Keys or key mechanisms not necessary to the essential functioning of the saxophone, but that make playing easier. The most common optional keys on saxophone are the high F-sharp key (commonly available on all saxophones) and the low A key (commonly available on baritone saxophones). Optional keys make certain aspects of technique and pitch easier. For example, the high F-sharp key greatly enhances the quality and response of high F-sharp and many of the altissimo notes. In addition, a baritone saxophone with a low A key is almost essential because players are often required to play low A-natural in the standard literature and there is no practical way to play a low A-natural without the optional key. See also Construction and Design, page 357

Overblow: See Overblow, page 55

Overtones: See Overtones, page 55

Pad Height: See Key/Pad Height, page 45

Parts, Saxophone: The parts of a saxophone are identified in figure 4.25.

Pitch Adjustment: See Intonation, page 382; Tuning/Tuning Note Considerations, page 417

Pitch Tendencies: Generally, the tendency for any note to deviate from a specified standard, usually the equal tempered scale based on a reference frequency of A=440. That is, when players talk about the pitch tendencies of their instruments, they are almost always talking about how sharp or flat certain notes are in reference to a modern, equal-tempered tuner. The term pitch tendency is most commonly used to refer to pitch deviations that are an inherent part of an instrument's design. In many instances, pitch tendencies are consistent on a given instrument (e.g., most clarinets or most trumpets) regardless of the make or model of the instrument. For example, most saxophones are sharp on fourth-line D-natural. The pitch tendencies of the saxophone are discussed under Intonation in this chapter. See also Intonation, page 382; Temperament, page 61; Tuning/Tuning Note Considerations, page 417

Plastic Reeds: See Synthetic Reeds, page 283; Reeds, Single, page 265

Plateau Model/System: Also called a "closed-hole system," a system where the tone holes are covered by pads rather than by the fingertips. Because the tone holes are so large, saxophones are built entirely on the plateau system. See also Plateau Model/System, page 56

Playing Position: See Hand/Holding/Instrument/Playing Positions and Posture, page 367

Posture: See Hand/Holding/Instrument/Playing Positions and Posture, page 367

Preparing the Right Hand: See Crossing The Break, page 358

Rails, Reed: The side edges of a single reed. See also Reeds, Single, page 265

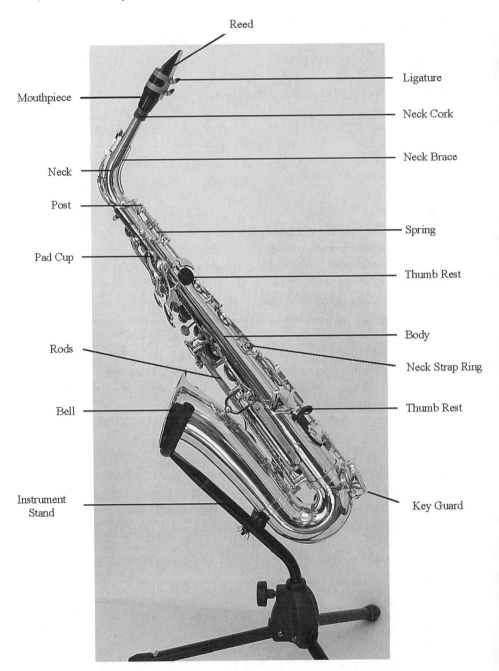

Reed

Ligature

Mouthpiece

Neck Cork

Neck Brace

Neck

Post

Spring

Pad Cup

Thumb Rest

Body

Rods

Neck Strap Ring

Bell

Thumb Rest

Instrument
Stand

Key Guard

FIGURE 4.25. *Parts of a Saxophone*

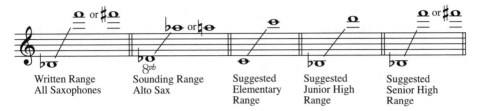

Written Range   Sounding Range   Suggested   Suggested   Suggested
All Saxophones   Alto Sax   Elementary   Junior High   Senior High
                                       Range   Range   Range

FIGURE 4.26. *Range*

Rails/Side Rails, Mouthpiece: See Side Rails, Mouthpiece, page 281

Range: In general, the distance from the lowest note to the highest note on a given instrument. In addition, players and teachers often refer to the different registers (roughly by octave) of the saxophone in terms of range: low range, middle range, high range, and altissimo range. The written and sounding ranges of the saxophones appear in the following section and are summarized in figure 4.26. See also Register/Registers, page 401; Transpositions, page 416

Key Questions

Q: What ranges are recommended for elementary, junior high/middle school, and senior high students?

A: A student's range varies according to experience and ability level. Once the fundamentals of tone production and embouchure formation are mastered, range can be extended systematically. Suggested ranges for each level are as follows.
    Elementary: Low C-natural to high C-natural
    Junior High: Low B-flat to high D-natural
    Senior High: Low B-flat to high F (or F-sharp)

Reed: Information regarding reeds is under Reeds, Single, and other related terms in the chapter 3. See Reeds, Single, page 265

Reed/Mouthpiece Angle: The mouthpiece enters the mouth at a slightly upward angle. See also Instrument Angle, page 375

Register/Registers: Groups of notes that share certain tonal characteristics usually related to pitch range, timbre, and/or manner of production. Players vary in their description of registers. Some players and teachers use the term "register" interchangeably with the term "range" to describe the playing ranges of the instrument. Furthermore, players and teachers also use terms such as "high" and "low" indiscriminately, or at least relatively, depending upon the musical context. Ultimately, delineating registers commonly used by junior high students, senior high students, college students, and professional players is a subjective process that varies according to the criteria used for delineation. Nonetheless, it seems reasonable to divide the saxophone range into four registers. These registers are listed in the following section and are notated in figure 4.27. See also Range, page 401

1. Low Register—From low B-flat (or low A-natural) to first-space F-sharp.
2. Middle Register—From second-line G-natural to G-sharp above the staff.
3. High Register—From A-natural (above the staff) to high F-natural (or F-sharp).
4. Altissimo Register—All notes above high F-natural (or F-sharp).

Releases/Cutoffs: See Releases/Cutoffs, page 56

Resistance: In general, the counteraction of the reed, mouthpiece, and instrument to the incoming air stream. The amount of resistance provided by the instrument and reed/mouthpiece combination dictates the amount of air and support needed to start and maintain a steady tone. That is, the reed, mouthpiece and, to a lesser degree the saxophone, all contribute to the resistance felt by the player. Reeds in particular affect resistance significantly. Generally speaking, harder reeds cause more resistance than softer reeds. A certain amount of resistance is needed to maintain a steady, rich tone quality and good pitch. When reeds are too soft, the tone is thin and "quivery," and pitch is difficult to control. When reeds are too hard, the tone is airy, response is poor, pitch control suffers, and players' embouchures tire quickly. Reeds need to be

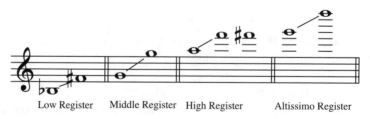

FIGURE 4.27. *Register/Registers*

hard enough to push back against the lower lip pressure in order to create a stable tone but not so hard that players have to fight against the reed. The appropriate reed strength is directly dependent on the mouthpiece being used and the ability of the player to control the reed/mouthpiece combination during play. That is, players with well-developed embouchures can control a larger mouthpiece and a harder reed more effectively than players with less developed embouchures.

The amount of resistance is also significantly affected by the lay or facing of a mouthpiece. As a general rule, long-lay mouthpieces (with more open facings) will have more resistance than short-lay mouthpieces (with more closed facings), all things being equal. Players who use long-lay mouthpieces will generally use softer reeds or have significantly stronger embouchure control than players who use short-lay mouthpieces. See also Breathing/Breath Support/Air Control, page 10; Mouthpiece/Mouthpieces, page 392; Response, page 405

Key Questions

Q: How much resistance is ideal for different age levels?

A: In general, beginners should use beginner-level mouthpieces with soft reeds because they provide less resistance, which helps players produce a tone easily. As players' embouchures develop and strengthen, harder reeds and advanced mouthpieces can provide the additional resistance needed to produce a warm, rich characteristic saxophone tone. Several factors affect the best reed choice for beginning saxophone players, including age, physical maturity, experience on another instrument, the mouthpiece, other physical equipment, and climate conditions. In general, younger, less physically developed players should begin on softer reeds (number 1½ or 2), while older, more physically developed players can start on slightly harder reeds (number 2 or 2½).

Teaching Tips Regarding Resistance/Response

1. Single reed players need a certain amount of resistance from the reed/mouthpiece combination. As their embouchures and support strengthens, the ability of the reed to push back against the supporting embouchure and create the resistance that holds the tone steady declines. The tone becomes unsteady or "shaky," soft, and thin. Using a harder reed helps solve this problem. Have students move up ½ reed strength at a time until an acceptable balance is found.

2. Double-cut reeds are generally a little harder than single-cut reeds. If students are using a number 2 strength single-cut reed (a good choice for beginners) having them move to a number 2 double-cut reed after a few months of playing may help improve tone quality and response.

3. As a rule, students should begin with a number 2 (fifth- or sixth-graders) or 2½ (seventh-graders) single-cut reed. After a few months, they should move to a number 2½ or 3 double-cut reed. After a year or so, students should move to a number 3 or 3½ double-cut reed. By the end of their second year, students should consider purchasing a more advanced mouthpiece, and they should be playing on a number 3 or 3½ double-cut reed.

4. Teachers are often reluctant to have students move up in reed strength in a progressive manner. As a result, students often play with beginner-level tone qualities for too long. Slightly harder, more resistant reeds will improve tone quality and pitch control. These reeds may feel too hard at first; however, as players' embouchures strengthen and adapt to the harder reed strength, the improvements in tone quality and pitch control will be obvious. If the new reed strength is too hard, students' embouchures will not readily adapt and the tone will be weak and airy. In this case, adjust by using a slightly softer reed.

5. It is important to note that a reed strength number represents a range of reed strengths. That is, not all number 2 reeds will have the same degree of resistance. In a numerical context, a number 2 reed may have a reed strength anywhere between a number 1½ and a 2½. Try several reeds of a particular strength designation before determining whether a reed strength number is too hard or too soft overall.

6. As students mature, they should switch to more advanced mouthpieces, which typically have bigger chambers. These mouthpieces provide the potential for a much bigger, richer tone quality. Initially, students may find that they need to use slightly softer reeds on advanced mouthpieces. For example, if a student is using a number 3½ reed on a student-line mouthpiece, he or she may need to use a number 3 reed on an advanced mouthpiece for a brief period of time. Although the exact reed strength varies from player to player, most advanced players use a number 3, 3½, or 4 double-cut reed.

Resonance Keys: Keys sometimes added to regular fingerings to improve the tonal response, tone quality, and/or pitch of certain notes. For example, when playing high C-sharp, players sometimes depress the index finger of the right hand (4) to make the tone more resonant and to improve pitch. See also Speaker Keys, page 406

Response: The way a reed vibrates as a result of the player's air stream and embouchure. The term response is also used to refer to the ease with which the notes "speak" or sound. Some notes respond more easily than others, depending on how much of the tube is closed and how much air speed is needed to set the reed in vibration. Notes in the extreme high or low range tend not to respond as well as notes in the middle range. The quality and condition of the saxophone, the reed/mouthpiece combination, and a player's ability to control the air speed and air volume greatly affect reed response. See also Resistance, page 402

Selecting an Instrument: See Instrument Brands, page 376; Instrument Selection, page 33

Shank, Mouthpiece: A term sometimes used to describe the part of a mouthpiece that fits over the neck cork and runs into the mouthpiece bore. Saxophonists often refer to this area as the mouthpiece throat. Shank is a term more commonly associated with brass mouthpieces. See also Mouthpiece/Mouthpieces, page 392

Shoulders: The areas that surround the heart of a single reed. The shoulders extend back toward the heel of the reed. See also Reeds, Single, page 265

Side Rails, Mouthpiece: The two edges along the sides of the mouthpiece table that extend from the bottom of the mouthpiece window to the tip rail. The side rails should have even, uniform dimensions and should be free from nicks and scrapes. Damaged side rails make the tone difficult to control and often cause squeaking and poor tone quality. See also Mouthpiece/Mouthpieces, page 392

Single-Cut Reeds: Reeds that have one visible slice or cut from the stock to form the vamp. That is, the bark has been removed from the U-shape to the tip. All of the outer bark surrounding the U-shape to the heel of the reed is intact. The standard reeds made by Rico and LaVoz are single-cut reeds. See also Reeds, Single, page 265; Double-Cut Reeds, page 214

Slap Tongue: A tonguing technique that produces a "slapping" or "popping" effect on the attacks. Slap tonguing is sometimes used as a special effect in both jazz and contemporary literature and is produced by pressing the tongue hard against the reed to close or nearly close the tip opening, building up air pressure, and then releasing the tongue quickly. See also Extended/Contemporary Techniques, page 29

Soprano Saxophone: See Instrument Family and Playing Considerations, page 376

Sounding Range: See Instrument Family and Playing Considerations, page 376; Range, page 401; Transpositions, page 416

Spat Keys: A term sometimes used to describe the cluster of keys operated by the left-hand little finger. The saxophone spat keys include the G-sharp key, the C-sharp key, the B key, and the B-flat key. To operate these keys efficiently and effectively, players develop muscle strength and control in the left-hand little finger. Practicing low-note scale exercises can facilitate this development.

Speaker Keys: Generally, a term used for keys that help notes respond or speak when depressed. Speaker keys can be special keys (e.g., bassoon flick keys) or they can be regular keys (e.g., an octave key). On saxophone, the two octave keys are the most obvious speaker keys. See also Resonance Keys, page 405

Spit Valve/Water Key: A key mechanism designed to help drain excess moisture from the crook (i.e., the U-shaped tubing past the neck) of the baritone saxophone. The soprano, alto, and tenor saxophones do not have water keys.

Spring Hook Tool: See Spring Hook Tool, page 59

Springs: See Springs, page 59

Squeaks: Undesirable, accidentally produced partials that sometimes sound during normal play. Squeaks can be caused by several factors. Some of the most common causes of squeaks include poor or dry reeds, poor embouchure formation, overblowing, or accidentally hitting side keys. Squeaking is a common problem for beginners as they learn to control their embouchures and the instrument. A more detailed discussion regarding the causes of squeaks is in "Practical Tips" at the end of this chapter.

Staggered Breathing: See Staggered Breathing, page 59

Stamina: See Endurance/Stamina, page 28

Stands: See Instrument Stands, page 39

Starting Note/Range, The Best: Most players will have excellent results starting on third-line B-natural (1) and working their way downward note by note to second line G-natural (1-2-3). This note range is ideal for several reasons. First, it is relatively easy to produce a tone in this range. Second, the fingerings in this range are relatively simple and intuitive. Third, this range provides teachers with the opportunity to point out that as more holes are covered, the tones get lower. These relationships make this range ideal for simple ear training exercises. Finally, adding one finger at a time in a comfortable range enables players to depress the keys properly. That is, players learn to depress the keys more efficiently when they proceed in a logical step-by-step manner. This starting note range is shown is figure 4.28. It is interesting to note that because band method books must accommodate beginners on a variety of instruments, they often do not have players start on the above sequence of notes.

Stock: The part of a reed that has the bark on it. See also Reeds, Single, page 265

Subtone: A technique used primarily in jazz playing where players drop the jaw and support the reed to a greater degree with the lower lip and surrounding muscles. Subtone results in an airy or "breathy" tone quality and is used on all saxophones, although it is especially effective on alto, tenor, and baritone saxophones in the lower register. See also Extended/Contemporary Techniques, page 29

Swab: See Swab, page 59; Care and Maintenance, page 353

Synthetic Reeds: See Synthetic Reeds, page 283

Table, Mouthpiece: The flat underside of a mouthpiece on which the reed lies. It is imperative that the mouthpiece table be flat and smooth. A warped and/or damaged table makes the tone difficult to control and often causes squeaks. See also Mouthpiece/Mouthpieces, page 392

Starting Note Range

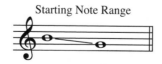

FIGURE 4.28. *Starting Note Range*

Technique: In general, the manner and ability with which players use the technical skills involved in playing an instrument. Most commonly, the term is used to describe the physical actions involved in playing an instrument, and often specifically refers to technical passages. Virtually every pedagogical aspect of woodwind playing (acoustical, physical, and mental) affects technique. General technical considerations for all woodwind instruments are in chapter 1. The following suggestions and considerations apply specifically to the saxophone. When appropriate, readers are directed to relevant terms in the book where particular topics are addressed in detail. See also Alternate Fingerings/Alternates, page 336; Technique, page 60

General Technical Considerations/Concerns for Saxophone Players

1. Saxophone keys are heavy and cumbersome compared to flute, oboe, and clarinet keys, and they are farther from the tone holes. As a result, playing fast, technical passages cleanly can be difficult on saxophone. Fortunately, the keys are comfortably spaced, and saxophonists do not have to worry about covering the tone holes with their fingers.

2. Although it is easier to produce a sound initially on the saxophone than it is on other woodwind instruments, proper embouchure formation and air control is crucial to technical fluidity. Because of the saxophone's construction (a brass instrument body that uses a cane reed to produce a tone), it has great tonal and pitch flexibility. When this flexibility is coupled with proper playing positions and air control, players can create a wide variety of articulations and musical effects, and they can execute technical passages smoothly and efficiently. However, this flexibility coupled with poor playing positions and air control is detrimental to technical proficiency.

3. Players often have trouble with the left-hand palm keys and the right-hand side keys in the upper range because reaching these keys requires the hands and/or fingers to shift slightly away from "home" position. Specifically, the left and right hands tend to rock back and the wrists tend to bend inward excessively when depressing these keys, causing the fingers to pull away from the keys. In many instances, players actually straighten or lock the fingers and lose track of the "home" keys altogether. Working with the palm/side keys in this range slowly and deliberately to develop finger coordination, timing, and proper placement is extremely important to technical development.

Specific Technical Considerations/Concerns for Saxophone Players

1. Alternate Fingerings/Alternates—Saxophone players use several alternate fingerings. The choice of fingerings should be determined by musical considerations including tone quality, intonation, and smoothness of the phrase. Although new fingerings may seem awkward initially, developing control over all fingerings including alternates is crucial to technical proficiency. See Alternate Fingerings/Alternates, page 336

2. Right- and Left-hand Key Clusters (Little-Finger Keys)—Saxophone players often struggle with the little-finger keys, especially on the left hand. Playing passages that involve the little fingers slowly and deliberately to develop finger coordination and dexterity is extremely important to technical development. Most saxophones are equipped with rollers that enable players to slide or roll the little finger more easily from one key to another in the key cluster. Learning to slide or roll properly from one key to another in the key cluster is crucial to proper technique. Playing smoothly to or from low B-flat, B-natural, and C-sharp is particularly problematic. Working on the little-finger keys slowly and deliberately to develop finger coordination and control is extremely important to technical development.

3. Octave Key—A common problem for saxophone players is not using the octave key when playing fourth-line D-natural and above. Players discover that they can bite (firm the embouchure considerably) to make the notes respond in the correct octave. Proper use of the octave key is critical for proper tone, intonation, and response. Not using the octave key causes problems in these areas and impedes technical proficiency. See also Octave Key, page 398

4. Left Thumb—A common problem among saxophone players is improper left thumb position. The proper position of the left thumb is at an angle with the thumbnail pointing at approximately 2 o'clock, so that the thumb can reach the octave key with a simple rocking motion, rather than a "jumping" motion. Using a jumping motion and having the left thumb out of position is extremely detrimental to technique, especially in rapid passages.

5. Right Thumb—Players often develop the habit of placing the thumb too far under the thumb rest, making it difficult to operate

the keys properly. Not placing the thumb properly under the rest hinders technical proficiency, especially in rapid passages. The thumb should be placed under the rest between the thumbnail and first joint.

6. Fingers Too Far From Keys—Saxophone players are notorious for letting their fingers "fly" too far from the keys. This habit causes poor finger coordination and slows technique overall. The fingers should come off of the keys only to the extent necessary to let the tone hole open up all the way. Developing efficient finger movement and keeping fingers close to the keys at all times will significantly improve technical proficiency.

7. Crossing the Break/Preparing the Right—Crossing the break can be very problematic on saxophone. The primary considerations are with finger coordination and finger/hand position, rather than with tonal response and covering tone holes. The main challenge with crossing the break is moving from an open fingering (where few keys are depressed) to a closed fingering (where many keys are depressed), requiring coordination of hands and fingers. For example, the interval from open C-sharp to fourth-line D-natural requires players to coordinate finger movement from a note that involves no fingers (open C-sharp) to a note that involves seven fingers (D-natural). Maintaining proper hand positions, keeping the fingers close to the keys at all times, and minimizing excess finger motion will help make crossing the break easier. See also Crossing the Break, page 358

8. High Range—Saxophone players are frequently required to play in the high range of the instrument. Developing control of embouchure, air, and fingers in the high range is essential to technical fluidity and proficiency. Suggestions for playing in the high range are listed as follows. See also Altissimo/Extended Range, page 341

   A. Saxophone players need to make very few adjustments in embouchure, air, and oral cavity throughout the range of the instrument compared to other woodwind instruments. That is, the same basic embouchure and open oral cavity used in the low range is also appropriate for the high range. This fact is the primary reason that players who start on clarinet and switch to saxophone often experience so much difficulty with tone quality and pitch on saxophone.

B. Saxophonists do make slight adjustments in embouchure, air, and the oral cavity to compensate for pitch tendencies. In addition, it is not uncommon to make slight changes in air and oral cavity focus on the lowest and the highest notes. See Altissimo/ Extended Range, page 341

C. Saxophonists often have trouble coordinating the left- and right-hand palm/side keys when playing high notes. Slow, deliberate practice will help players gain control of and coordinate these palm/side keys.

9. Skips and Leaps—Executing skips and leaps can be challenging. As with crossing the break, coordinating the fingers becomes key to executing skips and leaps effectively. Maintaining proper hand positions, keeping the fingers close to the keys at all times, and minimizing excess finger motion will help players execute skips and leaps cleanly. Suggestions for executing skips and leaps effectively are listed as follows. See also Crossing the Break, page 358

A. The primary technical consideration with skips and leaps is that players often make unnecessary changes in embouchure, air, and oral cavity from note to note. Again, there is no need to make such changes on saxophone.

B. Occasionally, when slurring to top-space G-natural or G-sharp above the staff, these pitches will "crack." It may be necessary to firm the embouchure very slightly to facilitate pitch placement on these notes. Finger/thumb coordination can also cause these slurs to crack. That is, if the thumb is too late activating the octave key (relative to the movement of the fingers), then the note may crack.

C. The octave key mechanism on the neck of the saxophone is susceptible to damage. If it is not working properly, it can cause the pitch to "crack," especially when slurring up to top-space G-natural or G-sharp or when slurring down from high D-natural (or above) to top-space G-natural or G-sharp.

Temperament: See Temperament, page 61

Tenor Saxophone: See Instrument Family and Playing Considerations, page 376

Throat/Bore, Mouthpiece: A term used to describe the part of a mouthpiece that fits over the neck cork and runs into the mouthpiece chamber. Most saxophone players use the term "throat" when describing this part of the mouthpiece. "Bore" is a term more commonly associated with brass mouthpieces. See also Mouthpiece/Mouthpieces, page 392

Thumb Rests: Places where the right and left thumbs are placed while in the playing position. The left thumb rest is next to the octave key. The left thumb should be angled across the thumb rest so that the thumb can bend or rock slightly at the knuckle to operate the octave key. The right thumb rest is on back of the saxophone below the neck strap ring and across from the side B-flat key. The right thumb should be perpendicular to the thumb rest and should contact the thumb rest at some point between the end of the thumb and the middle joint, depending on the size of the hand. Adjustable thumb rests are available as well. These thumb rests can be adjusted to better fit players' hands. See also Hand/Holding/Instrument/Playing Positions and Posture, page 367

Timbre: See Tone Quality, page 415

Tip Opening: The opening between the tip of the reed and the mouthpiece tip rail. The tip opening is a significant factor in determining the amount of resistance a mouthpiece will offer and the type of tone produced on an instrument. As a rule, a wider tip opening increases the amount of resistance the mouthpiece/reed combination will have. However, a wider tip opening also increases the potential for a bigger, fuller tone. Conversely, a narrower tip opening lessens the amount of resistance a mouthpiece/reed combination will have and reduces the potential for a bigger, fuller tone. See also Mouthpiece/Mouthpieces, page 392; Resistance, page 402

Tip Rail, Mouthpiece: The narrow flat area at the end of the mouthpiece table. The tip rail should be smooth and flat, and it should be free from nicks and scrapes. A damaged tip rail makes the tone difficult to control and often causes squeaking and poor tone quality because the reed is unable to close properly against the mouthpiece. Tip rails that are too wide produce a dead tone with little flexibility. Tip rails that are too narrow or uneven tend to be bright and inconsistent, and are more likely to squeak. See also Mouthpiece/Mouthpieces, page 392

Tip, Reed: The very thin area of a single reed that extends from the end of the reed slightly back. Generally, the tip of a reed closes off against the mouthpiece tip rail. See also Reeds, Single, page 265

Tone Holes: See Tone Holes, page 63

Tone Production: The term used to describe how tone is produced on an instrument. General considerations for woodwind tone production are discussed under Tone Production in chapter 1. Specific considerations for saxophone tone production and some of the terms included within the saxophone chapter that address tone production appear in the following section.

Tonal Concept/Tone Quality

Develop a concept of "good" saxophone tone and the type of tone quality desired. Listening to advanced players and high quality recordings can help develop appropriate tonal concepts. In addition, taking lessons from a knowledgeable teacher who provides an exemplary model during lessons is invaluable. See also Tone Production, page 63

1. Use appropriate equipment (instrument, mouthpiece, reed, ligature, etc.). Players should play on equipment that matches their level of performance and experience. As players mature, they should experiment with several advanced mouthpieces, ligatures, reeds, and necks under the guidance of a knowledgeable teacher to find the right combination for them.

2. Strive for a consistent tone quality and evenness of scale in all ranges, and develop control of the air stream at all dynamic levels. Maintain an open throat and oral cavity in all registers as if saying the syllable "ah" or "oh." Although the direction of the air stream may change slightly in the extreme high range (slightly higher) and in the extreme low range (slightly lower), the concept of focusing warm air around the reed as if saying "who" throughout the entire range of the instrument is a sound teaching concept on saxophone. That is, even in the high range, there is no need to close the oral cavity or tighten the embouchure.

Embouchure

Maintain proper embouchure formation at all times. Proper mechanics of embouchure are critical to tone production. Although many fine players' embouchures vary slightly from a classic or standard embouchure, the fundamental characteristics have withstood the test of time. Achieving a mature, characteristic tone on any wind instrument requires time and practice to develop the physical and aural skills necessary for proper tone production. A brief summary of embouchure considerations for good tone production appears in the following list. See also Embouchure, page 361

1. The mouth corners are drawn inward toward reed.
2. The lips surround the mouthpiece as if saying "oh" or "who." A drawstring analogy is often used to describe this rounded position.
3. The lower lip is slightly curled over the bottom teeth, and the jaw is lowered slightly. The lower lip remains against the reed, supported by the bottom teeth/jaw and surrounding muscles. Players should not put too much pressure on the lower lip with the teeth.
4. The chin remains flat, but not tight. The cheeks should not be puffed.
5. The upper teeth rest on top of the mouthpiece.
6. Maintain a consistent embouchure.

Breathing and Air

A thorough discussion of breathing and air is in chapter 1. See Breathing/Breath Support/Air Control, page 10; Tone Production, page 63

Vibrato

While vibrato is not a factor in tone production for beginners, it is a factor in tone production for more advanced players. Typically, vibrato is added after the fundamentals of good tone production have been mastered. Considerations for vibrato are listed as follows. See also Vibrato, page 418

1. Add vibrato to a full, well-centered tone according to the musical style being performed.
2. Use vibrato to enhance tone quality, not to cover up poor tone quality.
3. Use a jaw vibrato.

Specific Tonal Considerations/Concerns for Saxophone Players

1. Embouchure/High Notes—Players tend to bite or pinch in the high range, especially when they start on clarinet and switch to saxophone. As a rule, the alto saxophone embouchure should remain relatively the same throughout the entire range of the instrument. That is, the embouchure used in the high range is basically the same as it is in the middle and low ranges.

2. Tonal Control—Young players have a tendency to play with a loud, raucous tone quality. Players can think of surrounding the reed

with warm air as if saying "who" and using a steady, consistent air stream.

3. Mouthpiece Placement—Young players tend to take too much mouthpiece in the mouth. Only about one-third of the beak (or slightly more) should be inserted into the mouth.

4. Reed—Players need to use appropriate reed strengths. Harder reeds are more resistant than softer reeds. A certain amount of resistance is needed to maintain a steady, rich tone quality and proper intonation. When reeds are too soft, the tone is thin and "quivery" and pitch is difficult to control. When reeds are too hard, the tone is airy, response is poor, pitch control suffers, and players' embouchures tire quickly. Reeds need to be hard enough to push back against the lower lip pressure in order to create a stable tone but not so hard that players have to "fight" the reed. See also Reeds, Single, page 265

Tone Quality: The characteristic sound associated with an instrument regarding tone color or timbre, and consistency, focus, and control of the air stream. The tone quality of the saxophone varies from dark and mellow to bright and edgy, depending to a large degree on the reed/mouthpiece combination. From a mechanical standpoint, tone quality is dependent upon several factors involving the design of the instrument, the materials used in instrument construction, and, most important, the reed/mouthpiece combination, which is discussed under Reeds, Single, in chapter 3 and Mouthpiece/Mouthpieces in chapter 1. From a player's standpoint, tone quality is largely dependent upon two factors: (1) the use of air, which is discussed in detail under Tone Production and Breathing/Breath Support/Air Control, and (2) the embouchure and oral cavity, which is discussed in detail under Tone Production and Embouchure. Common terms associated with tone quality and common terms used to describe tone quality are identified and described under Tone Quality in chapter 1. See also Breathing/Breath Support/Air Control, page 10; Tone Quality, page 68

Key Questions

Q: Should I work on tone quality or intonation first?

A: Tone quality. If players cannot play with a good, consistent tone quality, working on intonation is counterproductive.

Tonguing: See Tonguing, page 71

Transpositions: The relationship between the written and sounding ranges of an instrument. Saxophones are transposing instruments. That is, saxophones do not sound as written. Members of the saxophone family, with only a few exceptions, are either in the keys of B-flat or E-flat. What follows is a list of saxophone transpositions. A summary of notated transpositions is shown in figure 4.29. See also Range, page 416

Saxophone Transpositions

1. The B-flat soprano saxophone sounds a major second lower than written. As a result, when it plays a written third-space C-natural, it sounds a concert B-flat one whole step lower than the written C-natural. The B-flat soprano saxophone sounds one octave higher than the B-flat tenor saxophone.

2. The E-flat alto saxophone sounds a major sixth lower than written. As a result, when it plays a written third-space C-natural, it sounds a concert E-flat a major sixth lower than the written C-natural. The E-flat alto saxophone sounds one octave higher than the E-flat baritone saxophone.

3. The B-flat tenor saxophone sounds an octave and a major second lower than written. As a result, when it plays a written third-space C-natural, it sounds a concert B-flat a major ninth below the written C-natural. The tenor saxophone sounds one octave lower than the B-flat soprano.

4. The E-flat baritone saxophone sounds an octave and a major sixth lower than written. As a result, when it plays a written third-space C-natural, it sounds a concert E-flat an octave and a major sixth below the written C-natural. The baritone saxophone sounds one octave lower than the E-flat alto saxophone.

FIGURE 4.29. *Saxophone Transpositions*

5. The B-flat bass saxophone sounds two octaves and a major second lower than written. As a result, when it plays a written third-space C-natural, it sounds a concert B-flat two octaves and a major second below the written C-natural. The bass saxophone sounds one octave lower than the B-flat tenor saxophone and two octaves lower than the B-flat soprano saxophone.

Triple-Tonguing: A technique that enables performers to tongue triple patterns rapidly. See also Multiple-Tonguing, page 52

Tuning/Tuning Note Considerations: Tuning any instrument is a process that involves making mechanical adjustments (e.g., pulling out or pushing in a mouthpiece, slide, or instrument joint) so that the instrument will produce pitches that are in tune with a predetermined standard (e.g., A = 440). Tuning notes refer to specific pitches that are good to tune to on any given instrument. Considerations have been given to the notes most commonly used for tuning wind groups. Adjusting pitch and adjusting for pitch tendencies of the saxophone are discussed under Intonation. Considerations for tuning the saxophone appear in the following list.

Tuning the Saxophone

1. Most saxophones are designed to be in tune (using A=440 as a standard) when the mouthpiece is positioned approximately two-thirds the way onto the neck cork, depending on the mouthpiece and the saxophone. The only way to determine the precise placement is to use a tuner, and even then, slight adjustments will be made from day to day.

2. Players can raise or lower the pitch by adjusting the position of the mouthpiece. Pulling the mouthpiece out flattens the pitch, whereas pushing the mouthpiece in sharpens the pitch. Generally, only small adjustments (no more than three-eighths of an inch) should be made for tuning purposes. The need to make larger adjustments is often an indication of problems in other areas such as embouchure or air focus. Occasionally, a particular mouthpiece may be ill suited for a particular instrument. In such instances, it is not uncommon to see a mouthpiece pulled out or pushed in near the end of the cork. Such placements negatively affect the overall intonation of the instrument, resulting in an uneven scale from note to note. Playing in tune under these circumstances is virtually impossible.

3. The position of the neck is not used to tune the instrument. The neck should be inserted into the receiver as far as it will go.

Tuning Note Considerations: Alto and Baritone

1. Concert B-flat (written G-natural)—An excellent tuning note in both octaves. The upper octave note is a little better for the alto, and the lower octave note is a little better for the baritone.
2. Concert A-natural (written F-sharp)—An excellent tuning note in both octaves and probably the best tuning note on the instrument. The upper octave note is a little better for the alto, and the lower octave note is a little better for the baritone.
3. Concert F-natural (written D-natural)—A poor tuning note in all three octaves. The lower octave note tends to be a little flat, and the middle and upper octave notes tend to be quite sharp.

Tuning Note Considerations: Soprano and Tenor

1. Concert B-flat (written C-natural)—A pretty good tuning note in the lower octave and an "okay" tuning note in the middle octave. The third-space C-natural tends to be a bit flat, so it may be better to tune to the low C-natural, depending on the instrument. Avoid tuning to the high C-natural.
2. Concert A-natural (written B-natural)—A pretty good tuning note in the middle octave (third-line B-natural) and a poor tuning note in both the lower and upper octaves because both octaves tend to be quite sharp. Generally, the third-line B-natural (concert A-natural) is a better tuning note than third-space C-natural (concert B-flat).
3. Concert F-natural (written G-natural)—A good tuning note in both octaves. Second-line G-natural is probably the best tuning note on soprano and tenor.

Vamp: The area of the reed from which the bark has been removed starting at the U-shaped cut and extending toward the heart of the reed. In other words, the vamp is the sloped area of the lay between the shoulders and the heart. See also Reeds, Single, page 265

Vibrato: Two types of vibrato are commonly used in woodwind playing: jaw vibrato and diaphragmatic vibrato. Jaw vibrato results in regular pitch fluctuations around a tonal center, whereas diaphragmatic vibrato results in regular intensity (loudness) fluctuations around a tonal center. Nearly all saxophone players use a jaw vibrato. Steps for developing vibrato are under Vibrato in chapter 1. See also Vibrato, page 74

Water Key: See Spit Valve/Water Key, page 406

Window, Mouthpiece: The open area of a mouthpiece cut out of the mouthpiece table and opposite the baffle. The flat side of the reed covers the window. The term "window" is also sometimes used to refer to the opening between the throat and the chamber. See also Mouthpiece/Mouthpieces, page 392

Written Range: The written range for all saxophones is the same regardless of key or size; it is the sounding ranges that vary from instrument to instrument. Furthermore, all saxophone music is written in the treble clef. The basic written range of all saxophones is from low B-flat (below the staff) to high F-natural above the staff. Most intermediate and professional model saxophones have a high F-sharp key that extends this range upward one half step to high F-sharp. Many baritone saxophones have a low A-key that extends the instrument's range downward one half step to low A-natural, and some sopranos have a high G-key that extends the instrument's range upward one half step to high G-natural. Suggested ranges for different playing levels are under Range. See also Instrument Family and Playing Considerations, page 376; Range, page 401; Transpositions, page 416

PRACTICAL TIPS

Saxophone Basic Fingerings

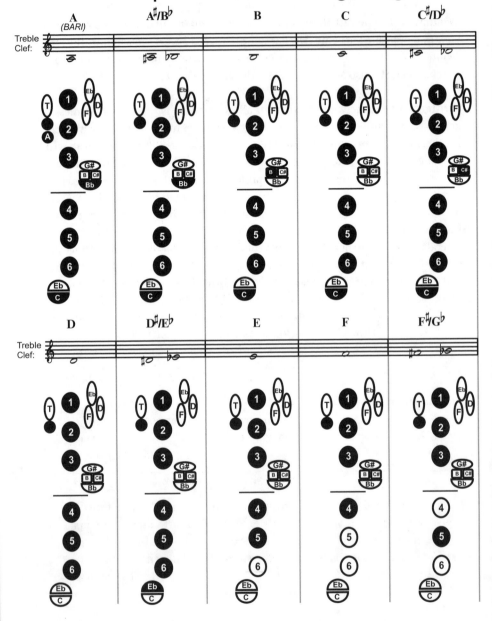

Saxophone Basic Fingerings

Saxophone Basic Fingerings

Saxophone Basic Fingerings

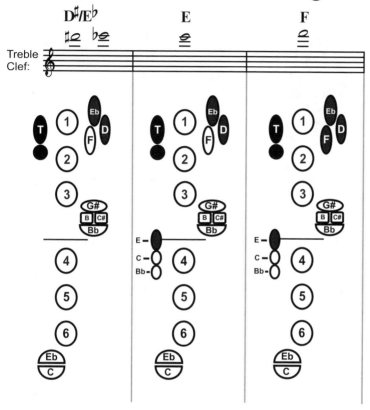

Saxophone Alternate Fingerings

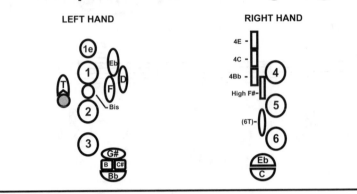

LEFT HAND	RIGHT HAND

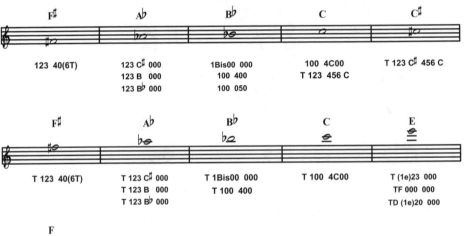

F♯	A♭	B♭	C	C♯
123 40(6T)	123 C♯ 000	1Bis00 000	100 4C00	T 123 C♯ 456 C
	123 B 000	100 400	T 123 456 C	
	123 B♭ 000	100 050		

F♯	A♭	B♭	C	E
T 123 40(6T)	T 123 C♯ 000	T 1Bis00 000	T 100 4C00	T (1e)23 000
	T 123 B 000	T 100 400		TF 000 000
	T 123 B♭ 000			TD (1e)20 000

F
T (1e)20 000

Saxophone Altissimo Fingerings

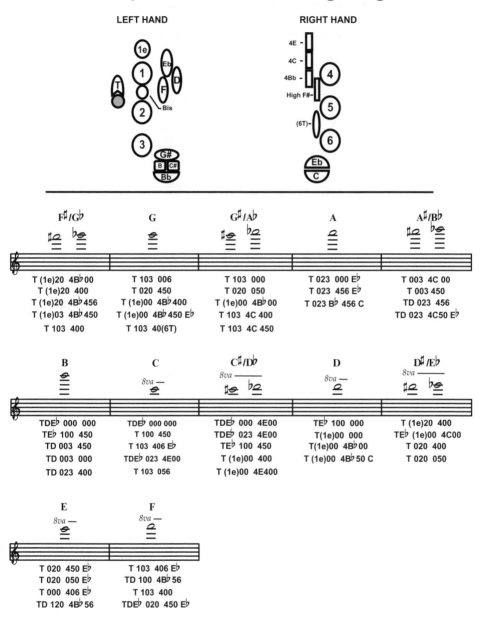

Saxophone Special Trill Fingerings

Trills performed with regular fingerings are not included

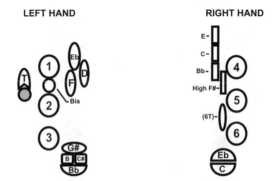

Saxophone Special Trill Fingerings
Trills performed with regular fingerings are not included

C# to D	D# to E	D# to E	Eb to F	F to F#
123 C# 456 C	123 456 Eb	123 456 Eb	123 456 Eb	123 40 (6T)

F# to G#	G# to A	Ab to Bb	A to Bb	Bb to B
123 G# 050	123 G# 000	123 G# Bb 00	120 Bb 00	120 Bb 00
		1Bis 23 G# 000	1Bis 20 000	100 400
				1Bis 00 000

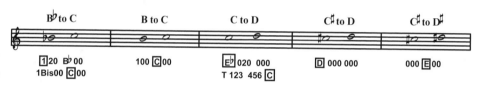

Bb to C	B to C	C to D	C# to D	C# to D#
120 Bb 00	100 C 00	Eb 020 000	D 000 000	000 E 00
1Bis00 C 00		T 123 456 C		

D# to E	Eb to F	F to F#	F# to G#	G# to A
T 123 456 Eb	T 123 456 Eb	T 123 40 (6T)	T 123 G# 050	T 123 G# 000

Saxophone Special Trill Fingerings

Trills performed with regular fingerings are not included

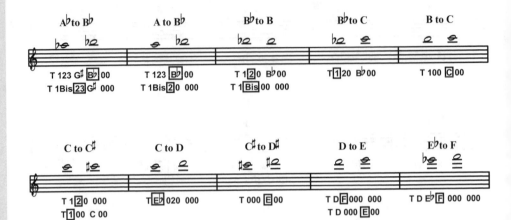

Ab to Bb
T 123 G♯ B♭ 00
T 1Bis 23 G♯ 000

A to Bb
T 123 B♭ 00
T 1Bis 2 0 000

Bb to B
T 1 2 0 B♭ 00
T 1 Bis 00 000

Bb to C
T 1 20 B♭ 00

B to C
T 100 C 00

C to C♯
T 1 2 0 000
T 1 00 C 00

C to D
T E♭ 020 000

C♯ to D♯
T 000 E 00

D to E
T D F 000 000
T D 000 E 00

Eb to F
T D E♭ F 000 000

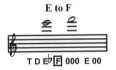

E to F
T D E♭ F 000 E 00

COMMON TECHNICAL FAULTS AND CORRECTIONS

Many problems in wind playing result from basic faults in the following areas: (1) instrument assembly, (2) embouchure formation, and (3) hand/holding/playing positions and posture. The following section provides information on how to correct technical faults frequently encountered in saxophone performance. Headings appear in alphabetical order.

Assembly

FAULT 1:   Improperly aligning the neck of the instrument with the bell and body.

CORRECTION: Align the neck with the center of the bell or slightly to the left of center. Make sure that the tightening screw is loose while the neck is being positioned and/or adjusted. When the neck is positioned properly, tighten the screw snugly. Do not overtighten.

FAULT 2:   Not pushing the neck onto the body far enough.

CORRECTION: Make sure that the end of the neck and the neck receiver at the top of the instrument body are clean. Loosen the tightening screw and insert the neck straight (not at an angle) into the body with a gentle back-and-forth twisting motion. Push the neck in all the way, align the neck properly, and tighten the screw snugly.

FAULT 3:   Pushing the mouthpiece too far/not far enough onto the neck.

CORRECTION: After tuning properly, mark a short line on the cork with a pencil or pen, and use this line as a guide to place the mouthpiece each time the saxophone is assembled. Although the precise placement of the mouthpiece may vary slightly from day to day, this line provides an excellent reference point.

FAULT 4:   Improperly aligning the mouthpiece.

CORRECTION: Make sure that the reed side of the mouthpiece (mouthpiece table) faces the floor. The mouthpiece angle is correct when the player can keep his or her head straight (not tilted to one side) when playing. The mouthpiece should be pushed onto the neck cork to the predetermined tuning line or mark. Usually, about two-thirds of the cork will be covered;

however, the exact placement of the mouthpiece on the neck cork can vary widely from one instrument and/or mouthpiece to another. Check the mouthpiece placement regularly with a tuner.

FAULT 5:   Handling the instrument carelessly and putting unnecessary pressure on the keys and rods.

CORRECTION: Handle the saxophone by grasping the bell firmly with the left hand. Avoid touching the rods and keys. Attach the saxophone to the neck strap immediately. Do not walk around with the saxophone detached from the neck strap. Carry the saxophone in the case or keep it hooked to the neck strap. Assembling the saxophone while seated or standing next to the playing location will minimize unnecessary handling.

FAULT 6:   Handling the neck improperly, and placing unnecessary pressure on the octave key mechanism.

CORRECTION: Avoid touching the octave key mechanism on the neck during assembly. Hold the neck such that the palm of the hand is above (not touching) the octave key mechanism. The neck is held securely along the sides of the neck between the right thumb and fingers. After making sure that the tightening screw is loose, insert the neck into the main body with a gentle back-and-forth twisting motion and align the neck properly. Tighten the screw snugly.

FAULT 7:   Applying unnecessary pressure to the neck (or actually bending the neck) when placing the mouthpiece onto the neck cork.

CORRECTION: When placing the mouthpiece on the neck, support the neck with the left hand. Place the left thumb on the underneath side of the neck just behind the cork, and hold the neck securely between the thumb and index fingers. Gently wrap the other fingers around the neck without touching the octave key mechanism. Make sure the neck cork is well greased, and use a gentle back-and-forth twisting motion while pushing the mouthpiece straight onto the neck cork. Do not pull downward on the neck when placing the mouthpiece onto the neck.

FAULT 8:   Improperly aligning the reed on the mouthpiece table.

CORRECTION: Center the reed on the mouthpiece table between the side rails and slightly below the tip rail. As a general rule, a very small amount of black (tip rail) should be showing above the tip of the reed. Pushing the reed up slightly past the tip slightly can improve the tone quality of soft reeds and raise the pitch slightly.

FAULT 9:   Improperly placing the ligature and setting the tension.

CORRECTION: Place the ligature slightly below the U-shaped cut of the reed and tighten the ligature just enough to hold the reed in place. Do not overtighten. Overtightening the ligature affects tone quality and reed response, and it will strip the ligature threads quickly.

FAULT 10:   Sliding the ligature over the reed/mouthpiece assembly.

CORRECTION: Make sure that the ligature is placed over the mouthpiece before placing or positioning the reed on the mouthpiece table. While holding up the ligature toward the tip of the mouthpiece with the left hand, slide the reed between the ligature and the mouthpiece table, and position the ligature slightly below the U-shaped cut. Align the reed properly and tighten the ligature screws enough to hold the reed in place. Using this method of placing the reed on the mouthpiece will help prevent chipped reeds.

Embouchure Formation

FAULT 1:   Not rolling enough bottom lip over the teeth.

CORRECTION: Generally, the red part of the bottom lip is not visible (or may be barely visible) at the point where the reed contacts the bottom lip; however, the amount of bottom lip over the teeth varies from player to player.

FAULT 2:   Taking too much mouthpiece into the mouth.

CORRECTION: The mouthpiece should be inserted into the mouth about one-third (probably too little) to one-half (probably too much) the length of the beak. The exact position depends upon the player and the mouthpiece, and slight adjustments can be made based on tone quality and response.

FAULT 3:   Mouth corners are drawn back in a smiling position.

CORRECTION: The embouchure should be rounded as if saying "who" or "oh." Using the drawstring analogy often helps players understand this roundness.

FAULT 4:   Embouchure too tight or biting.

CORRECTION: The embouchure should be relaxed as if saying "who" or "oh." Think of blowing warm air into and through the saxophone and lower the jaw slightly. The bottom lip forms a cushion for the reed. That is, the lips and teeth should not bite the reed by being stretched too tightly. The top lip should rest naturally on top of the mouthpiece.

FAULT 5:   Air escaping through the mouth corners.

CORRECTION: Air escapes when the surrounding muscles are not supporting inwardly toward the mouthpiece. Players can think of surrounding the reed with even pressure from all sides (a drawstring effect) and form a seal around the mouthpiece so that air does not escape through the mouth corners. Forming a proper embouchure will eliminate this problem.

FAULT 6:   Puffing the cheeks.

CORRECTION: The mouth corners provide support inwardly toward the mouthpiece, and the chin should remain flat. Focus the air stream around the reed and through the tip opening.

FAULT 7:   Top teeth not resting on the mouthpiece.

CORRECTION: Rest the top teeth lightly on top of the mouthpiece without biting into the mouthpiece. If players find this placement uncomfortable, a thin rubber pad can be placed on top of the mouthpiece.

FAULT 8:   Top teeth putting too much pressure on top of the mouthpiece.

CORRECTION: The top teeth should rest on top of the mouthpiece lightly without biting the mouthpiece. Too much pressure results when players force the head downward. Players should maintain proper position of the head during play.

Hand/Holding/Instrument Playing Positions and Posture

FAULT 1:   Elbows too far from or too close to the body while playing.

CORRECTION: Elbows should be held out from the body in a relaxed, comfortable position.

FAULT 2:   Elbows resting on knees while playing.

CORRECTION: Elbows should be held out from the body in a relaxed, comfortable position. Younger, smaller players sometimes rest their arms on their knees when they get tired. Take frequent breaks to eliminate fatigue and encourage proper playing positions at all times.

FAULT 3:   Holding the saxophone at an improper angle, causing the right and/or left wrist to bend excessively.

CORRECTION: Generally, the mouthpiece/neck assembly is centered with the main body of the saxophone. However, the neck can be turned slightly in either direction for comfort and stability. Players who stand while playing, or who position the saxophone between the legs while in the seated position, often turn the neck slightly to the left. Players who sit while playing and hold the saxophone in the side position, often turn the neck slightly to the right. Regardless of the playing position, the wrists should remain relatively straight if the saxophone is held at the proper angle.

FAULT 4:   Tilting the head too much to one side.

CORRECTION: The head remains straight at all times. Players who hold the saxophone in the side position are prone to tilting their heads while playing. Turning the mouthpiece to the right will compensate for the angle of the saxophone.

FAULT 5:   Slouching.

CORRECTION: Sit up (or stand) straight, keep the chin in a normal position (not down or up), keep the eyes straight ahead, and keep the shoulders and back straight but relaxed.

FAULT 6:   Resting the bell of the saxophone on the chair.

CORRECTION: Sit farther forward on the chair so that the bell cannot rest on the chair and adjust the neck strap so that the mouthpiece enters the mouth at the proper angle.

FAULT 7:   Improperly positioning the bell.

CORRECTION: Both holding positions (side and front) require that the bell of the saxophone be drawn slightly back toward the body. Maintaining a proper bell position allows the mouthpiece to enter the mouth at the appropriate angle and enables players to maintain proper hand/holding/instrument/playing positions and posture.

FAULT 8:   Not placing the left thumb on the thumb rest at the proper angle.

CORRECTION: Keep the left thumb on the thumb rest at an angle (approximately 2 o'clock) that will allow the thumb to operate the octave key with a small rocking motion.

FAULT 9:   "Locking" or straightening fingers.

CORRECTION: Fingers should be slightly curved so that a C-shape is formed between the thumb and fingers.

FAULT 10:   Allowing the right-hand or left-hand little finger to droop or float out of position.

CORRECTION: The right-hand and left-hand little fingers should remain close to the D-sharp key and G-sharp keys respectively in a ready position to minimize finger movement and facilitate technical proficiency.

FAULT 11:   Pushing the right thumb too far under the thumb rest.

CORRECTION: As a rule, the right thumb contacts the thumb rest between the thumbnail and the knuckle. Depending on the make or type of saxophone and the placement of the thumb rest, the thumb may contact the thumb rest slightly below the knuckle. The right thumb serves as a balance point for the saxophone but does not support the weight of the instrument.

FAULT 12:   Bending the right wrist.

CORRECTION: The right wrist should remain relatively straight; however, a slight bend is normal. An excessively bent wrist is often the result of the bell being angled too far to the right. Turn the saxophone slightly to the left and adjust the neck accordingly if needed.

FAULT 13:   Holding fingers too far from keys.

CORRECTION: Fingers remain as close as possible to the keys while playing to eliminate unnecessary motion. Keeping the fingers close to the keys promotes smooth, clean, and fast technique.

FAULT 14:   Improperly adjusting the neck strap.

CORRECTION: Adjust the neck strap so that the mouthpiece comes directly to the mouth when the instrument is in proper playing position. The neck strap is improperly adjusted if players have to reach up or down for the mouthpiece. The adjustment mechanism on the neck strap can slide out of place during use because of the saxophone's weight. As a result, players typically need to make small adjustments periodically to maintain the position of the neck strap.

COMMON PROBLEMS, CAUSES, AND SOLUTIONS FOR SAXOPHONE

Problems in wind instrument playing relate to some aspect of sound. That is, incorrect assembly is not a problem; poor tone quality or squeaking is a problem. Incorrect assembly is simply one common cause of such problems. Understanding this distinction makes it easier to apply effective solutions to problems. The following section provides information on solving problems frequently encountered in saxophone performance. The main headings are: Articulation Problems, Intonation Problems, Performance/Technical Problems, and Tone Quality and Response Problems.

Articulation Problems

PROBLEM: Audible dip or scoop in pitch during initial attacks.

CAUSE 1:   Excessive movement of the embouchure (especially the jaw and tongue) while tonguing.

SOLUTION 1:   Use light, quick movements of the tongue and maintain a consistent embouchure. Use a "tu" syllable not a "twa" syllable. Practice tonguing in front of a mirror and use the visual feedback to help eliminate jaw movement.

CAUSE 2:   Embouchure not set properly before the attack.

SOLUTION 2:   Allow enough time to be physically and mentally set before the attack. That is, the embouchure must be set properly for the note being played. When the embouchure is too tight or too loose for a particular note at the point of attack, players will make an immediate adjustment or shift to correct the pitch. This shift causes an audible dip or scoop in the attack.

PROBLEM: Heavy, thick, and/or sluggish attacks.

CAUSE 1:   Too much tongue contacting the reed on the attacks coupled with a slow tonguing action.

SOLUTION 1:   Minimize tongue movement. Use a light, quick tonguing action and make sure the tip of the tongue strikes the tip of the reed. Think of moving only the tip of the tongue during the tonguing process and use a "tu" attack for normal tonguing.

CAUSE 2:   Tonguing too far down on the reed.

SOLUTION 2:   The tip of the tongue strikes the tip of the reed. Make sure the tongue is pulled back or arched slightly in the mouth to begin the tonguing process. This position places the tongue slightly higher in the mouth to start. Think of moving only the tip of the tongue quickly and lightly.

CAUSE 3:   Tongue disrupting the air stream.

SOLUTION 3:   If the tongue is too low or too high in the mouth, or if the tongue moves too slowly, the air stream is disrupted, causing sluggish attacks. Make sure the tongue is pulled back or arched slightly in the mouth to begin the tonguing process, and increase the quickness of the tongue strike against the tip of the reed.

PROBLEM: Mistimed attacks (tongue, embouchure, air).

CAUSE 1:   Tongue and air stream not coordinated.

SOLUTION 1:   Practice coordinating the tongue and the air stream by attacking one note at a time. Think of starting the tongue and the air at the same time on attacks. Although it is the release of the tongue from the reed that actually starts a tone, the air stream and the tongue must work together.

CAUSE 2:   Embouchure not set properly before the attack.

SOLUTION 2: Allow enough time to be physically and mentally set before the attack. That is, the embouchure must be set properly for the note being played. An embouchure that is too tight or too loose for the note being played can delay the response of the attack.

CAUSE 3: Too much embouchure movement during attacks.

SOLUTION 3: The embouchure must be set properly for the note being played. Maintain embouchure formation and avoid using a "jawing" action. Think of moving only the tip of the tongue.

CAUSE 4: Player not set to play.

SOLUTION 4: Maintain proper playing positions (physical readiness), and internally hear the pitches before playing them (mental readiness).

PROBLEM: Inability to execute clean slurs.

CAUSE 1: Inconsistent air stream.

SOLUTION 1: Do not change the air stream from note to note. Instead, blow a consistent stream of air and simply move the fingers. On saxophone, it is generally not necessary to adjust the air stream for various pitches in slurred passages; however, adjustments in air speed and air volume should be made as necessary to accommodate the dynamic level.

CAUSE 2: Too much embouchure movement throughout a slurred passage.

SOLUTION 2: Use the same embouchure throughout the entire passage. Making large shifts in embouchure for various notes disrupts the air stream and is completely unnecessary on saxophone.

CAUSE 3: Fingers not coordinated.

SOLUTION 3: Keep the fingers close to the keys and depress them quickly and smoothly from note to note. Avoid excess finger movement, and avoid "slapping" the keys.

CAUSE 4: Player not set to play.

SOLUTION 4: Maintain proper playing positions (physical readiness), and internally "hear" the pitches before playing them (mental readiness).

PROBLEM: Inability to execute clean releases.

CAUSE 1:   Inappropriate use of tongue cutoffs.

SOLUTION 1:   Use breath releases rather than tongue cutoffs in most musical contexts because tongue cutoffs tend to be harsh and abrupt. Tongue cutoffs are appropriate in some jazz styles.

CAUSE 2:   Putting the tongue back on the reed too hard on tongue cutoffs.

SOLUTION 2:   When tongue cutoffs are appropriate (e.g., some jazz styles), be sure that players do not use too much tongue, which distorts the attacks. When tongue cutoffs are called for, the tongue should make a modest amount of contact on the tip of the reed.

CAUSE 3:   Not stopping the air at the point of release.

SOLUTION 3:   Practice maintaining an open air column from the diaphragm into the instrument, and stop the air by suspending it mid-stream as if lightly gasping. Using the throat as a valve and/or pushing the air on releases both prevent clean releases.

CAUSE 4:   Not "lifting" on the release.

SOLUTION 4:   Think of gasping lightly on the release and directing the air stream upward. Thinking this way helps stop the flow of air quickly while maintaining an open air column. Make sure to maintain a consistent embouchure during the release.

CAUSE 5:   Closing off the embouchure and/or throat, or using the embouchure and/or throat as a valve for stopping the air.

SOLUTION 5:   Be sure that the embouchure and throat remain unchanged on breath releases. It is the air that is stopped to release a tone. Think of gasping lightly on the release and directing the air stream upward. Thinking this way helps stop the flow of air quickly while maintaining an open air column, an open throat, and a proper embouchure.

PROBLEM: Inability to execute a controlled accent.

CAUSE 1:   Not balancing the air stream and tongue appropriately.

SOLUTION 1:   On most accents, do not increase the weight of the tongue on the attack. Rather, the accent is produced by a sudden increase in air. On an accented note, "lift off" with the air; that is, think of gasping lightly and directing the air stream upward on the release. As a rule, do not use tongue cutoffs on accented notes.

CAUSE 2: Too much tongue on releases in staccato passages with repeated accents.

SOLUTION 2: Think of tonguing each note consistently and evenly, and the releases will take care of themselves. In rapid patterns, the release of each note (except the first) in the pattern becomes the attack for each subsequent note.

Intonation Problems

PROBLEM: Pitch generally flat in all registers.

CAUSE 1: Mouthpiece pulled out too far.

SOLUTION 1: Determine the appropriate mouthpiece placement by using a tuner, and put a line or mark on the neck cork with a pen. Position the mouthpiece at this line each time the instrument is assembled, and then make small adjustments as needed.

CAUSE 2: Embouchure too loose.

SOLUTION 2: Think of surrounding the reed with warm air as if saying "who," and firm the embouchure slightly. Think of decreasing the imaginary circle of air into the instrument, while still maintaining an open air stream. That is, use a slightly more focused air stream.

CAUSE 3: Too much air, or overblowing.

SOLUTION 3: Use a controlled, steady air stream, and slow the air stream slightly. Form the embouchure as if saying "who" or "oh," and surround the reed with warm air.

CAUSE 4: Not compensating for the natural tendency of the saxophone to go flat in loud passages.

SOLUTION 4: Raise the direction of the air stream slightly to compensate for the drop in pitch and use a more focused oral cavity. It may be necessary to firm the embouchure slightly on pitches that are significantly flat, especially in the fortissimo dynamic range.

CAUSE 5: Air stream directed downward too much.

SOLUTION 5: Surround the reed with warm air as if saying "who" or "oh" and maintain a consistent air stream. For a more narrow focus, think of blowing air through and around the tip opening.

CAUSE 6:   Poor, slouching posture.

SOLUTION 6:   When seated, sit up straight (but avoid being rigid or tense) with feet flat on the floor. Sit toward the front edge of the chair. When standing, stand straight (avoid being tense or rigid) and position the feet about shoulder width apart. Standing with the left leg in front of the right leg may add stability and comfort, especially on tenor and baritone. Do not "lock" the knees when standing. This position may also enable players to take in more air during inhalation.

CAUSE 7:   Holding the saxophone at an incorrect angle.

SOLUTION 7:   Adjust the neck strap properly. The bell of the saxophone should be brought back so that the mouthpiece enters the mouth at a slightly upward angle. If the mouthpiece enters at an improper angle, the embouchure's ability to support the reed properly is comprised and the pitch will be flat.

CAUSE 8:   Head tilted downward or forward too much.

SOLUTION 8:   Adjust the neck strap so that the mouthpiece comes directly to the mouth. Players should not have to reach upward or downward for the mouthpiece. Reaching for the mouthpiece affects the embouchure's ability to support the reed properly and causes the pitch to be flat.

CAUSE 9:   Pads are too close to the tone holes.

SOLUTION 9:   Have a knowledgeable repair technician adjust the pads to the proper height.

CAUSE 10:   Reed is too soft.

SOLUTION 10:   Using harder reeds will offer more resistance and raise the pitch. Softer reeds tend to play flat.

CAUSE 11:   Neck not inserted all the way into the body.

SOLUTION 11:   After loosening the neck screw, place the neck into the body of the instrument as far as it will go. Tighten the neck screw so that the neck stays in place. Do not over tighten.

PROBLEM: Pitch generally sharp in all registers.

CAUSE 1:   Mouthpiece pushed in too far.

SOLUTION 1: Determine the appropriate mouthpiece placement by using a tuner, and put a line or mark on the neck cork with a pen. Position the mouthpiece at this line each time the instrument is assembled, and then make small adjustments as needed.

CAUSE 2:   Embouchure too tight, or biting.

SOLUTION 2: Relax the embouchure, lower the jaw slightly, and surround the reed with warm air as if saying "who" or "oh." "Oh" is slightly more open than "who." Let the tone quality dictate which syllable is more appropriate. Make sure the mouth corners are drawn inward rather than pulled back and that the lower lip is not stretched too tightly over the teeth. It may be helpful to think of increasing the imaginary circle of air into the instrument. That is, use a slightly more open air stream.

CAUSE 3:   Not using enough air.

SOLUTION 3: Use a controlled, steady air stream, and increase air speed.

CAUSE 4:   Not compensating for the natural tendency to go sharp as less air is used.

SOLUTION 4: Lower the direction of the air stream slightly to compensate for the rise in pitch and use a more open oral cavity. It may be necessary to relax the embouchure slightly on pitches that are significantly sharp, especially in the pianissimo dynamic range.

CAUSE 5:   Air stream directed upward too much.

SOLUTION 5: Surround the reed with warm air as if saying "who" or "oh" and maintain a consistent air stream. It may help to think of blowing air through and around the tip opening.

CAUSE 6:   Holding the saxophone at an incorrect angle.

SOLUTION 6: Adjust the neck strap properly. The bell of the saxophone should be brought back so that the mouthpiece enters the mouth at a slightly upward angle. When the mouthpiece angle causes too much lower lip pressure on the reed, the pitch goes sharp.

CAUSE 7:   Pads are too far from tone holes.

SOLUTION 7: Have a knowledgeable repair technician adjust the pads to the proper height.

CAUSE 8:   Reed is too hard.

SOLUTION 8:   Using softer reeds will offer less resistance and lower the pitch.

PROBLEM: Pitch is inconsistent throughout the playing range.

CAUSE 1:   Inconsistent air stream.

SOLUTION 1:   Do not change the air stream from note to note. Instead, blow a consistent stream of air and simply move the fingers. On saxophone, it is generally not necessary to adjust the air stream for various pitches in slurred passages; however, adjustments in air speed and air volume should be made as necessary to accommodate the dynamic level.

CAUSE 2:   Inconsistent embouchure.

SOLUTION 2:   Form a good basic embouchure and make sure that there is enough bottom lip over the teeth. Practice playing long tones to develop the embouchure muscles, and concentrate on keeping the embouchure consistent at all times. Use a mirror on a regular basis to check embouchure formation until proper habits are formed.

CAUSE 3:   Lack of proper breath support.

SOLUTION 3:   Work on breathing exercises with and without the saxophone to help develop breath support. Take full breaths and practice playing long tones at all dynamic levels. Focus on maintaining a consistent air speed appropriate for each dynamic level. Practice extensively at softer dynamic levels because it is harder to maintain proper breath support at softer dynamic levels than it is at louder dynamic levels. In addition, breath support is often compromised when playing technical passages, because players tend to focus on technique at the expense of proper breath support. Practice maintaining breath support in technical passages.

CAUSE 4:   Slouching.

SOLUTION 4:   When seated, sit up straight (but avoid being rigid or tense) with feet flat on the floor. Sit toward the front edge of the chair. When standing, stand straight (avoid being tense or rigid) and position the feet about shoulder width apart. Standing with the left leg in front of the right leg may add stability and comfort, especially on tenor and baritone. Do not "lock" the knees when standing. This position may also enable players to take in more air during inhalation.

CAUSE 5:   Shifting the angle at which the saxophone is held.

SOLUTION 5:   Adjust the neck strap properly. The bell of the saxophone should be brought back so that the mouthpiece enters the mouth at a slightly upward angle. If the mouthpiece enters at an improper angle, the embouchure's ability to support the reed properly is comprised and the pitch will be flat and inconsistent.

PROBLEM: Pitch is inconsistent throughout the playing range.

CAUSE 1:   Inconsistent air stream.

SOLUTION 1:   Do not change the air stream from note to note. Instead, blow a consistent stream of air and simply move the fingers. On saxophone, it is generally not necessary to adjust the air stream for various pitches in slurred passages; however, adjustments in air speed and air volume should be made as necessary to accommodate the dynamic level.

PROBLEM: Playing out of tune without adjusting.

NOTE: A detailed account of adjusting pitch can be found under Intonation in chapter 1.

CAUSE 1:   Inability to hear beats or roughness.

SOLUTION 1:   Focus on hearing the beats or pulsations that occur when pitches are out of tune. Play long tone unisons with other players and listen for beats. Deliberately playing extremely flat and sharp to accentuate the beats will help players learn to hear beats.

CAUSE 2:   Not knowing how to adjust pitch on the instrument.

SOLUTION 2:   There are several ways to adjust pitch involving the mouthpiece position, embouchure, throat, oral cavity, air stream, and alternate fingerings. Players need to learn how each of these factors affects pitch.

CAUSE 3:   The physical skills necessary to adjust pitch on the instrument are not developed.

SOLUTION 3:   Practice adjusting pitch every day and continue developing embouchure skills. Relax and tighten the embouchure, focus the air stream upward and downward, open and close the throat and oral cavity, and try alternate fingerings. Learn "what does what" so that appropriate adjustments can be made when necessary.

Performance/Technical Problems

PROBLEM: Sloppy playing in tongued technical passages.

CAUSE 1: Tongue and fingers not coordinated.

SOLUTION 1: Practice simple interval exercises slowly with a metronome, and make sure that the tongue and fingers move together. Keep the fingers close to the keys during these exercises to avoid excessive finger movement. As control is gained, progress to more difficult exercises and continue to practice with a metronome. Gradually speed up the exercises, but make sure that proper finger-tongue coordination is maintained.

CAUSE 2: Tonguing speed too slow.

SOLUTION 2: Using a metronome, start by practicing a variety of simple rhythm patterns on isolated pitches at a slow tempo. Gradually increase the speed and difficulty of the exercises. Use a "tip to tip" (tip of the tongue to the tip of the reed) technique and keep the tongue motion light and quick. Periodically, practice tonguing slightly faster than is comfortable. Develop control and rhythmic precision by changing the tempo frequently.

PROBLEM: Sloppy playing overall.

CAUSE 1: Poor Hand/Holding/Instrument/Playing Positions and Posture.

SOLUTION 1: Make sure that the playing basics are maintained at all times. A detailed discussion of these playing basics is located under Hand/Holding/Instrument/Playing Positions and Posture.

CAUSE 2: Poor instrument action.

SOLUTION 2: Make sure the key mechanisms have been properly adjusted, cleaned, and oiled. Excessively heavy or uneven action is usually a result of poorly adjusted key mechanisms, poorly adjusted pads, and/or bent key mechanisms. In addition, make sure the springs are in proper working condition. Weak springs sometimes bobble or bounce, which inhibits technical fluidity.

CAUSE 3: Using awkward fingerings.

SOLUTION 3: Use alternate fingerings when appropriate to maximize technical fluidity. Preparing the right hand when crossing the break and using basic chromatic fingerings contributes significantly to clean playing.

PROBLEM: Speed of the fingers seems slow in technical passages.

CAUSE 1: Tenseness in the fingers and hands.

SOLUTION 1: Practice tough passages slowly at first to gain control, and focus on staying relaxed; trying too hard or forcing the fingers to move during technical passages slows down the fingers. Gradually increase the tempo of the passage, and develop the habit of staying relaxed at all tempos.

PROBLEM: An excessive amount of key noise can be heard when the keys are depressed.

CAUSE 1: Key mechanisms need to be oiled.

SOLUTION 1: If excessive key noise is heard during regular play, oil the mechanisms. As a rule, key mechanisms should be oiled lightly once a month or so. Clacking sounds are often caused by metal-to-metal contact, which results in excessive wear of the key mechanisms.

CAUSE 2: Pushing keys down too hard or "slapping" the keys.

SOLUTION 2: Use only enough finger pressure to seal the pads against the tone holes. Stay relaxed, and think of playing smoothly and efficiently. Keeping the fingers close to the keys will help eliminate the tendency to "slap" the fingers down.

CAUSE 3: Corks or felts are missing.

SOLUTION 3: If the corks or felts that prevent metal-to-metal contact (and help regulate proper key height) fall off, replace them and adjust pad height appropriately.

PROBLEM: Skips and leaps not clean.

CAUSE 1: Fingers not coordinated.

SOLUTION 1: Practice simple interval exercises slowly with a metronome, and focus on moving the tongue and fingers together. Keep the fingers close to the keys during these exercises to avoid excessive finger movement. It may also help to slur all exercises because tonguing often covers up poor finger coordination. As control is gained, progress to more difficult exercises and continue to practice with a metronome. Gradually speed up the exercises, making sure that proper finger-tongue coordination is maintained.

CAUSE 2:   Air stream not maintained properly.

SOLUTION 2:   Maintain a consistent air stream at all dynamic levels. Improper use of air in passages involving skips and leaps causes coordination problems between the tongue, fingers, and air stream. Players tend to focus on skips and leaps at the expense of proper breath support. Focus on maintaining breath support in all technical passages.

CAUSE 3:   Improper left thumb (octave key) action.

SOLUTION 3:   Make sure that the left thumb is positioned on the thumb rest at an angle such that the thumbnail is directed at approximately 2 o'clock. This position allows the thumb to reach the octave key with a simple rocking motion, rather than a jumping motion. Using a jumping motion and having the left thumb out of position hinders technique, especially in rapid passages.

PROBLEM: Poor finger-tongue coordination.

CAUSE 1:   Poor playing habits resulting from playing too fast, too soon.

SOLUTION 1:   Practice simple interval exercises slowly with a metronome, and focus on moving the tongue and fingers together. Keep the fingers close to the keys during these exercises to avoid excessive finger movement. Slur all exercises because tonguing often covers up poor finger coordination. As control is gained, progress to more difficult exercises. Continue to practice with a metronome, and continue to slur the exercises.

CAUSE 2:   Air stream not maintained properly.

SOLUTION 2:   Improper use of air in technical passages causes coordination problems between the tongue, fingers, and air stream. Maintain a consistent air stream at all dynamic levels. Players tend to focus on technique at the expense of proper breath support. Focus on maintaining breath support at all times until proper support becomes automatic.

PROBLEM: Uneven finger movement within the beat.

CAUSE 1:   Poor control of individual fingers.

SOLUTION 1:   Playing fast is one thing; playing with control is another. Make sure proper hand positions are maintained. Use a metronome and practice exercises that isolate each finger. Practice these exercises slowly and deliberately at first and gradually increase tempo, while always focusing on control. The ring fingers and the little fingers are particularly problematic, so work on these fingers extensively.

Cause 2:	Poor coordination of cross fingerings.

Solution 2:　When more awkward fingerings are mixed with less awkward fingerings in technical passages, uneven finger movement within the beat often occurs. Make sure proper hand positions are maintained. Use a metronome and practice exercises that isolate problematic combinations of fingerings. Practice these exercises slowly and deliberately at first and gradually increase tempo, while always focusing on control.

Tone Quality and Response Problems

Problem:	The tone is small and weak.

Cause 1:	Lack of sufficient air, air speed, and/or breath support.

Solution 1:　Use more air, increase air speed, and keep the air stream consistent. Take full breaths and practice playing long tones at all dynamic levels. Focus on maintaining a consistent air speed appropriate for each dynamic level. Practice extensively at softer dynamic levels because it is harder to maintain proper breath support at softer dynamic levels than it is at louder dynamic levels.

Cause 2:	Embouchure too tight or "Biting."

Solution 2:　Relax the embouchure, lower the jaw slightly, and think of saying "who" or "oh" and surround the reed with warm air. Think of increasing the size of the imaginary circle of air into the instrument. That is, use a slightly more open air stream.

Cause 3:	Tight or closed throat.

Solution 3:　Relax or open the throat as if saying "ah." Saying the syllable "ah" and shifting to an "oh" syllable while exhaling will open the throat and oral cavity and keep the embouchure round.

Problem:	An unfocused tone quality.

Cause 1:	Improper direction of the air stream.

SOLUTION 1:   Direct the air stream toward the tip opening. Surround the reed with warm air as if saying "who" or "oh" to relax the embouchure. "Oh" is slightly more open than "who." The resulting tone quality dictates which syllable is most appropriate.

CAUSE 2:   Embouchure too loose.

SOLUTION 2:   Think of surrounding the reed with warm air as if saying "who," and firm the embouchure slightly. Think of decreasing the imaginary circle of air into the instrument. That is, use a slightly more focused air stream.

CAUSE 3:   Mouthpiece is not centered in the mouth.

SOLUTION 3:   The mouthpiece remains centered in the mouth at all times. Use a mirror on a regular basis to check mouthpiece placement until proper habits are formed.

CAUSE 4:   Not enough bottom lip over the teeth, making embouchure control inconsistent.

SOLUTION 4:   Put more of the lower lip over the teeth and listen for improved tone quality. Very little red (if any) should be showing at the point where the lip contacts the reed.

CAUSE 5:   Mouthpiece enters the mouth at an incorrect angle.

SOLUTION 5:   Adjust the neck strap properly. Do not reach upward or downward for the mouthpiece. The bell of the saxophone should be brought back so that the mouthpiece enters the mouth at a slightly upward angle. If the mouthpiece enters at an improper angle, the embouchure's ability to support the reed properly is impaired and the tone will be unfocused.

PROBLEM: Lack of tone control.

CAUSE 1:   Embouchure is inconsistent.

SOLUTION 1:   Form a good basic embouchure and make sure that there is enough bottom lip over the teeth. Practice playing long tones to develop the embouchure muscles, and focus on keeping the embouchure consistent at all times. Use a mirror on a regular basis to check embouchure formation until proper habits are formed. Sometimes a player's embouchure is unstable because the reed is too soft to provide sufficient resistance against the embouchure pressure, resulting in a quivery tone. Using a harder reed may help stabilize the embouchure.

CAUSE 2:   Inconsistent breath support and/or control of the air stream.

SOLUTION 2:   Practice breathing exercises with and without the saxophone to help develop breath support. Take full breaths and practice playing long tones at all dynamic levels. Focus on maintaining a consistent air speed appropriate for each dynamic level. Practice extensively at softer dynamic levels because it is harder to maintain proper breath support at softer dynamic levels than it is at louder dynamic levels. Maintain breath support in technical passages. That is, breath support is often compromised when playing technical passages because players tend to focus on technique at the expense of proper breath support.

CAUSE 3:   Inconsistent hand/holding/instrument/playing positions and posture.

SOLUTION 3:   Develop and follow a daily routine so that maintaining proper positions becomes habit. Proper placements of the left and right thumbs and proper adjustment of the neck strap are particularly important for tone control. A detailed discussion of these playing basics is located under Hand/Holding/Instrument/Playing Positions and Posture.

CAUSE 4:   Inconsistent throat and/or tongue positions.

SOLUTION 4:   The throat should remain open as if saying "ah," and the tongue should remain relatively flat and relaxed in the mouth when slurring and drawn back slightly (arched) in the mouth when tonguing. Unnecessary movement and tension of the throat and tongue disrupts the air stream and can affect tone control, tone quality, and pitch.

CAUSE 5:   Mouthpiece does not enter the mouth straight on.

SOLUTION 5:   Make sure the mouthpiece and neck are centered with the lips so that the mouthpiece enters the mouth at a straight angle. Often, placing the music stand too far off to one side causes the mouthpiece to enter the mouth at a diagonal.

CAUSE 6:   The mouthpiece is turned or twisted when it enters the mouth, causing players to tilt their heads.

SOLUTION 6:   Turn the mouthpiece so that it stays parallel to the lips. Keep the head straight at all times whether the saxophone is held in front or to the side.

CAUSE 7:   Mouthpiece baffle is too high.

SOLUTION 7:   Use a medium baffle. A mouthpiece with a high baffle tends to be very hard to control and has a bright sound. A mouthpiece with a medium baffle will be much easier to control and will result in a much warmer tone quality.

PROBLEM: Lack of dynamic control.

CAUSE 1:   Insufficient control of the air stream and/or insufficient breath support throughout the dynamic range.

SOLUTION 1:   Practice playing long tones at one dynamic level over a set number of counts. When long tones can be played evenly at one dynamic level, practice playing long tones at different dynamic levels. Later, practice playing crescendi and decrescendi on long tones evenly over a set number of counts from one dynamic level to another. The softest and loudest dynamic levels can be particularly problematic. As a result, practicing at softer and louder dynamic levels is particularly important for tonal control.

CAUSE 2:   Making unnecessary embouchure adjustments when changing dynamics.

SOLUTION 2:   Keep the embouchure relatively stable and consistent regardless of the dynamic level. Exceptions include (1) in the pianissimo range, relax the embouchure slightly to compensate for the tendency of the pitch to go sharp; and (2) in the fortissimo range, firm the embouchure slightly to compensate for the tendency of the pitch to go flat.

CAUSE 3:   Using inappropriate reed strengths.

SOLUTION 3:   Use reeds that are commensurate with playing experience. Reeds that are too hard are difficult to control and tend to respond poorly or "cut out" at softer dynamic levels. Reeds that are too soft restrict the ability to play loudly.

PROBLEM: The low notes do not respond well.

CAUSE 1:   Leaks in the pads.

SOLUTION 1:   Check for leaks and replace any worn out pads. The larger pads on the lower keys tend to leak more than do smaller pads. Check the larger pads often for leakage.

CAUSE 2:   Reed is too hard.

SOLUTION 2:   Use a slightly softer reed. Softer reeds provide less resistance and improve response in the low range.

CAUSE 3:   Not enough air and/or air stream too slow.

SOLUTION 3:   Use more air and increase air speed on the initial attacks for low notes. Once the note has responded, less air is needed to keep the tone sounding. Find a balance and adjust air accordingly.

CAUSE 4:   Embouchure too tight or biting.

SOLUTION 4:   Relax the embouchure and lower the jaw slightly in the low range. Think of using an "ah" syllable and maintain an open throat and oral cavity. Focus for the particular note being played. Low notes do require more air than high notes.

PROBLEM: The high notes do not respond well.

CAUSE 1:   Reed is too soft.

SOLUTION 1:   Choose a reed that provides enough resistance to vibrate at the higher frequencies. Soft reeds tend to "close off" under embouchure pressure in the high range. Move up in reed strength.

CAUSE 2:   Embouchure too tight, or biting.

SOLUTION 2:   Relax the embouchure, lower than jaw slightly, and think of using a warm air steam. There is no need to tighten the embouchure in the high range. Use the same basic embouchure in the high range that is used in the middle range, and then focus the oral cavity slightly for the particular note being played.

CAUSE 3:   Overblowing.

SOLUTION 3:   Focus for the note being played and use a controlled air stream. There is no need to blow harder in the high range; however, slight adjustments in the oral cavity do need to be made. Practice playing familiar tunes in the high range to develop control.

PROBLEM: A loud, raucous, squawky tone.

CAUSE 1:   Too much mouthpiece in the mouth.

SOLUTION 1:   Take less of the mouthpiece in the mouth. Only about one-third of the beak (or slightly more) should be inserted into the mouth. Players with a pronounced underbite tend to look as if they are not taking

enough mouthpiece in the mouth, whereas players with an overbite tend to look as if they are taking too much mouthpiece in the mouth. Let the tone quality be the determining factor for the best mouthpiece placement.

CAUSE 2:   Too much air with an unfocused embouchure.

SOLUTION 2:   Use a proper embouchure. Think of surrounding the reed with warm air as if saying "who." It may also help to think of decreasing the imaginary circle of air into the instrument. That is, use a slightly more focused air stream. Focus the throat and oral cavity for the pitch being played.

CAUSE 3:   Improper focus of the air stream.

SOLUTION 3:   Think of blowing air through and around the tip opening. Think of surrounding the reed with air as if saying "who." Experiment with air direction until the best tone quality is achieved.

PROBLEM: A thin, pinched tone.

CAUSE 1:   Embouchure is too tight.

SOLUTION 1:   Relax the embouchure and surround the reed with warm air as if saying "who" or "oh." "Oh" is slightly more open than the "who." Let the tone quality dictate which syllable is more appropriate. Make sure that the mouth corners are drawn inward rather than back and that the lower lip is not stretched too tightly over the teeth. It may be helpful to think of increasing the imaginary circle of air into the instrument. That is, use a slightly more open air stream.

CAUSE 2:   Reed is too soft.

SOLUTION 2:   Discard old reeds and move up in reed strength. Using reeds that are too soft causes players to "bite," resulting in a thin, pinched tone. As reeds wear out they tend to soften. A reed that is too hard may break in after being played.

CAUSE 3:   Too little mouthpiece in the mouth.

SOLUTION 3:   Take more mouthpiece in the mouth. Players tend to bite and/or to close off the tip opening when too little mouthpiece is taken into the mouth. About one-third of the beak (or slightly more) should be inserted into the mouth. The exact amount of mouthpiece in the mouth is determined by the tone quality.

CAUSE 4: Improper focus of the air stream.

SOLUTION 4: Direct the air stream toward the tip opening. Focusing the air stream at too high an angle can result in a thin tone. Focusing the air stream at too low an angle can result in a spread tone. Think of surrounding the reed with a steady stream of warm air as if saying "who," and think of blowing the air stream through the instrument.

CAUSE 5: Using beginning level mouthpieces.

SOLUTION 5: Use a more advanced mouthpiece. Beginner-level mouthpieces respond easily for beginners, but they do not provide enough resistance for mature players. They tend to sound thin, small, and pinched. Mature players need more advanced mouthpieces. Advanced mouthpieces are made from better materials, and they are available in a wide variety of chambers and tip openings so that they can be matched to the player's level.

CAUSE 6: Instrument is improperly positioned, putting excessive pressure on the reed.

SOLUTION 6: Reposition the instrument so that the mouthpiece enters the mouth at a slightly upward angle.

CAUSE 7: Not using a sufficient amount of air and/or the air stream is too slow, and the player is "biting" to compensate.

SOLUTION 7: Increase air speed and the amount of air being used, while maintaining an appropriate embouchure.

PROBLEM: Grunting or guttural noises can be heard during normal play.

CAUSE 1: Closing the throat or glottis when coughing or swallowing is normal; however, players sometimes develop the habit of closing the throat to stop the air and opening it to release the air, which results in a grunting sound. Closing the throat and using it as a valve to control air flow negatively affects releases, tone quality, and pitch.

SOLUTION 1: Maintain an open throat as if saying "ah" and learn to control the flow of the air from the diaphragm.

PROBLEM: A reedy/buzzy tone.

CAUSE 1:   Reed is too soft.

SOLUTION 1:   Move up in reed strength. Soft reeds can sound reedy/buzzy. Players can also move the reed up slightly past the tip to improve the tone quality and pitch of soft reeds. Players who have played for two or three years should use medium (number 3) or medium hard (number 3½) reeds.

CAUSE 2:   Reed is in poor condition.

SOLUTION 2:   Use a reed that has good balance and a good cut. Also, make sure the reed has not been damaged.

CAUSE 3:   Poor mouthpiece/reed combination.

SOLUTION 3:   Replace beginning mouthpieces with more advanced mouthpieces after a few years of playing. In addition, use double-cut reeds (3 or 3 ½) with advanced mouthpieces for a more mature sound.

PROBLEM: An airy tone quality.

CAUSE 1:   Reed is too hard.

SOLUTION 1:   Use a softer reed. As a rule, beginners should use soft reeds (1 ½ or 2), intermediate players should use medium reeds (2 ½ or 3), and advanced players should use medium hard or hard reeds (3 ½ or 4), depending on the mouthpiece being played.

CAUSE 2:   Air escaping from the mouth corners.

SOLUTION 2:   Focus on keeping the mouth corners inward toward the mouthpiece, and use a proper embouchure at all times. Air escapes from the mouth corners when the surrounding muscles are not supporting inwardly toward the mouthpiece. Letting air escape from the mouth corners can become a habit.

CAUSE 3:   Leaks in the instrument.

SOLUTION 3:   Have a repair technician check for leaks and replace any worn out and/or leaking pads.

CAUSE 4:   The height of the pads above the tone holes is incorrect.

SOLUTION 4:   Adjust the pad height and play the instrument after each adjustment to determine if appropriate adjustments have been made. Pad height should be adjusted by a knowledgeable repair technician.

PROBLEM: The tone sounds dead and lifeless, and the pitch is flat.

CAUSE 1:   The reed is too old and/or too soft.

SOLUTION 1:   Discard the reed and use a new one. Reeds do wear out relatively quickly, even though they may still look good. As a rule, after a reed has been played on consistently for a couple of weeks, it begins to deteriorate. Visible signs of aging include a "dirty" or "dingy" look to the reed with nicks or chips in the tip. Old reeds that have been left on the mouthpiece consistently also may have black spots on them as well as an unpleasant musty odor.

PROBLEM: Squeaks/squeaking.

CAUSE 1:   Reed is too dry and/or is warped.

SOLUTION 1:   Reeds should be soaked thoroughly before playing. To prevent reeds from drying out and warping during rehearsals, wet them periodically with the mouth or water. During prolonged periods of resting, a mouthpiece cap can prevent reeds from drying out. Store reeds in a reed guard or reed case immediately after playing to help prevent warping.

CAUSE 2:   Unfocused/unstable embouchure.

SOLUTION 2:   Practice long tones to strengthen the embouchure muscles, and concentrate on eliminating unnecessary embouchure movement, especially when playing skips and leaps. The embouchure should remain relatively constant at all times.

CAUSE 3:   Reed poorly constructed and/or in poor condition (cracked, chipped, unbalanced, etc.).

SOLUTION 3:   Use a good reed that has not been damaged. Although a sound can be produced on a cracked or chipped reed, such reeds do not allow the reed to close off against the mouthpiece tip rail, which can cause squeaks. Store reeds in a reed guard or reed case immediately after playing to help prevent damage.

CAUSE 4:   Poorly constructed and/or damaged mouthpiece.

SOLUTION 4:   Replace the mouthpiece. The side rails and tip rail of the mouthpiece should be even, smooth, and free of chips or cracks. In addition, hairline cracks in the beak of the mouthpiece cause squeaks and can be very difficult to detect.

CAUSE 5:   Too much mouthpiece in the mouth.

SOLUTION 5:   Take less of the mouthpiece in the mouth. Only about one-third of the beak (or slightly more) should be inserted into the mouth. Too much mouthpiece in the mouth causes squeaks, and it results in a "squawky" harsh sound.

CAUSE 6:   Hitting side keys.

SOLUTION 6:   Maintain proper hand position. Inadvertently hitting the left-hand palm keys with the side of the left hand or the B-flat side key with the side of the right hand can cause squeaks. Maintain a "C" shape with the hands and fingers to avoid hitting these keys accidentally.

CAUSE 7:   Leaks in the instrument.

SOLUTION 7:   Have a repair technician check for leaks and replace any worn out and/or leaking pads.

CAUSE 8:   Saxophone out of adjustment.

SOLUTION 8:   Have the saxophone adjusted so that the keys work properly. The keys work together in a precise manner to produce each tone. If the keys are not opening and closing properly, squeaks can occur. The octave key on the neck is a particular "problem" key because the small connecting rod on the body of the saxophone protrudes slightly from the body, making it susceptible to damage. When this rod bent outward, the octave key remains open causing squeaks.

PROBLEM: Gurgling sounds on certain pitches.

CAUSE 1:   Water has accumulated in one of the octave vent holes, or in one of the palm key tone holes.

SOLUTION 1:   Remove the water by blowing a fast, narrow stream of air into the appropriate vent or tone hole. Some players use cigarette paper or a pipe cleaner to remove water from vent holes. Care must be taken not to scratch or damage the vent holes.

CAUSE 2:   Water has accumulated in the mouthpiece and/or the neck.

SOLUTION 2:   Suck the excess condensation from the mouthpiece regularly. During long periods of play, take the neck and mouthpiece off the instrument and swab them thoroughly.

CAUSE 3: Poor reed/mouthpiece combination. Not all reeds fit onto every mouthpiece properly, and not all mouthpieces fit onto the neck properly. An improper fit can cause gurgling sounds, especially in the low range. These gurgling or warbling sounds are not the result of excess water.

SOLUTION 3: Try a different reed/mouthpiece combination or replace the neck cork to accommodate the mouthpiece.

PROBLEM: A slightly delayed response of certain notes during slurred intervals, or the wrong pitch is sounding even though the fingering is correct.

CAUSE 1: Pad or pads sticking. Pads absorb moisture during normal play. This moisture attracts dirt and food particles. These particles collect in and around the tone holes and on the pads (particularly in the creases), causing pads to stick. In addition, sugar from certain beverages also causes pads to stick. The G-sharp key and the low C-sharp key are notorious for sticking.

SOLUTION 1: Clean the pads and tone holes. For a "quick fix," place a thin sheet of tissue paper, cigarette paper, or a dollar bill (preferably a clean one) between the sticking pad and tone hole. Close the pad lightly and pull the paper through. Cleaning pads in this way is fairly common among advanced players. Various types of "no-stick" powder are also available. These powders do work for a very short period of time; however, they are often quite messy, and they create more problems in the long run because they simply add to the particles already collected on the pads and inside the tone holes. Generally, powders should not be used to free sticking pads. Ultimately, the instrument may need to be taken apart and cleaned thoroughly by a repair technician, and sticking pads may need to be replaced. Players should not eat or drink (except water) while playing to avoid pad and instrument damage.

CAUSE 2: The crease in the pad is too deep, causing the pad to bind against the tone hole edge.

SOLUTION 2: Replace the pad.

CAUSE 3: The outside layer of a pad is torn, causing the pad to bind against the tone hole edge.

SOLUTION 3: Replace the pad.

CAUSE 4: A rod is bent.

SOLUTION 4: Have a repair technician straighten the rod. Bent rods can cause key mechanisms to stick. Often, players can feel a bump or hitch in the mechanism, indicating that a bent rod is the source of the problem.

CAUSE 5: A spring has come off, a spring is broken, or a spring is loose or worn out.

SOLUTION 5: Put springs back into place using a spring hook tool. A pencil, small screwdriver, or crochet hook can also be used to replace springs in some cases, but they are not nearly as effective. Spring-hook tools are easy to use and inexpensive and are an excellent investment. Loose or worn springs can sometimes be tightened by reseating them and/or by bending them gently in the appropriate direction. Broken springs must be replaced.

CAUSE 6: Pivot (post) screws are loose. Pivot screws work themselves loose periodically, creating problems with the alignment of key mechanisms. The area around pivot screws can also get gummed up by accumulating dirt and other foreign materials, resulting in sticky key mechanisms.

SOLUTION 6: Clean pivot screws and surrounding areas. Place a drop of key oil on the screws and threads, and tighten the screws snugly. Placing a small amount of nail polish on screw heads and rods that frequently work themselves loose will help hold them in place.

5

Oboe

Acoustical Properties: The acoustical and physical tonal characteristics of an instrument that affect its sound quality. The oboe is one of the oldest woodwind instruments. Traditionally made of wood, the oboe is a conical tube closed at one end (i.e., the double reed end) and open at the other (i.e., the bell end). The vibration of a double reed produces its characteristic timbre, and the key design is similar to other woodwind instruments. These design characteristics result in a tone that produces a full complement of partials. The oboe overblows the octave. That is, most of the fingerings used in the lower octave will produce a note one octave higher when one of its two (or three) octave keys is depressed. Only the first (fundamental) and second partials are used for the majority of the normal playing range. See also Acoustical Basics, page 3; Construction and Design, page 479; Harmonics, page 32

Key Questions

Q: If the oboe overblows the octave, and most of the fingerings used in the lower octave can also produce a note one octave higher, why are many of the fingerings different from one octave to the next?

A: Different fingerings are used because they produce a better tone quality, are better in tune, and/or are more responsive.

Q: Why does the oboe have more than one octave key?

A: To improve tone quality and intonation, and to provide players with greater technical flexibility. Most oboes have a semi-automatic octave key design, which involves two octave keys. In this design, players depress the first octave key for the range of notes between (and including) fourth-space E-natural to G-sharp above the staff. The second or side octave key is depressed for high A-natural through high C-natural above the staff.

Some oboes have a fully-automatic octave key mechanism. In this design, players depress only one octave key for all notes in the upper range. Although having one octave key may sound like a better option, its complicated design is often difficult to adjust properly, and it limits the number of alternate fingerings. Finally, some professional oboes actually have three octave keys rather than the traditional two. The third octave key facilitates playing in the extreme altissimo range (i.e., high E-natural and above).

Action: See Action, page 3

Adjusting Pitch: The process of raising or lowering the pitch of notes. A general discussion of adjusting pitch is under Intonation in chapter 1. Specific suggestions for adjusting pitch on oboe are under Intonation in this chapter.

Air Stream: Physically, the stream of air pushed from the lungs by the diaphragm and abdominal muscles through the trachea and oral cavity into and through a musical instrument. Although the physical nature of exhaling is basically the same for everyone, the ways the air stream is used to play particular instruments vary widely. A general discussion of the air stream and breathing is under Air Stream and Breathing/Breath Support/Air Control in chapter 1. In addition, the effects of the air stream on pitch are under Intonation in this chapter. Specific comments regarding the oboe air stream appear below.

Unlike other woodwind players who generally use a warm air stream, oboe players generally blow a cold, focused air stream through a small aperture in the reed. The air stream must be consistent and steady, and there must be sufficient air speed and air volume to support the tone. In addition, the direction of the air stream changes according to range, and these changes are made in conjunction with embouchure changes. That is, the air must be focused slightly upward as the scale ascends and slightly downward as the scale descends, and the embouchure must firm and loosen accordingly. Strive for a consistent tone quality and evenness of scale in all ranges and develop control of the air stream at all dynamic levels. Maintain an open throat and oral cavity in all registers as if saying the syllable "oo." In the high range, players tend to use a smaller, firmer "oo" syllable or even an "ee" syllable to focus tone more effectively. Considerable disagreement exists as to the appropriateness of particular syllables. Teachers and players should experiment with a variety of syllables and use what yields the best results. The idea of focusing the air around the reed and making slight adjustments throughout the normal playing range of the instrument is a sound teaching concept on oboe.

Players must use a tuner and listen carefully to determine the appropriate adjustments in air and embouchure.

The direction of the air stream may be moved up or down to adjust the pitch of individual tones. For example, the low range of most oboes tends to be flat, while the high range tends to be sharp. Raising the air stream sharpens the pitch, while lowering the air stream flattens the pitch. Adjustments to the air stream can be made with slight movements of the embouchure and/or oral cavity (e.g., use a more open syllable and/or lower the jaw slightly). See also Air Stream, page 4; Breathing/Breath Support/Air Control, page 10; Intonation, page 505

Alternate Fingerings/Alternates: Fingerings not considered standard or basic that can be used to enable or enhance musical performance. Alternate fingerings are most often used to minimize awkward fingerings or to improve intonation in specific musical contexts. The choice of when and which alternate fingerings to use should ultimately be determined by the musical result. That is, does using the alternate fingering improve the musicality of the performance?

Developing command of alternate fingerings is important so that players can use the most appropriate fingering in a given situation. Learning alternate fingerings can be awkward at first. Practicing patterns, passages, scales, and other exercises in which alternate fingerings can be incorporated is helpful. Practice alternate fingerings slowly and deliberately, focusing on only one or two alternate fingerings at a time.

The alternate fingerings described below are appropriate for players who are fundamentally sound. Examples of when to use these alternates are shown in figure 5.1. When appropriate, suggestions and comments regarding alternate fingerings have been included. A complete fingering chart that includes alternate fingerings is in "Practical Tips" at the end of this chapter. See also Intonation, page 505; Technique, page 551

Common Alternate Fingerings for Oboe

1. Alternate Forked-F—An alternate fingering used in arpeggiated passages involving D-natural to F-natural. Forked-F (1-2-3 4-6) is also used when playing to or from low notes (E-flat and below) and when playing to or from the half-holed notes (D-flat, D-natural, and D-sharp). On some oboes, the E-flat key will need to be depressed as a resonance key. On other oboes (usually professional models), it will not be necessary to depress this key.

FIGURE 5.1. *Alternate Fingerings*

2. Alternate Left-F—An alternate fingering available on some intermediate and professional oboes. The left-F key is in the left-hand little finger key cluster near the low B-flat key. Left-F (1-2-3 4-5-F-side key) is often used when playing from first-space F-natural to low D-natural.

3. Alternate Left-E-flat (first-line and top-space)—There are two E-flat fingerings. Both fingerings involve depressing the index, middle, and ring fingers of both hands (1-2-3 4-5-6); however, players have a choice as to which little finger (left or right) will be used to complete the fingering for each note. If the left-hand little finger is used, the fingering is called left E-flat. If the right-hand little finger is used, the fingering is called right E-flat. Right E-flat is considered the regular fingering.

   Left E-flat is used when playing from D-flat to E-flat and back to D-flat. If the right-hand little finger (the standard fingering) is used in these contexts, the right-hand little finger is required to slide from the E-flat key to the D-flat key. The left-hand little finger can be used instead for the E-flat to avoid this awkward slide. When the left-hand E-flat fingering is used, it depresses the alternate E-flat immediately below the G-sharp key, eliminating the need for the right-hand little finger to depress the E-flat key. The only difference in upper and lower alternate fingerings is that the upper note is half-holed.

4. Alternate Right-A-flat (second-space and above the staff)—There are two A-flat fingerings. Both fingerings involve depressing the index, middle, and ring fingers of the left hand (1-2-3); however, players have a choice as to whether to use the little finger of the left hand or the side of the right-hand index finger to complete the fingering for each note. If the left-hand little finger is used to depress the A-flat key, the fingering is called left A-flat. If the side of the right-hand index finger is used to depress the A-flat side key, the fingering is called right (or side) A-flat. Left A-flat is considered the regular fingering. Right A-flat is used when playing from notes that use the left-hand little finger (low B-flat, B-natural, left E-flat, or left F-natural) to A-flat.

5. Alternate D-natural (fourth-line)—Alternate D-natural is normally used when trilling from C-natural to D-natural; however, it can also be used in rapid passages when playing from C-natural to D-natural and back to C-natural. The standard fingering for C-natural is the index finger of the left hand (1) and the index finger of the right hand (4). The standard fingering for D-natural is ½-2-3 4-5-6. Shifting from two keys to six keys using standard fingerings creates coordination problems. To simplify the performance of this interval, D-natural can be fingered using only 1-4, and either the left-hand D-natural trill key between the first and

second tone holes, or the right-hand D-natural trill key between the fourth and fifth tone holes of the right hand. In both cases, the D trill key is fingered with the middle finger of the left (2) or right hand (5).

6. Alternate C-sharp/D-flat—Alternate C-sharp is normally used when trilling from C-natural (third-space) to C-sharp (third-space); however, it can also be used in rapid passages when playing from C-natural to C-sharp and back to C-natural. The standard fingering for C-natural is the index finger of the left hand and the index finger of the right hand (1-4). The standard fingering for C-sharp is ½-2-3 4-5-6-C-sharp key. Shifting from two keys to seven keys using standard fingerings creates coordination problems. To simplify the performance of this interval, C-sharp can be fingered using only the index finger of the right hand (4). C-sharp can also be fingered using only 1-4 and the C-sharp trill key located between the second and third tone holes of the left hand. The C-sharp trill key is depressed using the ring finger (3) of the left hand.

7. Alternate Low B-natural and B-flat—When playing from a low B-natural or B-flat to a low C-sharp/D-flat, players can play the B-natural or B-flat using the C-sharp key, rather than the C key, which is used in the normal fingering.

Leaving Fingers Down to Facilitate Technical Playing

1. Players sometimes leave the left-hand G-sharp key (little finger) down when playing certain intervals because leaving it does not affect the other pitches. For example, when playing from top-line F-sharp to G-sharp to F-sharp to D-sharp, the G-sharp key can be left down.

2. When playing from E-flat to A-flat or from A-flat to E-flat (in both octaves), players sometimes depress both the E-flat and the A-flat keys at the same time with the left-hand little finger to effect a smoother transition between the two notes.

3. When playing forked-F, depressing the D-sharp key (right-hand little finger) may improve tone quality, pitch, and response. However, adding the D-sharp key may also raise the pitch too much.

4. When playing from C-sharp to D-sharp (or vice versa), players can leave the D-sharp key down while playing the C-sharp.

Key Questions

Q: When should students begin using alternate fingerings?

A: Students who are fundamentally sound can begin using alternate fingerings when opportunities arise to incorporate them into rehearsals and performances. By the time students are in high school, they should be using alternate fingerings regularly.

Q: Is it better to adjust pitch by making embouchure adjustments or by using special fingerings or adding keys?

A: It depends on the musical context. Generally, if using alternate fingerings improves the musicality of a performance, then use them.

Altissimo/Extended Range: In general, a term sometimes used for the notes in the high range and/or the extreme high range of an instrument. On oboe, the altissimo range extends from high E-natural upward to about double high C-natural. In the standard literature for oboe, the altissimo range is most commonly heard in advanced works. Players typically begin working on the altissimo range after they have developed excellent control and facility throughout the normal range of the instrument. Producing altissimo notes successfully involves making several adjustments including using altissimo fingerings, adjusting the embouchure formation, and changing the speed, focus, and direction of the air stream. Some suggestions for developing the altissimo range are outlined below.

Suggestions for Developing the Altissimo Range

1. Work on altissimo after developing a good, consistent tone quality throughout the normal range of the instrument.
2. Use a slightly harder reed than normal.
3. Try a variety of altissimo fingerings to determine which ones work best for a particular instrument.
4. Embouchure/Oral Cavity Suggestions
   A. Take slightly more reed in the mouth.
   B. Firm the embouchure, decreasing the aperture size overall. In addition, try dropping the jaw slightly (while maintaining a firm embouchure) to open the oral cavity.
   C. Pull the lips back slightly.
   D. Close the throat as if saying "ee."
   E. Arch and pull tongue back slightly.

5. Air Stream Comments/Suggestions
   A. The air must move faster than in the normal range.
   B. Focus the air stream as if saying "hee."
   C. Altissimo success hinges on the ability to make the air move fast on a narrowly focused plane. That is, faster air speed is essential to play in the altissimo range.
6. Start with high C-natural (normal range) and work up to the altissimo range one note at a time.
7. Start notes with the air rather than with the tongue, and slur from one note to the next until control is gained in the initial stages.

Key Questions

Q: Do high school students really need to have control over the altissimo range?

A: No. Very few pieces appropriate for high school instrumental music programs include the altissimo range. In addition, working on the altissimo range too soon can create bad habits such as biting and overblowing.

Q: When should students begin learning altissimo?

A: Advanced students who are fundamentally sound can begin working on the altissimo range at the high school level, preferably under the guidance of a knowledgeable teacher.

Anchor Tonguing: See Anchor Tonguing, page 6

Articulated Keys: Keys that automatically open or close more than one tone hole or key mechanism by design. Articulated keys enhance technique and help produce a more even scale throughout the instrument's playing range. All oboes have an articulated G-sharp key (left-hand little finger) and an articulated E-flat/C key (right-hand little finger). Some intermediate and most professional oboes also have an articulated C-sharp/B key, which enables the C-sharp key to close automatically when playing from or to low B-flat or B-natural. The articulated C-sharp key mechanism helps players trill from low B-natural to low C-sharp.

Articulation: See Articulation/Articulative Styles, page 6

Assembly: The way an instrument is put together. Proper assembly is important to playability, instrument care, and maintenance. Teaching students to carefully assemble their instruments using a defined assembly procedure can help significantly reduce wear and tear. The oboe can be assembled efficiently and safely using the steps listed below. Figures 5.2, 5.3, and 5.4 can be used to guide the assembly process. See also Hand/Holding/Instrument Playing Positions and Posture, page 493

1. The oboe should be assembled while standing (when the case is securely resting on a chair or table) or while kneeling (when the case is sitting on the floor). Oboes should not be assembled in the player's lap. Although oboes are small, the parts can easily be dropped and damaged.

2. If the corks feel dry, apply cork grease them before continuing with the assembly process. Rub the cork grease into the cork with

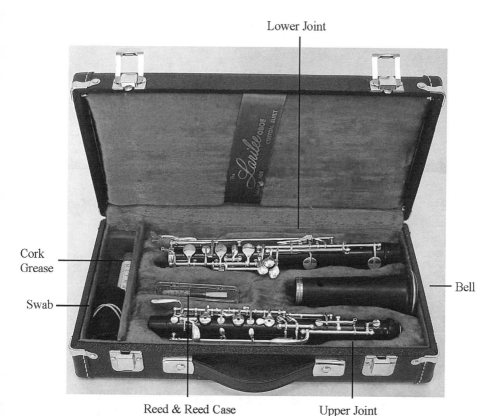

FIGURE 5.2. *Oboe before Assembly*

FIGURE 5.3. *Assembled Oboe (with B-flat Key)*

the thumb and index finger. If the corks are new, it may be necessary to apply cork grease every time the instrument is assembled for the first few weeks. As the corks become conditioned, they will not need to be greased as often.

3. Grasp the bell with the left hand, making sure that the thumb closes the pad cup. Closing this pad cup raises the bridge key and keeps the linkage mechanism from being damaged during the assembly process.

FIGURE 5.4. *Assembled Oboe (without B-flat Key)*

4. Grasp the lower joint (the larger of the two main joints) with the right hand in a manner that does not put excessive pressure on key mechanisms and attach the bell to the lower joint with a back-and-forth twisting motion. Align the bridge keys (if the bell has a low B-flat key) as shown in figure 5.5. Some teachers allow students to determine for themselves the best way to grasp the lower joint, while others teach their students to place the right hand and

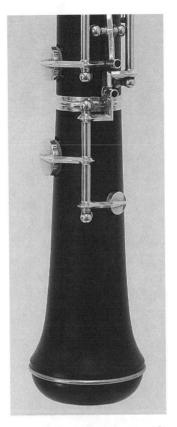

FIGURE 5.5.　*B-flat Bell Bridge Key Alignment*

fingers on the keys in playing position. The important thing is to avoid placing excess pressure on the keys and key mechanisms.

5. Grasp the upper joint (the smaller of the two main joints) so that the left hand and fingers are in playing position on the keys and attach the upper joint to the lower joint with a back-and-forth twisting motion. Avoid putting excessive pressure on the keys, and make sure that the bridge keys are properly aligned as shown in figure 5.6. There should not be excessive movement between the joints. If the joints are loose and/or the cork is cracked and worn, the corks should be replaced. It is important to maintain a proper seal so that the instrument responds appropriately.

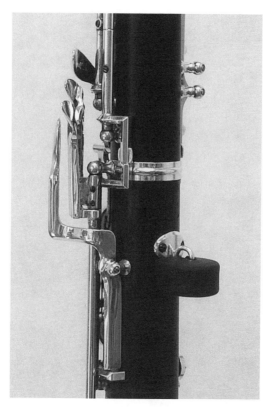

Figure 5.6. *Bridge Key Alignment*

6. Holding the cork portion of the reed between the thumb and index finger, place the reed into the upper joint with a slight back-and-forth motion. Make sure that the reed is pushed in all the way. The blades of the reed should be positioned parallel with the teeth and floor as shown in figure 5.7. Although double reeds do not technically have a top and a bottom blade, experienced players often develop a preference for having a particular blade on top, depending on how a reed sounds and responds.

Attacks: A detailed discussion of attacks is under Attacks in chapter 1. See also Releases/Cutoffs, page 56; Tonguing, page 71

Back Pressure: Air pressure that builds up inside the oral cavity and lungs during normal play. Although all wind players experience back pressure to a degree

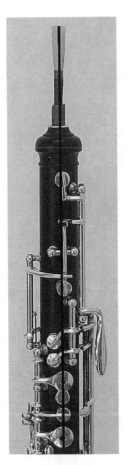

FIGURE 5.7. *Reed Alignment*

during play, oboe players experience a great deal of back pressure because the tip opening or reed aperture is quite small. During play, oboists take in more air than can possibly pass through the tip opening, causing the excess air to back up inside the oral cavity. As a result, players often find themselves struggling to get rid of excess air. Although nothing can totally eliminate back pressure, it can be reduced by playing on good reeds, developing proper breathing habits, learning to use air efficiently, and phrasing properly.

Balance and Blend Considerations: In general, woodwind instruments are less homogeneous than brass instruments. As a result, they do not always blend together as well as brass instruments in ensemble settings. To enhance blend, some instrumental teachers recommend using the same brand and/or model of instruments. In addition, some teachers encourage players within instrument sections to play on the same or comparable mouthpieces and/or reeds for a more homogeneous sound. Blend between two or more oboes can be enhanced by using high quality reeds and by using wooden oboes.

In a typical wind band with fifty to sixty players, one or two oboe players are often recommended as a good number for balance considerations. The number of oboe players in any wind group depends largely on the type of sound desired, the number of instruments available, and the strength of oboe players in the program.

Bass Oboe: See Instrument Family and Playing Considerations, page 502

Beats: See Beats, page 10

Bell Tones: See Bell Tones, page 10

Blanks, Reed: See Reed Blanks, page 518

Bocal: The curved, conical metal tube that fits into the main body of the English horn and onto which the reed is placed. Bocals are available in a variety of lengths to accommodate pitch and tone quality concerns. Bocals are generally numbered 1 through 3, with 1 being the shortest. There is a direct relationship between the length of a bocal and pitch. Specifically, shorter bocals sharpen the pitch, while longer bocals flatten the pitch. Bocals affect virtually every aspect of English horn playing including pitch, tone quality, and response. In addition, a bocal may play better in one range than it does in another, and it may play better on one instrument than it does on another. English horn bocal makers include Dallas Bocal Company, Fox, Howell, Laubin, Lickman, Loreé, Chudnow, Hiniker, and Symer. Bocals are inconsistent from one company to another in terms of bocal design, length, and numbering systems. For example, two number 2 bocals made by different makers may play quite differently when played on the same instrument.

Boehm System: A fingering system designed by Theobald Boehm (1794–1881) commonly associated with woodwind instruments, especially flute and clarinet. Although Boehm system oboes have been manufactured, modern oboes typically employ a conservatory or conservatoire system.

Bore, Instrument: In general, a term used to describe the inside shape and dimensions of an instrument's tube. The bassoon has a conical bore. See also Acoustical Properties, page 459; Conical, page 478; Cylindrical, page 483

Break: The point at which there is a register shift on an instrument. Typically, a break involves moving from an open fingering (with few tone holes closed) to a closed fingering (with most tone holes closed), and usually involves a vent key, such as an octave or register key. The primary break occurs at fourth-line D-flat, where players begin using the half-hole technique. For example, playing from third-space C-natural to fourth-line D-flat and vice versa involves crossing the break. A secondary break occurs at fourth-space E-natural, where players must begin to use the first octave key. For example, playing from fourth-line D-natural to fourth-space E-natural involves crossing the secondary break. Another secondary break occurs at high A-natural (above the staff), where players must switch from the first octave key to the second (side) octave key. For example, playing from high G-sharp to high A-natural involves crossing this break. See also Crossing the Break, page 481; Technique, page 551

Breathing/Breath Support/Air Control: See Breathing/Breath Support/Air Control, page 10; Circular Breathing, page 23

Butt, Reed: A term sometimes used for the bottom end or heel of oboe reed cane. See also Reeds, Double, page 531

Cane/Cane Color: The material from which a reed is constructed, and the color, tint, or cast that a particular reed has. A detailed discussion of cane is under Reeds, Double in this chapter. See also Reeds, Double, page 531

Care and Maintenance: Taking proper care of the oboe is essential for achieving high performance levels. Most of the maintenance suggestions below are relevant to secondary school students, and many of them simply involve establishing a daily routine. See also Care and Maintenance Accessories, page 614

Routine Maintenance

1. Assemble and disassemble the oboe properly each day.

2. Grease the corks regularly so that excess pressure can be avoided during the assembly/disassembly processes.

3. Maintain proper hand/holding/instrument position while playing. When resting, hold the oboe in a safe position. The basic resting position is to stand the instrument straight up and rest the bell on the leg. Angling the oboe horizontally across the lap is another relatively common resting position; however, this position allows excess condensation to run down onto the pads.

4. Carry the instrument securely in an upright position to minimize the chance of banging the instrument into music stands, chairs, or other instruments.

5. When putting the instrument in its case, lay the sections down gently in their proper locations, then swab out the moisture one joint at a time. When swabbing out joints, insert and pull the swab from the large end to the small end of each joint several times.

6. When playing for extended periods of time, remove the moisture that sometimes collects in the tone holes, especially the octave vent holes in the upper joint. Players often blow forcefully into these vent holes to remove excess water. If this action does not work, they often use a feather or cigarette paper to remove excess moisture. The bell does not collect much moisture and generally does not need to be swabbed.

7. Rest the oboe in an upright position. When the oboe is rested in a horizontal or semi-horizontal position, water tends to run into tone holes, especially when the tone holes are face down.

8. Remove excess water on pads off with a piece of ungummed cigarette paper, a dollar bill, or other absorbent material. Ultimately, pads that get wet constantly will need to be replaced more often than other pads because the excess moisture causes them to harden and lose their proper seal.

9. Wipe off the outside of the oboe with a dry, soft cloth to remove excess moisture, fingerprints, dust, and so on.

10. Blow out the excess moisture from the reed by blowing gently on the cork end of the reed and/or by "sucking" out the excess moisture from the tip end of the reed. Store reeds in a reed guard or reed case immediately after playing to avoid damaging them.

11. Keep cases humidified. Many advanced players humidify their instrument cases by using a "Damp-it" or other product made for oboes. The general idea is that the damp material keeps the wood from drying out and cracking. Some players simply place orange peels in their cases as a means of controlling the humidity inside the case. Other players prefer to take their oboes into more humid areas (e.g., the laundry room) approximately once

a month or so to humidify the wood. These humidifying techniques are not needed for plastic instruments.

Key Questions

Q: Some sources suggest that swabs should be pulled from the small end
to the large end of each joint so that the swab does not get stuck. How should
students swab their oboes?

A: Pulling the swab from the small end compresses the swab, preventing it from absorbing moisture properly throughout the length of the joint.
Students should pull the swab from the large end to the small end of the joint
because the swab absorbs moisture more efficiently; however, students must
not force the swab through the small end of the joint because it can get stuck.

Other Maintenance

1. Remove the dust from under the key mechanisms once every couple of weeks or so with a small, soft paintbrush.

2. If excessive key noise is heard during regular play, oil the mechanisms with woodwind key oil. These clacking sounds are generally
   caused by metal-to-metal contact, which results in excessive wear
   of the key mechanisms. As a rule, the key mechanisms should be
   oiled lightly once a month or so.

3. Clean out the tone holes every month or so to remove excess dirt,
   lint, and grime that has collected over time. A toothpick or pipe
   cleaner can be used for this purpose. Care must be taken not to
   damage the tone holes and the key mechanisms during the cleaning process.

4. With wooden oboes, oil the bore, the exterior of the oboe, and the
   bell with bore oil once or twice a year. Make sure that the oil does
   not get on the pads. When oiling the bore, place a small amount
   of oil on a soft cloth and run the cloth through each joint several
   times as if swabbing the instrument.

5. Once or twice a year, wipe the corks with a soft, clean cloth. Cork
   grease tends to attract dirt, creating a build-up on the corks. Some
   players use alcohol to clean cork, but alcohol should be used only
   by knowledgeable players. After cleaning the corks, apply a small
   amount of cork grease and rub it in well using the thumb and
   index finger.

Considerations

1. A well-made and well-fitted case is essential to maintaining instrument condition. Some oboe cases also include case covers, which add additional protection. Insulated case covers are also available to further protect the oboe from temperature changes.

2. Avoid subjecting oboes to extreme temperature and humidity changes. Oboes are more likely to crack or split when exposed to extreme temperature and humidity changes, especially when cold instruments are warmed up too quickly. In addition, pads, corks, and felts have a tendency to loosen as the oboe contracts and expands in response to temperature and humidity. Never leave the instrument in an uncontrolled environment.

3. If an instrument is cold, let it warm up gradually. Do not warm up oboes by blowing warm air into them. The sudden change in temperature could make the inside of the oboe expand faster than the outside, causing it to crack.

4. Small cracks that have not gone through to the bore or that do not go through a tone hole should be repaired immediately. Larger cracks or splits, especially those that go through tone holes, may or may not be able to be repaired properly.

5. Do not clean keys with silver polish or other similar polish. Polish damages key mechanisms, ruins pads, and gums up tone holes.

6. Apply cork grease if the joints are tighter than normal during assembly and disassembly. Wrap cigarette paper or Teflon tape around the corks if the joints are too loose. Humidity affects cork. As a result, there will be times when the joints will feel tighter or looser than others during assembly and disassembly. As the humidity increases, cork expands; as humidity decreases, cork contracts. These differences are normal.

Cases, Instrument: Generally, the cases that come with most oboes are the best cases for everyday use, especially for young players. These hard cases protect the instrument well and are designed to fit particular instruments. This design secures the instrument properly in the case and provides adequate storage for reeds and cleaning accessories. Nonetheless, there is a variety of instrument cases on the market today designed to suit a variety of needs. Some of the more popular cases for oboe are insulated for added protection from temperature and humidity changes. Generally, the outer shell consists of synthetic-covered rigid plastic or wood, molded plastic, or leather. The interiors are typically lined with high-density foam padding. Commercially made oboe cases are available under such brand names as Altieri, Bam, Chiltern, Gewa, Howarth, Marigaux, Harris, Gator, Lorée, Orly, ProTec, SKB, and Wiseman.

Key Questions

Q: Are all cases well constructed and designed?

A: No. Students should not purchase cases without checking them out thoroughly. Many cases do not protect instruments properly. Inspect each case for adequate padding, sturdy and secure hinges and handles, and a proper fit for the instrument. A case that does not fit the instrument well or a poorly constructed case will not adequately protect the instrument, which may result in damaged equipment.

Q: Why do some oboe players put orange peels in their cases?

A: To keep their oboes from drying out and to maintain a more consistent humidity level in their cases.

Q: Should players keep case humidifiers in their cases?

A: Yes and no. Case humidifiers should be used in dry climates; however, they are not always necessary in humid climates. Using humidifiers unnecessarily can actually damage the instrument.

Cases, Reed: See Reed Cases/Holders, page 520

Channels, Reed: See Reeds, Double, page 531

Choosing an Instrument: See Instrument Selection, page 33

Clefs: The treble clef is used to notate music for oboe and English horn.

Conical: A term used to describe the cone-shaped tubing often used in instrument construction that is relatively narrow on one end (e.g., the reed end) and gradually widens toward the bell. Oboes and English horns are conical. See also Acoustical Basics, page 3; Acoustical Properties, page 459; Cylindrical, page 483

Conservatory System: A key design most commonly used on oboes. A "simplified conservatory" system is typically used for beginning oboes and generally does not include a left-hand F key, low B-flat, or any other extra key work. A "modified conservatory" oboe is typically considered an intermediate instrument and is equipped with all of the "essential" key work, including the left-hand F key, the low B-flat key, the B-natural/C-sharp articulation, and the F resonance key. The modified conservatory model may include some "extras" such as a double ring E-flat to E-natural (i.e., split D) key and third octave key. These oboes may also be made of plastic or wood, and are typically appropriate for all but very serious players. A "full conservatory" system, sometimes called a Gillet system, has forty-five key mechanisms not including optional keys. Professional oboes are considered "full conservatory" models. These models usually have a full complement of key work, including the left F key, low B-flat key, B-natural/C-sharp articulation, F resonance key, split D ring, a third octave key, alternate C-key (banana key), and several trill keys (e.g., B-flat/B, C/D, B/C-sharp). The exact key work on any given model varies. Oboe keys are typically made of nickel silver and may be either silver or gold-plated.

Most conservatory system oboes have semi-automatic octave keys, so that the first octave key automatically closes when the second octave key is depressed; however, some oboes have a fully-automatic octave key system in which only one octave key is used. In addition, some full conservatory oboes have an open-hole system in which rings are used instead of plates for the tone holes, similar to the clarinet. In these open-hole designs, players must cover tone holes with their fingers. Other full conservatory oboes utilize a plate system or English thumbplate system for covering holes. These systems are designed for comfort and ease of play; however, even in these systems, the right-hand third key is almost always an open hole. See also Construction and Design, page 479

Construction and Design: The oboe is pitched in C, and the English horn is pitched in F a fifth below concert pitch. Sound is produced with a double reed. Oboes and English horns are typically made of wood (intermediate and professional models) or plastic (beginning models); however, composite materials such as Green Line are sometimes used. Wooden oboes are typically made from grenadilla wood (African blackwood); however, rosewood, cocobolo, ebony, and violet wood are sometimes used. Oboes have both open and closed tone holes. Beginning models have more closed holes (plateau system), and advanced models have more open holes (conservatory system).

Oboes are available in a wider variety of key configurations than any other instrument except bassoon. The difference between a beginning instrument and a professional instrument is significant, not only in the materials used, but in the features available. A beginning oboe, or "simplified conservatory" model is typically not equipped with a left F key, low B-flat, or any other extra key work. A beginning oboe may be made of wood; however, plastic is more common. The "modified conservatory" oboe is typically considered an intermediate instrument, and is equipped with all of the "essential" key work, including the left F key, the low B-flat key, the B-natural/C-sharp articulation, and the F resonance key. The modified conservatory model may also include some "extras" such as a split D ring and third octave key. Intermediate oboes are often made of wood, but they may also be made of plastic. Intermediate oboes are appropriate for all but the most serious players.

Professional oboes are almost always made of wood (typically grenadilla) and are considered "full conservatory" models. These oboes usually have a full complement of key work, including the split D ring, a third octave key, and several trill keys. Considerable inconsistency exists regarding the exact key work on any given model of oboe. A list of key work and other options available for oboe appears below.

Low B-flat and vent key	Articulated C-sharp key
F-sharp key tab	B-flat/B, C/D, B/C-sharp trill keys
Left F key	Metal-lined tenon sockets
Third octave key	"Philadelphia D" key
Split D ring	Grenadilla body (part or all)
Metal-lined tenons	Resin (part or all)
Adjustable thumb rest	Delrin inserts in tone holes
F resonance key	Low B-flat key

Another consideration with oboes, especially wooden oboes, is age. Oboes do not age as well as some other instruments. Over time and with use, the bore dimensions can change slightly, altering the tonal characteristics of the instrument in undesirable ways. Oboes are also highly susceptible to cracking, more so than any other wooden instrument. Cracking most often occurs during the first year of play. As a result, players should "break in" the oboe slowly over a period of time. If an oboe cracks, it should be fixed as soon as possible by a knowledgeable repair technician.

Although the oboe does not have a mouthpiece, the quality and construction of the reed has a significant impact on tone quality, response, and intonation. The majority of advanced players make their own reeds (or finish reed blanks), or at least make significant modification to commercial reeds. Finding a good "fit" between the reed, the instrument, and the player is critical to proper tonal and technical development. See also Acoustical Basics, page 3; Acoustical Properties, page 459; Reeds, Double, page 531

Cracks: See Care and Maintenance, page 474

Crossing the Break: Technically, playing from any note below fourth-line D-flat (half-hole) to fourth-line D-flat or above is crossing the break; however, crossing the break usually refers to performing intervals close in proximity to fourth-line D-flat. For example, playing from third-space C-natural (1-4) to D-flat (½-2-3 4-5-6-D-flat key) involves crossing the break. Common examples of crossing the break appear in figure 5.8. The main challenge with crossing the break is moving from an open fingering (where few keys are depressed) to a closed fingering (where many keys are depressed), requiring coordination of hands and fingers. In addition, crossing the break requires the left-hand index finger to execute the half-hole technique. A secondary break occurs at fourth-space E-natural, where players must begin using the first octave key. For example, playing from fourth-line D-natural to top-space E-natural involves crossing the secondary break. Another secondary break occurs at high A-natural (above the staff), where players must switch from the first octave key to the second (side) octave key. Playing from high G-sharp to high A-natural involves crossing this break. See also Break, page 474 Technique, page 551

Preparing the Right Hand/Suggestions for Crossing the Break

1. Oboe players do not "prepare the right hand" like clarinet players do; however, when players alternate between from C-natural to D-flat or D-natural repeatedly in a passage, they can use the long C-natural fingering instead of the regular fingering (1-4). That is, players can finger the third-space C-natural ½-2-3 4-5-6-C key. Playing to D-flat or D-natural from this alternate C-natural is technically simpler.

Teaching Tips for Crossing the Break

1. Make sure students keep their fingers close to the keys and in the ready position at all times. Proper finger position will improve finger coordination.

2. Practice these intervals slowly at first, and work on one interval at a time. When students can play from C-natural to D-flat, C-natural

FIGURE 5.8. *Crossing the Break*

to D-natural, and C-natural to D-sharp in isolation, have them
put two or more intervals together.

3. When learning to play these intervals, tonguing each note can
    improve response; however, tonguing can also mask problems
    with finger coordination. As a result, it is important that students
    practice these intervals using slurs across the break. Students
    will often make changes in air, embouchure, throat, and so on
    to compensate for poor finger coordination when playing across
    the break. Such compensations are unnecessary and should
    be discouraged. In addition, maintaining a steady air stream
    and a consistent embouchure when playing across the break is
    essential.

Crow/Double Crow: The characteristic buzzing sound produced when double
reed players play or blow on the reed alone. After soaking the reed thoroughly
for about five minutes, the reed's ability to produce a crow or double crow can
be tested. Most good reeds produce these sounds when players blow into or
play on the reed alone. Although the terms are often used interchangeably, a
crow contains only one pitch, and a double crow contains two. To produce a
crow, players should put the tip of the reed in the mouth and blow gently until
a tone (crow) is produced. To produce a double crow, players should place most
of the reed into the mouth, blow gently at first without much lip pressure, and
then increase air speed until the reed "crows." A good double crow is one that
contains both a high and a low pitch. Many oboe players tune the pitch of the
"crow" to a concert C. Occasionally, players use the term "cackle" instead of
"crow" in describing the sound produced by the reed alone.

Cut: A term sometimes used to describe the manner in which double reed blanks
are prescraped, particularly in the tip and channel areas. Some players use "cut"
as a general term to describe the manner in which double reeds are scraped and
trimmed in the reed-making process. The term "cut" is more commonly associated with the U-shaped area of a single reed from where the bark has been
removed. See also Reeds, Double, page 531

Cutting Block: Typically, a small, round block of plastic or wood used in double reed making. A cutting block is a must in any reed-making kit. It provides a
raised, even surface for clipping the reed tip. See Reed Making and Adjustment,
page 521

Cylindrical: A term used to describe the cylinder-shaped tubing often used in instrument construction. Unlike conical tubing, which is relatively narrow on one end and gradually widens toward the other, cylindrical tubing remains the same diameter along the entire length of tubing. Oboe bores are slightly conical, not cylindrical. See also Acoustical Basics, page 3; Acoustical Properties, page 459; Conical, page 478

Diaphragm: See Breathing/Breath Support/Air Control, page 10; Diaphragm, page 26

Dizziness/Lightheadedness: See Dizziness/Lightheadedness, page 26

Double Crow: See Crow/Double Crow, page 482

Double Reeds: See Reeds, Double, page 531

Double-Tonguing: A technique that enables performers to tongue duple patterns rapidly. See Multiple-Tonguing, page 52

Doubling Considerations: Oboe players are sometimes required to double on English horn. Suggestions and considerations regarding the similarities and differences in the oboe and English horn are under Instrument Family and Playing Considerations.

Dutch Rush: Also called reed rush, horsetail, file grass, and shave grass, a natural fiber that can be used to smooth cane and to remove small amounts of cane in reed making. See also Reed Making and Adjustment, page 521

Dynamic Considerations: See Dynamic Considerations, page 26; Intonation, page 505

Embouchure: The oboe can be a somewhat difficult instrument on which to initially create a sound for several reasons. First, the oboe is more resistant than other woodwind instruments. Second, the embouchure is difficult to control at very soft and loud dynamic levels. Third, oboe players experience more back pressure than other wind players. Finally, appropriate embouchure adjustments on oboe require embouchure development and experience and are extremely challenging for beginners. For these reasons and more, players often start on another instrument and switch to oboe after they have gained some experience.

The basic oboe embouchure is the same throughout the range of the instrument; however, embouchure adjustments are necessary for achieving tonal consistency and pitch accuracy. The embouchure is generally more relaxed in the low range, with slightly less upper and lower lip rolled over the teeth. The embouchure is generally firmer in the high range, with slightly more upper and lower lip rolled over the teeth. The steps for forming a fundamentally sound oboe embouchure are described below. Proper oboe embouchures are shown in figures 5.9 through 5.12. Proper English horn embouchures are shown in figures 5.13 and 5.14. General embouchure considerations for the English horn are described under Instrument Family and Playing Considerations. See also Instrument Family and Playing Considerations, page 502

1. Separate the lips slightly and place the tip of the reed on the center of the lower lip.

2. Rest the tip of the reed on the center of the lower lip.

3. Close the lips lightly and roll the lips inward over the teeth as the reed is inserted into the mouth so that both the upper and the lower lips cushion and support the reed. Most of the reed (about two-thirds) is taken into the mouth, and the reed remains centered.

4. Lower the chin/jaw slightly and position the lips as if saying "oo." This position enables the lips to seal around the reed in a draw-string manner. The reed should be supported equally in all directions. As a rule, very little or none of the red part of the lips should be visible; however, because the size and shape of players' lips vary, the amount of the red part showing varies from player to player. Generally, a player with thin lips will have less red showing than a player with thick lips.

5. Avoid bunching the chin and puffing the cheeks.

Key Questions

Q: How does the oboe embouchure compare to the bassoon embouchure?

A: The oboe embouchure is much firmer than the bassoon embouchure. Generally, the top lip is rolled over the teeth slightly more with an oboe embouchure than it is with a bassoon embouchure; therefore, a little less of the top lip will be visible. In addition, fewer embouchure changes are required on oboe throughout the range than on bassoon.

FIGURE 5.9. *Embouchure*

FIGURE 5.10. *Embouchure in the Low Range*

FIGURE 5.11. *Embouchure in the Middle Range*

FIGURE 5.12. *Embouchure in the High Range*

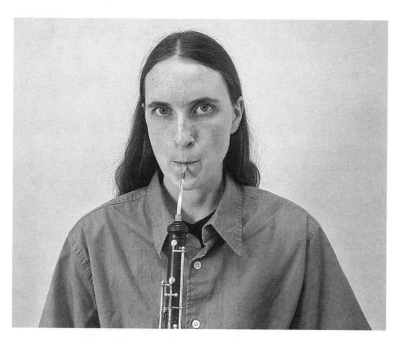

FIGURE 5.13. *English Horn Embouchure (Front View)*

FIGURE 5.14. *English Horn Embouchure (Side View)*

Q: How much of the lips is rolled over the teeth?

A: The amount of red showing varies according to the shape and thickness of the player's lips. As a rule, only a little bit of the red portion of the lips should be visible when the embouchure is formed correctly in the normal playing range. Generally, players with thin lips will have less red showing than will players with thick lips.

Q: Does the embouchure change throughout the playing range?

A: Yes. Although the basic embouchure remains the same, slight changes in the embouchure are necessary to adjust pitch and tone quality. For example, it is common to use a looser embouchure in the low range than in the high range. In fact, in the high range, the red part of the lips is often not visible. As a general rule, as oboe players ascend, they gradually firm their embouchures, and as they descend, they gradually relax their embouchures.

All of these adjustments are relatively slight. Radical changes in embouchure should be avoided.

Q: How much pressure should the teeth exert on the lips?

A: A small amount. Most of the pressure on the reed is applied and supported by the facial muscles. The idea of surrounding the reed with equal pressure from all sides is a sound teaching concept. Teachers often use the analogy of a drawstring to explain the oboe embouchure.

Q: How much of the reed should be inserted into the mouth?

A: Whatever amount yields the best tone quality; however, the general rule is that about two-thirds of the reed should be inserted in the mouth.

Q: What can be done to strengthen the embouchure?

A: Strengthen the embouchure muscles by practicing long tones and long tone exercises regularly and by extending practice time gradually over a period of weeks. Also, avoid excessively long practice sessions. Distributed practice is more effective than massed practice.

Q: Is the same basic embouchure used for English horn?

A: Yes. However, on English horn, the embouchure is slightly more open and relaxed because of the larger reed. Furthermore, English horn players may need to focus the air downward slightly more in the low range and upward slightly more in the high range than oboe players.

Teaching Tips for Embouchure Formation

1. Have students play "Mary Had a Little Lamb" on the reed alone. The position of the reed in the mouth for the middle tone should provide a good starting point.

2. When teaching embouchure, tell students that the embouchure should remain fairly consistent throughout the middle range (first-space F-natural through about third-space C-natural); however, as a rule, players need to firm the embouchure as they ascend and relax the embouchure as they descend. For example, a low C-natural will be more relaxed than a third-space C-natural and much more relaxed than a high C-natural. Telling beginners that

changes are needed will help focus pitches properly and contribute to good intonation.

3. Teachers should not see excessive movement of the embouchure, even when students use vibrato. Students sometimes develop the habit of moving the embouchure when vibrato is used. This movement negatively affects tone quality, tonal consistency, and pitch.

4. The idea of applying equal pressure all around the reed, sometimes called the "drawstring effect," is a sound teaching concept on oboe because it enables students to understand the need for a round embouchure.

5. Students with moderate to severe overbites will need to bring their jaw forward so that an even amount of pressure can be applied to both blades.

6. Students with moderate to severe underbites will need to bring their jaw back so that an even amount of pressure can be applied to both blades.

7. Students can use a mirror to check their embouchure formations and reed placement. Using a mirror regularly in the beginning stages will help students develop proper playing habits.

Endurance/Stamina: See Endurance/Stamina, page 28

English Horn: See Instrument Family and Playing Considerations, page 502

Exhalation/Exhaling: See Breathing/Breath Support/Air Control, page 10

Extended/Contemporary Techniques: In general, ways of producing sounds on an instrument that are not traditionally characteristic of the instrument or not typically called for in standard literature. A detailed discussion of these techniques is found under Extended/Contemporary Techniques in chapter 1. See also Extended/Contemporary Techniques, page 29

F Resonance Key: An additional key that opens automatically when the forked-F fingering is used to improve the tone quality of the F-natural, eliminating the need to add the E-flat key (little finger) on the right hand. Although older oboes may not have an F resonance key, it has become standard on oboes today.

Family: See Instrument Family and Playing Considerations, page 502

Fish Skin: A material sometimes used as a quick fix to prevent air from leaking out of the sides of the reed. Fish skin is wrapped around the reed to help seal the area that is leaking. Many players use Teflon tape (also called plumbers tape) instead of fish skin. Teflon tape is an inexpensive and readily available alternate to fish skin and can be found at any hardware store.

Flutter Tonguing: A technique that involves rolling or fluttering the tongue rapidly while producing a tone. Flutter tonguing uses the same motion of the tongue that is used when pronouncing a rolling "r." Players who cannot roll their tongues may use a throat growl as a substitute. See also Extended/Contemporary Techniques, page 29

Fork F: An alternate fingering for F-natural that requires the fingerings on the right hand to be in a "fork" position (index and ring fingers are down and the middle finger is up). The fingering for Fork F is 1-2-3 4-6 (plus the octave key in the upper register). See Alternate Fingerings/Alternates, page 461

Fork F Resonance Key: See F Resonance Key, page 490

French Reed: Generally, a reed that is lighter in the heart, and thinner in the shoulders and tip area. French reeds are made to sound vibrant and bright, unlike German reeds, which generally sound dark and heavy. See also German Reed, page 491; Reeds, Double, page 531

Fundamental: See Fundamental, page 32

German Reed: Generally, a reed that is heavy in the heart, and thicker in the shoulders and tip area. German reeds are made to sound dark and heavy, unlike French reeds, which sound relatively bright and thin. See also French Reed, page 491; Reeds, Double, page 531

Gouge: A term used in several ways to describe double reed cane. Gouge can refer to the general state of unfinished cane, the manner in which cane is removed, and/or the process of removing cane. Gouged cane is cane that has been soaked and run through a gouging machine, which cuts and shaves the cane into a more workable form. See also Reeds, Double, page 531

Grain, Reed: The natural fibers in reed cane. The grain or fibers of a reed can be fine, coarse, or a combination of the two. By comparing several reeds, players can

FIGURE 5.15. *Half-Hole Position*

easily learn to see the variations in the grain. Reeds that contain too many coarse grains typically do not respond well, feel rough on the lip, and produce an unsatisfactory tone quality. Reeds that contain too many fine grains are often inconsistent and tend to wear out very quickly. See also Reeds, Double, page 531

Grattage: A French word used to describe the manner in which a reed is scraped. See also Reeds, Double, page 531

Half-Hole Technique: A performance technique that typically involves covering half (or part) of a tone hole with one finger. This traditional technique works only with an open tone hole. On oboe, most instruments are now designed with a half-hole key for the first hole on the upper joint (index finger), eliminating the need to cover the tone hole directly. The purpose of this key is to help players execute half-holes. On oboe, the three D's (D-flat, D-natural, and D-sharp) are half-holed by rolling the index finger downward slightly, uncovering the small vent hole normally covered by the index finger as shown in figure 5.15. Opening the vent hole helps these pitches respond in the appropriate register, much like the octave key does on other pitches. Musical examples of when to use the half-hole technique are shown in figure 5.16. See also Extended/Contemporary Techniques, page 29

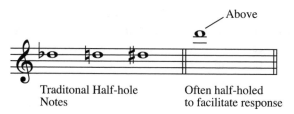

FIGURE 5.16. *Half-Hole Notes*

Key Questions

Q: Does the index finger roll upward or downward when using the half-hole technique?

A: Downward.

Q: Are half-holes used for anything other than the three D's?

A: Yes. The half-hole is also used for the high D-natural and D-sharp above the staff. It is also sometimes used for high E-natural, F-natural, and above, depending on the instrument. At the advanced level, using half-holes enables players to play quarter tones in contemporary literature. In addition, half-holes are sometimes used when executing certain trills. Using half-holes in these situations is an advanced technique, usually beyond most high school players.

Teaching Tips for Half-Holes

1. Students quickly learn that the three D's will respond without using half-holes, and they often choose not to half-hole these pitches. Not using the half-hole technique on the three D's is problematic. Using half-holes on the three D's improves tone quality, intonation, and response. Only in fast technical passages can these pitches not be half-holed. In such passages, not using half-holes may improve technical fluidity, and the differences in tone quality, intonation, and response will not be noticed.

2. The index finger rolls downward when using the half-hole technique; it does not slide. In addition, the index finger maintains contact with the instrument at all times during this process.

Hand/Holding/Instrument/Playing Positions and Posture: Holding the oboe properly and maintaining good hand position and playing position are key factors in developing good technique, facility, and ease of playing. In addition, maintaining proper positions will reduce muscle fatigue and help players avoid physical problems, such as carpal tunnel syndrome. Suggestions for hand/holding/instrument/playing positions and posture are listed below.

Left-Hand Position

1. The left hand is on top (upper joint) with the thumb positioned both on the wood (or plastic) just below the octave key and slightly touching the octave key. The thumb is positioned at a slightly upward angle so that it can operate the octave key with a simple rocking motion. The thumb remains in constant contact with the instrument, even when it is engaging the octave key.

2. The fingers curve slightly around the oboe as if forming an open "C." The fingers remain no more than three-eighths of an inch from the keys or tone holes.

3. Because the keys/tone holes are positioned slightly farther apart on oboe than they are on flute or clarinet, the fingers need to be spread farther apart to cover the holes properly. As a result, the fingers typically cross the instrument at a slightly downward angle.

4. The index, middle, and ring fingers are positioned on or above the first, second, and third tone holes (1-2-3) respectively. Open tone holes are covered with the pads of the fingers, rather than the tips of the fingers.

5. The index finger is angled so that the first finger joint is slightly touching or over the second octave key. This position makes it easier to use this octave key when needed. The index finger remains in position to cover the first tone hole and to execute half-holes on the three D's (D-flat, D-natural, and D-sharp) at all times.

6. The little finger touches the B key lightly and remains ready to operate the little-finger keys (G-sharp, B, B-flat, E-flat, and F). Some teachers suggest resting the little finger on the G-sharp key; however, the B key is a better choice because it is more centrally located in the key group or cluster.

7. The wrist remains virtually straight; however, a very slight inward bend is acceptable.

Right-Hand Position

1. The right hand is on the bottom (lower joint) with the thumb positioned on the back side of the oboe under the thumb rest. The thumb rest should contact the thumb between the thumbnail and the first joint, and the thumb should remain relatively straight.
2. The fingers curve slightly around the oboe as if forming an open "C." The fingers remain no more than three-eighths of an inch from the tone holes.
3. Because of key placement and design, the fingers cross the instrument at a slightly downward angle. This position improves technical playing.
4. The index, middle, and ring fingers are positioned on or above the fourth, fifth, and sixth tone holes (4-5-6), respectively. Open tone holes are covered with the pads of the fingers, rather than with the tips of the fingers.
5. The little finger touches the D-sharp/E-flat key lightly and remains ready to operate the little-finger keys (D-sharp, C, and C-sharp). Some teachers suggest resting the little finger on the C key; however, the D-sharp/E-flat key is a better choice because it is used more often, especially if the oboe does not have an F resonance key.
6. The wrist remains virtually straight; however, a very slight inward bend is acceptable. Proper hand positions are shown in figures 5.17 and 5.18.

Holding/Instrument Position

1. The weight of the oboe is supported by the right thumb. Balance of the instrument is controlled primarily by the right thumb, to a lesser degree by the left thumb, and by the embouchure when the instrument is being played.
2. The bell is held out from the body at about a 40- to 45-degree angle. As a general point of reference, the oboe is held out from the body just past the knees. Small adjustments to this position can be made based on the player's tone quality. As a rule, the oboe is held out from the body slightly farther than the clarinet.
3. The oboe is centered with the body.
4. The elbows are held away from the body in a relaxed manner. Proper oboe playing positions are shown in figures 5.19 and 5.20. Proper English horn playing positions are shown in figures 5.21 and 5.22.

FIGURE 5.17. *Thumb Positions*

FIGURE 5.18. *Hand Position*

FIGURE 5.19. *Playing Position (Front View)*

Posture

1. Sit up straight (but avoid being rigid or tense) with feet flat on the floor. Sit toward the front edge of the chair while in the seated playing position. If the instrument touches the front of the chair, move farther forward on the chair.

2. Avoid being tense or tight in the playing position because tension negatively affects both the mental and physical aspects of playing the oboe.

3. Keep the head straight and relaxed. Bring the reed to the mouth. Do not reach for the reed.

4. Ensure proper placement of the music stand. The music stand should be in a position that enables each player reading from

FIGURE 5.20. *Playing Position (Side View)*

the stand to read the music comfortably and easily and to see the teacher/director while maintaining proper playing positions. The most common problem is for music stands to be too low. The most detrimental problem is for music stands to be placed too far to one side, forcing players to abandon good playing positions. Players who share music stands often experience this problem.

5. Maintain proper instrument angle. The oboe is held out from the body at about a 40- to 45-degree angle. When the instrument is too close or too far from the body, players cannot support the reed properly, resulting in poor tone quality, poor tone control, and poor intonation.

6. Adjust the neck strap (if used) properly, especially on English horn. When the neck strap is too low, players have to reach down for the reed. When the neck strap is too high, players have to reach up for the reed. In both situations, the head and neck are forced

FIGURE 5.21. *English Horn Playing Position (Front View)*

out of position, causing problems with tone quality, breath support, and technique.

7. Ensure proper right thumb placement to avoid pain and fatigue. Make sure that the thumb rest contacts the thumb between the nail and first joint. In addition, pain and discomfort may be relieved by placing a pad on the thumb rest at the point of contact. Pads designed for this purpose are available at most music stores. In recent years, it has become somewhat more common to see oboe players using neck straps. As long as the correct instrument angle is maintained, neck straps that help support the instrument can help reduce fatigue and injury, especially when playing for extended periods of time.

FIGURE 5.22. *English Horn Playing Position (Side View)*

Harmonics: See Harmonics, page 32

Heart: The center portion of the reed blades extending from just behind the tip toward the shoulders. When held up to a light, the heart can be seen as a symmetrically shaped shaded area. Hearts are clearly visible in German but not in French reeds; however, French reeds are cut and shaped in such a way that the blades appear to be evenly shaded. The heart of a German reed can be seen and felt as a slight hump running down the middle of the blades and extending toward the edges (rails) of the blade. No such heart is apparent on a French reed. See also Reeds, Double, page 531

Heel: A term sometimes used to describe the butt end of a reed, or the end of the cane opposite the tip. See also Reeds, Double, page 531

History: Double reed instruments have been around in one form or another for thousands of years and were common among the ancient civilizations of Mesopotamia and Egypt. Double reed instruments are believed to have originated in the Eastern cultures and introduced to European cultures during the Middle

Ages. Some predecessors of the oboe include the bombarde (French) or pommer (German) and the more familiar krummhorn. Although it is not known who invented the oboe, it appears to have been invented in the 1650s. Originally believed to be used indoors as a softer, mellower sounding alternative to the one-piece shawm, the first oboes had three sections and only two keys. Unlike the shawm, which held a double reed inside a wooden pirouette, the oboe reed was mounted freely, much like modern oboes. Pitched in C, oboes are cone shaped and generally made of grenadilla wood, and were a standard part of orchestral ensembles by the beginning of the seventeenth century. More keys, including an octave key, were added in the eighteenth and nineteenth centuries, increasing the oboe's range and its flexibility. A variety of fingering systems has been developed through the years including the thumb-plate system, the Conservatoire system, and the plateau system. The conservatory model oboe, originally designed by François Lorée and George Gillet, is commonly used by professionals today. The oboe d'amore, pitched in A, was popular during the Baroque period. Basically an alto oboe that employed a bocal similar to the English horn bocal, the oboe d'amore was replaced by the oboe pitched in C. The English horn, invented in the mid-eighteenth century, was designed to extend the range of the oboe downward. Because of the wider-spaced key arrangement, English horns use key mechanisms with pads, much like the mechanisms used on saxophones. The baritone oboe or bass oboe as it is often called, is pitched one octave below the oboe. It was invented in the 1740s and is rarely used today. In the early 1900s, Wilhelm Heckel invented the Heckelphone, a close relative of the oboe. The Heckelphone was basically a baritone or bass oboe with a larger reed and bulb-shaped bell that enhanced playing in the low range. Like baritone oboes, Heckelphones did not last and are rarely used today. In addition, there are also piccolo oboes; however, they are rarely used except in double reed ensemble music.

Instrument Angle: The oboe is held out from the body at about a 40- to 45-degree angle. When the oboe is held too close to the body, the tone tends to be small and pinched because the pressure on the bottom blade of the reed is increased. When the oboe is held too far from the body, the tone tends to be out of focus or spread because the pressure on the bottom blade of the reed is decreased. In both instances, problems result from uneven embouchure pressure being applied to the reed.

Key Questions

Q: How does the instrument angle of the oboe compare to the instrument angle of the clarinet?

A: As a rule, the oboe is held farther from the body than the clarinet is.

Q: Do all players hold the oboe at the same angle?

A: No. Experienced players may find that holding the instrument out slightly more or slightly less from the body improves their tone quality. However, beginners should be taught to hold the instrument at about a 40- to 45-degree angle (just past the knees). Later, as players gain experience, they can experiment to see if a slightly different angle improves their tone quality.

Instrument Brands: Several brands of oboes are available. Some makers carry several models to accommodate a wide range of playing skills and budgets. Other makers carry models that are particularly suited to certain skill levels, budgets, and playing situations. Used instruments are also a good option for many players, and used instruments made by reputable manufacturers are available. When searching for an inexpensive or used instrument, beware of "off" brands and instrument models (even with reputable brands) that have not performed up to a high standard. The list below includes several reputable oboe manufacturers. Although this list is not exhaustive, it does provide a good starting point for research. See also Instrument Selection, page 33

Oboe Manufacturers

Buffet; Bulgheroni; Covey; Fossati; Fox; Howarth; Josef; Jupiter; Laubin; Loree; Marigaux; MCW; Patricola; Rigoutat; Selmer; and Yamaha.

Instrument Family and Playing Considerations: The oboe pitched in C is the oboe commonly used in ensembles today. The English horn pitched in F is also commonly played in advanced ensembles. Other types of oboes that are available, but not regularly heard, include the oboe d'amore pitched in A and historical instruments, such as the Baroque oboe, the Classical oboe, the Viennese oboe, and the Heckelphone. Figure 5.23 shows an oboe, an oboe d'amore, and an English horn. Unusual members of the oboe family that are rarely heard include the bass oboe (pitched one octave below the traditional oboe), the piccolo oboe or musette (pitched in E-flat or F), and the contrabass oboe (pitched two octaves below the traditional oboe). Considerations for playing the English horn are described below.

English Horn

1. Embouchure—The English horn embouchure is similar to the oboe embouchure; however, the English horn embouchure is slightly more relaxed overall, especially in the low range.

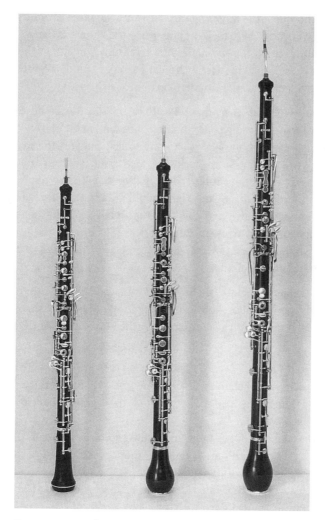

FIGURE 5.23. *Oboe Family*

2. Air Stream—The air stream needs to be slightly warmer on English horn. In addition, the English horn requires more air than does the oboe.

3. Reed—English horn reeds and oboe reeds are not interchangeable. English horn reeds are generally slightly thicker overall, and they sometimes have a wire similar to a bassoon reed wire. In addition, English horn reeds are designed to be placed on a bocal like a bassoon reed, and not in a reed well like an oboe reed.

4. Technique—The fingerings are basically the same as oboe finger-ings; however, because of its larger size and key work, many players find the English horn slightly more cumbersome than the oboe. As a result, playing fast technical passages will be slightly more difficult on English horn than on oboe.

5. Hand/Holding/Instrument Position and Posture—The English horn is larger and heavier than an oboe, and many players choose to use a saxophone-like neck strap to help support the weight of the instrument. Using a neck strap also lessens the pressure on the right thumb significantly, reducing the risk of injury and increas-ing the flexibility of the right hand. In addition, floor pegs or chair pegs are also available for English horn to help support the weight of the instrument. Such devices can be particularly helpful for young players; however, advanced players may find that these devices limit mobility.

6. Instrument Angle—The English horn is held a little closer to the body than the oboe; however, the angle of the bocal causes the reed to enter the mouth at approximately the same angle as the oboe.

7. Assembly—The basic steps for assembling the English horn are listed below.
   A. Attach the bell to the lower joint with a slight twisting motion. Depress the pad cup to avoid damaging the bridge key mechanism.
   B. Attach the upper joint to the lower joint/bell assembly with a slight back-and-forth twisting motion, making sure that the bridge keys are aligned properly.
   C. Insert the bocal into the well or receiver such that the bend is upward and aligned with the center of the tone holes or keys.
   D. Slide the reed over the end of the bocal all the way. The flat part of the reed faces downward.

8. Intonation—See Intonation, page 505

Instrument Parts: See Parts, Oboe, page 515

Instrument Position: See Hand/Holding/Instrument Playing Positions and Posture, page 493

Instrument Ranges: See Range, page 517

Instrument Selection: See Instrument Brands, page 502; Instrument Selection, page 33

Instrument Sizes: See Instrument Family and Playing Considerations, page 502

Instrument Stands: See Instrument Stands, page 39

Intonation: Generally, the degree of "in-tuneness" in a melodic and a harmonic context. In ensemble playing, the most important factors in achieving intonation accuracy are: (1) hearing intonation problems, (2) understanding what adjustments need to be made to correct intonation problems, and (3) having the skills to make the necessary adjustments. A detailed general discussion of intonation is in chapter 1. Specific suggestions for helping players better understand the pitch tendencies of the oboe and how to make appropriate pitch adjustments are outlined separately in this section. See also Intonation, page 41; Temperament, page 61; Tuning/Tuning Note Considerations, page 561

General Comments for Adjusting Pitch

Adjusting pitch is the process of raising or lowering the pitch of notes. Comments and suggestions for adjusting pitch are outlined below.

1. Embouchure/Air Stream—The embouchure and air stream can be altered in several subtle ways to adjust or humor pitches. As players progress, they learn to make sure embouchure adjustments for certain pitches are part of standard technique. Common embouchure/air stream/oral cavity adjustments are described below.
   A. To lower or flatten the pitch, focus the air stream downward. As a rule, the farther downward the air stream is directed, the flatter the pitch will be. The air stream may be focused downward by making slight changes in the oral cavity (i.e., a slightly more open focus) and/or by making slight adjustments in embouchure (i.e., a slightly lowered jaw).
   B. To raise or sharpen the pitch, focus the air stream upward. As a rule, the farther upward the air stream is directed, the sharper the pitch will be. The air stream may be focused upward by making slight changes in the embouchure and/or oral cavity. These changes involve creating a slightly smaller focus in the oral cavity and/or raising the jaw slightly.

C. To sharpen the pitch, firm the embouchure slightly; to flatten the pitch, loosen the embouchure slightly. The embouchure can be firmed by increasing lip pressure around the reed and loosened by decreasing lip pressure around the reed. Changes in embouchure tension and air speed are facilitated by thinking of using a cold or a warm air stream. A warm air stream tends to decrease air speed and relax the embouchure, which flattens the pitch. A cold air stream tends to increase air speed and firm the embouchure, which sharpens the pitch. Typically, oboe players use a colder air stream than other woodwind players do; however, thinking of using a warmer air stream will help relax the embouchure, thus opening up the tone and flattening the pitch.

D. Make only slight changes in air stream and embouchure when adjusting pitch. Large-scale changes affect tone quality, control, and focus.

2. Throat/Oral Cavity—A tight, restricted throat causes the pitch to go sharp. An open throat results in the best tone quality on oboe. Relax the throat as if saying "ah," and the pitch will drop. Changes and adjustments in the oral cavity affect both tone quality and pitch, and are usually accomplished by having students think of saying certain syllables such as "oh," "oo," "ah," and "ee" in the altissimo register. The use of such syllables is effective in altering pitch and tone quality; however, be aware that using syllables often causes accompanying changes in embouchure and air flow as well. Understanding the relationships and balances between embouchure, air stream, throat, and oral cavity is important for both players and teachers.

3. Alternates/Adding Keys—If slight changes in air stream and embouchure do not bring the desired pitches in tune, adding keys to regular fingerings or using alternate fingerings may help bring certain pitches in tune. On the other hand, adding keys and using alternates to adjust pitch is not always practical. As a general rule, tonal considerations, technical considerations and tempo largely dictate the appropriateness of such adjustments. Finally, adding keys or using alternates to adjust pitch often negates the need to make changes in air stream or embouchure.

4. Dynamics/Air Speed—Changes in dynamics/air speed affect pitch, sometimes significantly. Considerations regarding dynamics/air speed are described below.

A. When playing loudly and increasing air speed, the pitch tends to go sharp. Adjust by focusing the air stream downward and/ or loosening the embouchure slightly. Proper air speed and control is maintained at all times. Do not overblow.

B. When playing softly and decreasing air speed slightly, the pitch tends to go flat. Adjust by focusing the air stream upward and/ or firming the embouchure slightly. Even at softer dynamic levels, the air stream must move fast enough to sustain and support the pitch. Not using enough air or using an air stream that is too slow causes the pitch to go flat.

5. Mechanical—Mechanical design characteristics that affect intonation are described below.

A. If the pitch is flat overall, check to make sure that the reed is pushed in all the way. As a rule, the reed should be pushed into the reed well as far as it will go.

B. Pad height affects pitch. If pads are too low, the pitch will be flat. If pads are too high, the pitch will be sharp. Make sure instruments are properly adjusted.

C. Leaks and other mechanical problems affect pitch. Check the oboe regularly for leaks, loose and/or broken springs, and missing corks or felts. Maintaining the instrument in good repair is essential for good intonation.

6. Reeds—Hard reeds tend to play sharp, especially when playing softly. In addition, players tend to firm up the embouchure to control a harder reed, which further raises pitch. Soft reeds tend to play flat, especially when playing loudly. When players try to relax and maintain a good embouchure, tone and pitch are very difficult to control because the reed does not provide enough resistance against the embouchure pressure. When players bite too hard, the reed aperture or tip opening closes, resulting in a small, pinched tone or no tone at all. Players should use a reed strength that provides a modest amount of resistance in the middle register.

7. Position of the Reed in the Mouth—If the reed is inserted too far into the mouth, the pitch will be sharp. If the reed is not inserted far enough into the mouth, the pitch will be flat. About two-thirds of the reed should be inserted into the mouth. Players often adjust pitch by making slight adjustments in the amount of reed taken in the mouth.

8. Instrument Angle—When the oboe is held too close to the body, the tone tends to be small and pinched, and the pitch tends to be sharper because the pressure on the reed is increased. When the oboe is held too far from the body, the tone tends to be out of focus or spread and the pitch tends to be flatter because the pressure on the reed is decreased. In both instances, problems result from uneven embouchure pressure being applied to the reed. Exaggerated instrumental angles in or out from the body cause flatness in pitch because the reed is not supported properly. The oboe is held out from the body at about a 40- to 45-degree angle, which is slightly farther away from the body than a clarinet is held.

9. Instrument Family—The English horn shares the same general pitch tendencies as the oboe and can be adjusted in the manner described above; however, because the English horn is larger, it uses a larger reed. As a result, the English horn is generally less sensitive to pitch adjustments than the oboe, so players may have to exaggerate the adjustments they would normally make on oboe. In addition, unlike oboes, English horns have bocals. Pulling the bocal out will lower the pitch slightly, and pushing the bocal in will raise the pitch slightly. Bocals are also manufactured in different lengths, similar to bassoon bocals. Bocals are generally numbered 1 through 3, with 1 being the shortest. There is a direct relationship between the length of a bocal and pitch. Specifically, shorter bocals sharpen the pitch, and longer bocals flatten the pitch.

Tuning the Oboe

A detailed description of how to tune the oboe is under Tuning/Tuning Note Considerations in this chapter.

Pitch Tendencies

Pitch tendencies refers to the tendency for certain notes on an instrument to deviate from a specified standard, usually the equal tempered scale based on a reference frequency of A = 440. That is, when players talk about the pitch tendencies of their instruments, they are almost always talking about how sharp or flat certain notes are in reference to a modern, equal-tempered tuner. Comments and suggestions regarding pitch tendencies are outlined below. A summary of these tendencies is presented in figures 5.24 and 5.25.

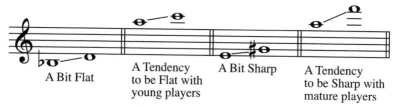

FIGURE 5.24. *Intonation Tendencies (General)*

FIGURE 5.25. *Intonation Tendencies (Specific)*

General Range/Register Tendencies—Flat Pitches

1. The low notes tend to be flat (between low B-flat and D-natural below the staff).
2. The notes using the side octave key (high A-natural through high C-natural) tend to be flat if players do not make appropriate embouchure adjustments.
3. Inexperienced players sometimes play flat in the high/altissimo register because their embouchures are not developed properly for playing in that range and because their concepts of adjusting pitch are not developed.

Adjustments for Numbers 1, 2, and 3

Adjustment 1—Take slightly more reed into the mouth and increase air speed.

Adjustment 2—Focus the air stream upward slightly.

Adjustment 3—Firm the embouchure. Do not bite or pinch the reed excessively and close the tip opening.

Adjustment 4—For the low notes, think of using an "oo" syllable to help focus the oral cavity. For the high notes, think of using an "ee" syllable to help focus the oral cavity.

General Range/Register Tendencies—Sharp Pitches

1. The notes in the range from first-line E-natural to second-line G-sharp tend to be sharp.
2. The notes in the high register (above high A-natural) tend to be sharp.

   Adjustments for Numbers 1 and 2

   Adjustment 1—Relax the embouchure slightly (lower the jaw slightly) and open the oral cavity but maintain embouchure focus.

   Adjustment 2—Take slightly less reed in the mouth and decrease air speed slightly.

   Adjustment 3—Focus the air stream downward slightly.

   Adjustment 4—Use a more open syllable such as "oh" or "ah' to help lower the pitch.

Specific Pitch Tendencies—Making Adjustments for Problem Pitches

1. Third-line B-natural and third-space C-natural tend to be sharp.
2. Top-space E-natural and G-natural above the staff tend to be very sharp.

   Adjustments for Numbers 1 and 2

   Adjustment 1—Relax the embouchure slightly (lower the jaw slightly) and open the oral cavity, but maintain embouchure focus.

   Adjustment 2—Use a more open syllable such as "oh" or "ah' to help lower the pitch.

   Adjustment 3—Focus the air stream downward slightly.

   Adjustment 4—Take slightly less reed in the mouth and decrease air speed.

3. Third-line B-flat tends to be a bit flat.
4. Low C-sharp/D-flat is very flat.

   Adjustment 1—Focus the air stream upward slightly.

   Adjustment 2—Take slightly more reed into the mouth and increase air speed.

   Adjustment 3—Firm the embouchure slightly, but do not bite or pinch the reed.

   Adjustment 4—Think of using an "oo" syllable to help focus the oral cavity.

Adding Fingers to Adjust for Intonation Problems

Players can depress keys in addition to the regular fingering to adjust pitch. An outline of basic fingering adjustments appears below.

1. Adding the right-hand ring finger (6) to the regular third-space C-natural fingering tends to darken and flatten third-space C-natural.
2. Adding the right-hand ring finger (6) to the regular high C-natural may flatten high C-natural; however, on some instruments, adding this key may actually raise the pitch.
3. Adding the E-flat key (right-hand little finger) to fork F will raise the pitch.
4. Adding the right-hand middle finger (5) and/or the ring finger (6) to the high D-natural (above the staff) will lower the pitch.

Using Alternate Fingerings to Adjust Intonation

It is common for players to use alternate fingerings to adjust pitch. An outline of basic alternates and their typical relationships to the corresponding regular fingerings appears below.

1. Fork F is slightly flatter than regular F-natural or left F.
2. Alternate C-sharp (third-space trill) and D-natural (fourth-line trill) is sharper than regular D-natural.
3. There is no difference in pitch between alternate E-flat, alternate A-flat and the regular fingerings for these notes.
4. There is no difference in pitch between left F-natural and regular F-natural.

Key/Pad Height: See Key/Pad Height, page 45

Lightheadedness: See Dizziness/Lightheadedness, page 26

Long-Scrape Reed: A reed that has about two-thirds (or more) of the reed scraped from the tip toward the binding, as opposed to a short-scrape reed, which is scraped only about halfway or less. Most oboe reeds are long-scrape reeds.

Low B-flat Key: An auxiliary key that extends the range of the instrument downward one half step from low B-natural to low B-flat. Oboes with a low B-flat key have an extra tone hole and key mechanism on the bell and have a slightly longer bell to accommodate this additional key. Low B-flat keys are found on virtually all intermediate and professional model oboes and on some beginning instruments. The low B-flat key is operated by the left-hand little finger. When depressed, it closes the low B-flat tone hole on the bell of the oboe. In addition to extending the range downward one half step, the addition of the low B-flat key provides increased resonance for low B-natural and low C-natural.

Mandrel: A tapered metal tool for holding reeds while they are being scraped or filed. Mandrels are also used to help shape and form the reed in the finishing process. See also Reed Making and Adjustment, page 521

Multiphonics: See Extended/Contemporary Techniques, page 29

Multiple-Tonguing: See Multiple-Tonguing, page 52

Neck Strap: A strap positioned around the player's neck that attaches to a strap ring on the oboe via a clip or hook. Neck straps are typically made of nylon or leather and are adjustable so that the instrument can be positioned properly. Traditionally, oboe players have not used neck straps; however, neck straps are becoming more popular because they take most of the instrument's weight off of the right thumb, reducing fatigue and the risk of injury. Neck straps are necessary for the English horn because of its weight and size. Playing the English horn without the neck strap can be cumbersome and uncomfortable. It can also promote poor playing habits and make the instrument more susceptible to damage. Most English horns are equipped with a ring for the neck strap, and many players, both experienced and inexperienced, use a neck strap to reduce fatigue and maintain good playing position. In addition, floor pegs or chair pegs are also available for English horn to help support the weight of the instrument. Such devices can be particularly helpful for young players; however, advanced players may find that these devices limit mobility.

Oboe d'amore: The oboe d'amore became popular during the Baroque period. Although the oboe d'amore was replaced by the oboe pitched in C, it is still fairly common today. Pitched in A, the oboe d'amore is basically an alto oboe that uses a bocal similar to an English horn bocal. See also Instrument Family and Playing Considerations, page 502

Octave Keys: Most oboes are designed with a semi-automatic octave key, which actually involves two octave keys as shown in figure 5.26. In this design, players depress the first octave key for range of notes between and including fourth-space E-natural to G-sharp above the staff. The second octave key is engaged when

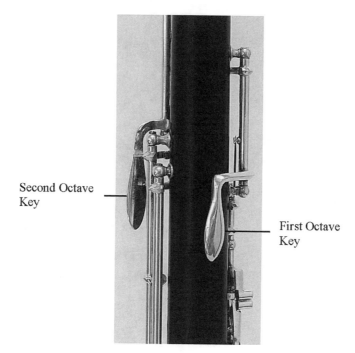

Second Octave Key

First Octave Key

FIGURE 5.26. *Two Octave Keys*

playing high A-natural to high C-natural above the staff. No octave keys are used for high C-sharp above the staff to high D-sharp. The first or third octave key can be used for high E-natural and above, depending on the instrument. Some oboes have a fully-automatic octave key mechanism. In this design, players depress only one octave key for all notes in the upper range. Although having one octave key may sound like a better option, its complicated design is often difficult to adjust properly, and it limits the number of alternate fingering possibilities. Finally, some professional oboes actually have three octave keys rather than the traditional two as shown in figure 5.27. The third octave key is positioned above and overlaps the first octave key. It is used when playing in the altissimo range (i.e., high E-natural and above) and is only needed for advanced literature. The various octave key configurations available for oboe are summarized below. Notated examples of when to use the octave keys are shown in figure 5.28.

First Octave Key (semi-automatic design)

1. The first octave key is used for the range of notes between and including fourth-space E-natural to G-sharp above the staff. This

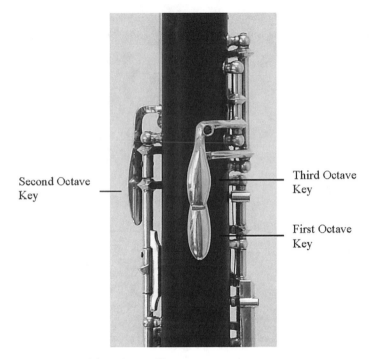

FIGURE 5.27. *Three Octave Keys*

octave key is operated by a slight rocking motion of the left thumb at the joint, and not by sliding or rolling the thumb.

Second Octave Key (semi-automatic design)

1. The second octave key is used for the range of notes between high A-natural and high C-natural. This octave key is operated by shifting or moving the index finger inward and contacting the octave key on the side of the upper index finger joint of the left hand.

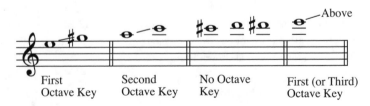

FIGURE 5.28. *Using the Octave Keys*

2. On instruments with a semi-automatic design, it is not necessary to lift the first octave key (i.e., remove the thumb from the first octave key) when operating the second octave. The second octave key automatically closes the first octave key when engaged.

3. On older model oboes that are not made with a semi-automatic design, it is necessary to release the first octave key when operating the second octave key to avoid having both octave keys open at the same time.

Third Octave Key (found on some professional oboes)

1. The third octave key is used for the range of notes above and including high E-natural. This octave key is operated by shifting or moving the left thumb slightly above the first octave key.

Octave Key (automatic design)

1. Used for all notes above and including fourth-space E-natural, this octave key is operated by a slight rocking motion of the thumb at the joint and not by sliding or rolling the thumb.
2. There is no side octave key on oboes made with a fully-automatic design.

Optional Keys/Key Mechanisms: Keys or key mechanisms that are not necessary to the essential functioning of the oboe but that make playing easier. Optional keys on the oboe include: low B-flat key, left F key, split D ring, B-flat (bell) resonance key, third octave key, and an F resonance key. See also Conservatory System; Construction and Design, page 479

Overblow: See Overblow, page 55

Overtones: See Overtones, page 55

Pad Height: See Key/Pad Height, page 45

Parts, Oboe: The parts of an oboe are identified below in figure 5.29.

Pitch Adjustment: See Intonation, page 505; Tuning/Tuning Note Consideration, page 561

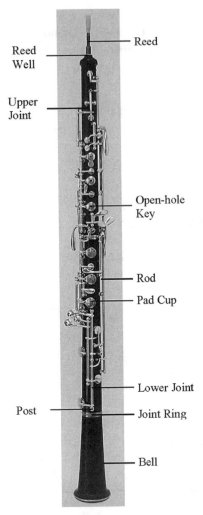

Reed
Well

Reed

Upper
Joint

Open-hole
Key

Rod

Pad Cup

Lower Joint

Post

Joint Ring

Bell

FIGURE 5.29. *Parts of an Oboe*

Pitch Tendencies: Generally, the tendency for any note to deviate from a specified standard, usually the equal tempered scale based on a reference frequency of A = 440. That is, when players talk about the pitch tendencies of their instruments, they are almost always talking about how sharp or flat certain notes are in reference to a modern, equal tempered scale. The term "pitch tendency" is most commonly used to refer to pitch deviations that are an inherent part of an instrument's design. In many instances, pitch tendencies are consistent on a given instrument (e.g., most clarinets or most trumpets) regardless of the make or model of the instrument. For example, most oboes tend to play sharp in the high register. The pitch tendencies of the oboe are discussed under Intonation in this chapter. See also Temperament, page 61; Tuning/Tuning Note Considerations, page 561

Pivoting: A term used to describe the shifts or rolling actions that occur when playing from low B-flat to B-natural and when playing from low C-natural to C-sharp. When pivoting from low B-flat to B-natural, it may be possible to leave the little finger on both keys and merely roll the finger off of the B-flat key rather than making a large motion and losing contact with the B-flat key. When pivoting from C-natural to C-sharp, players can try to rock or pivot between the two keys in the manner described above; however, it may be necessary to actually shift or slide the finger from one key to another in this instance.

Plaque: A small piece of metal, plastic, or wood inserted into the tip opening to provide a solid surface against which the blades can be scraped or sanded. Plaques are made in a variety of shapes and sizes to accommodate a player's preferences. See also Reeds, Double, page 531

Plateau Model/System: Also called a closed-hole system, a system where the tone holes are covered by pads rather than by the fingertips. Most oboes employ a plateau system or closed-hole system where the tone holes are covered predominantly by keys/pads, which have small vent holes rather than open holes. The right-hand ring finger key is an exception and is open on almost all oboes. See also Plateau/Model System, page 56

Playing Position: See Hand/Holding/Instrument/Playing Positions and Posture, page 493

Posture: See Hand/Holding/Instrument/Playing Positions and Posture, page 493

Preparing the Right Hand: See Crossing the Break, page 481

Rails, Reed: The side edges of a double reed. See also Reeds, Double, page 531

Range: In general, the distance from the lowest note to the highest note on a given instrument. In addition, players and teachers often refer to the different registers (roughly by octave) of the oboe in terms of range: low range, middle range, high range, and altissimo range. The written and sounding ranges of the oboe and

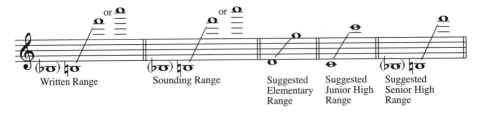

FIGURE 5.30. *Range*

English horn appear below and are summarized in figure 5.30. See also Register/Registers, page 545; Transpositions, page 559

Key Questions

Q: What ranges are recommended for elementary, junior high/middle school, and senior high students?

A: A student's range varies according to experience and ability level. After the fundamentals of tone production and embouchure formation are mastered, range can be extended systematically. Suggested ranges for each level are presented below.

Elementary: Low D-natural to high G-natural (above the staff)
Junior High: Low C-natural to high C-natural (above the staff)
Senior High: Low B-natural (B-flat if equipped) to high F-natural (above the staff)

Reed: See Reeds, Double, page 531

Reed Angle: The reed enters the mouth at an upward angle. The oboe is held out from the body at about a 40- to 45-degree angle, which is a slightly farther away from the body than the clarinet is held. See also Hand/Holding/Instrument Playing Positions and Posture, page 493; Instrument Angle, page 501

Reed Blanks: Unfinished reeds that have been shaped and tied. Reed blanks are sold to musicians interested in making, or more accurately scraping and refining, their own reeds. Companies also offer cane that has been split, gouged, and/or shaped. Uncut cane or tube cane is also readily available to players who want to make their own reeds.

Reed Care: Taking proper care of reeds is an important part of playing. It can also be challenging (and expensive), especially for beginners. The suggestions below will help prevent reed damage.

Handling Reeds

Most physical damage to reeds results from trying to position or reposition the reed on the instrument. Damage also occurs frequently from hitting the reed against something or someone in a normal rehearsal setting. It is advisable to develop proper habits for handling reeds in the beginning stages.

1. Hold the instrument properly when at rest. This position protects the reed.
2. Develop the habit of handling the reed at the ball (bassoon), tube, or cork end of the reed.
3. Make adjustments in reed alignment without touching the blades in any way. Adjust at the ball (bassoon), tube, or cork end of the reed.
4. Remove the reed from the instrument and soak it in a container of water when resting for extended periods of time.

Extending Reed Life

In addition to developing proper habits in handling reeds, other steps can also be taken to extend reed life and keep reeds in optimal playing condition. The suggestions below may help extend the life and maintain the playing quality of double reeds.

1. Rotate Reeds—Rather than playing on the same reed every day, alternate three or four reeds.

2. Rinse Reeds and Wipe off Excess Moisture Before Storing Them— This process will minimize the amount of dust and other materials that typically cling to wet surfaces and will help keep reeds clean. In addition, remove excess moisture from inside the reed by gently blowing air through the reed from the tube end.

3. Avoid Eating and Drinking (Except Water) During Practice Sessions—Eating and drinking causes foreign substances to collect on the inside and outside of the reed and will inhibit reed performance.

4. Do Not Handle Reeds with Dirty Hands—Handle reeds with clean hands to avoid buildup of oil and grime. Even with clean hands and careful handling, reeds will occasionally look dirty, especially when they are older. That is, some discoloration occurs with normal use.

5. Clean Reeds—Blow a mouthful of clean water through the reed (from the tube end) after each playing session to help prevent buildup on the inside of the reed. Periodically soaking reeds in hydrogen peroxide (or one of the products designed to clean reeds, such as ReedLife) for five minutes and then rinsing the reed with clean water will help remove buildup on the inside and outside of the reed and may extend reed life.

Reed Cases/Holders: Devices designed to hold and protect one or more reeds. Reed cases for double reed players are particularly important because they contribute to the playability and longevity of reeds. Double reeds typically come in plastic cases. These cases are not recommended for storage because they do not provide adequate ventilation for the reed. In addition, plastic cases do not allow reeds to dry evenly on both sides, which negatively affects performance and shortens reed life. Most commercially made reed cases are made of wood, plastic, and/or leather and are designed to hold reeds securely in place. Most cases hold several reeds, from as few as three to as many as twenty-four or more.

Key Questions

Q: Should all of my students have reed cases for their reeds?

A: Yes. Reeds are an expensive investment, and they are very delicate. Their protection, care, and management are critical components of oboe and bassoon playing. Reed cases should be considered standard equipment for all oboe and bassoon players.

Reed Knife: A knife specifically designed to shape and adjust reeds. Reed knives can be purchased at many local music stores and are useful for removing large or small amounts of cane. In addition, a wide variety of blade designs and shapes is available to suit a player's needs. The two most common knife designs include beveled knives (used for removing large amounts of cane) and hollow-ground knives (used for removing small amounts of cane). In an emergency, a single-edged razor blade can also be used in place of a reed knife; however, it is not as convenient, and it is significantly harder to control than a reed knife. Skillful use of a reed knife (or knives) takes practice. Commercially made double reed knives are available under such brand names as Albion, Charles, Forrests, Fox, Hodge, Landwell, Prestini, and Rigotti. See also Reed Making and Adjustment, page 521

Key Questions

Q: Do oboe and bassoon students need reed knives?

A: No. First, commercially made reeds suitable for most high school players are readily available. Players usually play on several reeds and find the ones that work well for them. Second, even advanced high school players who like to adjust their reeds typically make only minor adjustments to reeds. Minor adjustments can be made easily using fine-grit sandpaper (400 or 600). Finally, although double reed players have more need for a reed knife than other reed players, issues regarding knives in school settings may preclude students from having them.

Reed Making and Adjustment: Making double reeds is a complex process that requires specific tools and materials in addition to at least a modest amount of training and supervision. The information provided below does not discuss the details of reed making and is not intended to teach someone how to make reeds. Rather, its purpose is to provide a more in-depth understanding of reeds, reed adjustment, and the reed-making process. Adjusting double reeds is a relatively complicated task. It requires some of the tools and materials discussed below and a fair amount of experience, preferably gained from working with more experienced players and/or teachers. The more players experiment with reeds, reed adjustment, and reed making, the better their adjustments are likely to be. The information and suggestions discussed below should help players make reed adjustments with a reasonable expectation of success. Double reed tools for bassoon and oboe are shown in figures 5.31 and 5.32.

Tools and Materials

1. Reed Knife—Reed knives can be purchased at many local music stores and are useful for removing large or small amounts of cane. A single-edge razor blade can also be used instead of a reed knife, but it is not as convenient and it lacks the control of a reed knife.

2. Dial-Indicator/Micrometer—A tool used by some reed makers to determine the thickness throughout various areas of a reed or cane to aid in making or duplicating reeds. A dial indicator can measure cane or finished reeds to a hundredth of a millimeter, and is one of several high-tech tools available for reed making. Other such tools include hardness testers and tools to measure cane flexibility ("flextor tools").

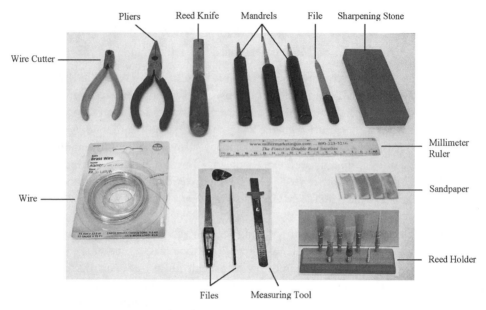

FIGURE 5.31. *Bassoon Reed Tools*

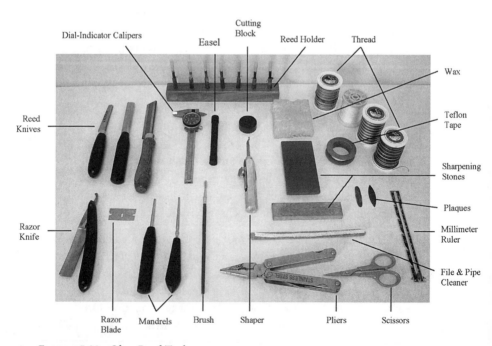

FIGURE 5.32. *Oboe Reed Tools*

3. Tip Cutter—A knife designed specifically to trim the tip end of a reed. Although a tip cutter is a handy tool, many players simply use a straight-edge reed knife.

4. Teflon/Plumbers Tape—Tape sometimes used to seal an oboe reed. When used, the tape is wrapped around the shoulder area of the reed.

5. Millimeter Ruler—A ruler used to measure the length of the reed. Most oboe reeds are about 70mm long, although they may be as long as 75mm or as short as 68mm.

6. Sharpening Stone—A stone designed for sharpening reed knives.

7. Wire—On bassoon and English horn, wire wrapped around the two blades for stability and adjusting purposes. In reed making, #22 gauge wire is common. Wires are not typically used on oboe reeds but may be used on rare occasions for stability and/or to help seal a reed.

8. Thread—On oboe, thread is used to bind the reed to the staple. On bassoon, thread is wrapped around the binding or "ball" to seal the reed and stabilize the bottom wire. Threads are made of polyester and nylon and are available in several thicknesses and a wide variety of colors.

9. Files—Players can purchase special files for making and adjusting reeds. Reed files vary from smooth to coarse and are typically used to finish reeds. As a general rule, reed knives are used to remove a lot of cane quickly in the initial shaping process, and reed files are used when less cane needs to be removed in the refinement process. Reed makers differ dramatically in how they make and adjust reeds and in their usage of knives, files, and other reed making tools. Files are most commonly used by bassoon players to shape and finish bassoon reeds. Flat files are typically used for large-scale shaping, and thin needle files are typically used for finishing work. Needle files are available in a variety of shapes, including squares, rounds, and half rounds. Some files have a blunt tip, and others have a pointed tip. The choice of files depends on what adjustments need to be made and on the experience and needs of the reed maker.

10. Shaper—A tool designed to shape an oboe reed. A shaper is used to guide the removal of excess cane from a piece of gouged cane (which has straight edges) until the gouged cane matches the shaper's shape or design.

11. Mandrel—A tapered metal tool for holding reeds while they are being tied, scraped, or filed, and for helping shape and form reeds in the finishing process. There are basically two types of mandrels: (1) long, for holding and forming the reed in the initial stages of reed making; and (2) short, for holding and finishing the reed in the latter stages of reed making. Mandrels are tapered to about one-eighth of an inch.

12. Plaque—A small piece of metal, plastic, or wood inserted into the tip opening to provide a solid surface against which the blades can be scraped or sanded. Plaques are made in a variety of shapes and sizes to accommodate a player's preferences.

13. Cutting Block/Billot—A small, round piece of hard wood or plastic used as a cutting surface when cutting and shaping the tip of a reed. Cutting blocks are designed with either a flat or a slightly convex surface.

14. Easel—A cylindrical piece of hard wood with stop ends and a center line cut into it that is used to help shape a double reed.

15. Reamer—A bassoon reed tool designed to clean and shape the reed tube so that the reed will fit properly onto the bocal. Several types of reamers are available today and vary in the number of cutting edges and in the way they are tapered. The most important factor in choosing a reamer is that it be tapered to match the end of the bocal to ensure a proper fit.

16. Pliers—Pliers are used predominantly on bassoon reeds to adjust the wires, but they can also be used to help shape the tube and throat. Pliers specifically made for double reeds are available; however, virtually any pair of needle-nosed pliers will suffice.

17. Sandpaper/Dutch Rush—Materials used to remove small amounts of cane from a reed. Although both wet and dry sandpaper can be used to adjust reeds, wet sandpaper is more practical. A very fine paper such as number 400 or 600 should be used. The finer paper provides more control by enabling smaller amounts

of cane to be removed safely. Dutch rush (also called reed rush, horsetail, file grass, and shave grass) can also be used to remove small amounts of reed; however, because it removes so little cane, Dutch rush is typically used to finish or polish the lay of a reed and to close reed pores. Dutch rush is available commercially, but it is fairly easy to find growing around swampy areas throughout the United States. Dutch rush should be wetted and flattened before using.

General Suggestions for Adjusting Double Reeds

Most reed adjustments can be made in two general ways: (1) removing cane from various parts of the reed by scraping the blades with a reed knife and/or by sanding the blades with fine sandpaper or Dutch rush; and (2) squeezing the sides of the reed (adjusting the wire on bassoon) to open, close, and/or reshape the reed in some way. Which tool and method to use for adjusting reeds is largely dependent upon how much and where the reed needs adjustment. In addition, most players prefer to soak their reeds before making any adjustments and to keep them soaked throughout the adjustment process. The general suggestions listed below are intended to provide an overview of reed adjustment. Experienced reed makers and/or players each develop individual preferences for reed adjustments to suit their needs and tastes.

1. Before adjusting any reed, make sure it has good face validity. That is, make sure the reed looks good. For example, check the cane color, grain, heart, lay, tip, throat, tube, wires (bassoon), binding, and heel.

2. Perform the light test. Hold the reed up to the light and make sure the heart looks good. As a rule, it is a waste of time working on a reed that looks unusually uneven or poorly cut or if the cane appears to be of poor quality.

3. Before assuming that a reed needs adjusting, make sure it is thoroughly soaked in water (five minutes or so) before being tested. Generally, reeds that are played on before being thoroughly soaked do not play well.

4. Give reeds a chance to break-in before making large-scale adjustments. Make small adjustments over several days and play on the reed after each adjustment. As a rule, do not make too many adjustments in one playing session.

5. When it is possible to make adjustments by squeezing the reed lightly rather than by scraping the reed, do so. The effects of squeezing the reed can usually be undone. Scraping cane from the lay thins the reed, and this action cannot be undone.

6. Close the pores on new reeds by inserting a shaped plaque into the reed and gently rub the lay (both blades) from shoulder to tip with the fingertip or thumb. Not closing the pores can cause problems with tone quality, control, and responsiveness. The reed should be soaked thoroughly before closing the pores, and the finger or thumb should be kept slightly moist during this process. Some players prefer to use Dutch rush or a fine sandpaper (wet/dry 600 grit) instead of their fingers. Sanding the lay lightly with Dutch rush or very fine sandpaper and then rubbing it with the thumb will close the pores and will make the reed feel very smooth against the lips.

7. As a rule, make large adjustments with a reed knife and small adjustments with fine sandpaper or Dutch rush.

General Suggestions for Scraping/Sanding Double Reeds

Use a plaque when scraping or sanding reeds. Insert the plaque between the blades until the reed blades grip the plaque to support the reed while scraping. Make sure the plaque is centered with the blades. The plaque helps support the reed evenly across the width of the reed, which helps players sand or scrape the reed in a more uniform manner. The suggestions below are intended to help players understand the basic techniques or methods of scraping double reeds.

1. Direction—Scrape or sand from the shoulders to the tip. That is, scrape with the grain rather than against it, and scrape away from the body.

2. Spine/Ridge—Avoid scraping the spine or center "hump" of the blades.

3. Channels/Windows—Many effective adjustments can be made in the windows. It is important to maintain symmetry when scraping in these areas and to gradually thin the windows from the spine toward the rails. It is sometimes possible to use the plaque as a guide. That is, when the plaque is in place between the blades, the

color of the plaque should be seen evenly through the reed blades. Scrape with the grain rather than against the grain.

4. Tip—The tip is the thinnest portion of the reed. It should have a slight ridge or spine (German reed); however, this ridge should be visible only when the reed is held up to the light. The tip gradually thins toward the edges from the center point or ridge. When scraping the tip, use very light strokes and straight knife angles.

Specific Suggestions for Adjusting Double Reeds

1. Characteristic—The reed feels/responds too hard.

Adjustment 1—Before doing anything, make sure the reed is thoroughly soaked. Then, check the tip opening. If the opening is too large on oboe or bassoon, squeeze the reed lightly from the top and bottom with the fingers to close the opening slightly. As a general rule, the oboe reed tip opening should be about the width of a nickel; however, this width can vary depending on the strength of the reed and the experience of the player. On bassoon, if the opening is still too large, squeeze the first wire from the top and bottom with a pair of pliers until the desired tip opening is achieved. The tip opening should be about one-sixteenth of an inch wide in the middle, and should taper down (top blade) or up (bottom blade) evenly to the corners. Players should check the tube for roundness after adjusting the first wire. It may be necessary to squeeze the second wire from the sides to reshape the tube properly.

Adjustment 2—If the reed still feels/responds too hard and the tip opening looks good, produce a "crow" on the reed alone. If the "crow" sounds sharp, high pitched, and/or tight, the lay needs to be thinned. Generally, hard reeds are increasingly less responsive in the low range than they are in the middle range, where they may respond quite well. Hard reeds HG also tend to play sharp overall. Thinning the lay (shoulders, channels, heart) evenly and symmetrically will help correct these problems. Use a plaque when scraping or sanding reeds and avoid removing too much cane at one time. Most players use a reed knife to make adjustments; however, small adjustments are often made using fine-grit sandpaper. Make adjustments and then play on the reed. Remove cane from the area behind the tip to the shoulder and play on the reed before removing cane from the tip area and the area slightly back of the tip. This process can be repeated several times over a period of days.

Adjustment 3—If the reed still feels hard, the tip area can be carefully thinned in the manner described in number 4 above until the desired results are achieved. Be very careful when thinning the tip. Symmetry must be maintained or the reed will not respond properly.

2. Characteristic—The reed feels too soft.

    Adjustment 1—Before doing anything, make sure the reed is thoroughly soaked. Then, check the tip opening. If the opening is too small, squeeze the reed lightly from the sides with the fingers to increase the size of the tip opening slightly. This action is usually a short-term solution at best.

    Adjustment 2—Clip a very small amount off the tip with a reed knife and cutting block.

    Adjustment 3—If the reed still feels soft, clip more cane from the tip until the desired results are achieved. Monitor pitch with the clipped reed because if the reed becomes too short, the pitch will go sharp.

3. Characteristic—The tone quality is poor and difficult to control, and the response is inconsistent throughout the range, even though the reed looks good.

    Adjustment 1—Before doing anything, make sure the reed is thoroughly soaked. Then, check the blades for balance and "sameness." Ideally, both blades should be the same on both sides of the spine or ridge in terms of thickness and shape at respective points along both blades. Many players divide each blade into two halves, left and right, and work to make each half a mirror image of the other. Three basic tests can help determine if the two blades are not balanced.

    First, hold the reed (preferably soaked) up to a light and look at both blades as described earlier. Checking the shape of the heart and lay can often reveal inconsistencies in the thicknesses of the blades and where these inconsistencies are.

    Second, with the reed thoroughly soaked, insert a plaque between the blades. Push the plaque lightly back against each blade to help determine if one blade is thicker than the other. The thicker blade will provide more resistance than the thinner blade. In addition, it may be possible to see the plaque through both blades of the reed. If the plaque, or parts of the plaque, can be seen better through one blade than it can through the other, then that blade is thinner in those areas.

Finally, with the reed thoroughly soaked, squeeze the center of both blades between the thumb and index fingers to help determine if one blade is thicker than the other. The reed must be turned over and squeezed several times for comparison purposes to ascertain which of the two blades is thicker. After testing the reed, scrape cane from the thicker blade in the appropriate locations to obtain balance and consistency.

Adjustment 2—Test the reeds to see if there is leakage from the sides of the reed. If there is leakage, put Teflon tape around the shoulder area to help seal the reed.

4. Characteristic—The reed plays sharp, even though the reed looks good and is the appropriate length.

Adjustment 1—Thin the lay of the reed as mentioned in number 1 above.

Adjustment 2—Increase the size of the tip opening slightly by squeezing the sides of the reed or by adjusting the first wire (bassoon).

Adjustment 3—Thin the tip slightly as mentioned in number 4 above.

5. Characteristic—The reed plays flat, even though the reed looks good.

Adjustment 1—Reeds that play flat usually produce a thin, small tone as well. These characteristics are caused by cane that is too thin, too soft, and/or too old. Squeezing the sides of the reed to increase the size of the tip opening (and/or adjusting the first wire on bassoon) may help produce a better tone quality for a short period of time. However, there is not much players can do with these types of reeds.

Adjustment 2—Clip a very small amount of the reed tip with a reed knife and cutting block and check the pitch. If the reed becomes too short, the overall pitch will be sharp.

6. Characteristic—Low notes do not respond well.

Adjustment 1—Check the tip opening. Usually an opening that is too large causes response problems. Squeeze the blades together and hold for a brief period of time.

Adjustment 2—Thin the back part of the reed evenly at the shoulders.

Adjustment 3—Insert a plaque and thin the tip area lightly by sanding.

7. Characteristic—Reed is buzzy.

Adjustment 1—Thin the sides of the reed and make sure all sides are uniform.

Adjustment 2—Reshape the tip corners and work for evenness and consistency.

8. Characteristic—Tone lacks depth.

Adjustment 1—The reed is not vibrating well beyond the tip. Blend the tip with the heart by scraping/sanding back of the tip into the windows and heart areas.

Adjustment 2—Reshape the tip corners and work for evenness and consistency.

Reed Testing: The only true test of any reed is to soak it thoroughly and play on it. Reeds will often "break in" over time, so it is important to play on a reed a few times before making reed adjustments or determining its fate. Nonetheless, the tests below can help determine the quality of a reed.

"Crow" or "Double Crow"

After soaking the reed thoroughly for about five minutes, the reed's ability to produce a "crow" or "double crow" can be tested. Most good reeds produce a crow or double crow sound when players blow into or play on the reed alone. Although the terms "crow" and "double crow" are often used interchangeably, a crow is characterized by only one pitch, while a double crow is characterized by two or more pitches. To produce a crow, put the tip of the reed in the mouth and blow gently until a tone (crow) is produced. To produce a double crow, place the reed in the mouth to the wrapping, blow gently at first without much lip pressure, and then increase air speed until the reed crows. A good double crow is one that produces both high and low sounds. Many players tune the pitch of the crow to a third-space E-flat (bassoon) or high C-natural above the staff (oboe).

Testing for Leaks along the Side Seams of the Tube

After soaking the reed thoroughly for about five minutes, the reed can be tested for air leaks along the seams. To do this, players can plug the heel (or staple) end of the tube with their finger while blowing normally into the reed. On oboe, if air escapes through the seams, seal the leaks with Teflon tape or plumbers tape. On bassoon, if air escapes through the seams, tighten the first wire. The reed must be soaked thoroughly when performing this test; otherwise, leaks may be caused by a reed that is too dry.

The "Pop" Test

After soaking the reed thoroughly for about five minutes, a "pop" test can be performed to test for air leaks. To perform a "pop" test, plug the end of the reed with the finger while sucking out all of the air inside the reed. This process will cause the blades of the reed to close. When the reed is pulled out of the mouth, the blades will stay closed for a second or so and then "pop" open. Reeds that stay closed are too soft. Squeezing the sides of the reed and/or the first wire (bassoon) will increase the size of the tip opening and will help improve the sound of the reed, at least for a while. Reeds that will not close at all are probably too hard, or do not seal on the sides. Hard reeds can be scraped or sanded down until they are softer. In addition, if the tip opening is too large, the first wire (bassoon) can be squeezed downward (with the fingers or pliers) slightly to help response. Players should check the tube for roundness after adjusting the first wire. It may be necessary to squeeze the second wire from the sides to reshape the tube properly. Again, it is important that the reed be soaked thoroughly when performing this test.

Reed Tools: See Reed Making and Adjustment, page 521

Reed Well/Receiver: On oboe, the part of the top joint into which the reed is inserted. On bassoon, the receiver is the part of the tenor joint into which the bocal is inserted. Reed wells or receivers vary from instrument to instrument, so players need to find out which type of reed tubes and bocals fit best for their particular instruments.

Reeds, Double: Physically, the vibrating mechanism that sets the air column in vibration on reed instruments. Reeds are largely responsible for determining the type of tone quality and response, and the amount of tone control that players can achieve. Traditionally made of cane and more recently synthetic materials, reeds are the single most important factor in determining tonal characteristics on reed instruments. Beginners and many intermediate players typically use commercial reeds. However, commercial reeds are very expensive, and they do not offer enough individualization for experienced players. Because the reed is such an important component of double reed playing, virtually all experienced players make and adjust their own reeds to some degree. By learning to make and adjust reeds according to their individual tastes, performers are able to make reeds that provide the desired responsiveness and tone quality.

PHYSICAL DEMANDS OF A REED

A musical tone is produced when air sets the reed in vibration. The tone produced by the vibrating reed is determined by the length of the air column and the instrument to which the reed is attached. This length varies according to the fingering being used at any given time. Research shows that the blades of a double reed actually close off the reed aperture periodically when a tone is being produced, resulting in short bursts of air being emitted into the instrument rather than a continuous air stream. This fact illustrates the importance of proper reed balance during performance. Because the vibrating reeds literally beat against each other during vibration, the balance, cut, symmetry, size of tip opening, and overall construction of the reed all affect its responsiveness.

REED VIBRATION

During performance, the reed vibrates continually at ever-changing frequencies. These changes are often extreme. For example, to produce a low C-natural on the oboe, the reed must vibrate at approximately 260 hertz (Hz). An octave leap (third-space C-natural) would require the reed to vibrate twice as fast (approximately 520 Hz), and a two-octave leap (high C-natural) would require the reed to vibrate at approximately 1040 Hz. On bassoon, to produce a low B-flat, the reed must vibrate at approximately 58 Hz. An octave leap would require the reed to vibrate twice as fast (approximately 116 Hz), and a two-octave leap would require the reed to vibrate at approximately 232 Hz. The ideal reed would vibrate equally well at all frequencies; however, this ideal is difficult, if not impossible, to achieve. Nonetheless, players continually strive to make and adjust reeds that approach this ideal.

REED CANE

Reeds are made from a cane called Arundo donax, a tall reed that resembles bamboo. Arundo donax has a hard outer layer, called the "bark" or "rind," that provides strength and stability for the reed tube, and a softer inner layer that, when exposed by scraping away the bark, is flexible and will vibrate easily. It also contains a chemical called "lignin" which adds to the material's elastic and flexible quality, and the material dampens quickly. Several factors affect the quality of the cane, including the climate, soil, irrigation, fertilization and time of harvest. It is generally believed that the best cane is grown in southern France.

Cane plants can reach twenty feet in height and are harvested every couple of years. Once cut, their branches are removed. The cane is then dried or sunned to a golden color. The cane plants are aged for as long as two years before being used for reeds.

Reed cane consists of many fibers, which are like hollow tubes held together by an absorbent pithlike substance. Several qualities inherent in any piece of cane can affect the quality and type of reed that it may produce, including age, hardness, stiffness, resiliency, density, grain, and flexibility.

Reed makers use a variety of methods to determine whether a particular piece of cane will result in a "good" reed. The most preferred cane color has yellow or purple-yellowish bark. Green to deep green cane is generally considered not properly aged. Brown cane is considered to be older but may still yield good reeds, and white or gray cane is considered past its usefulness. Reed makers may also assess the quality of the cane while they are working on reeds, gauging how the material feels while using machines and hand tools. Regardless of which testing methods a reed maker uses, exactly which pieces of cane to use is a matter of personal preference, and different reed makers will prefer different pieces of cane, depending on the playing characteristics they prefer.

Cane of various lengths, widths, and thicknesses is available for oboe, English horn, and bassoon. Players generally choose the cane that best suits their needs for reed making. Advanced players sometimes start making their reeds from tube cane, which is literally a piece of cane that is still in its basic hollow tube shape; however, most players start with gouged cane. Gouged cane is cane that has been soaked and run through a gouging machine, which cuts and shaves the cane into a more workable form. Terminology commonly used to describe double reeds is listed below. Oboe reed cane and parts used to make oboe reeds are shown in figure 5.33, and a comparison of reed sizes is shown in figure 5.34. The parts of an oboe reed and a bassoon reed are identified in figure 5.35.

Parts of a Reed

1. Binding/Wrapping/Tie—The string, thread, and/or wire (bassoon) used to bind reeds together. The thread is generally made of cotton or nylon and then sometimes covered with lacquer, wax,

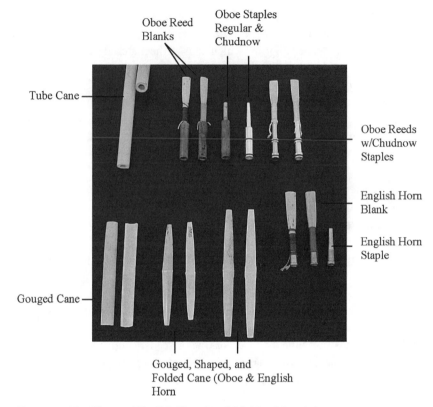

Tube Cane

Oboe Reed Blanks

Oboe Staples Regular & Chudnow

Oboe Reeds w/Chudnow Staples

English Horn Blank

English Horn Staple

Gouged Cane

Gouged, Shaped, and Folded Cane (Oboe & English Horn

FIGURE 5.33. *Oboe and English Horn Reed-Making Materials*

or a liquid plastic coating made for double reeds. The wires used in bassoon making are generally made of brass, iron, or silver. Wires are not typically used on oboe reeds like they are on bassoon reeds; however, a wire is sometimes added for stability and to help seal the reed. On bassoon, a plastic tube is sometimes used in place of string as a binding material. The string and the third wire form a ball shape near the heel end of the reed. On both oboe and bassoon, a wrapping (Teflon tape, fish skin, or plumbers tape) is sometimes wrapped around the throat of a reed to help seal it. The reed in figure 5.36 has been wrapped with Teflon tape.

2. Channels/Windows—The areas of the lay between the heart and the rails. The channels extend from the shoulders toward the tip

FIGURE 5.34. *Reed Comparisons: Oboe, Oboe d'Amore, English Horn, Bassoon, and Contrabassoon*

and comprise a significant portion of the reed in terms of reed adjustment.

3. First Wire—On bassoon, the wire just behind or in back of the shoulder that is often used to adjust bassoon reeds.

4. Heart—The center portion of the blades extending from just behind the tip toward the shoulders. When held up to a light, the heart can be seen as a symmetrically shaded U-shaped area. Hearts are clearly visible in German but not in French reeds. French reeds are cut and shaped in such a way that the blades appear to be evenly shaded. The heart of a German reed can be seen and felt as a slight hump or ridge running down the middle of the blades and extending toward the edges (rails) of the blade. No heart as such is apparent on a French reed.

5. Heel/Butt/Boot—The end of the reed (cane) farthest from the tip.

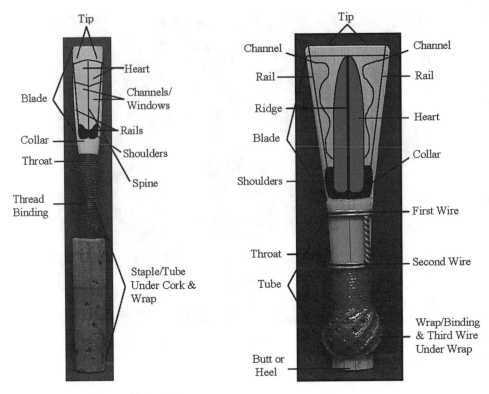

FIGURE 5.35. *Double Reed Parts*

6. Lay—A general term used to describe the scraped or shaped part of the reed that extends from the tube at the shoulders to the tip. Some players refer to various portions of the lay more specifically, especially in relationship to reed adjustment. These portions include the tip, rails/sides, heart, and channels/windows. On a short-scrape reed, only about half (or less) of the reed is scraped from the tip toward the binding. On a long-scrape reed, about two-thirds (or more) of the reed is scraped from the tip toward the binding.

7. Rails/Sides—A term used by some players to describe the very narrow areas or strips of the lay that run along the edges of a reed from the shoulder to the tip.

FIGURE 5.36. *Teflon Tape Around Reed*

8. Second Wire—On bassoon, the wire just ahead or in front of the binding.

9. Shoulders—The back portions of a reed that extend from the tube (or from where the exposed part of the cane begins) toward the lay. Each blade has two shoulders, one on each side of the spine. Some players refer to the top part of the shoulder area as the "collar."

10. Spine/Ridge/Hump—The hump or center ridge of the lay that runs from the shoulder to the tip or just back of the tip.

11. Staple/Tube—On oboe, a metal tube (usually silver or brass) onto which the cane part of a reed is tied. Staples have an oval opening on one end (the end onto which the cane is tied) and a circular opening on the other end (the end to which the cork

is attached). Staples vary in design, so players must determine which type of staple is best suited for their particular instrument.

12. Stock—The part of the reed that has the bark on it.

13. Third Wire—On bassoon, the wire under the binding nearest the heel. The third wire is not visible on a finished bassoon reed.

14. Throat—On oboe, a term sometimes used to describe the reed opening at the oval end of the staple. On bassoon, the throat is the part of the reed tube between the first and second wires where the end of the bocal ultimately stops.

15. Tip—The very thin area of a reed (both blades) that extends from the end of the reed slightly back.

16. Tip Opening/Reed Aperture—The oval-shaped opening formed by the two blades of a double reed.

17. Tube/Body—The round tube-shaped part of a double reed. On bassoon, the tube extends from the heel end of the reed just past the first wire where the reed begins to be shaped. On oboe, the tube is also called the staple.

Playing Characteristics of a Good Reed

1. Responds freely and easily over the entire range of the instrument.
2. Plays all octaves of the instrument reasonably well in tune without significant adjustments in embouchure or lip pressure.
3. Responds well in all dynamic ranges of the instrument.
4. Produces an appropriate amount of resistance to wind pressure.
5. Facilitates all types of articulations throughout the range of the instrument.

What to Look for When Selecting Reeds

1. Binding—The thread should look evenly and neatly distributed, and the binding should fit snuggly. On bassoon, a loose binding is an indication that the cane shrank after the third wire was tightened and covered.

2. Cane Color—Cane that has a golden-yellowish cast is desirable. Reeds that are bright yellow, have a slight greenish cast, or have

dark brown streaks in the lay may indicate that the cane was not aged properly or was of poor quality. Brown spots or flecks in the stock are common and should appear somewhat evenly spaced on the cane.

3. Grain—The grain of a reed can be fine, medium, or coarse. Reeds that contain predominately coarse grains typically do not respond well, feel rough on the lip, and tend to produce an unsatisfactory tone quality. Reeds that contain fine grains are often inconsistent and tend to wear out quickly. Cane that has a predominantly medium grain with fine and coarse grains interspersed evenly throughout will generally yield better, more consistent results. Also, the grain should run straight from the heel to the tip.

4. Heart—Generally, the quality of the heart is dependent upon the symmetry and likeness of both blades. One common test that can be performed to see if the heart is symmetrical is to hold the reed up to the light so that the various light and dark shades can be seen. Ideally, a U-shaped (or W-shaped, depending on reed-making style) area of darkness extending from behind the tip back into the center of the blade is visible. This area should be centered with the sides of the reed and should be surrounded by evenly spaced, lighter areas near the tip and on both sides. The lighter areas represent softer (thinner) sections and the darker (thicker) areas represent harder sections of the reed. If these areas are symmetrical, the reed has a reasonably good chance of producing a good tone quality. Unfortunately, although this light test is a relatively reliable check, cane is not always consistent in color. That is, a reed may look "bad" and play well, or a reed may look "good" and play poorly. The reeds in figures 5.37 and 5.38 are highlighted with a bright light. Darker and lighter areas are plainly visible, and the symmetry of the reeds (or lack of it) can also be seen. The reed blank on the far right shows very little light because of its thickness; however, the heart, ridge, grain, and other features of the finished reeds can be seen. When figures 5.37 and 5.38 are compared, the similarities and differences in the two blades of each reed are apparent.

5. Lay—To a large extent, the lay determines the reed's potential for a good tone quality. It is important that the lay is even, smooth,

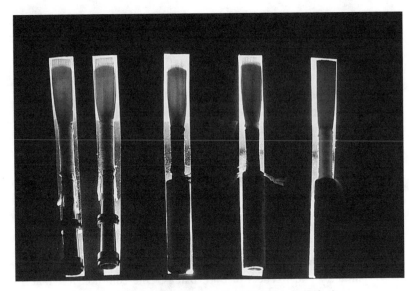

FIGURE 5.37. *Light Highlighting Areas of Five Oboe Reeds (Side 1)*

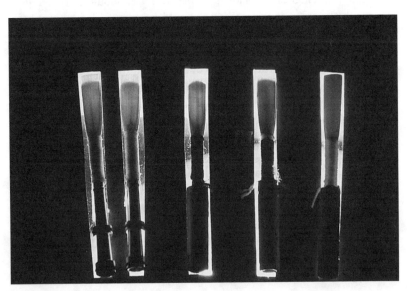

FIGURE 5.38. *Light Highlighting Areas of Five Oboe Reeds (Side 2)*

and symmetrically tapered from the center to the edges on both blades.

6. Spine/Ridge/Hump—The hump slopes evenly along and down both sides of the blade and blends into the heart and tip. A short, thick hump increases resistance and decreases response, whereas a long, thin hump decreases resistance and increases response.

7. Tip—The tip of a reed is crucial to producing a good tone quality. Its thickness and flexibility must be the same across the width of the reed on both blades. The center of the tip is slightly thicker than the edges, which thin out evenly on the sides and corners. Holding the reed up to the light can provide information about the thickness, shape, and consistency of the tip. The tip opening should be symmetrical. From the center, the top and bottom blades curve downward or upward, respectively, in an even and consistent manner until they meet at the edges of the reed.

8. Throat—On oboe, the area where the cane meets the staple. On bassoon, the throat is the area underneath the first wire. On both instruments, the area inside the throat should be symmetrically shaped. Some throats are almost round while others are elliptical, depending on how the reed was made. The shape and symmetry of the inside throat area can be observed by looking through the heel end of the tube while holding the tip of the reed toward a light. The throat area (inside and outside) should be rounded, not angular. On bassoon, the symmetry of throat is particularly important because it enables the wire to shape the throat evenly when tightened properly.

9. Tube/Body—The inside and outside of the tube should be round from the back portion of the wrapping to the heel. On oboe, tubes (or staples) that are not round may not fit properly into the reed well. On bassoon, tubes that are not round indicate poor workmanship and/or poor cane. Irregularly shaped tubes will leak when inserted onto the bocal.

10. Wires—On bassoon, the wires are important because they not only hold the reed together, but they are mostly responsible for shaping the tube, throat, and ultimately, the entire reed. The first and second wires should fit snugly around the reed. That is, the

wires should make contact with the cane all around the reed. The wires should be twisted on neatly and securely but should not dig or cut into the cane.

Reed Strength

There are basically two systems for identifying reed strength. The first is a numbering system. For example, one company employs a numbering system in which reeds are numbered as follows: 1 (very soft), 2 (soft), 3 (medium soft), 4 (medium), 5 (medium hard) and 6 (hard). The second system does not use numbers. Instead it simply uses words to designate reed strength. For example, one company designates its reeds as soft, medium soft, medium, medium hard, and hard when identifying reed strength.

Unfortunately, both systems are unreliable and inconsistent to some degree primarily because a reed strength designation does not indicate a specific reed hardness, but rather a range of hardness. For example, a medium strength reed may actually be closer to a medium soft or medium hard strength reed depending on the individual reed. As a result, there is no guarantee that three medium strength reeds will play the same. In fact, there is a great chance that they will be significantly different. The only way to know how a reed responds is to play on it, and even then it will most likely change over time. Despite these inconsistencies, designating reed strength in some manner does provide players with a general idea of how hard a reed is likely to be.

Problematic Reed Types

Double reeds may display one or more problematic playing characteristics that are used to categorize reeds, including dead, hard, hollow, soft, and uncontrollable. Because reeds are often inconsistent, it is important to evaluate a reed's performance over time before determining its ultimate fate. Playing consistency is a key factor in determining which reeds will work well, which reeds may work well with adjustments, and which reeds will probably never work well. It is important to note that a reed that does not respond well on a particular day may still not be a bad reed. In fact, a reed may perform poorly on any particular day due to relatively minor factors such as weather conditions or because the reed was not soaked properly before playing. Experienced players rarely discard reeds after the first playing. Some players keep reeds for years, hoping they will be playable at some point. Various problematic reed types are described below. Figure 5.39 shows a reed with slipped blades, loose thread, a damaged tip, and damaged side rails.

FIGURE 5.39. *Common Reed Problems: Slipped Blades, Loose Thread, Damaged Tip and Sides*

1. Dead/Lifeless Reeds—After a reed has been played on for an extended period of time, tone quality and control begin to deteriorate. That is, the reed just does not seem to vibrate properly. Older reeds often sound dull and lifeless. At this point, nothing can be done to bring the reed back, and it should be discarded. Sometimes, even a new reed can have these qualities, especially if the cane it is made from is too old or of poor quality. Reeds with many dark brown streaks seem particularly prone to these tendencies.

2. Hard Reeds—Hard reeds are characterized by a consistently "airy" sound, and typically have response problems (especially in the low range) that make proper articulation difficult. Hard reeds also require much more air to produce a tone, which can result in

breath control difficulties and poor phrasing. Hard reeds tend to be consistent over time; however, they do tend to soften somewhat after they have been played on a few times. As a result, a reed that is a little too hard when first played may be just about right after it is broken in. If a reed does not soften adequately after a reasonable breaking-in period (some reeds actually feel harder after being played on a few times), it may need to be sanded or scraped.

3. Hollow/Unbalanced Reeds—Some reeds may respond well and may even yield a consistent tone quality, yet lack a "core" to the sound. That is, the tone sounds hollow. A hollow sound is generally the result of an unbalanced reed. More specifically, the heart of the reed is usually thin in areas and/or not symmetrical. With these types of reeds, virtually nothing can be done to give fullness to the sound, and the reed should be discarded.

4. Soft Reeds—Soft reeds are characterized by a consistently thin, pinched, reedy tone and are often accompanied by intonation problems. Players will often pinch the reed to the point of closing off the tip opening completely, which stops the flow of air into the instrument. Try opening the reed tip slightly by squeezing the sides of the reed lightly (oboe and bassoon) or by adjusting the first wire with pliers (bassoon). If these actions do not help, it may be necessary to trim the reed tip. Care should be taken not to trim the tip too much because pitch, tone quality, and response may be negatively affected. Sometimes a reed that is too soft can be firmed slightly by thoroughly soaking the reed and drying it in the case for several days; however, the results of this process are usually short-lived.

5. Squeaky/Uncontrollable Reeds—Squeaky/uncontrollable reeds tend to crack and/or feel as if they are going to squeak or break, making control of the tone difficult. Uncontrollable reeds are often cracked or chipped, may be unbalanced (thicker on one side than the other, cut unevenly, etc.), and/or have some other inherent flaw. If a reed squeaks or is uncontrollable occasionally, and the reed looks good, problems are usually caused by warping and/or by not soaking the reed sufficiently. During periods of low humidity, reeds tend to dry out quickly, causing the blades to warp (usually unevenly). Warping causes poor reed response, poor tone quality, and squeaks or chirps. Storing reeds in well-constructed

reed cases and soaking reeds thoroughly before playing helps extend reed life.

Reed Length

Oboe reeds vary in length from about 68mm to about 72mm. Most reeds are about 70mm long. Bassoon reeds vary in length from about 2 inches (short model reed) to about 2 and three-eighths inches (long model reed). Most reeds are about 2 and an eighth inches long.

Register/Registers: Groups of notes that share certain tonal characteristics usually related to pitch range, timbre, and/or manner of production. Players vary in their description of registers. Some players and teachers use the term "register" interchangeably with the term "range" to describe the playing ranges of the instrument. Furthermore, players and teachers also use terms such as "high" and "low" indiscriminately, or at least relatively, depending upon the musical context. Ultimately, delineating registers commonly used by junior high students, high school students, college-level players, and professional players is a subjective process that varies according to the criteria used for delineation. Nonetheless, it seems reasonable to divide the oboe range into four registers. These registers are listed below and are notated in figure 5.40. See also Range, page 517

1. Low Register—From low B-flat to first-space F-sharp.
2. Middle Register—From second-line G-natural to G-sharp above the staff.
3. High Register—From A-natural (above the staff) to high D-sharp.
4. Altissimo Register—High E-natural and above.

Releases/Cutoffs: See Releases/Cutoffs, page 56

Resistance: In general, the counteraction of the reed and oboe to the incoming air stream. The amount of resistance provided by the instrument and reed dictates

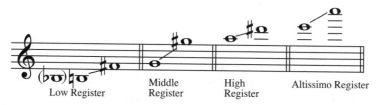

FIGURE 5.40. *Register/Registers*

the amount of air and support needed to start and maintain a steady tone. That is, the reed and, to a lesser degree, the oboe both contribute to the resistance felt by the player. Reeds in particular affect resistance significantly. Generally, harder reeds cause more resistance than softer reeds. A certain amount of resistance is needed to maintain a steady, rich tone quality and good pitch. When reeds are too soft, the tone is thin and "quivery," and pitch is difficult to control. When reeds are too hard, the tone is airy, response is poor, pitch control suffers, and players' embouchures tire quickly. Reeds need to be hard enough to push back against the embouchure pressure in order to create a stable tone, but not so hard that players have to fight against the reed. The appropriate reed strength is directly dependent on the ability of the player to control the reed during play. That is, players with well-developed facial muscles can control a harder reed with a larger tip opening or reed aperture than players with less-developed facial muscles.

The amount of resistance is also significantly affected by the tip opening. As a general rule, large tip openings will have more resistance than small tip openings. Players who use reeds with large tip openings will generally use softer reeds or have significantly stronger embouchure control than players who use reeds with small tip openings. See also Breathing/Breath Support/Air Control, page 10; Reeds, Double, page 531; Response, page 547

Key Questions

Q: How much resistance is ideal for different age levels?

A: Beginners should use soft reeds (soft or medium soft) because they provide less resistance, which helps students produce a tone more easily. As players' embouchures develop and strengthen, harder reeds (medium or medium hard) can provide the additional resistance needed to produce a warm, rich characteristic oboe tone. Advanced players typically use a medium hard or hard reed, although it can be difficult to determine the exact reed strength used by the overwhelming number of advanced players who make and adjust their own reeds.

Teaching Tips Regarding Resistance/Response

1. Oboe players need a certain amount of resistance from the reed. As their embouchures and support strengthen, the ability of the reed to push back against the supporting embouchure and create the resistance that holds the tone steady declines. The tone becomes unsteady or shaky, soft, and thin. Using a harder reed helps solve

this problem. Have students move up one reed strength at a time until an acceptable balance is found.

2. As a rule, students should begin with a soft or medium soft reed. After a few months, they should move to a medium strength reed. After a year or so, students should move to a medium hard strength reed. By the end of their second year, students should be playing on a medium hard or hard strength reed depending on their embouchures, their playing abilities, and their practice habits.

3. Advanced students should play on handmade reeds. Their quality is usually superior to store-bought reeds.

4. Teachers are often reluctant to have students move up in reed strength in a progressive manner. As a result, oboe students often play with beginner-level tone qualities for too long. Slightly harder, more resistant reeds will improve tone quality and pitch control. Slightly harder reeds may feel too hard at first; however, as students' embouchures strengthen and adapt to the harder reed strength, the improvements in tone quality and pitch control will be obvious. If a new reed strength is too hard, students' embouchures will not readily adapt, and the tone will be weak and airy. In this case, adjust by using a slightly softer reed.

Resonance Keys: Keys sometimes added to regular fingerings to improve the tonal response, tone quality, and/or pitch of certain notes. See also F Resonance Key, page 490

Response: The way a reed vibrates as a result of the player's air stream and embouchure. The term "response" is also used to refer to the ease with which the notes "speak" or sound. Some notes respond more easily than others, depending on how much of the tube is closed and how much air speed is needed. Notes in the extreme high or low range tend not to respond as well as notes in the middle range. The quality and condition of the oboe, the reed, and a player's ability to control the air speed and air volume greatly affect reed response. See also Resistance, page 545

Secondary Break: A term used by advanced players to describe playing from a note below fourth-space E-natural to fourth-space E-natural or above. That is, a secondary break occurs at fourth-space E-natural, where players begin using the first octave key. For example, playing from fourth-line D-natural to fourth-space

FIGURE 5.41. *Secondary Break*

E-natural involves crossing the secondary break. Another secondary break occurs at high A-natural (above the staff), where players must switch from the first octave key to the second (side) octave key. For example, playing from high G-sharp to high A-natural involves crossing this break. Examples of crossing the secondary breaks are shown in figure 5.41. The primary break occurs on D-flat, D-natural, and D-sharp. This break involves moving from an open fingering (where few keys are depressed) to a closed fingering (where many keys are depressed), requiring coordination of hands and fingers. The three D's involve using the half-hole technique. See also Crossing the Break, page 481

Selecting an Instrument: See Instrument Brands, page 502; Instrument Selection, page 33

Shaper: A metal tool that helps shape oboe reeds. Specifically, cane is soaked thoroughly and then folded onto the shaper and clamped securely in place, after which the cane is shaved using a wedge knife or a single-edge razor blade. Cane that has been shaped properly is ready for tying and is sometimes referred to as gouged, shaped, and folded. See also Reeds, Double, page 531

Short-Scrape Reed: A reed that has less bark scraped from the lay than a normal reed, typically only slightly more than one-half of the blades. A short-scrape reed leaves a great deal of bark on the blades, providing a more penetrating tone, appropriate for some musical contexts (e.g., solo playing, outdoor playing). A short-scrape reed must be soaked considerably longer than a normal reed (approximately twenty minutes in warm water) for optimal response. Most oboe reeds are long-scrape reeds.

Shoulders: The back area of the lay toward the wire or thread. Some players refer to this area as the collar. See also Reeds, Double, page 531

Slap Tongue: A tonguing technique that produces a "slapping" or "popping" effect on the attacks. Slap tonguing is sometimes used as a special effect in both jazz and contemporary literature and is produced by pressing the tongue hard against the reed to close or nearly close the tip opening, building up air pressure, and then releasing the tongue quickly. See also Extended/Contemporary Techniques, page 29

Sounding Range: See Instrument Family and Playing Considerations, page 502; Range, page 517; Transpositions, page 559

Speaker Keys: Generally, a term used for keys that help notes respond or "speak" when depressed. Speaker keys can be special keys (e.g., F resonance key) or they can be regular keys (e.g., an octave key). On oboe, the octave keys are the most obvious speaker keys. See also Resonance Keys, page 547

Spine: The center ridge or hump of a double reed blade that essentially divides a well-made reed into two symmetrical sides. See also Reeds, Double, page 531

Spring Hook Tool: See Spring Hook Tool, page 59

Springs: See Springs, page 59

Squeaks: Undesirable, accidentally produced partials that sometimes sound during normal play. Squeaks can be caused by several factors. Some of the most common causes of squeaks include: (1) fingers not covering tone holes properly, (2) poor or dry reeds, (3) poor embouchure formation, and/or (4) overblowing or hitting side keys. A more detailed discussion of squeaks can be found in "Practical Tips" at the end of this chapter.

Staggered Breathing: See Staggered Breathing, page 59

Stamina: See Endurance/Stamina, page 28

Stands: See Instrument Stands, page 39

Staple, Reed: The metal tube onto which the cane is fastened. Some staples come with cork already attached, and some staples do not have cork on them. Staples vary in length; however, 46mm and 47mm are standard staple sizes. See also Reeds, Double, page 531

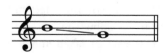

FIGURE 5.42. *Starting Note Range*

Starting Note/Range, The Best: Most students will have excellent results start-ing on third-line B-natural and working their way downward note by note to sec-ond line G-natural. This note range is ideal for several reasons. First, it is relatively easy to produce a tone in this range. Second, the fingerings in this range are rela-tively simple and intuitively logical. Third, this range provides teachers with the opportunity to point out that as more holes are covered, the tones get lower. These relationships make this range ideal for simple ear training exercises. Finally, add-ing one finger at a time in a comfortable range enables students to cover each tone hole properly. That is, players learn to cover the tone holes more efficiently when they proceed in a logical step-by-step manner. This starting note range is shown is figure 5.42. It is interesting to note that because band method books must accom-modate beginners on a variety of instruments, they often do not have players start on the above sequence of notes.

Key Questions

Q: Should I start my students on oboe?

A: No. Generally, the oboe is not a good starting instrument for several reasons. First, producing a good tone on oboe is more problematic than it is on flute, clarinet, or saxophone. Second, the design of the oboe requires the fingers to be slightly farther apart, making correct hand position difficult (if not impossible) for young players with small hands. Third, the ability to control the air stream and the amount of back pressure produced on oboe present formidable challenges, even to experienced players. Asking a stu-dent to deal with these challenges from the beginning along with all of the other demands of playing a musical instrument can be overwhelming.

Q: What instrument should I start my students on before switching them to oboe?

A: Students can switch to oboe if they are highly motivated, regardless of what instrument they start on; however, only students who have devel-oped proper mechanics of tone production and technique on their start-ing instruments should switch to oboe. In addition, students switching must have fairly long fingers or they will not be able to finger the instru-ment properly. Clarinetists will probably have an easier time switching to oboe than saxophonists or flutists. The fingerings are the same in many instances; however, the firmer embouchure used on clarinet is more condu-cive to playing oboe than the more relaxed embouchure used on saxophone.

The flute embouchure is least like the oboe embouchure. In addition, the back pressure on oboe is more similar to the back pressure on clarinet than it is on saxophone or flute.

Stock: The part of a reed that has bark on it. See also Reeds, Double, page 531

Swab: See Swab, page 59; Care and Maintenance, page 474

Synthetic Reeds: Reeds made from synthetic, man-made materials instead of traditional cane. A variety of synthetic reeds are available today. These reeds last longer and are more durable than cane reeds. In addition, they do not need to be moist to respond; therefore, they do not dry out. However, the sound produced by synthetic reeds is not the same quality as the sound produced by cane reeds, and the vast majority of players prefer cane reeds. Despite the sound difference, many players find synthetic reeds useful in some situations. For example, synthetic reeds are useful when players are doubling on other instruments and the oboe must respond immediately with little or no preparation. Some teachers prefer to start beginners on synthetic reeds because they are more affordable, consistent, and durable. Some of the most commonly used synthetic reeds are marketed under the names Advantage, Americane, Emerald, Fox, Graham Standard, Karacha, Legere, and Olivieri. See also Reeds, Double, page 531

Technique: In general, the manner and ability with which players use the technical skills involved in playing an instrument. Most commonly, the term is used to describe the physical actions involved in playing an instrument, and often specifically refers to technical passages. Virtually every pedagogical aspect of woodwind playing (acoustical, physical, and mental) affects technique. General technical considerations for all woodwind instruments are in chapter 1. The Considerations/Concerns points offered here apply specifically to problems related to oboe technique. When appropriate, readers are directed to relevant terms in the book where particular topics are addressed in detail. See also Alternate Fingerings/Alternates, page 461; Technique, page 60

General Technical Considerations/Concerns for Oboe Players

1. Oboe keys are small, light, and close to the tone holes, which enables technical speed; however, the keys are also spaced slightly farther apart than are flute and clarinet keys. In addition, the oboe fingerings are a bit more awkward than flute, clarinet, or saxophone fingerings. Finally, some regular oboe fingerings in the

normal range do not follow an intuitive or logical pattern. As a result, technically difficult passages are more problematic on oboe than on flute, clarinet, or saxophone.

2. The amount of back pressure that oboe players experience is greater than on all other woodwind instruments. As a result, oboe players often struggle with excess air. That is, instead of running out of air, players actually experience a buildup of excess air. Particularly during long, rapid technical passages, players often do not have time to release excess air. An important part of technical development on oboe is to learn how to release excess air to avoid stress that can manifest itself in tenseness in the hands, fingers, and other parts of the body.

3. The amount of embouchure and air control needed for pitch placement on oboe is significant. Oboe players make subtle changes in embouchure and air constantly. During large skips and leaps, these changes can be pronounced. If these changes in embouchure and air are not executed properly, the air stream is disrupted and technical fluidity is inhibited.

Specific Technical Considerations/Concerns for Oboe Players

1. Half-Hole Technique (Left-hand Index Finger)—The left-hand index finger must roll down slightly to execute the half-hole technique on D-flat, D-natural, and D-sharp (the three D's). Not executing the half-hole technique properly is a common problem on oboe. See also Half-Hole Technique, page 492

2. Right- and Left-Hand Key Clusters (Little-Finger Keys)—Oboe players often struggle with the left- and right-hand little-finger keys. Working on the little-finger keys or key clusters slowly and deliberately to develop finger coordination is extremely important to technical development. Learning to shift or slide properly from one key to another in these key clusters is also crucial to proper technique. See also Pivoting, page 517

3. Incorrect Use of the Octave Keys—Players often do not utilize the two (and possibly three) octave keys at the correct times. The first octave key is used from top-space E-natural to A-flat above the staff, and the second octave key is used from A-natural above the staff to high C-natural above the staff. No octave key is used

for high C-sharp to high D-sharp. Altissimo E-natural and above requires the first octave key (or the third octave key on some professional oboes). See also Octave Keys, page 512

4. Left Thumb—Players often develop the habit of "jumping" the left thumb from its resting position to the octave key rather than using a simple rocking motion. Not placing the thumb at the appropriate angle (about 1 o'clock) and using a rocking motion is extremely detrimental to technique, especially in rapid passages.

5. Right Thumb—Players often develop the habit of placing the right thumb too far under the thumb rest, making it difficult to place and move the fingers properly on the instrument. This position is extremely detrimental to technique, especially in rapid passages. The thumb should be placed under the rest between the thumbnail and first joint so that the fingers can move freely.

6. Crossing the Break—Crossing the break can be as problematic on oboe as it is on other woodwind instruments. The primary technical considerations are with finger coordination and finger/hand position. The main challenge with crossing the break is playing from an open note (where few keys are depressed) to a closed note (where most keys are depressed). These intervals require precise coordination of hands and fingers. Maintaining proper hand positions, keeping the fingers close to the keys at all times, and minimizing excess finger motion will improve crossing the break. See also Crossing the Break, page 481

7. High Range—As the notes get higher, players need to increase air speed, firm their embouchures, and focus the air and oral cavity to achieve the proper tonal response. The response of notes above high G-natural becomes increasingly more difficult as the range ascends. In addition, the fingerings for notes above high C-natural become increasingly more difficult and less intuitive. Practicing scales, arpeggios, and etudes can help smooth out fingering problems in the high register.

8. Alternate Fingerings/Alternates—Like other woodwind players, oboe players learn to use alternate fingerings to improve technical proficiency. The choice of fingerings should be determined by musical considerations including tone quality, intonation, and smoothness of the phrase. Although new fingerings seem

awkward initially, developing control over all fingerings is crucial to technical facility. See also Alternate Fingerings/Alternates, page 461

9. Skips and Leaps—Skips and leaps can be particularly challenging for oboe players. As with crossing the break, coordinating the fingers and making proper embouchure adjustments are critical to executing skips and leaps effectively. Maintaining proper hand positions, keeping the fingers close to the keys at all times, and minimizing excess finger motion will help players execute skips and leaps cleanly. Suggestions for executing skips and leaps effectively are listed as follows. See also Crossing the Break, page 481

    A. The primary technical consideration with skips and leaps is to make proper adjustments in embouchure, air, and oral cavity from note to note. Within the middle register (e.g., first-line E-natural to third-space C-natural), these adjustments are relatively subtle; however, from the low register to the high register (e.g., low C-natural to high B-natural), these adjustments are significant.

    B. As a rule, when ascending to higher pitches (e.g., high B-natural or C-natural), the embouchure needs to be firmer, the air speed needs to be faster, and the air stream and oral cavity need to be more focused. When descending to lower pitches, players must reverse these adjustments.

    C. The adjustments in embouchure, air, and oral cavity must be balanced. That is, increasing air speed significantly without changing the embouchure or air direction may help a higher pitch to sound, but it will also create problems with pitch and tone quality. Likewise, increasing embouchure tension without making appropriate changes in air speed, direction, and focus will also create problems with pitch and quality. As a rule, players must balance the adjustments in embouchure tension, air speed, air direction, and the oral cavity, rather than making large-scale changes in one or two of these variables.

    D. Learning to make appropriate adjustments to embouchure (firmness, looseness, shape), air (direction, speed, and focus), and oral cavity (focus) is crucial to playing skips and leaps smoothly and efficiently. The appropriateness of any adjustment should be determined by the tone quality and pitch placement that result.

10. Trill Fingerings—Oboe players are required to trill fairly often. A special trill fingering chart is in "Practical Tips" at the end of this chapter.

Temperament: See Temperament, page 61

Third Octave Key: In addition to the two traditional octave keys, some professional model oboes have a third octave key. The third octave key is above and overlaps the first octave key. It facilitates playing in the altissimo range (high E-natural and above) and is only needed for advanced literature. See also Octave Keys, page 512

Thumb Rests: Metal or plastic rests attached to the back of the oboe under which the right thumb is positioned while the instrument is being played. Thumb rests may be coated with plastic or rubber for comfort. Adjustable thumb rests are available as well. These thumb rests can be adjusted up or down to better fit players' hands. See also Hand/Holding/Instrument/Playing Positions and Posture, page 493

Tip Opening/Reed Aperture: The opening between the two blades of a double reed. The tip opening is a significant factor in determining the amount of resistance a reed will offer and the type of tone produced on an instrument. As a general rule, a reed with a large tip opening will produce more resistance and a bigger tone quality. Conversely, a reed with a small tip opening will produce less resistance and a smaller tone quality. In addition, large tip openings have a greater dynamic potential than small tip openings. See also Resistance, page 545; Response, page 547

Teaching Tips Regarding Tip Opening

1. The "correct" size for a tip opening varies from reed to reed and from player to player and is largely dependent upon the relationships between the tip opening, reed strength, and embouchure pressure. Following are some suggestions regarding these relationships. Ultimately, it is the tone quality and response that determine whether a particular tip opening is appropriate.
   A. A harder reed generally requires a slightly smaller tip opening and/or more embouchure pressure.
   B. A softer reed generally requires a slightly larger tip opening and/or slightly less embouchure pressure.

    C. Players who consistently play with a small, thin tone need to use a slightly harder reed and/or a reed with a larger tip opening. If the tone is tight or pinched, a looser embouchure is needed.

    D. Players who consistently play with an unfocused or raucous tone need to use a slightly softer reed and/or a reed with a smaller tip opening. If the tone is loose and uncontrolled, a firmer embouchure is needed.

Tip, Reed: The wide end of the reed opposite the heel. The tip of a reed is crucial to good tone quality. Its thickness and flexibility must be even across the width of the reed and the same on both blades. Holding the reed up to the light can provide some idea about the consistency of the tip regarding thickness and shape. See also Reeds, Double, page 531

Tone Holes: See Tone Holes, page 63

Tone Production: The term used to describe how tone is produced on an instrument. General considerations for woodwind tone production are discussed under Tone Production in chapter 1. Specific considerations for oboe tone production and some of the terms that address tone production appear separately.

Tonal Concept/Tone Quality

Develop a concept of "good" oboe tone and the type of tone quality desired. Listening to advanced players and high-quality recordings can help develop appropriate tonal concepts. In addition, taking lessons from a knowledgeable teacher who provides an exemplary model during lessons is invaluable. See Tone Production, page 63

1. Use appropriate equipment (i.e., instrument and reed). Students should play on equipment that matches their level of performance and experience. As students mature, they should learn to make and adjust reeds under the guidance of a knowledgeable teacher. In oboe playing, the reed is the primary factor in determining tone quality.

2. Strive for a consistent tone quality and evenness of scale in all ranges and develop control of the air stream at all dynamic levels. Maintain an open throat and oral cavity in all registers as

if saying the syllable "oo." In the high range, players tend to use a smaller, firmer "oo" syllable or even an "ee" syllable to focus tone more effectively. Considerable disagreement exists as to the appropriateness of particular syllables. Teachers and players should experiment with a variety of syllables and use what yields the best results.

EMBOUCHURE

Maintain proper embouchure formation at all times. Proper mechanics of embouchure are critical to tone production. Although many fine players' embouchures vary slightly from a classic or standard embouchure, the fundamental characteristics have withstood the test of time. Achieving a mature, characteristic tone on any wind instrument requires time and practice to develop the physical and aural skills necessary for proper tone production. A brief summary of embouchure considerations for good tone production appears in the following list. See also Embouchure, page 483

1. The mouth corners are drawn inward toward the reed.
2. The lips surround the reed evenly in all directions as if saying "oo." A drawstring analogy is often used to describe this rounded position.
3. The lips roll inward over the teeth so that both the upper and the lower lips cushion and support the reed. About two-thirds of the reed is taken into the mouth, and the reed remains centered.
4. The chin remains flat. Avoid bunching the chin and puffing the cheeks.
5. As a general rule, as oboe players ascend, they need to gradually firm their embouchures, and as they descend, they need to relax their embouchures. These adjustments are relatively slight. Large-scale changes in embouchure should be avoided.

BREATHING AND AIR

A thorough discussion of breathing and air is in chapter 1. See Breathing/Breath Support/Air Control, page 10; Tone Production, page 63

VIBRATO

While vibrato is not a factor in tone production for beginners and intermediate players, it is a factor in tone production for more advanced players. Typically, vibrato is added once the fundamentals of good tone production have been mastered. Oboists use a diaphragmatic vibrato, although some oboists prefer to call it a throat vibrato. Considerations for vibrato are listed as follows. See also Vibrato, page 562

1. Add vibrato to a full, well-centered tone according to the musical style being performed.
2. Use vibrato to enhance tone quality, not to cover up poor tone quality.

Specific Tonal Considerations/Concerns for Oboe Players

1. High Notes—As notes get higher, players need to increase air speed, firm their embouchures, and narrow the focus of the air stream and oral cavity to achieve proper tonal response, tone quality, and pitch. Notes above high G-natural become increasing more difficult to play with good tone quality and intonation. In addition, the fingerings for high notes become increasingly complex and less intuitive. There is frequently more than one fingering for the same note. Players typically experiment to find the fingering that works best for them.

2. Technical Considerations—Players must half-hole the three D's (D-flat, D-natural, and D-sharp). Players sometimes half-hole notes improperly or do not half-hole notes at all. In addition, players often do not utilize the two (or three) octave keys at the correct times. The first octave key is used from top-space E-natural to A-flat above the staff and on high E-natural and above on oboes not equipped with a third octave key. The second octave key is used from A-natural above the staff to high C-natural above the staff. When equipped, the third octave key is used on high E-natural and above. See also Half-Hole Technique, page 492

3. Embouchure—As a general rule, the embouchure is more relaxed in the low range and firmer in the high range. Furthermore, in the low range, the jaw is dropped down and back slightly, and less of the upper and lower lips tend to be rolled over the teeth. The oboe embouchure is firmer than other woodwind embouchures;

however, the embouchure should never be considered "tight." See also Embouchure, page 483

4. Reed—A certain amount of resistance is needed to maintain a steady, rich tone quality and proper intonation. When reeds are too soft or the reed aperture too small, the tone is thin and "quivery" and pitch is difficult to control. When reeds are too hard or the reed aperture too large, the tone is airy, response is poor, pitch control suffers, and players' embouchures tire quickly. Reeds need to be hard enough to push back against the embouchure pressure in order to create a stable tone, but not so hard that players have to fight the reed. See also Reeds, Double, page 531

5. Reed Placement—Young players are often inconsistent with the amount of reed they take into the mouth, which is detrimental to tone production and pitch. Taking too much reed in the mouth causes the pitch to be sharp, and taking too little reed in the mouth causes the pitch to be flat. In both cases, producing a steady tone is almost impossible.

6. Back Pressure—Adjusting to the amount of back pressure experienced when playing oboe is challenging. Instead of running out of air, oboe players actually experience a buildup of excess air, which negatively affects tone production. Developing proper breathing habits and gaining playing experience help players learn how to use air more efficiently; however, nothing can eliminate the back pressure that players experience during play. See also Back Pressure, page 471

Tone Quality: The characteristic sound associated with an instrument regarding tone color or timbre, and consistency, focus, and control of the air stream. The tone quality of the oboe is often described as reedy or nasally. Compared to other woodwind instruments, the oboe's tone is much more reedy. From a mechanical standpoint, tone quality is dependent upon the design of the instrument; the materials used in instrument construction; and, most important, the reed, which is discussed under Reeds, Double. From a player's standpoint, tone quality is largely dependent upon two factors: (1) the use of air, which is discussed in detail under Tone Production and Breathing/Breath Support/Air Control, and (2) the embouchure and oral cavity, which is discussed in detail under Tone Production and Embouchure. Common terms associated with tone quality and common terms used to describe tone quality are identified and described under

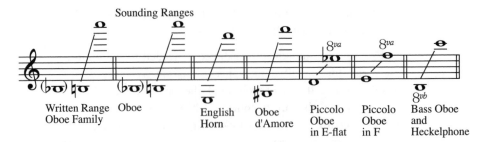

FIGURE 5.43. *Oboe Family Transpositions*

Tone Quality in chapter 1. See also Breathing/Breath Support/Air Control, page 10; Tone Quality, page 68

Key Questions

Q: Should I work on tone quality or intonation first?

A: Tone quality. If players cannot play with a good, consistent tone quality, working on intonation is counterproductive.

Tonguing: See Tonguing, page 71

Transpositions: The relationship between the written and sounding ranges of an instrument. The oboe is non-transposing instrument. That is, the oboe sounds as written. However, the English horn and the oboe d'amore are transposing instruments. What follows is a list of transpositions for the oboe family. A summary of notated transpositions is shown in figure 5.43. See also Range, page 517

Oboe, English Horn, and Oboe d'amore Transpositions

1. The oboe is a non-transposing instrument. It is pitched in C and sounds as written. In other words, when an oboe plays a written C-natural, it sounds a concert C-natural.
2. The English horn is pitched in F and sounds a perfect fifth lower than written. As a result, when it plays a written third-space C-natural, it sounds a concert F-natural, a perfect fifth lower than the written C-natural.
3. The oboe d'amore is pitched in A and sounds a minor third lower than written. As a result, when it plays a written third-space

C-natural, it sounds a concert A-natural a minor third lower than the written C-natural.

Piccolo Oboe, Baritone/Bass Oboe and Heckelphone Transpositions

1. The piccolo oboe is a transposing instrument. It is pitched in either E-flat or F above the regular oboe in C and sounds higher than written. When an E-flat oboe plays a written C-natural, it sounds a concert E-flat, a minor third higher than written. When an F oboe plays a written C-natural, it sounds a concert F-natural, a perfect fourth higher than written.

2. The bass oboe, sometimes called a baritone oboe, is a transposing instrument. It is pitched in C and sounds one octave below the regular oboe in C, and one octave below the written pitch. When a bass oboe plays a written C-natural, it sounds a concert C-natural one octave below the written pitch.

3. The Heckelphone is a transposing instrument. Like the bass oboe, it is pitched in C one octave below the regular oboe in C. Therefore, it also sounds one octave below the written pitch. When it plays a written C-natural, it sounds a concert C-natural one octave below the written pitch.

Triple-Tonguing: A technique that enables performers to tongue triple patterns rapidly. See also Multiple-Tonguing, page 52

Tube/Body, Reed: See Staple, page 549

Tuning/Tuning Note Considerations: Tuning any instrument is a process that involves making mechanical adjustments (e.g., pulling out or pushing in a mouthpiece, slide, or instrument joint) so that the instrument will produce pitches that are in tune with a predetermined standard (typically A = 440). Tuning notes refer to specific pitches that are good to tune to on any given instrument. Considerations have been given to the notes most commonly used for tuning wind groups. Adjusting pitch and adjusting for pitch tendencies of the oboe are discussed under Intonation. Considerations for tuning the oboe appear in the following section.

Tuning the Oboe

1. Oboes are designed to be in tune (at A = 440) when the reed is pushed into the reed well all the way. Unlike the other woodwind instruments, which can be adjusted by pulling a mouthpiece and/ or instrument joint, the pitch of the oboe is almost exclusively dependent upon the quality and design of the reed and the player's embouchure.

2. Small adjustments in sharpness can be made by pulling the reed out slightly; however, this type of adjustment is usually made only when absolutely necessary.

Tuning Note Considerations

1. Concert B-flat—An "okay" tuning note in the middle octave; however, it tends to be a bit flat. The upper and lower octave B-flats should not be used as tuning notes.
2. Concert A-natural—Second-space A-natural is a good tuning note, and one of the best tuning notes on the instrument. The upper octave A-natural should not be used as a tuning note.
3. Concert F-natural—The first-space F-natural (regular fingering, not fork) is an "okay" tuning note. Do not use fork F or top-line F-natural as tuning notes.

FINGERING CHARTS

Oboe Basic Fingerings

Oboe Basic Fingerings

Oboe Basic Fingerings

Oboe Basic Fingerings

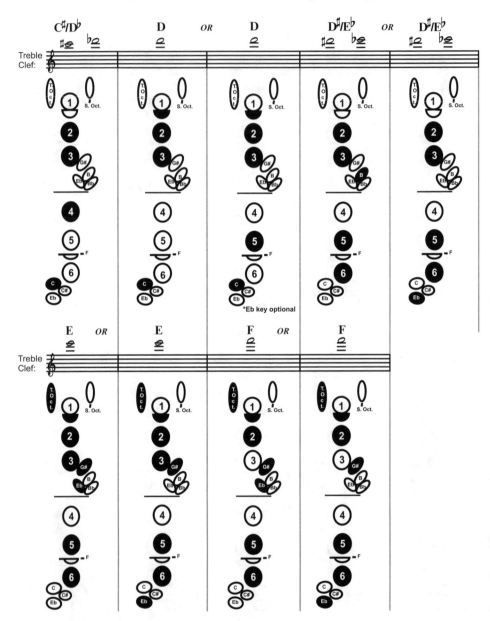

Oboe Alternate Fingerings

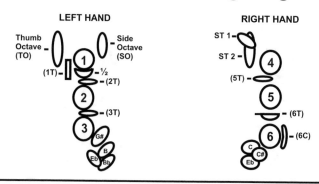

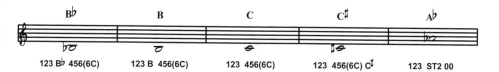

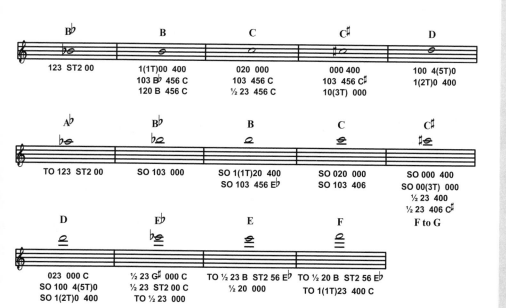

B♭	B	C	C♯	A♭
123 B♭ 456(6C)	123 B 456(6C)	123 456(6C)	123 456(6C) C♯	123 ST2 00

B♭	B	C	C♯	D
123 ST2 00	1(1T)00 400	020 000	000 400	100 4(5T)0
	103 B♭ 456 C	103 456 C	103 456 C♯	1(2T)0 400
	120 B 456 C	½ 23 456 C	10(3T) 000	

A♭	B♭	B	C	C♯
TO 123 ST2 00	SO 103 000	SO 1(1T)20 400	SO 020 000	SO 000 400
		SO 103 456 E♭	SO 103 406	SO 00(3T) 000
				½ 23 400
				½ 23 406 C♯

D	E♭	E	F	F to G
023 000 C	½ 23 G♯ 000 C	TO ½ 23 B ST2 56 E♭	TO ½ 20 B ST2 56 E♭	
SO 100 4(5T)0	½ 23 ST2 00 C	½ 20 000	TO 1(1T)23 400 C	
SO 1(2T)0 400	TO ½ 23 000			

Oboe Altissimo Fingerings

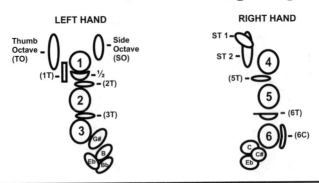

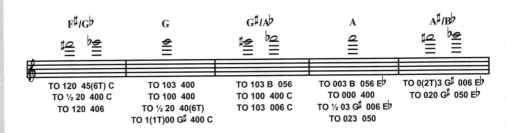

F♯/G♭	G	G♯/A♭	A	A♯/B♭
TO 120 45(6T) C	TO 103 400	TO 103 B 056	TO 003 B 056 E♭	TO 0(2T)3 G♯ 006 E♭
TO ½ 20 400 C	TO 100 400	TO 100 400 C	TO 000 400	TO 020 G♯ 050 E♭
TO 120 406	TO ½ 20 40(6T)	TO 103 006 C	TO ½ 03 G♯ 006 E♭	
	TO 1(1T)00 G♯ 400 C		TO 023 050	

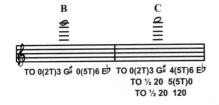

B	C
TO 0(2T)3 G♯ 0(5T)6 E♭	TO 0(2T)3 G♯ 4(5T)6 E♭
	TO ½ 20 5(5T)0
	TO ½ 20 120

Oboe Special Trill Fingerings

Trills performed with regular fingerings are not included

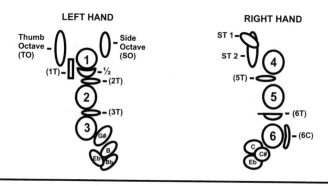

Oboe Special Trill Fingerings

Trills performed with regular fingerings are not included

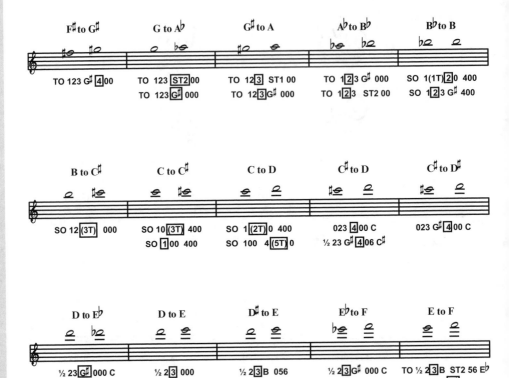

Common Technical Faults and Corrections

Many problems in wind playing result from basic faults in the following areas: (1) instrument assembly, (2) embouchure formation, and (3) hand/holding/playing positions and posture. The following section provides information on how to correct technical faults frequently encountered in oboe performance. Headings appear in alphabetical order.

Assembly

Fault 1:   The bridge keys between the bell and the lower joint are not properly aligned.

Correction: Make sure that the pad cup on the bell is depressed during assembly so that the bridge key is raised to avoid bending the linkage mechanism, and align the bridge key between the lower joint and bell during assembly.

Fault 2:   Improper reed placement.

Correction: Push the reed in all the way and position it parallel to the floor. The reed angle is correct when the player's head is straight (not tilted to one side) when playing.

Fault 3:   Careless handling of the instrument and unnecessary pressure on the keys and rods.

Correction: Avoid unnecessary pressure on rods and keys by holding the upper and lower joints the way they are held when the instrument is being played. In other words, depress 1-2-3 (left hand) on the upper joint, and depress 4-5-6 (right hand) on the lower joint. Make sure that the corks are well greased. Assembling the oboe while seated or standing next to the playing location will minimize unnecessary handling.

Fault 4:   Improper alignment of the bridge keys between the lower and upper joints.

Correction: Make sure that the bridge keys between the upper and lower joints are aligned properly. Improper alignment causes notes not to speak properly and hinders proper hand position.

Fault 5:   Not greasing corks sufficiently.

CORRECTION: Grease corks weekly (more if necessary) to make assembly easier. Dry corks can cause players to use excessive pressure on the key mechanisms during assembly.

Embouchure Formation

FAULT 1:   Not enough bottom or top lip over teeth.

CORRECTION: Generally, the red part of the lips is not visible (or is barely visible) during play; however, the amount of lips over the teeth varies from player to player.

FAULT 2:   Taking too much or too little reed into the mouth.

CORRECTION: As a rule, about two-thirds of the reed should be inserted into the mouth. The exact placement depends on the player and the reed, and should be determined by the position that yields the best tone quality and response.

FAULT 3:   Mouth corners are drawn back in a smiling position.

CORRECTION: Although the mouth corners should remain somewhat firm, the embouchure should be rounded as if saying "who." Players can think of surrounding the reed with even pressure from all sides (a drawstring effect) and forming a rounded seal around the reed.

FAULT 4:   Embouchure too tight.

CORRECTION: The embouchure should be relatively firm (but not tight), and it should remain in a rounded position. The lips form a cushion for the reed without excess pressure (biting). Unlike other woodwind instruments, the oboe requires players to use a cold air stream during play.

FAULT 5:   Air escaping through the mouth corners.

CORRECTION: Air escapes when the surrounding muscles are not supporting inwardly toward the reed. Players can think of surrounding the reed with even pressure from all sides (a drawstring effect) and forming a seal around the reed so that air does not escape through the mouth corners. Forming a proper embouchure will eliminate this problem.

FAULT 6:   Puffed cheeks.

CORRECTION: The mouth corners provide support inwardly toward the reed, and the chin should remain flat.

Hand/Holding/Instrument Playing Positions and Posture

FAULT 1: Elbows too far from or too close to the body while playing.

CORRECTION: Elbows should be held out from the body in a relaxed, comfortable position.

FAULT 2: Elbows resting on knees while playing.

CORRECTION: Elbows should be held out from the body in a relaxed, comfortable position. Younger, smaller players sometimes rest their arms on their knee when they get tired. Take frequent breaks to eliminate fatigue and encourage proper playing positions at all times.

FAULT 3: Holding the oboe at an improper angle.

CORRECTION: The oboe should be centered with the body and held out at about a 40- to 45-degree angle. The oboe is generally held out away from the body slightly more than the clarinet. The exact placement is determined by the tone quality, pitch, and response. The angle of the oboe is the same, whether the player is standing or sitting. On English horn, the bell is brought back toward the body slightly more than the oboe because of the bocal angle.

FAULT 4: Head tilted to one side.

CORRECTION: The head should remain straight at all times. Make sure that the reed is parallel to the floor and not improperly twisted or turned to one side.

FAULT 5: Slouching posture.

CORRECTION: Sit up straight, keep the chin in a normal position (not up or down), keep the eyes straight ahead, and keep the shoulders and back straight but relaxed.

FAULT 6: Resting the bell on the knees or holding the bell with the knees.

CORRECTION: Sit farther forward on the chair and keep the feet flat on the floor with the knees about shoulder width apart. The bell should extend beyond the knees at about a 40- to 45-degree angle.

FAULT 7:   Not positioning the left thumb properly.

CORRECTION: The left thumb should be placed at a slight angle (about 1 o'clock) so that it can operate the octave key with a slight turn of the thumb.

FAULT 8:   Lifting the left thumb off of the instrument when engaging the octave key.

CORRECTION: The left thumb should remain in contact with the instrument at all times, even when engaging the octave key.

FAULT 9:   Fingers are straight or "locked."

CORRECTION: Fingers should be slightly curved so that a C-shape is formed between the thumb and fingers.

FAULT 10:   The right-hand little finger is floating out of position.

CORRECTION: The right-hand little finger should remain close to the C key to minimize finger movement and facilitate technical proficiency.

FAULT 11:   The right thumb is pushed too far underneath the thumb rest.

CORRECTION: Make sure that the right thumb is positioned underneath the thumb rest between the nail and the knuckle.

FAULT 12:   The wrists are bent.

CORRECTION: The wrists should remain relatively straight. If the elbows and instrument are in the proper position, wrist position is generally not a problem.

FAULT 13:   The left-hand little finger is allowed to droop or to float out of position.

CORRECTION: The left-hand little finger should remain close to the B key in a ready position to minimize finger movement and improve technical proficiency.

FAULT 14:   Fingers too far from keys.

CORRECTION: Fingers should remain as close to the keys as possible without distorting tone quality and/or pitch. Keeping fingers close to keys or tone holes minimizes movement and improves technique.

FAULT 15:   The left-hand index finger is angled improperly.

CORRECTION: The left-hand index finger must be placed so that it can half-hole when necessary by rocking slightly rather than by using a less efficient sliding motion.

COMMON PROBLEMS, CAUSES, AND SOLUTIONS FOR OBOE

Problems in wind instrument playing relate to some aspect of sound. That is, incorrect assembly is not a problem; poor tone quality or squeaking is a problem. Incorrect assembly is simply one common cause of such problems. Understanding this distinction makes it easier to apply effective solutions to problems. The following section provides information on solving problems frequently encountered in oboe performance. The main headings are: Articulation Problems, Intonation Problems, Performance/Technical Problems, and Tone Quality and Response Problems.

Articulation Problems

PROBLEM: Audible dip or scoop in pitch during initial attacks.

CAUSE 1:   Excessive movement of the embouchure (especially the jaw) while tonguing.

SOLUTION 1:   Use light, quick movements of the tongue and maintain a consistent embouchure. Use a "tu" syllable not a "twa" syllable. Practice tonguing in front of a mirror and use the visual feedback to help eliminate jaw movement.

CAUSE 2:   Embouchure not set properly before the attack.

SOLUTION 2:   Allow enough time to be physically and mentally set before the attack. That is, the embouchure must be set properly for the note being played. When the embouchure is too tight or too loose for a particular note at the point of attack, players will make an immediate adjustment or shift to correct the pitch. This shift causes an audible dip or scoop in the attack.

PROBLEM: Heavy, thick, and/or sluggish attacks.

CAUSE 1:   Too much tongue on the attacks coupled with a slow tonguing action.

SOLUTION 1:   Minimize tongue movement. Use a light, quick tonguing action. Thinking about striking only the bottom blade with the tongue can help avoid striking the reed too hard during the attack. Think of moving only the tip of the tongue during the tonguing process and use a "tu" attack for normal tonguing.

CAUSE 2:   Tonguing too far down on the reed.

SOLUTION 2:   The tip of the tongue strikes the tip of the reed. Make sure the tongue is pulled back or arched slightly in the mouth to begin the tonguing process. This position places the tongue slightly higher in the mouth to start. Thinking about striking only the bottom blade with the tongue can help players avoid striking the reed too hard during the attack.

CAUSE 3:   Tongue disrupting the air stream.

SOLUTION 3:   If the tongue is too low or too high in the mouth, or if the tongue moves too slowly, the air stream is disrupted, causing sluggish attacks. Make sure the tongue is pulled back or arched slightly in the mouth to begin the tonguing process, and increase the quickness of the tongue strike against the tip of the reed.

PROBLEM: Mistimed attacks (tongue, embouchure, air).

CAUSE 1:   Tongue and air stream not coordinated.

SOLUTION 1:   Practice coordinating the tongue and the air stream by attacking one note at a time. Think of starting the tongue and the air at the same time on attacks. Although it is the release of the tongue from the reed that actually starts a tone, the air stream and the tongue must work together.

CAUSE 2:   Embouchure not set properly before the attack.

SOLUTION 2:   Allow enough time to be physically and mentally set before the attack. That is, the embouchure must be set properly for the note being played. An embouchure that is too tight or too loose for the note being played can delay the response of the attack and cause excess jaw movement.

CAUSE 3:   Too much embouchure movement during attacks.

SOLUTION 3:   The embouchure must be set properly for the note being played. Maintain embouchure formation and avoid using a "jawing" action. Think of moving only the tip of the tongue.

CAUSE 4:   Player not set to play.

SOLUTION 4:   Maintain proper playing positions (physical readiness), and internally "hear" the pitches before playing them (mental readiness).

PROBLEM: Inability to execute clean slurs.

CAUSE 1:   Inconsistent air stream.

SOLUTION 1:   Do not change the air stream from note to note. Instead, blow a consistent stream of air and simply move the fingers. On oboe, it is generally not necessary to adjust the air stream for various pitches in slurred passages unless they contain large intervals; however, adjustments in air speed and air volume should be made as necessary to accommodate the dynamic level.

CAUSE 2:   Too much embouchure movement throughout a slurred passage.

SOLUTION 2:   Use the same embouchure throughout the entire passage. Making large shifts in embouchure for various notes disrupts the air stream and is completely unnecessary on oboe.

CAUSE 3:   Fingers not coordinated.

SOLUTION 3:   Keep the fingers close to the keys and depress them quickly and smoothly from note to note. Maintain proper hand position, avoid excess finger movement, and avoid "slapping" the keys.

CAUSE 4:   Player not set to play.

SOLUTION 4:   Maintain proper playing positions (physical readiness), and internally hear the pitches before playing them (mental readiness).

PROBLEM: Inability to execute clean releases.

CAUSE 1:   Inappropriate use of tongue cutoffs.

SOLUTION 1:   Use breath releases rather than tongue cutoffs in most musical contexts because tongue cutoffs tend to be harsh and abrupt. Tongue cutoffs are appropriate in some jazz styles.

CAUSE 2:   Putting the tongue back on the reed too hard on tongue cutoffs.

SOLUTION 2:   When tongue cutoffs are appropriate (e.g., some jazz styles), be sure that players do not use too much tongue, which distorts the attacks. The tongue should make a modest amount of contact on the tip of the bottom blade. Thinking about striking only the bottom blade with the tongue can help avoid striking the reed too hard during the attack. The rest of the "attack" consists of a sudden increase in air.

CAUSE 3:   Not stopping the air at the point of release.

SOLUTION 3:   Practice maintaining an open air column from the diaphragm into the instrument, and stop the air by suspending it midstream as if lightly gasping. Using the throat as a valve and/or pushing the air on releases both prevent clean releases.

CAUSE 4:   Not "lifting" on the release.

SOLUTION 4:   Think of gasping lightly on the release and directing the air stream upward. Thinking this way helps stop the flow of air quickly while maintaining an open air column. Make sure to maintain a consistent embouchure during the release.

CAUSE 5:   Closing off the embouchure and/or throat, or using the embouchure and/or throat as a valve for stopping the air.

SOLUTION 5:   The embouchure and throat remain unchanged on breath releases. It is the air that is stopped to release a tone. Think of gasping lightly on the release and directing the air stream upward. Thinking this way helps stop the flow of air quickly while maintaining an open air column, an open throat, and a proper embouchure.

PROBLEM: Inability to execute a controlled accent.

CAUSE 1:   Not balancing the air stream and tongue appropriately.

SOLUTION 1:   On most accents, the weight of the tongue is not increased on the attack. Rather, the accent is produced by a sudden increase in air. On an accented note, "lift off" of the air; that is, think of gasping lightly and directing the air stream upward on the release. As a rule, do not use tongue cutoffs on accented notes.

CAUSE 2:   Too much tongue on releases in staccato passages with repeated accents.

SOLUTION 2: In rapid patterns, the release of each note (except the first) in the pattern becomes the attack for each subsequent note. As a result, think of tonguing each note consistently and evenly, and the releases will take care of themselves.

Intonation Problems

PROBLEM: Pitch generally flat in all registers.

CAUSE 1: Reed is improperly made and/or too long.

SOLUTION 1: Play with the reed pushed all the way into the reed well. If the overall pitch is flat, try a slightly shorter reed.

CAUSE 2: Too little reed in the mouth.

SOLUTION 2: Insert about two-thirds of the reed into the mouth. The reed is centered in the mouth.

CAUSE 3: Too little air and/or air stream too slow.

SOLUTION 3: Use a controlled, steady air stream, and increase the speed and volume of the air stream slightly. Practice proper breathing techniques.

CAUSE 4: Not compensating for the natural tendency of the oboe to go flat in soft passages.

SOLUTION 4: Raise the direction of the air stream slightly to compensate for the drop in pitch and use a more focused oral cavity. It may be necessary to firm the embouchure slightly on pitches that are significantly flat, especially in the pianissimo dynamic range.

CAUSE 5: Air stream directed downward too much.

SOLUTION 5: Form a drawstring embouchure as if saying "oo." Maintain a consistent air stream. Focus the air slightly upward.

CAUSE 6: Slouching.

SOLUTION 6: When seated, sit up straight (but avoid being rigid or tense) with feet flat on the floor. Sit toward the front of the chair to avoid hitting the oboe against the chair. Do not rest the elbows on the lap. When standing, stand straight (avoid being tense or rigid) and position the feet about shoulder width apart. Poor posture restricts proper breath support and promotes embouchure problems.

CAUSE 7: Holding the oboe out too far from the body.

SOLUTION 7:   Hold the oboe at a 40- to 45-degree angle away from the body. Holding the oboe in too close or out too far will cause the reed to enter the mouth at an incorrect angle, upsetting the balance of the embouchure's pressure on the reed and negatively affecting pitch.

CAUSE 8: Head tilted downward or forward too much.

SOLUTION 8:   Keep the head, eyes, and chin straight. Reaching for the reed negatively affects the embouchure's ability to support the reed properly and causes the pitch to be flat.

CAUSE 9: Pads are too close to the tone holes.

SOLUTION 9:   Have a knowledgeable repair technician adjust the pads to the proper height.

CAUSE 10: Reed is too soft.

SOLUTION 10:   Use harder reeds to gain more resistance and raise the pitch.

CAUSE 11: Lower lip and/or jaw drawn down too far.

SOLUTION 11:   Bring the lower lip/jaw up farther until the overall pitch is accurate and consistent. Players should surround the reed with even pressure from all directions.

PROBLEM: Pitch generally sharp in all registers.

CAUSE 1: Reed is improperly made and/or too short.

SOLUTION 1:   Try a slightly longer reed. The oboe is designed to be played with the reed pushed all the way into the reed well. Small adjustments in sharpness can be made by pulling out the reed slightly; however, this type of adjustment is usually made only when absolutely necessary.

CAUSE 2: Embouchure too tight.

SOLUTION 2:   Relax the embouchure as if saying "oo" until the overall pitch is accurate and consistent. Think of using a warmer air stream.

CAUSE 3: Too much air.

SOLUTION 3:   Use less air and a controlled air stream. Develop proper breathing techniques.

CAUSE 4:   Not compensating for the natural tendency to go sharp as more air is used.

SOLUTION 4:   Gradually lower the direction of the air stream to compensate for the rise in pitch and use a more open oral cavity. It may be necessary to relax the embouchure slightly on pitches that are significantly sharp, especially in the fortissimo dynamic range.

CAUSE 5:   Air stream directed upward too much.

SOLUTION 5:   Form a drawstring embouchure as if saying "oo." Maintain a consistent air stream. Focus the air slightly downward.

CAUSE 6:   Too much reed in the mouth.

SOLUTION 6:   Make sure that about two-thirds of the reed is inserted in the mouth. The reed is centered in the mouth.

CAUSE 7:   Pads are too far from tone holes.

SOLUTION 7:   Have a knowledgeable repair technician adjust the pads to the proper height.

CAUSE 8:   Reed is too hard.

SOLUTION 8:   Use softer reeds to decrease resistance and lower the pitch.

PROBLEM: Pitch is inconsistent throughout the playing range.

CAUSE 1:   Inconsistent air stream.

SOLUTION 1:   Do not change the air stream drastically from note to note. Instead, blow a consistent stream of air and make small adjustments based on the pitches being played. Adjustments in air speed, air volume, and air direction should be made as necessary to accommodate the dynamic level and pitches involved.

CAUSE 2:   Inconsistent embouchure.

SOLUTION 2:   Form a good basic drawstring embouchure using an "oo" syllable, and make sure that enough of the lips cover the teeth. In general, very little of the red part of the lips should be showing. Practice playing long tones to develop the embouchure muscles, and concentrate on keeping the embouchure consistent yet relaxed at all times. Use a mirror on a regular basis to check embouchure formation until proper habits are formed.

CAUSE 3: Lack of proper breath support.

SOLUTION 3: Work on breathing exercises with and without the oboe to help develop breath support. Practice playing long tones at all dynamic levels. Focus on maintaining a consistent air speed appropriate for each dynamic level. Practice extensively at softer dynamic levels because it is harder to maintain proper breath support and good intonation at softer dynamic levels than it is at louder dynamic levels. In addition, breath support is often compromised when playing technical passages because players tend to focus on technique at the expense of proper breath support. Practice maintaining breath support in technical passages.

CAUSE 4: Slouching.

SOLUTION 4: Sit up straight (but avoid being rigid or tense) with feet flat on the floor. Sit toward the front of the chair to avoid hitting the oboe against the chair. Do not rest the elbows in the lap. When standing, stand straight (avoid being rigid or tense) and position the feet about shoulder width apart.

CAUSE 5: Shifting the angle at which the oboe is held.

SOLUTION 5: The oboe is held at about a 40- to 45-degree angle from the body. Holding the oboe in too close or out too far will cause the reed to enter the mouth at an incorrect angle, upsetting the balance of the embouchure's pressure on the reed and negatively affecting pitch.

CAUSE 6: Reed is too old and/or affected by environmental conditions.

SOLUTION 6: Use a reed that has not lost its response characteristics. Reeds have a limited life, and a reed can go from having excellent response characteristics to having poor response characteristics relatively quickly. Before discarding a reed that plays poorly, let it rest a few days and try it again. Sometimes environmental factors such as humidity and temperature affect reed response and pitch.

CAUSE 7: Reed is unbalanced.

SOLUTION 7: Adjust the reed to balance both blades as much as possible. Make small adjustments and test the reed after each adjustment. Many players adjust reeds over several days to accurately gauge their playing characteristics and to ensure that the reeds are not ruined (too much cane removed) during the adjustment process.

PROBLEM: Playing out of tune without adjusting.

NOTE: A detailed account of adjusting pitch can be found under Intonation in chapter 1.

CAUSE 1: Inability to hear beats or roughness.

SOLUTION 1: Focus on hearing the beats or pulsations that occur when pitches are out of tune. Play long tone unisons with other players and listen for beats. Deliberately playing extremely flat and sharp to accentuate the beats will help players learn to hear beats.

CAUSE 2: Not knowing how to adjust pitch on the instrument.

SOLUTION 2: Learn how to adjust pitch on oboe. The oboe does not have the same overall pitch adjustment mechanisms as other woodwind instruments (that is, the reed is not designed to be pulled out from the reed well to adjust pitch). Reed length, embouchure, throat, oral cavity, air stream, and alternate fingerings can all be used to adjust the pitch.

CAUSE 3: The physical skills necessary to adjust pitch on the instrument are not developed.

SOLUTION 3: Practice adjusting pitch every day and continue developing embouchure skills. Relax and tighten the embouchure, focus the air stream upward and downward, open and close the throat and oral cavity, and try alternate fingerings. Learn "what does what" so that appropriate adjustments can be made when necessary.

Performance/Technical Problems

PROBLEM: Sloppy playing in tongued technical passages.

CAUSE 1: Tongue and fingers not coordinated.

SOLUTION 1: Practice simple interval exercises slowly with a metronome, and make sure that the tongue and fingers move together. Keep the fingers close to the keys during these exercises to avoid excessive finger movement. As control is gained, progress to more difficult exercises and continue to practice with a metronome. Gradually speed up the exercises, but make sure that proper finger-tongue coordination is maintained.

CAUSE 2: Tonguing speed too slow.

SOLUTION 2: Using a metronome, start by practicing a variety of simple rhythm patterns on isolated pitches at a slow tempo. Gradually increase the speed and difficulty of the exercises. Use a "tip to tip" (tip of the tongue to the tip of the reed or bottom blade) technique and keep the tongue

motion light and quick. Periodically, practice tonguing slightly faster than is comfortable. Develop control and rhythmic precision by changing the tempo frequently.

PROBLEM: Sloppy playing overall.

CAUSE   1:   Poor   Hand/Holding/Instrument/Playing   Positions   and Posture.

SOLUTION 1:   Make sure that the playing basics are maintained at all times. A detailed account of these playing basics can be found under Hand/Holding/Instrument/Playing Positions and Posture.

CAUSE 2:   Poor instrument action.

SOLUTION 2:   Make sure the key mechanisms have been properly adjusted, cleaned, and oiled. Excessively heavy or uneven action is usually the result of poorly adjusted key mechanisms, poorly adjusted pads, and/ or bent key mechanisms. In addition, make sure the springs are in proper working condition. Weak springs sometimes bobble or bounce, which inhibits technical fluidity.

CAUSE 3:   Using awkward fingerings.

SOLUTION 3:   Use alternate fingerings and prepare the right hand when appropriate to maximize technical fluidity.

PROBLEM: Speed of the fingers seems slow in technical passages.

CAUSE 1:   Tenseness in the fingers and hands.

SOLUTION 1:   Practice tough passages slowly at first to gain control, and focus on staying relaxed; trying too hard or forcing the fingers to move during technical passages slows down the fingers. Gradually increase the tempo of the passage and develop the habit of staying relaxed at all tempos.

PROBLEM: An excessive amount of key noise can be heard when the keys are depressed.

CAUSE 1:   Key mechanisms need to be oiled.

SOLUTION 1:   If excessive key noise is heard during regular play, oil the mechanisms. As a rule, the key mechanisms should be oiled lightly once a month or so. Clacking sounds are often caused by metal-to-metal contact, which results in excessive wear of the key mechanisms.

CAUSE 2: Pushing keys down too hard or "slapping" the keys.

SOLUTION 2: Use only enough finger pressure to seal the pads (or fingers) against the tone holes or to cover the tone holes properly with the finger pads. Stay relaxed and think of playing smoothly and efficiently. Keeping the fingers close to the keys will help eliminate the tendency to "slap" the fingers down.

CAUSE 3: Corks or felts are missing.

SOLUTION 3: Sometimes the corks or felts that prevent metal-to-metal contact (and also help regulate proper key height) fall off. In such cases, the clacking is quite noticeable, and the affected key or keys will often appear out of line with the rest of the keys in the stack. Replace missing corks or felts and adjust height appropriately.

PROBLEM: Skips and leaps not clean.

CAUSE 1: Fingers and/or tongue not coordinated.

SOLUTION 1: Practice simple interval exercises slowly with a metronome, and focus on moving the tongue and fingers together. Keep the fingers close to the keys and tone holes during these exercises to avoid excessive finger movement. It may also help to slur all exercises because tonguing often covers up poor finger coordination. As control is gained, progress to more difficult exercises and continue to practice with a metronome. Gradually speed up the exercises, making sure that proper finger-tongue coordination is maintained.

CAUSE 2: Air stream not maintained properly.

SOLUTION 2: Maintain a consistent air stream at all dynamic levels. Players tend to focus on skips and leaps at the expense of proper breath support. Improper use of air in passages with skips and leaps causes coordination problems between the tongue, fingers, and air stream. Focus on maintaining breath support in all technical passages.

CAUSE 3: Improper left thumb action.

SOLUTION 3: The left thumb is positioned at a slightly upward angle so that it can operate the octave key with a simple rocking motion. The thumb remains in constant contact with the instrument even when it is engaging the octave key.

PROBLEM: Poor finger-tongue coordination.

CAUSE 1:   Poor playing habits resulting from playing too fast, too soon.

SOLUTION 1:   Practice simple interval exercises slowly with a metronome, and focus on moving the tongue and fingers together. Keep the fingers close to the keys and tone holes during these exercises to avoid excessive finger movement. Slur all exercises because tonguing often covers up poor finger coordination. As control is gained, progress to more difficult exercises. Continue to practice with a metronome, and continue to slur the exercises.

CAUSE 2:   Air stream not maintained properly.

SOLUTION 2:   Maintain a consistent air stream at all dynamic levels. Improper use of air in technical passages causes coordination problems between the tongue, fingers, and air stream. Players tend to focus on technique at the expense of proper breath support. Focus on maintaining breath support at all times until proper support becomes automatic.

PROBLEM: Uneven finger movement within the beat.

CAUSE 1:   Poor control of individual fingers.

SOLUTION 1:   Playing fast is one thing; playing with control is another. Use a metronome and practice exercises that isolate each finger. Practice these exercises slowly and deliberately at first and gradually increase tempo, while always focusing on control. The ring fingers and the little fingers are particularly problematic, so work on these fingers extensively.

CAUSE 2:   Poor coordination of cross fingerings and half-hole fingerings.

SOLUTION 2:   When more awkward fingerings are mixed with less awkward fingerings in technical passages, uneven finger movement within the beat often occurs. Use a metronome and practice exercises that isolate problematic combinations of fingerings. Practice these exercises slowly and deliberately at first and gradually increase tempo, while always focusing on control.

Tone Quality and Response Problems

PROBLEM: The tone is small and weak.

CAUSE 1:   Lack of sufficient air, air speed, and/or breath support.

SOLUTION 1: Use more air, increase air speed, and keep the air stream consistent. Take full breaths and practice playing long tones at all dynamic levels. Focus on maintaining a consistent air speed appropriate for each dynamic level. Practice extensively at softer dynamic levels because it is harder to maintain proper breath support at softer dynamic levels than it is at louder dynamic levels.

CAUSE 2: Embouchure too tight.

SOLUTION 2: Relax the embouchure. Think of saying "oo" and surround the reed with air. Think of increasing the size of the imaginary circle of air into the instrument. That is, use a slightly more open air stream.

CAUSE 3: Tight or closed throat.

SOLUTION 3: Relax or open the throat as if saying "ah." Saying the syllable "ah" and shifting to an "oo" syllable while exhaling will open the throat and oral cavity and keep the embouchure round.

CAUSE 4: The reed tip opening is too small

SOLUTION 4: Increase the size of the tip opening by squeezing inward on the sides of the reed, or try a different reed.

CAUSE 5: Not enough reed in the mouth.

SOLUTION 5: Take more reed in the mouth. About two-thirds of the reed should be inserted into the mouth.

PROBLEM: An unfocused tone quality.

CAUSE 1: Improper direction of the air stream.

SOLUTION 1: Direct the air stream toward the tip opening. Surround the reed with air and make sure that the embouchure formation is appropriate.

CAUSE 2: Embouchure too loose.

SOLUTION 2: Firm the mouth corners slightly while maintaining a flat chin. The lips form an "O" shape and support the reed equally from all directions. Think of decreasing the imaginary circle of air into the instrument. That is, use a slightly more focused air stream.

CAUSE 3: Reed is not centered in the mouth.

SOLUTION 3:   Use a mirror regularly to check reed placement until proper habits are formed.

CAUSE 4:   Not enough bottom lip over the teeth, making embouchure control inconsistent.

SOLUTION 4:   Put more of the lower lip over the teeth and listen for improved tone quality. Very little red (if any) should be showing at the point where the lip touches the reed.

CAUSE 5:   Reed enters the mouth at an incorrect angle.

SOLUTION 5:   Adjust the holding position so that the reed enters the mouth at a slightly upward angle, while the head stays straight. Reed angle is directly affected by instrument angle. The oboe is held at about a 40- to 45-degree angle from the body. Holding the oboe in too close or out too far will cause the reed to enter the mouth at an incorrect angle, upsetting the balance of the embouchure's pressure on the reed and negatively affecting pitch. If the reed enters at an improper angle, the embouchure's ability to support the reed properly is impaired, and the tone will be unfocused.

PROBLEM: Lack of tone control.

CAUSE 1:   Embouchure is inconsistent.

SOLUTION 1:   Form a good basic embouchure, and make sure that there is enough bottom lip over the teeth. Practice playing long tones to develop the embouchure muscles, and focus on keeping the embouchure consistent and stable at all times. Use a mirror regularly to check embouchure formation until proper habits are formed. Sometimes, a player's embouchure is unstable because the reed is too soft to provide sufficient resistance against the embouchure pressure, resulting in a "quivery" tone. Using a harder reed may help stabilize the embouchure.

CAUSE 2:   Inconsistent breath support and/or control of the air stream.

SOLUTION 2:   Practice breathing exercises with and without the oboe to help develop breath support. Practice playing long tones at all dynamic levels. Focus on maintaining a consistent air speed appropriate for each dynamic level. Practice extensively at softer dynamic levels because it is harder to maintain proper breath support at softer dynamic levels than it is at louder dynamic levels. Maintain breath support in technical passages. That is, breath support is often compromised when playing technical passages, because players tend to focus on technique at the expense of proper breath support.

CAUSE 3:   Inconsistent hand/holding/instrument/playing positions and posture.

SOLUTION 3:   Develop and follow a daily routine so that maintaining proper positions becomes habit. Make sure that the oboe is held out from the body at about a 40- to 45-degree angle. A detailed discussion of these playing basics is under Hand/Holding/Instrument/Playing Positions and Posture.

CAUSE 4:   Inconsistent throat and/or tongue positions.

SOLUTION 4:   The throat should remain open as if saying "ah," and the tongue should remain relatively flat and relaxed in the mouth when slurring and drawn back slightly (arched) in the mouth when tonguing. Unnecessary movement and tension of the throat and tongue disrupts the air stream and can affect tone control, tone quality, and pitch.

CAUSE 5:   The reed enters the mouth diagonally.

SOLUTION 5:   Make sure the oboe is centered with the lips so that the reed enters the mouth at a straight angle. Often, placing the music stand too far off to one side causes the reed to enter the mouth at a diagonal.

CAUSE 6:   The reed is turned or twisted when it enters the mouth, causing players to tilt their heads.

SOLUTION 6:   Turn the reed so that it stays parallel to the lips. Keep the head, eyes, and chin straight at all times.

PROBLEM: Lack of dynamic control.

CAUSE 1:   Insufficient control of the air stream and/or insufficient breath support throughout the dynamic range.

SOLUTION 1:   Practice playing long tones at one dynamic level over a set number of counts. When long tones can be played evenly at one dynamic level, practice playing long tones at different dynamic levels. Later, practice playing crescendi and decrescendi on long tones evenly over a set number of counts from one dynamic level to another. The softest and loudest dynamic levels can be particularly problematic. As a result, practicing at softer and louder dynamic levels is particularly important for tonal control.

CAUSE 2:   Making unnecessary embouchure adjustments when changing dynamics.

SOLUTION 2:   Keep the embouchure relatively stable and consistent regardless of the dynamic level. Exceptions include (1) in the pianissimo range, firm the embouchure slightly to compensate for the tendency of the pitch to go flat; and (2) in the fortissimo range, relax the embouchure slightly to compensate for the tendency of the pitch to go sharp.

CAUSE 3:   Using inappropriate reed strengths.

SOLUTION 3:   Use reeds that are commensurate with playing experience. Reeds that are too hard are difficult to control and tend to respond poorly or "cut out" at softer dynamic levels. Reeds that are too soft restrict the ability to play loudly.

PROBLEM: The low notes do not respond well.

CAUSE 1:   Leaks in the pads.

SOLUTION 1:   Check for leaks and replace any worn out pads.

CAUSE 2:   Reed is too hard.

SOLUTION 2:   Use a slightly softer reed for less resistance and good response in the low range.

CAUSE 3:   Not enough air and/or air stream too slow.

SOLUTION 3:   Use more air and increase air speed on the initial attacks for low notes. Once the note has responded, less air is needed to keep the tone sounding. Find a balance and adjust the air accordingly.

CAUSE 4:   Too much air and/or air stream too fast.

SOLUTION 4:   Use less air and decrease air speed. Overblowing in the low range causes the low notes to lose focus or crack and is a common problem with beginners.

CAUSE 5:   Embouchure too tight.

SOLUTION 5:   Relax the embouchure slightly in the low range. Think of using an "ah" syllable, and maintain an open throat and oral cavity. Focus for the particular note being played. As a rule, low notes do require more air than high notes.

CAUSE 6:   Oboe is being held too far from or too close to the body.

SOLUTION 6:   Hold the oboe at about a 40- to 45-degree angle from the body. Holding the oboe in too close or out too far will cause the reed to enter the mouth at an incorrect angle, upsetting the balance of the embouchure's pressure on the reed and impeding low note response.

CAUSE 7: Too much reed in the mouth.

SOLUTION 7: Insert about two-thirds of the reed into the mouth. The reed is centered in the mouth.

PROBLEM: The high notes do not respond well.

CAUSE 1: Reed is too soft.

SOLUTION 1: Move up in reed strength. The reed needs to provide enough resistance to vibrate at the higher frequencies. In addition, soft reeds "close off" more easily under embouchure pressure in the high range than do hard reeds.

CAUSE 2: Embouchure too tight.

SOLUTION 2: Relax the embouchure. Although firming the embouchure in the high range is normal, there is no need to tighten the embouchure excessively in the high range. Use the same basic embouchure in the high range that is used in the middle range, and then focus the oral cavity slightly for the particular note being played.

CAUSE 3: Overblowing.

SOLUTION 3: Focus for the note being played and use a controlled air stream. There is no need to blow harder in the high range; however, slight adjustments in the oral cavity may need to be made for certain pitches to facilitate response, tone quality, and intonation. Practice playing familiar tunes in the high range to develop control.

CAUSE 4: Not enough air and/or air stream too slow.

SOLUTION 4: Increase air stream and/or air speed. Work on breathing exercises with and without the oboe to develop better breathing techniques.

CAUSE 5: Embouchure too loose.

SOLUTION 5: Firm the embouchure slightly around the reed. For most players, very little of the red part of the lips should show when the embouchure is correctly formed.

CAUSE 6: Not using the octave keys correctly.

SOLUTION 6:   Always use the correct octave keys for the fingerings that require them. Practice using octave keys until it becomes automatic.

PROBLEM: A loud, raucous, squawky tone.

CAUSE 1:   Too much reed in the mouth.

SOLUTION 1:   Take less reed in the mouth. About two-thirds of the reed should be inserted into the mouth.

CAUSE 2:   Too much air with an unfocused embouchure.

SOLUTION 2:   Use a proper embouchure and a cold air stream for the best tone quality. Think of surrounding the reed with air as if saying "oo." It may also help to think of decreasing the imaginary circle of air into the instrument. That is, use a slightly more focused air stream. Focus the throat and oral cavity for the pitch being played.

CAUSE 3:   Improper focus of the air stream.

SOLUTION 3:   Think of blowing air through and around the tip opening. Think of surrounding the reed with air as if saying "who." Experiment with air direction until the best tone quality is achieved.

PROBLEM: A thin, pinched tone.

CAUSE 1:   Embouchure is too tight.

SOLUTION 1:   Relax the embouchure and surround the reed with cool air as if saying "oo." Let the tone quality dictate which syllable is more appropriate. Make sure the mouth corners are drawn inward rather than back and that the lower lip is not stretched too tightly over the teeth. It may be helpful to think of increasing the imaginary circle of air into the instrument. That is, use a slightly more open air stream.

CAUSE 2:   Reed is too soft.

SOLUTION 2:   Discard old reeds and/or move up in reed strength. Using reeds that are too soft causes players to "bite," resulting in a thin, pinched tone. As reeds wear out they tend to soften. A reed that is too hard may break in after being played.

CAUSE 3:   Too little reed in the mouth.

SOLUTION 3:   Take more reed in the mouth. About two-thirds of the reed should be inserted into the mouth.

CAUSE 4:   Improper focus of the air stream.

SOLUTION 4:   Direct the air stream toward the tip opening. Think of surrounding the reed with a steady stream of cold air as if saying "who," and
think of blowing the air stream through the instrument. Focusing the
air stream at too high an angle can result in a thin tone. Focusing the air
stream at too low an angle can result in a spread tone.

CAUSE 5:   Instrument is being held too close to or too far from the body,
putting excessive pressure on the reed.

SOLUTION 5:   Reposition the instrument so that the reed enters the mouth
at a slightly upward angle. The oboe should be held at a 40- to 45-degree
angle.

CAUSE 6:   Not using a sufficient amount of air and/or the air stream is too
slow.

SOLUTION 6:   Increase air speed and the amount of air being used, and
work on breathing exercises to develop proper breathing techniques.

CAUSE 7:   Tip opening in the reed is too small.

SOLUTION 7:   For a short-term fix, squeeze the reeds from the sides. The
only effective long-term solution is to get a different reed.

PROBLEM: Grunting or guttural noises can be heard during normal
play.

CAUSE 1:   Closing the throat or glottis when coughing or swallowing is
normal; however, players sometimes develop the habit of closing the throat
to stop the air and opening it to release the air, which results in a grunting
sound. Closing the throat and using it as a valve to control air flow negatively affects releases, tone quality, and pitch.

SOLUTION 1:   Maintain an open throat as if saying "ah" and learn to control the flow of the air from the diaphragm. Do not engage the throat in
any way when articulating.

PROBLEM: A reedy/buzzy tone.

CAUSE 1:   Reed is too soft.

SOLUTION 1:   Move up in reed strength. Soft reeds can sound reedy/
buzzy. Players who have played for two or three years should use medium
or medium hard reeds.

CAUSE 2:   Reed is in poor condition.

SOLUTION 2:   Use a reed that has good balance and a good cut. Also, make sure the reed has not been damaged.

CAUSE 3:   Improper focus of air stream.

SOLUTION 3:   Relax the embouchure and surround the reed with cool air. Maintain a consistent air stream. A reedy/buzzy tone can also be improved by relaxing the embouchure and opening the throat/oral cavity appropriately.

CAUSE 4:   Too much reed in the mouth.

SOLUTION 4:   Take less reed in the mouth. About two-thirds of the reed should be inserted into the mouth.

PROBLEM: An airy tone quality.

CAUSE 1:   Reed is too hard.

SOLUTION 1:   Use a softer reed. As a rule, beginners should use soft reeds (soft or medium soft), intermediate players should use medium reeds (medium soft, medium, or medium hard), and advanced players should use medium hard reeds (medium hard or hard).

CAUSE 2:   Air escaping from the mouth corners.

SOLUTION 2:   Form a proper embouchure. Air escapes from the mouth corners when the surrounding muscles are not supporting inwardly toward the reed. Letting air escape from the mouth corners can become a habit. Make sure that the mouth corners are drawn in toward the reed and that even pressure is used all the way around the reed.

CAUSE 3:   Leaks in the instrument.

SOLUTION 3:   Have a repair technician check for leaks and replace any worn out and/or leaking pads.

CAUSE 4:   The height of the pads above the tone holes is incorrect.

SOLUTION 4:   Adjust the pad height and play the instrument after each adjustment to determine if appropriate adjustments have been made. Pad height should be adjusted by a knowledgeable repair technician.

PROBLEM: The tone sounds dead and lifeless, and the pitch is flat.

CAUSE 1:   The reed is too old and/or too soft.

SOLUTION 1:   Discard the reed and use a new one. Reeds do wear out relatively quickly, even though they may still look good. As a rule, after a reed has been played on consistently for a couple of weeks, it begins to deteriorate. Visible signs of aging include a dirty or dingy look to the reed with nicks or chips in the reed tip.

PROBLEM: Squeaks/squeaking.

CAUSE 1:   Reed is too dry and/or is warped.

SOLUTION 1:   Soak the reed thoroughly before playing. To prevent reeds from drying out and warping during rehearsals, wet them periodically with the mouth or with water. During prolonged periods of resting, reeds should be soaked in water. Store reeds in a reed guard or reed case immediately after playing to help prevent warping.

CAUSE 2:   Unfocused/unstable embouchure.

SOLUTION 2:   Practice long tones to strengthen the embouchure muscles, and concentrate on eliminating unnecessary embouchure movement, especially when playing skips and leaps. The embouchure should remain relatively constant and stable at all times. Sometimes, a player's embouchure is unstable because the reed is too soft to provide sufficient resistance against the embouchure pressure, resulting in a "quivery" tone. Using a harder reed will provide the necessary resistance.

CAUSE 3:   Reed poorly constructed and/or in poor condition (cracked, chipped, unbalanced, etc.).

SOLUTION 3:   Use a good reed that has not been damaged. Although a sound can be produced on a cracked or chipped reed, such reeds do not allow the blades to close off against each other, which can cause squeaks. Store reeds in a reed guard or reed case immediately after playing to help prevent damage.

CAUSE 4:   Too much reed in the mouth.

SOLUTION 4:   Take less reed in the mouth. About two-thirds of the reed should be inserted into the mouth.

CAUSE 5:   Hitting keys unintentionally.

SOLUTION 5:   Maintain proper hand position and finger placement. Cover tone holes with the pads of the fingers. Move the fingers and hands as little as possible when moving from note to note.

CAUSE 6:   Leaks in the instrument.

SOLUTION 6:   Have a repair technician check for leaks and replace any worn out and/or leaking pads.

CAUSE 7:   Oboe out of adjustment.

SOLUTION 7:   Have the oboe adjusted so that the keys work properly. The keys work together in a precise manner to produce each tone. If the keys are not opening and closing properly, squeaks can occur. Sometimes a visual check will indicate the obvious point of the problem.

PROBLEM: Gurgling sounds on certain pitches.

CAUSE 1:   Water has accumulated in one or more of the tone holes or vent holes.

SOLUTION 1:   Remove the water by blowing a fast, narrow stream of air into the appropriate tone hole (i.e., usually the first open tone hole). Some players use cigarette paper, feathers, Q-tips, or other absorbent implements to remove water from the tone holes. Care must be taken that such implements do not scratch or damage the tone holes. During long periods of play, disassembling the instrument and swabbing it out thoroughly may be helpful.

CAUSE 2:   Poor reed.

SOLUTION 2:   Suck the excess condensation from the reed regularly. Reeds that are cracked, warped badly, worn out, or otherwise damaged, and reeds that fit improperly onto the reed well sometimes cause a gurgling sound, especially in the low range.

PROBLEM: A slightly delayed response of certain notes during slurred intervals, or the wrong pitch is sounding even though the fingering is correct.

CAUSE 1:   Pad or pads sticking. Pads absorb moisture during normal play. This moisture attracts dirt and food particles. These particles collect in and around the tone holes and on the pads (particularly in the creases), causing pads to stick. In addition, sugar from certain beverages also causes pads to stick.

SOLUTION 1:   Clean the pads and tone holes. For a quick fix, place a thin sheet of tissue paper, cigarette paper, or a dollar bill (preferably a clean one) between the sticking pad and tone hole. Close the pad lightly, and pull the paper through. Cleaning pads in this way is fairly common among advanced players. Various types of "no-stick" powder are also available.

These powders do work for a very short period of time; however, they are often quite messy, and they create more problems in the long run because they simply add to the particles already collected on the pads and inside the tone holes. Generally, powders should not be used to free sticking pads. Ultimately, the instrument may need to be taken apart and cleaned thoroughly by a repair technician, and sticking pads may need to be replaced. Players should not eat or drink (except water) while playing to avoid pad and instrument damage.

CAUSE 2: The crease in the pad is too deep, causing the pad to bind against the tone hole edge.

SOLUTION 2: Replace the pad.

CAUSE 3: The outside layer of a pad is torn, causing the pad to bind against the tone hole edge.

SOLUTION 3: Replace the pad.

CAUSE 4: A rod is bent.

SOLUTION 4: Have a repair technician straighten the rod. Bent rods can cause key mechanisms to stick. Often, players can feel a bump or hitch in the mechanism, indicating that a bent rod is the source of the problem.

CAUSE 5: A spring has come off, a spring is broken, or a spring is loose or worn out.

SOLUTION 5: Use a spring-hook tool to put springs back into place. A pencil, small screwdriver, or crochet hook can also be used to replace springs in some cases, but they are not nearly as effective. Spring-hook tools are easy to use, inexpensive, and are an excellent investment. Loose or worn springs can sometimes be tightened by reseating them and/or by bending them gently in the appropriate direction. Broken springs must be replaced.

CAUSE 6: Pivot (post) screws are loose. Pivot screws work themselves loose periodically, creating problems with the alignment of key mechanisms. The area around pivot screws can also get gummed up by accumulating dirt and other foreign materials, resulting in sticky key mechanisms.

SOLUTION 6: Clean pivot screws and surrounding areas. Place a drop of key oil on the screws and threads, and tighten the screws snugly. Placing a small amount of nail polish on screw heads and rods that frequently work themselves loose will help hold them in place.

6

Bassoon

Acoustical Properties: The acoustical and physical tonal characteristics of an instrument that affect its sound quality. Traditionally made of wood, the bassoon is a conically shaped tube closed at one end (the double reed end) and open at the other (the bell end). This construction, along with the vibration of a double reed, produces its characteristic timbre. These design characteristics result in a tone that produces a full complement of partials. The bassoon overblows the octave. That is, some of the fingerings used in the lower octave (e.g., A-natural through D-natural) will produce a note one octave higher when the instrument is overblown or when the whisper key is opened. Only the first (fundamental) and second partials are used for the majority of the normal playing range. See also Acoustical Basics, page 3; Construction and Design, page 618; Harmonics, page 32

Action: See Action, page 3

Adjusting Pitch: The process of raising or lowering the pitch of notes. A general discussion of adjusting pitch is under Intonation in chapter 1. Specific suggestions for adjusting pitch on bassoon are under Intonation in this chapter.

A-flat to B-flat Trill Key: An auxiliary key designed to facilitate trills between A-flat and B-flat. This key is below the E key (pan key) next to the F-sharp and G-sharp alternate keys and is operated by the right thumb. See also Alternate Fingerings/Alternates, page 599

Air Stream: Physically, the stream of air pushed from the lungs by the diaphragm and abdominal muscles through the trachea and oral cavity into and through a musical instrument. Although the physical nature of exhaling is basically the same for everyone, the ways the air stream is used to play particular instruments vary widely. A general discussion of the air stream and breathing is under Air

Stream and Breathing/Breath Support/Air Control in chapter 1. In addition, the effects of the air stream on pitch are under Intonation in this chapter. Specific comments regarding the bassoon air stream appear separately.

Bassoon players should surround the reed with warm air as if saying "who" or "oh" and think of pushing the air through the instrument. "Who" is most appropriate for players who need a more focused air stream, while "oh" is most appropriate for players who need a more open air stream. Considerable disagreement exists as to the appropriateness of particular syllables. Teachers and players should experiment with a variety of syllables and use what yields the best results. Ultimately, adjustments in the embouchure and the air stream are dictated by tone quality and intonation concerns.

On bassoon, the direction of the air stream changes according to range, and these changes are made in conjunction with embouchure changes. There is a direct relationship between air and embouchure. Specifically, players need to focus the air slightly upward as the scale ascends and slightly downward as the scale descends, and the embouchure must firm and loosen accordingly. The idea of focusing the air around the reed and making slight adjustments throughout the normal playing range of the instrument is a sound teaching concept on bassoon. Players should use a tuner and listen carefully to determine the appropriate adjustments in air and embouchure. See also Air Stream, page 598; Breathing/Breath Support/Air Control, page 10; Intonation, page 148

Alternate Fingerings/Alternates: Fingerings not considered standard or basic that can be used to facilitate or enhance musical performance. Alternate fingerings are most often used to minimize awkward fingerings or to improve intonation in specific musical contexts. The choice of when and which alternate fingerings to use should ultimately be determined by the musical result. That is, does using the alternate fingering improve the musicality of the performance?

Developing command of alternate fingerings is important so that players can use the most appropriate fingering in a given situation. Learning alternate fingerings can be awkward at first. Practicing patterns, passages, scales, and other exercises in which alternate fingerings can be incorporated is helpful. Practice alternate fingerings slowly and deliberately, focusing on only one or two at a time.

The alternate fingerings described in the following section are appropriate for players who are fundamentally sound. Examples of when to use these alternates are shown in Figure 6.1. When appropriate, suggestions and comments regarding alternate fingerings have been included. A complete fingering chart that includes alternate fingerings is in "Practical Tips" at the end of this chapter. See also Intonation, page 648; Technique, page 668

Examples of Alternate F♯/G♭ and Alternate G♯/A♭

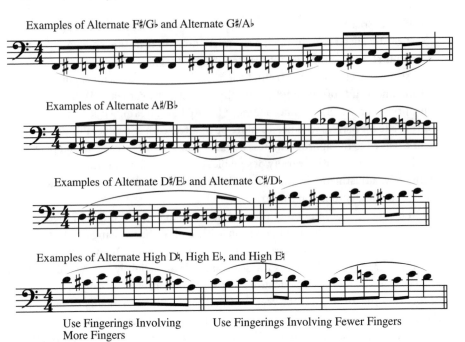

Examples of Alternate A♯/B♭

Examples of Alternate D♯/E♭ and Alternate C♯/D♭

Examples of Alternate High D♮, High E♭, and High E♮

Use Fingerings Involving   Use Fingerings Involving Fewer Fingers
More Fingers

FIGURE 6.1. *Alternate Fingerings*

RIGHT THUMB

The right thumb operates four keys on the back of the boot joint. These include: (1) the E (pan) key, (2) the F-sharp key, (3) the G-sharp, and (4) the B-flat keys. The E (pan) key is the standard fingering for E-natural below the staff; however, there are three common alternate fingerings for F-sharp, G-sharp, and B-flat. These fingerings use the right thumb and are described as follows.

1. Alternate F-sharp/G-flat (below the staff/first-line)—An alternate fingering used to avoid sliding the right thumb across thumb keys (e.g., when playing from F-sharp to A-sharp, both of which involve the right thumb). The regular fingering for F-sharp is W-1-2-3 4-5-6 plus the F-sharp key (right thumb). The alternate F-sharp fingering is W-1-2-3 4-5-6 plus the alternate F-sharp key (right-hand little finger). As a rule, when possible, players should avoid sliding the thumbs and little fingers. The same alternate fingering is used in both octaves, except that the upper octave G-flat is half-holed, and the whisper key is optional.

2. Alternate G-sharp/A-flat (first-line/first-space)—An alternate fingering used to simplify finger movement and to avoid sliding the right-hand little finger across two keys (e.g., when playing from F-natural to G-sharp, both of which involve the right-hand little finger). The regular fingering for G-sharp is W-1-2-3 4-5-6 plus the G-sharp key (right-hand little finger). The alternate G-sharp fingering is W-1-2-3 4-5-6 plus the alternate G-sharp key (right thumb). As a rule, players should avoid sliding the thumbs and little fingers whenever possible. The same alternate fingering is used in both octaves, except that the upper octave G-sharp is half-holed, and the whisper key is optional. On many newer instruments, the little-finger keys have rollers similar to those commonly found on the saxophone. These rollers make it easier to move from one key to another in the cluster. As a result, players have the option of rolling between keys (required when regular fingerings are used) or using alternate fingerings.

3. Alternate A-sharp/B-flat (first-space/second-line)—An alternate fingering used primarily in chromatic passages (e.g., when playing from A-natural to A-sharp to B-natural). The regular fingering for A-sharp is W-1-2-3 4-5 plus the A-sharp key (right thumb). The alternate A-sharp fingering is W-1-2-3 4-5-6x (the 6x key is positioned just above the regular 6 key and is operated by the right-hand ring finger). The same alternate fingering is used in both octaves, except that the whisper key is not used in the upper octave.

Left Thumb

The left thumb operates as many as eight keys alone and in combination. These main keys include the whisper key and the D, C, B, B-flat keys. The left thumb is also used to operate the following flick keys: (1) the A flick key, which is used for top-line A-natural and B-flat above the staff, (2) the C flick key (sometimes referred to as the B flick key), which is used for B-natural and C-natural above the staff), and (3) the D flick key, which is used for D-natural above the staff. The following alternate fingerings described involve the left thumb.

1. Alternate D-sharp/E-flat (third-line/third-space)—An alternate fingering used to simplify finger movement when playing between certain intervals (e.g., when playing from D-sharp to D-natural). The regular fingering for D-sharp is W-1-3. The alternate D-sharp

fingering is W-C-sharp key (both keys depressed at the same time by the left thumb) plus 1-2.

2. Alternate C-sharp/D-flat (above the staff)—An alternate fingering used to enable players to operate the flick key in certain slurred passages. The regular fingering for C-sharp involves depressing the C-sharp key and the D key simultaneously with the left thumb plus 1-2-3. When the left thumb is depressing these two keys, it cannot be used to "flick" other notes appropriately. In intervals involving notes that need to be flicked (e.g., from C-sharp to high D-natural), fingering the C-sharp 1-2-3 5-6-F key (right-hand little finger) is a better fingering because it leaves the left thumb free to operate the flick keys.

High Range Alternates

There are several alternate fingerings for notes in the high range that advanced players can learn to use in specific contexts. These alternates are included in the bassoon fingering chart in "Practical Tips" at the end of this chapter. Three of the most common high range alternates appear as follows.

1. Alternate High D-natural (above the staff)—The regular fingering for high D-natural is 1-2. This note can also be fingered 1-2 5-6-F key. This alternate can be used when playing from a note that involves several keys in the basic fingering. For example, when playing from high E-flat above the staff (1-2 5-6) to high D-natural (1-2 5-6-F key), this alternate simplifies finger movement between the two notes.

2. Alternate High E-flat (above the staff)—The regular fingering for high E-flat is 1-2 (4)-5-6. This note can also be fingered 1-2-C-sharp key. This alternate can be used when playing from a note that involves only a few keys in the basic fingering. For example, when playing from high D-natural above the staff (1-2) to high E-flat (1-2-C-sharp key), this alternate simplifies finger movement between the two notes.

3. Alternate High E-natural (above the staff)—The regular fingering for high E-natural is 1-3-D-sharp key (4)-5-6. This note can also be fingered 1-D-sharp key. This alternate can be used when playing from a note that involves only a few keys in the basic fingering. For example, when playing from high D-natural above the staff (1-2)

to high E-natural (1-D-sharp key), this alternate simplifies finger movement between the two notes.

Key Questions

Q: When should students begin using alternate fingerings?

A: Students who are fundamentally sound can begin using alternate fingerings when opportunities arise to incorporate them into rehearsals and performances. By the time students are in high school, they should be using alternate fingerings regularly.

Q: Is it better to adjust pitch by making embouchure adjustments or by using special fingerings or adding keys?

A: It depends on the musical context. Generally, if using alternate fingerings improves the musicality of a performance, then use them.

Altissimo/Extended Range: In general, a term used for the notes in the high range and/or the extreme high range of an instrument. The normal bassoon range typically extends to high C-natural. Notes higher than C-natural are commonly referred to as altissimo notes. In the standard literature for bassoon, the altissimo range is most commonly heard in advanced works. Players typically begin working on the altissimo range after they have developed excellent control and facility throughout the normal range of the instrument. Producing altissimo notes successfully involves making several adjustments including using altissimo fingerings, adjusting the embouchure formation, and changing the speed, focus, and direction of the air stream. Some suggestions for developing the altissimo range appear as follows.

Suggestions for Developing the Altissimo Range

1. Work on altissimo after developing a good, consistent tone quality throughout the normal range of the instrument.
2. Use a slightly harder reed than normal.
3. Try a variety of altissimo fingerings when possible and choose the best fingering for the instrument.
4. Embouchure/Oral Cavity Suggestions
   A. Put slightly more reed in the mouth.
   B. Firm the embouchure, decreasing the aperture size overall.
   C. Pull the lips back slightly.

D. Experiment with different oral cavity and/or throat positions by using a variety of syllables. For example, arch and pull the tongue back slightly as if saying "ee" when ascending.

5. Air Stream Comments/Suggestions
   A. Move the air faster than in the normal range.
   B. Focus the air stream as if saying "ee."
   C. Focus the air stream on a narrow plane; faster air speed is essential to play in the altissimo range.

6. Start with high C-natural (normal range) and work up to the altissimo notes one note at a time.

7. When first working on altissimo, use breath attacks and slur from one note to the next. Once control is gained, try tonguing the notes. Make sure that the tongue is light and quick; it should disrupt the air stream minimally.

Key Questions

Q: Do high school students really need to have control over the altissimo range?

A: No. Very few pieces appropriate for high school instrumental music programs include the altissimo range. In addition, working on the altissimo range too soon can foster bad habits such as biting and overblowing.

Q: When should students begin learning altissimo?

A: Advanced students who are fundamentally sound can begin working on the altissimo range at the high school level, preferably under the guidance of a knowledgeable teacher.

Anchor Tonguing: See Anchor Tonguing, page 6

Articulated Keys: Keys that automatically open or close more than one tone hole by design. Despite having a complicated key system, the bassoon actually has fewer true articulated keys than other woodwind instruments; most of the bassoon's keys open and close only one tone hole. However, the bassoon does have some articulated keys. For example, when the E (pan) key is depressed, the whisper key closes automatically. As a result, players do not have to use the whisper key below low F-natural (i.e., from low E-natural downward). Articulated keys are designed to improve technique.

Articulation: See Articulation/Articulative Styles, page 6

Arundo Donax: See Cane/Cane Color, page 614

Assembly: The manner in which an instrument is put together before being played. Proper assembly is important to playability, instrument care, and maintenance. Teaching students to carefully assemble their instruments using a defined assembly procedure can help significantly reduce wear and tear on the instrument. The bassoon can be assembled efficiently and safely using the steps listed here. Figures 6.2 and 6.3 can be used to guide the assembly process. See also Hand/Holding/Instrument Playing Positions and Posture, page 634

1. The bassoon should be assembled while standing (when the case is securely resting on a chair or table) or while kneeling (when the case is sitting on the floor). The instrument is too big, too heavy, and too cumbersome to be laid across the lap and assembled.

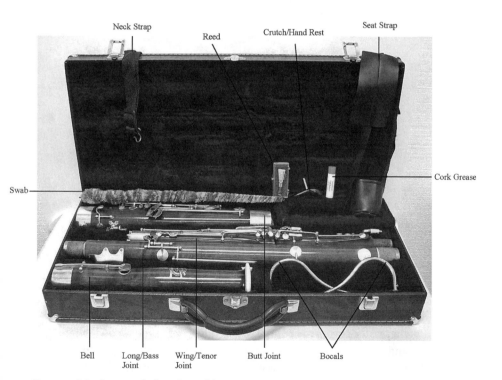

FIGURE 6.2. *Bassoon before Assembly*

FIGURE 6.3. *Bassoon Assembled*

2. Before handling the bassoon, place the reed in a cup of water so
   that water covers the entire lay and tube (i.e., to the second wire)
   and soak thoroughly for about five minutes. The wrapping does
   not need to be soaked; however, many players immerse the entire
   reed in water.

3. If the corks feel dry, apply cork grease to them before continuing with the assembly process. Rub the cork grease into the cork with the thumb and index finger. If the corks are new, it may be necessary to apply cork grease every time the instrument is assembled for the first few weeks. As the corks become conditioned, they will not need to be greased as often.

4. Grasp the boot joint with the right hand, making sure that the smaller opening is positioned to the right. Rest the boot joint (holes up) in the bottom of the case while holding the joint securely with the right hand.

5. Grasp the wing (tenor) joint with the left hand (thumb in the curved groove below key cluster) and insert the joint into the smaller opening of the boot joint with a back-and-forth twisting motion. Make sure that the bridge key is aligned properly and that the curved groove is aligned with the larger hole in the boot.

6. Grasping the long (bass) joint with the left hand (make sure that the finger holes are away from you and the thumb keys are toward you), insert the joint into the larger hole in the boot joint with a back-and-forth twisting motion. Lock the two joints together with the joint lock. The proper position of the butt joint in comparison with the tenor and bass joints is shown in figure 6.4.

7. Grasp the bell with the left hand so that the tenon is raised (depress the key mechanism) and insert the bell into the long joint with a back-and-forth twisting motion. Make sure the bridge keys are aligned properly as shown in figure 6.5.

8. Attach the hand rest (crutch) as shown in figure 6.6 and adjust its height according to hand size. When in the playing position, the finger pads should be in a position to cover the tone holes comfortably. Some players prefer to have the "ball" side up, whereas others prefer to have the "ball" side down. Players can choose the position that feels more comfortable.

9. Grasp the bocal between the thumb and index finger just above the cork (this positioning will not bend the bocal), and insert the bocal into the wing (tenor) joint with a back-and-forth twisting motion so that the vent hole can be closed by the whisper key pad. The proper bocal position is shown in figure 6.7. Be especially careful

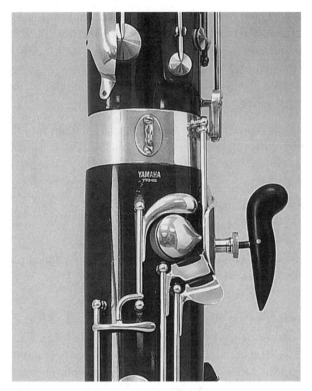

FIGURE 6.4. *Boot Joint Alignment*

not to damage the whisper key mechanism extending upward from the wing joint when inserting the bocal into the wing joint.

10. Place the reed onto the bocal with a back-and-forth twisting motion until it stops. The blades of the reed should be positioned parallel with the teeth and floor. Although double reeds do not technically have a top and a bottom blade, experienced players often develop a preference for having a particular blade on top, depending on how a reed sounds and responds.

Attacks: A detailed discussion of attacks is under Attacks in chapter 1. See also Releases/Cutoffs, page 56; Tonguing, page 71

Back Pressure: Air pressure that builds up inside the oral cavity and lungs during normal play. Although players of all wind instruments experience back

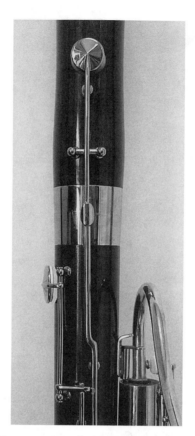

FIGURE 6.5. *Bell/Bridge Key Alignment*

pressure to a degree, back pressure is particularly common on double reed instruments because the tip opening or aperture of the reeds is so small. In the course of normal playing, players use much more air than can possibly go through the tip opening, causing the excess air to back up inside the oral cavity. As a result, players often find themselves struggling to get rid of excess air. Although nothing can totally eliminate back pressure, playing on good reeds, developing proper breathing habits, learning to use air efficiently, and phrasing properly all help lessen back pressure.

Balance and Blend Considerations: In general, bassoons do not project well and are easily masked in ensemble settings; however, bassoons typically blend well with both woodwind and brass instruments. When two or more bassoons are

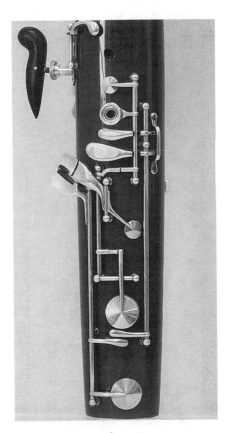

Figure 6.6. *Crutch Position*

playing in an ensemble, blend may be improved by using the same type of instrument and/or reed.

In a typical wind band with fifty to sixty players, one or two bassoons are often recommended as a good number for balance considerations. The number of bassoon players in any wind group depends largely on the number of instruments available, the type of sound desired, and the strength of bassoon players in the program.

Beats: See Beats, page 10

Bell Tones: See Bell Tones, page 10

Binding: Also called "wrapping," the string wrapped around the tube below the second wire of a bassoon reed. On modern bassoon reeds, the binding

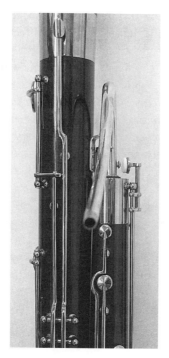

Figure 6.7. *Whisper Key Pad Alignment*

covers the third wire of the reed with a Turk's Head knot. See Reeds, Double, page 531

Blanks, Reed: See Reed Blanks, page 518

Body/Tube: The round tube-shaped part of a double reed that extends from the heel end of the reed just past the first wire where the reed begins to be shaped.

Bocal: The curved, conically shaped metal tube that fits into the wing (tenor) joint and onto which the reed is placed. Because of the bassoon's large size and the extremely short distance the bocal can be moved before the pad no longer covers the whisper key, only very slight adjustments in pitch can be made by pulling out the bocal. That is, the bocal cannot be pulled out or pushed in to sharpen or flatten the pitch to any significant degree. The bocal is inserted all the way into the bassoon, and its length (as well as the reed length) ultimately determines the overall pitch of the instrument. Bocals are available in a variety of lengths to accommodate pitch and tone quality concerns. Bocals are generally numbered 0 through 4, with 0 being the shortest. There is a direct relationship between the length of a bocal and pitch. Specifically, shorter bocals sharpen the pitch, while longer bocals flatten the pitch. Many bassoons come with two bocals, typically a number 1 and a number 2 as shown in figures 6.8 and 6.9; however, it is common for advanced players to have several bocals.

In a sense, bocals are to bassoon players what barrels are to clarinetists or necks are to saxophonists. Bocals affect virtually every aspect of bassoon playing, including pitch, tone quality, and response. In addition, a particular bocal may play better in one range than it does in another, or better on one instrument than another. For example, many professional players use a very specific bocal to play in the extreme altissimo range.

Bocal design, length, and numbering systems are not always consistent from one manufacturer to the next. Two number 2 bocals made by different companies may play quite differently when played on the same instrument. For example, bocals made by Fox tend to be one number off from the norm. That is, a number 3 Fox bocal is equivalent to most other number 2 bocals. Some systems for delineating bocals also use letters in conjunction with the traditional numbers. The letters typically provide information regarding the type of metal from which the bocal is made, the thickness of the metal, and/or the bocal model.

FIGURE 6.8. *Bassoon Bocal*

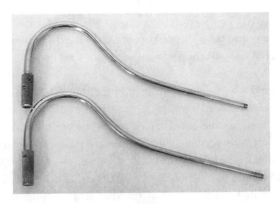

FIGURE 6.9. *Bassoon Bocals*

Key Questions

Q: Are there standard bocals that are appropriate for young students?

A: Yes. The Heckel 2CC and the Fox 3CVC are excellent choices for most bassoonists; however, bocals should be tried first to determine whether they are appropriate for the individual player.

Bocal Receiver: The part of the tenor joint into which the bocal is inserted.

Bocal/Reed Angle: The reed/bocal enters the mouth almost straight on or at a slightly downward angle. Adjust the seat and/or neck strap to bring the bocal to the mouth and avoid raising or lowering the head, or craning the neck forward to reach the reed.

Bore, Instrument: In general, a term used to describe the inside shape and dimensions of an instrument's tube. The bassoon has a conical bore. See also Acoustical Properties, page 598; Conical, page 618; Cylindrical, page 622

Break: The point at which there is a register shift on an instrument. Typically, a break involves moving from an open fingering (with few tone holes closed) to a closed fingering (with most tone holes closed), and usually involves a vent key, such as an octave key or register key. The bassoon has two breaks. The first break occurs on the three G's (G-flat, G-natural, and G-sharp). That is, when players play from a note below G-flat to one of the three G's, they are playing across the first break. The first break is a true break in that the fingering for the F-natural below the break involves virtually no fingers (except the whisper key), and the fingerings for the three G's involve most of the fingers. Part of the challenge with this break is that the three G's involve the half-hole technique, where the left-hand index finger (1) covers only half of the tone hole. Another break occurs at top-line A-natural because this is the first note played with the whisper key open. It is not necessarily a true break, but rather a break in terms of instrument response. Pitches over both breaks require a vent hole for proper response. Not venting these pitches can cause them to crack.

The term "break" is also used to describe the manner in which octave keys, register keys, or flick keys function to produce the higher partial. That is, all of these keys work by disrupting or breaking the air column at strategic locations along the instrument tube. It is this disruption that causes the upper register to respond appropriately. See also Crossing the Break, page 619; Technique, page 668

Breathing/Breath Support/Air Control: See Breathing/Breath Support/Air Control, page 10; Circular Breathing, page 23

Buffet (French) System Bassoon: The Buffet system bassoon evolved as a result of several small improvements to key work over time. Buffet system bassoons differ from Heckel system bassoons in several respects. Buffet system bassoons have: (1) narrower bores, (2) different key work, (3) greater ease of response in the high register, and (4) a more distinctive "reedier" tone quality. Buffet system bassoons are common in some European counties, including France, Italy, and Spain, but are rarely played in the United States. See also Heckel (German) System Bassoon, page 643

Butt, Reed: A term sometimes used for the bottom end or heel of bassoon reed cane. See also Reeds, Double, page 531

Cane/Cane Color: The material from which a reed is constructed, and the color, tint, or cast of a particular reed. A detailed discussion of cane is under Reeds, Double, in chapter 5. See also Reeds, Double, page 531

Care and Maintenance: Taking proper care of the bassoon is essential for achieving high performance levels. Most of the following maintenance suggestions are relevant to secondary school students, and many of them simply involve establishing a daily routine. See also Care and Maintenance Accessories, page 23

Routine Maintenance

1. Assemble and disassemble the bassoon properly each day.

2. Grease the corks regularly so that excess pressure can be avoided during the assembly/disassembly processes.

3. Maintain proper hand/holding/instrument position while playing. When resting, hold the bassoon in a safe position. The basic resting position is to lay the instrument across the lap with the tone holes up.

4. Carry the instrument securely in an upright position to minimize the chance of banging the instrument into music stands, chairs, or other instruments. Advanced players often remove the bocal and reed when carrying the instrument.

5. When placing the instrument in its case, lay the sections down gently in their proper locations, then swab out the moisture one joint at a time. Most of the moisture collects in the boot and wing joints. When swabbing the wing joint, insert and pull the swab

from the large end to the small end of each joint several times. When swabbing the boot joint, a piece of cloth attached through the eye of a cleaning rod can be inserted from the upper side and pushed down to the bottom of the boot joint and then pulled back up. This procedure should be repeated several times. Many players use an extra piece of absorbent cloth (chamois or microfiber) along with the traditional wool swabs that come with the instrument for this purpose. The bass joint and bell do not collect much moisture and do not need to be swabbed daily.

6. When playing for long periods of time, remove the bass joint and dump the excess water from the boot joint to avoid getting water in the tone holes. Occasionally, water gets into the smaller tone holes or vent holes and affects tone production. Players can blow forcefully into the tone holes to remove excess water. If this action does not work, a feather or soft pipe cleaner may be used to remove water from tone holes.

7. Rest the bassoon in an upright position. When the bassoon is rested in a horizontal or semihorizontal position, water tends to run into tone holes.

8. If water runs onto the low G-natural and G-sharp keys, dry the pads off with a piece of paper, a dollar bill, or a blotter to prolong their life. These pads usually need to be replaced more often than other pads because the excess moisture causes them to harden and lose their proper seal.

9. Wipe off the outside of the bassoon with a dry, soft cloth to remove excess moisture, fingerprints, dust, and so on.

10. Blow out excess moisture from the bocal by blowing forcefully on the cork end of the bocal. Once a week or so, the bocal should be washed with warm soapy water and wiped out with a bocal cleaner. The whisper key can be cleaned periodically as well with a toothpick or broom fiber. Avoid using metal objects to clean this vent hole because they can scratch and/or enlarge the hole, which affects the overall playability of the instrument.

11. Blow out the excess moisture from the reed by blowing gently on the heel end of the reed and/or by sucking out the excess moisture from the tip end of the reed. Store reeds in a reed guard or reed case immediately after playing to avoid damaging them.

Other Maintenance

1. Remove the dust from under the key mechanisms once every couple of weeks or so with a small, soft paintbrush.

2. If excessive key noise is heard during regular play, oil the mechanisms. As a rule, the key mechanisms should be oiled lightly once a month or so. These clacking sounds are often caused by metal-to-metal contact, which can cause excessive wear to the key mechanisms over time.

3. Every couple of months polish the wood with furniture polish or a polish made for polishing bassoons to help preserve and maintain the finish.

4. Clean the tone holes every month or so to remove excess dirt, lint, and grime that has collected over time. A toothpick or pipe cleaner can be used for this purpose. Care must be taken not to damage the tone holes and the key mechanisms during the cleaning process.

5. Oil the bore with bore oil once or twice a year. Place a small amount of oil on a soft cloth and run the cloth through each joint several times in the same manner as swabbing the instrument. Make sure that the oil does not get on the pads.

6. The bass and bell joints do not need to be oiled as often. These joints can be wiped out periodically with a clean, soft cloth.

7. Once or twice a year, wipe off the corks with a soft, clean cloth. Cork grease tends to attract dirt and creates a buildup on the corks. Some players use alcohol to clean cork, but alcohol should be used only by knowledgeable players. After cleaning the corks, apply a small amount of cork grease and rub it in well using the thumb and index finger.

Considerations

1. Buy a well-made and well-fitted case to maintain instrument condition. Some bassoon cases also include case covers, which add protection.

2. Avoid subjecting the bassoon to extreme temperature and humidity changes. Pads, corks, and felts have a tendency to loosen as the instrument contracts and expands in response to temperature and humidity. In addition, bassoons are more likely to crack or split

when exposed to extreme temperature and humidity changes, especially when cold instruments are warmed up too quickly. Never leave the instrument in an uncontrolled environment.

3. If an instrument is cold, let it warm up gradually. Do not warm up bassoons by blowing warm air into them. The sudden change in temperature could make the inside of the bassoon expand faster than the outside, causing it to crack.

4. Repair immediately any small cracks that have not gone through to the bore or that do not go through a tone hole. Larger cracks or splits, especially those that go through tone holes, may or may not be able to be repaired properly.

5. Do not clean keys with silver polish or other similar polish. Polish damages key mechanisms, ruins pads, and gums up tone holes.

6. Make allowances for humidity. As the humidity increases, cork expands; as humidity decreases, cork contracts. As a result, there will be times when the joints will feel tighter or looser than others during the assembly and disassembly processes. These differences are normal. If the cork is too tight, apply cork grease. If the cork fits too loosely, wrap Teflon tape or cigarette paper around the cork to make it fit better.

Cases, Instrument: Generally, the cases that come with most bassoons are the best cases for everyday use, especially for young players. These hard cases protect the instrument well and are designed to fit particular instruments. This design secures the instrument properly in the case and provides adequate storage for reeds, bocals, straps, and basic cleaning accessories. Aftermarket bassoon cases (gig bags) are available. Gig bags may be made of a variety of materials. Generally, the shell consists of synthetic-covered rigid plastic or wood, molded plastic, or leather. The interiors are typically constructed from lined high-density foam padding. Other features of gig bags may include shoulder straps, carrying handles, and accessory pockets. Commercially made bassoon cases are available under such brand names as Bam, Bonna, Fox, Howarth, Pro Tec, Renard, and Wiseman.

Key Questions

Q: Are all cases well constructed and designed?

A: No. Students should not purchase cases without checking them out thoroughly. Many cases do not protect instruments properly. Inspect each case for adequate padding, sturdy and secure hinges and handles, and a proper fit for the instrument. A case that does not fit the instrument well or a poorly constructed case will not adequately protect the instrument, which may result in damaged equipment.

Q: Should players keep case humidifiers in their cases?

A: Yes and no. Case humidifiers should be used in dry climates; however, they are not always necessary in humid climates. Using humidifiers unnecessarily can actually damage the instrument.

Cases, Reed: See Reed Cases/Holders, page 520

Chipping: A term used by some players to describe the process of thinning the tip of a double reed with a reed knife.

Choosing an Instrument: See Instrument Selection, page 33

Cleaning Rods: See Care and Maintenance, page 614

Clefs: Bassoon music is generally written in bass clef; however, tenor clef and treble clef are also common, especially in the high range.

Conical: A term used to describe the cone-shaped tubing often used in instrument construction that is relatively narrow on one end (the reed end) and gradually widens toward the bell. The bassoon is conical. See also Acoustical Basics, page 3; Acoustical Properties, page 598; Cylindrical, page 622

Construction and Design: The bassoon is pitched in C and is a non-transposing instrument. The contrabassoon sounds one octave lower than the bassoon. Bassoons are typically made of wood or plastic. Keys are usually nickel silver with either nickel or silver plating. Two fingering systems are available for bassoon, French and German. In the United States, the German system is overwhelmingly the most popular. Most bassoons are still handmade, and they are generally very expensive. It is standard practice in school music programs to purchase bassoons. Typically, only students who are serious about pursuing music beyond high school purchase their own bassoons.

Playing the bassoon challenges younger players for several reasons. First, the bassoon's key design is more awkward and less intuitive than other woodwind instruments. Second, players with small hands will find it difficult (if not impossible) to reach all of the keys. Third, the bassoon is heavier and more awkward to hold than other woodwind instruments.

Some student-line and intermediate instruments are designed with smaller players in mind. Not only is the key work often simplified in most student models, but the keys may be moved closer together (i.e., "short reach" bassoons) to eliminate wide stretches. Student-line and intermediate instruments are generally equipped with a crook lock. This mechanism locks the bassoon into the low register by automatically closing the whisper key when notes below the low E-natural are played. Student-line and intermediate instruments may be made of plastic or wood.

Professional instruments are typically made of wood (usually maple) and have a full complement of key work (28 keys). The extra keys are intended to enhance technical playing and tonal response. More expensive instruments are often equipped with more rollers and key guards to make playing easier and to protect the key work. In addition, lining in the bore of the boot joint designed to prevent moisture damage is available on many instruments. Virtually all new instruments are equipped with a hand rest or crutch. Inexperienced players should use a hand rest; however, experienced players may or may not use a hand rest, depending on personal preference.

Bocals are another significant design component of the bassoon. The design and length of the bocal significantly affect pitch and tone quality. Players can improve the tonal characteristics of their instruments significantly and less expensively by investing in a new bocal rather than purchasing a new instrument. Advanced players often have more than one bocal for different playing situations. Many bassoons come with two bocals of different lengths so that the pitch of the instrument can be adjusted without changing the reed. The choice of bocals is a matter of personal preference.

Although bassoons do not have mouthpieces, the quality and construction of the reed greatly affect the tonal characteristics and pitch of a bassoon. Most advanced players make their own reeds or finish reed blanks, but some choose to modify commercial reeds. Finding a good fit between the reed, the bocal, the instrument, and the player is critical to proper tonal and technical development. See also Acoustical Basics, page 3; Acoustical Properties, page 598; Reeds, Double, page 531

Contrabassoon: See Instrument Family and Playing Considerations, page 645

Crossing the Break: Technically, playing from any note below fourth-space G-flat to fourth-space G-flat or above is crossing the break; however, crossing the break usually refers to performing intervals close in proximity to fourth-space G-flat. For example, going from fourth-line F-natural to G-flat, third-space E-natural to G-flat, E-natural to G-flat, E-natural to G-natural, third-line D-sharp to G-flat, D-sharp to G-natural, and so on is commonly referred to as "crossing the break." Crossing the break can be problematic on the bassoon because players are required to play from an open note (where few keys are depressed) to a closed note (where most keys are depressed). These intervals require precise coordination of hands and fingers. In addition, crossing the break involves moving to a fingering that requires a half-hole on the left-hand index finger. Preparing the right hand simplifies the problems inherent in crossing the break, while causing only slight changes in tone quality and intonation. Another break occurs at top-line A-natural because this is the first note played with the whisper key open (i.e., vented by opening up a small hole in the bocal). It is not necessarily a true break, but is considered a break in terms of instrument response. Both breaks require a vent hole to help pitches respond, and not venting these pitches properly causes them to break or crack badly. Suggestions for crossing the break and preparing the right hand appear in the following list. See also Alternate Fingerings/Alternates, page 599; Break, page 613; Technique, page 668

Preparing the Right Hand/Suggestions for Crossing the Break

1. When playing intervals back and forth across the break, the appropriate fingers can be left down. For example, when playing from one of the three G's to F-natural and back to one of the three G's, the right-hand fingers (4-5-6) can be left down when playing the F-natural.

Crossing the Break: Other Problematic Intervals

1. Playing across the break from F-natural to A-natural and above can also be problematic because these notes require venting the whisper key. Because preparing the right hand is not a practical option with these intervals, it is important to maintain proper hand position and to practice precise finger coordination. Common examples of crossing the break appear in figure 6.10.

Teaching Tips for Crossing the Break

1. Make sure students keep their fingers close to the keys and in the ready position at all times. Proper finger position will improve finger coordination.

2. Practice playing intervals around the break slowly at first, and work on one interval at a time.

Prepare the right hand by depressing the appropriate right-hand keys on the lower note in each grouping

FIGURE 6.10. *Crossing the Break*

3. When learning to play these intervals, have students slur across the break. Although tonguing each note can improve response, it can also mask problems with finger coordination. Students will often make changes in air, embouchure, throat, and oral cavity to compensate for poor finger coordination when playing across the break. Such compensations are unnecessary and detrimental to technical development. In addition, maintaining a steady air stream and a consistent embouchure when playing across the break is essential.

Crow/Double Crow: The characteristic buzzing sound produced when double reed players play or blow on the reed alone. After soaking the reed thoroughly for about five minutes, the reed's ability to produce a crow or double crow can be tested. Most good reeds produce these sounds when players blow into or play on the reed alone. Although the terms are often used interchangeably, a crow contains only one pitch, and a double crow contains two. To produce a crow, players should put the tip of the reed in the mouth and blow gently until a tone (crow) is produced. To produce a double crow, players should place the reed in the mouth almost to the first wire, blow gently at first without much lip pressure, and then increase air speed until the reed "crows." A good double crow is one that contains both a high and a low pitch. Many bassoon players tune the pitch of the crow to a concert E-flat. Occasionally, players use the term "cackle" to describe the sound produced by the reed alone.

Cut: A term sometimes used to describe the manner in which double reed blanks are prescraped, particularly in the tip and channel areas. Some players use "cut" as a general term to describe the manner in which double reeds are scraped and trimmed in the reed-making process. The term is more commonly associated with the U-shaped area of a single reed from where the bark has been removed. See also Reeds, Double, page 531

Cutting Block: Typically a small, round block of plastic or wood used in double reed making. A cutting block is a must in any reed-making kit. It provides a raised, even surface for clipping the tip of the reed. See also Reed Making and Adjustment, page 521

Cylindrical: A term used to describe the cylinder-shaped tubing often used in instrument construction. Unlike conical tubing, which is relatively narrow on one end and gradually widens toward the other, cylindrical tubing remains the same diameter along the entire length of tubing. Bassoon bores are slightly conical, not cylindrical. See also Acoustical Basics, page 3; Acoustical Properties, page 598; Conical, page 618

D Speaker Key: A key used to extend the bassoon's range. The D key is above the C speaker key on the wing joint and is operated by the left thumb. The D key enhances a player's ability to slur up to high D-natural and E-flat, and it facilitates the response of notes above high C-natural. At one time, the high D speaker key was largely an optional key, and many professionals had this key added to their instruments. Today, it is a standard key on most bassoons.

Dial Indicator: A tool used by some double reed makers to determine the thickness of various areas of a reed to aid in making or duplicating reeds. See also Reed Making and Adjustment, page 521

Diaphragm: See Breathing/Breath Support/Air Control, page 10; Diaphragm, page 26

Dizziness/Lightheadedness: See Dizziness/Lightheadedness, page 26

Double Bassoon: Another name for the contrabassoon. See Instrument Family and Playing Considerations, page 645

Double Crow: See Crow/Double Crow, page 621

Double Reeds: See Reeds, Double, page 531

Double-Tonguing: A technique that enables performers to tongue duple patterns rapidly. See also Multiple-Tonguing, page 52

Doubling Considerations: Bassoon players are sometimes required to double on contrabassoon. The contrabassoon sounds one octave lower than the bassoon. It also uses a much larger reed, and its keys/tone holes are spaced farther apart than they are on bassoon. Playing the contrabassoon requires more air and a more open throat/oral cavity than does playing the bassoon. Players also have to adjust their hand positions to accommodate the wider spacing of the keys/tone holes. See also Instrument Family and Playing Considerations, page 645

Dutch Rush: Also called reed rush, horsetail, file grass, and shave grass, a natural fiber that can be used to smooth cane and to remove small amounts of cane in the reed making process. See Reed Making and Adjustment, page 521

Dynamic Considerations: See Dynamic Considerations, page 26; Intonation, page 648

E Speaker Key: An optional key found on some professional model bassoons used to extend range. The E key is above the D speaker key on the wing joint and is operated by the left thumb. The E key enhances a player's ability to play high E-natural. Although advanced players prefer having the high E key, it is not needed for high school and most college playing.

Embouchure: The basic bassoon embouchure is relatively easy to form; however, developing an even tone quality throughout the range of the bassoon and controlling intonation are challenging. These challenges, coupled with the instrument's size and relatively awkward fingering system, make the bassoon unsuitable for most beginners. Players often start on another instrument and switch to bassoon after they have gained some experience. Therefore, most players will have the additional challenge of "unlearning" embouchure habits from another instrument while learning the bassoon embouchure. In practical terms, these old habits will likely result in an embouchure that is too tight and pinched, because the bassoon requires a more relaxed, rounded embouchure than other woodwind instruments.

Although the same basic embouchure is used throughout the middle range, embouchure adjustments are necessary in the lower and upper ranges. As a general rule, the embouchure is more relaxed in the low range and firmer in the high range. In addition, the jaw is dropped down and back farther in the very low range. Playing with an even tone quality and playing in tune throughout the range requires more embouchure and air adjustments on bassoon than on other wind instruments. The steps for forming a fundamentally sound bassoon embouchure are described in the following list. Proper embouchures are shown in figures 6.11 through 6.14. See also Instrument Family and Playing Considerations, page 645

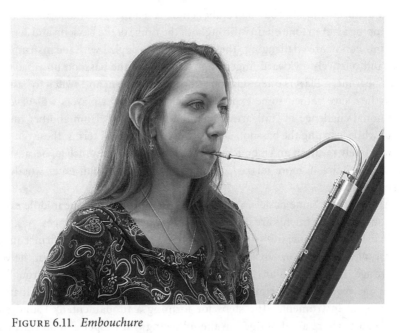

Figure 6.11. *Embouchure*

FIGURE 6.12. *Embouchure in the Low Range*

FIGURE 6.13. *Embouchure the Middle Range*

FIGURE 6.14. *Embouchure in the High Range*

1. Separate the lips slightly by lowering the jaw. Bring the jaw down and back, forming an overbite. The overbite formation is essential to achieving a good bassoon tone quality and is unique to the bassoon. Some teachers refer to this formation as an "offset" embouchure. Sometimes, saying the syllable "ah" and then rounding the embouchure into the syllable "oh" helps players achieve proper placement of the jaw and lips.

2. Rest the tip of the reed on the center of the lower lip.

3. Close the lips lightly and roll the lips inward over the teeth so that both the upper and the lower lips cushion and support the reed. Allow the reed to be drawn into the mouth as the lips are rolled over the teeth. Most of the reed is inserted into the mouth, so that the upper lip is almost touching the wire. The bottom lip is slightly farther back on the reed (bottom blade) than the upper lip (top blade) when the embouchure is properly formed.

4. Position the lips as if saying "oh." This position enables the lips to seal around the reed in a drawstring manner. The reed is supported equally in all directions. As a rule, very little or none of the

red part of the lips should be visible; however, because the size and shape of players' lips vary, the amount of red showing varies from player to player. Generally, a player with thin lips will have less red showing than will a player with thick lips.

5. Avoid bunching the chin and puffing the cheeks. Remember, the jaw will be drawn back and downward in an overbite formation.

Key Questions

Q: How does the bassoon embouchure compare to the oboe embouchure?

A: The bassoon embouchure is much looser. Generally, a little more of the top lip is visible with a bassoon embouchure, but virtually none of the red part of the bottom lip is visible. In this regard, the bassoon embouchure more closely resembles a saxophone embouchure. In addition, more embouchure changes are required on bassoon throughout the entire range than on oboe, or on any other woodwind instrument for that matter. The ear and embouchure must be trained to make proper adjustments.

Q: How much pressure should the teeth exert on the lips?

A: A small amount. Most of the pressure on the reed is applied and supported by the facial muscles. The idea of surrounding the reed with equal pressure from all sides is a sound teaching concept. Teachers often use the analogy of a drawstring to explain the bassoon embouchure.

Q: How much of the reed should be inserted into the mouth?

A: Whatever amount yields the best tone quality and intonation. The top lip should almost touch the first wire.

Q: What can be done to strengthen the embouchure?

A: Strengthen the embouchure muscles by practicing long tones and long tone exercises regularly and by extending practice time gradually over a period of weeks. Also, avoid excessively long practice sessions. Distributed practice is more effective than massed practice.

Teaching Tips for Embouchure Formation

1. The bassoon embouchure should remain basically the same throughout the middle register. Slight embouchure adjustments

need to be made as the range expands upward and downward. Larger adjustments are required in the low and high ranges.

2. A "jawing" effect is very common on bassoon. Teachers should see very little jaw movement. Regular or excessive jaw movement often indicates that the embouchure tension is incorrect (generally, it is too tight). Excess jaw movement is detrimental to tone quality, intonation, articulation, and technique.

3. The idea of applying equal pressure all around the reed, sometimes called the drawstring effect, is a sound teaching concept because it enables students to understand the need for a round embouchure.

4. Students with moderate to severe underbites may face significant challenges with the bassoon embouchure, which requires an overbite formation.

5. Students can use a mirror to check their embouchure formations and placement of the reed. Using a mirror regularly in the beginning stages will help students develop proper playing habits.

End Pin/Spike: An adjustable metal rod attached to the instrument and designed to help support the weight of the instrument. End pins are standard on most contrabassoons; however, even with end pins, players must still balance the instrument. Contrabassoon stands designed to support the entire weight of the instrument may be more appropriate for young players and are an alternative to balancing the instrument on an end pin.

Endurance/Stamina: See Endurance/Stamina, page 28

Exhalation/Exhaling: See Breathing/Breath Support/Air Control, page 10

Extended/Contemporary Techniques: In general, ways of producing sounds on an instrument that are not traditionally characteristic of the instrument or not typically called for in standard literature. A detailed discussion of these techniques is found under Extended/Contemporary Techniques in chapter 1. See also Extended/Contemporary Techniques, page 29

Extension: A device inserted into the bell of the bassoon that extends the range of the bassoon downward, usually to a low A-natural. The replacement bell extension or "A bell" enables players to play all of the notes in the low range (including low B-flat) with better intonation than do options that do not include a bell extension (e.g., alternate fingerings or embouchure adjustments).

Family: See Instrument Family and Playing Considerations, page 645

Files: A variety of files can be used to shape and finish bassoon reeds. Flat files are typically used for large-scale shaping, and thin needle files are typically used for finishing work. Needle files are available in a variety of shapes, including squares, rounds, and half rounds. Some files have a blunt tip, and others have a pointed tip. The choice of files depends on what adjustments need to be made and on the experience and needs of the reed maker. See Reed Making and Adjustment, page 521

First Wire: See Reeds, Double, page 531

Fish Skin: A material sometimes used as a quick fix to prevent air from leaking out of the sides of the reed. Fish skin is wrapped around the reed to help seal the area that is leaking. Many players use Teflon tape (also called plumbers tape) instead of fish skin. Teflon tape is an inexpensive and readily available alternative to fish skin and can be found at any hardware store.

Flick Keys/Flicker Keys/Speaker Keys/Flip Keys/Flicking: Keys depressed and released quickly in a "flicking" motion to facilitate the response of the notes between top-line A-natural and high D-natural above the staff. The flick keys are on the wing (tenor) joint and are operated by the left thumb. The acoustical function of the bassoon's flick keys is similar to the function of the octave keys on saxophone and oboe or to the register key on clarinet in that all of these keys break or disrupt the air column in strategic locations along the instrument tube. It is this break that causes the upper register notes to respond appropriately. On bassoon, the notes in the middle register from fourth-space G-flat to D-natural above the staff use the same basic fingerings as the notes one octave lower. Using the half-hole technique helps the three G's (G-flat, G-natural, and G-sharp) respond in the appropriate octave, but does not help the response of the notes from A-natural to D-natural. As a result, flick keys are used to help these notes respond cleanly in the appropriate octave. In addition to facilitating octave jumps, flick keys are vital to improving the response of these notes in slurred passages involving other intervals. It should also be mentioned that high E-flat also uses a flick key; however, the fingering for this E-flat is not the same as the fingering for E-flat one octave lower. For this reason, the range of pitches from A-natural to D-natural is commonly considered to be the flick key range.

Key Questions

Q: Should my students be using flick keys, or are they optional?

FIGURE 6.15. *Flick Key Examples*

A: Using flick keys is a standard practice in bassoon playing and should not be considered optional. Your students should be using flick keys, especially when slurring up to the pitches between high A-natural and high D-natural. Some players use flick keys only when executing slurred ascending intervals to these pitches, whereas others use flick keys in virtually every situation involving these pitches. Using flick keys whenever possible helps these pitches respond with clarity and precision.

Q: When should students begin using the flick keys?

A: When the music contains intervals (especially slurs) to A-natural, B-flat, B-natural, C-natural, D-natural, or E-flat (e.g., E-natural to A-natural; F-natural to B-flat; G-natural to C-natural).

Q: How many flick keys are there, and when should they be used?

A: There are four flick keys: A-natural, C-natural, D-natural, and E-flat (the C-sharp key). Flick keys should be used any time a player is ascending to A-natural, B-flat, B-natural, C-natural, D-natural, or E-flat. Examples of when to use flick keys are shown in figure 6.15.

Q: Which flick keys are used for which notes?

A: For A-natural and B-flat, use the A flick key. Sometimes, the C flick key may actually make the B-flat respond better and/or be better in tune. Players can experiment to see which key works best on their instruments.

For B-natural and C-natural, use the C flick key.

For D-natural, use the D flick key (or C flick key if the bassoon has no D key).

For E-flat, use the E-flat flick key (i.e., the C-sharp key). See figure 6.16.

Q: What is the correct technique for flicking?

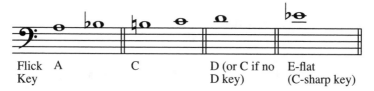

Flick   A   C   D (or C if no   E-flat
Key   D key)   (C-sharp key)

FIGURE 6.16. *Flick Keys*

A: Immediately before (approximately one count) the appropriate key is flicked, the left thumb is removed from the whisper key (the pitch will remain in the correct octave because it is already being sounded) and positioned over or slightly above the appropriate flick key. The thumb then flicks the key using either a straight-on motion or a slightly downward motion at the precise moment the fingers shift to the note to be flicked. Upward flicking movements should be avoided because they result in excess finger motion and poor hand position.

Q: What happens when flick keys are not used?

A: Generally, the upper pitches do not respond cleanly without using flick keys. Players who do not use flick keys often compensate by biting the reed and/or forcing the air stream. Such practices negatively affect tone quality and pitch. Biting can also cause the response of the upper notes to be delayed, creating problems with rhythmic accuracy and consistency.

Flutter Tonguing: A technique that involves rolling or fluttering the tongue rapidly while producing a tone. Flutter tonguing uses the same motion of the tongue that is used when pronouncing a rolling "r." Players who cannot roll their tongues may use a throat growl as a substitute.

French Reed: A style of bassoon reed that is lighter in the heart and thinner in the shoulders and tip area than is a German reed. French reeds are cut and shaped in such a way that the blades appear to be evenly shaded and are often used on French (Buffet) system bassoons. French reeds are made to sound vibrant and bright, unlike German reeds, which generally sound dark and heavy. See also German Reed, page 632; Reeds, Double, page 531

French System Bassoon: See Buffet/French System Bassoon, page 614

Fundamental: See Fundamental, page 32

German Reed: A style of bassoon reed that is heavy in the heart and thicker in the shoulders and tip area than is a French reed. The heart of a German reed can be seen and felt as a slight hump running down the middle of the blades and extending toward the edges (rails) of the blades. German reeds are cut and shaped in such a way that the heart appears as a dark, symmetrically shaded area when held up to a light. German reeds are made to sound dark and heavy, unlike French reeds, which sound relatively bright and thin. German reeds are far more common than French reeds among bassoon players because they produce a bigger, darker tone. Most commercial reeds are German reeds. See also French Reed, page 631; Reeds, Double, page 531

German System Bassoon: See Heckel (German) System Bassoon, page 643

Grain, Reed: The natural fibers in reed cane. The grain or fibers of a reed can be fine, medium, coarse, or a combination of the three. By comparing several reeds, players can easily learn to see variations in the grain. Reeds that contain predominately coarse grains typically do not respond well, feel rough on the lip, and produce an unsatisfactory tone. Reeds that contain very fine grains are often inconsistent and tend to wear out quickly. See also Reeds, Double, page 531

Half-Hole Technique: A performance technique that typically involves covering half (or part) of a tone hole with one finger. A key covered by a key/pad mechanism cannot be covered using a traditional half-hole technique, although the key can be pressed halfway down. On bassoon, the three G's (G-flat, G-natural, and G-sharp) are half-holed by only partially covering the first tone hole with the left-hand index finger. Although not common, some bassoons are now designed with a half-hole key for the first hole on the wing joint (left-hand index finger), much like the half-hole key on oboe. The purpose of this key is to enhance a player's ability to execute half-holes. This key has not proved to be any more effective than traditional techniques, however, and it limits a player's flexibility on how much of the hole can be covered. Musical examples of when to use the half-hole technique are shown in figure 6.17.

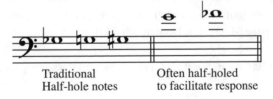

FIGURE 6.17. *Half-Hole Notes*

Key Questions

Q: Is it important to cover exactly one-half of the hole with the index finger?

A: No. The term "half-hole" is not entirely accurate or reflective because more or less than half of the hole may be covered depending on the pitch being played and the response characteristics of individual instruments. As a rule, players find that less of the hole needs to be covered for the G-flat (F-sharp) than for the G-natural, and less of the hole needs to be covered for the G-natural than for the G-sharp (A-flat). It is important to remember that instruments vary regarding how much of the hole should be covered to obtain the best musical result.

Q: How can my students determine how much of the hole to cover?

A: Through trial and error. Have students slur from F-natural to F-sharp (G-flat) several times, while covering different amounts of the hole each time. If an inappropriate amount of the hole is covered, the F-sharp will crack or break when the student tries to slur up to it from F-natural. Keep experimenting until the upper note no longer cracks. Repeat this process for G-natural (i.e., slur from F-natural to G-natural) and G-sharp (i.e., slur from F-natural to G-sharp).

Q: Does the index finger roll upward or downward when using the half-hole technique?

A: Downward.

Q: Are half-holes used for anything other than the three G's?

A: Yes. At the advanced level, using half-holes enables players to play quarter tones in contemporary literature. In addition, half-holes are sometimes used to facilitate the performance of trills and certain notes in the high range. Using half-holes in these situations is an advanced technique, usually beyond most high school players.

Teaching Tips for Half-holes

1. Students quickly learn that the three G's will respond without using half-holes, and they often choose not to half-hole these pitches. Not using the half-hole technique on the three G's is problematic. Using the half-hole technique improves tone quality,

intonation, and response. Only in fast technical passages can these pitches not be half-holed. In such passages, not using half-holes may help improve technical fluidity, and the differences in tone quality, intonation, and response will not be noticed.

2. The index finger rolls downward when using the half-hole technique; it does not slide. In addition, the index finger maintains contact with the instrument body at all times during this process.

3. Students often do not cover enough of the hole when they try to half-hole. It is important to understand that covering less than half of the hole often causes many more problems with tone quality, intonation, and response than does covering too much of the hole.

4. Make sure that students keep the whisper key closed on the three G's. Students often lift off of the whisper key when use the half-hole technique. Help students understand that they use the half-hole technique to vent a note (i.e., one of the three G's), and that when they open the whisper key at the same time, they are in effect venting the note twice. Notes do not need to be vented twice.

Hand Rest/Crutch: An adjustable device that helps maintain proper position of the right hand. A hand rest also provides a balance point or base point for the right hand, which improves technical playing. Some teachers and players consider the hand rest optional, depending on the size of a player's hands. For example, if a player has small hands, he or she may not be able to reach the tone holes/keys if a hand rest is used. In addition, some professional players do not use hand rests because they feel that they limit flexibility. However, in most cases, a hand rest should be considered a standard part of the bassoon.

Hand/Holding/Instrument/Playing Positions and Posture: Holding the bassoon properly and maintaining good hand position and playing position are key factors in developing good technique, facility, and ease of playing. In addition, maintaining proper positions will reduce muscle fatigue and help to avoid physical problems, such as carpal tunnel syndrome. Suggestions for appropriate hand/holding/instrument/playing positions and posture are listed in the following section. Basic hand position is shown in figure 6.18.

Figure 6.18. *Hand Position*

Left-Hand Position

1. The left hand is on top with the thumb centered over the whisper key at a straight angle. The thumb remains relaxed so that it can operate the thumb keys as shown in figure 6.19. The bassoon rests against the left hand at the base of the first finger.
2. The fingers curve slightly around the bassoon as if forming an open "C" or as if holding a ball. The fingers remain no more than three-eighths of an inch from the keys or tone holes.
3. Because the tone holes are spread farther apart than on other woodwind instruments, the fingers need to be spread farther apart to cover the holes properly. As a result, the fingers typically cross the instrument at a downward angle, as shown in figure 6.20. In addition, the index finger is arched slightly to allow the player to easily half-hole the three G's (G-flat, G-natural, and G-sharp) when necessary.
4. The index, middle, and ring fingers are positioned on or above the first, second, and third tone holes (1-2-3), respectively. Open tone holes are covered with the pads of the fingers rather than the tips of the fingers.

FIGURE 6.19. *Left Thumb Position*

FIGURE 6.20. *Left-Hand Position*

5. The little finger touches the D-sharp key lightly and remains ready to operate the little-finger keys (D-sharp and C-sharp keys).
6. The wrist remains virtually straight; however, a slight inward bend is acceptable.

Right-Hand Position

1. The right hand is on bottom. The height of the hand rest (or crutch) is adjusted so that the fingers can cover the tone holes comfortably, and so that the thumb can operate the thumb keys with minimal effort, as shown in figure 6.21.
2. The fingers curve slightly, and they cross the instrument at a slightly downward angle as shown in figure 6.22.
3. The right thumb rests above (or lightly touches) the E (pan) key, as shown in figure 6.23.
4. The index, middle, and ring fingers are positioned on or above the fourth, fifth, and sixth tone holes (4-5-6), respectively. Open tone holes are covered with the pads of the fingers rather than the tips of the fingers.

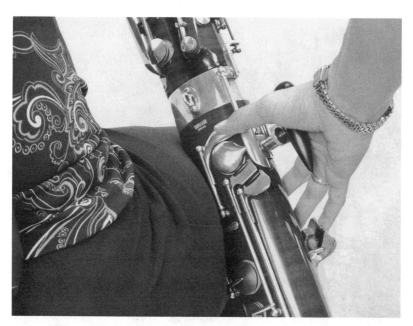

FIGURE 6.21. *Right-Hand Position on Crutch*

FIGURE 6.22. *Right-Hand Position*

FIGURE 6.23. *Right Thumb Above E (Pan) Key*

5. The little finger touches the F key lightly and remains ready to operate the little finger keys (F-natural, F-sharp, and G-sharp).
6. The wrist remains virtually straight.

Holding/Instrument Position

1. The weight of the bassoon is supported by a seat strap or a neck strap. Balance of the instrument is controlled primarily by the base of the left hand and,to a lesser degree, by the embouchure when the instrument is being played.
2. Keep the head straight and position the seat strap (or neck strap) so that the reed comes directly to the lips. Players should not have to reach up or down for the reed.
3. The bassoon rests against the right leg with the boot joint drawn back slightly so that the reed enters the mouth straight on or at a slightly upward angle.
4. The bassoon crosses the body at a diagonal, such that the player reads the music over the top (or slightly to the right) of the bocal and to the right of the wing joint. The bell is positioned slightly forward. The reed is turned slightly to the right (parallel to the floor) so that the head remains straight.
5. The elbows are held away from the body in a relaxed manner.
6. The position of the bocal can be adjusted only slightly because the whisper key must be in a position to seat properly over the vent hole. Proper playing positions are shown in figures 6.24 and 6.25. The proper playing position for the contrabassoon is shown in figure 6.26.

Posture

1. Sit up straight (but avoid being rigid or tense) with feet flat on the floor. Sit toward the right side of the chair to avoid hitting the bassoon against the chair. In the normal playing position, the B-flat and F-sharp keys on the back of the boot joint keys often rest against the side of the leg, causing the keys to get snagged on a player's clothing. In addition, the leg sometimes prevents these keys from opening properly. To prevent snagging, most instruments are equipped with a guard on these keys. These guards are especially important for younger players.

FIGURE 6.24. *Playing Position (Front View)*

2. Avoid being tense or tight in the playing position because tension impairs both the mental and physical aspects of playing the bassoon.

3. Keep the head straight and relaxed in the playing position. Bring the reed to the mouth. Do not reach for the reed.

4. Ensure proper placement of the music stand. Many posture problems result from poor placement of the music stand. The music stand should be in a position that enables each player reading from the stand to read the music comfortably and easily and to see the teacher/director while maintaining proper playing positions. The most common problem is for music stands to be too low. The most detrimental problem is for music stands to be placed too far to one side, forcing players to abandon good playing

FIGURE 6.25. *Playing Position (Side View)*

positions. Players who share music stands often experience this problem.

5. Maintain proper instrument angle to alleviate posture problems. When the instrument is too close or too far from the body, players cannot support the reed properly, resulting in poor tone quality, tone control, and intonation.

Key Questions

Q: Why are the keys/tone holes spread farther apart on bassoon?

A: Because the length of the instrument tube is so long, the tone holes need to be spaced farther apart to produce the correct pitch.

FIGURE 6.26. *Playing Position Contrabassoon*

Manufacturers have compensated for this need somewhat as a matter of practicality. A close inspection of the tones holes reveals that many of them are angled. These angles make it possible to get the appropriate notes to respond, while enabling players to reach the keys/tone holes relatively comfortably.

Teaching Tips for Hand/Holding/Instrument Playing Positions and Posture

1. The right thumb rests above (or lightly touches) the E (pan) key. Sometimes, a beginning student may have small hands and will need to rest the right thumb. It may be helpful to briefly rest the

thumb above the B-flat key on the instrument body to alleviate fatigue. By no means should this position become habit.

Harmonics: See Harmonics, page 32

Heart: The center portion of the reed blades extending from just behind the tip toward the shoulders. When held up to a light, the heart can be seen as a symmetrically shaped shaded area. Hearts are clearly visible in German but not in French reeds; however, French reeds are cut and shaped in such a way that the blades appear to be evenly shaded. The heart of a German reed can be seen and felt as a slight hump running down the middle of the blades and extending toward the edges (rails) of the blade. No such heart is apparent on a French reed. See also Reeds, Double, page 531

Heckel (German) System Bassoon: Bassoons made according to a key system designed by Carl Almenraeder (1786–1843) and Johann A. Heckel (1812–1877). Bassoons employing a German key system are by far the most common bassoons in use today and are the standard in the United States. The Heckel system bassoon differs from the Buffet (French) system bassoon (used by some European players) in several respects. The Heckel system bassoon is a larger bore instrument with more keys and an overall bigger, darker sound. See also Buffet (French) System Bassoon, page 614

Heel: A term sometimes used to describe the butt end of a reed, or the end of the cane opposite the tip. See also Reeds, Double, page 531

History: The history of the bassoon is unclear, and authors vary in their interpretations of its development. During the Middle Ages and throughout the Renaissance, double reed instruments called shawms were common. Shawms varied in size. The largest shawm, called a bass pommer or bombard, is generally considered to be one of the predecessors of the bassoon. In reality, the shawm was constructed more like an oboe or English horn. Although the shawm had both a double reed and a bocal, the main instrument body was designed from one straight tube. Another predecessor of the bassoon was the dulcian or bass curtal. Although the main instrument body was constructed from one piece, the curtal was designed with two parallel tubes or channels connected by a U-shaped bend, a design more similar to the modern-day bassoon. The bass curtal was the most common bass instrument in the late to mid-1600s. It was replaced by bassoon in the last half of the seventeenth century. Pitched in C, bassoons originally had three keys. Made of maple, the tube was cone-shaped. Because of its length (over eight feet), the tube was doubled for ease of playing. The bassoon was developed throughout the last half of the seventeenth century, and by the beginning of the eighteenth century comprised sections including the boot, the wing or tenor joint, the bass or long joint, and the bell. The bassoon continued to develop throughout the nineteenth century. In the 1850s, Charles-Joseph Sax (1791–1865) and his son Adolph Sax (1814–1894), two of the most well-known instrument makers in history, designed a bassoon with twenty-three keys. However, it is Johann A. Heckel (1812–1877) and his descendants who are most often credited with refining the bassoon and whose name, Heckel, is traditionally associated with high-quality bassoons. The bassoon steadily gained acceptance in the musical world and has been a standard part of the orchestra since the nineteenth century.

Instrument Angle: The bassoon is held such that the bell is slightly forward and to the left side of the player's body. The reed/bocal enters the mouth almost straight on, or at a slightly downward angle. When the bell is positioned too far forward or too far to the left side, the left hand is forced to support the weight of the instrument. Such extreme angles inhibit technical facility, tone quality, and pitch, and they can cause injuries if maintained over time.

> *Key Questions*
>
> Q: How does the instrument angle of the bassoon compare to the instrument angle of the oboe?
>
> A: As a rule, the bassoon reed enters the mouth at a greater angle (i.e., straighter) than the oboe reed.

Instrument Brands: Several brands of bassoons are available from which to choose. Some makers carry several models to accommodate a wide range of playing skills and budgets. Other makers carry models that are particularly suited to certain skill levels, budgets, and playing situations. Used instruments are also a good option for many players, and used instruments made by reputable manufacturers are available. When searching for an inexpensive or used instrument, beware of "off" brands and instrument models (even with reputable brands) that have not performed up to a high standard. The following list includes several reputable bassoon manufacturers. Although this list is not exhaustive, it does provide a good starting point for research. See also Instrument Selection, page 33

Bassoon Manufacturers

Amati; Fox; Heckel; Linton; Puchner; Selmer; Schreiber; and Yamaha

Instrument Family and Playing Considerations: The basic family of bassoons consists of the bassoon and contrabassoon (or double bassoon), which are shown in figures 6.27, 6.28, and 6.29.

FIGURE 6.27. *Bassoon in Instrument Stand*

FIGURE 6.28. *Bassoon*

Both the bassoon and the contrabassoon are used in bands and orchestras. The bassoon is a non-transposing instrument, and the contrabassoon sounds one octave lower than the bassoon. The main differences between the bassoon and contrabassoon are described as follows.

1. The contrabassoon is exactly twice as long as the bassoon and is typically supported by an end pin or an instrument stand.

Figure 6.29. *Contrabassoon*

2. The contrabassoon reed is much larger than the bassoon reed, requiring more air and a more open throat/oral cavity.
3. The tone holes are spaced farther apart on contrabassoon, requiring adjustments in hand position.
4. The contrabassoon has a tuning slide for overall pitch adjustments; bassoons do not have tuning slides.

5. The contrabassoon's key work is not as standardized as other instruments, and many old instruments are still in use today. As a result, a wide variety of fingerings can be used on contrabassoons. Some of these fingerings may or may not work on a particular instrument. Books that provide information on contrabassoon fingerings are listed in the reference section of this book.

Instrument Parts: See Parts, Bassoon, page 658

Instrument Position: See Hand/Holding/Instrument Playing Positions and Posture, page 634

Instrument Ranges: See Range, page 660

Instrument Selection: See Instrument Brands, page 644; Instrument Selection, page 33

Instrument Sizes: See Instrument Family and Playing Considerations, page 645

Instrument Stands: See Instrument Stands, page 39

Intonation: Generally, the degree of "in-tuneness" in a melodic and a harmonic context. In ensemble playing, the most important factors in achieving intonation accuracy are: (1) hearing intonation problems, (2) understanding what adjustments need to be made to correct intonation problems, and (3) having the skills to make the necessary adjustments. A detailed general discussion of Intonation is in chapter 1. Specific suggestions for helping players better understand the pitch tendencies of the bassoon and how to make appropriate pitch adjustments are outlined separately in this section. See also Intonation, page 41; Temperament, page 61; Tuning/Tuning Note Considerations, page 675

GENERAL COMMENTS FOR ADJUSTING PITCH

Adjusting pitch is the process of raising or lowering the pitch of notes. Comments and suggestions for adjusting pitch are outlined here.

1. Embouchure/Air Stream—The embouchure and air stream can be altered in several subtle ways to adjust or humor pitches. As

players progress, they learn to make embouchure adjustments for certain pitches as part of standard technique. Common embouchure/air stream/oral cavity adjustments are described as follows.

A. To lower or flatten the pitch, focus the air stream downward. As a rule, the farther downward the pitch is directed, the flatter the pitch will be. The air stream may be focused downward by making slight changes in the oral cavity (i.e., a slightly more open focus) and/or by making slight adjustments in embouchure (i.e., jaw lowered slightly).

B. To raise or sharpen the pitch, focus the air stream upward. As a rule, the farther upward the pitch is directed, the sharper the pitch will be. The air stream may be focused downward by making slight changes in the oral cavity (i.e., a slightly smaller focus) and/or by making slight adjustments in embouchure (i.e., jaw raised slightly).

C. As a rule, a firmer embouchure results in a sharper pitch, and a looser embouchure results in a flatter pitch. The embouchure can be firmed by increasing lip pressure around the reed and loosened by decreasing lip pressure around the reed. On bassoon, it is common to drop the jaw to help lower the pitch and to raise the jaw to help raise the pitch. Changes in embouchure tension and air speed are facilitated by thinking of using a cold or a warm air stream. A warm air stream tends to decrease air speed and relax the embouchure, which flattens the pitch. A cold air stream tends to increase air speed and firm the embouchure, which sharpens the pitch. Typically, bassoon players use a warm air stream except in the high range. In fact, the warm air stream used on bassoon in the normal range is more similar to the air stream used on the saxophone than any other instrument.

D. As a rule, only slight changes in air stream and embouchure should be made when adjusting pitch in a given range. Large-scale changes affect tone quality, control, and focus. However, on bassoon, larger adjustments in embouchure, air stream, and in the oral cavity are sometimes necessary for proper pitch placement, especially in the low and high ranges.

2. Throat/Oral Cavity—A tight, restricted throat causes the pitch to go sharp. Relax the throat as if saying "ah," and the pitch will drop.

In addition, the tone quality will improve noticeably. Changes and adjustments in the oral cavity affect both tone quality and pitch and are usually accomplished by having players think of saying certain syllables such as "oh," "oo," "ah," and "ee" in the altissimo register. The use of such syllables is effective in altering pitch and tone quality; however, be aware that using syllables often causes accompanying changes in embouchure and air flow as well. Understanding the relationships and balances between embouchure, air stream, throat, and oral cavity is important to players and teachers.

3. Alternates/Adding Keys—If slight changes in the air stream and embouchure do not bring the desired pitches in tune, adding keys to regular fingerings or using alternate fingerings may help bring certain pitches in tune. On the other hand, adding keys and using alternates to adjust pitch is not always practical. As a general rule, tonal considerations, technical considerations, and tempo largely dictate the appropriateness of such adjustments. Finally, adding keys or using alternates to adjust pitch often negates the need to make changes in air stream or embouchure.

4. Dynamics/Air Speed—Changes in dynamics/air speed affect pitch, sometimes significantly. Considerations regarding dynamics/air speed are described as follows.
   A. When playing loudly and increasing air speed, the pitch tends to go sharp. Adjust by focusing the air stream downward slightly and/or loosening the embouchure slightly. Proper air speed and control should be maintained at all times. Do not overblow.
   B. When playing softly and decreasing air speed, the pitch tends to go flat. Adjust by focusing the air stream upward slightly, focusing the oral cavity, and/or firming the embouchure slightly. Even at softer dynamic levels, the air stream must move fast enough to sustain and support the pitch. Not using enough air or using an air stream that is too slow causes the pitch to go flat.

5. Mechanical—Mechanical design characteristics that affect intonation are described as follows.

A. If the pitch is flat overall, check to make sure that the reed is pushed onto the bocal as far as it will go. As a rule, the reed should be pushed onto the bocal all the way.

B. Maintain proper pad height. If pads are too low, the pitch will be flat. If pads are too high, the pitch will be sharp. Make sure instruments are properly adjusted.

C. Check the bassoon regularly for leaks, loose and/or broken springs, and missing corks or felts. Maintaining the instrument in good repair is essential for good intonation.

6. Bocal—Because of the large size of the bassoon and the extremely short distance the bocal can be moved before the pad no longer covers the whisper key, only very slight adjustments in pitch can be made by pulling out the bocal. In addition, pulling out the bocal creates a gap in the instrument tube that some players believe affects tone quality. However, the length of the bocal affects pitch dramatically. If the pitch of a bassoon is extremely sharp or flat, players will almost certainly have to purchase another bocal. Bocals are available in a variety of lengths to accommodate pitch and tone quality concerns. There is a direct relationship between the length of a bocal and pitch. Specifically, shorter bocals sharpen the pitch, whereas longer bocals flatten the pitch. Many bassoons come with two bocals, a number 1 and a number 2; however, it is common for advanced players to have several bocals.

7. Reeds—Hard reeds tend to play sharp, especially when playing softly. In addition, players tend to firm up the embouchure to control a harder reed, which further raises pitch. Players should use a reed that provides a modest amount of resistance in the middle register. Soft reeds tend to play flat, especially when playing loudly. In situations where players try to relax and maintain a good embouchure, tone and pitch are very difficult to control because the reed does not provide enough resistance against the embouchure pressure. In situations where players "bite" too hard, the reed tip opening closes, resulting in a small, pinched tone or no tone at all.

8. Position of the Reed in the Mouth—If the reed is inserted too far into the mouth, the pitch will be sharp. If the reed is not inserted

far enough into the mouth, the pitch will be flat. When the reed is inserted properly into the mouth, the top lip should be almost touching the first wire. Players sometimes adjust pitch by making slight adjustments in the amount of reed taken in the mouth.

9. Instrument Angle—When the bassoon reed enters the mouth at too small an angle (i.e., similar to a clarinet), the tone tends to be smaller and pinched, and the pitch tends to be sharper because the pressure on the reed is increased. When the bassoon reed enters the mouth at too great of an angle (i.e., the reed comes down into the mouth) the tone tends to be out of focus or spread, and the pitch tends to be flatter because the pressure on the reed is decreased. In both instances, problems result from uneven embouchure pressure being applied to the reed. Exaggerated instrument angles in or out from the body cause a flatness in pitch because the reed is not supported properly. As a rule, the bassoon reed enters the mouth straight on or almost straight on; however, bassoon players vary in this regard. It seems that the way the reed enters the mouth varies according to one's training and experience. Some players prefer a slightly downward angle, whereas others prefer a slightly upward angle.

Tuning the Bassoon

A detailed description of how to tune the bassoon is under Tuning/Tuning Note Considerations in this chapter.

Pitch Tendencies

Pitch tendencies refers to the tendency for certain notes on an instrument to deviate from a specified standard, usually the equal tempered scale based on a reference frequency of A = 440. That is, when players talk about the pitch tendencies of their instruments, they are almost always talking about how sharp or flat certain notes are in reference to a modern, equal tempered scale. Comments and suggestions regarding pitch tendencies are outlined in the following list. A summary of these tendencies is presented in figures 6.30 and 6.31.

General Range/Register Tendencies—Flat Pitches

1. Bassoons tend to play flat in the range above the staff (between C-natural and high F-natural).

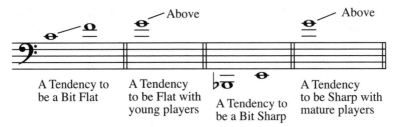

FIGURE 6.30. *Intonation Tendencies (General)*

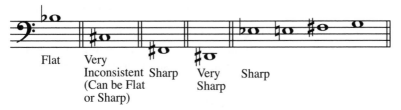

FIGURE 6.31. *Intonation Tendencies (Specific)*

2. Inexperienced players sometimes play flat in the high/altissimo register because their embouchures are not developed properly for playing in that range and because their concepts of adjusting pitch are not developed.

> Adjustment 1—Take slightly more reed into the mouth and increase air speed.
>
> Adjustment 2—Focus the air stream upward slightly.
>
> Adjustment 3—Think of using a slightly firmer "oo" syllable to help focus the oral cavity.
>
> Adjustment 4—Firm the embouchure slightly, but do not bite or pinch the reed.

General Range/Register Tendencies—Sharp Pitches

1. Bassoons tend to play sharp in the low range (between low B-flat and E-natural below the staff).

2. Experienced players sometimes play sharp in the high/altissimo register (high B-natural and above) because they tend to

overcompensate or bite the reed too much rather than adjusting air speed and focus.

> Adjustment 1—Relax the embouchure slightly (lower the jaw slightly) and open the oral cavity, but maintain embouchure focus.
>
> Adjustment 2—Use a more open syllable such as "oh" or "ah" to help lower the pitch.
>
> Adjustment 3—Focus the air stream downward slightly.
>
> Adjustment 4—Take slightly less reed in the mouth and decrease air speed slightly.

Specific Pitch Tendencies—Making Adjustments for Problem Pitches

1. B-flat above the staff tends to be flat.
2. Second-space C-sharp can be sharp or flat depending on the bassoon. Use a tuner to determine how sharp or flat C-sharp is and adjust accordingly. If flat, adjust as follows. If sharp, see the adjustments for numbers 3 through 6.

> *Adjustments for Numbers 1 and 2*
>
> > Adjustment 1—Take slightly more reed in the mouth and increase air speed.
> >
> > Adjustment 2—Focus the air stream upward slightly.
> >
> > Adjustment 3—Firm the embouchure slightly, but do not bite or pinch the reed.
> >
> > Adjustment 4—Think of using a slightly firmer "oo" syllable to help focus the oral cavity.

3. Low F-sharp below the staff tends to be sharp.
4. Low D-natural below the staff is a very sharp note.
5. Third-space E-flat and E-natural tend to be sharp.
6. Fourth-line F-sharp and top-space G-natural tend to be sharp.

> *Adjustments for Numbers 3, 4, 5, and 6*
>
> > Adjustment 1—Relax the embouchure slightly (lower the jaw slightly) and open the oral cavity, but maintain embouchure focus.
> >
> > Adjustment 2—Use a more open syllable such as "oh" or "ah" to help lower the pitch.
> >
> > Adjustment 3—Focus the air stream downward slightly.
> >
> > Adjustment 4—Take slightly less reed in the mouth

Adding Fingers to Adjust for Intonation Problems

Players can depress other keys in addition to the regular fingering to adjust pitch. An outline of basic fingering adjustments appears as follows.

1. Low D below the staff is a very sharp note. Adding the low B-flat key (left thumb) will flatten the pitch.
2. Low E-natural below the staff tends to be sharp. Adding the low C-sharp key will lower the pitch.
3. If the second-space C-sharp is flat, adding the E (Pan) Key (right thumb) to the regular fingering will raise the pitch.
4. The third-space E-flat tends to be slightly sharp, especially with a hard reed. Adding the B-flat key (right thumb) and the index finger (4) or middle finger (5) to the regular fingering will lower the pitch.
5. On top-space G-natural, adding the E-flat key or the D-flat key (with the left-hand little finger) as a resonator key will lower the pitch. This addition also helps the tone quality match the G-flat/ F-sharp better.

Using Alternate Fingerings to Adjust Intonation

It is common for players to use alternate fingerings to adjust pitch. A list of basic alternates and their typical relationships to the corresponding regular fingerings appears here.

1. The fingering for fourth-line F-sharp involving the left-hand little finger F-sharp key is generally sharper than the fingering involving the right-hand little finger F-sharp key.
2. The regular fingering for C-sharp above the staff is often sharp. Try fingering this note C-sharp key-1-2-3-B-flat key 4-5-6-F key.
3. On high-B-flat, using the C flick key rather than the A flick key may raise the pitch slightly.

Joint Lock: A mechanism designed to lock the wing joint and the bass joint together when the instrument is assembled.

Key/Pad Height: See Key/Pad Height, page 45

Knife, Reed: See Reed Knife, page 520

Lay: The scraped or shaped portion of the bassoon reed that extends from the tube (at the shoulders) to the tip. Some players refer to various portions of the lay more specifically, especially when discussing reed adjustment. These portions include the tip, channels, rails, spine, back, heart, and collar. To a large extent, the lay determines the reed's potential for a good tone quality. It is important that the lay is even, smooth, and symmetrically tapered from the center to the edges on both blades. See also Reeds, Double, page 531

Leg Strap: A strap designed to be wrapped around the leg to help support the weight of the bassoon. Because of the versatility and functionality of seat straps, very few players use leg straps today. See also Seat Strap, page 664

Lightheadedness: See Dizziness/Lightheadedness, page 26

Locking Mechanism: See Whisper/Piano Key Locking Mechanism, page 678

Low A Extension: Some bassoons are made with a longer bell joint that extends the range of the bassoon downward one half step from B-flat to A-natural. Bassoons with low A extensions are unnecessary because virtually all of the music written for high school and college playing does not contain low A-naturals.

Mandrel: A tapered metal tool for holding reeds while they are being scraped or filed. Mandrels are also used to help shape and form the reed in the finishing process. See also Reed Making and Adjustment, page 521

Multiphonics: See Extended/Contemporary Techniques, page 29

Multiple-Tonguing: See Multiple-Tonguing, page 52

Mutes: Generally, devices that alter tone quality when placed into the bells of instruments. Mutes (or virtually any soft object) inserted into the bell of the bassoon tends to have a muting effect. Mutes are rarely used and are generally effective only in the lower register.

Neck Strap: A strap positioned around the player's neck that attaches to a strap ring on the bassoon via a clip or hook. Instrument height is adjusted by sliding the strap up or down so that the reed comes naturally to the mouth. Unlike seat straps, which support the bassoon from the boot joint, neck straps are hooked to a ring closer to the middle of the instrument (above the boot joint) on the long (bass) joint as seen in figure 6.32. Neck straps can adversely affect instrument angle if not properly used and adjusted. Neck straps also put more stress on the right hand because the right hand must push against the boot joint (via the hand

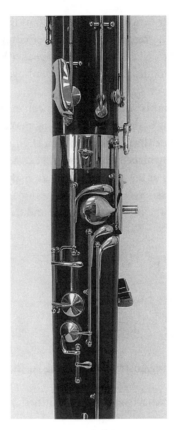

FIGURE 6.32. *Neck Strap Ring*

rest) to help balance the instrument. As a result, players who use neck straps must use a hand rest. See also Seat Strap, page 664

Octave Keys: On instruments such as the saxophone and oboe, a key mechanism that enables players to play upper octave notes. The bassoon does not have octave keys; however, the bassoon does use vent holes or keys to facilitate the response of upper octave notes. For example, the three upper octave G's (G-flat, G-natural, and G-sharp) are fingered the same as the lower octave G's except that they are half-holed. Using the half-hole technique vents these notes, which improves response. In a sense, the half-hole functions like an octave key. In addition, the notes from A-natural to D-natural use the same basic fingerings in both octaves except that the whisper key is opened in the upper octave. This vent hole helps notes respond in the upper octave and also functions like an octave key. In addition, flick keys improve the response of the upper octave notes from A-natural to D-natural. See also Flick Keys/Flicker Keys/Speaker Keys/Flip Keys/Flicking, page 629; Half-Hole Technique, page 632; Whisper Key, page 677

Optional Keys/Key Mechanisms: Keys or key mechanisms that are not standard to the essential functioning of the bassoon, but that make playing easier. Optional keys on the bassoon include the plateau key, high D, E, and F keys, E/F-sharp trill key, A-flat/B-flat trill key, whisper key locks, and extra rollers for the little finger keys. Although these keys or key mechanisms can make certain aspects of technique and pitch easier, bassoons without these optional keys are fully functional and capable of producing the full range of notes and trills. See also Construction and Design, page 618

Overblow: See Overblow, page 55

Overtones: See Overtones, page 55

Pad Height: See Key/Pad Height, page 45

Pan Key: See Hand/Holding/Instrument Playing Positions and Posture; page 634

Parts, Bassoon: The parts of a bassoon are identified in figure 6.33.

Pipe Resonances: The partials that are produced by the bore of the bassoon (including the bocal), particularly in the upper register. If the bore of the bassoon were perfectly conical, then the pipe resonances would be related by even harmonic ratios. That is, the second partial would be exactly twice the frequency of the fundamental, and the third partial would be exactly three times the frequency of the fundamental. However, the bassoon is not perfectly conical. The bassoon bore contains several modifications in shape to improve overall tuning and tone quality. In addition, the cone shape is effectively shortened at the reed end of the bocal because the reed is placed where the missing portion of the cone would be. As a result, the ratios of the pipe resonances are slightly stretched on the bassoon, with pitch discrepancies becoming very noticeable by the third partial. These pitch discrepancies necessitate the need to use seemingly arbitrary fingerings in the upper register.

Pitch Adjustment: See Intonation, page 648; Tuning/Tuning Note Considerations, page 675

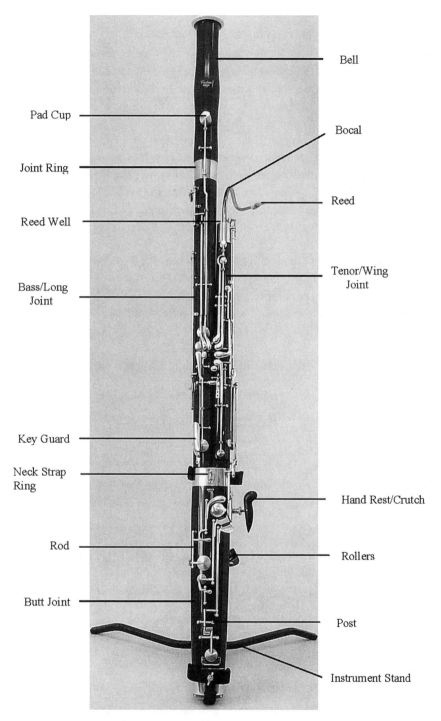

Bell

Pad Cup

Bocal

Joint Ring

Reed

Reed Well

Bass/Long
Joint

Tenor/Wing
Joint

Key Guard

Neck Strap
Ring

Hand Rest/Crutch

Rod

Rollers

Butt Joint

Post

Instrument Stand

FIGURE 6.33. *Parts of a Bassoon*

Pitch Tendencies: Generally, the tendency for any note to deviate from a specified standard, usually the equal tempered scale based on a reference frequency of A = 440. That is, when players talk about the pitch tendencies of their instruments, they are almost always talking about how sharp or flat certain notes are in reference to a modern, equal tempered scale. The term "pitch tendency" is most commonly used to refer to pitch deviations that are an inherent part of an instrument's design. In many instances, pitch tendencies are consistent on a given instrument (e.g., most clarinets or most trumpets) regardless of the make or model of the instrument. For example, most bassoons tend to play flat above the staff. The pitch tendencies of the bassoon are discussed under Intonation in this chapter. See also Intonation, page 648; Temperament, page 61; Tuning/Tuning Note Considerations, page 675

Plaque: A metal tool shaped to follow the contour of a reed that can be inserted between the two blades of a double reed to provide a solid surface on or against which the blades can be scraped or sanded. Plaques are made in a variety of shapes and sizes to accommodate a player's preferences. See also Reed Making and Adjustment, page 521

Playing Position: See Hand/Holding/Instrument/Playing Positions and Posture, page 634

Posture: See Hand/Holding/Instrument/Playing Positions and Posture, page 634

Preparing the Right Hand: See Crossing the Break, page 619

Rails, Reed: A term used by some players to describe the very narrow areas or strips of the lay that run along the edges of a reed from shoulder to tip. See also Reeds, Double, page 531

Range: In general, the distance from the lowest note to the highest note on a given instrument. In addition, players and teachers often refer to the different registers (roughly by octave) of the bassoon in terms of range: low range, middle range, and high range. The written and sounding ranges of the bassoon appear here and are summarized in figure 6.34. See also Register/Registers, page 661; Transpositions, page 675

Key Questions

Q: What ranges are recommended for elementary, junior high/middle school, and senior high students?

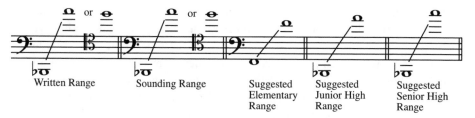

FIGURE 6.34. *Range*

A: A student's range varies according to experience and ability level. Once the fundamentals of tone production and embouchure formation are mastered, range can be extended systematically. It is important to remember that most elementary students do not start on bassoon. That is, they learn to play another instrument first and then switch to bassoon after gaining experience. For that reason, the suggested elementary range on bassoon is more demanding than on other woodwind instruments. Suggested ranges for each level are presented as follows.

Elementary: Low F-natural to high F-natural (above the staff)
Junior High: Low B-flat to high A-natural (above the staff)
Senior High: Low B-flat to high C-natural (above the staff)

Reamer: A tool designed to clean and shape the reed tube so that the reed will fit properly onto the bocal. Several types of reamers are available today and vary in the number of cutting edges and in the way they are tapered. The most important factor in choosing a reamer is that it be tapered to match the end of the bocal to ensure a proper fit. See also Reed Making and Adjustment, page 521

Reed/Bocal Angle: The reed enters the mouth almost straight on, or at a slightly upward angle. Keep the head straight and bring the reed to the mouth, making the necessary adjustments with the seat strap (or neck strap). See also Instrument Angle, page 644

Reeds: Information regarding reeds is under Reeds, Double, and other related terms in chapter 5. See Reeds, Double, page 531

Register/Registers: Groups of notes that share certain tonal characteristics usually related to pitch range, timbre, and/or manner of production. Delineating registers is somewhat arbitrary on any instrument; however, delineating registers on bassoon is particularly problematic for several reasons. First, its four-octave range is larger than most wind instruments. Second, the instrument's design makes it more difficult to produce an even tone quality throughout any given range with any degree of consistency. This fact becomes quite obvious when you watch professional players play because they seem to be adjusting air and embouchure constantly. Third, delineating registers commonly used by junior high students, senior high students, college-level players, and professional players is a subjective process that varies according to the criteria used for delineation. Nonetheless, it seems reasonable to divide the bassoon range into five registers. These registers are listed here and are notated in figure 6.35. See also Range, page 660

1. Low Register—From low B-flat to E-natural (below the staff).
2. Middle Register—From F-natural (below the staff) to fourth-line F-natural.
3. Half-Hole Register—The three G's (G-flat, G-natural, and G-sharp).
4. High Register—From high A-natural (top-line) to G-natural above the staff
5. Altissimo Register—From high G-sharp upward about one octave.

Releases/Cutoffs: See Releases/Cutoffs, page 56

Resistance: In general, the counteraction of the reed, bocal, and bassoon to the incoming air stream. The amount of resistance provided by the instrument and reed dictates the amount of air and support needed to start and maintain a steady tone. That is, the reed, bocal, and (to a lesser degree) the bassoon, all contribute to the resistance felt by the player. As a rule, smaller bocals tend to be less resistant than more open bocals; however, smaller bocals also tend to produce smaller, brighter tones. Reeds in particular affect resistance significantly. Generally, harder

FIGURE 6.35. *Register/Registers*

reeds cause more resistance than softer reeds. A certain amount of resistance is needed to maintain a steady, rich tone quality and good pitch. When reeds are too soft, the tone is thin and quivery, and pitch is difficult to control. When reeds are too hard, the tone is airy, response is poor, pitch control suffers, and players' embouchures tire quickly. Reeds need to be hard enough to push back against the embouchure pressure to create a stable tone, but not so hard that players have to fight against the reed. The appropriate reed strength is directly dependent on the ability of the player to control the reed during play. That is, players with well-developed facial muscles can control a harder reed with a larger tip opening or reed aperture than players with less-developed facial muscles.

The amount of resistance is also significantly affected by the tip opening. As a general rule, large tip openings will have more resistance than small tip openings. Players who use reeds with large tip openings will generally use softer reeds or have significantly stronger embouchure control than players who use reeds with small tip openings. See also Breathing/Breath Support/Air Control, page 10; Reeds, Double, page 531; Response, page 664

Key Questions

Q: How much resistance is ideal for different age levels?

A: Beginners should use soft or medium soft reeds because they provide less resistance, which helps produce a tone more easily. As players' embouchures develop and strengthen, harder reeds can provide the additional resistance needed to produce a warm, rich characteristic bassoon tone.

Teaching Tips Regarding Resistance/Response

1. Bassoon players need a certain amount of resistance from the reed, the bocal, and the bassoon. As their embouchures and support strengthen, the ability of the reed to push back against the supporting embouchure and create the resistance that holds the tone steady declines. The tone becomes unsteady or shaky, soft, and thin. Using a harder reed helps solve this problem. Have students move up one reed strength at a time until an acceptable balance is found.

2. As a rule, students should begin with a soft or medium soft reed. After a few months, students can move to a medium soft or medium reed. After a year or so, students can move to a medium or medium hard reed. By the end of their third or fourth year, students should

begin experimenting with reed making and adjustment under the guidance of an experienced bassoon teacher.

3. Teachers are often reluctant to have students move up in reed strength in a progressive manner. As a result, students often play with beginner-level tone qualities for too long. Slightly harder, more resistant reeds will improve tone quality and pitch control. Slightly harder reeds may feel too hard at first; however, as players' embouchures strengthen and adapt to the harder reed strength, the improvements in tone quality and pitch control will be obvious. If a new reed strength is too hard, players' embouchures will not readily adapt, and the tone will be weak and airy. In this case, adjust by using a slightly softer reed.

Resonance Keys: Keys sometimes added to regular fingerings to improve the tonal response, tone quality, and/or pitch of certain notes. See also Flick Keys/ Flicker Keys/Speaker Keys/Flip Keys/Flicking, page 629; Whisper Key, page 677

Response: The way a reed vibrates as a result of the player's air stream and embouchure. The term "response" is also used to refer to the ease with which the notes "speak" or sound. Some notes respond easier than others, depending on how much of the tube is closed and how much air speed is needed. Notes in the extreme high or low range tend not to respond as well as notes in the middle range. The quality and condition of the bassoon, the reed, the bocal, and a player's ability to control the air speed and air volume greatly affect reed response. See also Resistance, page 662

Seat Strap: A beltlike strap with a hook or ring attached to one end designed to hold and support the weight of the bassoon in the playing position. Seat straps are laid across a player's chair and then sat on by the player. In essence, it is the player's weight that helps hold the bassoon in place by not allowing the strap to move. Instrument height is adjusted by sliding the strap to the left or to the right so that the reed comes naturally to the mouth. When using seat straps, the left hand is responsible for balancing the instrument while the seat strap supports the vast majority of the instrument's weight. If players use a seat strap, they can use or not use a hand rest; however, a hand rest is virtually always used with a neck strap. Some professional players prefer not using a hand rest because they believe the right thumb has greater freedom without the hand rest. Neck straps can be used to support the bassoon, but they are not as common as seat straps, and they necessitate the need to use a hand rest. See also Neck Strap, page 656

Second Wire: The wire in front of the binding and between the first and third wires. See also Reeds, Double, page 531

Secondary Break: The bassoon has two breaks. The first (primary) break occurs on the three G's (G-flat, G-natural, and G-sharp). For example, when players play from a note below G-flat to one of the three G's, they are playing across the first break. A secondary break occurs at top-line A-natural, where players must first open the whisper key. Although this break does not require switching from closed to open fingers, it is a break in terms of instrument response. Pitches over both breaks require a vent hole for proper response. Not venting these pitches properly can cause them to crack. Examples of the secondary break are shown in figure 6.36. See also Break, page 613; Crossing the Break, page 619

Selecting an Instrument: See Instrument Brands, page 644; Instrument Selection, page 33

Short-Scrape Reed: A reed that has less bark scraped from the lay than a normal reed, typically slightly more than one-third of the portion between the tip and the first wire. A short-scrape reed leaves a great deal of bark on the blades, providing a more penetrating tone, appropriate for some musical contexts (e.g., solo playing, outdoor playing). A short-scrape reed must be soaked considerably longer than a normal reed (approximately twenty minutes in warm water) for optimal response. Most bassoon reeds are long-scrape reeds.

Shoulders: The back area of the lay toward the wire or thread. Some players refer to this area as the collar. See also Reeds, Double, page 531

Slap Tongue: A tonguing technique that produces a slapping or popping effect on the attacks. Slap tonguing is sometimes used as a special effect in both jazz and contemporary literature and is produced by pressing the tongue hard against the reed to close or nearly close the tip opening, building up air pressure, and then releasing the tongue quickly. Slap tonguing is more common on single reed instruments than it is on double reed instruments. See also Extended/Contemporary Techniques, page 29

The Whisper Key is Released on Notes Above G-sharp

FIGURE 6.36. *Secondary Break*

Sounding Range: See Instrument Family and Playing Considerations, page 645; Range, page 660; Transpositions, page 675

Speaker Keys: Generally, a term used for keys that help notes respond or "speak" when depressed. Speaker keys can be special keys (e.g., bassoon flick keys), or they can be regular keys (e.g., an octave key). On bassoon, the whisper key is the most obvious speaker key. See also Flick Keys/Flicker Keys/Speaker Keys/Flip Keys/Flicking, page 629; Whisper Key, page 677

Spine: The center ridge or hump of a double reed blade that essentially divides a well-made reed into two symmetrical sides. See also Reeds, Double, page 531

Spring Hook Tool: See Spring Hook Tool, page 59

Springs: See Springs, page 59

Squeaks: Undesirable, accidentally produced partials that sometimes sound during normal play. Squeaks can be caused by several factors. Some of the most common causes of squeaks for beginners include poor or dry reeds, poor embouchure formation, fingers not covering tone holes properly, or hitting side keys. A more detailed discussion of squeaks can be found in "Practical Tips" at the end of this chapter.

Staggered Breathing: See Staggered Breathing, page 59

Stamina: See Endurance/Stamina, page 28

Stands: See Instrument Stands, page 39

Starting Note/Range, The Best: Most students will have excellent results starting on fourth-line F-natural and working their way downward note by note to low F-natural. This note range is excellent for several reasons. First, it is relatively easy to produce a tone in this range. Second, the fingerings in this range are relatively simple and intuitively logical. Third, this range provides teachers with the opportunity to point out that as more holes are covered, the tones get lower. These relationships make this range ideal for simple ear training exercises. Finally, adding one finger at a time in a comfortable range enables students to cover each tone hole properly. The more tone holes students have to cover, the less likely they are to cover them properly. This starting note range is shown is figure 6.37. It is interesting to note that because band method books must accommodate beginners on a variety of instruments, they often do not have players start on the above sequence of notes.

FIGURE 6.37. *Starting Note Range*

Key Questions

Q: Should I start my students on bassoon?

A: No. Generally, the bassoon is not a good starting instrument for several reasons. First, producing a good tone on bassoon is more problematic than it is on flute, clarinet, or saxophone. Second, the design of the bassoon requires the fingers to be farther apart, making correct hand position difficult (if not impossible) for young players with small hands. In addition, the fingerings on bassoon are often counterintuitive and awkward. Third, the instrument is large and heavy, making it awkward and cumbersome to control. Dealing with these challenges from the beginning along with all of the other demands of playing a musical instrument can overwhelm a student.

Q: What instrument should I start my students on before switching them to bassoon?

A: Students can switch to bassoon from any instrument if they are highly motivated; however, only students who have developed proper mechanics of tone production and technique on their starting instruments should switch to bassoon. In addition, students switching to bassoon must have fairly long fingers or they will not be able to finger the instrument properly. Saxophonists will probably have an easier time switching to bassoon than clarinetists or flutists will. The looser embouchure used in playing the saxophone is more conducive to playing bassoon than the relatively firmer embouchure of the clarinet, and the flute embouchure is very different.

Stock: The part of a reed that has the bark on it. See also Reeds, Double, page 531

Swab: See Swab, page 59; Care and Maintenance, page 614

Synthetic Reeds: Reeds made from synthetic, man-made materials instead of traditional cane. A variety of synthetic reeds are available today. These reeds last longer and are more durable than cane reeds. In addition, they do not need to be moist to respond; therefore, they do not dry out. However, the sound produced by synthetic reeds does not have the same quality as that produced by cane reeds, and the vast majority of players prefer cane reeds. Despite the sound difference, many players find synthetic reeds useful in some situations. For example, some players choose to have a synthetic reed on hand in case other reeds do not respond well. Synthetic reeds are also a reasonable choice when playing outdoors or in varying climate conditions where reed response may be a problem. Some teachers prefer to start beginners on synthetic reeds because they are more affordable, consistent, and durable. See also Reeds, Double, page 531

Technique: In general, the manner and ability with which players use the technical skills involved in playing an instrument. Most commonly, the term is used to describe the physical actions involved in playing an instrument and often specifically refers to technical passages. Virtually every pedagogical aspect of woodwind playing (acoustical, physical, and mental) affects technique. General technical considerations for all woodwind instruments are in chapter 1. The following suggestions and considerations apply specifically to the bassoon. When appropriate, readers are directed to relevant terms in the book where particular topics are addressed in detail. See also Alternate Fingerings/Alternates, page 599; Technique, page 668

General Technical Considerations/Concerns for Bassoon Players

1. The bassoon key system is more awkward than other instrument systems. The keys are spaced far apart, the fingerings are often complicated, the thumbs are much more actively involved in regular fingerings, and players are required to cover tone holes in many instances with the pads of their fingers, as clarinet players do. In addition, many bassoon fingerings in the normal range do not follow an intuitive or logical pattern. As a result, technically difficult passages are more problematic on bassoon than on other woodwind instruments. Finger coordination is a primary concern of bassoonists.

2. The amount of back pressure that bassoon players experience is greater than all other woodwind instruments except oboe and clarinet; however, the amount of back pressure is less consistent on bassoon. In the low range, there is very little back pressure, whereas in the high range, there is a considerable amount of back pressure. Players must adjust to these variances to play with technical fluidity.

3. The amount of embouchure and air control needed for pitch placement and the variations in embouchure, air, and the oral cavity are

greater on bassoon than any other woodwind instrument. Bassoon players make changes in these variables constantly throughout the normal range. When playing large skips and leaps, these changes are substantial. If these changes in embouchure and air are not executed properly, the air stream is disrupted and technical fluidity is negatively affected.

Specific Technical Considerations/Concerns for Bassoon Players

1. Whisper Key—A common problem with young players is that they do not use the whisper key correctly because they discover that the notes respond with or without it. The whisper key should be kept closed by the left thumb below top-line A-natural downward to low F-natural. Improper use of the whisper key inhibits response, tone quality, and technical proficiency. See also Whisper Key, page 677

2. Half-Hole Technique (Left-Hand Index Finger)—The left-hand index finger must roll down slightly to execute the half-hole technique on G-flat, G-natural, and G-sharp (the three G's). Not executing the half-hole technique properly is a common problem on bassoon. See also Half-Hole Technique, page 632

3. Jaw Movement during Articulation—Bassoon players are notorious for "jawing" during the tonguing process. Jawing results in poor attacks, poor tonguing, and poor response, all of which inhibit technical proficiency. However, because playing large skips and leaps often requires significant changes in embouchure, it is common to see more jaw movement from bassoon players than other woodwind players. See also Tonguing, page 71

4. Left Thumb—The use of the left thumb is crucial to technical proficiency on bassoon. The thumb is used to operate several keys independently, and sometimes, two or more keys simultaneously. See also Flick Keys/Flicker Keys/Speaker Keys/Flip Keys/Flicking, page 629; Whisper Key, page 677

5. Flick Keys—Players often do not use the flick keys properly. Using flick keys improves the response of the notes between top-line A-natural and high D-natural above the staff, which promotes technical proficiency. The flick keys are operated by the left thumb. See also Flick Keys/Flicker Keys/Speaker Keys/Flip Keys/Flicking, page 629; Whisper Key, page 677

6. Right Thumb—Although the use of the right thumb is not as involved as the left thumb in fingering technical passages, the right thumb is also used to operate several keys independently. The right thumb is used primarily to operate the E (pan) key; however, it also operates the A-sharp key, the F-sharp key, and the G-sharp key. See also Flick Keys/Flicker Keys/Speaker Keys/Flip Keys, page 629; Whisper Key, page 677

7. Hand Rest Height—The height of the hand rest has a significant effect on technique. If adjusted too low, the fingers will hang over the keys, and if adjusted too high, the fingers will not reach the keys. A properly adjusted hand rest provides a balance point or base point for the right hand, which improves technical proficiency. On the other hand, some advanced players do not use a hand rest because they believe that it limits mobility. That is, although using a hand rest is important for beginners, advanced players may find that not using a hand rest may, in fact, increase technical proficiency by providing greater flexibility. See also Hand Rest/Crutch, page 634

8. Alternate Fingerings/Alternates—Like other woodwind players, bassoon players use alternate fingerings. The choice of fingerings should be determined by musical considerations including tone quality, intonation, and smoothness of the phrase. Although new fingerings seem awkward initially, developing control over all fingerings is crucial to technical proficiency. See also Alternate Fingerings/Alternates, page 599

9. Trill Fingerings—Bassoons are not required to trill that often, but the execution of trills is more difficult on bassoon than on other woodwind instruments. A special trill fingering chart is in "Practical Tips" at the end of this chapter.

Temperament: See Temperament, page 61

Third Wire: On a bassoon reed, the wire nearest the heel. The third wire is covered (typically with string) in a Turk's Head knot. This knot forms the ball end of the reed. See also Reeds, Double, page 531

Throat, Reed: The part of the reed tube between the first and second wires where the end of the bocal ultimately stops. See also Reeds, Double, page 531

Tip Opening/Reed Aperture: The opening between the two blades of a double reed. The tip opening is a significant factor in determining the amount of resistance a reed will offer and the type of tone produced on an instrument. The tip opening should be symmetrical. The widest point (about one-sixteenth of an inch) is in the center. From the center, the top and bottom blades curve downward or upward, respectively, in an even and consistent manner until they meet at the edges of the reed. As a rule, a reed with a large tip opening will produce more resistance and a bigger tone quality. Conversely, a reed with a small tip opening will produce less resistance and a smaller tone quality. In addition, reeds with large tip openings have a greater dynamic potential than reeds with small tip openings. See also Reeds, Double, page 531; Resistance, page 662; Response, page 664

Teaching Tips Regarding Tip Opening

1. The "correct" size for a tip opening is largely dependent upon the relationships between the tip opening, reed strength, and embouchure pressure. What follow are some suggestions regarding these relationships. Ultimately, it is the tone quality and response that determine whether a particular tip opening is appropriate.
   A. A harder reed generally requires a slightly smaller tip opening and/or more embouchure pressure.
   B. A softer reed generally requires a slightly larger tip opening and/or slightly less embouchure pressure.
   C. Players who consistently play with a small, thin tone need to use a slightly harder reed and/or a reed with a larger tip opening. If the tone is tight or pinched, a looser embouchure is needed.
   D. Players who consistently play with an unfocused or raucous tone need to use a slightly softer reed and/or a reed with a smaller tip opening. If the tone is loose and uncontrolled, a firmer embouchure is needed.

Tip, Reed: The wide end of the reed opposite the heel. The tip of the reed is crucial to producing a good tone quality. Its thickness and flexibility must be even across the width of the reed and the same on both blades. Holding the reed up to the light can provide some idea about the consistency of the tip regarding thickness and shape. See also Reeds, Double, page 531

Tone Holes: See Tone Holes, page 63

Tone Production: The term used to describe how tone is produced on an instrument. General considerations for woodwind tone production are discussed under Tone Production in chapter 1. Specific considerations for bassoon tone production and some of the terms included in this chapter that address tone production appear in Tonal Concept/Tone Quality.

Tonal Concept/Tone Quality

Develop a concept of "good" bassoon tone and the type of tone quality desired. Listening to advanced players and high-quality recordings can help develop appropriate tonal concepts. In addition, taking lessons from a knowledgeable teacher who provides an exemplary model is invaluable. See Tone Production, page 63

1. Use appropriate equipment (e.g., instrument, bocal, reed). Players should play on equipment that matches their level of performance and experience. As players mature, they should learn to make and adjust reeds under the guidance of a knowledgeable teacher. The reed is the primary factor in determining tone quality. The bocal also affects tone quality and pitch to a marked degree.

2. Strive for a consistent tone quality and evenness of scale in all ranges and develop control of the air stream at all dynamic levels. Maintain an open throat and oral cavity in all registers as if saying the syllable "ah" or "oh." Even in the high range, there is no need to close the oral cavity; however, an "oo" syllable may be used for better focus if the tone is spread. Considerable disagreement exists as to the appropriateness of particular syllables. Teachers and players should experiment with a variety of syllables and use what yields the best results.

Embouchure

Maintain proper embouchure formation at all times. Proper mechanics of embouchure are critical to tone production. Although many fine players' embouchures vary slightly from a classic or standard embouchure, the following fundamental characteristics have withstood the test of time. Achieving a mature, characteristic tone on any wind instrument requires time and practice to develop the physical and aural skills necessary for proper tone production. A brief summary of embouchure considerations for good tone production appears as follows. See also Embouchure, page 623

1. Draw the mouth corners inward toward the reed.

2. Surround the reed evenly with the lips in all directions as if saying "oh." A drawstring analogy is often used to describe this rounded position. The bassoon embouchure is much more relaxed than the oboe embouchure.

3. Roll the lips inward over the teeth so that both the upper and the lower lips cushion and support the reed. Most of the reed is taken into the mouth, so that the upper lip is almost touching the first wire. The reed remains centered in the mouth.

4. Drop the jaw down and back, forming an overbite. This position is crucial for achieving a good tone quality.

5. Avoid bunching the chin and puffing the cheeks.

6. Maintain a consistent embouchure in the middle register. As a rule, the embouchure is quite loose in the low range and much firmer in the high range. Slight changes in embouchure and air stream are common throughout the instrument's range to help focus for specific pitches. In fact, more embouchure adjustments are necessary on bassoon than on any other woodwind instrument.

BREATHING AND AIR

A thorough discussion of breathing and air is in chapter 1. See also Breathing/Breath Support/Air Control, page 10; Tone Production, page 63

VIBRATO

While vibrato is not a factor in tone production for beginners and intermediate players, it is a factor in tone production for more advanced players. Typically, vibrato is added after the fundamentals of good tone production have been mastered. Considerations for vibrato are listed here. See also Vibrato, page 677

1. Add vibrato to a full, well-centered tone according to the musical style being performed.
2. Use vibrato to enhance tone quality, not to cover up poor tone quality.
3. Use a combination of diaphragmatic and jaw vibrato.

Specific Tonal Considerations/Concerns for Bassoon Players

1. High Notes—As notes get higher, players need to increase air speed, firm their embouchures, and narrow the focus of the air stream and oral cavity to achieve proper tonal response, tone quality, and pitch. Notes above high D-natural become increasingly more difficult to play with good tone quality and intonation. In addition, the fingerings for high notes become increasingly complex and less intuitive. There is frequently more than one fingering for the same note. Players typically experiment to find the fingering that works best for them.

2. Technical Considerations—Players must half-hole the three G's (G-flat, G-natural, and G-sharp) appropriately. Players sometimes half-hole notes improperly or do not half-hole notes at all. In addition, players should keep the whisper key closed for all notes below top-line A-natural because it improves tonal response and consistency. See also Half-Hole Technique, page 632; Whisper Key, page 677

3. Embouchure—As a general rule, the embouchure is more relaxed in the low range and firmer in the high range. In addition, the jaw is dropped down and back, forming an overbite. This overbite formation is slightly exaggerated in the very low range. Playing with an even tone quality and playing in tune throughout the range requires more embouchure and air adjustments on bassoon than on any other wind instrument. See also Embouchure, page 623

4. Reed—A certain amount of resistance is needed to maintain a steady, rich tone quality and proper intonation. When reeds are too soft or the reed aperture is too small, the tone is thin and "quivery" and pitch is difficult to control. When reeds are too hard or the reed aperture is too large, the tone is airy, response is poor, pitch control suffers, and players' embouchures tire quickly. Reeds need to be hard enough to push back against the embouchure pressure to create a stable tone, but not so hard that players have to fight the reed. See also Reeds, Double, page 531

5. Reed Placement—Many players do not take enough of the reed in the mouth, which negatively affects tone production in all ranges. The top lip should almost touch the first wire, while the lower lip is drawn down and back. Taking too little reed in the mouth causes the pitch to be flat and the tone quality to be inconsistent.

6. Back Pressure—Bassoons produce more back pressure than all other woodwind instruments except oboe; however, the amount of back pressure is less consistent on bassoon. In the low range, there is very little back pressure, whereas in the high range, there is a considerable amount of back pressure. Players must adjust to these variances to play with technical fluidity.

Tone Quality: The characteristic sound associated with an instrument regarding tone color or timbre, and consistency, focus, and control of the air stream. From a mechanical standpoint, tone quality is dependent upon several factors involving the design, construction, quality, and condition of the instrument. From a player's standpoint, tone quality is largely dependent upon two factors: (1) the use of air, which is discussed under Tone Production and Breathing/Breath Support/Air Control, and (2) the embouchure and oral cavity, which is discussed under Tone Production and Embouchure. Common terms associated with tone quality and common terms used to describe tone quality are identified and described under Tone Quality in chapter 1. See also Breathing/Breath Support/Air Control, page 10; Tone Quality, page 68

Key Questions

Q: Should I work on tone quality or intonation first?

A: Tone quality. If players cannot play with a good, consistent tone quality, working on intonation is counterproductive.

Tonguing: See Tonguing, page 71

Transpositions: The relationship between the written and sounding ranges of an instrument. The bassoon is a non-transposing instrument. That is, the bassoon sounds as written. For example, when a bassoon player plays a fourth-line F-natural, the sounding pitch is a fourth-line F-natural. The contrabassoon sounds one octave lower than written and one octave lower than the bassoon. A summary of transpositions is shown in figure 6.38. See also Range, page 660

Triple-Tonguing: A technique that enables performers to tongue triple patterns rapidly. See also Multiple-Tonguing, page 52

Tuning/Tuning Note Considerations: Tuning any instrument is a process that involves making mechanical adjustments (e.g., pulling out or pushing in

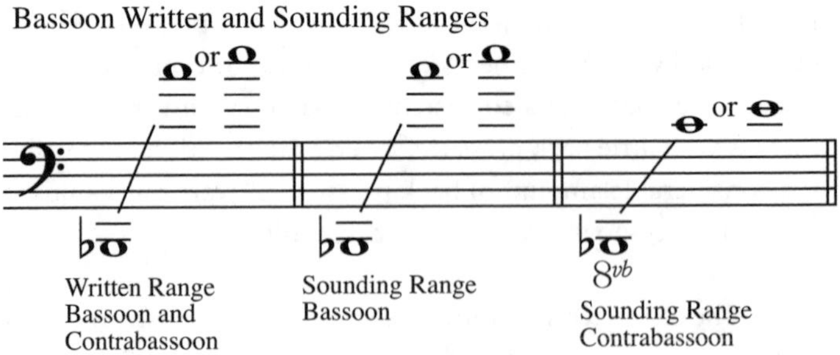
Bassoon Written and Sounding Ranges
or
or
or
8vb
Written Range
Bassoon and
Contrabassoon
Sounding Range
Bassoon
Sounding Range
Contrabassoon

FIGURE 6.38. *Bassoon Transpositions*

a mouthpiece, slide, or instrument joint) so that the instrument will produce pitches that are in tune with a predetermined standard (e.g., A = 440). Tuning notes refer to specific pitches that are good to tune to on any given instrument. Considerations have been given to the notes most commonly used for tuning wind groups. Adjusting pitch and adjusting for pitch tendencies of the bassoon are discussed under Intonation. Considerations for tuning the bassoon appear in this section under "Tuning the Bassoon."

Tuning the Bassoon

1. The design of the bassoon makes it an extremely inflexible instrument to tune mechanically. It does not have a mouthpiece or instrument joint to pull out or push in to adjust pitch, nor does it have a tuning slide. Instead, pitch is largely determined by the bocal/reed combination.

2. The bocal can be pulled out slightly, which may flatten the pitch; however, because the bassoon is so large and the distance the bocal can be moved is so short, only very slight adjustments in pitch can be made by pulling out the bocal. As a result, repositioning the bocal has a minimal effect on pitch.

3. If the pitch is extremely sharp or flat, players will almost certainly have to use another bocal. Bocals are available in a variety of lengths to accommodate pitch and tone quality concerns. Bocals are generally numbered 0 through 4, with 0 being the shortest. There is a direct relationship between the length of a bocal and pitch. Specifically, shorter bocals raise the pitch, whereas longer bocals lower the pitch.

4. The reed is a major factor in both tone production and pitch. For this reason, students should study with a knowledgeable player/ teacher and learn how to make and adjust their own reeds.

Tuning Note Considerations

1. Concert B-flat—An "okay" tuning note in the middle octave (i.e., above the staff). The upper and lower octave B-flats should not be used as tuning notes.
2. Concert A-natural—An excellent tuning note in the middle octave (i.e., top-line A-natural), and one of the best tuning notes on the instrument. The upper and lower octave A-naturals should not be used as tuning notes.
3. Concert F-natural—A poor tuning note in all three octaves. The low octave tends to be a little sharp, the middle octave tends to be flat, and the upper octave is difficult to control.

U Joint: The U-shaped tube at the bottom of the boot joint that connects the wing and bass joints. Water collects in the U joint after the instrument is played, and many players remove the bass joint and dump the excess water. The U joint should be swabbed out thoroughly after the instrument has been played.

Vibrato: Two types of vibrato are commonly used in woodwind playing: jaw vibrato and diaphragmatic vibrato. Jaw vibrato results in regular pitch fluctuations around a tonal center, whereas diaphragmatic vibrato results in regular intensity (loudness) fluctuations around a tonal center. Nearly all bassoon players use a combination of jaw and diaphragmatic vibrato. Steps for developing vibrato are in chapter 1 under Vibrato. See also Vibrato, page 74

Whisper Key: Sometimes referred to as the piano or pianissimo key, a key operated by the left thumb that opens and closes a small vent hole on the bassoon. The whisper key was designed by Wilhelm Heckel (1856–1909) and first appeared on bassoons at the end of the nineteenth century. Now a standard key on all bassoons, the whisper key improves the quality of the notes in the high range (i.e., top-line A-natural and above) when left open. The whisper key is kept closed by the left thumb below top-line A-natural downward to low F-natural. Below low F-natural, the whisper key is automatically closed by the E (pan) key. Keeping the whisper key closed for all notes below top-line A-natural improves the player's ability to play softly, and it improves tone quality and intonation. It should also be mentioned that on some instruments, certain notes in the high range may

FIGURE 6.39. *Whisper Key*

actually sound better with the whisper key down (closed). Players should experiment with each note to see how their particular instruments respond. Examples of when to use the whisper key are shown in figure 6.39.

Whisper/Piano Key Locking Mechanism: A mechanism designed to lock the whisper (piano) key closed when playing rapid passages between low F-natural (below the staff) and fourth-space G-sharp. This mechanism frees the left thumb from having to hold down the whisper key in this range, which improves technical playing. The whisper key lock is usually attached to the boot joint and is operated by the right thumb, but may be attached to the wing joint. Bassoons using a conservatory system do not operate the whisper key locking mechanism in this way. Instead, the whisper key locking mechanism is operated with the little finger of the left hand.

Wires: The means by which the two blades of a bassoon reed are held together. Bassoon reeds have three wires. Two are visible, and one is covered by the binding or wrapping. The first wire is the wire closest to the tip of the reed, the second wire is just above the binding between the first and second wires, and the third wire lies underneath the binding near the heel of the reed. The first and second wires may be adjusted to control the positioning of the blades and the size and shape of the tip opening, which affects tonal characteristics and response. See also Reeds, Double, page 531

Wrapping: See Binding, page 610

Written Range: The written range for the bassoon and contrabassoon is the same, even though the contrabassoon sounds one octave lower than the bassoon. The bassoon is a non-transposing instrument spanning over four octaves, from low B-flat (one octave below second-line B-flat in the bass clef) to third-space C-natural in the treble clef. Advanced players extend this range upward to F-natural or higher. Suggested ranges for different playing levels are under Range. See also Instrument Family and Playing Considerations, page 645; Range, page 660; Transpositions, page 675

Bassoon Basic Fingerings

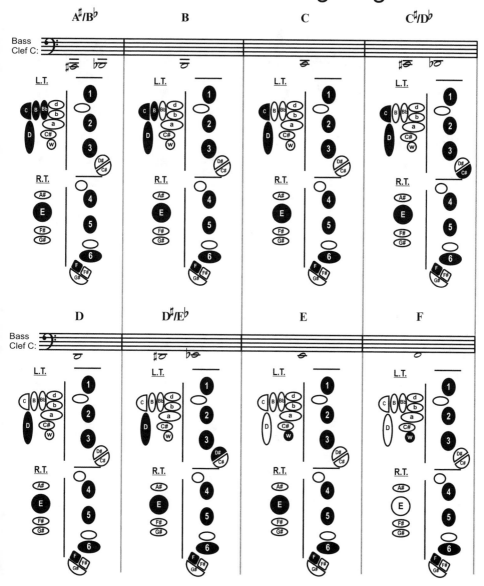

Bassoon Basic Fingerings

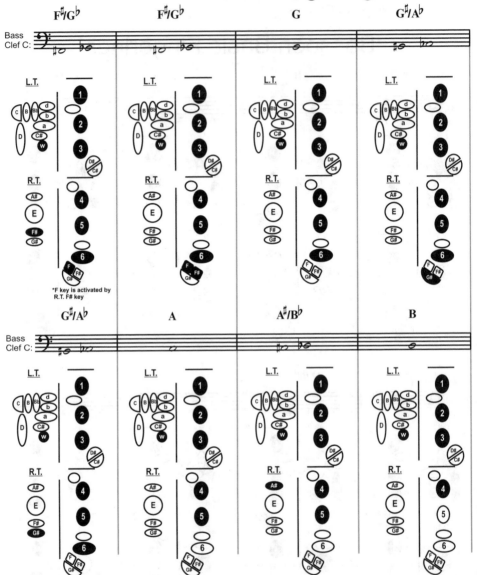

*F key is activated by R.T. F# key

Bassoon Basic Fingerings

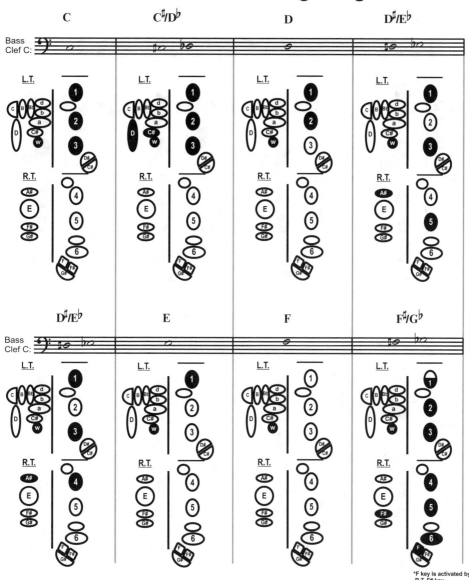

*F key is activated by
R.T. F# key

Bassoon Basic Fingerings

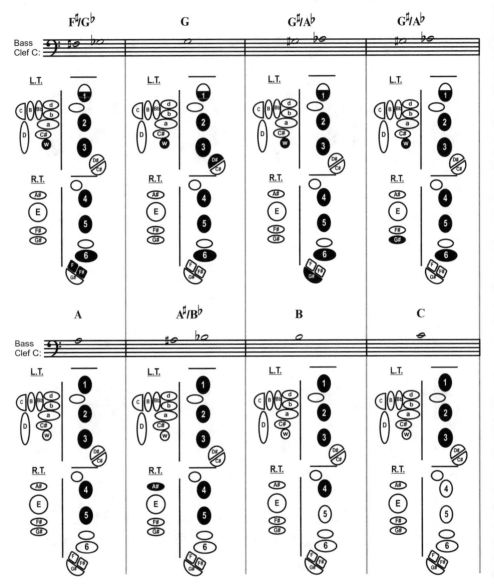

Bassoon Basic Fingerings

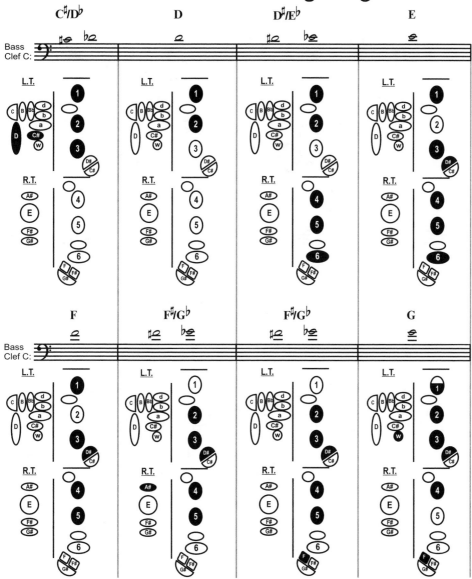

Bassoon Alternate Fingerings

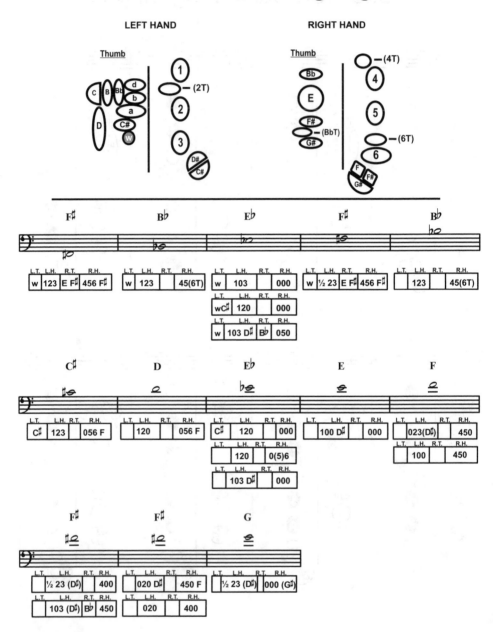

Bassoon Altissimo Fingerings

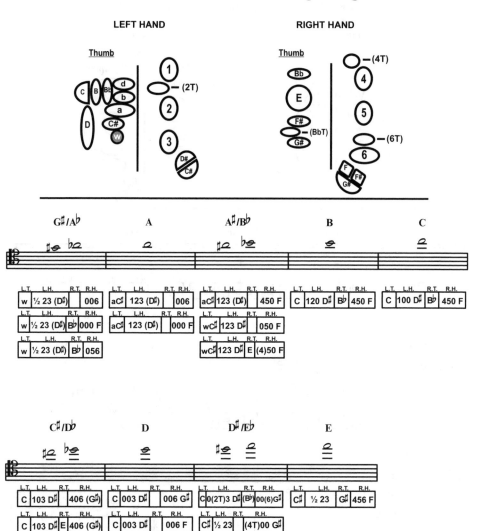

Bassoon Special Trill Fingerings

Trills performed with regular fingerings are not included

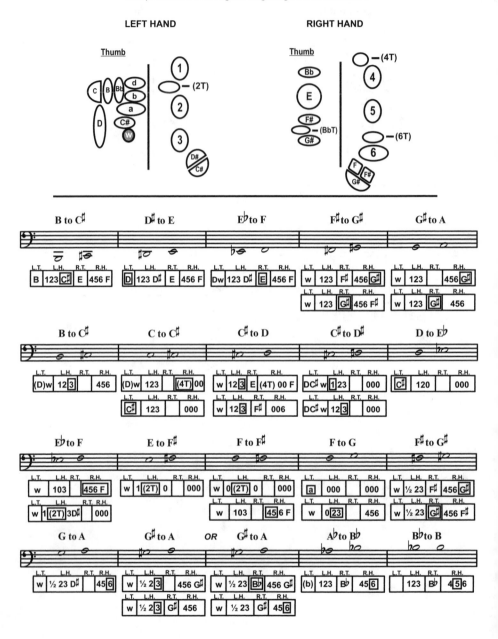

Bassoon Special Trill Fingerings

Trills performed with regular fingerings are not included

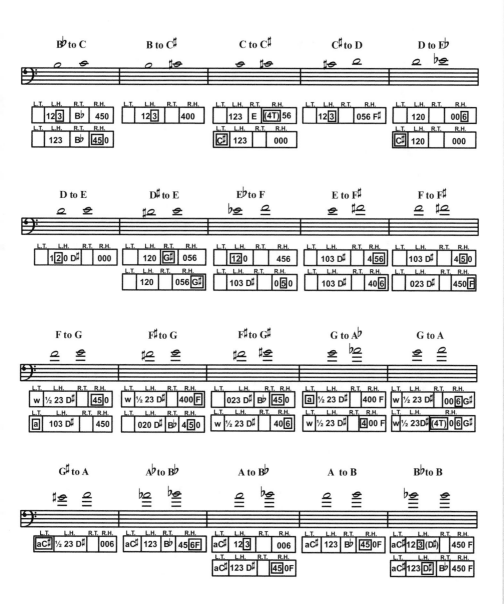

Common Technical Faults and Corrections

Many problems in wind playing result from basic faults in the following areas: (1) instrument assembly, (2) embouchure formation, and (3) hand/holding/playing positions and posture. The following section provides information on how to correct technical faults frequently encountered in bassoon performance. Headings appear in alphabetical order.

Assembly

FAULT 1:   The bridge keys between the tenor and the boot joints are not properly aligned.

CORRECTION: Align the bridge keys so that the whisper key can close properly.

FAULT 2:   Improper reed alignment.

CORRECTION: Push the reed in all the way and position it parallel to the floor. The reed angle is correct when the player's head is straight (not tilted to one side) when playing.

FAULT 3:   Handling the instrument carelessly and putting unnecessary pressure on the keys.

CORRECTION: During assembly, handle the sections of the bassoon in a way that avoids all unnecessary contact with the keys. Assemble the bassoon in this manner every day so that handling the instrument safely becomes habit.

FAULT 4:   Improper alignment of the wing (tenor) and the long (bass) joints.

CORRECTION: Make sure that the curved side (i.e., the groove) of the tenor joint is aligned with the hole in the boot joint during assembly and that the locking mechanism (if so equipped) is engaged properly.

FAULT 5:   Not greasing corks sufficiently.

CORRECTION: Grease corks weekly (more if necessary) to facilitate assembly. Dry corks can cause players to use excessive pressure on the key mechanisms during assembly.

FAULT 6: Handling the bocal near the reed end.

CORRECTION: Handle the bocal between the thumb and index fingers near the cork to avoid bending the bocal. Pulling or twisting on the reed end of the bocal can bend and damage it and render it unplayable. Damaged bocals resulting from careless handling is a common problem with young players.

FAULT 7: Not inserting the bocal properly.

CORRECTION: Insert the bocal so that the vent hole can be covered appropriately by the whisper key pad.

Embouchure Formation

FAULT 1: Not enough bottom lip over teeth.

CORRECTION: Be flexible on this point. Generally, the red part of the lips is not visible (or is barely visible) during play; however, the amount of lips over the teeth varies from player to player.

FAULT 2: Taking too little reed in the mouth.

CORRECTION: Take enough reed into the mouth so that the top lip touches (or almost touches) the first wire. The exact placement depends on the player and the reed, and should be determined by the position that yields the best tone quality and response.

FAULT 3: Mouth corners are drawn back in a smiling position.

CORRECTION: Round the mouth corners as if saying "oh." A drawstring analogy is often used to describe this rounded position. In addition, the jaw is drawn down and back more on bassoon than it is on other woodwind instruments, so the analogy can be misleading if proper jaw position is not also explained.

FAULT 4: Embouchure too tight.

CORRECTION: Ensure that the embouchure is rounded and relaxed. The jaw should be drawn down and back to accentuate the natural overbite position. The bassoon embouchure is much more relaxed than the oboe embouchure.

FAULT 5:   Air escaping through the mouth corners.

CORRECTION: Form a proper embouchure. Air escapes when the surrounding muscles are not supporting inwardly toward the reed. Players should form a seal around the reed so that air does not escape through the mouth corners.

FAULT 6:   Puffed cheeks.

CORRECTION: Keep the jaw down and back, and keep the chin relatively flat. Focus the air stream around and through the tip opening of the reed.

Hand/Holding/Instrument Playing Positions and Posture

FAULT 1:   Elbows too far from or too close to the body while playing.

CORRECTION: Hold the elbows out from the body in a relaxed, comfortable position. The elbows may be held out slightly farther on bassoon than on other woodwind instruments to facilitate proper hand/finger position on the keys.

FAULT 2:   Left elbow resting on the knee while playing.

CORRECTION: Hold the elbows out from the body in a relaxed, comfortable position. Younger, smaller players sometimes rest their left arm on their knee when they get tired. Take frequent breaks to eliminate fatigue, and encourage proper playing positions at all times. Players who angle the bassoon too far across their bodies must support more of the instrument's weight with their left hand, which results in fatigue. These players compensate by resting the left elbow on the knee. Holding the instrument at a proper angle will reduce the need to support the elbow on the knee and it will help reduce fatigue.

FAULT 3:   Holding the bassoon at an improper angle.

CORRECTION: Make sure the bassoon crosses the player's body diagonally with the boot joint resting against the right hip and drawn back near the edge of the chair. Holding the bassoon at an extreme diagonal angle (too horizontal) causes the left hand to support too much of the instrument's weight, causing fatigue and limiting technical proficiency.

FAULT 4:   Head tilted to one side.

CORRECTION: Make sure that the reed is parallel to the floor and not improperly twisted or turned to one side. The head should remain straight at all times.

FAULT 5:   Slouching.

CORRECTION: Sit up straight, keep the chin in a normal position (not up or down), keep the eyes straight ahead, and keep the shoulders and back straight but relaxed.

FAULT 6:   Reed entering the mouth at an inappropriate angle.

CORRECTION: Make sure that the boot joint is positioned back sufficiently and that the head stays straight. The reed should enter the mouth almost straight in. Most players prefer a slightly upward angle, while some prefer a slightly downward angle. The exact angle that the reed should enter the mouth is determined by the tone quality.

FAULT 7:   Improper positioning of the left thumb.

CORRECTION: Position the left thumb so that it can operate the B-natural and the B-flat keys by rolling rather than by jumping. The D and C keys can then be operated by the ball of the thumb.

FAULT 8:   Fingers are straight or locked.

CORRECTION: Emphasize that fingers should be slightly curved so that an open C-shape is formed between the thumb and fingers. The fingers are spread farther apart on bassoon than on other woodwind instruments because of the size of the bassoon and because of the position of the keys and tone holes.

FAULT 9:   The right-hand little finger is floating out of position.

CORRECTION: Ensure that the right-hand little finger lightly touches or rests just above the F key in a ready position to minimize finger movement and promote technical proficiency.

FAULT 10:   The right thumb is improperly positioned.

CORRECTION: Position the right thumb so that it is close to or actually touching the E (pan) key.

FAULT 11: The wrists are bent.

CORRECTION: Keep the wrists relatively straight. If the elbows and instrument are properly positioned, wrist position is generally not a problem.

FAULT 12: The left-hand little finger is allowed to droop or float out of position.

CORRECTION: Position the left-hand little finger so that it lightly touches or rests just above the D-sharp key in a ready position to minimize finger movement and promote technical proficiency.

FAULT 13: Fingers too far from keys or tone holes.

CORRECTION: Keep fingers as close to the keys and tone holes as possible without distorting tone quality and/or pitch. Keeping the fingers close to the keys or tone holes minimizes finger movement and promotes proper playing technique.

FAULT 14: The left-hand index finger is angled improperly.

CORRECTION: Position the left-hand index finger so that it can half-hole when necessary by rocking slightly rather than by using a less efficient sliding motion. If the rocking motion for executing the half-hole technique is awkward or difficult, position the left-hand index finger at a greater or lesser angle.

FAULT 15: Seat strap adjusted improperly.

CORRECTION: Make sure the seat strap is adjusted so that the reed can be brought to the mouth almost straight on or at a slightly upward angle. That is, players should not have to reach for the reed.

COMMON PROBLEMS, CAUSES, AND SOLUTIONS FOR BASSOON

Problems in wind instrument playing relate to some aspect of sound. That is, incorrect assembly is not a problem; poor tone quality or squeaking is a problem. Incorrect assembly is simply one common cause of such problems. Understanding this distinction makes it easier to apply effective solutions to problems. The following section provides information on solving problems frequently encountered in bassoon performance. The main headings are: Articulation Problems, Intonation Problems, Performance/Technical Problems, and Tone Quality and Response Problems.

Articulation Problems

> **PROBLEM:** Audible dip or scoop in pitch during initial attacks.

> **CAUSE 1:** Excessive movement of the embouchure (especially the jaw) while tonguing.

SOLUTION 1: Use light, quick movements of the tongue and maintain a consistent embouchure. Use a "tu" syllable, not a "twa" syllable. Practice tonguing in front of a mirror, and use the visual feedback to help eliminate jaw movement.

> **CAUSE 2:** Embouchure not set properly before the attack.

SOLUTION 2: Allow enough time to be physically and mentally set before the attack. That is, the embouchure must be set properly for the note being played. When the embouchure is too tight or too loose for a particular note at the point of attack, players will make an immediate adjustment or shift to correct the pitch. This shift causes an audible dip or scoop in the attack.

> **PROBLEM:** Heavy, thick, and/or sluggish attacks.

> **CAUSE 1:** Too much tongue on the attacks coupled with a slow tonguing action.

SOLUTION 1: Minimize tongue movement. Use a light, quick tonguing action. Thinking about striking only the bottom blade with the tongue can head off a tendency to strike the reed too hard during the attack. Think of moving only the tip of the tongue during the tonguing process, and use a "tu" attack for normal tonguing.

> **CAUSE 2:** Tonguing too far down on the reed.

SOLUTION 2: The tip of the tongue strikes the tip of the reed. Make sure the tongue is pulled back or arched slightly in the mouth to begin the tonguing process. This position places the tongue slightly higher in the mouth to start. Thinking about striking only the bottom blade with the tongue can prevent players from striking the reed too hard during the attack.

CAUSE 3:   Tongue disrupting the air stream.

SOLUTION 3:   If the tongue is too low or too high in the mouth, or if the tongue moves too slowly, the air stream is disrupted, causing sluggish attacks. Make sure the tongue is pulled back or arched slightly in the mouth to begin the tonguing process, and increase the quickness of the tongue strike against the tip of the reed.

PROBLEM: Mistimed attacks (tongue, embouchure, air).

CAUSE 1:   Tongue and air stream not coordinated.

SOLUTION 1:   Practice coordinating the tongue and the air stream by attacking one note at a time. Think of starting the tongue and the air at the same time on attacks. Although it is the release of the tongue from the reed that actually starts a tone, the air stream and the tongue must work together.

CAUSE 2:   Embouchure not set properly before the attack.

SOLUTION 2:   Allow enough time to be physically and mentally set before the attack. That is, the embouchure must be set properly for the note being played. An embouchure that is too tight or too loose for the note being played can delay the response of the attack and cause excessive jaw movement.

CAUSE 3:   Too much embouchure movement during attacks.

SOLUTION 3:   Set the embouchure properly for the note being played. Maintain embouchure formation and avoid using a "jawing" action. Think of moving only the tip of the tongue.

CAUSE 4:   Player not set to play.

SOLUTION 4:   Maintain proper playing positions (physical readiness), and internally "hear" the pitches before playing them (mental readiness).

PROBLEM: Inability to execute clean slurs.

CAUSE 1:   Inconsistent air stream.

SOLUTION 1:   Do not change the air stream from note to note unless larger intervals are involved. Instead, blow a consistent stream of air and simply move the fingers. Adjustments in air speed and air volume should be made as necessary to accommodate the dynamic level.

> CAUSE 2:   Too much embouchure movement throughout a slurred passage.

SOLUTION 2:   Use the same embouchure throughout the entire passage. Making large shifts in embouchure for various notes disrupts the air stream and is completely unnecessary on bassoon.

> CAUSE 3:   Fingers not coordinated.

SOLUTION 3:   Keep the fingers close to the keys and depress them quickly and smoothly from note to note. Maintain proper hand position, avoid excess finger movement, and avoid "slapping" the keys.

> CAUSE 4:   Player not set to play.

SOLUTION 4:   Maintain proper playing positions (physical readiness), and internally hear the pitches before playing them (mental readiness).

> PROBLEM: Inability to execute clean releases.

> CAUSE 1:   Inappropriate use of tongue cutoffs.

SOLUTION 1:   Use breath releases rather than tongue cutoffs in most musical contexts because tongue cutoffs tend to be harsh and abrupt. Tongue cutoffs are appropriate in some jazz styles.

> CAUSE 2:   Putting the tongue back on the reed too hard on tongue cutoffs.

SOLUTION 2:   When tongue cutoffs are called for (e.g., some jazz styles), make sure the tongue makes only a modest amount of contact with the tip of the bottom blade. Thinking about striking only the bottom blade with the tongue can help avoid striking the reed too hard during the attack. The rest of the "attack" consists of a sudden increase in air.

> CAUSE 3:   Not stopping the air at the point of release.

SOLUTION 3:   Practice maintaining an open air column from the diaphragm into the instrument, and stop the air by suspending it mid-stream as if lightly gasping. Using the throat as a valve and/or pushing the air on releases both prevent clean releases.

> CAUSE 4:   Not "lifting" on the release.

SOLUTION 4:   Think of gasping lightly on the release and directing the air stream upward. Thinking this way helps stop the flow of air quickly while maintaining an open air column. Make sure to maintain a consistent embouchure during the release.

CAUSE 5:   Closing off the embouchure and/or throat, or using the embouchure and/or throat as a valve for stopping the air.

SOLUTION 5:   Keep the embouchure and throat unchanged on breath releases. It is the air that is stopped to release a tone. Think of gasping lightly on the release and directing the air stream upward. Thinking this way helps stop the flow of air quickly while maintaining an open air column, an open throat, and a proper embouchure.

PROBLEM: Inability to execute a controlled accent.

CAUSE 1:   Not balancing the air stream and tongue appropriately.

SOLUTION 1:   On an accented note, "lift off" of the air; that is, think of gasping lightly and directing the air stream upward on the release. On most accents, the weight of the tongue is not increased on the attack. Rather, the accent is produced by a sudden increase in air. As a rule, do not use tongue cutoffs on accented notes.

CAUSE 2:   Too much tongue on releases in staccato passages with repeated accents.

SOLUTION 2:   Think of tonguing each note consistently and evenly, and the releases will take care of themselves. In rapid patterns, the release of each note (except the first) in the pattern becomes the attack for each subsequent note.

Intonation Problems

PROBLEM: Pitch generally flat in all registers.

CAUSE 1:   Too little reed in the mouth.

SOLUTION 1:   The top lip should almost touch the first wire.

CAUSE 2:   Bocal is too long.

SOLUTION 2:   Use a shorter bocal. For example, if the bocal is a number 2, try using a number 1 bocal. Larger numbered bocals will be longer, which will result in a flatter overall pitch.

CAUSE 3:   Too little air.

SOLUTION 3:   Use a controlled, steady air stream, and increase the speed and volume of the air stream slightly. Form a drawstring embouchure as if saying "oh," and surround the reed with warm air. Practice proper breathing techniques.

CAUSE 4:   Embouchure is too loose.

SOLUTION 4:   Firm the mouth corners slightly while maintaining a flat chin. The lips form an "O" shape, and the lower lip remains firm but not too tight, forming a cushion for the reed. Think of decreasing the imaginary circle of air into the instrument. That is, use a slightly more focused air stream.

CAUSE 5:   Air stream directed downward too much.

SOLUTION 5:   Form a drawstring embouchure as if saying "oh" and surround the reed with warm air. Maintain a consistent air stream. Focus the air slightly upward.

CAUSE 6:   Slouching.

SOLUTION 6:   Sit up straight (but avoid being rigid or tense) with feet flat on the floor. Sit toward the right side of the chair to avoid hitting the bassoon against the chair. If the instrument is resting against the leg, it can prevent the B-flat and F-sharp keys from opening and closing properly.

CAUSE 7:   Reed enters the mouth at an incorrect angle.

SOLUTION 7:   Adjust the seat strap properly. The bassoon reed enters the mouth almost straight on or at a slightly upward angle. If the reed enters at an improper angle, the embouchure's ability to support the reed properly will be compromised, and the pitch will be flat.

CAUSE 8:   Head tilted downward or forward too much.

SOLUTION 8:   Adjust the seat strap so that the reed comes directly to the mouth. Keep the head, eyes, and chin straight. Players should not have to reach upward or downward for the reed. Reaching for the reed negatively affects the embouchure's ability to support the reed properly and causes the pitch to be flat.

CAUSE 9:   Pads are too close to the tone holes.

SOLUTION 9:   Have a knowledgeable repair technician adjust the pads to the proper height.

CAUSE 10:   Reed is too soft.

SOLUTION 10:   Use harder reeds. Soft reeds tend to play flat. Using harder reeds are more resistant and raise the pitch.

CAUSE 11:   Reed is improperly made and/or too long.

SOLUTION 11:   Try a slightly shorter reed if the overall pitch is flat. The bassoon is designed to be played with the reed pushed all the way onto the bocal.

CAUSE 12:   Reed is pulled out too far.

SOLUTION 12:   Push the reed onto the bocal all the way.

CAUSE 13:   Not compensating for the natural tendency of the bassoon to go flat in soft passages.

SOLUTION 13:   Raise the direction of the air stream slightly to compensate for the drop in pitch and use a more focused oral cavity. It may be necessary to firm the embouchure slightly on pitches that are significantly flat, especially in the pianissimo dynamic range.

PROBLEM: Pitch generally sharp in all registers.

CAUSE 1:   Reed is improperly made and/or too short.

SOLUTION 1:   Try a slightly longer reed. The bassoon is designed to be played with the reed pushed all the way onto the bocal. Small adjustments in sharpness can be made by pulling out the reed slightly; however, this type of adjustment is usually made only when absolutely necessary.

CAUSE 2:   Embouchure too tight.

SOLUTION 2:   Relax the embouchure. Try a drawstring embouchure using the syllable "oh" and make sure that the lower lip/jaw is drawn down and back forming an overbite with the upper jaw. Some players find that thinking of yawning helps to relax a tight embouchure. It may be helpful to think of increasing the imaginary circle of air into the instrument. That is, use a slightly more open air stream.

CAUSE 3:   Too much air.

SOLUTION 3:   Use less air, a controlled air stream, and work on proper breathing techniques.

CAUSE 4:   Not compensating for the natural tendency to go sharp as more air is used.

SOLUTION 4:   Gradually lower the direction of the air stream to compensate for the rise in pitch, and use a more open oral cavity. It may be necessary to relax the embouchure slightly on pitches that are significantly sharp, especially in the fortissimo dynamic range.

CAUSE 5:   Air stream directed upward too much.

SOLUTION 5:   Form a round embouchure as if saying the syllable "oh," and surround the reed with warm air. Maintain a consistent air stream. It may help to think of blowing air through and around the tip opening.

CAUSE 6:   Too much reed in the mouth.

SOLUTION 6:   Take less reed in the mouth. A proper embouchure requires taking most of the reed into the mouth, but the upper lip should not touch the first wire. In addition, an overbite formation is essential to achieving a good tone quality and intonation on bassoon.

CAUSE 7:   Pads are too far from tone holes.

SOLUTION 7:   Have a knowledgeable repair technician adjust the pads to the proper height.

CAUSE 8:   Reed is too hard.

SOLUTION 8:   Using softer reeds will offer less resistance and lower the pitch.

CAUSE 9:   Bocal is too short.

SOLUTION 9:   Use a longer bocal. If the bocal is a number 1, try using a number 2 bocal. Lower numbered bocals will be shorter and will raise the overall pitch.

PROBLEM: Pitch is inconsistent throughout the playing range.

CAUSE 1:   Inconsistent air stream.

SOLUTION 1:   Do not change the air stream drastically from note to note unless large intervals are involved. Instead, think of blowing a consistent stream throughout the passage and making only slight adjustments for tonal and pitch considerations. However, adjustments in air speed and air volume should be made as necessary to accommodate the dynamic level.

CAUSE 2:   Inconsistent embouchure.

SOLUTION 2:   Form a good basic drawstring embouchure using an "oh" syllable, and make sure that enough of the lips covers the teeth. Practice playing long tones to develop the embouchure muscles, and concentrate on keeping the embouchure consistent yet relaxed at all times. Use a mirror to check embouchure formation regularly until proper habits are formed.

CAUSE 3:   Lack of proper breath support.

SOLUTION 3:   Work on breathing exercises with and without the bassoon to help develop breath support. Take full breaths and practice playing long tones at all dynamic levels. Focus on maintaining a consistent air speed appropriate for each dynamic level. Practice extensively at softer dynamic levels because it is harder to maintain proper breath support and good intonation at softer dynamic levels than it is at louder dynamic levels. In addition, breath support is often compromised when playing technical passages because players tend to focus on technique at the expense of proper breath support. Practice maintaining breath support throughout technical passages.

CAUSE 4:   Slouching.

SOLUTION 4:   Sit up straight (but avoid being rigid or tense) with feet flat on the floor. Sit toward the right side of the chair to avoid hitting the bassoon against the chair. If the instrument is resting against the leg, it can prevent the B-flat and F-sharp keys from opening and closing properly.

CAUSE 5:   Shifting the angle at which the bassoon is held.

SOLUTION 5:   Make sure that the bassoon crosses the body diagonally and that the boot joint is brought back slightly. Keep the head, eyes, and chin straight and always bring the reed to the mouth. Allow adequate time after long periods of rest to position the instrument properly for the next entrance.

CAUSE 6:   Reed is too old and/or affected by environmental conditions.

SOLUTION 6:   Use a reed that has not lost its response characteristics. Reeds have a limited life, and a reed can go from having excellent response characteristics to having poor response characteristics relatively quickly. Before discarding a reed that plays poorly, let it rest a few days and try it again. Sometimes humidity and temperature affect reed response and pitch.

CAUSE 7:   Reed is unbalanced.

SOLUTION 7:   Adjust the reed to balance both blades as much as possible. Make small adjustments and test the reed after each adjustment. Many players adjust reeds over several days to accurately gauge their playing characteristics and to ensure that the reeds are not ruined (too much cane removed) during the adjustment process.

PROBLEM: Playing out of tune without adjusting.

NOTE: A detailed of adjusting pitch is under Intonation in chapter 1.

CAUSE 1:   Inability to hear beats or roughness.

SOLUTION 1:   Focus on hearing the beats or pulsations that occur when pitches are out of tune. Play long tone unisons with other players and listen for beats. Deliberately playing extremely flat and sharp to accentuate the beats will help players learn to hear beats.

CAUSE 2:   Not knowing how to adjust pitch on the instrument.

SOLUTION 2:   Learn how to adjust pitch on bassoon. Reed position, embouchure, throat, oral cavity, air stream, fingerings, and changes in bocal size all affect pitch.

CAUSE 3:   The physical skills necessary to adjust pitch on the instrument are not developed.

SOLUTION 3:   Practice adjusting pitch every day and continue developing embouchure skills. Relax and tighten the embouchure, focus the air stream upward and downward, open and close the throat and oral cavity, and try alternate fingerings. Learn "what does what" so that appropriate adjustments can be made when necessary.

Performance/Technical Problems

PROBLEM: Sloppy playing in tongued technical passages.

CAUSE 1:   Tongue and fingers not coordinated.

SOLUTION 1:   Practice simple interval exercises slowly with a metronome, and make sure that the tongue and fingers move together. Keep the fingers close to the keys and tone holes during these exercises to avoid excessive finger movement. As control is gained, progress to more difficult exercises and continue to practice with a metronome. Gradually speed up the exercises, but make sure that proper finger-tongue coordination is maintained.

CAUSE 2:   Tonguing speed too slow.

SOLUTION 2:   Using a metronome, start by practicing a variety of simple rhythm patterns on isolated pitches at a slow tempo. Gradually increase the speed and difficulty of the exercises. Use a "tip to tip" (tip of the tongue to the tip of the bottom blade) technique and keep the tongue motion light and quick. Periodically practice tonguing slightly faster than is comfortable. Develop control and rhythmic precision by changing the tempo frequently.

PROBLEM: Sloppy playing overall.

CAUSE 1:   Poor Hand/Holding/Instrument/Playing Positions and Posture.

SOLUTION 1:   Make sure that the playing basics are maintained at all times. A detailed of these playing basics is under Hand/Holding/ Instrument/Playing Positions and Posture.

CAUSE 2:   Poor instrument action.

SOLUTION 2:   Make sure the key mechanisms have been properly adjusted, cleaned, and oiled. Excessively heavy or uneven action is usually a result of poorly adjusted key mechanisms, poorly adjusted pads, and/ or bent key mechanisms. In addition, make sure the springs are in proper working condition. Weak springs sometimes bobble or bounce, which inhibits technical fluidity.

CAUSE 3:   Using awkward fingerings.

SOLUTION 3:   Use alternate fingerings and prepare the right hand when appropriate to maximize technical fluidity.

PROBLEM: Speed of the fingers seems slow in technical passages.

CAUSE 1:   Tenseness in the fingers and hands.

SOLUTION 1:   Practice tough passages slowly at first to gain control, and focus on staying relaxed; trying too hard or forcing the fingers to move during technical passages slows down the fingers. Gradually increase the tempo of the passage, and develop the habit of staying relaxed at all tempos.

PROBLEM: An excessive amount of key noise can be heard when the keys are depressed.

CAUSE 1: Key mechanisms need to be oiled.

SOLUTION 1: If excessive key noise is heard during regular play, oil the mechanisms. As a rule, the key mechanisms should be oiled lightly once a month or so. Clacking sounds are often caused by metal-to-metal contact, which results in excessive wear of the key mechanisms.

CAUSE 2: Pushing keys down too hard or "slapping" the keys.

SOLUTION 2: Use only enough finger pressure to seal the pads (or fingers) against the tone holes or to cover the tone holes properly with the finger pads. Stay relaxed, and think of playing smoothly and efficiently. Keeping the fingers close to the keys will help eliminate the tendency to "slap" the fingers down.

CAUSE 3: Corks or felts are missing.

SOLUTION 3: Replace missing corks or felts and adjust height appropriately. Sometimes the corks or felts that prevent metal-to-metal contact (and also help regulate proper key height) fall off. In such cases, the clacking is quite noticeable, and the affected key or keys will often appear out of line with the rest of the keys in the stack.

PROBLEM: Skips and leaps are not clean.

CAUSE 1: Fingers and/or tongue not coordinated.

SOLUTION 1: Practice simple interval exercises slowly with a metronome, and focus on moving the tongue and fingers together. Keep the fingers close to the keys and tone holes during these exercises to avoid excessive finger movement. It may also help to slur all exercises because tonguing often covers up poor finger coordination. As control is gained, progress to more difficult exercises and continue to practice with a metronome. Gradually speed up the exercises, making sure that proper finger-tongue coordination is maintained.

CAUSE 2: Air stream not maintained properly.

SOLUTION 2: Maintain proper use of air in passages involving skips and leaps to avoid coordination problems between the tongue, fingers, and air stream. Maintain a consistent air stream at all dynamic levels. Players tend to focus on skips and leaps at the expense of proper breath support. Focus on maintaining breath support in all technical passages.

CAUSE 3:   Improper left thumb action.

SOLUTION 3:   Proper use of the left thumb is crucial to technical proficiency on bassoon. The thumb is centered over the whisper key at a straight angle, and it remains relaxed so that it can operate the thumb keys.

PROBLEM: Poor finger-tongue coordination.

CAUSE 1:   Poor playing habits resulting from playing too fast, too soon.

SOLUTION 1:   Practice simple interval exercises slowly with a metronome, and focus on moving the tongue and fingers together. Keep the fingers close to the keys and tone holes during these exercises to avoid excessive finger movement. Slur all exercises because tonguing often covers up poor finger coordination. As control is gained, progress to more difficult exercises. Continue to practice with a metronome, and continue to slur the exercises.

CAUSE 2:   Air stream not maintained properly.

SOLUTION 2:   Maintain proper use of air in technical passages to avoid coordination problems between the tongue, fingers, and air stream. Maintain a consistent air stream at all dynamic levels. Players tend to focus on technique at the expense of proper breath support. Focus on maintaining breath support at all times until proper support becomes automatic.

PROBLEM: Uneven finger movement within the beat.

CAUSE 1:   Poor control of individual fingers.

SOLUTION 1:   Use a metronome and practice exercises that isolate each finger. Practice these exercises slowly and deliberately at first and gradually increase tempo, while always focusing on control. The ring fingers and the little fingers are particularly problematic, so work on these fingers extensively.

CAUSE 2:   Poor coordination of cross fingerings and half-hole fingerings.

SOLUTION 2:   Many bassoon fingerings involve awkward finger movements. When more awkward fingerings are mixed with less awkward fingerings in technical passages, uneven finger movement within the beat often occurs. Use a metronome and practice exercises that isolate problematic

combinations of fingerings. Practice these exercises slowly and deliberately at first and gradually increase tempo, while always focusing on control.

Tone Quality and Response Problems

PROBLEM: The tone is small and weak.

CAUSE 1:   Lack of sufficient air, air speed, and/or breath support.

SOLUTION 1:   Use more air, increase air speed, and keep the air stream consistent. Take full breaths and practice playing long tones at all dynamic levels. Focus on maintaining a consistent air speed appropriate for each dynamic level. Practice extensively at softer dynamic levels because it is harder to maintain proper breath support at softer dynamic levels than it is at louder dynamic levels.

CAUSE 2:   Embouchure too tight.

SOLUTION 2:   Relax the embouchure. Think of saying "oh" and surround the reed with warm air. Think of increasing the size of the imaginary circle of air into the instrument. That is, use a slightly more open air stream.

CAUSE 3:   Tight or closed throat.

SOLUTION 3:   Relax or open the throat as if saying "ah." Saying the syllable "ah" and shifting to an "oh" syllable while exhaling will open the throat and oral cavity and keep the embouchure round.

CAUSE 4:   The reed tip opening is too small

SOLUTION 4:   Increase the size of the tip opening by squeezing inward on the first wire, or try a different reed.

CAUSE 5:   Not enough reed in the mouth.

SOLUTION 5:   Take more reed in the mouth. The top lip should almost touch the first wire.

PROBLEM: An unfocused tone quality.

CAUSE 1:   Improper direction of the air stream.

SOLUTION 1:   Direct the air stream toward the tip opening. Surround the reed with warm air as if saying "who" or "oh" to relax the embouchure. "Oh" is slightly more open than "who." The resulting tone quality dictates which syllable is most appropriate.

CAUSE 2: Embouchure too loose.

SOLUTION 2: Firm the mouth corners slightly while maintaining a flat chin. The lips form an "O" shape, and the lower lip remains firm but not too tight, forming a cushion for the reed. Think of decreasing the imaginary circle of air into the instrument. That is, use a slightly more focused air stream.

CAUSE 3: Reed is not centered in the mouth.

SOLUTION 3: For most players, the reed should be centered in the mouth. Use a mirror regularly to check reed placement until proper habits are formed.

CAUSE 4: Not enough bottom lip over the teeth, making embouchure control inconsistent.

SOLUTION 4: Put more of the lower lip over the teeth and listen for improved tone quality. Very little red (if any) should be showing at the point where the lip touches the reed.

CAUSE 5: Reed enters the mouth at an incorrect angle.

SOLUTION 5: Make sure that the reed enters the mouth straight or at a slight angle, while the head stays straight. Reed angle is often affected by the height of the neck strap or by the position of the seat strap. The neck strap or seat strap is adjusted so that players do not have to reach up or down for the reed when they are in proper playing position. If the reed enters at an improper angle, the embouchure's ability to support the reed properly is impaired, and the tone will be unfocused.

PROBLEM: Lack of tone control.

CAUSE 1: Embouchure is inconsistent.

SOLUTION 1: Form a good basic embouchure and make sure that there is enough bottom lip over the teeth. Practice playing long tones to develop the embouchure muscles, and focus on keeping the embouchure consistent and stable at all times. Use a mirror regularly to check embouchure formation until proper habits are formed. Sometimes, a player's embouchure is unstable because the reed is too soft to provide sufficient resistance against the embouchure pressure, resulting in a quivery tone. Using a harder reed may help stabilize the embouchure.

CAUSE 2: Inconsistent breath support and/or control of the air stream.

SOLUTION 2: Practice breathing exercises with and without the bassoon to help develop breath support. Take full breaths and practice playing long tones at all dynamic levels. Focus on maintaining a consistent air speed appropriate for each dynamic level. Practice extensively at softer dynamic levels because it is harder to maintain proper breath support at softer dynamic levels than it is at louder dynamic levels. Maintain breath support in technical passages. That is, breath support is often compromised when playing technical passages because players tend to focus on technique at the expense of proper breath support.

CAUSE 3: Inconsistent hand/holding/instrument/playing positions and posture.

SOLUTION 3: Develop and follow a daily routine so that maintaining proper positions becomes habit. Proper placements of the left and right thumbs, and proper adjustment of the seat/neck strap are particularly important for tone control. A detailed account of these playing basics is under Hand/Holding/Instrument/Playing Positions and Posture.

CAUSE 4: Inconsistent throat and/or tongue positions.

SOLUTION 4: The throat should remain open as if saying "ah," and the tongue should remain relatively flat and relaxed in the mouth when slurring and drawn back slightly (arched) in the mouth when tonguing. Unnecessary movement and tension of the throat and tongue disrupts the air stream and can affect tone control, tone quality, and pitch.

CAUSE 5: The reed enters the mouth diagonally.

SOLUTION 5: Make sure the bocal is centered with the lips so that the reed enters the mouth at a straight angle. Often, placing the music stand too far off to one side causes the reed to enter the mouth at a diagonal.

CAUSE 6: The reed is turned or twisted when it enters the mouth, causing players to tilt their heads.

SOLUTION 6: Turn the reed so that it stays parallel to the lips. Keep the head, eyes, and chin straight at all times.

PROBLEM: Lack of dynamic control.

CAUSE 1: Insufficient control of the air stream and/or insufficient breath support throughout the dynamic range.

SOLUTION 1:   Practice playing long tones at one dynamic level over a set number of counts. When long tones can be played evenly at one dynamic level, practice playing long tones at different dynamic levels. Later, practice playing crescendi and decrescendi on long tones evenly over a set number of counts from one dynamic level to another. The softest and loudest dynamic levels can be particularly problematic. As a result, practicing at softer and louder dynamic levels is particularly important for tonal control.

CAUSE 2:   Making unnecessary embouchure adjustments when changing dynamics.

SOLUTION 2:   As a rule, the embouchure remains relatively stable and consistent regardless of the dynamic level. Exceptions include (1) in the pianissimo range, firm the embouchure slightly to compensate for the tendency of the pitch to go flat, and (2) in the fortissimo range, relax the embouchure slightly to compensate for the tendency of the pitch to go sharp.

CAUSE 3:   Using inappropriate reed strengths.

SOLUTION 3:   Reeds that are too hard are difficult to control and tend to respond poorly or to "cut out" at softer dynamic levels. Reeds that are too soft restrict the ability to play loudly.

PROBLEM: The low notes do not respond well.

CAUSE 1:   Leaks in the pads.

SOLUTION 1:   Check for leaks and replace any worn-out pads. The pads on the boot joint tend to leak more than other pads do because of the moisture that collects in the bottom of the joint. Check the larger pads on the boot joint often for leakage.

CAUSE 2:   Reed is too hard.

SOLUTION 2:   Using a slightly softer reed will offer less resistance and improve response in the low range.

CAUSE 3:   Not enough air and/or air stream too slow.

SOLUTION 3:   Use more air and increase air speed on the initial attacks for low notes. Once the note has responded, less air is needed to keep the tone sounding. Find a balance and adjust the air accordingly.

CAUSE 4: Too much air and/or air stream too fast.

SOLUTION 4: Use less air and decrease air speed. Overblowing in the low range causes the low notes to lose focus or crack and is a common problem with beginners.

CAUSE 5: Embouchure too tight.

SOLUTION 5: Relax the embouchure slightly in the low range. Think of using an "ah" syllable, and maintain an open throat and oral cavity. Focus for the particular note being played. As a rule, low notes do require more air than high notes.

PROBLEM: The high notes do not respond well.

CAUSE 1: Reed is too soft.

SOLUTION 1: Move up in reed strength. The reed needs to provide enough resistance to vibrate at the higher frequencies. In addition, soft reeds "close off" more easily under embouchure pressure in the high range than hard reeds.

CAUSE 2: Embouchure too tight.

SOLUTION 2: Relax the embouchure. Although firming the embouchure in the high range is normal, there is no need to tighten the embouchure excessively in the high range.

CAUSE 3: Overblowing.

SOLUTION 3: Focus for the note being played and use a controlled air stream. There is no need to blow harder in the high range; however, slight adjustments in the oral cavity may need to be made for certain pitches to improve response, tone quality, and intonation. Practice playing familiar tunes in the high range to develop control.

CAUSE 4: Not enough air and/or air stream too slow.

SOLUTION 4: Increase air stream and/or air speed. Work on breathing exercises with and without the bassoon to develop better breathing techniques.

CAUSE 5: Embouchure too loose.

SOLUTION 5: Firm the mouth corners slightly while maintaining a flat chin. The lips form an "O" shape, and the lower lip remains firm but not too

tight, forming a cushion for the reed. Think of decreasing the imaginary circle of air into the instrument. That is, use a slightly more focused air stream.

CAUSE 6:   Not using half-holes on the three G's.

SOLUTION 6:   Use the half-hole technique when fingering the three G's. Practice using the half-hole technique until it becomes automatic.

CAUSE 7:   Not using flick keys from high A-natural to high D-natural.

SOLUTION 7:   Always use the flick keys from high A-natural to high D-natural. Practice using flick keys until it becomes automatic.

PROBLEM: A loud, raucous, squawky tone.

CAUSE 1:   Too much reed in the mouth.

SOLUTION 1:   Take less reed in the mouth, and make sure that the jaw is not positioned too far forward. The mouth corners should be drawn in toward the reed, and the jaw should be down and back, forming an overbite.

CAUSE 2:   Too much air with an unfocused embouchure.

SOLUTION 2:   Use a proper embouchure. Think of surrounding the reed with warm air as if saying "oh." It may also help to think of decreasing the imaginary circle of air into the instrument. That is, use a slightly more focused air stream. Focus the throat and oral cavity for the pitch being played.

CAUSE 3:   Improper focus of the air stream.

SOLUTION 3:   Think of blowing air through and around the tip opening. Think of surrounding the reed with air as if saying "oh." Experiment with air direction until the best tone quality is achieved.

PROBLEM: A thin, pinched tone.

CAUSE 1:   Embouchure is too tight.

SOLUTION 1:   Relax the embouchure and surround the reed with warm air as if saying "who" or "oh." "Oh" is slightly more open than "who." Let the tone quality dictate which syllable is more appropriate. Make sure the mouth corners are drawn inward rather than pulled back and that the lower lip is not stretched too tightly over the teeth. It may be helpful to think of increasing the imaginary circle of air into the instrument. That is, use a slightly more open air stream.

CAUSE 2: Reed is too soft.

SOLUTION 2: Discard old reeds and/or move up in reed strength. Using reeds that are too soft causes players to "bite," resulting in a thin, pinched tone. As reeds wear out they tend to soften. A reed that is too hard at first may break in after being played.

CAUSE 3: Too little reed in the mouth.

SOLUTION 3: Take more reed in the mouth. The top lip should be almost touching the wire.

CAUSE 4: Improper focus of the air stream.

SOLUTION 4: Focusing the air stream at too high an angle can result in a thin tone. Focusing the air stream at too low an angle can result in a spread tone. Direct the air stream toward the tip opening. Think of surrounding the reed with a steady stream of warm air as if saying "oh," and think of blowing the air stream through the instrument.

CAUSE 5: Instrument is being held too close to the body, putting excessive pressure on the reed.

SOLUTION 5: Reposition the instrument so that the reed enters the mouth at a slightly upward angle (almost straight in).

CAUSE 6: Not using a sufficient amount of air and/or the air stream is too slow.

SOLUTION 6: Increase air speed and the amount of air being used, and work on breathing exercises to develop proper breathing techniques.

CAUSE 7: Tip opening in the reed is too small.

SOLUTION 7: Adjust the first wire with pliers to increase the size of the tip opening. If this solution does not work, use a different reed.

PROBLEM: Grunting or guttural noises can be heard during normal play.

CAUSE 1: Closing the throat or glottis when coughing or swallowing is normal; however, players sometimes develop the habit of closing the throat to stop the air and opening it to release the air, which results in a grunting sound. Closing the throat and using it as a valve to control air flow negatively affects releases, tone quality, and pitch.

SOLUTION 1:   Maintain an open throat as if saying "ah" and learn to control the flow of the air from the diaphragm. Do not engage the throat in any way when articulating.

PROBLEM: A Reedy/Buzzy Tone

CAUSE 1:   Reed is too soft.

SOLUTION 1:   Move up in reed strength. Soft reeds can sound reedy/buzzy. Players who have played for two or three years should use medium or medium-hard reeds.

CAUSE 2:   Reed is in poor condition.

SOLUTION 2:   Use a reed that has good balance and a good cut. Also, make sure the reed has not been damaged.

CAUSE 3:   Improper focus of air stream.

SOLUTION 3:   Relax the embouchure and surround the reed with warm air as if saying "oh." Maintain a consistent air stream. A reedy/buzzy tone can also be improved by relaxing the embouchure and opening the throat/oral cavity appropriately.

PROBLEM: An airy tone quality.

CAUSE 1:   Reed is too hard.

SOLUTION 1:   Use a softer reed. As a rule, beginners should use soft reeds (soft or medium soft), intermediate players should use medium reeds (medium soft, medium, or medium hard), and advanced players should use medium hard reeds (medium hard or hard).

CAUSE 2:   Air escaping from the mouth corners.

SOLUTION 2:   Form a proper embouchure to eliminate this problem. Air escapes from the mouth corners when the surrounding muscles are not supporting inwardly toward the reed. Letting air escape from the mouth corners can become a habit. Make sure that the mouth corners are drawn in toward the reed and that the jaw is drawn down and back, forming an overbite.

CAUSE 3:   Leaks in the instrument.

SOLUTION 3:   Have a repair technician check for leaks and replace any worn out and/or leaking pads.

CAUSE 4:	The height of the pads above the tone holes is incorrect.

SOLUTION 4: Adjust the pad height and play the instrument after each adjustment to determine if appropriate adjustments have been made. Pad height should be adjusted by a knowledgeable repair technician.

PROBLEM:	The tone sounds dead and lifeless, and the pitch is flat.

CAUSE 1:	The reed is too old and/or too soft.

SOLUTION 1: Discard the reed and use a new one. Reeds do wear out relatively quickly, even though they may still look good. As a rule, after a reed has been played on consistently for a couple of weeks, it begins to deteriorate. Visible signs of aging include a dirty or dingy look to the reed with nicks or chips in the reed tip.

PROBLEM:	Squeaks/squeaking.

CAUSE 1:	Reed is too dry and/or is warped.

SOLUTION 1: Reeds should be soaked thoroughly before playing. To prevent reeds from drying out and warping during rehearsals, wet them periodically with the mouth or with water. During prolonged periods of resting, reeds should be soaked in water. Store reeds in a reed guard or reed case immediately after playing to help prevent warping.

CAUSE 2:	Unfocused/unstable embouchure.

SOLUTION 2: Practice long tones to strengthen the embouchure muscles, and concentrate on eliminating unnecessary embouchure movement, especially when playing skips and leaps. The embouchure should remain relatively constant and stable at all times. Sometimes, a player's embouchure is unstable because the reed is too soft to provide sufficient resistance against the embouchure pressure, resulting in a quivery tone. Using a harder reed will provide the necessary resistance.

CAUSE 3:	Reed poorly constructed and/or in poor condition (cracked, chipped, unbalanced, etc.).

SOLUTION 3: Use a good reed that has not been damaged. Although a sound can be produced on a cracked or chipped reed, such reeds do not allow the blades to close off against each other, which can cause squeaks. Store reeds in a reed guard or reed case immediately after playing to help prevent damage.

CAUSE 4:   Too much reed in the mouth.

SOLUTION 4:   Take less reed in the mouth. A proper embouchure requires taking most of the reed into the mouth, but the upper lip should not touch the first wire. In addition, an overbite formation is essential to achieving a good tone quality and intonation on bassoon.

CAUSE 5:   Not properly covering tone holes.

SOLUTION 5:   Maintain proper hand position. The bassoon requires the fingers to spread apart to cover the tone holes. The hand position is often awkward at first; however, if the tone holes are not properly covered, squawks are likely to occur.

CAUSE 6:   Leaks in the instrument.

SOLUTION 6:   Have a repair technician check for leaks and replace any worn out and/or leaking pads.

CAUSE 7:   Bassoon out of adjustment.

SOLUTION 7:   Have the bassoon adjusted so that the keys work properly. The keys work together in a precise manner to produce each tone. If the keys are not opening and closing properly, squeaks can occur. Sometimes a visual check will indicate the obvious point of the problem. The whisper key can be particularly problematic if not adjusted properly.

PROBLEM: Gurgling sounds on certain pitches.

CAUSE 1:   Water has accumulated in one or more of the tone holes or vent holes.

SOLUTION 1:   Remove the water by blowing a fast, narrow stream of air into the appropriate tone hole (i.e., usually the first open tone hole). Some players use cigarette paper, feathers, Q-tips, or a pipe cleaner to remove water from the tone holes. Care must be taken that such implements do not scratch or damage the tone holes. During long periods of play, disassembling the instrument and swabbing it out thoroughly may be helpful.

CAUSE 2:   Poor reed.

SOLUTION 2:   Suck the excess condensation from the reed regularly. Gurgling sounds can be caused by reeds that are cracked, warped badly, worn out, or otherwise damaged, and by reeds that fit improperly onto the bocal.

PROBLEM: A slightly delayed response of certain notes during slurred intervals, or the wrong pitch sounds even though the fingering is correct.

CAUSE 1: Pad or pads sticking. Pads absorb moisture during normal play. This moisture attracts dirt and food particles. These particles collect in and around the tone holes and on the pads (particularly in the creases), causing pads to stick. In addition, sugar from certain beverages also causes pads to stick.

SOLUTION 1: Clean the pads and tone holes. For a quick fix, place a thin sheet of tissue paper, cigarette paper, or a dollar bill (preferably a clean one) between the sticking pad and tone hole. Close the pad lightly, and pull the paper through. Cleaning pads in this way is fairly common among advanced players. Various types of "no-stick" powder are also available. These powders work for only a very short period of time, and they are often quite messy. They create more problems in the long run because they simply add to the particles already collected on the pads and inside the tone holes. Generally, powders should not be used to free sticking pads. Ultimately, the instrument may need to be taken apart and cleaned thoroughly by a repair technician, and sticking pads may need to be replaced. Players should not eat or drink (except water) while playing to avoid pad and instrument damage.

CAUSE 2: The crease in the pad is too deep, causing the pad to bind against the tone hole edge.

SOLUTION 2: Replace the pad.

CAUSE 3: The outside layer of a pad is torn, causing the pad to bind against the tone hole edge.

SOLUTION 3: Replace the pad.

CAUSE 4: A rod is bent.

SOLUTION 4: Have a repair technician straighten the rod. Bent rods can cause key mechanisms to stick. Often, players can feel a bump or hitch in the mechanism, indicating that a bent rod is the source of the problem.

CAUSE 5: A spring has come off, a spring is broken, or a spring is loose or worn out.

SOLUTION 5: Use a spring-hook tool to put the spring back into place. A pencil, small screwdriver, or crochet hook can also be used to replace springs in some cases, but they are not nearly as effective. Spring-hook tools are easy to use and inexpensive. Loose or worn springs can sometimes be tightened by reseating them and/or by bending them gently in the appropriate direction. Broken springs must be replaced.

CAUSE 6:   Pivot (post) screws are loose. Pivot screws work themselves loose periodically, creating problems with the alignment of key mechanisms. The area around pivot screws can also get gummed up by accumulating dirt and other foreign materials, resulting in sticky key mechanisms.

SOLUTION 6:   Clean pivot screws and surrounding areas. Place a drop of key oil on the screws and threads and tighten the screws snugly. Placing a small amount of nail polish on screw heads and rods that frequently work themselves loose will help hold them in place.

CAUSE 7:   Not using flick keys appropriately between high A-natural and high D-natural.

SOLUTION 7:   Use flick keys appropriately to help notes respond and sound better in tune. Practicing using flick keys until it becomes automatic.

General Resources for Instrumental Music Teachers

ACOUSTICS RESOURCES

Backus, J. (1977). *The acoustical foundations of music* (2d ed.). New York: Norton.

Benade, A. H. (1976). *Fundamentals of musical acoustics.* New York: Oxford University Press.

Fletcher, N. H., & T. D. Rossing (1998). *The physics of musical instruments* (2d ed.). New York: Stringer-Verlag.

Hall, D. E. (1991). *Musical acoustics* (2d ed.). Pacific Grove, CA: Brooks/Cole Publishing.

Nederveen, C. J. (1998). *Acoustical aspects of woodwind instruments.* Dekalb: Northern Illinois University Press.

Rossing, T. D. (1994). Musical instruments. In *Encyclopedia of applied physics,* Vol. 11, pp. 129–171. New York: VCH Publishers.

WOODWIND PEDAGOGY BOOKS

Bartolozzi, B. (1982). *New sounds for woodwinds* (2d ed.). London: Oxford University Press.

Colwell, R., & T. W. Goolsby (2001). *The teaching of instrumental music* (3d ed.). Englewood Cliffs, NJ: Prentice-Hall.

Dietz, W. (1998). *Teaching woodwinds: A method and resource handbook for music educators.* New York: Schirmer.

Merriman, L. (1978). *Woodwind research guide: A selective bibliography of materials pertaining to the literature, development, and acoustics of woodwind instruments.* Evanston, IL: The Instrumentalist Co.

Rehfeldt, P. (1998). *Playing woodwind instruments: A guide for teachers, performers, and composers.* Long Grove, IL: Waveland Press.

Saucier, G. A. (1981). *Woodwinds: Fundamental performance techniques.* New York: Schirmer.

Sawhill, C., & B. McGarrity (1962). *Playing and teaching woodwind instruments.* Englewood Cliffs, NJ: Prentice-Hall.

Westphal, F. (1990). *Guide to teaching woodwinds* (5th ed.). Dubuque, IA: Brown.
Woodwind anthology: A compendium of woodwind articles from The Instrumentalist. (1984). Evanston, IL: The Instrumentalist Co.

GENERAL PEDAGOGY WEB SITES

Alexander Technique	www.alexandertechnique.com
Band Director Resources	www.banddirector.com
JSTOR (Woodwind and Brass Information)	www.links.jstor.org
Music Education Resources	www.menc.org
Music Teachers Information	www.mtna.org
Bandworld	www.bandworld.org

CD RECORDINGS AVAILABLE THROUGH WEB SITES

www.amismusicalcircle.com
www.bassoonmaster.com
www.cdconection.com
www.cduniverse.com
www.classicaldirectory.com
www.classicsax.com
www.forrestsmusic.com
www.howarth.uk.com
www.mmimports.com
www.musiciansnews.com/windbrass
www.oboeclassics.co.uk
www.reedmusic.com
www.testament.com.uk
www.tutti.co.uk
www.ukcd.net
www.walkingfrog.com
www.weinermusic.com
www.woodwindsonline.com
www.bostonrecords.com
www.tower.com
www.amazon.com

REEDS, SINGLE

Armato, B. (1996). *Perfect a reed—and beyond: Reed adjusting method.* Ardsley, NY: PerfectaReed.

Bowen, G. H. (1981). *Making and adjusting clarinet reeds.* Hancock, MA: Sounds of Woodwinds.

Grabner, W. (1999). *Making clarinet reeds by hand.* Highland Park, IL: ClarinetXpress.

Guy, L. (1997). *Selection, adjustment, and care of single reeds* (2d ed.). Stony Point, NY: Rivernote Press.

Kirck, G. T. (1983). *The reed guide: A handbook for modern reed working for all single reed woodwind instruments.* Decatur, IL: Reed-Mate.

Opperman, K. (2002). *Handbook for making and adjusting single reeds: For all clarinets and saxophones* (rev. ed.). Oyster Bay, NY: M. Baron.

Reed, R. (2004). *The saxophone reed: The advanced art of adjusting single reeds.* West Conshohocken, PA: Infinity Publishing.

Rehfeldt, P. (1983). *Making and adjusting single reeds.* Lakeside, AZ: Mill Creek.

Reeds, Double

Berman, M. (1988). *The art of oboe reed making.* Toronto: Canadian Scholars Press.

Eubanks, M. G. (1986). *Advanced reed design and testing procedure for bassoon.* Portland, OR: Arundo Research.

Hedrick, P., & E. Hedrick (1972). *Oboe reed making: A modern method.* Oneonta, NY: Swift-Dorr.

Ledet, D. (1982). *Oboe reed styles—theory and practice.* Bloomington: Indiana University Press.

Light, J. (1983). *The oboe reed book: A straight-talking guide to making and understanding oboe reeds.* Des Moines, IA: Drake University Press.

Pesavento, A. (1972). *Design and adjustment principles of the bassoon reed: A manual for the intermediate player.* Indianapolis: Lang.

Popkin, M. A., & L. Glickman (1969). *Bassoon reed making—including bassoon repair, maintenance and adjustment and an approach to bassoon playing.* Evanston, IL: The Instrumentalist Co.

Schleiffer, E. (1974). *The art of bassoon reed making.* Oneonta, NY: Swift-Dorr.

Weait, C. (1980). *Bassoon reed-making: A basic technique* (2d ed.). New York: McGinnis & Marx.

Weber, D. (1990). *The reed maker's manual: Step-by-step instructions for making oboe and English horn reeds.* Phoenix, AZ: D. B. Weber and F. B. Capps.

Additional Resources for Flute

Flute Pedagogy Books

Debost, M. (1996). *The simple flute from A to Z.* London: Oxford University Press.

Dick, R. (1989). *The other flute: A performance manual of technique* (2d ed.). New York: Oxford University Press.

Floyd, A. S. (1990). *The Gilbert legacy: Methods, exercises and techniques for the flutist.* Cedar Falls, IA: Winzer.

Howell, T. (1974). *The avant-garde flute: A handbook for composers and flutists.* Berkeley: University of California Press.

Harrison, H. (2002). *How to play the flute: Everything you need to know to play the flute.* New York: St. Martin's Griffin.

Kincaid, W., and C. Polin (1970). *The art and practice of modern flute technique* (3d ed.). New York: MCA.

Krell, J. C. (1997). *Kincaidiana: A flute player's notebook* (2d ed.). Santa Clarita, CA: National Flute Association.

Mather, R. (1980). *The art of playing the flute.* Iowa City, IA: Romney.

Meylan, R. (1988). *The flute.* Portland, OR: Amadeus.

Neuhaus, M. (1986). *The flute fingering book.* Naperville, IL: Flute Studio Press.

O'Neill, J. (1994). *The jazz method for flute.* London: Schott.

Pellerite, J. (1972). *A modern guide to fingerings for the flute* (2d ed.). Bloomington: Zalo.

Pheland, J., & L. Burkart (2000). *The complete guide to the flute and piccolo.* Boston: Conservatory.

Powell, A. (2002). *The flute.* New Haven, CT: Yale University Press.

Putnik, E. (1970). *The art of flute playing.* Evanston, IL: Summy-Birchard.

Rockstro, R. S. (1928/1890). *The flute.* London: Musica Rara.

Stoune, M. C. (1998). *The flutist's handbook: A pedagogy anthology.* Santa Clarita, CA: National Flute Association.

Toff, N. (1996). *The flute book: A complete guide for students and performers.* New York: Oxford University Press.

Flute Literature Resources

Flute World graded catalogue (14th ed.). (1998). Franklin, MI: Flute World.

Pellerite, J. (1978). *A handbook of literature for the flute* (3d ed.). Bloomington, IN: Zalo.

Rainey, T. (1985). *The flute manual: A comprehensive text and resource book for both the teacher and student.* Lanham, MD: University Press of America.

Rasmussen, M. (1966). *Teacher's guide to the literature of woodwind instruments.* Milford, NH: Brass and Woodwind Quarterly.

Vester, F. (1967). *Flute repertoire catalog.* London: Musica Rara.

———. (1985). *Flute music of the eighteenth century.* London: Musica Rara.

Voxman, H. (1975). *Woodwind solo and study material music guide.* Evanston, IL: The Instrumentalist Co.

Wain, R. (1979). *Music library catalog: National flute association* (2d ed.). Tucson: University of Arizona Press.

Wilkins, W. (1974). *The index of flute music including the index of baroque flute sonatas.* Magnolia, AR: The Music Register.

Flute Journals/Magazines

Flute Talk—The Instrumentalist Co.

Flutist Quarterly—National Flute Association (NFA)

Web Sites

National Flute Association (NFA)   www.nfaonline.org
www.flute.com

ADDITIONAL RESOURCES FOR OBOE

Oboe Pedagogy Books

Browne, G. (2000). *The art of cor anglais.* Sycamore, IL: Sycamore.
Burgess, G., & B. Haynes (2004). *The oboe.* New Haven, CT: Yale University Press.
Goossens, L., & E. Roxburgh (1977). *Oboe.* New York: Schirmer.
Joppig, G. (1988). *The oboe and the bassoon.* Trans. Alfred Clayton. Portland, OR: Amadeus Press.
Light, J. (1994). *Essays for oboists: More "straight talk" about achieving success as an oboist (or any other wind player).* Des Moines, IA: Alborada Publications.
Mayer, R. M. (1969). *Essentials of oboe playing.* Des Plaines, IL: Karnes.
Rothwell, E. (1977). *The oboist's companion.* Vol. 3. New York: Oxford University Press.
———. (1983). *Oboe technique* (3d ed.). New York: Oxford University Press.
Sprenkle, R., & D. Ledet (1961). *The art of oboe playing.* Evanston, IL: Summy-Birchard.

Oboe Literature Resources

Gifford, V. (1983). *Music for oboe, oboe d'amore, and English horn: A bibliography of materials in the Library of Congress.* Westport, CT: Greenwood.
Haynes, B. (1985). *Music for oboe, 1650–1800: A bibliography* (rev. ed.). Berkeley, CA: Fallen Leaf Press.
McMullen, W. W. (1994). *Soloistic English horn literature from 1736–1984.* Stuyvesant, NY: Pendragon Press.
Stanton, R. E. (1972/1974). *The oboe player's encyclopedia.* 2 vols. Oneonta, NY: Swift-Dorr.
Wilkins, W. (1976). *Index of oboe music including an index of baroque trio sonatas.* Magnolia, AR: The Music Register.

Oboe Journals

Double Reed News—British Double Reed Society (BDRS)
The Double Reed—International Double Reed Society (IDRS)

Web Sites

International Double Reed Society   www.idrs.org
The British Double Reed Society   www.bdrs.org.uk
Windplayer Online   www.windplayer.com

ADDITIONAL RESOURCES FOR CLARINET

Clarinet Pedagogy Books

Brymer, J. (1977). *Clarinet*. New York: Schirmer.

Campione, C. (2001). *Campione, on clarinet: A complete guide to clarinet playing and instruction*. Fairfield, OH: J. Ten-Ten Publications.

Drushler, P. (1978). *The altissimo register: A partial approach*. Rochester, NY: Shall-u-mo.

Gold, C. V. (1983). *Contemporary clarinet technique: A study of the altissimo register*. Greensboro, NC: Spectrum Music.

Guy, L. (2000). *Embouchure building for clarinetists* (3d ed.). Stony Point, NY: Rivernote Press.

Lawson, C. (1995). *The Cambridge companion to the clarinet*. New York: Cambridge University Press.

———. (2000). *The early clarinet: A practical guide*. New York: Cambridge University Press.

Pino, D. (1980). *The clarinet and clarinet playing*. New York: Scribners.

Rehfeldt, P. (1978). *New directions for clarinet*. Berkeley: University of California Press.

Ridenour, T. (1986). *Clarinet fingerings: A comprehensive guide for the performer and educator*. Kenosha, WI: Leblanc.

———. (2002). *The educator's guide to the clarinet: A complete guide to teaching and learning the clarinet* (2d ed.). Duncanville, TX: T. Ridenour.

Stein, K. (1958). *The art of clarinet playing*. Evanston, IL: Summy-Birchard.

Thurston, F. (1985). *Clarinet technique* (4th ed.). London, NY: Oxford University Press.

Weston, P. (1982). *The clarinetist's companion*. Corby, Northants (United Kingdom): Fentone Music.

CLARINET LITERATURE RESOURCES

Gee, H. (1981). *Solos de concours, 1897–1980*. Bloomington: Indiana University Press.

Gilbert, R. (1972). *The clarinetist's solo repertoire: A discography*. New York: Richard Gilbert.

———. (1973 and 1975). *The clarinetist's solo repertoire: A discography* (2 vols.). New York: Grenadilla Society.

———. (1996). *The clarinetists' discography III and 1996 supplement*. New York: Grenadilla Society.

Gillespie, J. (1973). *Solos for unaccompanied clarinet: An annotated bibliography of published works*. Detroit: Information Coordinators.

Heim, N. M. (1984). *Clarinet literature in outline*. Hyattsville, MD: Norcat Music Press.

Opperman, K. (1960). *Repertory of the clarinet*. New York: Ricordi.

Wilkins W. (1975). *The index of clarinet music*. Magnolia, AR: The Music Register.

Clarinet Journals

The Clarinet—International Clarinet Association (ICA)

Web Sites

Clarinet Info Page	www.sneezy.org/clarinet
Clarinet Pages	www.woodwind.org/clarinet
ClassicWeb Clarinet Page	www.classicweb.com/Clarinet.htm
International Clarinet Association	www.clarinet.org
The Orchestral Clarinetist	www.clarinetxpress.com/ orchestralclarinet.html
World Clarinet Alliance	www.wka-clarinet.org

ADDITIONAL RESOURCES FOR SAXOPHONE

Saxophone Pedagogy Books

Harvey, P. (1981). *The saxophonist's bedside book.* Alexandria, VA: Fentone Music.

Ingham, R. (1998). *The Cambridge companion to the saxophone.* Cambridge: Cambridge University Press.

Mauk, S. (1986). *A practical approach to playing the saxophone: For class or individual instruction.* Ithaca, NY: Lyceum.

Mordnes, E. J. (2004). *101 saxophone tips: Stuff all the pros know and use.* New York: Hal Leonard.

Teal, L. (1963). *The art of saxophone playing.* Evanston, IL: Summy-Birchard.

Saxophone Literature Resources

Dawson, J. (1981). *Music for saxophone by British composers: An annotated bibliography.* Medfield, MA: Dorn.

Dorn, K. (1972). *Over 560 more compositions for the saxophone.* San Diego, CA: Dorn Publications.

Gee, H. (1986). *Saxophone soloists and their music 1844–1985: An annotated bibliography.* Bloomington: Indiana University Press.

Harvey, P. (1995). *Saxophone.* London: Kahn & Averil

Hemke, F. L. (1975). *A comprehensive listing of saxophone literature* (rev. ed.). Elkhart, IN: Selmer.

Londeix, J. M. (1994). *150 years of music for saxophone: Bibliographical index of music and educational literature for the saxophone.* Cherry Hill, NJ: Roncorp.

———. (2003). *A comprehensive guide to saxophone repertoire 1844–2003.* Cherry Hill, NJ: Roncorp.

Schleuter, S. L. (1993). *Saxophone recital music: A discography.* Westport, CT: Greenwood.

Wilkins, W. (1979). *The index of saxophone music.* Magnolia, AR: The Music Register.

Saxophone Journals

Saxophone Journal—Dorn Publications
The Saxophone Symposium—North American Saxophone Alliance (NASA)

Web Sites

North American Saxophone Alliance (NASA)	www.saxalliance.org
Sax on the Web	www.saxontheweb.net
The International Saxophone Home Page (ISHP)	www.saxophone.org
The Saxophone Journal	www.dornpub.com/ saxophonejournal.html

ADDITIONAL RESOURCES FOR BASSOON

Bassoon Pedagogy Books

Biggers, C. A. (1977). *The contra-bassoon*. Bryn Mawr, PA: Elkan-Vogel.
Camden, A. (1962). *Bassoon Technique*. London: Oxford University Press.
Cooper, L., & H. Toplansky (1968). *Essentials of bassoon technique*. Union, NJ: Howard Toplansky.
Klimko, D. J. (1974). *Bassoon performance practices and teaching in the United States and Canada*. Moscow, ID: School of Music Publications.
Langwill, L. (1965). *The bassoon and contrabassoon*. New York: Norton.
Popkin, M. (1969). *Bassoon reed making including bassoon repair, maintenance and adjustment, and an approach to bassoon playing*. Evanston, IL: The Instrumentalist Co.
Spencer, W. & F. A. Mueller (1969). *The art of bassoon playing* (2d ed.). Evanston, IL: Summy-Birchard.

Bassoon Literature Resources

Beebe, J. (1990). *Music for unaccompanied solo bassoon: An annotated bibliography*. Jefferson, NC: McFarland.
Fletcher, K. K. (1988). *The Paris conservatoire and the contest solos for bassoon*. Bloomington: Indiana University Press.
Koenigsbeck, B. (1994). *Bassoon bibliography*. Monteux, France: Musica Rara.
Risdon, H. (1963). *Musical literature for the bassoon*. Seattle: Berdon.
Wilkins, W. (1975). *The index of bassoon music*. Magnolia, AR: The Music Register.

Bassoon Journals

Double Reed News—British Double Reed Society (BDRS)
The Double Reed—International Double Reed Society (IDRS)

Web Sites

International Double Reed Society	www.idrs.colorado.edu
Resources and Information for Bassoonists	www.bassoon.org
British Double Reed Society (BDRS)	www.bdrs.org.uk
Windplayer Online	www.windplayer.com

PROFESSIONAL ASSOCIATIONS/ORGANIZATIONS

American Bandmasters Association
(ABA)
1521 Pickard
Norman, OK 73072-6316
405-321-3373
www.americanbandmasters.org

American School Band Directors
Association (ASBDA)
P.O. Box 146
Otsego, MI 49078-0146
616-694-2092
www.asbda.com

British Double Reed Society
(BDRS)
Christopher Rosevear
The Old School
Bagwell Lane, Winchfield
Hook RG27 8DB, UK

Conductors' Guild, Inc.
103 High St., Room 6
West Chester, PA 19382-3262
610-430-6010
www.conductorsguild.org

International Association of Jazz
Educators (IAJE)
P.O. Box 724
Manhattan, KS 66505-0724

913-776-8744
www.iaje.org

International Clarinet Association
(ICA)
P.O. Box 1310
Lyons, CO 80540 USA
801-867-4335
www.clarinet.org

International Double Reed Society
(IDRS)
Norma Hooks
2423 Lawndale Road
Finksburg, MD 21048-1401
410-871-0658
www.idrs.org

National Association of College
Wind and Percussion Instructors
Richard K. Weerts, Executive
Secretary-Treasurer
Division of Fine Arts
Truman State University
Kirksville, Missouri 63501
www.nacwpi.org

National Band Association (NBA)
P.O. Box 121292
Nashville, TN 37212-1292
615-343-4775
www.nationalbandassociation.org

National Flute Association (NFA)
26951 Ruether Avenue, Suite H
Santa Clara, CA 91351
www.nfaonline.org

North American Saxophone Alliance
    (NASA)
Kenneth Tse, Membership Director

School of Music
University of Iowa
Iowa City, IA 52242
www.saxalliance.org

PROFESSIONAL JOURNALS/MAGAZINES

American Music Teacher (AMT)
Music Teachers National Association
    (MTNA)
The Carew Tower
441 Vine Street, Suite 505
Cincinnati, OH 45202-2814

Bandworld Magazine
ABC/BW/WIBC
407 Terrace St.
Ashland, OR 97520

Double Reed News
British Double Reed Society
    (BDRS)
Christopher Rosevear
The Old School
Bagwell Lane, Winchfield
Hook RG27 8DB, UK

Flutist Quarterly
National Flute Association (NFA)
26951 Ruether Ave., Suite H
Santa Clarita, CA 91351

The Instrumentalist Magazine
200 Northfield Road
Northfield, IL 60093

International Journal of Music
    Education (IJME)
ISME International Office
P.O. Box 909
Nedlands 6909, WA
Australia

Jazz Education Journal
International Association for Jazz
    Education (IAJE)
P.O. Box 52
St. Bonaventure University
St. Bonaventure, NY 14778

Journal of Band Research
American Bandmasters
    Association (ABA)
Troy State University Press
Managing Editor
Troy, AL 36082

Journal of Music Teacher Education
    (JMTE)
Music Educators National
    Conference (MENC)
1806 Robert Fulton Drive
Reston, VA 20191

Music Educators Journal (MEJ)
Music Educators National
    Conference (MENC)
1806 Robert Fulton Drive
Reston, VA 20191

Music Magazine
American Federation of
    Musicians (AFM)
1501 Broadway, Suite 600
New York, NY 10036

Saxophone Journal
Dorn Publications
P.O. Box 206
Medfield, MA 02052 USA

School Band and Orchestra Magazine
50 Brook Road
Needham, MA 02494
781-453-9310

Teaching Music (TM)
Music Educators National
    Conference (MENC)
1806 Robert Fulton Drive
Reston, VA 20191

The Clarinet
International Clarinet Association
    (ICA)
1406 Lowden Avenue
Wheaton, IL 60187

The Double Reed
International Double Reed Society
    (IDRS)
Norma Hooks
2423 Lawndale Road
Finksburg, MD 21048-1401
410-871-0658

The Music Trader
23916 SE Kent-Kangley Road
Maple Valley, Washington 98038
425-413-4343

The Saxophone Symposium
North American Saxophone Alliance
    (NASA)
Thomas Smialek, Editor
Penn State University, Hazelton
76 University Drive
Hazelton, PA 18202-1291

Wind Player Magazine
P.O. Box 2750
Malibu, CA 90265
800-946-3305

The Woodwind Quarterly
26911 Maple Valley—Black Diamond
    Hwy SE
Maple Valley, WA 98038
425-413-4343

Index

acoustical basics, 1
  See also harmonics
acoustical properties, 81 (fl), 188 (cl), 335
    (sx), 459 (ob), 598 (bsn)
  See also acoustical basics; construction
    and design; harmonics
action, 1
adjusting pitch, 4 (com), 82 (fl), 189 (cl),
    336 (sx), 460 (ob), 598 (bsn)
  See also intonation
A-flat to B-flat trill key, 598 (bsn)
  See also alternate fingerings/alternates
air column, 4
  See also acoustical basics
air stream, 4 (com), 82 (fl), 189 (cl), 336
    (sx), 460 (ob), 598 (bsn)
  and circular breathing, 23
  and dizziness/lightheadedness, 26
  and dynamics, 26
  and intonation, 41
  and mouthpieces, 50
  See also breathing/breath support/air
    control; articulation/articulative
    styles; tone production
Albert system, 190
alternate fingerings/alternates, 83 (fl), 190
    (cl), 336 (sx), 461 (ob), 599 (bsn)
  See also intonation; technique
altissimo/extended range, 86 (fl), 195 (cl)
    341 (sx), 465 (ob), 603 (bsn)
alto clarinet, 203
  embouchure, 236

hand/holding/instrument playing
    positions and posture, 224
transposition, 293
written range, 296
  See also instrument family and playing
    considerations
alto flute, 123, 125
transposition, 151
written range, 155
  See also instrument family and playing
    considerations
alto sax, 335
  air stream, 336
  embouchure, 361
  hand/holding/instrument playing
    positions and posture, 367
  transposition, 416
  written range, 419
  See also instrument family and playing
    considerations
anchor tonguing, 6
  See also tonguing
arm, 87
articulated keys, 88 (fl), 198 (cl), 343 (sx),
    466 (ob), 604 (bsn)
articulation. *See* articulation/articulative
    styles
articulation/articulative styles, 6
  See also attacks; breathing/breath
    support/air control; releases;
    tonguing
arundo donax, 266

assembly, 88 (fl), 198 (cl), 344 (sx), 466
    (ob), 605 (bsn)
    See also hand/holding/instrument/
    playing positions and posture
attacks, 9 (com), 90 (fl), 348 (sx)
    See also articulation/articulative styles;
    releases; tonguing

B foot joint, 93
    See also foot joint
back pressure, 202 (cl), 349 (sx), 471 (ob),
    608 (bsn)
    oboe vibrato and tonal
    considerations, 558
baffle, 47 (com), 203 (cl), 349 (sx)
    See also mouthpiece/mouthpieces
balance and blend considerations, 90 (fl),
    203 (cl), 349 (sx), 472 (ob), 609 (bsn)
baritone saxophone, 381
    air stream, 336
    construction and design, 357
    embouchure, 363
    low A key, 391
    playing position, 373, 376
    transposition, 416
    written range, 419
    See also instrument family and playing
    considerations
barrel, 204, 211
    and tuning, 241
    See also tuning rings
bass clarinet, 204
    embouchure, 217
    transposition, 293
    written range, 296
    See also instrument family and playing
    considerations
bass flute, 93
    transposition, 151
    See also instrument family and playing
    considerations
bass oboe, 501
    transposition, 560
    See also instrument family and playing
    considerations
bass saxophone, 376
    transposition, 417

    See also instrument family and playing
    considerations
bassoon, 598
    embouchure, 623
    hand/holding/instrument playing
    positions and posture, 634
    transposition, 675
    written range, 678
    See also instrument family and playing
    considerations
beak, 47 (com), 204 (cl), 351 (sx)
    See also mouthpiece/mouthpieces
beats, 10
    and temperament, 61
    See also intonation
bell tones, 10
Bennett. *See* flute scales
binding, 610
    See also reeds, double
bis, 94 (fl), 351 (sx)
    See also alternate fingerings/alternates
blanks, reed, 205
    See also reeds, single
bocal, 473 (English horn), 611 (bsn)
    assembly, 504 (English horn), 607 (bsn)
    pitch adjustment, 508 (English horn),
    676 (bsn)
    position of, 504 (English horn), 639
    (bsn)
bocal receiver, 504 (English horn), 613
    (bsn)
bocal/reed angle, 504 (English horn), 613
    (bsn)
body, 94
    See also materials in flute making; parts,
    flute; wall thickness
body/tube, 611
Boehm system, 94 (fl), 205 (cl), 473 (ob)
bore, instrument, 94, 613
    See also acoustical properties; conical;
    cylindrical
bore, mouthpiece, 205
    See also mouthpiece/mouthpieces
bore/throat, mouthpiece, 205 (cl), 351 (sx)
    See also mouthpiece/mouthpieces
break, 94 (fl), 205 (cl), 352 (sx), 474 (ob),
    613 (bsn)

See also crossing the break; technique
breath attacks. *See* attacks
breathing/breath support/air control, 10
Briccialdi key, 95
Buffet (French) system bassoon, 614
    See also Heckel (German) system
      bassoon
butt, reed, 206 (cl), 474 (ob), 614 (bsn)
    reed parts, 267, 268, 535, 536
    See also heel; reeds, double; reeds, single

C foot joint, 95
    See also B foot joint; foot joint
C-sharp trill key, 95 (fl)
cane/cane color, 206 (cl), 353 (sx), 474 (ob),
    614 (bsn)
    See also reeds, double; reeds, single
care and maintenance, 23 (com), 95 (fl),
    206 (cl), 353 (sx), 474 (ob), 614 (bsn)
care and maintenance accessories, 23, 614
cases, instrument, 97 (fl), 209 (cl), 356
    (sx), 477 (ob), 617 (bsn)
cases, reed. *See* reed holders/guards/cases
chamber, 48 (com, 210 (cl), 357 (sx)
    See also mouthpiece/mouthpieces
chimney. *See* riser
chipping, 618
choosing an instrument. *See* instrument
    selection
circular breathing, 23
clarinet, 188
    embouchure, 215
    hand/holding/instrument playing
      positions and posture, 224
    transposition, 292
    written range, 296
    See also instrument family and playing
      considerations
cleaning/tuning rod, 98
    See also cork stopper
clefs, 98 (fl), 210 (cl), 357 (sx), 478 (ob), 618
    (bsn)
closed G-sharp key, 98 (fl)
    See also open G-sharp key
closed-hole model. *See* plateau model
conical, 25 (com), 99 (fl), 210 (cl), 357 (sx),
    478 (ob), 618 (bsn)
    See also acoustical basics

construction and design, 99 (fl), 211 (cl),
    357 (sx), 479 (ob), 618 (bsn)
    See also acoustical basics; acoustical
      properties
contemporary techniques. *See* extended/
    contemporary techniques
contra-alto clarinet, 232
    embouchure, 217
    hand/holding/instrument playing
      positions and posture, 226
    transposition, 233
    written range, 296
    See also instrument family and playing
      considerations
contrabass clarinet, 232
    embouchure, 217
    hand/holding/instrument playing
      positions and posture, 226
    transposition, 233
    written range, 296
    See also instrument family and playing
      considerations
Cooper scale. *See* flute scales
cork stopper, 100
cracks, 208, 209, 475, 480
cross-fingering, 25
crossing the break, 100 (fl), 212 (cl), 358
    (sx), 481 (ob), 619 (bsn)
    See also break; technique
crow/double crow, 482 (ob), 621 (bsn)
    See also double crow
cut, 482 (ob), 621 (bsn)
    See also reeds, double
cutting block, 482 (ob), 621 (bsn)
    See also reed making and
      adjustment
curved head joint, 102
    See also head joint
curved lip plate, 102
cut, reed, 214 (cl), 360 (sx)
    See also reeds, single
cylindrical, 25 (com), 102 (fl), 214 (cl), 360
    (sx), 483 (ob), 622 (bsn)
    See also acoustical basics
    See also acoustical properties

D speaker key, 622 (bsn)
Deveau scale. *See* flute scales

dial indicator, 622
  See also reed making and adjustment
diaphragm, 26
  See also breathing/breath support/air
    control
dizziness/lightheadedness, 26
double bassoon, 622
double crow. *See* crow/double crow
  See also reeds, double
double reeds. *See* reeds, double
double-cut reeds, 214
  See also reeds, single
double-lip embouchure, 215
  See also embouchure
double-tonguing. *See* multiple-tonguing
doubling considerations, 622 (bsn)
  See also instrument family and playing
    considerations
drawn tone holes, 103
  See also soldered tone holes; tone
    holes
Dutch rush, 215
  See also reeds, single
dynamic considerations, 26
  See also intonation

E speaker key, 623 (bsn)
E-flat soprano clarinet, 233
  embouchure, 217
  transposition, 233
  written range, 296
  See also instrument family and playing
    considerations
embouchure, 104 (fl), 215 (cl), 361 (sx),
    483 (ob), 623 (bsn)
  See also instrument family and playing
    considerations
embouchure hole, 110
  See also lip plate; riser
embouchure plate. *See* lip plate
end cap, 110
  See also cork stopper
end pin/spike, 220, 628
end rail. *See* tip rail, mouthpiece
endurance/stamina, 28
exhalation/exhaling. *See* Breathing/Breath
    Support/Air Control

extended/contemporary techniques, 29
    (com), 110 (fl), 221 (cl), 366 (sx), 490
    (ob), 628 (bsn)
extension, 628

F resonance key, 490 (ob)
facing/lay, 222 (cl), 366 (sx)
  See also mouthpiece/mouthpieces
family. *See* instrument family and playing
    considerations
files, 629
  See also reed making and adjustment
fingering charts, 156 (fl), 297 (cl), 420 (sx),
    563 (ob), 679 (bsn)
first wire. *See* reeds, double
fish skin, 491
flick keys/flicker keys/speaker keys/flip
    keys/flicking, 629 (bsn)
flute, 81
  embouchure, 104
  hand/holding/instrument playing
    positions and posture, 113
  transposition, 151
  written range, 155
  See also instrument family and playing
    considerations
flute scales, 111
flutter tonguing, 32 (com), 111 (fl), 222
    (cl), 366 (sx), 491 (ob), 631 (bsn)
foot joint, 111
fork F, 491 (ob)
  See also alternate fingerings/alternates
fork F resonance key. *See* F resonance key
French case, 111
  See also cases, instrument
French model flute, 111
  See also plateau model flutes
French reed, 491 (ob), 631 (bsn)
  See also German reed; reeds, single
F-sharp key, 221 (cl), 366 (sx)
  See also alternate fingerings/alternates
fundamental, 32
  See also bell effect; harmonics

German reed, 222 (cl), 491 (ob), 632 (bsn)
  See also reeds, single
gizmo key, 113 (fl)

gold. *See* materials in flute making
gouge, 491
   See also reeds, double
grain, reed, 222 (cl), 491 (ob)
   See also reeds, double; reeds, single
grattage, 492
   See also reeds, double

half-hole key, low clarinets, 223 (cl)
half-hole technique, 492 (ob), 632 (bsn)
   See also extended/contemporary
      techniques
half-holes, 113 (fl), 222 (cl), 367 (sx)
   See also extended/contemporary
      techniques
hand rest/crutch, 634
hand/holding/instrument/playing
      positions and posture, 113 (fl), 224
      (cl), 367 (sx), 493 (ob), 634 (bsn)
harmonics, 32
head joint, 121
head joint angle, 121
   See also instrument angle
heart, 230 (cl), 500 (ob), 643 (bsn)
   See also reeds, double; reeds, single
heel, 230 (cl), 500 (ob), 643 (bsn)
   See also reeds, double; reeds, single
high C facilitator. *See* gizmo key
high F-sharp key, 375 (sx)
high G-key, 375 (sx)
history, 121 (fl), 230 (cl), 375 (sx), 500 (ob),
      643 (bsn)

inline G, 121 (fl)
   See also offset G
instrument angle, 122 (fl), 230 (cl), 375
      (sx), 501 (ob), 644 (bsn)
instrument brands, 122 (fl), 232 (cl), 376
      (sx), 502 (ob), 644 (bsn)
   See also instrument selection
instrument family and playing
      considerations, 122 (fl), 232 (cl), 376
      (sx), 502 (ob), 645 (bsn)
instrument position. *See* hand/holding/
      instrument playing positions and
      posture
instrument ranges. *See* range
instrument selection, 33

instrument stands, 39
intonation, 41 (com), 129 (fl), 238 (cl), 382
      (sx), 505 (ob), 648 (bsn)
inverted ligature, 246
   See also ligatures

joint lock, 655

key cups, 136
key/pad height, 45
knife. *See* reed knife

lay, 655
   See also reeds, double
lay, mouthpiece. *See* facing/lay
   See also mouthpiece/mouthpieces
lay, reed, 247
   See also reeds, single
leg strap, 656
   See also seat straps
ligature, 247, (cl), 390 (sx)
   See also ligature
lightheadedness. *See* dizziness/
      lightheadedness
lip plate, 136
   See also riser
locking mechanism. *See* whisper/piano
      key locking mechanism
long-scrap reed, 511 (ob), 665 (bsn)
low A extension, 656 (bsn)
low A key, 391 (sx)
low B key, 136 (fl)
   See also B foot joint
low B-flat key, 511 (ob)

mandrel, 512 (ob), 656 (bsn)
   See also reed making and adjustment
materials in flute making, 136
mouthpiece/mouthpieces, 45 (com), 247
      (cl), 392 (sx)
mouthpiece/reed angle, 249 (cl), 397 (sx)
   See also instrument angle
multiphonics. *See* Extended/
      Contemporary Techniques
multiple-tonguing, 52
mutes, 397 (sx), 656 (bsn)

neck, 249 (cl), 397 (sx)

neck strap, 249 (cl), 398 (sx), 512 (ob), 656 (bsn)
    See also seat strap
nickel silver. *See* materials in flute making

oboe, 459
    embouchure, 483
    hand/holding/instrument playing positions and posture, 493
    transposition, 559
    written range, 562
    See also instrument family and playing considerations
oboe d'amore, 503, 512
    See also instrument family and playing considerations
octave key(s), 137 (fl), 250 (cl), 398 (sx), 512 (ob), 657 (bsn)
offset G, 137 (fl)
    See also inline G
open G-sharp key, 137 (fl)
open-hole model. *See* French model flute
optional keys/key mechanisms, 137 (fl), 250 (cl), 398 (sx), 515 (ob), 658 (bsn)
    See also construction and design
overblow, 55
overtones, 55
    See also acoustical properties; harmonics

pad height. *See* key/pad height
pads, 55
pan key, 637 (bsn)
parts
    bassoon, 658
    clarinet, 250
    flute, 138
    oboe, 515
    saxophone, 399
piccolo
    air stream, 83
    embouchure, 109
    transposition, 151
    written range, 155
    playing position, 119
    See also instrument family and playing considerations
pipe resonances, 658

pitch adjustment. *See* intonation
    See also tuning/tuning note considerations
pitch tendencies, 56 (com), 138 (fl), 250 (cl), 399 (sx), 516 (ob), 660 (bsn)
    See also intonation; temperament
pivoting, 517
plaque, 517 (ob), 660 (bsn)
    See also reeds, double
plastic reeds. *See* synthetic reeds
plateau model flutes, 138
    See also French model flute; plateau model/system
plateau model/system, 56 (com), 252 (cl), 399 (sx), 517 (ob)
platinum. *See* materials in flute making
playing position. *See* hand/holding/instrument/playing positions and posture
poly-cylindrical bore, 252 (cl)
posture. *See* hand/holding/instrument/playing positions and posture
preparing the right hand. *See* crossing the break

rails, reed, 252 (cl), 399 (sx), 660 (bsn)
    See also reeds, double; reeds, single
rails/side rails, mouthpiece. *See* side rails, mouthpiece
range, 140 (fl), 252 (cl), 401 (sx), 517 (ob), 660 (bsn)
    See also register/registers; transpositions
reamer, 661
    See also reed making and adjustment
reed. *See* reeds, single; reeds, double
reed blanks, 253, 518
    See also reeds, single
reed angle, 518 (ob), 613 (bsn)
    See also hand/holding/instrument playing positions and posture; instrument angle
reed care, 253 (cl), 518 (bsn)
reed clipper/trimmer, 255
reed cases/holders, 255 (cl/sx), 520 (ob/bsn)
reed holders/guards/cases, 255 (cl/sx), 520 (ob/bsn)
reed knife, 256 (cl), 520 (ob)

See also reed making and adjustment

reed making and adjustment, 256 (cl/sx), 521 (ob/bsn)

reed testing, 530

reed tools. *See* reed making and adjustment

reed well/receiver, 531 (ob)

reed/bocal angle, 661 (bsn)
See also instrument angle

reed/mouthpiece angle, 265 (cl), 401 (sx)
See also instrument angle

reeds
double, 531
single, 265
See also synthetic reeds

register key, 278

register/registers, 140 (fl), 279 (cl), 401 (sx), 545 (ob), 661 (bsn)
See also range

releases/cutoffs, 56 (com)
See also articulation/articulative styles; attacks; breathing/breath support/air control; resistance; response

resistance, 141 (fl), 280 (cl), 402 (sx), 545 (ob), 662 (bsn)

resonance keys, 280 (cl), 405 (sx), 547 (ob), 664 (bsn)
See also speaker keys

response, 142 (fl), 280 (cl), 405 (sx), 547 (ob), 664 (bsn)
See also resistance

ring inserts. *See* tuning rings

riser, 142

rolled tone holes, 142
See also tone holes

seat strap, 664
See also neck strap

second wire, 665
See also reeds, double

secondary break, 281 (cl), 547 (ob), 665 (bsn)
See also break; crossing the break

secondary throat tones, 281
See also throat tones

selecting an instrument. *See* instrument selection; instrument brands

serial number, 58

shank, mouthpiece, 281

See also mouthpiece/mouthpieces

shaper, 548
See also reeds, double

short-scrape reed, 548 (ob), 665 (bsn)

shoulders, 281 (cl), 548 (ob), 665 (bsn)
See also reeds, single

side rails, mouthpiece, 281
See also mouthpiece/mouthpieces

single-cut reeds, 282 (cl), 405 (sx)
See also reeds, single

slap tongue, 142 (fl), 282 (cl), 405 (sx), 548 (ob), 665 (bsn)
See also extended/contemporary techniques

soldered tone holes, 142
See also tone holes

soprano saxophone, 377
air stream, 336
embouchure, 363
playing position, 373, 376
transposition, 416
written range, 419
See also instrument family and playing considerations

sounding range. *See* range
See also instrument family and playing considerations; transpositions

spat keys, 406 (sx)

speaker keys, 282 (cl), 406 (sx), 548 (ob), 666 (bsn)
See also resonance keys

spine, 548 (ob)
See also reeds, double

spit valve/water key, 406 (sx)

split E mechanism, 143 (fl)

spring hook tool, 59

springs, 59

squeaks, 282 (cl), 406 (sx), 549 (ob), 666 (bsn)

staggered breathing, 59

stamina. *See* endurance/stamina

stands. *See* instrument stands

staple, 549
See also reeds, double

starting note/range, the best, 143 (fl), 283 (cl), 407 (sx), 549 (ob), 666 (bsn)

sterling silver. *See* materials in flute making

stock, 283
  See also reeds, single
stopper. *See* cork stopper
subtone, 407 (sx)
  See also extended/contemporary
    techniques
swab, 59
synthetic reeds, 283 (cl), 550 (ob)
  See also reeds, single

table, mouthpiece, 284 (cl), 407 (sx)
  See also mouthpiece/mouthpieces
technique, 60 (com), 144 (fl), 284 (cl), 408
    (sx), 551 (ob), 668 (bsn)
temperament, 61
  See also harmonics; intonation
tenor sax, 379
  air stream, 336
  embouchure, 363
  playing position, 373, 376
  transposition, 416
  written range, 419
  See also instrument family and playing
    considerations
third octave key, 554 (ob)
  See also octave keys
third wire, 670
  See also reeds, double
throat tones, 287
throat, reed, 670
  See also reeds, double
throat/bore, mouthpiece, 288
  See also mouthpiece/mouthpieces
thumb rests, 147 (fl), 288 (cl), 412 (sx), 554
    (ob)
  See also hand/holding/instrument/
    playing positions and posture
timbre. *See* tone quality
tip opening, 45 (com), 288 (cl) 412 (sx),
    555 (ob), 671 (bsn)
  and back pressure, 349, 472
  and endurance/stamina, 28
  and mouthpiece facing/lay, 49, 50
  and resistance, 545, 662
  and wires, 678
  See also mouthpiece/mouthpieces
tip opening/reed aperture, 555 (ob), 671
    (bsn)

See also tip opening
tip rail, mouthpiece, 49 (com), 288 (cl),
    412 (sx)
  See also mouthpiece/mouthpieces
tip, reed, 289 (cl), 555 (ob), 671 (bsn)
  See also reeds, double; reeds, single
tone holes, 63 (com), 147 (fl)
tone production, 63 (com), 160 (fl), 289
    (cl), 413 (sx), 556 (ob), 672 (bsn)
  See also tone quality
tone quality, 68 (com), 150 (fl), 291 (cl),
    415 (sx), 559 (ob), 675 (bsn)
  See also tone quality
tonguing, 71
  See also articulation/articulative styles;
    attacks
transpositions, 151 (fl), 292 (cl), 416 (sx),
    559 (ob), 675 (bsn)
  See also range
trill keys, 151
triple-tonguing. *See* multiple-tonguing
tube/body, reed. *See* staple
tuning rings, 294
tuning/tuning note considerations, 152
    (fl), 294 (cl), 417 (sx), 561 (ob), 675
    (bsn)

U joint, 677

vibrato, 74 (com), 154 (fl), 296 (cl), 418
    (sx), 562 (ob), 677 (bsn)

wall thickness, 155
water key. *See* spit valve/water key
whisper key, 677 (bsn)
whisper/piano key locking
    mechanism, 678
window, mouthpiece, 296
  See also mouthpiece/mouthpieces
wing lip plate, 155
wires, 523, 533, 541, 562, 678
  See also reeds, double
wrapping, 678
  See also binding
written range, 155 (fl), 296 (cl), 419 (sx),
    562 (ob), 678 (bsn)
  See also instrument family and playing
    considerations; range; transpositions